T0326901

Ramon Llull
Romance of Evast and Blaquerna

# Ramon Llull
# Romance of Evast and Blaquerna

Introduction by Albert Soler and Joan Santanach
Translation and notes by Robert D. Hughes

BARCINO·TAMESIS

BARCELONA/WOODBRIDGE 2016

First published 2016
by Tamesis (Serie B: TEXTOS, 60)
in association with Editorial Barcino

LLLL institut
ramon llull
Catalan Language and Culture

The translation of this work has been supported by a grant from the Institut Ramon Llull

ISBN 978 1 85566 304 6
COPYRIGHT DEPOSIT: B. 21337-2016

Tamesis is an imprint of Boydell & Brewer Ltd
PO Box 9, Woodbridge, Suffolk IP12 3DF, UK
and of Boydell & Brewer Inc.
668 Mt Hope Avenue, Rochester, NY 14620, USA
www.boydellandbrewer.com

Editorial Barcino, S. A.
Acàcies 15. 08027 Barcelona, Spain
www.editorialbarcino.cat

Printed by Fotoletra
Passeig de Sant Joan, 198
08037 Barcelona, Spain

Cover illustration:
Mural paintings from the Pia Almoina, Lleida
Detail, ca. 1330, n. inv. 3
© Museu de Lleida: diocesà i comarcal, 2016
Photo: Antoni Benavent

# Contents

# Introduction

## 1. RAMON LLULL AND HIS COMPLEX RELATION TO LITERATURE

With his *Romance of Evast and Blaquerna* (hereafter *Blaquerna*),[1] composed in Montpellier around 1283, Ramon Llull completed the most ambitious novel until that point ever written. It was so both in terms of its plot structure and its narrative realisation. What Llull wished to accomplish was a 'total novel', namely, a fiction which accounted for everything that was primordial within both individual and collective life; for everything that was of paramount importance within the public spheres of Church, politics, estate or profession; for everything that was essential to the internal and moral dimensions of the individual. Llull thus wrote the novel with the aim of constructing a work which might be of interest to all manner of persons, whether lay, religious, educated or uneducated, members of the knightly class, merchants, artisans or the populace in general.

Ramon Llull's relation to literature, however, was complex. A good number of his books are treatises devoted to philosophical, scientific and theological questions, though there are certain among them wherein literary expression carries significant weight. Poetic works, novels and dialogues likewise form part of his oeuvre, though in no case are we dealing with works which fit easily into the moulds established by the—essentially profane—tradition that preceded him. It was chiefly upon such a tradition that Llull cast suspicion.

---

1. The form *Blaquerna*, lacking an 'n' after the initial *a*, is the one which features in the oldest codices of the work's textual tradition, as well as in the contemporary manuscripts of other Lullian works wherein it is mentioned (the *Doctrina pueril* (or *Book of Instruction for Children*), the *Liber super Psalmum Quicumque*, *Fèlix, o Llibre de meravelles* (*Fèlix, or the Book of Wonders*), and the *Liber de fine*). It is likewise the form which appears in the catalogue of the *Electorium* elaborated by Thomas Le Myésier, a disciple of Llull. Although it became customary in texts copied within the Crown of Aragon, the variant *Blaquerna*, the 'n' of which was added for reasons of euphony and whose etymology, moreover, was false, did not begin to spread until the mid-fourteenth century. On this matter, see Badia, Santanach & Soler 2016, 105, n. 14.

After his conversion in around 1263, the troubadour literature which he had cultivated previously, as well as any other manifestation characteristic of profane literature, such as chivalric narrative, became for him the subject of criticism and rejection. It should come as no surprise, therefore, that no troubadouresque compositions of his have been preserved or that in one of the earliest works he wrote following his conversion, namely, the extremely lengthy *Llibre de contemplació en Déu* (*Book of Contemplation upon God*), dating from approximately 1272-1274, he should have set out to replace the entire preceding lyric tradition—which incited its readers to succumb to lust as well as other sins—with new moral and pious formulae much closer in kind to the *Llibre de contemplació* itself.[2] Llull, in fact, lays down this book as a model and starting-point for the new literature, one that contrasts with worldly values and is correctly oriented towards their true spiritual counterparts, and must needs arise as an alternative to the prior tradition as a whole.

In subsequent works, this highly belligerent attitude was replaced by a tacit—and tactical—acceptance of romance literature; or rather, by the practical use of particular points of reference. In the *Llibre del gentil e dels tres savis* (*Book of the Gentile and the Three Wise Men*), for instance, written between 1274 and 1276, Llull reclaimed the Classical dialogue form, this being one which enabled him to contrast divergent ideological and religious viewpoints. The prologue to the *Llibre de l'orde de cavalleria* (*Book of the Order of Chivalry*), composed during those same years, constitutes the first instance of a chivalric tale's being originally written in the Catalan language. Herein our author narrates the chance encounter of a young squire—who, while travelling to court, has fallen asleep on his palfrey—with an elderly knight, who has since become a hermit. Following a pleasant dialogue, the hermit offers the aspiring knight a book wherein is described that in which chivalry consists and that to which it forms a response. This book, of course, is the Lullian treatise itself.

In *Blaquerna*, Llull goes one step further. Within this text, he constructs a lengthy and sustained account wherein narration becomes inseparable from doctrine. *Blaquerna*'s plot-line is relatively simple: it recounts the story of a boy from a well-to-do family who, having ex-

---

2. Llull concentrates such proposals within Ch. 118 of this work; see Llull 2009a: 136-140.

pressed profound spiritual concerns, leaves his home in order to become a hermit. A sequence of circumstances causes him temporarily to forgo his vocation and lead him to profess as a monk in an abbey. Later on he finds himself having successively to accept the roles of abbot, bishop and pope. Only at the end of his life, once already old, can he step down from his pontifical throne and succeed in becoming a hermit. The narrative also includes the lives of Blaquerna's parents, Evast and Aloma, as well as of Natana, the girl whom the former had put forward to him as his betrothed, who becomes a nun and an abbess. Llull, however, associates the story of these four characters with the renewal of the entire world, Christian as well as non-Christian, something which, from a narrative point of view, constitutes a major challenge.

## 2. A NOVEL OF LENGTHY GESTATION: 1276-1283. THE QUESTION OF THE TITLE

At the end of the *Book of the Order of Chivalry*, Llull makes an assertion regarding his wish to write a book about the clergy which, since it cannot be identified with any title from that particular period, may be interpreted as a reference to a 'proto-*Blaquerna*', understood as a work focused upon the clerical estate:

> [...] since we must now write a book about the Order of the Clergy, this is why we are making the *Book of the Order of Chivalry* so brief. [3]

A short time later, while he was working on the *Doctrina pueril* (*Book of Instruction for Children*), a text written directly after the chivalric tract, the project must have begun to crystallise within him according to the form it ultimately ended up assuming. [4] In fact, in the final chapter of that work, namely, 'On Paradise', he states that he is no longer able to carry on speaking about celestial glory and that, therefore, 'I must abandon it, and we shall speak about the *Book of Evast and Blaquerna*'. [5] In any case, in some of the opening chapters of the novel, as

---

3. See Llull 1988: 221; for a commentary upon this passage, see Soler 1990. English translation from Llull 2013a: 81-82.

4. See Santanach 2000.

5. See Ch. 100, § 11, therein, in Llull 2005: 284.

well as in certain sections of the *Doctrina pueril*, there are clear indications of the—up to a certain point—simultaneous composition of the two works.[6]

The work's composition would have extended to at least the year 1283, since that was the date when the General Chapter of the Dominican Order held in Montpellier took place, as is mentioned in Chapter 90, § 7:

> In a town called Montpellier, in which this *Book of Evast and Blaquerna* was written, there was a very important General Chapter of the Preachers. At the chapter were bishops and other prelates, as well as friars from all the Christian territories.

Finding himself in Montpellier in 1283, therefore, Llull took the opportunity, as we read above, to work on the composition of *Blaquerna* —a fact which does not preclude his having written passages thereof in other locations.[7]

The composition of the work, therefore, would have extended from the year 1276 to at least 1283. Possible interruptions to the writing of the romance, conceivably resulting from the foundation of the monastery of Miramar, which occurred in 1276, or caused by the circumstances the Crown of Aragon had to face during those years.[8]

Whatever the case may be, by the second half of the 1280s *Blaquerna* had been completed. Proof of this lies in the fact that in Chapter 76, favourable comments are made concerning the Apostolic Brethren, a sect condemned as heretical in March 1286. Moreover, Llull must have already finished the novel when he sojourned for the first time in Paris, for the reason that the French version of *Blaquerna* fea-

---

6. Although they are not the only ones, the similarities observable between one of the final chapters of the catechetical treatise, namely, Ch. 91, 'On how one should raise one's son', and the upbringing administered to Blaquerna in Ch. 2 of *Blaquerna*, are particularly representative of this proximity, to the extent that one can conceive of the likelihood that during the latter's composition Llull had the former readily to hand or, of course, that both texts were quite possibly composed simultaneously.

7. The mention of a second Dominican Chapter General, which would have been held in the city of Bologna in 1285, has likewise been interpreted as a datable reference. Such mention, which we encounter in Ch. 86, § 7, is less explicit and, in any case, would refer to a meeting yet to be held.

8. For the lengthy composition of the work, see Domínguez 1986: 122 and Soler 1990: 275-276.

tures among the Lullian works belonging to his contact from those days in the French capital, namely, Peter of Limoges, this version being essentially the same as the one written in Catalan. Nor is it otiose to recall that the Latin version of the 'Llibre d'amic e amat' (or 'Book of the Lover and the Beloved') forms part of the manuscript Llull sent to the nobleman Pietro Gradenigo as a result of the latter's election to the post of Doge of Venice on 25th November 1289.[9]

It should be mentioned, moreover, that it has frequently been assumed that the 'Book of the Lover and the Beloved' was written, prior to *Blaquerna*, as a direct result of the mystical experiences of Ramon Llull himself, experiences often related to his sojourns at the impressive locale of Miramar. And the fact is that various generations of critics have been surprised that Llull should have offered a short self-contained work, consisting of brief, poetical prose statements (customarily called 'versicles'), within a novel. Nothing exists, however, to support such an interpretation; evidence, both material and content-specific, *is* available to us, on the other hand, evidence which indicates that Llull wrote his mystical opuscule as a further chapter of the romance. Among the material evidence lies the fact that although the Latin manuscripts of the 'Book of the Lover and the Beloved' circulated independently from the rest of *Blaquerna*, they explicitly relate the opuscule to the novel. Among the content-specific evidence, it is worth pointing out that the metaphor of the lover and the beloved already appears, though in an as yet incompletely defined form, within Chapters 79, 80 and 83 of the novel, and that in Chapter 88 reference is made to a 'Book of the Lover and the Beloved', which fails to match up with that in which the opuscule actually consists.[10]

Despite the resemblances suppressed and later reinstituted during the composition of the text, the foregoing situation should not have unduly affected the outlines of the work as these had initially been sketched. The consistency observable therein as regards the unfolding of the action from the first through to the final chapter (Chapter 115) force one to rule out the possibility of substantial mod-

---

9. For the date of *Blaquerna*, see above all Bonner 1977 and 1986, as well as Soler 1991. The foregoing observations, moreover, have enabled scholars definitively to rule out the hypotheses which situated the partial or complete composition of *Blaquerna* after the year 1294 and after the abdication of Pope Celestine V. For a reliable synthesis of the various dating proposals offered by Llull specialists up to the time of his writing, see Oliver 1959.

10. On this question, see below, n. 39, and Soler 1992.

ification. The unity of purpose and content present throughout the
five books demonstrates that, from the very outset of the work's composition, its plot was fully defined, the proposals for the renewal of
the order of matrimony being situated in the first book and the grad-
ual progress of the chief protagonist through the ecclesiastical hierarchy being located in the four remaining books.[11]

In contrast to the stability we observe in terms of content and the
general outlines of the plot throughout the composition of the work,
there is evidence pointing to the fact that, as his writing of the work
progressed, its genre—or, at the very least, the designation applicable
to the work's genre—became progressively clearer to Llull. In fact,
the first allusions Llull makes to the novel refer to it by means of the
more general and neutral designation of the *Llibre d'Evast e Blaquerna*
(*Book of Evast and Blaquerna*), as we find in the text's opening invocation. Llull had already used such a designation previously, in fact, in
his first documented explicit reference thereto, namely, that of Chapter 100, § 11 of the *Doctrina pueril.* He likewise employs this title in
Chapter 90, § 7 of the novel in question, in the passage wherein he
affirms that it was in the city of Montpellier that 'this *Book of Evast and
Blaquerna* was written'.

At the end of the work, however, the term '*llibre*' (or 'book') in relation to the title disappears. On various occasions we find instead the
noun *romanç* (or 'romance'). He uses it three times in the final chapter, namely, Chapter 115, and even a fourth time in the colophon.
Such a change is not gratuitous and should be viewed in relation, as
we have said, to the genre of the novel. Far from being a theoretical
treatise on the clerical order, as the title included in the *Book of the
Order of Chivalry* had insinuated, *Blaquerna* is a narrative fiction whose
reference points regarding genre are to be sought in the romance
narratives of French origin read by laypeople, above all courtiers, to
whom Llull addressed the work: the same public, that is, for whom he
had designed the tale of the squire and the elderly hermit which
opens his treatise on chivalry, a public capable of appreciating the
recreation of the chivalric universe, for instance, that is carried out in
the sylvan adventures of the youthful Blaquerna in Book Two, wherein
appear remote palaces concealed amid the dense forest and the pro-

---

11. For the unitary structure of the work, see likewise Oliver 1959: 327-328, as well
as Bonner 1986: 145-146.

tagonist has encounters with knights-errant, damsels and squires. The French *roman en prose* establishes itself as the closest narrative reference point available to Llull for his work of fiction—the first to enjoy such characteristics, lest we forget, using Catalan in its written form —irrespective of the fact that the spirit which inspired the latter diverged therefrom in numerous regards.[12] The Catalan adaptation of the term, then, becomes a means of indicating to the reader the narrative genre within which the work aims to insert itself.

The proposal for the reform of Christendom put forward in *Blaquerna*, fully realised as it is, must be related to the optimism which Llull's books written prior to 1287-1289 exude. To situate the entire human race upon the path to salvation was, in fact, Ramon Llull's goal. The desire to reorder the whole of humanity remained unshakable throughout his life, although what did change was his attitude when having to contend therewith as well as the expectations of immediate fulfilment which at some point, or so it would seem, he had set himself. He came to realise that, all things considered, the task would be more complicated than he had imagined.

During the aforementioned years, namely, at the end of the 1280s, Llull made his first foray out of the territories of the former Crown of Aragon. He travelled to Rome and to Paris with the aim of explaining his projects in those places, seeking support therefrom and, above all, familiarising its dignitaries with the Art, that is to say, his system for discovering the truth. Until that point, we have no evidence to suggest that he had travelled any further than the city of Montpellier, which at that time formed part of the Kingdom of Majorca.

The trip to Rome and to Paris failed to elicit anything besides indifference and incomprehension on the part of those to whom he addressed himself, whether the Papal Court or the university community. Prior to such events, while Llull was writing *Blaquerna*, he counted on the fact that his projects, with the Art at their forefront,

---

12. For the term *romanç* as a loan-word from the French *roman*, and for the chivalric referents of the novel, see Riquer 1984: I, 269-270, 277-280. Clearly, Arthurian referents are not the only ones of which Llull makes use from the literary repertoire of the romance genre: troubadour referents are likewise accommodated therein, and not only in the poetic compositions of Chs. 76 and 115 or in the versicles of the 'Book of the Lover and the Beloved', but also in other chapters, such as Ch. 64, a true narrative correlate for a *tenso* regarding the beauty of their respective ladies as maintained by Abbot Blaquerna and a knight-troubadour. For the work's narrative models, see below, § 6 of this introduction.

would not only impose themselves with a certain ease, but also that they would even be welcomed with enthusiasm. Some rather remarkable initial successes favoured such confidence. The most emphatic of these, no doubt, was the foundation in 1276 of a school for languages at the monastery of Miramar on the island of Majorca, a school subsidised by James II and intended for the training of missionaries. Such languages were to be employed by them in the demonstration of the Christian articles of faith to Muslims.

## 3. STRUCTURE AND NARRATIVE DEVELOPMENT OF *BLAQUERNA*

The romance is structured according to five books, devoted to five different estates, through which, with the exception of the first, Blaquerna passes during the course of his intense and highly active life's journey. The protagonist's passage through various estates facilitates his detection therein of wrongful opinions and behaviour, as well as the fact that he must adopt measures designed to correct these latter. Initially as a result of Blaquerna's own example, and subsequently, when he achieves high office and earns responsibility, of his moral authority, such measures become widespread and are introduced everywhere with unquestionable success.

The central role of each of the reforms described in *Blaquerna* is manifestly indicated by the distribution of the chapters within a catechetical framework:

| Book | Chapters | Estate represented | Protagonist | Catechetical framework or significant content |
|------|----------|--------------------|-------------|-----------------------------------------------|
| First | 1-18 | Married life | Evast, Aloma | The Seven Deadly Sins |
| Second. Part One | 19-41 | Religious life (female) | Natana | The five senses and the seven virtues |
| Second. Part Two | 42-66 | Religious life (male) | Blaquerna | *Ave Maria* |
| Third | 67-77 | Episcopal order | Blaquerna | Beatitudes |
| Fourth | 78-95 | Papal dominion | Blaquerna | *Gloria* |
| Fifth | 96-115 | Eremitic life | Blaquerna | 'The Book of the Lover and the Beloved', the 'Art of Contemplation' |

Such an expedient enables Llull to distinguish between a linear narrative thread (i.e. the story of each of the protagonists: Evast and Aloma, Natana, and Blaquerna), which drives the action forward, and the various condensations of that narrative which indicate reform in the strict sense (i.e. the chapters included within a particular framework).

### 3.1. BOOK ONE: ON MATRIMONY

Book One of the novel is devoted to the matrimonial estate and focuses upon the characters of Evast and Aloma, that is to say, Blaquerna's parents, who find their exemplary married life rewarded by the birth of a son. In Chapter 2, Llull reformulates the theme of the hero's childhood, customary in Romance narratives, and he turns it into an unusual account of the daily attentions Blaquerna receives in terms of nourishment, clothing and play when he is an infant, and likewise in terms of his subsequent primary and higher education. The fact is that this chapter constitutes the transformation into narrative material of the theoretical contents of Chapter 91, 'On how one should raise one's son', from the *Doctrina pueril.*

Of great note in this part of the work is the creation of the character of Aloma, a lady who holds her own opinions, shows tenacity and is endowed with a capacity for expressing emotion which contributes to making her a complex and plausible character like any other. Aloma is capable, for example, of going up against the authoritarian will of her husband, who wishes to dissolve their marriage in order to devote himself to the religious life (Chapter 4), and of getting her own way; she reveals an immense practical sense when confronted with Blaquerna's intention of leaving the world and devoting himself to the life of a hermit (Chapter 6), by contriving a plan to tempt him by means of the youthful Natana's amorous feelings towards him; she also shows the most human of reactions when bidding farewell to her son (Chapter 8), who is setting off for his hermitage, as well as at the death of her husband Evast (Chapter 18).

Once they have accepted Blaquerna's vocation and fulfilled their duty as parents, Evast and Aloma decide to devote themselves to a joint life of poverty, sexual continence and charity in the midst of the city in which they live (Chapter 9) and, on account of the resolute

opposition of Aloma, without the annulment of their marriage
(Chapter 4). In this way, Llull offers us the first fictitious recreation of
the style of penitential life for which certain laypeople, better known
as Beguins (male) and Beguines (female), opted during that period.
The couple's example would provoke all kinds of reactions among
their fellow townsfolk, this being something which would enable the
reader to acquaint him or herself with the colourful city life in the
closing years of the thirteenth century from an unusual perspective,
namely, that of the poor. These chapters (11-18) are assigned the
names of each of the Seven Deadly Sins and indicate the reform of
the order of matrimony and, in addition, of those who resided in cities though did not practise celibacy.

## 3.2. BOOK TWO: ON RELIGION

Book Two is devoted to the religious life and consists of two, well
differentiated parts. In the first of these, we are given an account of
the story of Natana, the young girl whom Aloma had used in the
hope of preventing Blaquerna's departure and who, inspired by the
latter's example, decides to enter a religious order, in spite of her
mother's opposition. As recounted, her entry therein (Chapter 20)
follows the well-known hagiographic model of Saint Clare of Assisi,
who had died but thirty years previously, and forms the starting-
point for a monastic life full of perfection which would lead Natana
to the position of abbess (the maximum responsibility for governance to which a lady could aspire) and to the consequent reform of
the monastery.

Natana's reforming task is clearly very Lullian and, therefore, reveals an unbounded confidence in the capacity of human reason to
progress towards the primary purpose for which it was created, namely, the knowledge and service of God. In this instance, such confidence is applied to the personal development of the ladies devoted to
the religious life, an estate traditionally disregarded in this respect.
When, in Chapter 39, a nun casts doubt upon the appropriateness of
the subtle reasonings the abbess addresses to her charges, therefore,
the reply she receives is specific:

So, while the abbess was uttering these words of great subtlety, a sister told
her that it was not lawful for such subtle words to be spoken to a woman.
So the abbess replied by saying that since the intellect was capable of understanding them, it was fitting that the will should wish the intellect to
be exalted thereby so that it may understand, and that consequently the
will might better be able to contemplate and understand God and His
works (§ 2).

From the second part of Book Two onwards, the story focuses once
and for all upon Blaquerna, following the episodes in which Evast,
Aloma and Natana have acted as protagonists. The chapters narrating his experiences within the forest (42-52) adopt as their narrative
model the French *roman en prose*.

In the Middle Ages, the enormous and continuous mass of forest
which extended across the whole of Europe represented the limits of
organised society and was a dangerous and hostile place; the *roman*
presented an idealised forest as the space wherein young knights
sought adventure, endeavoured to perfect themselves ethically, came
into contact with a wondrous realm and could seek the wise counsel
of aged hermits. Llull proposes a new vision of this novelesque framework: the story of a young hermit, rather than a youthful knight, who
enters the forest in search of a singular and extreme adventure, of a
spiritual nature. Within the forest, Blaquerna comes across allegorical figures (the Ten Commandments, Faith, Truth, Intellect, Devotion and Worth) which occupy the equivalent position of the
wondrous in chivalric narratives; it is these figures which reveal to
him the unfortunate and desperate situation of the world he has left
behind and cause him to become aware of the need to avoid remaining impassive in the face of this reality.

His initiation experiences within the forest cause Blaquerna to
adopt a strictly Lullian ideology which enables him to overcome prej-
udices, such as the belief that faith loses its merit when it is rationally
demonstrated; thus, Intellect recommends to him and instructs him
in the Lullian Art (Ch. 44, § 3).

Within the forest, moreover, Blaquerna also encounters a knight-
augur, a shepherd in distress, an abducted damsel, a disillusioned
minstrel and even the emperor, who has become lost while pursuing
a wild boar during a hunt. The chance encounter with the emperor
(Chapter 48) helps a character as distinguished as himself to become
involved in a plan for universal reform. The unfolding of this plan

will lead to a situation whereby, in the final chapter of the novel, the two most eminent dignitaries within Christianity, namely, the pope and the emperor, both already having stepped down from their posts, end up coinciding in a life of contemplation.

After all these encounters, Blaquerna shows himself to be prepared to forsake his lonely path and to return to the world on the first occasion he is needed; in this instance, by an abbey in which a false lay penitent, named Narpan, has installed himself and is corrupting the entire community (Chapter 52). Blaquerna ends up taking his vows in this monastery. The first thing he then does is to convince the community of the need to set up a school, in which can be learned, in the space of a year, not only the *trivium* (i.e. grammar, logic and rhetoric), but also 'the principles and the art pertaining to the four general sciences which are the most necessary, namely, theology, natural philosophy, medicine and law' (Chapter 56); it should be noted that shortly before *Blaquerna*, Llull had written four books concerning the principles of the aforesaid sciences, basing these latter upon his Art.

In the progression that will lead him to become abbot, Blaquerna fulfils the role of sacristan to the monastery; this post allows him a certain amount of spare time for contemplation, time which serves to compensate him for his thwarted eremitical project, and regarding which, moreover, he takes the opportunity to warn his readers about possible hallucinations brought on by fasting, vigils or obsessions (Chapter 59). Everything seems to indicate that the experience narrated in this chapter functions as preparation for the intellectually well-ordered contemplation which will be introduced in Book Five.

### 3.3. BOOK THREE: ON PRELACY

Blaquerna will accede to the rank of abbot and bishop following the resignation of his predecessors. In Book Three, when he has already become bishop, Blaquerna shares out among his eight canons an identical number of offices, organised according to the framework offered by the eight Beatitudes. Blaquerna's canons form a team resolved to carry out an in-depth reform of the society within which they live. Thus the Canon of Persecution (which corresponds to the Beatitude of 'Blessed are those who are persecuted for the sake of righteousness'; Matt 5:10) exercises his office with an uncommonly radical evangelism, using a style of apostleship fully engaged with the lives of the most disadvantaged:

> It came about one day that he was passing in front of a tavern where a large number of gamblers, goliards and scoundrels had assembled, and in that place were drinking, singing, dancing and playing instruments. The canon entered the tavern and bought some wine, and he danced with the gamblers and recited these verses concerning Our Lady [...] When he had recited these verses, he asked them to be seated, to drink and to recount certain agreeable tales. While the canon was among these people, the people who passed along the road derided him and reproached him for being in the company of such worthless men. Yet the canon did all he could to ensure that he was loved by those with whom he was keeping company, and they all took pleasure in his companionship, and made him their leader, and listened to his words, which he uttered in relation to Jesus Christ and the Apostles and to disdain for this world. He regaled them with such soothing words and placed himself in the company of such men so many times a week that he thereby converted many of them to virtuous habits and worthy conduct, and was not discouraged from so doing by reason of public censure (Ch. 76, 1 and 5).

In his resolute conduct, the canon promotes acts of protest and succeeds in denouncing, where necessary, the inconsistencies of the very bishop Blaquerna who has appointed him and even the injustices tolerated by the king. The fact is that *Blaquerna* exudes a radical approach towards all matters ecclesiastical and social that verges upon and, occasionally, exceeds the limits of what the Church of its day was in a position to accept, and thus situates itself alongside movements espousing lofty spiritual sensibility. Llull would not show equivalent audacity in any other work; the desire to make himself heard within influential ecclesiastical and political milieux would lead him to opt for prudence.

### 3.4. BOOK FOUR: ON THE PAPAL ESTATE

Book Four recounts Bishop Blaquerna's accession to the papal throne while in Rome for the purpose of addressing a series of questions to the pontiff, at the very time when this latter unexpectedly passes away. One day, a singular character makes an appearance at the new pon-

tiff's Court. There is no doubt from his appearance that he is an out-
cast: his head is shaven (the distinguishing mark of a fool), and he is
outlandishly dressed, bringing with him as his sole possessions a sparrowhawk and a dog. To the reader's surprise, the character is called
Ramon and bears the soubriquet 'the Fool'. In front of the Papal
Court, and using the animals in his company, he behaves like a buf-
foon and performs apparently meaningless acts. At the request of the
uncomprehending pope, Ramon explains that he has come on behalf of the emperor whom Blaquerna had met in the forest (Chapter
48), which emperor, having converted him to a truly evangelical life,
had commissioned him to travel throughout the world performing
these strange and provocative acts which possess a double meaning:

> It happened one day that the pope invited all the cardinals to dine,
> and held a grand court that day. When they had eaten at the court, a
> man dressed as a fool arrived, shaven-headed and bearing in one hand
> a sparrowhawk and in the other a leash to which was attached a dog he
> was leading. He greeted his lord the pope and his cardinals and the
> entire court on behalf of his lord the emperor, and he said these
> words:
>
> 'I am Ramon the Fool, who has come to this court by command of the
> emperor in order to practise my craft and to seek my companions.' (Ch.
> 79, § 3).

One of the characteristic features of Llull's oeuvre consists in the progressively increasing presence of its author within his own texts. The
Ramon the Fool who appears in *Blaquerna* cannot be said to be Llull
himself; we have no evidence that Llull ever presented such an appearance, nor that he performed provocative acts at the Courts he
visited. What lies beyond doubt, however, is the fact that we are dealing with a counterfigure or antitype of Ramon Llull himself, an *alter
ego* formed on the basis of the type represented by the 'Fool of God'.

Llull wrote *Blaquerna* prior to gaining first-hand knowledge of the
Papal Court. In 1283, and from Montpellier, he was speaking from
hearsay about the Curia, and about its operational problems and vices. For this precise reason, however, Llull was thinking about the
Church and the papacy without restrictions, a fact which explains the
creative force of his novel. As he envisages matters, the task of organising the Roman Curia rests upon the verses of the *Gloria* and is en-

trusted to various cardinals. Its aim is to correct certain of the universally acknowledged vices occurring within the Papal Court (e.g. power struggles, nepotism, the economic rights enjoyed by those in regular attendance, the operational sluggishness of its agencies, etc.) and to turn it into a locus of exemplary evangelism. One of the pope's first interventions limits the number of cardinals to fifteen and organises the courts thereof, standardising their incomes and revenues, as well as the number of their servants and animals, while likewise prohibiting and preventing them from receiving funds from other parties than the Curia which might encourage corrupt practices (Chapter 79, §§ 7-8). The majority of the ecclesiastical reforms enjoying universal scope, as well as some of those which apply to the whole of Christendom, are a simple extension of those applied to the Curia; the foregoing reveals a Romanocentric conception of the Church, this being one which was very widespread in the late-medieval period; it is the same conception as that which originated from circles highly critical of the Church hierarchy, but which, in fact, entertained a profound fondness for the papacy.

An example of the numerous activities instigated by Rome consists in the creation of a chancellery of foreign affairs (Chapter 88) which seeks to confer a truly universal dimension upon papal policies. Here we encounter one of the most curious episodes within the work, for the reason that the—at times fictitious, at others plausible—information provided by the ambassadors constitutes an expression of the concern and curiosity regarding the geography and customs of far-off lands which spread throughout the thirteenth century within a Latin West full of travellers: merchants, pilgrims, missionaries and ambassadors. And, lest we forget, Marco Polo was a contemporary of Ramon Llull.

Some of the outcomes of Blaquerna's reforms are already visible during his pontificate. In general, it is a question of specific achievements: the introduction of peace between Christian princes in dispute, for example; or the conversion of a province inhabited by unbelievers; or of a Saracen king; or of the great Tatar Khan and 'many people within his Court'; or of all the Jews and Saracens residing in a country; or isolated conversions of Jews who become apologists for the Christian faith, and so on.

## 3.5. BOOK FIVE: ON THE EREMITIC LIFE. THE 'BOOK OF THE LOVER AND THE BELOVED' AND THE 'ART OF CONTEMPLATION'

The culmination of sanctity in *Blaquerna*, as much for the clergy as for the laity, lies in the thoroughgoing life of the hermit, led independently from any canonical regulations.[13] It is logical, therefore, that by the time we reach Book Five, when the pope considers his duties to have been fulfilled, he should decide to step down from the papal throne and finally withdraw to a hermitage. Though it be fictional, the case of a pope who hands in his resignation nevertheless comes to us as a surprise, given that, until our own times, such an idea has not even been able to be floated in ecclesiastical circles. It is worth adding, moreover, that only a few years after this novel had been written, a very real papal resignation took place, namely, that of Celestine V, Pietro da Morrone, a holy hermit who was elected pope on 5th July 1294 in extreme circumstances and who, after but a few months, abdicated on 13th December of the same year, overcome by the problems associated with his office. Ramon Llull knew Celestine V and dedicated various works to him.[14]

Once at his final hermitage (Chapter 99), another hermit asks Blaquerna to write a book which might serve as subject matter on which contemplatives could reflect: this book would be the very widely renowned 'Book of the Lover and the Beloved', which corresponds to Chapter 100 of the novel. This text enables us to enter into the inner life of the protagonist.

The didactic material addressed to contemplatives is not limited to the opuscule written by the protagonist, but rather also includes an applied method of spirituality, namely, the 'Art of Contemplation' (Chapters 101-114).

---

13. This assertion is valid both for Pope Blaquerna and for the emperor, since in Ch. 115, the closing one, it is suggested that they end up being reunited in the eremitical life. Lest we forget, moreover, the young Blaquerna who begins his adventures by seeking a hermitage wherein to devote himself to contemplation is a layman, given that he does not enter a religious order until Ch. 55 and is not ordained a priest until Ch. 59.

14. The similarity between the plot of *Blaquerna* and the story of the hermit from Morrone who is elected pope and who subsequently steps down from his post has given rise to much speculation and has caused scholars to imagine a second redaction of the novel following the events of 1294 or even the influence of Llull upon the decision of Celestine V. Today we know with absolute certainty that *Blaquerna*, in the form we have it, was already written by at least 1289, any coincidences being purely casual.

### 3.6. Narrative skill: short forms and grand narratives

Llull succeeds in carrying out a narrative project as risky as the one he does with a strength of conviction, as well as narrative skill and audacity which end up rendering that project fully defensible. Even though it may seem paradoxical, the basis of Llull's ability to construct a sustained, ambitious and complex narrative, and to succeed fully in doing so, lies in his narrative skill regarding the short forms he employs within the story recounted. Ramon Llull is a master of 'tales' (or *recontaments*), of *exempla*, of proverbs and of sententious discourse. These literary forms enable him to get to the heart of situations and characters without lingering over anecdotes.[15] As it unfolds, the novel abounds with a vast number of episodes (i.e. short tales comparable to *exempla*) which are particularly present in those parts thereof that are structured in accordance with a prayer or with specific aspects of the catechism; such parts play the role of suggesting by means of narrative condensation the reform of a section of society.

Llull, moreover, establishes a series of correspondences between episodes and *exempla* narrated in different parts of the novel which creates an interplay of—short—references and reiterations which amplify the narrative and all that it seeks to suggest. Paragraphs 14-17 of Chapter 83, for instance, treat for the second time characters and a theme already developed in Chapter 76 at greater length and in greater detail: as we have already pointed out, one of Blaquerna's collaborators becomes friends with taverngoers of the lowest kind and manages to turn them into active agents of the moral and spiritual reform that is being recommended. In Chapter 85, § 3, Llull takes up once again the theme of Chapter 46, 'On Diligence', in which the youthful Blaquerna who is seeking a hermitage within the forest comes across various characters who, in their anxious haste, are incapable of listening to him or of answering correctly that which he asks them. The question of the expediency of learning

---

15. 'That sole level of reality in whose regard, from the Lullian viewpoint, it is worth making assertions is an abstract level, stripped of all particularities, wherein the real coincides with the concept, a level in whose regard, by means of personified or similar characters, assertions can readily be made which aim to be true and referential' (Friedlein 2011: 306).

languages in order to facilitate mission is present throughout Book Four and makes repeated appearances in a number of chapters.[16]

An appropriate narrative rhythm is likewise achieved by introducing a number of humorous touches and instances of ironic detachment into the narration, elements which serve as a counterpoint to the transcendence of the tale being told. Particularly comic is an episode which will prove decisive, however, in terms of the story's unfolding. In Chapter 52, Blaquerna imagines himself to be under an obligation momentarily to put a halt to his quest for a hermitage in the forest in order to place himself in the service of a false penitent, called Narpan, in order to prevent the latter from corrupting by his wicked example the monks of an abbey. Pervading the shock tactics used by Blaquerna to combat Narpan's wicked ways are a number of absurdities; to begin with, he serves him a disgusting meal consisting of roast fox (§ 7). After this, he makes him sleep in a topsy-turvy bed (§ 8), made 'according to the work of penance', and he ends up dressing Narpan in an outlandish manner (§ 10), whereby the latter tells him 'that he felt very great shame at the fact that the abbot and the monks might see him dressed in this way'. A further comic scene occurs in Chapter 48, § 4, when Blaquerna sends no less than the emperor himself to graze: '"My lord", said Blaquerna, "there is a spring close by where you can drink fine water and you can eat the cool grass that surrounds the spring."' We also encounter the case of the mule driver who starved himself, though fed his ass (Chapter 72, § 1).

## 4. BLAQUERNA, A NOVEL EXHIBITING VARIOUS AXES OF INTERPRETATION

The range of interpretative perspectives of which *Blaquerna* admits on account of the multiplicity of themes treated therein, provides convincing proof that Llull achieved the narrative aims he set himself when composing the novel. In no instance does that range of interpretative axes amount to dispersion or a miscellany, but rather it assembles itself into a narrative unity that is perfectly bound together.

---

16. See, for example, Chs. 80, §§ 3, 4, 7, 9, 12; 85, §§ 1, 2; 87, § 1; 88, §§ 3, 5, 6; and 95, §§ 3, 6.

## 4.1. The ordering of Christendom and the ordering of intentions

The totality of Llull's works, thought and life is grounded upon a reality which underlies Medieval Europe and is likewise fundamental to the aim of understanding what he did, thought and wrote: Christendom. From the year 380 when, at the instigation of the Emperor Theodosius, the Christian religion was declared the official religion of the entire Roman Empire, every person born under that Empire's authority took on the duty associated with their 'office' of receiving baptism, and became simultaneously a subject of the state and of the Church.

Beyond all its local particularities, Christendom was a civilising entity which extended across a vast geographical area, reaching the entire population resident therein. It was constitutive of religious, social, political and cultural realities which determined all forms of life in this world as well as all forms of life one could expect in the world to come, given that it accounted for and governed both aspects of existence. The combination of social, cultural and religious features particular to Christendom articulated themselves as a system and offered a potent worldview held in common. The symbiosis between political and religious power located the institution of the Church at the axis and centre of the entire system. That Church, in fact, was the unavoidable mediator between physical and political subjects, as well as between the religious subject and God, and it determined the truths one was expected to believe, not to mention the ultimate norms one was expected to follow. Medieval Christendom constituted a world without any obvious gaps, a world destined, according to God's plan, to become widespread and to impose itself as the natural form of organisation for human society.

Such was the ideal framework within which Llull lived and such is the conception of the world that *Blaquerna* expresses. Actual Christendom, however, had succumbed to all sorts of strains and internal contradictions—confrontations and wars, for instance, between Christian princes, or between civic and ecclesiastical authorities— and had, at the same time, to face up to significant external threats, such as the spread of Muslims and Tatars. In this context, groups and initiatives appeared which called for the reform of Christendom as of its structures; such groups very frequently advocated a return to the Gospel origins of poverty and simplicity. The spiritual currents contemporary to Llull which sought to transform society employed terms such as the *renovatio*—or *reformatio*—*mundi*—or *ecclesiae*.[17]

The concept Ramon Llull uses in order to refer to the reform of society is 'ordering / organisation' (Cat. *ordenament*). The expression 'to set the world in order'—and other such similar ones, always within the same semantic field —implies that there was an original order which has been altered and needs to be restored. The work which expresses in the liveliest and most optimistic way the Lullian desire to reorder the world is, without doubt, *Blaquerna*. The term *ordenament* occurs therein on seventy-two occasions.[18] The various protagonists of the romance are responsible for the restoration of order within each of the estates wherein they play a part. The pope, at the top of the hierarchy governing all Christendom, is also the person who bears the greatest responsibility towards the restoration of such order; at the moment of his learning that he has been elected pope, Blaquerna expresses matters thus:

> Throughout the world it is well known that the pope, together with his fellow cardinals, could bring order to almost the whole of our world, if he so wished. And since the world is in such great discord and disorder, it is a fearful thing to be pope. And great fault would be revealed in a pope, were he not to make use of his authority to bring order to the world by conforming his will to all of the authority that God has invested in the papacy for the purpose of so ordering it (Ch. 78, § 10).

Behind this reflection lies the Lullian doctrine of the two intentions, which is one of the foundation stones of Llull's thought and a doctrine to which he devoted an entire monograph, namely, the

---

17. In his *Protestatio*, which he sent to Benedict XI on 2nd June 1304, denouncing the persecution to which he had been subject and proposing to the latter a plan for Church reform, Arnold of Villanova (Cat. Arnau de Vilanova), for example, addressed himself to the pope in the following terms: 'You, along with your colleagues, have been advised by Our Lord Jesus Christ diligently to endeavour *to restore the purity and sanctity of His religion* within all the Catholic estates, and especially the aforementioned' (see Perarnau 1991: 212).

18. *Ordenació* occurs eight times and *ordenança* once. The verb *ordenar*, in its various conjugated forms, is used on a hundred and thirty occasions.

*Llibre d'intenció* (*Book of Intentions*).[19] This doctrine distinguishes between a thing's final cause—the 'first intention', towards which the use man makes of creation must address itself—and the instruments which enable one to achieve that finality or goal, instruments which have to be treated as a 'second intention'. Any human action whatsoever must be directed, in the final instance, towards the first intention, namely, to know, love and praise God. Anything whatsoever that a person possesses must be no more than an instrument in the service of this ultimate goal. To subvert the order of intentions and to turn the instruments into goals constitutes the origin of the sin and disorder in which the world abides. The link between the idea of order and the doctrine of first and second intentions is so close that 'the world [is] more profoundly in difficulty and error on account of the privation of properly ordered intentions than of anything else' (V.30, 8; Llull 2013: 211).

The novel *Blaquerna* has been defined as 'the great exemplification of the *Llibre d'intenció*.[20] And, without doubt, the entire reordering of the world proposed within the novel is quite simply the correct ordering of the two intentions, within both the individual and the collective spheres:

> In entreaty to the cardinals, therefore, the pope asked them to assist him in exercising his office for the glory of God, in such a way that they might cause people to revert to the purpose for which the various offices and sciences were intended, namely, to give glory to God. For so flawed has the world become, that there scarcely exists anyone who directs his intention towards the very reason he has been created and the reason he performs the office he does (Ch. 80, § 1).

Ignorance of the proper use of material things by means of the first and second intention is the principal cause of the wicked state of the world, as a result of which what the agents assigned to reintroducing order in *Blaquerna* will do the most is to educate their peers, in keep-

---

19. See Llull 2013. For the doctrine of the two intentions, see Ruiz Simon 2002, as well as the appraisal thereof given in Bonner 2012: 80-81.

20. Ripoll 2012: 21. By interpreting *Blaquerna* along 'intentional' lines, we are merely following the article cited.

ing with what the *Llibre d'intenció* (Book 2, § 11; Llull 2013: 131-132; emphasis added) has already advised:

> May you know, my son, that it is very wrong and reprehensible to love money, food, children, possessions, honours and all other things by means of the first intention; and it is very reprehensible to love God by the second intention or to fail to love God either by the first or the second intention. So, since this is such a great defect and so many ills stem therefrom, *it is, therefore, very necessary to preach to and to teach people who ignorantly think that they love and know God with the first intention, yet love Him with the second.*[21]

An interpretation of the novel along 'intentional' lines is adopted in the final chapter of *Blaquerna*, wherein the protagonist entrusts the romance to a minstrel for the purpose of its dissemination, and characterises it as a work concerning the original purposes of the various offices and sciences (Chapter 115, § 1).[22]

Readers of a medieval narrative which set out a *renovatio mundi* would have felt no surprise at the fact that the motive force behind the universal reform might have had a supernatural origin: divine interventions, miracles, apparitions, and so on. Nevertheless, such is not the case with *Blaquerna*, which is an extraordinarily sober work in this respect, and it is so because the ordering of the world recounted

---

21. Natana perfectly exemplifies this desire to preach to and teach everyone the first and second intentions in a whole series of sermons and reflections she addresses to the community of which she is abbess, sermons and reflections which aim, first of all, to order the five physical senses, the seven virtues and the three powers of the soul as regards the lives led by the nuns (Chs. 26-39). If one is able virtuously to use one's sensory and intellectual faculties, it is because one does so in accordance with first and second intentions (see, for example, Ch. 32, §§ 1-2).

22. See how the same idea is expounded in the *Llibre d'intenció*: 'My son, if you have eyes may you be able to see, and if you have ears may you be able to hear, and if you have a memory may you be able to remember, so that, by means of your intellect, you may be able to understand and, by means of your will, to love what God has ordained within the world by virtue of the ordering of intentions. For, my son, the blacksmith, the carpenter and the shoemaker exercise within their office so many things, as do all the other artisans, in order that, individually with each of these things and collectively with them all, they might adhere to the ordering of intentions, for the reason that by such ordering one exercises virtues against the vices by frequently, lengthily, fervently and righteously fearing, knowing and loving God, etc.' (V.30, 9; Llull 2013: 212).

therein is based upon the spreading of the Lullian doctrine of first and second intentions.[23]

In Chapter 49, 'On Consolation', one can read about the very specific and practical way in which Blaquerna assists a shepherd who, through his own neglect, namely, by having fallen asleep, traumatically loses his son as a result of an attack by a wolf. Blaquerna comes across a person who is in a state of shock, and what he immediately does is to involve himself in the shepherd's drama;[24] following this, he gives him what in today's terms we would call emergency psychological treatment: he produces a reaction in the shepherd by suggesting to him a greater misfortune than the one he has suffered (§ 6) and by representing to him the very same excessive grieving as the shepherd himself had been undertaking (§ 7). Blaquerna does all this with a view to restoring the latter's intellect and causing it to govern the passions which have become unbridled by suffering. Only when the shepherd has set his intellectual abilities in order can Blaquerna put to him a line of argument based upon the doctrine of first and second intentions, to the effect that the shepherd had loved his son as an end in himself, when he should have loved him as a means whereby to love God (§ 8). The principle of consolation consists in an acceptance of the proper ordering of that which exists. There are no miraculous solutions, therefore (i.e. nothing resembling the child's being saved through the intervention of the Mother of God, for instance), nor is there any recourse to superhuman forces: the event narrated has the most dramatic reality as its starting-point and no other solution thereto is proposed than the responsibility the shepherd bears with regard to the correct ordering of his cognitive abilities and the extending of this therapeutic model to his wife as well as to other events.

---

23. Chapter 62 recounts a miracle which is performed through the intercession of the Mother of God, who fills the granary pit used for storing wheat, from which pit Blaquerna's abbey was accustomed to giving alms in times of famine. The foregoing constitutes one of the few exceptions to the principle governing the absence of supernatural interventions.

24. In § 4 he kills the wolf, an act which has a clear symbolic dimension.

## 4.2. THE ACTIVE AND THE CONTEMPLATIVE LIFE

*Blaquerna* sets forth, in narrative form, a profound reflection upon the apparent dichotomy that exists between action and contemplation, between involvement in the real world and the lure of one's internal life, and between the prophetic and the mystical aspects of Christian existence. The debate is as old as the Gospels themselves, where it is expounded in the episode of Martha and Mary (Lk 10:38-41): Jesus resolves the dilemma in favour of Mary, the sister who listens to Him, rather than of Martha, the sister who serves Him: He opts for contemplation, in other words. Llull likewise, in his oeuvre, reveals the same preference on many occasions, such as in the *Proverbis de Ramon*, where he states: 'The active life is the servant of the contemplative, and the contemplative, of God' (Chapter 251).

In *Blaquerna*, however, this position becomes much more nuanced. Llull subtly introduces an error amid the motives driving the young Blaquerna to become a hermit: his desire for a *fuga mundi* or, in other words, his quest for the comfort of solitude and isolation from a world he perceives to be full of wickedness and corruption:

> I am taking what I have learned along with me to the mountains and I wish to be by myself so that there may be no obstacle to my loving, knowing, praising and blessing God by means of what I have learned within the world. This, my lord, is the foremost reason for my leaving the world. There are plenty of other reasons too, among which is the following, namely, that I hardly ever see any person in the world who carries out his duty as regards honouring, loving and knowing God or who feels grateful towards Him for the good that he has received from Him; for almost the entire world has turned into vanity, wickedness, deceit and error. *I prefer, therefore, to live among the wild beasts, the trees and the birds, which are without sin, than to remain among so many people who are ungrateful and blameworthy with respect to the benefits they have received from God* (Ch. 7, § 5; emphasis added).

This, apparently secondary, reason invalidates any contemplative vocation: the first intention of the eremitical life has to be to know, love and praise God, and in no case at all to live a tranquil life far removed from the world! This initial error will be what prevents Blaquerna from fulfilling his desire to be a hermit until he has satisfied the various requirements that people and communities set before him throughout his journey.[25]

In other words, Llull corrects Blaquerna's purely contemplative choice using action, something for which he also argues in the *Proverbis de Ramon*: 'No hermit achieves as much good as a worthy preacher' (Chapter 251). To a certain extent, Llull behaved in precisely this manner as far as his own life was concerned.

It is revealing to compare the way in which Llull presents Blaquerna's eremitical vocation at the beginning and end of his novel. The youthful Blaquerna who enters the forest is someone who has received a rigorous education (Chapter 2, §§ 8-9) and has shown proof of his learning by means of the examination his father had set him concerning a practical case (Chapter 3). He proposes to travel to the wilderness (Cat. *desert*), following the example of Saint John the Baptist and the 'the Holy Fathers who have passed from this world' (Chapter 5, § 4);[26] during the preparations and lamentations undertaken prior to his departure, repeated reference is made to the extent of the self-denial for which Blaquerna is making ready (e.g. raw

---

25. In Ch. 88, §§ 16-17, of the *Arbre de filosofia d'amor* (*Book of the Philosophy of Love*), the characters of the Lover and the ladies of love commit the same error until they encounter a pilgrim who berates them: 'The pilgrim harshly rebuked the Lover and the ladies, telling them to return to the world in order to remain with people, so that they might not be idle. [...] The Lover and the ladies returned to the world and they travelled throughout distant lands in order to win honour for the Beloved. And they underwent great hardships and great languor and sadness; yet all of this they did in order to abide in the Beloved's love' (Llull 1980: 152). A similar thing occurs in the case of Evast, who in Chapter 4, § 13, 'decided to consent to Aloma's wish to do penance at home and not leave the house, in order to avoid seeing or hearing worldly vanities, which prevent the soul from remembering, understanding and loving God and His Honours'. This notwithstanding, the life that Evast and Aloma end up leading is not a life of reclusion, but rather of active charity.

26. Here we have a reference to the so-called Desert Fathers who, in the fourth century, after Christianity had been chosen as the official religion of the Empire and persecutions had ended, inhabited the deserts of Egypt and Syria in order to lead a life of prayer, solitude, manual work and the lending of assistance to the poor. The *De Vitis Patrum*, which Saint Rufinus of Aquileia translated from the Greek into Latin at the beginning of the fifth century, presents the desert as a locus of miracles and of confrontations with the Devil (the medieval Catalan version of this work can be found in Batlle 1986); Blaquerna speaks thereof to his parents in the same vein: 'your son Blaquerna wishes to follow the life and rule of Elijah and of Saint John the Baptist and of the Holy Fathers who have passed from this world, who lived lives of penance and austerity in the mountains and in the wilderness so that they might escape from the world and overcome their flesh and the Devil' (Ch. 5, § 4).

food, harsh weather, dangers), a feature which ties in with the hagiographical tradition regarding the discipline of being a hermit. To
travel to the wilderness and to become a hermit, according to the
hagiographic frameworks and ideas about eremitic sanctity, represented a fairly radical renunciation of culture; the hermit was an ascetic who took all forms of rejection of the world to their very limit.[27]
When Blaquerna finally departs, what he does is to enter deep within
a great forest (Chapter 8). An assimilation takes place, therefore, between the concepts of 'wilderness' and 'forest', one which is not uncommon within medieval spatial imagination. When we come across
Blaquerna again in the narrative (Chapter 42), after the parenthesis
formed by the stories of Evast, Aloma and Natana, the great forest is
presented as a place at once dangerous and inhospitable, containing
wild animals which prowl about, and a *locus amoenus*, boasting beautiful meadows, springs and trees, which facilitate rest and contemplation.[28]

While in the forest, Blaquerna will receive an initiation which will
lead him a long way away from this ascetic and counter-cultural ideal
of the hermit, given that allegorical characters such as the Ten Commandments, Faith, Intellect, Truth, Devotion and Worth transmit to
him characteristically Lullian teachings which impel him to commit
himself to the proper ordering of society and the Church (Chapters
42-51). When, already elderly, Blaquerna finally becomes a hermit,
after having been a monk, an abbot, a bishop and having abdicated
as pope, there no longer remains within his life anything of the initial
ideal, whose origins lay in a radical eremitic paradigm. Not a hint of
untrammelled asceticism: Blaquerna the hermit leads a very moder-
ate and well-ordered life, as is narrated in detail in Chapter 98.[29] He
is not a miracle-working hermit subject to heavenly visions, but rather
someone who lives a modest and austere life and who, very impor-
tantly, devotes himself to writing. The 'Book of the Lover and the
Beloved' is of his creation. Not only is it the case that Blaquerna is a

---

27. The fact, not without interest, is that, in undertaking his eremitic adventure,
the only thing Blaquerna takes away with him are the garments of one of Evast's servants and seven loaves of bread; there is no mention of books or of writing equipment
(Ch. 8, § 8). As Le Goff asserts, 'The wilderness is the location most distant from
learned culture' (1985: 72).

28. See, for example, Ch. 42, § 1; Ch. 43, § 1.

29. See also, Chs. 96, § 6, and 97, § 5.

Pope Emeritus of advanced age, but also that Llull wishes to point to this evolution in the figure of the hermit and to distance himself from hyper-ascetic hermits unable to write and all but disengaged from reality.

In the Middle Ages, hermits enjoyed great popular renown on account of the radical nature of their choice of life; we should not forget the fact that eremeticism did not enjoy canonical status nor constitute a sacred order, but rather a kind of life and, therefore, that many hermits were not members of the clergy. Blaquerna sets out on his life as a hermit without having received holy orders and is, to all intents and purposes, a layman. On the contrary, the ecclesiastical hierarchy regarded hermits with mistrust since, as members of the laity, they had only acquired the rudiments of an education and easily eluded the control of the Church. Proof of such mistrust lies in the fact that, between 1198 and 1431, only a single hermit, namely, Pietro da Morrone, who had been made Pope Celestine V, was canonised. The Church clearly feared the potential mental instability from which hermits could suffer, a situation inherent in the harsh lives they led, which harshness was precisely the reason they garnered a halo of sanctity in the eyes of the public.[30]

For Llull there has to be a necessary harmonisation between the active and the contemplative life, as is stated in versicle 56 of the 'Book of the Lover and the Beloved': there must be a movement of spiritual ascent, but also one of descent towards reality. Said otherwise, the contemplative life is the necessary foundation of the active life, although this latter constitutes a guarantee that the former does not drift towards a sterile and cosy narcissism. This position is expressed clearly in Chapter 62 of *Fèlix, o el Llibre de meravelles* (*Felix, or the Book of Wonders*; hereafter, *Felix*), which bears the title 'The Active and the Contemplative Life', by means of various examples and considerations with which Llull emphasises his point as follows:

> This is what the hermit told Felix so that he would have knowledge of the active and contemplative life. And when Felix had understood each of these lives, he said to the hermit:

---

30. See Vauchez 1988. It is significant that in the canonisation process relating to hermits, research was conducted into whether the person in question had been *phantastica* (i.e. prone to flights of fancy).

'I am in great wonder that Christ and the Apostles took on an active life in this world and not a contemplative life, if the contemplative life is nobler than the active life.'

'Sir,' said the hermit, 'Christ and the Apostles led an active life with reference to their bodies, and a contemplative life with reference to their souls [...].'[31]

## 4.3. THE START OF A NEW ERA: TIME IS OF GREATER IMPORTANCE THAN SPACE

The temporal and spatial indeterminacy of the story narrated in *Blaquerna* underlines the universal character of the actions undertaken by its protagonists. We do not know when the action occurs nor for how long. The very names of the characters therein are as exotic as those of a *roman courtois*, given that they are not Catalan, but rather are invented by the author or taken from place names or from other languages: 'Blaquerna' is the name of a sanctuary and of a palace in Constantinople (Istanbul); 'Aloma', the name of the protagonist's mother, seems to originate from the Arabic word for 'mother'; 'Evast', the father's name, 'Natana', that of Blaquerna's female counterpart, and 'Narpan', the false penitent, do not appear to have identifiable meanings or origins. Only a single character can be related to any concrete, historical person, namely, Ramon the Fool (Chapter 79), who is the literary counterfigure of Ramon Llull himself. Nor do we know the name of the city in which Evast and Aloma live, nor where Blaquerna's abbey or his bishopric are located. There is, of course, one name relating to an actual place: Rome.

Despite this absence of temporal determinacy, within *Blaquerna* there exists a theological conception of history. Expressed therein is an awareness of having reached a key moment in salvation history.

---

31. See § 7 (Llull 2011-2014: II, 98; English translation from *SW* II, 883). In Ch. 62, §§ 11-13, while in the presence of one of his monks who has fully devoted himself to the veneration of the Mother of God, Abbot Blaquerna utters an emotional lament with regard to the spiritual cooling elicited in him by the obligations inherent to the rank of abbot. The anecdote emphasises the unavoidable need to find time for contemplation in the midst of an active life. In Ch. 62, § 6, of *Felix* this idea is expressed aphoristically: the tribulations of the active life are 'the pleasure and fruit of the active life, from which the fruit of the contemplative life was born and produced seed and leaf' (Llull 2011-2014: II, 98; English translation from *SW* II, 882).

This fact is one of the important things learned by the protagonist, while in the forest, from the words of Faith, Truth's sister. Faith is introduced as follows in Chapter 43, § 3:

> This lady is my sister and Intellect is my brother, towards which latter I travel in order that he may go to those people whence I come and that by necessary reasons he may demonstrate to them the fourteen articles. For the time has come when they no longer wish to accept the authority of saints; nor are there miracles such as those whereby people unaware of myself or my sister were once enlightened. So, because people require necessary reasons and demonstrations, let my brother go, who, by God's power, is capable of proving the fourteen articles.

Long-gone, therefore, are the days in which one could wield authorities—or, in other words, texts—which might convince one's interlocutors by virtue of their prestige, as are the times when miracles might testify to God's supernatural power. Faith now lives in an era of arguments and necessary demonstrations. In the following chapter, Intellect, Faith's brother, points to the central position the Art occupies in this new age:

> *The time has come* when our knowledge has reached great heights, and unbelievers call for necessary arguments and demonstrations, yet shun faith. It is time we went, and made use of the demonstrative knowledge we possess [...] We have a new method of disputing with unbelievers, namely, by teaching them the *Brief Art of Finding Truth*; and when they have learned it, we shall be able to confound them using the Art and its principles (Ch. 44, § 3; emphasis added).

The formula 'the time has come' is present in both cases, and appears at other points in the novel,[32] a formula which reveals the significant shift instituted within history by the emergence of an era characterised by the Art, as well as by necessary arguments and demonstrations.

In *Felix*, Blaquerna the hermit himself—and it is significant that it is none other than he—expounds this historical schema in greater detail. First came the time of the Prophets, the time, that is, of authorities and, therefore, of belief and of faith. Next came the time of

---

32. In Chs. 5, § 1; 80, § 9; and 84, § 4.

Christ and the Apostles, the time, that is, of miracles; and, insofar as
miracles are physically visible demonstrations of things, this period
was likewise a time of faith. And then came the time of learned men
in need of necessary reasons:

> Blaquerna said: 'In the days of the prophets it was proper to convert
> people on the strength of belief, because people believed more easily,
> and in the times of Christ and the Apostles miracles were quite fitting,
> because people did not have a solid base in scriptures, and therefore
> liked miracles, which are physically visible demonstrations of things.
> Now we have reached a time when people prefer necessary reasons,
> since they are well grounded in the great sciences of philosophy and
> theology; and therefore people who, through philosophy, have fallen
> into errors contrary to the Holy Roman Faith, should be conquered by
> means of necessary reasons, and their false opinions refuted by means
> of necessary reasons, which reasons are based on philosophy and theol-
> ogy.' (Chapter 12, § 19; Llull 2011-2014: I, 143; English translation from
> *SW* II, 717-718).

This final epoch is the one characterised by the Art, a period which
*Blaquerna* aims to narrate. The work reveals the conviction that this
new epoch has arrived, that it entails a lengthy process and that it will
culminate in the construction of a new Christendom.[33]

The idea of process is highly important in *Blaquerna*. The novel's
narrative thread is linked to the biography of the protagonist, and
the reordering of the world he stimulates has a progressive character,
wherein each phase includes the preceding one. These latter facts
highlight the idea of a process of transformation within the novel, a

---

33. Apocalyptic movements—and Arnold of Villanova in particular, a precise contemporary of Llull—determined the date of the World's End and of the arrival of the
Antichrist in order to indicate the imminence thereof as well as the urgency of the reforms that needed to be undertaken. For the case of Arnold, see Mensa 1998. For the
Lullian theology of history, see Gayà 2014. Within *Blaquerna* there is but a single allusion to the Antichrist, a figure fundamental to all apocalyptic historical schemata, an
allusion which occurs in Ch. 86, § 3, wherein 'a master of theology, a master of philosophy and a master of medicine likewise made their petitions to the pope and his
cardinals requesting that concise and necessary principles be provided to each science
by means of an Art, so that no science might be in confusion as a result of the proliferation of writings, and that during the time of the Antichrist one might be better
prepared to put an end to his false opinions'. Noteworthy is the lack of determinacy
surrounding 'the time of the Antichrist', which Llull situates in a remote future.

process which reinforces the temporal axis over and above its spatial counterpart. In the renewal of which Llull dreams, time is more important than space: there is no question of conquering any kind of —physical or symbolic—space, but rather of setting processes in motion. Not only does the attainment of such renewal dispense with the miraculous, but it is achieved 'through lengthy persistence'. In Chapter 94, when considering the need to extend the use of Latin to the whole of Christendom in order to facilitate evangelisation, a cardinal speaks to the pope in the following terms:

> Once this has been achieved, it is necessary that women and men should be assigned to go to this city in order to learn Latin and that, when they return to their countries, they should teach it to their children as soon as these start learning to talk. Thus, through lengthy persistence, you will be able to ensure that there is but a single language, a single belief and a single faith in the entire world, *for which reason each pope in succession must be devoted to the above task, as is necessary if one wishes to attend to as important an enterprise as you have undertaken* (§ 3; emphasis added).

Clearly there is an objective, which consists in universal unity, and clearly in order to achieve this *pax universalis* there is a lot more work left to do; Blaquerna is not the pope charged with accomplishing all this, but simply the one to initiate a process. As a result, the novel, which focuses upon the protagonist's biography but whose ending remains open, does not give an account of the realisation of this movement towards reordering (or founding of Heaven on Earth, one might say), but only of the beginning of a new era. Of great significance is the fact that the protagonist's death does not feature within the narrative and that the venerable hermit reappears in other works. An approach such as this refutes the notion that *Blaquerna* is a 'utopian' novel, an epithet which has often been assigned to it.[34]

One of the most important characteristics of the process of renewal stimulated by Blaquerna is that it should be cooperative, integrative and widespread; it involves the necessary collaboration of a team of people, which extends its action, in the form of waves emanating from a central point at which is located the protagonist, by way

---

34. On this question, see Hillgarth 1981-1983 and Ripoll 2012: 21.

of a well-defined purpose and a connection with that protagonist's inner world.

## 4.4. Papacy and Empire: overcoming a permanent conflict

The idea that a pope will instigate unprecedented societal reform has reappeared periodically within the history of the West from the thirteenth century onwards;[35] it is the myth known by the name of the 'Angelic Pope', a theme of a millenarian kind which stated that, at the end of days, the actions of a pontiff, a single individual adopting comprehensive measures, would achieve the utopia of universal reform. The formation of such an idea constituted the culmination of a process which, in the thirteenth century, situated the pope in a position of spiritual and political eminence enjoying universal scope. The profound desire for renewal contained within the myth of the 'Angelic Pope', however, was also proof of the dissatisfaction the Church's situation generated within circles critical of that very ecclesiastical institution.

There likewise circulated a further—and also widespread—idea which accounted for the imminent appearance of a Last Emperor and gave expression to identical hopes for reform. Both themes, though lacking any basis in Holy Scripture, were characteristic of apocalyptic and millenarian trends, carrying as they did an obvious political charge within a Europe divided between supporters of the Empire (Ghibellines) and supporters of the Papacy (Guelphs). The two themes, in fact, namely, that of the pope and that of the emperor, were simultaneously both cause and effect of the identification of the Empire and the Papacy as outstanding forms of power, dominion and ministry; it is significant that, in spite of their having separate origins, both motifs succeeded in merging with one another throughout the thirteenth century.[36]

*Blaquerna* is a unique, unusual and highly precocious instance of the narrative unfolding of this idea, as well as being one of the oldest

---

35. One of the most recent manifestations of this myth occurred upon the accession to the papal throne of Pope Francis in 2013 (Soler 2015).

36. The principal bibliography concerning the Angelic Pope and the Last Emperor is the following: Töpfer 1992, Reeves 1961 and 1993, as well as McGinn 1989. For an interpretation of *Blaquerna* from the standpoint of these two themes, see Soler 1999.

witnesses to the merging of the two characters, namely, the Angelic Pope and the Last Emperor. Let us not forget that, by chance, Blaquerna meets the emperor, who has become lost in the forest (Chapter 48), and that the latter will receive instruction from the young hermit as to a new concept of Worth, instruction which consists in nothing other than an application of the doctrine of first and second intentions (§ 5); it is at this point that the emperor promises to introduce the order corresponding to true Worth into both his household and his empire (§ 13). The emperor will implicitly reappear at the Court of Pope Blaquerna by way of two of his envoys, the Minstrel of Worth (Chapter 78, §§ 4-5) and Ramon the Fool (Chapter 79, § 4), who will offer news of the reforms he has undertaken. In the closing chapter of the romance (Chapter 115) it is suggested that Blaquerna and the emperor will join together in leading the life of a hermit (see the final strophe of the poem and § 5).

In 1283, in the context of confrontations between Guelphs and Ghibellines, *Blaquerna* was, among other things, a political fiction of the most topical kind: a story which gave an account of the pope and the emperor's joint participation in a common project of universal reorganisation, as well as of their both ending up living as hermits, would not have gone unnoticed. Let us briefly recall the nature of the historical context.

James I of Aragon's two heirs, Peter the Great (Peter III of Aragon; Peter II of Catalonia-Aragon) and James II of Majorca, belonged to opposite sides—those of the Ghibellines and Guelphs, respectively —in terms of the confrontation Peter had with the papacy and with France. At the same time that Ramon Llull was composing *Blaquerna*, the matter ended up as an international conflict of considerable proportions. Llull had formed part of the Royal Court of Majorca and, both for strategic reasons and out of conviction, was closer to the papacy's cause than that of the Empire.

In 1262 King Peter had married Constance, heiress of the Sicilian king Manfred. This latter was the illegitimate son of the Emperor Frederick II of Hohenstaufen (1194-1250), who had likewise been King of Sicily, as well as the *bête noire* of the papacy in the first half of the thirteenth century. Manfred was deprived of his dominions in 1265 by the pope and by Charles I of Anjou, uncle of King Philip III the Bold of France. When, in 1282, Sicily rose up in arms against the Angevins—the revolt known as the Sicilian Vespers having taken place in Palermo on 31st March—and proposed Peter as monarch, the Catalan king accepted, on the assumption that he was doing nothing other than re-establishing the legitimate rights his wife held over the island. Between August and October of that year he achieved full domination of Sicily, as well as the expulsion of the Angevins, who retreated to Calabria. Peter thus turned himself into the leader of the Ghibelline party.

The reaction of Pope Martin IV, ally of the House of Anjou, was to excommunicate the Catalan king and, in 1284, to assign the Crown of Aragon to Charles of Valois, son of Philip III of France. In June 1285 an imposing French army, headed by King Philip, crossed the Pyrenees in order to assert the latter's ostensive rights over the Catalan-Aragonese Crown; the epidemic which decimated the French force, as well as the skill of the Sicilian admiral Roger of Lauria prevented the invasion from being a success. In this confrontation, James II of Majorca lent his support to Charles of Anjou and opposed his brother Peter. In 1285 itself, the pope, the Catalan and the French king, as well as Charles of Anjou, all died, though for different reasons. In November of that year, and immediately after Peter had died, the new Catalan king, Alfonso II, conquered the island territories of the Kingdom of Majorca and retained them for the Crown of Aragon until 1298, when he returned them to his uncle James II of Majorca, as a result of the Treaty of Anagni.

Ramon Llull could not remain unaffected by the entire conflict and to the events that derived therefrom. Thus, between 1285 and 1298, Llull did not set foot again upon the island of Majorca; and in 1287, during his first journey beyond the frontiers of the former Crown of Aragon, he repaired to Rome and Paris, that is to say, to the Papacy and to the French ally of the Majorcan king. *Blaquerna* contains a significant reference to one of the most spectacular episodes of the whole conflict, namely, the Duel of Bordeaux, involving personal combat between the Catalan and the Angevin kings, which was arranged to take place on 1st June 1283. Charles of Anjou had taken a bold decision: to challenge his opponent to enter the lists to do battle at Bordeaux, as a result of which contest the matter of who enjoyed the right to occupy the island's throne would be decided. Peter accepted, turned up at the appointment in disguise, drew up a deed testifying to his appearance and returned from whence he had come on confirming that the field of battle was not neutral (i.e. 'victory' was his). In the novel (Chapter 81, §§ 3-6), Llull presents the case of two kings in conflict who challenge each other to a duel; the pope's intervention succeeds in the prevention of personal combat and the deflection of the warlike energies of the two contenders towards a crusade. In other words, he proposes a compromise solution to a case which, from his point of view, constituted a scandal for Christendom, namely, that of two Christian kings involved in internal warfare.

In *Blaquerna*, both the resolution Llull offers regarding the specific case of the two kings in conflict with each other and the approach he adopts towards the debate surrounding the Papacy and the Empire are revelatory of his desire to overcome the conflict— ever present as this was in one way or another in all of Christendom's internal struggles—between its two most eminent authorities in accordance with the framework offered to him by the themes of the Angelic Pope and the Last Emperor. It is also significant that the solution proposed is not one consisting of the sharing of power, namely, of the occupation of spaces pertaining to power, but rather of a participation in processes whereby order is reintroduced in line with the doctrine of first and second intentions; it is important for this reason that both figures, that is to say, the pope and the emperor, should renounce their posts and give way to successors who will continue the virtuous circle they themselves have set in motion.

*Blaquerna* ends with a surprising piece of narrative artifice which emphasises this dynamic of continuance. In Chapter 115, after Blaquerna the hermit has commissioned a minstrel to devote himself to the oral dissemination of *Blaquerna* in town squares, monasteries and courts, with a view to reinstituting the original purposes for which the various offices were conceived (§ 1), we read the following:

> We have now narrated the *Romance of Evast and Blaquerna*. So the tale returns to the emperor whom Blaquerna encountered in the forest, which emperor had brought order to his empire so that Worth might be restored therein, and had bequeathed his empire to his son, for whom he had composed a book of instruction for princes regarding the governance of his household, his person and his realm. And once he had done all these things, he left the world and went in search of Blaquerna, so that together, living as hermits, they might contemplate Our Lord God (§ 2).

On the one hand, the novel is considered to have been fully narrated; on the other, however, the story ('the tale') continues by way of details concerning the emperor. A distinction of the kind we make in the present day between the 'plot' and 'story' of a narrative is suggested here, therefore, a distinction pointing to the existence of a story broader than the plot which has been narrated within *Blaquerna*; 'the tale' would thus consist in the complete story regarding the protagonist and, likewise, the emperor. An episode from that of the latter is, in fact, recounted once *Blaquerna* the romance has ended, namely, the emperor's encounter with a bishop who is travelling to Rome to try to ensure that Llull's *Art abreujada d'atrobar veritat* (*Brief Art of Finding Truth*) becomes a reference work at all universities; the emperor takes advantage of the fact that the bishop is on his way to the Papal Court by imparting certain verses to him which the Minstrel of Worth is to sing. In this poem's closing dedication there is an allusion to Blaquerna, which allusion causes the bishop to indicate the latter's whereabouts to the emperor and enables Llull to suggest a future meeting between the two characters (§§ 3-5). New episodes from Blaquerna's story, episodes concerning his life as a hermit, moreover, continue to appear in two subsequent works: *Felix, or the Book of Wonders* (1287-1289) and the *Liber super Psalmum 'Quicumque vult'* (1288).

In summation, the fact that the story of the pope and of the emperor is broader than the narrative offered by *Blaquerna* the romance, as well as the open-endedness of the book itself, are an expression of the broad and open nature of the process Llull seeks to narrate, a process which includes the ultimate merging of the two loftiest powers of Christendom within a single project aimed at lending order to humanity.[37]

## 4.5. A TOTAL NOVEL FOR A TOTALITY OF READERS

In Chapter 88 of *Blaquerna* reports are given of the journeys undertaken by the envoys that the cardinal of 'Domine, fili unigenite, Jhesu

---

37. For the implications of the open-endedness of certain of Llull's literary works, an open-endedness which should be related to the status the Art enjoys as an 'open system', see Bonner 2012: 329-332.

Christe' has sent *urbi et orbi* for the purpose of learning about the state of affairs prevailing in the world. As could be no different, coming from the pen of an author originating from a Mediterranean country, the news provided with reference to southern lands (§ 2) is much more precise and realistic than that which is presented in respect of the distant lands of the misty north (§ 3). The chief problem regarding the tramontane countries is that 'in those parts there were many people who held diverse beliefs, and that the devil kept them in error by means of certain illusions and deceptions': appearances of white bears which give indication of an abundance of fish; talking trees; hoopoes which unleash storms when one cuts branches from a tree; polytheism; nomadism, and so on. On learning of these devilish misconceptions, the Holy Father and his cardinals decide to send envoys to such lands:

> holy and devout men should be dispatched to these people, men who might know these people's languages and might preach to them by means of exemplary and moral tales, as well as by metaphors and analogies, until their sensory faculties were sufficiently well-ordered as to cause the analogies to ascend to the powers of the soul, as a result of which their intellectual faculties might be enlightened by the Holy Catholic Faith (Ch. 88, § 3).

The missionaries will avail themselves of exemplary tales and their moral counterparts, as well as of metaphors and analogies, with the aim of imposing order upon the sensory faculties (Cat. *sensualitats*)—rooted as these are in the imagination—of certain wretched peoples who live under the Devil's influence. A literature which is disorderly in its intentions can nourish mental disorder because it stimulates the imagination to invent aberrant fictions; if such fiction is in accord with man's first intention, however, it has therapeutic effects, namely, it captures the imagination, imposes order thereupon and leaves it in a position to assist—or, at least, not to impede—the intellectual faculties, that is to say, a person's higher cognitive capacities, in their task of receiving the illumination of faith.

The *Romance of Evast and Blaquerna* is, in its entirety, literature written in consideration of the first intention. And let it be said that it is not simply a collection of exemplary tales, but rather a narrative of

great scope, one that is solidly linked together and capable of constructing a complex significatory universe as a consequence of the
various possible axes of interpretation of which it admits. Llull was
fully aware of having created a literary artefact for all kinds of readers. In Chapter 115, the closing chapter, a minstrel is given the assignment by the hermit protagonist to travel throughout the world
reading *Blaquerna*, and he fulfils this task 'in the town squares, the
courts and the monasteries' (§ 1): in town squares, for the benefit of
the people; in courts, for that of the governing elites; and in monasteries, for that of religious. Included, thus, are all earthly states of
existence: laity and clergy, men and women.

As a romance, *Blaquerna* fits in with the reading habits of a seignio-
rial and knightly court, given that it makes reference, in many ways
and in many of its central and anecdotal episodes, to the exercise of
governance. From this perspective, it can be understood as a book of
instruction for princes. In addition, however, as an account showing
signs, in general, of hagiographical and, in particular, of Franciscan,
inspiration, it ties in with a specific religious sensibility to which the
Majorcan Royal Family had, over time, shown growing affection.
There are clear indications that, to begin with, *Blaquerna* was written
with the immediate context of the Majorcan court in mind, a court to
which Llull himself had belonged, and it is highly likely that the earliest readers of the novel also formed part of this circle. Otherwise, the
allusive character of Ramon the Fool, who appears for the first time
in Chapter 79, would be unintelligible. Ramon's madness or folly has
to be understood within the context of the Majorcan Royal Court and
of the change in circumstances that the historical Llull imposed upon
himself. In this respect, it is very noteworthy that in Chapter 65, § 3,
a highly favourable reference is made to King James II of Majorca as
founder and provider of the monastery of Miramar, a reference
which functions as a kind of dedication of the work to the king and
his Court.

Strictly speaking, however, *Blaquerna* was not conceived as a courtly work and still less as a work written for the Court of Majorca. Llull
himself undertook the task of taking the work to Paris, of having it
translated into French and of disseminating it within an entirely different context, one centred upon a Court but also upon a university,
a context wherein the specific references to local realities had become noticeably blurred, though in spite of which the work did not

lose its interest or meaning.[38] Within the novel, moreover, there are materials appropriate for religious, monks, clerics and also for members of the laity of both sexes and of every rank and office. In Chapter 2, for instance, treating the protagonist's upbringing, practical approaches to child-rearing (i.e. breast-feeding, cradling, the clothing of infants) are presented, approaches solely documented in medical texts, and uncommon in the *'enfances'* accounts regarding a hero's childhood, in the Lives of saints or in catechetical treatises (apart from Llull's own *Doctrina pueril*). Further on, in Chapter 24, Natana puts to full use an art of election which enables one to select with assurance a successor to the abbess of the convent in which she has enrolled, that successor ending up being herself; this system anticipates by five centuries the electoral methods used by Condorcet and de Borda (Günter & Pukelsheim 2001).

## 5. The 'Book of the Lover and the Beloved' and the 'Art of Contemplation'

The 'Book of the Lover and the Beloved' is dual-natured. It forms part of *Blaquerna* because it fulfils a fundamental role in the narrative unfolding of the novel; from this viewpoint, the 'Book of the Lover and the Beloved' is a work whose author is Blaquerna, a character within the fiction. The opuscule, however, is also a work which transmits an experience of contemplation that has a meaning all by itself and can be read, as it often has been, independently from the novel.

A challenge, therefore, likewise dual, is laid down before the reader, namely, to appreciate the role that the 'Book of the Lover and the Beloved' plays within *Blaquerna* and to understand that in which this contemplative experience recounted to him or her consists.

Forming part of the novel, as it does, the 'Book of the Lover and the Beloved' fulfils two functions. On the one hand, it serves to justify Blaquerna's life experiences insofar as it directly reflects his inner life: Blaquerna is the Lover who seeks his Beloved, a fact which uncovers a

---

38. One of the earliest copies of *Blaquerna* to have been preserved belonged to the Canon and Fellow of the Sorbonne, Peter of Limoges, a prominent intellectual. Within his very extensive library, the *Romanz d'Evast et de Blaquerne* was the only work he possessed in the vernacular tongue (Soler 1992-1993).

new dimension of the protagonist. Until that point, this protagonist of
the romance has been, psychologically speaking, flat. It's true that during the episodes within the forest he learns certain key Lullian concepts which will determine how his life evolves, but he is characterised
above all by being a compendium of all the perfections. Insofar as
Blaquerna is the Lover, however, his character acquires a rare profun-
dity, since the Lover is someone who doubts, suffers, sins, becomes upset, weeps, laughs, experiences delight, is reconciled, and so on.

On the other hand, however, the 'Book of the Lover and the Beloved' is a didactic work which Blaquerna writes at the request of a
hermit for the instruction of other hermits. The assignment sets out
from the observation this hermit, who has already appeared in Chapter 97, § 2, makes to the effect that the hermits of Rome 'underwent
many temptations in certain regards because they did not know how
to adopt a method best suited to their lives'. It is for this reason that
the hermit has gone to Blaquerna, namely, in order to 'ask him to
write a book concerning the eremitic life, so that by using this book
he might gain the ability and wisdom whereby to maintain the other
hermits in contemplation and devotion' (Chapter 99, § 1). The opuscule the protagonist of the romance writes is a work of spiritual guidance, a prayer book.[39]

Chapter 99 likewise narrates the process whereby the 'Book of the
Lover and the Beloved' was composed. The question Blaquerna pos-
es to himself as author is: by means of which subject matter and in
what manner should he write the work they have commissioned him
to undertake. As far as the manner is concerned, he invokes the inspiration of the Muslim Sufis of whom he had learned when he was
pope:

---

39. See Ruiz Simon 2015. In Ch. 88, §4 of *Blaquerna* mention is already made of a
'Book of the Lover and the Beloved'. There we are told of the journey to Barbary, in
the Maghreb, of an envoy who bears news of a '*Book of the Lover and the Beloved*, in which
it was recounted how devout men composed songs about God and love, and how, on
account of their love of God, they left the world and travelled around it enduring poverty'. As a result of the envoy's information, 'the *Book of the Lover and the Beloved* was
translated'. It goes without saying that the 'Book of the Lover and the Beloved' which
*Blaquerna* itself presents to us is not the translation of a Muslim book; nor has research
ever uncovered any Muslim work which might, in fact, be the work to which Llull refers. What Llull puts forward in Ch. 88 seems, rather, to be a narrative hint, in terms of
a Muslim version, towards that which will subsequently make up the opuscule written
by the protagonist in a Christian vein.

he remembered how, once, when he was pope, a Saracen had told him that, amidst all the others, the Saracens had certain pious men, among whom those held in highest esteem were certain people called 'Sufis'. And these people use words of love and brief exemplary tales which inspire great devotion in a person. These words need to be explained, and such explanations cause the intellect to ascend, and on account of such an ascent the will rises and grows in devotion (§ 3).

The allusion to Sufi mysticism seems to have the aim of adding certain specific connotations to the opuscule, rather than of linking it to any particular textual sources.[40] What is genuinely important about this passage is the didactic character it attributes to the words of the Sufis, which words, lacking clarity and requiring elucidation or commentary as they do, give a boost to the reader's intellect. The idea that an enigmatic argument provides a stimulus to the intellect constitutes a topic of which Llull makes frequent use and forms one of the foundation stones of his teachings.[41] The 'Book of the Lover and the Beloved', composed as it is of short narrative units packed with metaphors, paradoxes and the coincidence of opposites, has this same didactic character: it raises questions in the reader's mind and obliges him or her to lend impetus to the capacities of intellect, will and memory of which he or she disposes.

As far as the book's subject matter is concerned, Blaquerna opts to write a book concerning the 'Lover' and the 'Beloved':

While Blaquerna wept and worshipped, and when God had raised his soul to the furthest limits of its ability to contemplate Him, he felt that he had transcended method as a result of the great fervour and devotion

---

40. In any case, the question remains open, since this reference has been the subject of a lengthy polemic between those who have found possible sources of inspiration within the Muslim Sufi tradition and those who refute such. We side with Dominique Urvoy (1979) when he maintains that the passage should be interpreted as Llull's adoption of an attitude, rather than as a datum.

41. This idea is formulated, for example, in versicle 354 of the 'Book of the Lover and the Beloved'. See also the following passage from *Felix*: "'Sir,' said Felix to the saintly hermit, "I am in great wonder at your examples, for they don't seem to me to have anything to do with what I asked." ¶"Fair friend," said the hermit, "I consciously gave you these examples so that you would elevate your intellect in the effort to understand; for the more obscure the example, the greater is the understanding of the intellect which understands it."' (Ch. 14; English translation from *SW* II, 722). On this matter, see Santanach 2015.

he experienced. So he cogitated upon the fact that the power of love adheres to no method when the Lover very fervently loves his Beloved (Ch.
99, § 2).

If Blaquerna has recourse to the theme of the Lover and the Beloved,
it is because such a theme has previously appeared within the novel:
once in Chapter 79, § 4; six times in Chapter 80, §§ 1, 2, 7, 10; and once
in Chapter 83, § 14. In such instances, the theme is always connected
in one way or another with Ramon the Fool, who makes brief, and to a
certain extent enigmatic, utterances wherein the Lover and the Beloved feature. In certain cases he identifies with or occupies the place of
the Lover, as occurs in Chapters 79, § 4 and 80, § 7. What seems to be
of genuine interest is the fact that the theme is associated with his un-
conventional way of behaving: when being introduced at the Papal
Court, for instance, Ramon the Fool warns that 'I wish my words to
transcend method, on account of my great love' (Chapter 79, § 4).[42]
Likewise, during his contemplative experiences, Blaquerna feels himself carried away by the strength of the love that he feels for the Beloved; in the process of writing the book that follows these experiences,
however, he incorporates certain very specific rhetorical procedures:

> And this he did every day, incorporating new reasonings into his prayers,
> so that in many and various ways he might compose the *Book of the Lover
> and the Beloved*, and that those ways might be concise and might enable
> the soul to go over a great number of them in a short time (Ch. 100, § 1).

In sum, he seeks to achieve a density of content at the same time as a
brevity and variety of form.

For Llull, to write a book about the Lover and the Beloved is equivalent to writing a book about the art of loving, because the theme of
the Lover and the Beloved, within the Lullian oeuvre, is closely connected to that which he calls *amància*. Seven years after he had written
*Blaquerna*, namely, in 1290, Llull completed in Montpellier an applica-

---

42. Within the novel there are places in which love and devotion are related to
each other by way of an apparent lack of adherence to rhetorical convention: 'Blaquerna took his leave of Natana. Love, which adheres to no method, led Natana, through
her tears, to say the following words in the presence of Aloma and Anastasia' (Ch. 6, §
16); 'Aloma uttered these and many other devout words in which she followed no
method to the Queen of Heaven' (Ch. 8, § 5).

tion of his Art—in this instance of the version called the *Art inventiva*, written in the same year—to the human will in its activity of loving. In the same way as had already been applied to the intellect in its activity of understanding, for the purpose of developing a theory of *ciència* (i.e. 'science', or demonstrative knowledge), his *Art amativa* seeks to develop a theory of *amància*, a Lullian term of his own coinage equivalent to *ciència*, though bearing reference to the realm of love.[43] Llull sets forth the need to make balanced and harmonious use of the intellect and the will or, in other words, to link knowledge and love:

> These two aforesaid properties of *ciència* and *amància* are equally necessary, because God is equally worthy of being known and loved by his people (*Art amativa*; Llull 1933: 6).

The theme of the Lover and the Beloved would be taken up again in the *Art amativa*, as well as in two works which were an application thereof, namely, the *Flowers of Love and Flowers of Intelligence* (1294) and the *Tree of the Philosophy of Love* (1298). In these three works there are hundreds of versicles whose execution is similar to those we find in the opuscule composed by Blaquerna.[44] The Lover and the Beloved are thus the principal exemplificatory device adopted by the Lullian art of *fin'amor*.

Llull calls the versicles which make up this mystical opuscule 'moral metaphors', and the nucleus of the 'Book of the Lover and the Beloved' is very specifically constituted by a metaphor, one which enables the term 'Lover' to function as a new word bearing the sense of 'a believer' (i.e. a member of the faithful, or baptised Catholic), even as that term preserves the connotations characteristic thereof, namely, fidelity, unconditionality, companionship, assistance, fondness, affection, discretion, intimacy and confidentiality. It is likewise by way of metaphor that 'Beloved' signifies 'God', though here retaining the connotations characteristic of the word 'Beloved', namely, intimacy, preference, tacit understanding and the object of love.

---

43. '*Amància* refers to a will that loves, just as *ciència* refers to an intellect that understands' (*Taula d'esta Art*; Llull 1933: 389).

44. The total number of versicles pertaining to the Lover and the Beloved to be found in all four works comes close to one thousand. The theme of the Lover and the Beloved has its origins, in fact, in the *Book of Contemplation* (*Llibre de contemplació*), where it already appears, though as formulated suggests hesitancy. On this question, see Soler 1992.

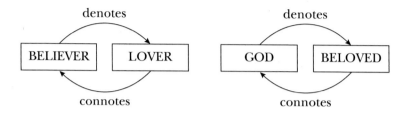

Thanks to this device, the ineffable relation between God and the believer becomes transformed into a story of friendship and acquires all the nuances pertaining to a story of love between friends. We acquaint ourselves with the plot of this story, by means of the assorted versicles which transmit it, in a way that is episodic, abstract and almost shorn of anecdote; paradoxically, however, it is precisely such essentialisation which enables the reader to absorb that story and to read into it his or her own contemplative adventure.[45]

The viewpoint from which this story is told is primarily that of the Lover; in this we encounter a reversal of the customary perspective, namely, that of Christian redemption, wherein man serves as an object of love on the part of God, whose love for the former enjoys temporal priority (1 Jn 4:10).[46] What the theme of the Lover and the Beloved seeks to underline is that God constitutes the plenitude towards which human desire addresses itself; the accent is placed upon this straining towards the plenitude of the being that is God. Versicle 322 expresses this thought very neatly:

> The Lover's memories and desires went on excursions and pilgrimages to the noble attributes of his Beloved, and there kept vigil. And they conveyed His countenance to him and filled his intellect with a radiance whereby his will increased his love.

---

45. The 'Book of the Lover and the Beloved' is conceived with a view to its being read as a term of reference for one's own inner experience. As has been emphasised by Ruiz Simon (2015: 71), Gregory the Great indicates to his readers, in his *Moralia in Job* I, 33, that: 'We should transform within ourselves what we read, because when our mind is moved by what it hears, our life concurs by putting into practice what that mind has heard.' As regards the versicles' content, a useful thematic catalogue is to be found in Dilla 1993.

46. For this reason, it has been aptly stated that Lullian contemplation is anthropocentric (Romano 2007: 388).

The meaning of the Lover's journey consists in his managing fully to become the Lover, a Lover permanently in the process of putting all his faculties to full use: his intellect paves the way towards comprehension of God, though it is his will, which loves, that drives the Lover, provided that his memory does not forget the Beloved.[47] Llull defines man as an animal that humanifies itself (Cat. *s'hominifica*), i.e., is in the process of becoming man; and we could say that the ultimate goal of man is to become the Lover.[48] The foregoing explains why Llull emphasises the irreducible difference that exists between the Lover and the Beloved—an otherness which respects the very natures of them both—as well as why his mysticism should show a clear preference for expressing itself in terms of a relationship between friends rather than one between spouses.[49] Versicle 251 reveals this in the most transparent way:

> The Beloved stands very far above Love, while the Lover stands very far below Love. So Love, which stands in the middle, lowers the Beloved down to His Lover and raises the Lover up to his Beloved.
>
> And from this lowering and raising does Love, whereby the Lover languishes and the Beloved is served, derive its life and origin.

It likewise explains why a proportion of the versicles constituting the 'Book of the Lover and the Beloved' should offer reflections upon the Divine Essence, that is to say, the Divine Virtues, an instance of which we encounter in versicle 37. The Divine Virtues are contemplated in themselves as well as in terms of the relation they bear to

---

47. An important part of the 'Book of the Lover and the Beloved' is devoted to commenting upon the behaviour of the three powers of the rational soul; see versicles 19 and 53, for example.

48. 'Man is a humanifying animal' (*Lògica nova* I, 5; Llull 1998: 14). 'Man is a humanifying and humanifiable being which participates in more creatures than any other' (*Arbre de ciència*; Llull 1957: 867).

49. Llull 'speaks wisely and beautifully about supreme otherness. An otherness which always respects the interpersonal nature of the relation between two different subjects, saves not only the super-eminence of God but also the humble nature of man. A revealing sentence from the *Tree of the Philosophy of Love* makes this point with the greatest clarity: "In terms of Love's essence, the Lover and the Beloved cannot be named without there being a genuine difference between them both"' (Torné 2015: 632).

each other, but also, at a lower level, as things that generate reflections within creation, as is seen in versicle 88.[50]

The story of the Lover draws one's attention to the dynamic nature of the human being and of its progressive growth, a dynamism which compels it to go beyond—ever beyond—itself, and which, for this reason, brings inevitable distress; suffering for love's sake is one of the book's recurrent themes (see versicles 8, 10 and 13, along with many others).

The aphorisms within the 'Book of the Lover and the Beloved' do not follow any thematic scheme or macrostructure according to which they are ordered. To the contrary, rather, given that the themes emerge by virtue of proximity, so that certain such themes suggest others, and are conveyed by means of an array of noteworthy literary devices, namely, dialogue, questions, description, definitions and short tales.

The most celebrated aspects of the 'Book of the Lover and the Beloved' are those which describe the—ever secondary—role created beings (e.g. the sun, clouds, the birds, paths) play in stimulating love for God, as well as the emotional state of the enamoured soul, tormented as this is by desire, forgetfulness, suffering, its own quest, its yearnings and its tears. It is here that Llull draws upon themes from the universal poetry of love, ranging from the *Song of Songs* to the Occitan troubadours, though always from the particular viewpoint of an urge towards the transcendent. The formulations Llull proposes for ancient motifs of universal scope are powerfully personal.

Beneath the apparently scattered themes, motifs and literary devices of the 'Book of the Lover and the Beloved', however, lies a solid structure of thought based upon the Lullian Art, the principles of which appear in a more or less explicit form in almost all of the versicles. Thus, for example, versicle 346 implicitly contains the principles *God - creature - operation* (corresponding to the 'blue triangle' of Figure T from the Art), here as they apply to the Incarnation, for the greatest work (or operation) of love that God can perform in a creature consists in a creature that is at once man and God:[51]

---

50. The role of the Divine Virtues (or attributes) in contemplation is explained above all in the 'Art of Contemplation', which follows the 'Book of the Lover and the Beloved' in *Blaquerna*.

51. Figure T enables one to determine the possible modes of relation that exist between other concepts of the Art. It consists of five triangles each containing three

'Tell us, Fool, what is the greatest and noblest love that exists in a creature?'

He replied: 'That which is one with the Creator.'

'Why?'

'Because the Creator does not have anything in which He can make a nobler creature.'

The 'Book of the Lover and the Beloved' presents various levels of difficulty as regards one's comprehension of the versicles contained therein. Some of its units employ obvious literary devices, as is the case with versicle 228, wherein we find a splendid maritime metaphor for love of long literary standing. Such units are addressed to the reader's sensory knowledge (i.e. knowledge arising from the senses and the imagination), having the sole aim of preparing him or her to gain access to a more elevated level of knowledge and love. This higher level consists in what the powers of the rational soul provide: 'Elevate your intellect and you shall elevate your love', as the *Proverbis de Ramon* (Llull 1928: 82) states. Thus, in versicle 30, Blaquerna gives an account of the theological concept of redemption transformed into a delightful tale of love:

> The Lover disobeyed his Beloved. The Lover cried. So the Beloved came to die, wearing His Lover's gown so that the Lover might retrieve what he had lost. And He gave him a greater gift than the one he had lost.

The 'gown' (Cat. *gonella*) was a long tunic, tied at the waist, and was the most common article of clothing in the Middle Ages; that the Beloved should have clothed Himself in the Lover's gown and come to die while wearing it, is a way of saying that He assumed his very nature in the Incarnation. Even though the question remains deliberately unanswered, it is not hard to guess that the great gift which the Lover receives following his Beloved's gesture is the grace of everlasting life. The same idea is expressed, in similar terms, in versicle

---

concepts: God, Creature, Operation; Difference, Concordance, Contrariety; Beginning, Middle, End; Majority, Equality, Minority; and Affirmation, Doubt, Negation. Llull could thus establish, for example, the concordance between two Dignities or the contrariety between a virtue and a vice.

254. If the reader has been able to grasp this admirable metaphor for redemption, he or she is already in a position to grasp versicle 305, wherein we find described, though with greater precision and by means of parallelisms, the history of salvation:

> The Beloved created and the Lover destroyed. The Beloved judged and the Lover wept. The Beloved redeemed and glorified the Lover. The Beloved completed His activities and the Lover remained eternally in his Beloved's company.

Finally, that reader will even be able interpret versicle 265, in which the formulation is much more conceptual and the aim clearly didactic:

> Love put the Lover's wisdom to the test by asking him whether the Beloved loved him more by assuming his nature or by redeeming him? But the Lover was dumbfounded, until he replied that Redemption accords with the prevention of unhappiness and Incarnation with the provision of happiness.
>
> But another question was posed with regard to his reply, namely, which constituted the greater love?

The first question contrasts the Incarnation with Redemption, and in doing so makes a subtle distinction: the former concerns the attainment of glory while the latter, the avoidance of eternal damnation. The reader will be able to answer the unresolved question, assuming he or she makes advances in the implicit process of intellectual refinement contained within the 'Book of the Lover and the Beloved'. And versicles such as numbers 211 and 232 will assist the reader in reaching an answer.

In the final instance, the process of stimulating the intellect which is designed to enable access to the contemplation of the ultimate truths of faith is based upon the elements and operations which go to form Ramon Llull's Art, both of which latter are present as much in the more literary versicles as they are in the more abstract ones.

Despite the fact that Llull indicates in the prologue to the opuscule that 'Blaquerna began his book, which he divided into as many versicles as there are days in a year' (Chapter 100, § 1), in none of the manuscripts to have been preserved do we find either 365 or 366

versicles. It should be added, moreover, that the versicles are not
numbered in any of the manuscript witnesses, and that in each of the
codices, once the respective quantities have been counted, a different number of units is obtained.[52] In the most up-to-date critical edition of the opuscule, the number of versicles to have been established
is 357 (Llull 2012: 60-63). The origins of this problem lie in the rather
imprecise system Llull used to delimit each unit, since he failed to do
so by means of a figure which might assist one in keeping track of the
relevant number thereof (Llull 2012: 59-60). Judging by the textual
data we possess, the structure to which the 'Book of the Lover and the
Beloved' aspired, therefore, was to remain unrealised. The anomaly
owes its explanation to the fact that the author considered the opuscule to be a fiction within the fiction that was the novel, which novel
did not require a more careful system of numbering for the versicles.[53]

In *Blaquerna*, Llull did not content himself with offering the results of the protagonist's contemplative experience so that one might
have access to his inner world—which is to say, the 'Book of the Lover
and the Beloved'—but rather desired that his reader might enter
into the very cognitive process whereby such experience came into
being. Here we are referring to the 'Art of Contemplation' which follows the opuscule. When Blaquerna was preparing to write his short
didactic work for the hermits of Rome, we are told that '[he] was at
prayer, so he considered the manner in which he was contemplating
God and His virtues. And when he had finished praying, he wrote
down that very manner whereby he had done so' (Chapter 100, § 1).

---

52. In the Catalan and Occitan witnesses the text to have been transmitted is the
same, the only difference resulting from the way the versicles are divided up. In the
French translations of the novel and in its Latin version, the *Liber amici et amati*, however, not only is the text divided up differently, but eight and two versicles, respectively,
are missing in comparison with the Catalan version.

53. From the time of the first printed editions of the 'Book of the Lover and the
Beloved' one can detect a preoccupation with the number of units the work contains.
The sixteenth-century editors were the first to introduce a system of numbering and, if
they added apocryphal texts to the opuscule, they did so, in part, for the purpose of
obtaining a satisfactory number of units. Modern editions which have already eliminated the supplementary texts present in the sixteenth-century editions, therefore,
have found themselves obliged to separate, on ill-defined grounds, certain versicles
which in the manuscripts appear to form a unit, in order to arrive at the figure of 366
such units which, in general, they offer.

The 'Art of Contemplation' give us an account of exactly what goes on within both Blaquerna's sensitive and his rational soul while he is at prayer; it thus narrates, in fact, the process prior to the composition of the 'Book of the Lover and the Beloved' and could have preceded the latter within *Blaquerna*.[54]

Even if the prologue to the 'Art of Contemplation' states that Blaquerna 'wrote a book about contemplation by way of an art' (Chapter 101, § 2), in reality, what we are offered in this regard is not a book written by the protagonist of the novel in the same sense as is the 'Book of the Lover and the Beloved', but rather a work in which an omniscient narrator describes the inner contemplative processes undergone by the character in question.[55] This narrator gives an account of Blaquerna's actions ('Blaquerna rose at midnight, gazed up at the heavens and the stars'; Chapter 102, § 1); of his thoughts (using indirect style: 'By virtue of the power that Blaquerna remembered in the Supreme Good, he was afforded the strength and ability to transmit his thoughts beyond the firmament'; Chapter 102, § 4; as well as direct style: 'Supreme Good, Who art great; Supreme Greatness, Who art good! Were You not eternal, You would not be such a great good'; Chapter 102, § 3); of the dialogues maintained by his memory, intellect and will (Chapter 102, § 7); and of the relations that come into being between his sensory faculties (e.g. his imagination) and their intellectual counterparts ('But before Blaquerna could altogether weep, his intellect lowered itself down to his imaginative faculty, and, using this, it began to think about and to doubt how it could be that before the world even existed, God might have possessed justice, generosity [...]'; Chapter 102, § 5); not to mention the interactions which are established between his will, his heart and his eyes ('his will, therefore, heated Blaquerna's heart so intensely that his eyes wept at great length'; Chapter 102, § 6). In terms of mod-

---

54. If the 'Art of Contemplation' is not presented to us before the 'Book of the Lover and the Beloved' it is surely because Llull intuited that, from the viewpoint of the novel's narrative economy, it was preferable to present the reader with the results of contemplation first of all and only later to explain to him or her how the former had come about.

55. We should identify this omniscient narrator with Llull himself, as is indicated in Ch. 101, § 6. In like manner, the title of Ch. 61 states that Blaquerna 'wrote the book *Ave Maria*', although, in what follows, we read a number of chapters whose themes focus upon the Mother of God, rather than a book whose author is Blaquerna.

ern psychology, we would say that the 'Art of Contemplation' is a
work of a meta-cognitive kind, whose aim is to render cognitive processes explicit.

In the 'Art of Contemplation' we come across a passage which
very ably illustrates the type of relation Llull considers that the reader
should establish vis-à-vis the two didactic works on the topic of contemplation contained within *Blaquerna*:

> So, when he had completed his prayer, he wrote down what he had con-
> templated, and then read what he had written down; yet he did not feel
> as much devotion while he was reading it as he had while he was contem-
> plating the same. Contemplation, therefore, is not so devout when one is
> reading a book as it is when one is actually contemplating the arguments
> written down in that book. The reason for this is that, during contempla-
> tion, the soul rises higher in order to remember, understand and love the
> Divine Essence than it does when it reads about what it has already con-
> templated, for devotion better befits contemplation than it does the writ-
> ten word (Ch. 104, § 12).

The written text, therefore, is expected to serve as but a form of tram-
poline for a—contemplative—mental activity which must needs be
autonomous: one can set out from 'arguments [which have been]
written down', rather than the written word itself, but must proceed
beyond such. By extension, we can say that Llull entertains this very
same idea in respect of his own oeuvre.[56]

---

56. Reading is even a 'sensual' (or sensory) form of prayer: 'like the person who,
in worship, names and utters Your Virtues and Your Honours while asking You for
grace, forgiveness and blessings' (*Llibre de contemplació*, Ch. 315, § 2; Llull 1960: 1005).
One must advance towards intellectual prayer, however: 'like the person who, during
prayer, remembers and understands and loves and contemplates You while remembering and understanding and loving Your Honours and Your Virtues' (§ 3). In this same
chapter of the *Book of Contemplation*, however, Llull acknowledges a third form of prayer
'composed of the two former types' (§ 1): 'It is called the third figure of prayer when
one performs good deeds and practises the virtues, for whenever one is righteous, and
merciful, and true, and humble and patient, and continent and devout, one worships
You and prays to You and invokes You, even if at that time one fails to remember You
or to understand You, yet remembers and understands and loves a different thing
righteously and virtuously' (§ 10; Llull 1960: 1006). Here we find a good synthesis of
the stand *Blaquerna* takes in support of the active life, connected as this latter there is
to an inner contemplative experience.

In the prologue to the 'Art of Contemplation' (Ch. 101, § 2), Llull gives details of the titles pertaining to the twelve chapters which make up the short work:

> Divine Virtues; Essence; Unity; Trinity; Incarnation; *Pater noster*; *Ave Maria*; Commandments; *Miserere mei Deus*; Sacraments; Virtues; and Vices.

He devotes a chapter, in fact, to each of these twelve parts, with the exception of the first, which he distributes across two separate chapters, namely, Chapters 102 and 103, according to whether the contemplation of the Virtues takes place individually or in groups thereof. In an entire branch of *Blaquerna*'s manuscript tradition, namely, the branch originating from the Occitan and French versions, however, an unexpected chapter devoted to the Passion of Jesus Christ appears. Despite the fact that this chapter has, at times, been considered apocryphal, we now possess sufficiently clear evidence that Llull decided to include this chapter in his 'Art of Contemplation' once *Blaquerna* had been put into circulation. This would explain why it only appears in certain manuscripts as well as why, unfortunately, it has not been preserved in any Catalan exemplar. The evident difference in style between the earlier chapters from the 'Art of Contemplation' and the one added—which is much longer than the others, for example—is, doubtless, attributable to the fact that this latter was written a few years after the novel was regarded as having been completed. It is significant in this respect that whereas in the rest of *Blaquerna*, including the 'Art of Contemplation', Llull refers to the Divine attributes, namely, the components of Figure A from his Art, using the term 'Virtues', in the chapter concerning Christ's Passion these are referred to as 'Dignities'. This discrepancy situates the chapter's composition later than that of the *Demonstrative Art* (1283), though no later than the year 1289. As Anthony Bonner (1996), has, in fact, explained, during the phase associated with the *Demonstrative Art* (1283-1289), Llull replaced the term 'Virtues' with that of 'Dignities' when it came to referring to the sixteen divine attributes. In the present edition, we offer the chapter concerning Christ's Passion as an appendix, here translated into English from the original Occitan version by which it was transmitted.

Documentation shows that Llull intervened in other works apparently already finished, works such as the *Doctrina pueril*, to which he added a chapter concerning chivalry, the peculiarity in this case being that the said chapter only circulated via the French and Latin versions thereof.[57]


## 6. NARRATIVE MODELS

In its basic formulation *Blaquerna* includes very clear narrative reference points of hagiographical origin: the Life of St Alexius; that of St Homobonus of Cremona; that of Saint Barlaam and Saint Josaphat; not to mention that of St Clare of Assisi; all of which Lives had circulated in various Catalan or Occitan versions, and at times in both languages (particularly in the *Legenda aurea* by Jacobus de Voragine). The similarities between the case of Alexius and his parents and that of Blaquerna and his own are plain to see. The parents of Alexius, as well as those of Blaquerna, are models of matrimonial sanctity. Alexius and Blaquerna are both children wished for by parents who were initially unable to have any (Chapter 1, §§ 15-18). Both Alexius' and Blaquerna's parents make a vow of chastity after they have had their respective children (Chapter 9, § 1). Alexius and Blaquerna receive a rigorous education (Chapter 2, §§ 8-9). Both leave their paternal homes, renouncing married life, in order to set out on a life of virtue and poverty (Chapter 8, § 8). Their parents lament the loss involved in the departure of their respective sons (Chapter 8, §§ 1 and 4).

The character of Evast, moreover, is inspired by that of St Homobonus of Cremona (d. 1197), who was the first ignoble layman to be canonised by the Church. Evast is a noble burgher obliged to operate as a merchant in order to prevent idleness (Chapter 1, §§ 1 and 12). Homobonus belonged to the middling bourgeoisie and devoted himself to the tailoring and sale of clothing; after his conversion he gave up business and immersed himself in works of charity, taking care of the sick and sharing out food among the poor, namely, the same things as Evast and Aloma do once they have established a rule of penitential life and conduct themselves as Beguins (Chapter 9, § 1).

---

57. For the authenticity of the chapter concerning the Passion of Jesus Christ in *Blaquerna* and of the chapter on chivalry in the *Doctrina pueril*, see Santanach 2005 and Llull 2009b: 67-70. For the Occitan text of the chapter 'On the Passion of Jesus Christ', the reader may consult Llull 2009b: 688-697.

Homobonus and Evast thus belong to a new category of saints, one which does not preclude either matrimony (though subject to sexual restrictions) or work conceived as charity, but rather considers these in a positive light.

For its part, Natana's vocation and her entry into a religious order is inspired by the case of St Clare. Neither Clare nor Natana, who are daughters of well-to-do families, accept the ease of married life as proposed to them by their parents (Chapter 19). Clare's friendship with St Francis of Assisi and that of Natana with Blaquerna play a decisive role in both of their religious vocations (Chapter 6). Clara and Natana flee their parental homes in secret, at night, though accompanied (Chapter 19, § 13). Each of them becomes a nun without delay (Chapter 20, §§ 3-6). In both instances their respective families fail to endorse the young women's religious vocation and seek to dissuade them, using force if necessary (Chapter 20, § 7). Clare and Natana overcome this opposition by means of their heroic virtue (Chapter 20, §§ 12-13), while their respective mothers, Ortolana and Anastasia, end up accompanying their daughters in the religious life (Chapter 20, § 15).

The model of Barlaam and Josaphat, a Christian adaptation of the legend of the Buddha, very widely circulated within Christian and Hebrew circles, makes many contributions to *Blaquerna*, among which the proposal that the eremitic life constitutes the ultimate model of spiritual perfection (Barlaam) is very worthy of note; a model, however, which contains a prior condition, given that the future hermit (Josaphat) has to carry out, as does Blaquerna, the repeated requests made of him concerning the reform of the reality which surrounds him. Various episodes from *Blaquerna* are inspired by situations whose origins lie in this legend, situations such as the temptation of marriage placed before Josaphat and Blaquerna as a strategy to dissuade them from their contemplative vocation, placed before them, however, so that it is not a question of the protagonists' struggles against their unbridled senses, but rather of a damsel who offers herself in marriage as a means of attaining her own salvation (Chapter 6).

The episode in the life of Natana wherein Anastasia attempts to discourage her daughter from becoming a religious and invites her to distract herself by gazing out of the window (Chapter 19, §§ 9-12), an attitude betraying idleness against which moralists expressed their reiterated advice, likewise has its reference point in the legend of Barlaam. What Natana sees on the street, however, is not only the pomp and gaiety in advance of a wedding ceremony, as her mother had intended, but rather the darker side of married life: the pain of giving birth; the cruel fates awaiting children; and widowhood. The experience bears marked similarities to the discovery made by prince Josaphat regarding the reality of death and illness, from which discovery his father had wished to spare him at all costs.

Beyond such specific episodes, in its prose versions, *Barlaam*, which is a very different text from the brief and schematic accounts given in the Lives of the saints, provides a model for lengthy and sustained prose fiction, containing as it does a narrative storyline crammed full of *exempla*, fiction, that is, which includes doctrinal statements and even religious dispute.[58]

Llull innovatively and unexpectedly combines this model biographical account with narrative themes whose origins lie in the chivalric novel. There are a great number of episodes in *Blaquerna* which evoke scenes typical of tales in which knights play the principal role (see Chapter 64, for example); it is in Chapters 42-51, however, in which the protagonist traverses forests in search of a hermitage that the influence of chivalric literature is most evident, taking concrete form in borrowed motifs, situations and characters.

Chapter 48, 'On Worth', stands out as a particularly well-wrought narrative section. Blaquerna, in the midst of the forest, meets by chance a minstrel disillusioned with the troubadour notion of Worth (Occ. *pretz*) and fully resolved, through spite, to censure it, in the manner of a Bernat de Ventadorn, who in his celebrated 'Quan vei la lauzeta mover' ('When I see the lark beat his wings'), decides to censure love and the female sex for the reason that his lady loves him not. While they are discussing the true meaning of Worth, the emperor in person—who has become lost during a hunt for a wild boar, a chivalric motif of long standing—arrives at the place where they are situated. The young hermit causes them to realise that neither the *pretz* of the one nor the daring of the other constitutes true Worth, which consists in nothing other than the practical application of the theological and cardinal virtues. After a short while, they all three arrive at a palace, where, as a notice hanging over the threshold an-

---

58. Badia 1992: 97-119; González-Casanovas 1992 and 1993.

nounces, Worth resides, banished from a society that cares little for her; in this particular instance of the motif of restricted access to a supernatural realm, Blaquerna alone is admitted to Worth's abode and he alone is permitted to address her and to receive instruction from her (§§ 8-10). We thus find that two paradigmatic figures of troubadouresque and chivalric Worth are barred from the palace of Worth itself, while a young hermit and model of religious virtues is indeed able to gain access; this young man, however, occupies within the narrative the position of the spiritual knight characteristic of the prose novels of the Grail cycle.

As far as the episode recounted in Chapter 48 is concerned, the similarities it reveals to an episode from the *Prose Tristan* would not have gone unnoticed, similarities which very probably indicate that Llull had the text to hand while writing his own. King Mark, who has become separated from his retinue during a hunt, finds himself alone in the middle of the Morois forest, and realising that it is getting dark he blows his horn. The blast is heard by Kahedin, who is in love with Queen Iseult, who herself has decided to depart from Tintagel after having inadvertently caused the madness of Tristan. When Kahedin arrives at where the king is situated, the latter hides himself in fear, believing that it is Tristan himself. Kahedin, exhausted, falls asleep. It does not take long before Palamedes, likewise a rival of Tristan for the love of Iseult, turns up and lets out a long lament against love, followed by a discussion on the same topic with Kahedin. King Mark, who has overheard it all, is discovered as a result of a fit of coughing on his part; he tries to pass himself off as a simple knight, but Kahedin recognises him. Following a disagreement with Palamedes which has no further consequences, Mark asks the knight for news regarding the Court of King Arthur, wherein resides the entire Worth of chivalry. The conversation provides material for the king to continue reflecting thereon once they have parted company.[59]

Even though the theme of Worth is not treated until the end, everything seems to indicate that this very theme suggested the entire episode to Llull. The similarities point in this direction: the king/emperor, who has become lost in a forest during a hunt, encounters two characters who have been debating a matter of fundamental im-

---

59. Löseth 1891: 70-71, no. 85.

portance (Love in the *Prose Tristan* and Worth in *Blaquerna*), after one
of the pair had registered grave complaints with regard to the concept under discussion; the king/emperor is recognised by one of the
two characters, yet it is the other who converses with him; and from
this encounter the king/emperor draws material whereby to reflect
upon the concept of Worth. Llull thus takes advantage of a point of
reference which culminates in a debate upon the concept of chivalric
Worth, in order to contrast therewith his own concept of Worth.[60]

There is yet another type of narrative source within *Blaquerna*,
which source makes a particular appearance in Chapters 69-76, dedicated as these are to the eight Beatitudes and devoted as they are to
the narration of the actions carried out by Bishop Blaquerna and his
canons in pursuit of the reform of his bishopric. This source consists
in the so-called legends concerning Saint Francis which arose in alternative spiritual circles throughout the thirteenth and fourteenth centuries, namely, the *Legend of Perugia*, the *Legend of the Three Companions*,
the *Mirror of Perfection* and the *Little Flowers of Saint Francis*. These texts
recount the life of St Francis while inserting therein brief episodes
which reveal the unusual, provocative and paradoxical nature of the
saint and his earliest followers. They do so in a narrative format to
which many anecdotes from *Blaquerna* come close, anecdotes such as
the one in which the canons charged with promoting the Beatitudes
'Blessed are those who weep' and 'Blessed are the meek' meet each
other at the butcher's shop and lament the image of the sacrifice of
the Paschal Lamb, Jesus Christ:

> One day, it came about that this canon was passing by a butcher's shop,
> when he saw the Canon of Meekness inside. This canon was watching how
> the butchers bound and slaughtered the lambs in such a way that they
> suffered no distress and calmly accepted their death. The Canon of
> Weeping asked the Canon of Meekness why he was in that place, and the
> latter replied to him, saying that he was there so that, by seeing the lambs
> slaughtered, he might remember his Lord, Jesus Christ, who let himself
> be bound and slaughtered just as calmly as the lambs, in order to save
> sinners (Ch. 71, § 1).

---

60. We should like to thank Lola Badia for bringing to our attention the close resemblance between these two episodes.

## 7. TRANSMISSION OF THE WORK

Three versions of *Blaquerna* produced during Llull's lifetime and at his own initiative have been preserved: the Catalan original and two translations, one into Occitan and the other into French. The French version was carried out on the basis of the Occitan one during Llull's first stay in Paris in around 1287-89. At this time he also had the 'Book of the Lover and the Beloved'—assigned the chapter number of 99 in the romance—translated into Latin, a text which he linked to a work written during that period, the *Liber super Psalmum 'Quicumque vult'*, whose protagonist is Blaquerna the hermit. The presence of Occitan as an intermediary language between the Catalan original and other languages is not exclusive to *Blaquerna*. It is likewise to be found in the tradition surrounding a work as close to the romance as is the *Doctrina pueril*, wherein the phenomenon should similarly be related to the earliest translations of the text, translations contemporary to Llull. In both works, the Occitan version constitutes the starting point for the French and the Latin translations.

Unlike the Occitan translation of *Blaquerna*, of which only one manuscript has been preserved, namely, MS. 478 from the Bibliothèque nationale de France, five manuscripts have been preserved of its French counterpart. Everything seems to indicate, therefore, that the latter enjoyed a fairly acceptable level of dissemination. One of these manuscripts belonged to Peter of Limoges, who, as has already been stated, was Ramon Llull's first contact in Paris; it is now preserved in the Bibliothèque nationale, bearing the catalogue number Fr. 24402. A second manuscript thereof, dating from the end of the thirteenth century, has been preserved, and is currently located at the Staatsbibliothek in Berlin, MS. Phill. 1911; Llull personally bequeathed this exemplar to the Charterhouse of Vauvert, most probably during his second stay in the French capital, from 1297 to 1299. This codex is a direct copy from the volume belonging to Peter of Limoges. As regards the other three manuscripts which complete the French tradition of *Blaquerna*, two date from the fourteenth century —one of which transmits the 'Book of the Lover and the Beloved' alone—and one from the year 1477. Eight medieval exemplars have been preserved of the *Liber amici et amati*. In 1289 Llull sent one of these codices, the current MS. Lat. VI, 200, belonging to the Biblioteca Marciana in Venice, to the Venetian Doge Pietro Gradenigo;

Llull included therein a selection of his works in addition to this mystical opuscule.

The manuscript tradition of *Blaquerna* which has been preserved in Catalan is considerably later than the earliest French, Occitan or Latin witnesses, some of which, as we have seen, were contemporary to Ramon Llull himself. The most complete codex thereof to have come down to us, albeit that its first signature as well as certain folios from its second are missing, is the current MS. Hisp. 67 from the Bayerische Staatsbibliothek in Munich, and dates from the turn of the fifteenth century. It was transcribed by an anonymous copyist likewise responsible for other Lullian manuscripts whose texts are in Catalan. Dating from the same period is a miscellaneous volume, namely, MS. 1025 from the Biblioteca Pública de Mallorca, a volume which contains Book Five of *Blaquerna*; we situate this exemplar within the Catalan tradition because it is written in this language, although it happens to be a case of a Catalan re-translation of an Occitan antecedent. The two witnesses known as the l'*Exposició d'amic e amat* are likewise in Catalan, witnesses which transmit the text of the opuscule together with a commentary thereon. In the first of these manuscripts it is stated that the *Exposició* was completed in Majorca in October 1492; as far as the copying of the second by Friar Joan Guàrdia is concerned, the task was concluded on 19th September 1646.[61]

One of the factors explaining the paucity of witnesses from the Catalan tradition of the work is the anti-Lullian campaign undertaken by the inquisitor Nicholas Eymerich (Cat. Nicolau Eimeric) at the end of the fourteenth century, a campaign which led to the destruction of numerous Lullian manuscripts. *Blaquerna* was not one of the works condemned in the *Directorium inquisitorum* (1376), although the 'Book of the Lover and the Beloved' indeed was (Llull 2012: 42).

The fact that some of the opening folios are missing from the base manuscript of *Blaquerna* caused the loss of a proportion of the initial text composing the novel, text which remains untransmitted by any Catalan medieval witness. The text of the novel to have been pre-

---

61. The first of these manuscripts forms part of a private collection in Barcelona; the second is to be found at the Arxiu Municipal in Palma de Mallorca, MS. 44. These commentaries derive from an earlier 'exposition' of the 'Book of the Lover and the Beloved', now lost, but which was written in Catalan in Valencia in March 1335; a Latin synthesis thereof dating from the sixteenth century is preserved in MS. N 250 sup. from the Biblioteca Ambrosiana in Milan.

served begins, therefore, almost at the end of the first paragraph of
Chapter 5, although a little bit further on a lengthy passage extending from the middle of paragraph 13 of the same chapter down to
almost as far as the end of paragraph 12 of Chapter 6 is likewise missing. In addition to the loss of the first four chapters, of passages from
the fifth and sixth, of the opening invocation and of the prologue,
the mutilation of the volume must also have resulted in the disap-
pearance of the table of contents one would expect the codex to have
contained immediately prior to the invocation. The most recent critical edition of the novel has chosen to reconstruct the text of these
chapters in modern Catalan, using the French medieval translation,
a Latin version from the end of the fifteenth or beginning of the sixteenth century, and the Catalan edition published by Joan Bonllavi
in 1521.[62]

The 'Book of the Lover and the Beloved' was printed for the first
time, in Paris, in 1505, under the editorship of the French humanist
Jacques Lefèvre d'Étaples. It consists in a Latin version produced
from a Catalan original wherein Lefèvre introduces a large number
of innovations, the most significant of which is the suppression of
forty-six original versicles and the addition of forty-nine newly devised ones. Despite the fact that this is the first edition to number the
versicles and arrive at a total figure for the units which corresponds to
that promised by Llull in the work's preamble, that is to say, the number of days in a year, this achievement is attributable above all to a
desire to recreate the text in a manner intended to offer 'stylistic im-
provements'. The version published by Lèfevre would become canonical, featuring, as it did, as the obligatory reference point for the
very numerous printed editions and translations of, as well as commentaries upon, the 'Book of the Lover and the Beloved' that were
produced from that time onwards until the twentieth century.[63]

The first printed edition of *Blaquerna* in its entirety dates from the
year 1521. The stimulus behind this event came from the priest and
Lullist Joan Bonllavi, born as he was in Rocafort de Queralt, though

---

62. On this question, see Llull 2009b: 63-66 and Appendix I therein.

63. For a commentary upon and inventory of these editions, see Llull 2012: 46-57
and Appendix II therein. The reader's attention should be drawn to the edition of the
*Liber amici et amati* prepared in Alcalá de Henares in 1517 under the auspices of Cardinal Jiménez de Cisneros, and most probably under the editorship of the Majorcan
Lullist Nicholas de Pax (Cat. Nicolau de Pacs).

at that stage a resident of Valencia. Bonllavi must have suggested the edition to Monsignor Gregori Genovart, Canon of the See of Majorca, to whom the prefatory letter with which the volume opens was addressed. Mgr. Genovart must have taken care of the expenses associated with the edition. Within the volume, we find, in addition to the novel, a second Lullian work, namely, the *Oracions e contemplacions de l'enteniment*. This much briefer opuscule offers an account of the process whereby the intellect ascends towards the Divine Dignities. Bonllavi must have decided to incorporate it at the end of the volume, immediately after the 'Book of the Lover and the Beloved' and the 'Art of Contemplation', which make up the bulk of Book Five of *Blaquerna*, by virtue of the affinities of content it presents as regards the book which treats of the eremitic life (i.e. Book Five itself).

The edition of 1521 consists in a volume of fairly generous proportions, in folio, printed in double columns. Each of the two works is preceded by a half title containing architectonic features, as well as further ornamentation characteristic of Renaissance tastes. The loss of the remaining Catalan witnesses copied by hand has been attributed to this very edition printed by Bonllavi. The latter's possible owners would have strongly favoured the printed text, a fact which might have contributed towards the disposal of manuscript exemplars.

In order to reduce the linguistic distance from which his contemporaries might perceive Llull's text, Bonllavi chose comprehensively to rewrite it and to draw them closer thereto. Not only did he carry out a linguistic modernisation of the work; he also adapted its style to the more rhetorical and Latinising tastes of the period.[64] To have done so, however, was not sufficient for him. In an effort at that time still very uncommon when it came to editing vernacular literature, he consulted earlier witnesses of *Blaquerna*, in order to present a text thereof free from corrupted readings. Bonllavi devoted special attention to the 'Book of the Lover and the Beloved'. In the matter of preparing the text thereof, he used not only the Occitan manuscript which has been preserved, wherein we find annotations by his own hand, but also the two Latin editions of the mystical work which had recently appeared, these having been published in Paris in 1505 and

---

64. Schmid 1988.

in Alcalá de Henares in 1517. This was the first time that philological methods had been applied to the task of establishing a Catalan text.[65]

Notwithstanding this, readers had to wait until 1914 before they possessed a truly philological edition of *Blaquerna*, edited by Salvador Galmés and Miquel Ferrà, one that was free, that is, from the influence of the editions of 1505 and 1521. Galmés himself improved upon the 1914 version in a later edition published between 1935 and 1954 in the 'Els Nostres Clàssics' collection. Most recently, in 2009 a new critical edition of *Blaquerna* appeared, the first to take into account the entirety of the novel's Catalan, Occitan, French and Latin manuscript and print traditions, in a volume edited by Albert Soler and Joan Santanach, which is the one used as the basis for the following translation.

Albert Soler and Joan Santanach

---

65. See Llull 2012: 52-53, and Soler 1995.

# Bibliography

## ABBREVIATIONS

EL  *Estudios Lulianos*

ENC  Els Nostres Clàssics

NEORL Nova Edició de les Obres de Ramon Llull, 5 vols., Palma de Mallorca: Patronat Ramon Llull, 1990 to present.

OE  Ramon Llull, *Obres essencials*, 2 vols., Barcelona: Selecta, 1957 and 1960 (Biblioteca Perenne).

ORL  Obres de Ramon Llull. Edició Original, 21 vols., Palma de Mallorca, 1906-1950.

SL  *Studia Lulliana* (*olim EL*)

BADIA, Lola (1992): *Teoria i pràctica de la literatura en Ramon Llull*, Barcelona: Quaderns Crema (Assaig, 10).

BADIA, Lola, SANTANACH, Joan and SOLER, Albert (in press): 'Ramon Llull no va escriure *Blanquerna*. Per a una correcta catalogació de la novel·la lul·liana', *Estudis Romànics*.

BATLLE, Columba M. (1986): *Les vides dels sants pares*, Publicacions de l'Abadia de Montserrat (Subsidia Monastis, 16).

BONNER, Anthony (1977): 'Problemes de cronologia lul×liana', *EL* XXI, 1-2, pp. 35-58.

BONNER, Anthony (1986): 'La data de *Blaquerna*', *EL* XXVI, 2, pp. 143-147.

BONNER, Anthony (1996): 'Més sobre el mot i el concepte de "dignitats" en Ramon Llull', *Estudis de Llengua i Literatura Catalanes* XXXII (= *Miscel·lània Germà Colón*, Barcelona: Publicacions de l'Abadia de Montserrat), pp. 5-14.

BONNER, Anthony (2012): *L'Art i la lògica de Ramon Llull. Manual d'ús*, trans. Helena Lamuela, Barcelona/Palma de Mallorca: Universitat de Barcelona/Universitat de les Illes Balears (Col·lecció Blaquerna, 9).

DILLA, F. Xavier (1993): 'Un catàleg temàtic del "Llibre d'amic e amat"', *SL* 33, pp. 99-126.

DOMÍNGUEZ, Fernando (1986): 'El "Libre d'amic e amat". Reflexions entorn de Ramon Llull i la seva obra literària', *Randa* 19, pp. 111-135.

FRIEDLEIN, Roger (2011): *El diàleg en Ramon Llull: l'expressió literària com a estratègia apologètica*, trans. Raül Garrigasait, Barcelona/Palma de Mallorca: Universitat de Barcelona/Universitat de les Illes Balears (Col·lecció Blaquerna, 8).

GAYÀ, Jordi (2014): 'Una teologia de la història, com a premissa del diàleg intercultural proposat per Ramon Llull', *Comunicació* 130, pp. 223-260.

GONZÁLEZ-CASANOVAS, Roberto J. (1992): 'Parabolic process in Barlaam and Llull's Blaquerna: object lessons and subject roles', in *Actes del sisè Col·loqui d'estudis catalans a Nord-Amèrica*, Barcelona: Publicacions de l'Abadia de Montserrat, pp. 215-228.

GONZÁLEZ-CASANOVAS, Roberto J. (1993): 'Preaching the Gospel in "Barlaam" and "Blanquerna": Pious Narrative and Parabole in Medieval Spain', *Viator. Medieval and Renaissance Studies* 24, pp. 215-231.

HILLGARTH, J. N. (1981-1983): 'Raymond Lulle et l'utopie', *EL*, 25, pp. 175-185.

LE GOFF, Jacques (1985): 'Le désert-fôret dans l'Occident médiéval', in *L'Imaginaire médiéval*, Paris: Gallimard, pp. 59-75.

LLULL, Ramon (1914): *Libre de Blanquerna*, Salvador Galmés and Miquel Ferrà (eds.), Palma de Mallorca: Comissió Editora Lulliana (Obres de Ramon Lull. Edició Original, IX).

LLULL, Ramon (1928): *Proverbis de Ramon. Mil proverbis. Proverbis d'ensenyament*, Salvador Galmés (ed.), Palma de Mallorca (ORL, XIV).

LLULL, Ramon (1933): *Art amativa. Arbre de filosofia desiderat*, Salvador Galmés (ed.), Palma de Mallorca (ORL, XVII).

LLULL, Ramon (1935-1954): *Libre de Evast e Blanquerna*, 4 vols., Salvador Galmés, Andreu Caimari and Rosalia Guilleumas (eds.), Barcelona: Editorial Barcino (Els Nostres Clàssics, 50-51, 58-59, 72 and 75).

LLULL, Ramon (1957): *Arbre de ciència*, in *OE* I, pp. 547-1046.

LLULL, Ramon (1960): *Llibre de contemplació*, in *OE* II, pp. 85-1269.

LLULL, Ramon (1988): *Llibre de l'orde de cavalleria*, Albert Soler Llopart (ed.), Barcelona: Editorial Barcino (ENC, A, 127).

LLULL, Ramon (1998): *Lògica nova*, Antoni Bonner (ed.), Palma de Mallorca: Patronat Ramon Llull (NEORL, IV).

LLULL, Ramon (2005): *Doctrina pueril*, Joan Santanach i Suñol (ed.), Palma de Mallorca: Patronat Ramon Llull (NEORL, VII),

LLULL, Ramon (2009a): *Llibre de contemplació*, Josep E. Rubio (ed.), Barcelona: Editorial Barcino (Biblioteca Barcino, 5).

LLULL, Ramon (2009b): *Romanç d'Evast e Blaquerna*, Albert Soler and Joan Santanach (eds.), Barcelona: Patronat Ramon Llull (Nova Edició de les Obres de Ramon Llull, VIII).

LLULL, Ramon (2011-2014): *Llibre de meravelles*, Lola Badia (ed.-in-chief), Xavier Bonillo, Eugènia Gisbert, Anna Fernàndez Clot and Montserrat Lluch (eds.), Palma de Mallorca: Patronat Ramon Llull (NEORL, X and XIII).

LLULL, Ramon (2012 [1995]): *Llibre d'amic e amat*, Albert Soler i Llopart (ed.), Barcelona: Editorial Barcino, 2nd ed. (ENC, B, 13).

LLULL, Ramon (2013): *Llibre d'intenció*, Maria I. Ripoll Perelló (ed.), Palma de Mallorca: Patronat Ramon Llull (NEORL, XII).

LLULL, Ramon (2013a): *The Book of the Order of Chivalry*, Noel Fallows (ed. and trans.), Woodbridge: The Boydell Press, 2013.

LÖSETH, E. (1891): *Le Roman en prose de Tristan, le roman de Palamèdes et la compilation de Rusticien de Pise. Analyse critique d'après les manuscrits de Paris*, Paris: Bouillon (Bibliothèque de l'École des Hautes Études, 82). Reprinted New York: Burt Franklin, 1970.

McGINN, B. (1989): '"Pastor angelicus": Apocalyptic Myth and Political Hope in the Fourteenth Century', in *Santi e santità nel secolo XIV: Società Internazionale di Studi Francescani. Atti del XV Convegno Internazionale, Assisi, 15-16-17 ottobre 1987*, Perugia: Università degli Studi di Perugia, Centro di Studi Francescani, pp. 219-251.

MENSA I VALLS, Jaume (1998): *Les raons d'un anunci apocalíptic: la polèmica escatològica entre Arnau de Vilanova i els filòsofs i teòlegs professionals (1297-1305)*, Barcelona: Facultat de Teologia de Catalunya (Col·lectània Sant Pacià, 61).

OLIVER, Antonio (1959): 'La fecha de la composición del "Libre de Blanquerna" de Ramon Llull', *EL*, 3, pp. 325-330.

PERARNAU, Josep (1991): 'L'*Ars catholica philosophiae* (primera redacció de la *Philosophia catholica et divina*) d'Arnau de Vilanova. Edició i estudi del text', *ATCA* 10, pp. 7-223.

REEVES, M. (1961): 'Joachimist Influences of the Idea of a Last World Emperor', *Traditio* 17, pp. 323-370.

REEVES, M. (1993): *The Influence of Prophecy in the Later Middle Ages: A Study in Joachimism*, Notre Dame/London: University of Notre Dame Press, 2nd edition.

RIPOLL, Maribel (2012): 'Una lectura no utòpica del *Romanç d'Evast e Blaquerna*', *SL* 52, pp. 3-24.

RIQUER, Martí de (1984 [1964]): 'Part antiga', Vols. 1-4, in Martí de Riquer, Antoni Comas and Joaquim Molas (eds.), *Història de la literatura catalana*, 12 vols., Barcelona: Editorial Ariel.

ROMANO, Marta M. M. (2007): 'Le facoltà dello spirito e della sensibilità nell'arte di contemplare di Raimondo Lullo', in *La contemplazione cristiana: esperienza e dottrina*, Laurent Touze (ed.), Vatican City: Libreria Editrice Vaticana, pp. 375-390.

RUIZ SIMON, Josep Maria (2002): '"En l'arbre són les fuyles per ço que y sia lo fruyt": apunts sobre el rerafons textual i doctrinal de la distinció lul·liana entre la intenció primera i la intenció segona en els actes *propter finem*', *SL* 42, pp. 3-25.

RUIZ SIMON, Josep Maria (2015): 'Les "metàfores morals" de l'ermità Blaquerna. A propòsit de la manera i la matèria del *Llibre d'amic e amat*', *eHumanista/IVITRA* 8, pp. 68-85.

SANTANACH I SUÑOL, Joan (2000): 'Notes per a la cronologia del cicle de l'*Ars compendiosa inveniendi veritatem*', *SL* XL, pp. 23-46.

SANTANACH I SUÑOL, Joan (2005): 'Manuscrits, còpies i traduccions. Ramon Llull i la transmissió de la *Doctrina pueril*', in *Actes de les I Jornades Internacionals Lul·lianes 'Ramon Llull al segle XXI' (Palma, 1, 2 i 3 d'abril de 2004)*, Maria Isabel Ripoll Perelló (ed.), Palma de Mallorca: Universitat de Barcelona/Universitat de les Illes Balears (Col·lecció Blaquerna, 5), pp. 297-324.

SANTANACH I SUÑOL, Joan (2015): 'Ramon Llull i l'obscuritat que il·lumina. Apunts sobre l'origen i la rendibilitat literària d'un recurs exegètic', *Anuario de Estudios Medievales* 45/1 (January-June 2015), pp. 331-354.

SCHMID, Beatrice (1988): *Les 'traduccions valencianes' del* Blanquerna *(València 1521) i de la* Scala Dei *(Barcelona 1523). Estudi lingüístic*, Barcelona: Curial/Publicacions de l'Abadia de Montserrat (Textos i Estudis de Cultura Catalana, 16).

SOLER I LLOPART, Albert (1990): 'Sobre el "Blaquerna", la clerecia i una obra misteriosa', *Catalan Review, Vol. 4, Homage to Ramon Llull*, pp. 263-277.

SOLER I LLOPART, Albert (1991): 'Encara sobre la data del "Blaquerna"', *SL* 31, pp. 113-123.

SOLER I LLOPART, Albert (1992): 'Orígens, composició i datació del "Llibre d'amic e Amat"', *SL* 32, pp. 135-151.

SOLER I LLOPART, Albert (1992-1993): 'Els manuscrits lul·lians de Pere de Llemotges', *Llengua & Literatura* 5, pp. 447-470.

SOLER I LLOPART, Albert (1995): 'Joan Bonllavi, lul·lista i editor eximi', *Estudis de Llengua i Literatura Catalanes* XXXI (= *Miscel·lània Germà Colón*, 4, Barcelona: Publicacions de l'Abadia de Montserrat), pp. 125-150.

SOLER I LLOPART, Albert (1999): 'Il papa angelico nel *Blaquerna* di Ramon Llull', *Studi Medievali*, 3rd series, 40, pp. 857-877.

SOLER I LLOPART, Albert (2015): 'El dinamisme renovador en l'Església: el papa Francesc, Ramon Llull i el papa Blaquerna', *Revista Catalana de Teologia* 40/2, pp. 657-674.

TÖPFER, B. (1992): *Il regno futuro della libertà: lo sviluppo delle speranze millenaristiche nel medioevo centrale*, Genoa: Marietti. Translation of *Das kommende Reich des Friedens*, Berlin: Akademie-Verlag GmbH, 1964.

TORNÉ, Josep (2015): 'Pensament i mística en Ramon Llull', *Revista Catalana de Teologia* 40/2, pp. 619-638.

URVOY, Dominique (1979): 'Les emprunts mystiques entre Islam et Christianisme et la véritable portée du *Libre d'Amic*', *EL* 23, pp. 37-44.

VAUCHEZ, André (1988): *La Sainteté en Occident aux derniers siècles du Moyen Âge. D'après les procès de canonisation et les documents hagiographiques*, Rome: École Française de Rome (Bibliothèque des Écoles françaises d'Athènes et de Rome, 241).

# Translator's Preface

My aim in translating the *Romance of Evast and Blaquerna* has been to produce a readable and plausible, if complex, modern rendering thereof (given that the source text is one of considerable complexity itself), while still preserving some of its more technical lexical features and, to a lesser degree, those of its syntax, where feasible. In this context, it is worth remembering that the sense of Old Catalan words is often closer to that of their classical (or, especially, vulgar) Latin equivalents than to those in Modern Catalan or indeed Modern English.

The tenses of verbs in this text, moreover, require at least some assistance as regards their transfer to an idiom ressembling that of Modern English, not least as regards the fact that in Old Catalan a present tense is often used where, in English, only a simple past will do; likewise, the Old Catalan imperfect tense often requires translation as an English pluperfect. Furthermore, the sequence of tenses in this text is not as rigorous or formalised as modern trends in English still demand. I have also tried to remain sensitive to the mood of verbs in the original text, given that the subjunctive and optative moods are prevalent therein, both of which are less common in English, the latter being mostly in abeyance or, where present, barely noticed. Such a decision may lend the text in its English form a more wistful and provisional sense than it has in the original Catalan, which text, both as regards its composition and content, manifests very directly a great definiteness in terms of conception, methods and objectives.

In the course of translating this work, I have allowed myself a certain latitude when rendering the most common verbs: 1) *esser*; 2) *estar*; 3) *tenir*; 4) *haver*; 5) *fer*; 6) *prendre*; and 7) *voler*, of all of whose literal senses the reader will no doubt be aware. In cases 1) and 2) the senses can, at times, be extended to include 'to live/reside/dwell/abide/lie', as well as 'to constitute' and 'to consist in', while 3)-6) can convey also senses such as: 'to enjoy' (e.g. good health), 'to entertain' (e.g. a thought), 'to harbour' (e.g. a desire), 'to exercise' (e.g. a function), 'to practise' (e.g. a virtue), 'to perform' (e.g. a role), 'to accomplish' (e.g. a task), 'to achieve' (e.g. a goal), 'to fulfil' (e.g. a purpose), 'to assume' or 'to adopt' (e.g. a role or position), and so on, as applicable. Likewise, in case 7), I have opted to translate the verb primarily as 'to wish', but also variously as 'to seek', 'to choose', 'to decide/determine/resolve' and 'to intend'. The same latitude is required, I believe, in the translation of certain commonly used adjectives and adverbs, namely, *gran, fort/fortment, bo, mal*, etc., of whose literal senses, once again, I need not remind the reader.

Certain aspects of vocabulary in any work by Ramon Llull will have a technical Lullian sense, the terms 'virtues', 'qualities', 'honours', 'dignities', for instance, all identifying, in their proper context, the divine attributes which, in Llull's Art or onto-theological system occupy the position of dynamic principles, which are present not only in the Godhead but also at every descending level of created reality, and are primitive and primary in terms of both the order of being and the order of knowledge. *Blaquerna*, however, contains fewer such technical terms than do many other of Llull's works, and we should bear in mind that the text in question is a fictional narrative aimed at a popular audience (albeit one that is hierarchically structured), to which that very text is designed to be of use in a highly practical way. Nevertheless, there are lexical elements within the text which would seem to have at least possible Lullian resonances: I am referring in particular, to give one example, to the verbs common in Llull's treatment of moral or ethical concerns, namely *vivificar* (lit. 'to vivify') and *mortificar* (lit. 'to mortify'), often closely associated with the virtues and the vices, respectively. One could, for Anglicising purposes, translate these terms as 'to enliven' and 'to deaden', but it seems preferable, under the influence of their (late-)Latin senses, to render these terms as 'to foster' and 'to curb/suppress', thus sacrificing some of the Lullian tonality, though, gaining, I feel, in clarity at the same time. Conversely, however, I feel that in the case of terms such as the adjective *contrari* or the noun *contrarietat*, as likewise with *concordant/concordança* and *desacord/acord*, it is necessary on most occasions to preserve their literal meaning given the importance of the triad of 'Difference, Concordance, Contrariety' in philosophical and theological terms within Figure T of Llull's Art.

The level of annotation within this volume is governed by the usu-
al constraints of the series within which it is published, though aims
to shed light all the same upon certain intellectual, cultural, ecclesiastical and ecclesiological traditions underlying much of Ramon
Llull's text, as well as upon historical events, institutions and person-
ages of significance thereto, not to mention upon Llull's own considered responses to such traditions. I have also sought, in as brief a
manner as possible, to highlight within the footnotes certain elements of Llull's 'Art of Finding Truth', given that this Art, in its various formulations, shapes and determines the vast majority of Llull's
oeuvre. It is within the footnotes, also, that the reader will find most
of my systematic and/or specific translation decisions explained.

I should first like to thank Anthony and Eve Bonner for agreeing
to read and make suggestions regarding my translation of the two
poems that feature within this book (the first in Chapter 76, the second at the very end, in Chapter 115), though, it must be said, all remaining faults are my own. I should also like to thank Drs Albert
Soler and Joan Santanach, the editors of the Catalan critical edition
in the NEORL series (for which, see 'Abbreviations'), from which version of the text I have made this translation, and to thank the latter,
my editor at Barcino, in particular, for commissioning me to undertake this task. My particular thanks, of course also go to both of the
latter for their very fine introduction to this volume, as well as to the
publisher's reader, Dr Marcel Ortín, for his attention to and astute
comments on my text.

Though in a general sense I am indebted towards the exemplary
translations into English of a number of Lullian works by Anthony
Bonner, I also feel bound to acknowledge a specific debt to previous
translators of *Blaquerna* or parts thereof. I am referring, first, to the
until now only existing translation into English produced almost a
century ago, in 1926, by Edgar Allison Peers, under the title *Blanquerna. A Thirteenth-Century Romance.*[1] The work has also very recently
been translated into readable, modern French by another experienced Catalanist and translator of Ramon Llull, namely, Patrick Gifreu.[2] Both of the above translations have many merits, not least in
the latter case the modernity of its tone and language, where feasible.

---

1. Llull (1987 (?)).
2. Llull (2007a).

Also of note are the two near-contemporaneous, though markedly distinct translations of the *Book of the Lover and the Beloved* (hereafter *Lover*), both well annotated, by Eve Bonner and, separately, by Mark D. Johnston.[3] I am very grateful to all of these translators for making my own task that little bit easier, if not somewhat more onerous given their very valid contributions. My translation, however, differs in numerous respects from the above, as one would expect. The reader will find these earlier translations listed in full within the Bibliography.

Robert D. Hughes
Prague, 1st September 2016

---

3. Bonner and Bonner (1993) and Llull (2003), respectively.

# Romance of Evast and Blaquerna

O Jesus Christ, great in honour, glorious God, Lord and Creator of the world and Saviour of the human race, and Our Lady, Holy Mary, glorious virgin, may you be the beginning, middle and end of this *Book of Evast and Blaquerna,* one written for the purpose of knowing, loving, praising and honouring God, our glorious Lord.[1]

## PROLOGUE

To signify the five wounds that Our Lord God Jesus Christ received on the true Holy Cross in order to redeem his people from the Devil's servitude, we wish to divide this book into five more so as to impart the principles and precepts regarding the way in which here within are signified five estates of people to whose advantage it is to possess this book. The first estate pertains to matrimony. The second pertains to religion. The third pertains to prelacy.[2] The fourth pertains to papal dominion. The fifth pertains to the eremitic life.

---

1. 'Beginning, Middle and End' have a second and third sense of 'origin, means and purpose' and 'principle, intermediary and goal', respectively, and as such are three of the principles from Llull's Art. Furthermore, remembering, knowing, loving, praising and honouring God constitute man's 'first intention' (or primary purpose) according to Ramon Llull.

2. Prelates (i.e. bishops, abbots and major superiors) form part of the one of the traditional 'estates' within a medieval realm, of which Llull identifies five, based upon a primary distinction between those in matrimony and those not.

**HERE BEGINS THE FIRST BOOK. ON MATRIMONY**

1. ON MATRIMONY

[1] In a city it came to pass that a tall and handsome young noble-man, the son of a respected burgher, had, after the death of his fa-ther, been left with a great abundance of worldly goods; and his father had brought him up to have very good habits. This young man was called Evast, and he was beautiful of body and noble of heart and his relatives most honourable. And he enjoyed such literacy that he fully understood Latin and could read all kinds of writings.

[2] Evast was the object of great longing within the city on the part of religious, and of certain other secular men who desired to draw near to him by way of matrimony.

[3] While Evast was thus sought after for their order by religious and for matrimony by secular men, he gave consideration one night to the orders of religion and of matrimony, and it became his inten-tion to enter that of religion, so as to spurn the vain delights of this world. He recalled, however, the great wealth his father had left him, and the fact that he was obliged to maintain the great household and the great alms his father had given while living this present life. For all these reasons, as well as because he was likewise the head of his entire family, he inclined towards entering into the order of matri-mony. And he decided to offer good instruction and a fine example, when married, to all those who were within the order of matrimony. And he desired to have children who might be servants of God, to whom he might leave his worldly goods, and that prior to his death he might serve God in one of the religious orders.

[4] When Evast had conceived and deliberated upon his inten-tion to love the order of matrimony, he told some of his relatives—above all those whom he greatly trusted—to seek for him within the city some maiden who was of noble descent, for through nobility of descent the heart is ennobled against wickedness and deceit. And he

wished to have a wife who was healthy and well-formed as regards her
body so that nature might enable her to lend bodily vigour to her
children. So Evast asked his relatives above all to seek a wife for him
who was well bred and humble, and that she and her own relatives
might consider themselves to be thoroughly pleased and honoured
by his approach.

[5] In that city there was a noble lady of very sound habits, who
had long been a widow and had a daughter called Aloma. It was widely known throughout the entire city that this maiden was very worthy
and that she ran and oversaw her mother's entire household. And
her good lady mother granted her authority so that she might be able
to run her own household when she was married; and she gave her a
great deal to do so that wicked thoughts which might incline her towards foul deeds should not enter her mind as a result of idleness.

[6] All the conditions Evast wished for in his wife were to be found
in Aloma, and those who had been seeking a wife on his behalf were
convinced of her virtuous habits. So, by God's will, was the marriage
of Evast and Aloma brought about.

[7] The day of their wedding was widely known throughout the
city, and many men and women wished to pay great honour to Evast
and Aloma on that day. Evast, however, wished to give an indication
of humility to the people, who, on wedding days, are opposed to humility and prefer pride and vainglory. On the day of their wedding,
therefore, Evast and Aloma went to the church accompanied by only
a few people, in order to signify humility, and so that there might be
no distraction from the sacrament of the Mass. Evast and Aloma wore
humble clothes; and there were holy and devout people in their company so that their prayers might better be heard and that God might
more pleasurably receive the offering that Evast and Aloma were
making to Him of their selves and of their possessions, which God
had entrusted to them.

[8] The entire day was one of prayer and devotion, in which a
great banquet was held for the poor of Jesus Christ, who praise and
bless God when one gives them alms.[3] And Jesus Christ is signified by

---

3. The 'Poor of (Jesus) Christ' are those who rely on alms to live, though, more
specifically, the term indicates a category of the poor which generally included widows
and orphans, as well as members of the monastic orders who, though they had taken a
vow of personal poverty, were nonetheless able to exercise ownership in common and
were, thus, in certain cases open to endowments.

them at weddings to which the poor are invited, while those who have no recollection of the Passion of the Son of God and consume the worldly goods that the poor lack and spend them on people who are under the sway of worldly vanities are shunned.

[9] On that day a saintly man celebrated Mass so that, by reason of his saintliness, God might set His grace upon Evast and Aloma. The saintly man who said Mass for them preached and explained the purpose for which matrimony is ordained, and he gave worthy instruction to Evast and Blaquerna and imparted to them the rule according to which they should live and fulfil the sacrament of marriage and the promise they had made to each other, so that by them might God be served and in them His grace made evident.

[10] On the day of their wedding, Evast and Aloma served the poor of Jesus Christ and, in remembrance of the humility of Our Lord Jesus Christ, they washed the hands and feet of thirteen paupers, and kissed their hands and feet and clothed their bodies in new garments. And it was announced throughout the city that any pauper who wished to receive alms for the love of Jesus Christ should go to eat at that wedding party.

[11] During the celebrations that day, Evast and Aloma's relatives and friends served the poor of Jesus Christ, and afterwards each of them went away to eat at their own house so as not to deprive the poor of their food. Evast and Aloma ate at the table alongside the thirteen paupers. And when they had eaten, Evast went away for the entire day to an acclaimed monastery of monks and there he remained in prayer and contemplation. Aloma went off to a different monastery of nuns in order to pray to God and praise Him.[4] Evast left instructions to give abundant quantities of food on the day of his wedding celebrations to both these monasteries as well as to all the other monasteries within the city.

[12] Evast suitably honoured Aloma in such a way as to foster within her love and fear, for these two things sit well in a wife's heart. And Evast put his wife in charge of the household, while he wished to devote himself to merchantry so that he might humble himself to perform some kind of office and that he might not remain idle and might preserve his worldly possessions so as to ensure the upkeep of

---

4. Note that here, in line with historical usage, the term 'monastery' is used interchangeably to designate enclosed orders both of men and of women.

his household. For by idleness a person becomes poor, haughty and lazy; while through burgherdom and arrogance certain men have succumbed to the reduction of their wealth and to poverty.

[13] There were no ill-bred servants in Evast and Aloma's household, lest the wicked habits thereof might occasion any dishonourable thoughts to develop in Aloma. Evast and Aloma went every day to see and to hear the holy sacrament of the Mass and, when they returned to their home, they gave alms from the wealth that God had entrusted to them. Following this, they tried to see how they might maintain their household. And on feast days and ferial days they willingly went to sermons and to the monks to hear God's word and to receive instruction whereby they might exist in a saintly state of life.

[14] The whole city benefited greatly from the honourable life led by Evast and Aloma, for both those in matrimony and those in religion drew a fine example and sound instruction therefrom. And they were loved and honoured by all the people in the city. And Evast and Aloma were held in such esteem in this city, that, in them, the men and women drew counsel, assistance and consolation as regards their needs.

[15] For a long time, Evast and Aloma remained together without having children. One day it happened that Aloma meditated upon the passing away of this present life, and she recalled that the reason she had entered into the order of matrimony was so as to have children who might be servants of God. At that point, her eyes filled with tears and her heart with sadness and sorrow because she did not have children. So she went into a garden that belonged to her house and, beneath a fine tree near a beautiful spring, she sat down and wept for a long time there while praying to the supreme God, Lord of all that exists, that through His compassion He might wish to give her a son who should be His servant, and that He might remove from her heart the grave sadness and concern to which she had succumbed on account of her desire to have children.

[16] While Aloma was weeping in this manner and praying to the God of Heaven that He might hear her prayers, Evast, as was his habit, came into the garden and saw Aloma, who was sorely weeping, and seeing her tears he was deeply shocked, so he said these words:

'Aloma, is there anything that I can do so that you may draw consolation? I am deeply shocked to see you weeping, as well as at the sorrow in your heart that your face signifies to me, for I have never detected any indication of sadness or displeasure in you until now. Aloma, my friend, why are you weeping? I thought that I knew your every desire, but it now seems to me that something has entered your mind which you have not revealed to me.'

[17] Aloma thought for a short while, yet was afraid of revealing her innermost feelings to her husband Evast, because she feared and loved him greatly. So that Evast might not become suspicious, however, nor begin to entertain any mistrustful thoughts towards her, Aloma decided to tell Evast the reason why she was weeping, and said:

'My lord Evast, ever since I have been under your authority I have not harboured within my heart any thought or desire which has had as much influence over me as does now the desire to have children. Because it would be a great loss if the wealth we possess were not to have any heir that was our son. And God does great favour and honour to a man when he gives him sons in whom his name and his family line are preserved. For this reason, when I think about death and I see that I have no children to whom this house might be left, I cannot hold back from crying and my heart will not be consoled by any other thing.'

[18] Evast replied to Aloma, saying:

'By God's power, all things are created in the service of man. Yet God does not wish to give man many things he desires, so that man might know His power and will, and so that man might have patience and subordinate his will to desiring the will of God. God does all these things and many others in order to increase the opportunities and ways whereby man might acquire great merit, on account of which divine justice is bound to give man great beatitude in the glory of Paradise. And, since this is the case, foolish is the mind, then, that fails to consider all these things. To want all that is desirable signifies pride, yet one can achieve greater virtue by exercising patience when one cannot have what one desires than the good that ensues when one satisfies one's desire by possessing that which deserves to be loved. And if all the people who exist were to love and serve God, then, having children would be a highly desirable thing to my mind, but since I'm afraid that they might not prove obedient to God, I'm equally afraid, therefore, of desiring to have children.'

[19] Evast presented many worthy arguments and many fine examples to Aloma in order to console her and to remove the sadness

from her heart. And because of the great love that Evast and Aloma felt for each other, Aloma was consoled by the words of her husband Evast, and said these words:

'I bless and adore that sovereign Lord who holds all things in His power. And blessed be He who makes me aware of my lowliness and of the fact that I am not worthy to possess all things; nor am I able to give Him thanks in the way that I should for the goods He has given me. My wishes and desires must remain subordinate to His will; and throughout my life I must desire all that which is pleasing and agreeable to God; and as a result of my foolish desires, I wish always to love God's great mercy and to place my hopes therein.'

## 2. ON BLAQUERNA'S BIRTH AND UPBRINGING

[1] Evast and Aloma always lived in charity, patience and humility. And on Sundays and on important feast days, Evast went to the monks' monasteries and, with them, celebrated in song and praised their Creator, and Aloma did likewise in the nuns' monasteries. And they went round all the hospices[5] serving the sick and, in secret, they visited the shamefaced poor, to whom they gave alms.[6] And they assigned certain offices to orphaned children so that these might not have, by reason of poverty, occasion to sin. While Evast and Blaquerna were performing these good works and many others, God, Who is the perfection of all goods, recalled Aloma's desire, as well as her humility and patience, and gave her a fine son, named Blaquerna.

[2] Evast and Aloma felt great joy and pleasure at the birth of Blaquerna. Evast went to church to render thanks to God and requested of Him that his son Blaquerna might be His servant every day of his life. The day that Blaquerna was born, Evast gave a great amount of alms to the poor of Jesus Christ. A week later Blaquerna received

---

5. Hospice: a place of lodging and shelter for travellers, pilgrims, the destitute and the sick, often run by members of a monastic order.

6. Loosely speaking, the 'shamefaced poor' are those suffering penury and want who cannot face the shame of begging; they are, therefore, to be distinguished from their so-called 'shameless' counterparts, namely, common beggars. As a class, the 'shamefaced poor' included the nobility who had come to live in reduced circumstances, merchants and citizens who had fallen on hard times, widows, women in childbirth, orphans and the sick.

baptism, and was blessed with godfathers and godmothers who lived saintly lives, so that by reason of their saintliness God might favour Blaquerna with His grace. That day, Evast had a saintly chaplain celebrate solemn Mass, and the chaplain administered the sacrament of baptism to Blaquerna, because such a sacrament ought not be administered by any wicked sinner who is unworthy of bestowing the said sacrament, which sacrament is the beginning of the path along which one proceeds towards everlasting rest.

[3] Blaquerna had a wetnurse who was healthy in body so that he might be suckled on healthy milk, for by reason of unhealthy milk infants become sickly and lack strength in their bodies. And the wetnurse was honourable and of good life, because one should avoid a wetnurse who is in a state of sin or who entertains vices within her, or who is of poor temperament, or whose natural condition or breath has been corrupted.

[4] Throughout the entire first year after Blaquerna was born, Aloma gave her son no other food than milk alone; for since they lack a strong digestive faculty,[7] during their first year infants cannot digest other foods, such as bread sops soaked in milk or oil that people give them or other similar foods that people coerce them to eat. Infants, therefore, have ringworm and boils under their armpits, as well as blisters and scabies, and their humours tend to rise upwards and destroy their brains and their sight, and to cause them many other maladies.

[5] Aloma clothed Blaquerna in such a way that in winter he might feel a certain amount of coldness and in the summer of heat, so that the elements of which the human body is composed might be in accord with the weather in which they carry out their activities and so that the body may be afforded a temperate quality, in order that ill humours might not become accustomed to rising upwards. Aloma frequently held her son Blaquerna in her arms. And when Blaquerna was of an age at which he could take steps and play with other infants, Aloma then let nature take its course in him until he was eight years old, and she did not force him into anything which was contrary to

---

7. The digestive faculty is, at least in Llull's understanding, one of four which make up the vegetative faculty, these four being the appetitive, retentive, digestive and expulsive powers. The generally ascending series of faculties is as follows: instrumentative, elementative, vegetative, sensitive (including a sixth sense, *affatus*, or speech), imaginative, and rational.

the things which nature demands of such infants. When Blaquerna was eight years old, his father Evast began teaching him to read and he caused him to be educated in accordance with the contents of the *Book of Instruction for Children*,[8] in which it is explained that, to start with, one should impart information to one's son in the vernacular and should give him instruction in and knowledge of the Articles of Faith, the Ten Commandments, and the Seven Sacraments of the Holy Church, as well as the seven virtues and the seven deadly sins, and the other things contained in the said book.

[6] One day it came to pass that Aloma gave her son, when he had to go to school, roasted meat for breakfast, and she gave him a pastry[9] that he could eat at school if he were to become hungry. When Evast learned of this, he rebuked Aloma harshly, telling her that one must not give children anything to eat in the morning apart from bread alone, lest they develop the habit of being greedy or sweet-toothed and lest they lose their appetite for eating at table when it is time for lunch. For, if they eat bread alone, children do not take such pleasure in doing so that they constrain nature's activities by eating a large amount. So, therefore, no food apart from bread alone should be given to children either first thing in the morning or at tea-time, and, what's more, bread should not be given to them unless they ask for it.

[7] Blaquerna was familiarised with all kinds of food so that his nature might not become accustomed to one such kind more than another. So neither strong nor too heavily diluted wine, nor spicy sauces which destroy one's natural heat, were permitted to him. A student was given to Blaquerna as a guardian and a teacher, and the student took him each morning before school to church and taught him to pray to God; and after Mass he took him to the music school so that Blaquerna might be able to assist with sung Mass.

[8] Blaquerna learned so much grammar[10] that he was able to understand and to speak Latin. After this he learned logic and rheto-

---

8. I.e. Llull's own *Doctrina pueril* (1274-76), whose Prologue details how a child's education should initially be conducted in the vernacular, and which goes on to discuss the Articles of Faith; the Ten Commandments; the Seven Sacraments; the seven virtues; and the seven deadly sins. Other themes covered by the *Doctrina pueril* include: the Seven Gifts of the Holy Spirit; the Eight Beatitudes; the Seven Joys of Our Lady; the Three Laws; and the Seven Arts.

9. *Flaó* (Cat.): a Catalan pastry, varying in shape according to region, often filled with cottage cheese; it can be either savoury or sweet.

10. I.e. Latin grammar.

ric, as well as natural philosophy so that he might more easily be able to acquire knowledge about the science of medicine in order to preserve the health of his body; and also about the science of theology so as to know, love, praise and serve God and so that his soul might dwell in the everlasting glory of Paradise.[11]

[9] When Blaquerna had studied the book called *The Book of the Principles and Degrees of Medicine*,[12] whereby he acquired sufficient knowledge to govern the health of his body, his father then had him study the science of theology, in which he heard explanations of Holy Scripture and answered theological questions.[13] While Blaquerna was learning in this fashion, Evast raised him with love and fear, for children should be brought up by means of these two virtues and, according to their age, likewise by means of fasting, prayer, confession and alms-giving, as well as humbleness in speech and dress and the company of virtuous people. And Evast taught other things similar to these to his son Blaquerna so that, when he had reached a suitable age, he might be, by habit and nature, of such a condition as to be highly pleasing to God and to people, and as not to prove resistant to acquiring the habits consonant with good behaviour.

### 3. ON THE QUESTION EVAST SET TO HIS SON BLAQUERNA

[1] Through the grace of divine light, Evast remembered the time during which he desired to enter a religious order. And he wished to test whether his son Blaquerna would be able to govern himself and

---

11. In the Middle Ages, instruction in the seven liberal arts was structured according to a division between the more elementary studies of the *trivium* (grammar, dialectic—i.e. logic—and rhetoric) and the more advanced subjects of the *quadrivium* (arithmetic, music, geometry and astronomy). Note also the primacy here attached to theology, viewed as a science. Science, here, was defined as deductive knowledge from self-evident first principles, as sketched out in Aristotle's *Posterior Analytics*.

12. I.e. Llull's own *Començaments de medicina* (1274-83), one of the so-called *Quattuor libri principiorum* (of the same date), these being texts concerning the principles of the four medieval sciences: medicine, philosophy, theology and law.

13. Scholastic method in the Theology faculty, which a student might enter only after receiving his Bachelor's degree from the Arts faculty, began with the reading and commentary upon (*lectio*) a sacred text by a presiding Master, followed by a period of reflection thereon (*meditatio*) by the students, after which any *quaestiones* occurring to the latter could be presented, *quaestiones* which the Master was expected to resolve in a *determinatio*.

run the household in such a way that it might be to God's honour, so
that Evast and Aloma might be able to enter religion and renounce
their worldly goods. While Evast was engaged in such reflections, his
son Blaquerna came back from school. He was very young, courteous
and pleasant in appearance, and he was eighteen years of age; he was
of very good bearing and was highly obedient to his father and his
mother.

[2] 'Beloved son', said Evast, 'I want you to answer this question for
me. In a castle close to this city, which castle lies at the entrance to a
great forest, it came to pass that a balister[14] went out to hunt red deer,
roe deer and other wild beasts in the forest, as was his custom. It so
happened that he wounded a deer with an arrow and that he followed
it all day, yet could not catch up with it or locate it. While the balister
was returning to the city, he came across a snarer who was carrying the
arrow in his hand. The balister asked the snarer where he had obtained that arrow, which belonged to him. The snarer replied that he
had found it in a dead deer he had come across and had sold to some
butchers. The question arose between the two as regards who should
receive the value the snarer had obtained for the deer, because the
balister said that he had slain it and that, were he not to have wounded
it, the snarer would not have found it dead. The snarer said that fortune had given it to him and that the balister had lost all hope of finding the deer, since he was on his way back to the city. Each of them',
said Evast, 'put forward strong arguments on his side. I now wish to
know how you might judge as regards to whom this deer should be
awarded, or whether it should be divided between the two of them.'

[3] Blaquerna replied to Evast:

'My lord, as well you know, occasion[15] is more powerful than fortune, because the ultimate end[16] for which the deer was wounded and
slain lies in occasion, while fortune is something which possesses no
end either in itself or in other people. And because the snarer found

---

14. A crossbowman.

15. In a general sense, the term 'occasion' can be considered equivalent to the
senses of 'ground', 'circumstance', or 'opportunity'. In Lullian metaphysics, at least at
the time of his *Llibre de contemplació en Déu* (*The Book of Contemplation on God*; hereafter
*LC*), 1273-74 (?), here ORL VIII, 540-41, the term is used interchangeably with 'cause',
and since such occasion/cause has greater affinity with Being (i.e. perfection) than
does fortune, which itself has greater affinity with non-being or privation, the former
carries positive connotations whereas the latter conspicuously does not.

16. Cat. *final intenció*: ultimate end or final cause (i.e. purpose).

the deer by fortune yet the deer was slain by occasion, and occasion coincides with the one who slew the deer, therefore, according to right and justice, in order to preserve the superiority occasion enjoys over fortune, one should award the deer to the balister. For, were it to be awarded to the snarer, offence would be caused to occasion, and fortune would be honoured with a distinction which ill befits it. And this is why, without a moment's hesitation, I award the value of the deer to the balister. The balister, however, ought first of all to prove that the arrow is his, for it is possible that the arrow might belong to another balister who could have slain the deer.'

[4] Evast asked Blaquerna whether it was fair that the snarer should return the deer to the balister or the value that he had obtained for it. Blaquerna answered by saying that the butcher was entitled to the deer:

'Because, as is customary in his trade, he had bought it believing that it belonged to the snarer, and because the snarer had sold it with the intention that the value should be his. An injustice would be done to the butcher, therefore, if he was prevented from obtaining the profit he was due to achieve from the deer. And the fact that the snarer should obtain recompense means that he should not incur a loss therefrom, which loss he would incur if he repaid the value to the butcher and returned the deer to the balister. For this reason, it is fair that he should only give the value of the deer back to the balister.'

[5] Evast said to Blaquerna:

'Tell me whether the balister is obliged to give anything to the snarer in return for the value of the deer.'

'My lord', said Blaquerna, 'there are two general kinds of law in this world, from which derive all the other particular laws. The first kind is in accordance with God; the second kind is in accordance with the world. And it is necessary that the kind of law that is regulated and ordered in accordance with God should be more subtle[17] and more scrupulous than the kind of law that is regulated and ordered in accordance with the world. On account of this difference between the two above laws are you able to know that, in keeping with the nobler and more necessary law, and out of consideration for charity, conscience and brotherliness, as well as out of courtesy against greed and envy, the balister should give something to the snarer for his ef-

---

17. In the sense of discerning.

forts. In order that the balister might come to acquire the aforesaid virtues independently through his free will by giving to the snarer some part of the value of the deer, however, it is ordained according to divine ordinance and according to worldly law that the balister should not be obliged by worldly law to give any part of the value of the deer to the snarer. For, were he obliged to do so, the liberty that corresponds to merit would not arise, by which liberty one can come to attain the aforesaid virtues; nor would worldly law be subject to heavenly law and, were it not to be so, God would have offended the nobler law in order to elevate the less noble, which is impossible and can be contradicted.'

[6] Evast said to Blaquerna:

'Tell me, son, whether the balister commits a sin if he fails to give anything to the snarer, a sin whereby he might warrant the torments of Hell.'

Blaquerna answered:

'My lord, there exists a distinction between deadly and venial sin; and if the snarer had any right to possess part of the value of the deer, the ordering of the two aforesaid rules would be contrary to justice and to God. But that is impossible. On account of this impossibility you can understand and know that the balister does not commit a deadly sin if he fails to give anything to the snarer. But since he does not wish to exercise courtesy or charity as would be fitting according to his conscience, he therefore commits a venial sin, whereby he does not warrant everlasting damnation, but rather, as a result, should enjoy less glory.'

[7] Evast asked his son Blaquerna all these questions and many others whose exposition would prove lengthy, yet Blaquerna answered them all with great perfection. When Evast realised that his son was enlightened with knowledge and good customs in such a way, he consequently became very happy and went into a chapel that he had at his house, a chapel in which Evast and Aloma would pray to God in private and attend Mass, and to which, on rising from the table, they would go to give thanks to God. The altar was dedicated to Saint Andrew, whom Evast and Aloma trusted to solicit grace and blessings on their behalf from God.

[8] When Evast was in the chapel, he knelt down before the altar and made the sign of the Holy Cross, as had become his custom, saying the following words:

'Glorious Lord God, Who has not forgotten his servant, who for so long has desired to serve You and honour You within a religious order! Blessed be You, Lord, and blessed be Your compassionate and humble mercy, which has sought to fulfil my desires as regards my son Blaquerna — to whom I have hoped and desired for such a long time to be able to entrust my worldly possessions, so that Aloma and I might be in a position to contemplate, love and serve You, in a religious order, while recalling Your Holy Passion and weeping for our sins, our faults and our trespasses. Lord, I worship Your goodness, Your greatness, Your power, Your wisdom and Your love, as well as the other Virtues in which You are one God in essence, Father and Son and Holy Spirit![18] Blessed be You, Lord, in Your Virtues and Your Qualities,[19] for You have given me a son so wise and of such worthy bearing, a son to whom from this day onwards I can leave and entrust responsibility for this household which You have commissioned me, Lord, to preserve.

4. ON THE DISPUTE EVAST HAD WITH ALOMA, WHO DID NOT WISH TO LET HIM ENTER RELIGION

[1] Evast gave considerable thought as to how he would reveal his inner feelings to Aloma and how he could induce her to enter a religious order, for he feared greatly that she might prevent him from doing so. The following day, after Mass, Evast and Aloma remained in the chapel while all the others went away, and Evast said the following words to Aloma:

'Aloma, friend, by God's power is our son Blaquerna filled with great wisdom and of worthy bearing, and has he already reached an age when we can entrust to him all our possessions and the running

---

18. God's 'Virtues' (some of which are listed here) are His perfect attributes, which under various names (Virtues, Qualities, Dignities) form the Principles of the Lullian Art. Throughout *Blaquerna* I have translated the terms *honors* and *honraments* in the most literal manner as 'Honours', since I believe they are precise equivalents to Llull's other protean designations for God's attributes such as are noted above. I have done so even at the risk of rather untranslatory repetition, as occurs in the case of phrases such as *honrar los honraments/honrar sos honraments*. As the reader will see, in Ch. 113, § 3 below, the term *honrament* is synonymous with the sense of 'quality'.

19. Cat. *en les teves virtuts i en els teus honors*. The coupling of (near-)synonymous terms is very common in medieval rhetoric. See previous note.

of this our household. It is time that Blaquerna had a wife and that
the two of us abandon this world and enter a religious order to live in
greater sanctity. And in the same way that, up to now, by our virtuous
lives we have been a light and a lesson to those who exist within the
order of matrimony, we should likewise by sanctity of life set a perfect
example to those who exist within religious orders. It is fitting, therefore, that we should take a part of our worldly wealth and for the love
of God give it to the poor of Jesus Christ, and that you should choose
the monastery of ladies that best pleases you and that I, with your
permission, might enter a religious order, which is something I have
desired for such a long time.'

[2] The words Evast had said to her seemed very unusual to Aloma, and they caused a marked change in her colour, while in her
heart she feared that Evast had taken a dislike to her whereby he
might wish to part company with her. So, before replying to him, she
began to think, and, as a result, Evast said to her:

'Aloma, why is it that you don't answer me? What is it that you are
thinking about? Did you hear what I said?'

'My lord', said Aloma, 'I heard what you said perfectly well, yet
you have made me suspect that you harbour some kind of ill will towards me as a result of which you wish to leave me. If you feel that I
have disappointed you in any respect, I beg you to take vengeance on
me in a different way and not to abandon me now that, at the end of
my days, I have greater need than ever of your help and guidance.'

[3] 'Aloma', said Evast, 'Rest assured that my will has never felt
anger towards you nor towards your deeds. I want you to know, rather, that all the days of my life, since the time it pleased God that we
might both be together, I have given thanks to Him, Who has given
me your company, because among the gifts that God grants to those
who love Him, the gift of good company is ever worthy of praise. Do
not think or fear, therefore, Aloma, that I am at all upset with you, but
rather I ask your forgiveness if I have ever done anything towards you
which may have caused you displeasure. But since we are at the end
of our lives, and since a religious order is more saintly than the order
in which we exist—and one must draw as close to God as one can, and
closer still, since we[20] have the opportunity to do so—I beg you, there-

---

20. The editors of the Catalan critical edition note the abrupt change of subject in
this clause.

fore, who have never disobeyed my requests or my words, now to obey the requests I make to you, so that we may both enter the contemplative life and leave the active life to our son Blaquerna. Let us do what we can so that by the grace of God Most High we may be together perpetually in the glory of God.'

[4] 'My lord Evast', said Aloma, 'I must answer your words with shame and fear, yet the God of glory knows that I have never entertained the thought or opinion that I might have to disobey you in any way nor that there might be disagreement between my will and yours. Given, however, that the beginning of our union was by order of matrimony and a beginning always bears relation to its end, namely, that we should always be together until the end, when death separates us; know, therefore, my lord, that in no way do I wish to be in conflict with the beginning of the first order in which God has placed me and in which God has preserved me and has kept me from committing any sin against that order. And to all the other things that you wish to do, wherein God may be served and you may take pleasure, I consent most willingly; however, on no account will I leave the order in which God has placed me. And, with all due respect, you should not counsel me to take up a different order towards which I do not feel as much devotion as I do towards the order in which I exist, for many men and many women despise their order and leave it due to a lack of devotion. And I beg you to tell me the reason why you have greater esteem for the order of religion than you do for the one in which you exist.'

[5] 'Aloma', said Evast, 'your answer saddens me greatly, although it might be the case that in order to please me you seek to demonstrate that you leave the order in which you exist against your will and take up the order of religion for love of me, so that I might feel more obliged towards you as a result. You do not have to seek a way of pleasing me more nor of obliging me any further, for I am very content with you and with your conduct; let us try to please God, Whose judgement we must all ultimately face. And may you know that since I am aware of your saintly life as well as aware of many defects in myself, I am of the opinion that you are more eager to pass into the holy order of religion than I am.'

[6] When Aloma heard that Evast suspected that she was only exempting herself in order to tempt him or to please him, her eyes filled with tears and she began to weep very profusely, so, sighing, she replied to him, saying:

'My lord, God alone is aware of people's most heartfelt thoughts, so may you know, in truth, that my heart has never borne as much pain or affliction as it does right now that it stands opposed to your will. For the good love that I have always entertained for you constrains me with such great force when I fail to obey your will that tears from my heart rise up to my eyes, and my eyes feel shame at being in your presence, and my anguished conscience makes me think that a moral flaw may exist where there is no imperfection at all. I, therefore, let you know, my lord, that I answer you in accordance with my will and with my order; and my will constrains and afflicts me because I fail to obey your will, and it makes me loathe separation and estrangement between you and me. So to be separated from you, therefore, would cause me harm, since my will wishes always to possess you and my eyes wish to behold you. It saddens me not to be able to carry out that which would please your will, at which pleasure my will would forever feel disconsolate and angry.'

[7] 'Aloma', said Evast, 'your demeanour and your good conduct please me greatly and, what's more, God wishes a man to love his virtuous wife. So, for all these reasons and for many more, I shall feel a great affliction in my heart if I part company with you. Because I am very happy whenever I see you and when I remember your worthy habits, and I am very happy when I hear people saying favourable things about you. However, because I must love my Creator and my Saviour more than any other thing, and because I desire to consecrate and administer His glorious body in Communion, the strength, therefore, of great desire causes me to forget the tribulation I shall suffer if I part company with you. Know, then, that in my heart lies a great affliction at the fact that I am the occasion of anything which may offend or displease you. And because love lends a person strength, as well as the power to endure and disdain many trials for its sake, I beg you, therefore, that in order to love and serve God, love may make the two of us suffer and endure the trials which will result from our parting.'

[8] 'My lord Evast', said Aloma, 'it is true that in this world there is no office as noble or beneficial as to consecrate and venerate the holy body of Our Lord God, Jesus Christ. And precisely because it is such a noble thing, it is not, therefore, permissible to attain to that holy mystery other than in a properly ordered manner;[21] nor, in or-

---

21. I.e. as an ordained cleric.

der to attain to such order, should one cause harm or tribulation to others, in whom that tribulation might generate anger or occasion for sin; nor is every man worthy of such a glorious office, and nor should he consider himself to be so. Thus, if you, My lord, desire to be a chaplain and to celebrate Mass, content yourself with going to church every day with the brothers and helping them celebrate Mass by reading the epistles, the readings, the responses and antiphons, and by replying to the chaplain who says Mass, as is already your custom. For though in your heart you may desire to be a chaplain, you do not consider yourself worthy to be such, since you are not so, given that God has not placed you in circumstances in which you may be thus, due to the fact that you are already in the order of matrimony. And every day I shall go to the nuns, as is already my custom, and I shall help them to sing and to respond to the Mass as well as to the honour of the holy sacrifice of the altar.[22] Let us do all we can; let us not, however, leave the order in which we exist.'

[9] 'Aloma', said Evast, 'it irks me to possess and to deal with worldly goods, because prayers are impeded thereby. And the desire to abandon carnal pleasures and to devote myself to prayer has entered my heart with such force, that there dwells within it nothing else but God alone. And I should like to carry out penance and satisfaction for the sins I have committed by eating, drinking, dressing up and lying in comfortable beds.[23] And I feel a powerful urge to preach the word of God and the Passion of His Son. And, given that religion is the estate most disposed towards all these things and to many others, I should therefore like to withdraw from the world and the order in which I exist so as to abide in the order wherein the blessed religious perform all the above things. So then, if you deprive me of as many blessings as I can obtain by belonging to a religious order, you will be opposing the increase of my happiness.'

[10] 'My lord', said Aloma, 'if you wish to withdraw from the world in order to serve God more fully and you wish to leave all your possessions to Blaquerna so that you and I might stay together, I am happy. Together in this chapel we shall be able to worship and offer prayers to God, and you will not have to deal with worldly goods or with the needs of our bodies, because Blaquerna will be able to take care of all

---

22. I.e. the Eucharist.
23. Cf. Mark 1:15.

of that. As a result, you need not enter a different order. If you wish
to undertake penance and lead an austere life, it will be much more
convenient for you to do so in your home than in a religious order,
and you will be able to undertake this in greater secrecy while in the
order of matrimony than in that of religion. Or if you wish to go to a
wilderness or to a mountain so that we may do penance there, I am
prepared to do so too.[24] And the more austere the life we lead and the
better we worship the King of Glory, the happier will be my soul
thereat. And let us practise chastity and abstain from knowing each
other in carnal pleasure. And instead of preaching you can, by saintly
life and virtuous example, preach to all those who are in the estate of
matrimony, and strengthen the religious as regards their order. And
you can do with me whatsoever you wish, as long as you do not command me to do anything that is contrary to the union which exists
between you and me.'

[11] 'Aloma', said Evast, 'it is a great virtue to be in a state of obedience and to grant and subject one's own will to others for the love
of Our Lord God.'

'My lord Evast, it is a great virtue to be master of one's own will,
which will each person knows better in himself than in another.'

'Aloma', said Evast, 'he attains great merit for himself who re-
nounces all things for the love of God and surrenders himself to the
service of God.'[25]

'My lord Evast', said Aloma, 'he has great merit who abides in the
world and possesses worldly goods sinlessly and surrenders himself to
serving the poor of Christ. And it is a great virtue to be wealthy in the
goods of this world and to be poor in spirit.[26] And if it is a virtue to
beg, for the love of God, it does not follow, therefore, that it is a vice

---

24. On deserts/wildernesses (Cat. *desert*) and mountains as sites of Christ's prayer,
see Lk 5:16 and Lk 6:12, respectively.

25. Cf. Matt 19:21. Well-known precedents for Evast's proposal are to be found in
the cases two late-antique wealthy Christian couples: Valerius Pinianus and his wife
Melania; and Meropius Pontius Paulinus and his wife Therasia. Both couples disposed
of a great deal of their worldly assets and distributed these to the poor, the former
couple, after their conversion, living a celibate married life and between them founding convents and monasteries, even for a while living in a hermitage. Paulinus, for his
part, became ordained, and settled with his wife at Cimitile, close to the shrine of St
Felix (regarding which latter saint, the reader should note the title of Llull's own *Fèlix,
o Llibre de meravelles* (*Felix, or the Book of Wonders*) (1287-89)).

26. Cf. Matt 5:3.

to give to the poor who beg, for the love of God. And it is dangerous to leave such great wealth to Blaquerna, who is young and whom you have still not tested as to whether he would be able to administer the wealth of this world. I would consider it good counsel, therefore, for you and I to carry out the penance which you desire within this household, yet if you think that we may venture out, I am happy to do so. Let us teach our son Blaquerna, then, how to be able to administer worldly wealth, so that it may be kept for the poor of Jesus Christ who each day receive provision from this household from the alms that you give them.'

[12] 'Aloma', said Evast, 'I have given you many true and compelling arguments whereby you must obey my requests. I beg you, moreover, not to exonerate yourself or to disobey me, but rather to satisfy me as regards that which I have desired for so long, and to refrain from causing sadness to enter my soul, as well as to prevent any resentment towards you from entering my will, since I have always loved you loyally.'

'My lord Evast', said Aloma, 'I have listened to your arguments and have tested within my heart whether I could consent to your pleas and commands, yet I cannot find any way of being able to consent to them. And because anger and ill will are often generated when one fails to obey the requests of another, from now on I beg you, therefore, to avoid speaking to me any further about this matter, for I should not give you a reply, and fear that ill will might arise between you and me. Let us, thus, return to what we were saying and speak about God and His works, as is our custom. And whenever you wish to do what I first proposed to you, I am prepared to follow your desires.'

[13] Evast was very unhappy at not being able to convert his wife Aloma to his desires. So, on many days and many occasions, he repeated the aforesaid things to her, and whenever he spoke to her about them he caused her to become annoyed and distressed, to no avail whatsoever. So Evast, therefore, felt pity for Aloma on account of the annoyance he had caused her, and he proposed thereafter not to speak to her about such matters, entrusting the entire affair to the will of God. So he decided to consent to Aloma's wish to do penance at home and not leave the house, in order to avoid seeing or hearing worldly vanities, which prevent the soul from remembering, understanding and loving God and His Honours.[27]

---

27. For the term 'Honours', see above, Ch. 3, § 8 and corresponding note.

[14] When Evast had conceived this desire, he summoned Aloma
the following morning after Mass, as was his custom, and Aloma immediately began to cry, thinking that he wished to say to her the
words that he was in the habit of telling her, and which had brought
sadness to her soul.

'Aloma', said Evast, 'do not cry, for since your resolve is so lofty
and strong that I cannot in any way bend it towards that which I have
so persistently requested from you, I now seek to bend my heart to
your will in order to obey your wishes. So let us ensure that we can
both privately lead a life of penance and austerity within this house
for the remainder of our lives, while it may please God. And let us
give full authority to our son Blaquerna over all our property, other
than as much income therefrom as is required to support our lives,
and let us give the rest to Blaquerna, as well as provide him with a
wife. So tomorrow, after Mass, let us summon him and inform him of
what we have said, put all our affairs into writing and set down the
rule according to which we commit ourselves to perform penance.'

Aloma was very content with these words, and she praised and
blessed God, Who had bestowed such an intention upon her husband Evast. And she told Evast that she was prepared to fulfil everything she had promised in her aforesaid words, and considered what
Evast had said to be desirable.


5. ON THE DISPUTE EVAST AND ALOMA HAD WITH THEIR SON
BLAQUERNA

[1] The following day, after Mass, Evast and Aloma summoned
Blaquerna and, in front of the altar, where the sign of the Cross stood,
Evast said the following words to Blaquerna:

'My beloved son Blaquerna, we must remember where we come
from and why we are created and to what we must return. And we
must acknowledge the benefits we have received from the Most High.
The time has come when we must scorn the world and renounce our
temporal goods: in old age and in the frailty of our bodies we have a
sign that death is drawing near to us. From now on it is time for Aloma and myself to lead an austere life and, throughout all our days, to
weep for our sins, say prayers and perform penance. Fair son, we bequeath to you, therefore, all our temporal goods, and as regards the

prayers and the other good works we shall perform, we include you therein. So, from now on, you may be master of all our property. Look after and run this household in such a manner that the benefits which accrue therefrom may not be dissipated and that accordingly we may receive provision towards our lives, and that the children you shall have may be brought up in such a way that they be pleasing to God.'

[2] When Evast had uttered these words and many others to his son Blaquerna, he took up his seal, while Aloma took up the keys to the house, and they wanted Blaquerna to accept the seal and the keys. Blaquerna, however, did not accept that which Evast and Aloma wished to give him, and he began to meditate upon and to gaze at the Cross. And he remembered the Holy Passion of Our Lord Jesus Christ, and how He and His Apostles had been poor in this world, and how He had scorned worldly wealth.[28] Blaquerna cogitated at length upon the aforesaid things before answering Evast. And, after he had finished cogitating, he said these words:

[3] 'My lord father', said Blaquerna, 'great is the honour you and Aloma wish to bestow upon your son Blaquerna, who is unworthy of receiving such great honour. And great confidence and faith do you have in him, that you wish to entrust so much to him without having put his loyalty, charity, justice and the other virtues to the test. May you receive God's gratitude and reward for the honour and kindness you show me, but in my regard may you know that, from now on, I do not seek to introduce into my heart any honour, riches or pleasures of this world, or any other things apart from God alone, Who has created and fashioned me so that I may be His tabernacle. A great wrong, therefore, would be done to God if anyone were to cast Him out from the residence in which He wishes to live, and my heart would be wronged if God were ejected therefrom.'

[4] Evast and Aloma felt very great wonder at the words uttered by Blaquerna, to whom Evast said:

'So, what is your intention? And the words that you utter, what deeds do they signify? Your words evoke great wonder in me! I beg you to tell me your intentions.'

'My lord', said Blaquerna, 'divine light stirs my soul to remember, understand and love poverty, the eremitic life and the renunciation

---

28. Here Llull is appealing to the Franciscan notion of the absolute poverty of Christ.

of this world, so that I may more perfectly contemplate and love the Son of God, Who came into this world for us sinners and Who suffered a very grievous Passion, according to that which the sign of the Cross signifies to my bodily eyes. And by reason of such signification, your son Blaquerna wishes to follow the life and rule of Elijah and of Saint John the Baptist and of the Holy Fathers who have passed from this world, who lived lives of penance and austerity in the mountains and in the wilderness so that they might escape from the world and overcome their flesh and the Devil, and so that nothing might prevent them from contemplating and loving the God of glory, Who is the beginning and end of all goods.'

[5] 'Blaquerna', said Evast, 'I am very happy and grateful at the holy devotion which has entered your heart. I have often hesitated to offer prayers to God that he might give me children because I feared that they might be sinners and act against God's commandments. But now I know that the desires that your mother Aloma entertained to have you as her son were worthy, since you wish to be God's servant. I do not reproach your devotion, but since you need to repay the debt to your father and to your mother for the benefits you have received from them, it is therefore incumbent upon you to remain within the world until Evast and Aloma have passed from this life, and in due course may you fulfil your devotion and your intention, which reside within you by virtue of divine power.'

[6] 'My lord Evast', said Blaquerna, 'I know only too well that I have received a natural benefit from you and from my mother Lady Aloma, and to the very best of your abilities you have seen to it that I am well bred and honourable. But above all benefit is that which I have received from God, and the ultimate reason[29] for which I am in this world is so as to know, love, praise and contemplate God. And since it is hazardous to be in this world, and all the more so for a young man, accordingly I wish to flee therefrom. I wish to go to God, Who calls me. For love of Him, I wish to leave father, mother, honours, wealth, happiness and everything else behind; since, as long as I have God in my heart, I shall not want for anything; and if God were

---

29. Cat. *final rahó*, Eng. 'final cause': one of the four Aristotelian causes; the other three are: material, efficient and formal. *Final rahó* is synonymous with *final intenció*, for which see above Ch. 3, § 3 and corresponding note. 'To know, love, praise and contemplate God' constitutes precisely the Lullian 'first' (and, therefore, ultimate) 'intention'.

not in my soul, who could provide fulfilment of that which my soul so desires?'

[7] 'Beloved son', said Evast, 'if you fail to obey my requests and my commands, you shall do wrong to Aloma and myself, as well as to the poor of Christ, who obtain abundant alms from the wealth of this house, which latter would be destroyed if you were to leave us. And you shall be to blame if Evast and Blaquerna, through lack of an administrator, have to forsake the penance they wish to undertake. And you shall be to blame for the hardships we suffer in our old age; and since blame and affront are displeasing to God, fair son, according to justice and charity, therefore, you cannot nor should not allow the wealth of this house to disappear, or be the occasion of our hardship, or hinder the benefits which shall follow from our penance.'

[8] 'My lord Evast', said Blaquerna, 'God wishes people to strive in His service unto death. It seems to me, therefore, that, given the age you have attained, Lady Aloma and yourself are capable of striving to obtain worldly wealth and to give alms therefrom. And the greater the contrast your age and years bear to the hardships of this world, provided the latter are borne in the service of God, the greater shall be your merit. Aloma and yourself should thus persist in the estate in which you live, and should not lose hope in God's help; nor should you imitate the ways of many people who renounce worldly goods in order to achieve repose, for such repose presents hardships and dangers to other people. When your lives near their end and your bodies lose their vigour, entrust your wealth to some loyal man so that he may do the same good therewith as do you; alternatively, divide up all your possessions between the poor of Christ. My lord, do not stand in the way of my happiness or put my desires at risk for the sake of corruptible and transitory worldly affairs; do not reproach me on account of that for which you should praise me; and let not your souls be saddened by that in which one should take delight.'

[9] 'Blaquerna', said Evast, 'try to practise penance and austerity amongst us before going to the wilderness in order to do so, and test your will as to whether it wishes to persist for long in that which it causes you to desire. What you seek to embark upon is no idle matter and you should not enter into it all of a sudden, for it very often happens that a man thinks that he will persist in leading an austere life before he has experience of the rigours and hardships that the body feels when enduring such denial, and when he experiences the hard-

ships he returns to the bodily pleasures and the vain delights in which he previously indulged, after which he becomes the object of people's disdain and reproach. Beloved son, do not be overhasty, restrain your will and heed my words.'

[10] 'Evast, my lord, to test and assay one's capacity to endure hardship and a life of austerity is nothing but indecisiveness generated by a lack of perfect devotion and love. For strength of devotion and love relieve hardship and austerity, and, the greater the hardship and austerity, the loftier and nobler are the degrees of devotion and love, as likewise are patience, fortitude, justice, hope and the other virtues. The only thing that can burden my soul, therefore, is that, in my regard, austerity and hardship should be less.'

[11] Evast presented many arguments to his son Blaquerna in order to rid the latter's heart of the thoughts and desires which had entered therein. The more he pleaded with him and the more arguments he placed before him, however, the more resolute and determined he found him. Evast ceased talking, therefore, from fear that his words might be displeasing to God and that, through divine grace, Blaquerna might have been inflamed by the Holy Spirit. While Evast was cogitating upon such matters, Aloma began to speak, tearfully and with great disturbance of mind, saying the following words to her son Blaquerna:

[12] 'Beloved son', said Aloma, 'what shall you eat when you are in your hermitage? How shall you clothe yourself, when the garments that you wear are in shreds? And who shall tend to you when you fall ill? Blaquerna, fair son, have pity upon your body, which I have very carefully nurtured. Take pity upon your father Evast and upon me, because on account of your absence and our fearfulness concerning your death or your hardships, our own hardships shall be increased, hopeful as we are that we shall draw consolation and assistance from you at the end of our lives. Yet now, when we hope to rejoice in you, and wish to provide you with a pleasantly disposed, very beautiful and well-bred maiden, from an honourable family, of considerable wealth, as your wife, you seek to leave us and to surrender your body to death, though you remain blameless, for you have not yet committed such grave sins that you ought to torment your body and ourselves, who have never done you harm or wrong.'

Aloma uttered these words and many others to her son, and she spoke her words with such devotion and amidst so many tears that accordingly Evast and Blaquerna began to weep, and all three of them wept for quite some time before Blaquerna was able to answer his mother Aloma.

[13] When Blaquerna had wept for a long while, and nature had repaid him her debt,[30] his soul had not forgotten his saintly devotion nor was his fortitude slow to strengthen his resolve against his bodily nature, so by the power of God Blaquerna said the following words to his mother Aloma and to Evast:

'With a tormented heart compelled by the force of love, I must oppose the desires of your soul. Love has taken hold of my will and makes me disobedient to yours, which has loved me very dearly for a long time. I am your son and have received my being from you and my father Evast. You have raised me to the very best of your abilities; you seek to give me all that you own; and you wish to place yourselves under my authority. But I am unable to serve you or to delight you by my presence, and it is only right that you should feel saddened by my bodily absence. I cannot reward you for the good that you have done me nor for the love that you have borne me. I do not belong to myself, for I belong to another who has taken hold of me. If I belonged to myself, I would give myself to you so as to serve and honour you all the days of my life. If God has taken hold of me and pulls me away from you and from the pleasures of this world, causing me to remain all alone in the great woods and forests, and among the wild beasts, and in places where there is a lack of available food, clothing and company, as well as of other things essential to man; then He, Who provides food and drink and clothing to the birds and beasts and preserves their health in such places, shall provide me with all that my body shall need to sustain its life, and my soul shall be able to contemplate His Honours and His glory. Should my body die through lack of what it requires, God shall have acted in accordance with His will towards that which belongs to Him; my soul shall have employed hope, charity and fortitude towards its Creator and towards the trials of its body, and the advantage to the soul shall be so great that the body's trials should be of no account. I shall pray for you to the glorious God every day of my life. And should God wish to grant me anything, on account of some merit, I shall beg Him to grant it to you. I

---

30. 'To pay one's debt to nature' in the medieval period meant 'to die'. The debt nature pays in reverse to Blaquerna comes in the form of tears.

ask your forgiveness for not being able to obey you and for being the source of your trials. I ask you as a favour to seek to forget me lest you suffer any tribulation on my account. Give me your blessing, for I wish to go to the place that God makes me desire.'

[14] When Blaquerna had said these words and many others which would take a long time to recount, he knelt down in front of Evast and Aloma and asked for their blessing, for he wished to go to the hermitage to serve God.

'Blaquerna, my son', said Aloma, 'do you really wish to depart right now?'

'Beloved mother', said Blaquerna, 'I wish to take leave of you this very moment and to go in the direction in which God and fortune shall guide me. I beg you, therefore, to give me your blessing and not to delay my journey, for the longer I am among you, the more you shall suffer by reason of my presence and I by reason of yours. And the further the desire withdraws from my soul, the greater affliction and languor my body feels as a result.'

'Fair son Blaquerna', said Aloma, 'since it is not proper for our farewells to be so brief, you shall stay with us the whole of this day and the whole of the night, so that the whole of this day and the whole of the night may be spent in tears, fondness and sorrow at your departure. And tomorrow morning, after Mass, Evast and I shall give you our blessing and say farewell to you for the rest of our lives; though may it please God that we can meet and know each other in His holy glory! And if in this current life your absence causes us tribulation and sorrow, may God delight us with your presence in everlasting glory.

## 6. ON THE TEMPTATION NATANA POSED TO BLAQUERNA

[1] When Aloma had finished speaking, she left the chapel and went to visit a widow called Anastasia, who had a very beautiful daughter named Natana. Great friendship existed between Aloma, Anastasia and Natana. When Aloma was in a room with Anastasia and Natana in complete privacy, she began to weep a great deal, and said:

'Alas, woe is me! How distraught I am for ever more at that from which I had most hoped to derive pleasure for all the days of my life! I have lost my son Blaquerna, whom I have loved above all things in this world! If I can receive no counsel and help from you as to how I might recover my son, my soul shall feel sorrow and sadness for the rest of my life.'

[2] Anastasia and Natana were deeply astonished and were moved to great compassion by Aloma's tears and words.

'O sister and friend', said Anastasia, 'do not weep, for if we can help you in any way, we shall do so very willingly and as best we can, so long as it may be done in such a way that, in consequence, no shame should fall upon us and that it not be misunderstood by people at large.'

Aloma replied to Anastasia and recounted the entire conversation that had taken place between Evast, Blaquerna and her, and how Blaquerna completely refused to obey their words and how he wished to take his leave of them the following morning and go off to the wilderness all alone to do penance for the remainder of his life.

'The assistance I ask of you, therefore, is that your daughter Natana should speak with my son Blaquerna to see whether she might make him change his mind and incline him towards the order of matrimony, so that he might be her husband. And all the property that Evast and I possess would belong to Natana and Blaquerna.'

[3] They agreed among themselves that Aloma should bring Blaquerna to Anastasia's house after lunch and that Aloma and Anastasia should leave Blaquerna and Natana by themselves in the room. They agreed likewise that Natana should say amorous words to Blaquerna whereby he might understand that she would like to be his wife and that she had loved him loyally[31] for a long time. Once they had settled these things, Aloma returned to her house and entered the chapel, where she found Evast and her son Blaquerna, who were weeping over the separation that was to come about between them.

'It is time for lunch', said Aloma, 'come and let us eat, for later there shall be occasion for us to weep as much as we wish.'

[4] They placed a great amount of food upon the table, though Evast, Aloma and Blaquerna ate little thereof. When they had eaten, Aloma took her cloak and asked Blaquerna to accompany her, for she wished to go to the house of a lady with whom she had to speak. Blaquerna accompanied Natana to Anastasia's house, and Aloma and her son Blaquerna entered the room where they found Anastasia

---

31. Cat. *amb bona amor*, a term used in 'courtly' love and opposed to *mala amor*.

and Natana all alone. Natana was very nobly dressed, and by nature and adornment very beautiful.

'Natana', said Aloma, 'keep my son Blaquerna company while I am talking to your mother Anastasia.'

Blaquerna and Natana remained all on their own in the room, while Aloma and Anastasia entered another such in order to speak.

[5] While Blaquerna and Natana were sitting next to each other, and Blaquerna was thinking about his journey, Natana began to say the following words to him:

'My lord Blaquerna, long have I wished to be able to tell you what I feel. I have loved you for a long time now and desire above all to be your wife. Love compels me to say these words. And if you, by reason of your family and wealth, are worthy of having a wealthier and more honourable wife, then may love—which causes me to hold you dear—assist me; and may my worthy intention assist me likewise, for I love you in order to be your wife rather than for the sake of any other disorderly thoughts. And may God fulfil my wish, which makes me desire to have children by you who may be servants of God and may resemble you in terms of the saintly life which you have achieved by the grace of God and by the instruction and example of Evast and Aloma, who are of greater saintliness than anyone within this city.'

[6] Natana was beautiful, and she said these and many other words to Blaquerna with caution, devotion and the appearance of great love. Blaquerna, however, did not forget his great wish, and the flame of the Holy Spirit, which had kindled his heart, was quick to come to his aid. So when Blaquerna had thought for a while about the words Natana had spoken to him, he said to her:

'I bless and adore that King of all Kings who is the hope and consolation of all sinners and who does not fail to remember His servants in their needs, because now I have begun to fall prey to temptations, and divine power aids me against false counsel. My heart rejoices at the fact that my temptations have commenced. Hope leads me to expect the same strength I feel now as regards this temptation when combatting the other temptations that are bound to assail me.'

Blaquerna greatly praised and blessed Our Lord God in this way before he answered Natana.

[7] Natana saw Blaquerna rejoicing and blessing the glorious God without responding to her words, so then she said to him:

'Blaquerna, why do you not answer me? What is it that you are saying? And what is it that brings joy to your soul?

Blaquerna said in reply to Natana:

'The Holy Spirit has enlightened my mind with the light of grace, which makes me wish for the eremitic life, in which I may have only God in my thoughts. When you, Natana, told me about your feelings, carnal pleasures began to tempt my soul through my bodily nature and the work of the Devil. So without delay my soul remembered once more its Lover and the divine light illumined my soul with divine love. This light makes me realise that God does not forget His servant; rather, it makes me despise your words so thoroughly that I am surprised, to judge by your demeanour, that thoughts as foolish as yours can have been acommodated in such a beautiful person as yourself, thoughts that counsel me to forsake the love of the supreme Lord for your own. Sometimes I have been unsure whether God would assist me in combatting certain temptations that shall assail me in the wilderness, but now I am no longer unsure about what I was previously so. Let any temptation whatsoever arise, since the sound principle from which I have set out leads me to disdain it.'

[8] The constancy of Blaquerna's resolve took Natana greatly by surprise, so she said to him:

'My friend, why do you not reply to my words?'

Blaquerna answered:

'If you wish to speak to me about God or to give me instruction as to how I can amply honour, love and serve Him, your words will be very pleasing to me, but from now on refrain from speaking vain words to me and let me think about my journey while my mother Aloma speaks to your mother Anastasia.'

[9] 'Blaquerna', said Natana, 'how will you be able to endure such an austere life for so long in the wilderness as you have resolved to do?'

[10] Blaquerna replied:

'Who caused Saint Catherine, Saint Eulalia and Saint Margaret and the other holy virgin martyrs to endure trials and death, all of whom for love of my beloved Jesus Christ let themselves be tortured, burned, hanged and put to death?[32] If they, who were young and fe-

---

32. Llull here refers to three female virgin martyrs of Christian tradition: St Catherine of Alexandria, martyred in the fourth century CE under the pagan emperor

male, by the grace of God underwent all these things and more such which they wished to endure, then shall I, who am a man, not be capable of enduring hunger, thirst, heat, cold and fear in my hermitage for love of my Lord? And is it not for me an incomparably greater virtue that I should trust in God's aid in the wilderness, than if, within this city, I were to trust in the aid of Evast and Aloma and in the riches of this world?'

[11] 'It often happens', said Natana, 'that with great courage one forms the intention of carrying out some bold act or of undergoing a certain ordeal and that, when one is amidst one's enemies and experiences the ordeal, then one refuses to go through with it and shies away from the ordeal which one believed one could undergo. Therefore, Blaquerna, when you are in the wilderness and you experience the austerity of life on account of the strange and meagre fare, and you remember Evast and Aloma and your other friends, and you reside among the wild beasts, under such circumstances shall you think differently from how you do now and shall you fear the things which you do not now fear.'

[12] 'Natana', said Blaquerna, 'I travel to the forests to contemplate my Lord Jesus Christ and his mother, glorious virgin, Our Lady, Holy Mary. And I travel in the company of faith, hope, charity, justice, prudence, fortitude and temperance. I require faith in order to believe the articles of the holy Catholic faith and to assist me in combatting the temptations that arise through ignorance. I travel in the company of hope in order to have confidence in the strength, the aid and the mercy of Him who wishes to have me all to Himself. Love leads my heart and conducts me to the wilderness, causing this city and other populated places to seem to me as if they are desolate and uninhabitable locations; love, indeed, enables one to master and overcome all things. Justice causes me to render to God my body and soul, since He is the creator and benefactor both of myself and of all things. Prudence enables me clearly to discern and to scorn this fleeting world full of deceit and error, and leads me to desire eternal happiness. Fortitude strengthens my heart with the strength of the Most

---

Maxentius; St Eulalia of Barcelona, thought to have been martyred at the age of thirteen by the emperor Diocletian in the early fourth century CE, though she is probably a figure of legend arising from the very similar fate suffered by St Eulalia of Mérida; Saint Margaret (or Margaret of Antioch), also possibly a figure of legend, was likewise a Christian martyr ostensibly put to death in 304 CE.

High. Temperance is mistress of my belly. If I cannot practise these virtues in the wilderness, therefore, I shall have to return; and if I were to fail to endure hunger, thirst, cold, heat, nakedness, fear, poverty and temptation in such a place, where would be the virtues and their operations without which I could not, nor would not wish to, live either there or anywhere else? Natana', said Blaquerna, 'you seek to scare me concerning those things I wish to endure on behalf of Him who underwent more grievous hardships on my account than these you mention to me.[33] And the desire to endure such hardships, as well as many others, causes me to leave my home and to travel to places where I may find and have them, for I do not wish to reside or remain in any place where I cannot find them.'

[13] 'Blaquerna', said Natana, 'I find your words very gratifying. And I should like to be with you at all times; so, please, take me away with you, so that together we may do penance in the place which you find most agreeable.'[34]

Blaquerna replied:

'It is not appropriate for you or anyone else to be with me; for I wish to have no companion other than God, the trees, the plants, the birds, the wild beasts, and streams, springs, meadows and riverbanks, and the sun, the moon and the stars, for none of these things prevents one's soul from contemplating God.'

[14] 'Blaquerna', said Natana, 'if I am with you and at times you feel a certain urge towards carnal pleasure, you shall have greater merit if you are able to observe abstinence and shall be more contrary to lust, which is a vice and is highly displeasing to God. And you shall possess greater fortitude if you control your flesh; and if you take me with you and feel confident that you can control your flesh, you shall possess greater hope accordingly. Thus, the greater the merit you can earn, the greater shall your wisdom be. So, the more forcefully you control yourself, the greater your love for God shall be. For all these reasons, therefore, and for many more, is it advisable for you to take me away with you.'

Blaquerna replied:

---

33. Note here that Christ is the ultimate point of comparison and model for the (lay) penitential life.

34. Here the figure of Natana is referring to the penitential life available to married couples in the thirteenth century as an expression of lay piety.

'The Law forbids one to tempt God.[35] Nor should one tempt one-self in the manner you have mentioned, for that is the way of pride and vainglory, and dangers lie therein, due to the frailty to which man has succumbed through the corruption of sin. However, when chance has it that one succumbs by some accident of circumstance wherein one has the opportunity to sin, it is then fitting for one to avail oneself of the virtues in the manner you have mentioned. On no account, therefore, would I take you away with me, but rather I coun-sel you to withdraw from the world and to have company with the fe-male religious from one of the orders in contemplating, remembering, understanding and loving the holy virtue of God, the foulness of this world and everlasting glory.'

[15] 'Blaquerna', said Natana, 'when we began to converse, love made me love your body and your fine features, but now, the virtue of your words has made my soul rise up to love the virtues of your soul. You have caused me to change my mind, you have enlightened my soul with divine virtue, you have given my heart to God, and whereas I desired to be your wife, you have given me Jesus Christ as my husband.'[36]

While Natana had been saying these words to Blaquerna, Aloma and Anastasia had been listening and had heard their conversation. Anastasia, however, was very angry at the words Natana had uttered, so she said to Aloma:

'Aloma, dear neighbour, I won't allow Blaquerna to speak to my daughter any more.'

So then Aloma and Anastasia entered the room and brought the conversation between Blaquerna and Natana to an end.

[16] Blaquerna took his leave of Natana. Love, which adheres to no method, led Natana, through her tears, to say the following words in the presence of Aloma and Anastasia:

'Blaquerna, do not forget me in your prayers, since your words make this room in which I am seem akin to me to the abode to which you desire to go.'

Blaquerna gave instruction to Natana as to how the seven virtues might preserve her virginity all the days of her life. Aloma and Blaquerna left Anastasia's house and returned home. Aloma told Ev-

---

35. Deut 6:16; and, in the context of prayer, Sir [Ecclus] 18:23.
36. Cf. Eph 5:23-31 and 2 Cor 11:2.

ast what had taken place between Blaquerna and Natana, as well as the reason she had taken Blaquerna to Anastasia's house. Evast informed Aloma that from that moment on they should not hinder Blaquerna's journey, for this journey was the work of God and it is a terrible thing to obstruct those who mean to serve God.

[17] Evast and Blaquerna spent the entire night with their son Blaquerna in the chapel. Who could possibly describe to you the tears and the devout words that passed between them? And who could tell you of the virtuous words Blaquerna spoke that night concerning God and His glory? And who could set down in writing the blessings Evast and Aloma gave to their son? And who could possibly prevent themselves from weeping if they were to hear their words?

## 7. On how Evast and Aloma provided an escort for their son Blaquerna

[1] The following day, after Mass, Evast informed his relatives and friends that they should come to bestow honour upon and to escort their son Blaquerna. Once they had all assembled, Evast described to them the divine blessing which had inspired his son Blaquerna to love the idea of going to be a hermit and to contemplate divine virtue in the wilderness and in uninhabited places. They all marvelled deeply at these words and they all begged Blaquerna to stay rather than to distress Evast or Aloma by his absence, saying that, after Evast had died, they would make Blaquerna their leader and ruler, as they had in the case of Evast. But Evast told them that this matter should not further be discussed, for so profoundly had Blaquerna conceived of his divine inspiration that on no account would he desist from his journey.

[2] 'My lord Evast', said Blaquerna, 'in order to avoid vainglory, and so that people do not deem to be vainglorious the honour that you and these lords wish to bestow upon me, and since I am not worthy to receive such great honour, if it please you I should prefer to take my leave from you, from Aloma and from these other lords at your house, and to set out unaccompanied on my journey with God's blessing.'

'Blaquerna', said Evast, 'one should not refrain from setting a commendable example merely on account of the vain talk of the people at large, an example which you set for all of us by loving and serving God and by despising this worldly life. For the worthy example that the people draw from you shall be more beneficial than what they say about it shall be damaging, and you shall gain more strength accordingly and shall reveal a greater contrast to vainglory, and in times to come you shall not consent to leave your hermitage on account of any temptation the devil may offer.'

[3] Evast and Aloma and a large number of people escorted Blaquerna, whose renown was great throughout the city. Blaquerna received many blessings from all the common people, and many sinners felt remorse for their sins, while many virtuous folk longed to increase their good works by honouring and serving God. Many people also felt great compassion for Evast and Aloma, who would never see Blaquerna again. Blaquerna too was deeply pitied for the hardship and austerity he would be required to endure in the lonely places in which he could not acquire the essential things his body would need to maintain bodily life.

[4] Blaquerna was white, ruddy and blonde. He was a beautiful sight to behold, for nature had given to his body all the features that, in a human body, are agreeable and pleasing to the eye. He was young in age and his soul had the fullness of virtues. In his heart resided, night and day, remembrance and love of divine dominion. The saintly intention his will so fervently desired stirred love and ardour towards God in all those who beheld him: the water in their hearts rose to their eyes through piety and devotion, and from those eyes ran tears.

[5] When Blaquerna and those who were escorting him were outside the city, he begged his father, his mother and the other lords to turn back. Aloma replied, however, saying that she would not part company from him on any account until she was at the forest which he would have to enter. Evast and all the others were of the same attitude, so they all continued to escort Blaquerna. While they were all doing so, Evast asked Blaquerna to tell him what was the foremost reason he had conceived the intention of becoming a hermit and of leaving the world.

'My lord', said Blaquerna, 'it has come about by God's will that you have had me instructed in theology and the other sciences, whereby I have acquired knowledge of God, Who is known by what is represented of His operation and power in creatures.[37] Since this

---

37. 'God, Creature, Operation' are principles from Llull's Art.

world is an obstacle to contemplating God and to considering His lofty power, I am therefore leaving the world behind. I am taking what I have learned along with me to the mountains and I wish to be by myself so that there may be no obstacle to my loving, knowing, praising and blessing God by means of what I have learned within the world. This, my lord, is the foremost reason for my leaving the world. There are plenty of other reasons too, among which is the following, namely, that I hardly ever see any person in the world who carries out his duty as regards honouring, loving and knowing God or who feels grateful towards Him for the good that he has received from Him; for almost the entire world has turned into vanity, wickedness, deceit and error. I prefer, therefore, to live among the wild beasts, the trees and the birds, which are without sin, than to remain among so many people who are ungrateful and blameworthy with respect to the benefits they have received from God.'

[6] When Blaquerna had finished speaking, Aloma begged Blaquerna to give her a single gift. Blaquerna replied by inquiring as to what gift she was asking for.

'Son', said Aloma, 'as a gift I'm not asking you to desist from your journey; rather, the gift I ask from you is one that you are able to give.'

'Ah, Aloma, mother and my mistress of mine!', said Blaquerna. 'You must surely realise that there is nothing which has remained in my power other than to follow the will of Him Who has inspired love in me when I cogitate upon His Honours. If the gift for which you ask, therefore, corresponds with God's will, then may all that I am able to give you be granted to you.'

'Son', said Aloma, 'I ask you to promise me that, before either you or I die, you will return to stay with me for a while, and then you may return to your hermitage. Or, if you do not wish to come to me, let your whereabouts be known via your messenger and I shall come to stay with you for as long as you find my company pleasant and agreeable.'

Blaquerna replied:

'You must surely realise, Aloma, that I do not have certain knowledge concerning either your or my life. So, if I were to promise you that I should come to you, yet I had died, you might think that I had not been true to you. And if I were to return to you, your trials, which you have endured on account of my departure, would be renewed. I cannot send you a messenger, for my entire life shall be solitary, lacking the company of any person. I am not capable, therefore, of all that which you ask of me, insofar as the divine will has ordered me to be obedient to its commandments.'

[7] 'Son', said Aloma, 'where is the place in which you will build your dwelling? And in which direction will you head?'

'Mother', said Blaquerna, 'I cannot talk with certainty about those things which I do not know. I must needs go through the forests and the high peaks to seek a particular place where there is water and some wild herbs whereby I may give sustenance to my body. Wherever the country, place or region may be is all in the hands of God, for in Him lies my hope, and I place my trust in Him to give me guidance in finding a suitable location where I may love and know him all the days of my life, and where I may pray to Him for your sake and for that of my father, Lord Evast.'

## 8. ON THEIR FAREWELLS

[1] While Blaquerna was talking in this manner to his mother Aloma, they arrived at the place where Blaquerna would have to enter the forest. Blaquerna and all the others came to a halt there. Blaquerna knelt down first of all in front of Evast and asked for his grace and blessing in place of his inheritance. Evast then knelt down and said a prayer to God for the sake of Blaquerna, using the following words:

'Divine Essence, Who art infinite in goodness, greatness, eternity, power, wisdom, love and perfection, and Who art virtue in all things without distinction, I worship You in terms of Your virtue and Your Virtues.[38] My son Blaquerna goes to serve and contemplate You in respect of Your Honours. I do not know the place where he will live, but I know very well that, wherever he may go, there You exist by essence, power and presence with regard to all Your Virtues, all Your powers and all Your perfections. Divine Essence which comprises all things, to You do I commend my son Blaquerna. Watch over him, since he has placed his devotion and hope in You; fill him with the love of serving You and reveal Your virtue to his intellect so that his

---

38. Once again, Llull enumerates some of God's attributes, which form the principles of his Art. Evast's encomium to God foreshadows the manner of Blaquerna's contemplation of God in the 'Art of Contemplation', for which, see below, Ch. 102.

will may love You more deeply; You, who art eternal, receive my son Blaquerna so that he might persist all the days of his life in cogitating upon Your blessedness. Do not attribute my faults to my son Blaquerna; if there are any sins or faults within him, may it please You that I do penance for them on his behalf. Do not forget the pleasure I feel in my heart at the fact that my son Blaquerna goes to serve You, even as this heart suffers at his absence. Simple Essence, pure act without end or beginning, You have given me my son Blaquerna; I have raised him to serve You as best I can; he is virginal in body and in mind; to You do I render him and to You do I commend him. To the grace of Your Trinity and to the blessings of the human nature You unite to the Son of the heavenly Father, Who dwells within You, I commend my son Blaquerna. The Queen of Heaven and Earth, Our Lady, Holy Mary; Saint Michael and all the angels; Abraham, Isaac, Jacob, Saint Joachim and all the patriarchs; Saint Peter and Saint Paul and all the Apostles; Saint Lawrence and Saint Vincent and all the martyrs; Saint Bernard, Saint Francis, Saint Dominic and all the confessors—may they all watch over and give succour to my son Blaquerna. Place my son Blaquerna in the hands of Elijah and Saint John the Baptist, who were hermits, so that through their merit You may watch over my son in his hermitage.'

[2] When Evast had finished his prayer, Blaquerna begged him to stand up so that he could pay his father the appropriate honour. Evast rose to his feet, and Blaquerna, while kneeling, kissed his father's hands and feet, and Evast kissed his son Blaquerna and made the sign of the Cross over his son's head and granted him his grace and blessing while weeping with great distress. When Blaquerna had received his father's blessing, he knelt down before his mother Aloma while asking for her grace and blessing through the bounty of the King of Glory.

[3] Blaquerna remained kneeling before his mother Aloma, his eyes gazing compassionately at her. Aloma was standing upright and gazed at the fair face of her son Blaquerna. The strength of her love and a sense of longing for her son stifled Aloma, who was unable to speak. Aloma and Blaquerna remained for a long time in this state wherein neither was able to say anything to the other.[39] Blaquerna,

---

39. Cf. below, Ch. 20, § 17; and Ch. 62, § 11 for a further reciprocal access of mutism brought on by profound love and devotion.

however, who wished to proceed with his journey, drew upon the strength of his resolve and said:

'It is time for my departure, so I must go.'

And he said to Aloma that he was awaiting her leave and blessing.

[4] By the power of God, Aloma was granted the ability to speak to her son Blaquerna, so she uttered these words:

'Beloved son, I must remember the Queen of Heaven, Mother of the Son of God, Jesus Christ, so that she might be of succour to you in all your needs.'

For this reason, therefore, Aloma knelt down, kissed the ground and raised her hands and eyes to the heavens, and with great devotion and many tears she uttered these words:

'O Queen, Glorious Virgin, in so many places are you honoured and invoked on account of your glorious Son! My son Blaquerna is going away all by himself, and I know not whereto. He goes to serve your Son and to remember, love and obey Him. Since he goes to honour and love your Son, would you not watch over, protect and love my son? You are in glory with your Son. Yet your Son causes mine to part from me and has me remain alone and disheartened. I shall love your Son because you love Him; will you love my son because he is loved by me? My soul is sad at the departure of my son, yet you are happy at the presence of yours. I had but a single son, yet your Son has stolen him from me: He makes him go to where he is at risk from wicked people and wild beasts; He shall cause him to live alone all the days of his life. He shall make him eat raw herbs, and his garments shall be the hair on his body, the hair on his head, and the air. Look down here and see how my son Blaquerna is fair of body and of heart; consider how the sun, the wind and his nakedness will darken and destroy the beauty of his features. When he is cold, who shall warm him? And when he is ailing, who shall tend him? When he is hungry, who shall feed him? When he is scared, who shall comfort him? If you were not to aid my son in the absence of my prayers, where would be your mercy and compassion? The sorrow I feel for my son, whom I see going to his death in misery and penance, and in the forests all alone I know not whereto, may it cause you to remember the sorrow that you felt for your Son, Whom you saw crucified and put to death. If your Son died, without sin, for the sake of love, what blame does my son bear, apart from love, which leads him to go to his death? Can any virtue which may be beneficial to my son emerge from what I understand concerning your Son and mine or from the hope I place in you?'

[5] Aloma uttered these and many other devout words in which she followed no method to the Queen of Heaven. While Aloma was engaged in adoration, Blaquerna looked up at the sun and saw that it was almost dark, so he said to Aloma that it was time that she and Evast and all the others returned to the city and that he should embark upon his journey. So Aloma stood up, therefore, and Blaquerna kissed her hands and her feet. And Aloma then kissed her son's eyes, mouth and face, and made the sign of the Cross over his head and gave him her grace and blessing and, once more kissing her son, she uttered the following words:

'Blaquerna, fair son, I commend and entrust you to the care and preservation of the Glorious Virgin and her virtues, whereby so many sinners receive aid and protection. May her mother Saint Anne and the holy man Joseph of Arimathaea, who requested the body of Jesus Christ, give you succour. I commend you to Saint Catherine, Saint Eulalia, Saint Mary Magdalen, Saint Margaret, Saint Clare and all the other female saints, and in their hands may you be placed. And by the sorrow and compassion that I now feel and shall continue to feel at your departure, may compassion also pervade everything which may help and protect you, so that it may aid you against your enemy and against the Devil. And you, my son, since you are so noble of heart, persevere with your saintly life in such a way that, by the grace and virtue of God, Evast and I may see you in never-ending glory.'

When Aloma had spoken these words, she hugged and kissed her son Blaquerna and fell to the ground in a faint.

[6] When Blaquerna had received the grace and blessing of Evast, and Aloma had returned to her senses, Blaquerna knelt down and tearfully lifted his gaze to heaven. He raised his thoughts and his hands to God, Whom he worshipped with respect to each of the fourteen articles of the holy Catholic faith, using the following words:

'Lord God, Who art Unity in Trinity and Trinity in Unity, in You I worship a Unity of Essence and a Trinity of Persons in the absence of any composition or any minority.[40] I worship, O Lord, the Father,

---

40. 'Majority, Equality and Minority' are three principles from Llull's Art. Majority and Minority, in this instance, are not applicable to God, for obvious reasons, though God enjoys majority over the created world.

Who by His infinite goodness, greatness, eternity, power, wisdom, love and perfection, generates a Son infinite in goodness, greatness, eternity, power, wisdom, love and perfection. This Son I love in Himself as well as in the Father, and the Father I worship in Himself as well as in the Son. I worship the Holy Spirit, who proceeds from the Father and the Son infinitely in goodness, greatness, eternity, power, wisdom, love and perfection. This Holy Spirit I worship in Himself as well as in the Father and the Son; and I worship the Father and the Son in the Holy Spirit. And I worship the three Persons and the aforesaid three essential virtues in the Divine Essence and in Its Unity; and the Essence or Unity I worship in the Persons or Virtues.'

'Lord God', said Blaquerna, 'I worship You as the Creator who has created the world and all that exists from nothing so that You may be known and loved and so that, in glory, we may be participants in Your blessedness and in You, our Glorifier. I worship You, Lord, as Redeemer and as Saviour. I worship Your conception through the workings of the Holy Spirit in the womb of the Holy Virgin Mary, whereby two natures were united in one Person called Jesus Christ. I worship You in Your Nativity and in the virginity of Our Lady, Holy Mary, who was a virgin prior to Your birth and remained so after that birth. I worship You, Lord, in Your Passion, which You suffered on the Cross in order to redeem mankind. And I worship Your soul, which descended into Hell in order to remove therefrom Adam, Noah, Abraham and the other prophets, who had desired Your Coming for so long. I worship You, Lord, since you were willing to revive and reveal to the Virgin Your glorified body so that it might give her comfort and offer us a sign of Resurrection. I worship You, Lord, since You ascended into Heaven to dwell forever in glory, seated at the right hand of the heavenly Father. I worship You and fear You, Lord, because You shall come on the Day of Judgement to judge the virtuous and the wicked, the former destined for perpetual glory, the latter for everlasting torment.'

[7] When Blaquerna had worshipped God in terms of the aforesaid articles, he worshipped and blessed Our Lady, Holy Mary, also blessing the angels and the Apostles and all the saints in glory. And he placed himself in the charge and safekeeping of God and the entire heavenly court, and offered thanks to God and to all the saints in Heaven. For a very long time he prayed to God for the sake of Evast and Aloma. His prayer and its method were so devout and pious that all those who were

with him wept, and they invoked the God of Heaven to give Blaquerna guidance so that he might live a long life under God's care.

[8] When Blaquerna had finished his prayer and had asked forgiveness from Evast and Aloma for the suffering they endured on his account, he took the wretched clothing worn by a messenger from Evast's household and gave him his own. And he took seven loaves to signify the seven virtues, so that he might have these latter with him all the days of his life. After this, he made the sign of the Cross in front of his eyes and turned to face the forest, setting off with these words:

'In the name of the Father, the Son and the Holy Spirit, one God, Who is the beginning, middle and end of our journey.'

[9] Evast and Aloma and all the others remained for such a long time in that place where Blaquerna had taken his leave, watching him as he receded, that he was eventually within the forest. So Aloma said:

'Alas, woe is me! I have lost sight of my son Blaquerna, whom I shall never see again in this present life.'

With great tears and sorrow Evast and Aloma and all the others returned to the city while speaking of Blaquerna and of the great devotion God had granted him above all other people that they had ever seen in their lives.


## 9. ON THE ESTATE OF EVAST AND ALOMA

[1] Evast and Aloma were in the chapel after Mass talking at length about the estate in which they abided, and they drew up and set in writing the Rule to which they should adhere all the days of their life. The Rule was as follows: At the beginning it was declared that, with the exception of all their expenses, they should entrust the entirety of their wealth to a devout religious, a lay brother, and that all their surplus income should be given to the poor of Christ.[41] They should wear only humble attire. They should eat meat only three days a week. They should not wear linen or lie upon sheets. They should not indulge in carnal pleasure. They should rise at Matins and say their

---

41. The renunciation of wealth undertaken by not only Blaquerna but also Evast and Aloma is reminiscent of the legend of St Alexius who, on the night of his wedding renounced both his bride and his patrimony in favour of embracing a life of poverty inspired by his love for God.

Hours. Following Mass, they should remain at prayer and discuss God. Prior to eating, they should wash the feet of thirteen paupers, at whose table they should eat. They should not leave the house at night. They should examine their conscience to see whether they might have erred against God or against their Rule, and they should both administer lashes to each other while accusing themselves of their faults. This was the Rule that Evast and Aloma adopted.[42]

[2] Evast and Aloma showed great concern to discover the brother to whom they wished to entrust their income, for they could not find anyone suitable in the whole environs of the city. So Aloma said to Evast that they should make some man their steward who was either Evast's or Aloma's relative. Evast, however, said that this was not advisable because relatives too greatly abuse the property people entrust to them, and they harbour opinions and desire that people make them their heirs. Evast did, however, remember a monk who was a priest: an elderly man, of good morals, from a foreign land. Evast begged the abbot to let him have this monk as his administrator so that he might be able to persevere in the aforesaid Rule, and to allow Evast and Aloma to say their confessions to him.[43] The monk was granted to Evast and Aloma and they abided in an estate which accorded with what was contained in the Rule they had adopted.

[3] While Evast and Aloma lived in the aforesaid manner and the entire city was set a worthy example by the virtuous instruction given by Evast and Aloma, it came to pass by the will of God that Evast fell severely ill and believed that, at any event, he would die from that illness. Evast called to his wife Aloma:

'Aloma', said Evast, 'I wish to write my Will with your counsel and in accordance with your wishes. I want you to tell me your opinion as to how I can make arrangements for my property so that God may be served thereby, and I ask you to let me know your wishes as regards what you intend to do after my death.'

---

42. The editors of the Catalan critical edition point to the rule for penitential life in operation at the time of *Blaquerna*'s composition, namely, Cardinal Hugolino's '*Memoriale propositi* fratrum et sororum de Penitentia in domibus propriis existentibus' (orally approved by Pope Honorius III in 1221; confirmed 1228).

43. According to the Rule of St Benedict, Ch. 1, there are four kinds of monks: the cenobite, the anchorite, the sarabaite (i.e. a heretical monk) and the gyrovague (i.e. a wandering monk: a term of criticism later directed at the Franciscans in particular).

Aloma was deeply distressed by Evast's illness, so she wept bitterly before she could answer him.

'My lord Evast', said Aloma, 'there will not be anything in all your wishes that I either would or should seek to oppose. So make arrangements for your property and for mine as you wish to, and make arrangements for me as you see fit, for, in any case, I submit my will to yours.'

[4] 'Aloma', said Evast, 'among the diverse things people do in this world for the love of God, it is laudable to give alms to the poor of Christ, which alms should be perpetual.[44] My intention, therefore, is to leave all my possessions for the building and endowment of a hospice wherein the homeless poor might be taken care of; and for you to be involved in helping with the administration of the hospice and in serving the poor, so that by your merit God might have pity on me, a sinner, and might keep Blaquerna and yourself in His favour. The priest and proctor[45] of this hospice should be this holy man who acts as overseer for us, and after his death another religious suited to managing the hospice should be sought, and this arrangement should prevail in the hospice under the above conditions.'

The arrangement, as well as Evast's words, greatly pleased Aloma, and she said that she was under his authority in order that she might obey all his commands. Evast wrote a Will in the aforesaid fashion, and he entrusted the hospice to the care of the prince of that country and likewise of the bishop and the city notables, in accordance with the above-stated formula. And he gave instruction that, after his death, he should be carried to the church in a humble manner without any pomp or ostentation, and that no relative of his should escort him to the church who might weep or show signs of sadness at what was in keeping with the course of nature and the workings of the divine will.

---

44. Perpetual alms were gifts given in perpetuity, i.e. they were not hereditary, on the understanding that the recipient, a religious house, say, contained no religious who were in possession of heirs.

45. Cat. *procurador*. In its most general sense, the English word 'proctor' indicates someone who acts on another's behalf or is appointed to take care of his or her affairs in the latter's absence, and is thus defined under Canon Law. This word, however, carries a range of senses including: 'a legal practitioner in ecclesiastical courts'; 'chief steward'; 'agent', 'representative' or 'proxy'; and 'deputy'. Clearly, the absent figure whom Llull represents in his frequent self-description as *procurador dels infeels* or 'proctor to the unbelievers', for which, see below Ch. 90, § 7, is the 'one true God'.

[5] Evast said his confession and received the body of Jesus Christ, saying the following words:

'I worship You, true flesh and true body of Jesus Christ, which is represented to my bodily eyes under the form of bread. I do not worship this bread; I worship and bless, rather, the Holy Body of Jesus Christ, who in this bread is represented to my spiritual eyes. I worship You, living Son of God, Who raised onto the Cross that body which I see spiritually, and which You united to Yourself. This body, so glorious, represents to my soul Your great and infinite power, which under the form of bread causes true flesh and true human being to exist; while your great humility causes it to stand before me, a sinner, so that I might receive grace and blessing therefrom. In You, glorified and glorious Holy Body, do I trust and place my hope, and in You do I believe and from You do I ask forgiveness. I receive You so that You may receive me into Your kingdom to know and contemplate Your virtue. And in Your virtue am I delivered from the hands of my mortal enemy.'

[6] When Evast had worshipped and received the Holy Body of Jesus Christ and had undertaken all that befits a devout Christian, he went to sleep. And, by the power of God and through the merits of Aloma and Blaquerna, who unfailingly prayed to God for him, God restored Evast to health. When Evast had recovered his health and was free from the illness, he reverted to the Rule under which he had become accustomed to living. One day he was looking in a box for a letter when he found the Will he had written, so he read it. Evast carefully considered the benefits that would arise from the arrangements he had made for after he had died. So Evast called to Aloma, saying:

'Were I to have died, the benefits that would have arisen accordingly to the poor of Christ are written here. And since God has chosen to lengthen my life, it is unfair that any loss should result therefrom to those who beg for love of Him. So, therefore, if you wish to do so, we may fittingly execute the Will during our lifetime, for, by chance, after our death others might not be as diligent as we shall be, or it might happen that we died sooner and consequently impeded the benefits that would have arisen from the arrangements and alms for the hospice.'

Evast's words greatly pleased Aloma, so she said to him that she was under obligation to obey his will in these matters as in all others.

## 10. ON THE HOSPICE

[1] Evast sold his house, from which sale he received a great deal of money, so he built a hospice in a very suitable location within the city. He also endowed the hospice with his entire income. And within this hospice Evast and Aloma acted for a long time as servants to the poor of Christ. Evast tended the sick men who lay in the hospice and Aloma the women. When they had tended the sick and it was time to eat, Evast and Aloma went begging together for the love for God[46] to collect what they were to eat that day, or they ate with someone who had invited them to share a meal for the love of God. They did not wish to eat or to spend on themselves anything which belonged to the hospice, and they begged for the love of God in order to acquire what they needed to sustain their lives.

[2] The example Evast and Aloma set and the worthy life they led were commendable, and on account of their merits God bestowed many favours on many people, answered the prayers of many sinners within that city, and healed many sick people in the hospice because of Evast and Aloma's own prayers. Many people were once sinners who, on account of Evast's praiseworthy example, practised penitence, and accordingly many people entered religion. And everything Evast and Aloma undertook constituted a rule, an example, an act of preaching or the gnawing of a conscience to all those who saw them. And because of what they did, they thus suppressed in sinners the seven deadly sins.

## 11. ON GLUTTONY

[1] One day it came to pass that Evast and Aloma had tended their patients and they went out to look for someone who might give them some food for the love of God, on account of their love for Whom they had given food to many sick people in the hospice. While Evast

---

46. To 'beg for the love of God' is a phrase which occurs repeatedly in the *Legenda trium sociorum* ('Legend of the Three Companions')—an account of the early years of the Franciscan Order, composed in 1241-47—, not least at *3 soc.*, 2, 3, 8 and 11; for these references (in English), see *FAED* 2, 66-110; (2) 69, (3) 73, (8) 83, (11) 94. In this same work, *3 soc.*, 3, St Francis, dressed as a wealthy layman, expresses the wish to exchange his clothes for those of a beggar and to go begging 'for the love of God', IBID., 94.

and Aloma were walking along a street close to the palace which housed the bishop of that city, the bishop himself came riding along in the company of numerous canons and clergy, having taken exercise outside the city so that he might be healthier and might develop a greater appetite for eating at table. It was the bishop's habit to take such exercise daily, and afterwards he would have Mass celebrated, following which he would go to eat. When the bishop saw Evast and Aloma, he invited them to dine with him, so on that day they ate together.

[2] When they had eaten and were due to give thanks to God, a burgher of that city, who had bought Evast's house, sent a cooked and larded peacock to the bishop, who had not yet risen from his table. The bishop resumed eating and sampled the peacock, sending some of it to Evast and Aloma, who were sitting humbly on the floor in front of him like paupers. All those to whom the bishop sent a portion of the peacock ate some, apart from Evast and Blaquerna, who did not wish to do so. The bishop asked Evast and Aloma why they were not eating the peacock.

'My lord', replied Evast, 'it is God's ordinance and will that a person should eat in order to satisfy the body according to its needs, yet what does not constitute a need for the body falls outside God's ordinance, can be the cause of illness and death, and concords with gluttony, which is contrary to temperance.[47] And since we have satisfied our bodies well enough, we, therefore, do not wish to go against God's will or against temperance, nor do we wish to be the cause of illness or death in ourselves, on account of the peacock or of any other foodstuff.'

[3] For the entire day, the bishop deeply considered the words Evast had spoken to him, and he remembered the noble estate and honour in which Evast and Aloma had abided and that they had forsaken the world and sold their house, which was one of the oldest and noblest in the city, as well as that it had been purchased by the man who had sent him the peacock. While the bishop was meditating in the aforesaid manner upon the great good that Evast and Aloma were performing, he felt a certain disturbance in his bowels due to the fact that he had eaten too much, a disturbance which frequently affected him when he had overeaten and as a result of which he had often

---

47. Temperance and gluttony are each a virtue and a vice, respectively, and feature among the seven virtues and seven vices in Llull's Art.

fallen ill. So deeply did the bishop consider the virtuous way of life led by Evast and Aloma, therefore, and so greatly did he reproach himself and know himself to be worthy of censure, that he subsequently celebrated Mass at Matins prior to taking his horse out for a ride. And he was punished for the vice whereby gluttony had held him in thrall to his stomach; and so strongly did he exercise temperance that on account of this virtue he acquired the others, and lived healthily for many years and accomplished great good.

## 12. ON LUST

[1] In that city where Evast and Aloma were doing penance, it came about that an elderly and lustful man married a young woman, while a lady already past her youth, because she loved carnal pleasure, married a handsome young man, who married her for the reason that she was a wealthy woman. The young lady and the young man were neighbours and they saw each other often, while the Devil, who strives as hard as he can to lead people astray, did his best to ensure that the young man and the young lady might be overcome by the sin of lust. While both of them were succumbing to this very sin, and had come to know each other carnally, it came to pass on a feast day that the elderly man and the youth, as well as their wives, were at church attending Mass. While they were so doing, it was raining outside and the weather was terrible. Evast and Aloma were standing in front of the doors of the couples' two houses; they were begging for alms for the sake of Jesus Christ, as had become their custom. From each of the houses emerged a serving girl, carrying rain-capes and clogs to the church for their lord and lady. One of the servants said to the other:

'Let's give alms to those two paupers so that they can carry the capes and clogs to the church, and we can avoid getting wet.'

Each of the servants considered this a good idea, so they gave some bread to Evast and Aloma, and told them to carry the capes and clogs to their lords and ladies.

[2] Evast carried the men's capes and clogs and Aloma those of the ladies. They entered the church, which was filled with people, and in the presence of everybody fulfilled their errand. All the people marvelled deeply at their great humility, those who marvelled most deeply thereat being the two men and the two ladies to whom

Evast and Aloma brought the capes. And because the saintly lives of
Evast and Aloma were well known throughout the city, and the honour and nobility in which they had been accustomed to living were
very considerable, the young man and the young lady decided that
never again should they know each other carnally nor succumb to the
sin of lust. The older lady repented of the intention she had entertained in marrying the young man, as did likewise the older man.
And because of the commendable example set by Evast and Aloma,
each of them desired chastity and the religious life.


13. ON GREED[48]

[1] It happened one day that Evast and Aloma were passing through
the main square so that some man might invite them to dine with him,
but they found no one who would do so. In that square was a very
wealthy money-changer who had a great deal of money laid out in
front of him and was an astoundingly greedy man. Evast and Aloma
begged him for the love of God to give them something to eat or some
money whereby they could purchase food from which they might have
lunch. The money-changer, who was deeply in thrall to the sin of greed,
replied by saying that he would not give them lunch or anything which
was his, and he rose from the table at which he had been sitting and
went to a cobbler to ask him to make him a pair of shoes.
    [2] Evast and Aloma walked along the streets begging for the love
of God when they happened to pass in front of the cobbler, who was
fitting the money-changer who had not wished to give them anything
with a pair of shoes. The cobbler called out to them both, saying:
    'It's time for lunch. I am a poor man and have a wife and children
who live on what I earn. There's a small amount of meat in the pot
and I'll waive the penny for the wine. In my house there's never
enough bread for everyone. For the love of God I beg one of you to
have lunch with me and to share in what God has enabled me to earn.'
    [3] Evast told Aloma to eat that day with the cobbler, and that he
would go to look for another place where he might eat. Aloma, however, who loved and honoured Evast deeply, told him that she would
go to look for another place, and that Evast should stay. Love and

---

48. Greed, here in the sense of miserliness.

charity obtained between Evast and Aloma and each felt pity for the other. The weather was very cold and it was raining hard, and it had taken considerable effort for Evast and Aloma to walk along the streets. While they were arguing, with each of them wishing to make the other one stay, Evast insisted that Aloma should remain with the cobbler at all costs. Aloma, who was ever obedient to Evast's will, stayed behind while Evast went off to seek alms for the love of God in a different place.

[4] While Evast and Aloma were revealing the love they felt towards each other and the cobbler was inviting one of them to dine with him even while letting his poverty be known, the money-changer was cogitating upon his great wealth, upon death and upon God's justice, and deep within himself he said the following words:

'Alas, wretched creature! How blind you have been right until now! Why have you been the slave and prisoner of the sin of greed? And of what worth is your money or your wealth without love? And where are the thanks you offer to God for the benefits He has given you? All you own is of less value than the goodwill the cobbler has shown towards the friends of God. With all of your money you could not buy the love and charity which obtains between Evast and Aloma.'

The money-changer cogitated very carefully upon the saintly lives of Evast and Aloma. And because of the worthy example they had set and the goodwill the cobbler had shown, the money-changer freed himself from thraldom to greed, and was subsequently generous and charitable towards the poor of Christ. And on account of the virtue of generosity present within him, he acquired many other virtues.

## 14. On pride

[1] While Aloma was eating with the cobbler and Evast was going around the town in search of a place to eat, he passed in front of the door of a very proud and wealthy man. That man was a draper[49] who was holding a great feast and wished to marry a daughter he had to a highly acclaimed knight of that city. Evast saw many paupers at the door of that house who were waiting for somebody to give them alms from the remnants of what was left on the table. Evast sat down among

---

49. In the historical sense of clothier and/or cloth merchant.

the other paupers, to whom he said many encouraging words, comforting and consoling them in their poverty, and reminding them of the poverty and humility of Jesus Christ and of the Apostles, who loved poverty.[50]

[2] When the time came such that all those in the house had eaten, a person brought the scraps from the table to the paupers. Each of them had his bowl and his plate in which to receive what was given to him for the love of God. Evast did not have anything in which to receive the cabbage that the person wished to give him; nor did he have a cup or a jug in which to pour the wine, so he begged a pauper to oblige him for the love of God by receiving his share in *his* bowl and *his* cup. Fellowship and brotherliness were established between Evast and the pauper, and they ate and drank together at the lord of the house's gate. While Evast and the pauper were eating, the lord of the house emerged therefrom with the other lords whom he had invited to dine with him, and he saw Evast sitting on the ground among the paupers.

[3] The draper and all the others were greatly astonished at Evast's humility. And on account of the profound humility that Evast displayed to the draper and the others, who recognised him and were aware of his saintly life, the draper remembered the pride he felt with respect to himself, and he remembered how he wished to be proud of his children, insofar as he sought to wed his daughter to a more highly acclaimed man than befitted her. So, by the power of God and by the virtuous example of Evast, the draper freed himself from his enslavement to pride, came to love humility and married his daughter to another draper.

15. ON SLOTH[51]

[1] Sloth had in its power a very wealthy man, who lived in the city where Evast and Aloma were performing their penance. That man

---

50. Pope Nicholas III promulgated the Bull *Exiit qui seminat* on the 14th August 1279 in order to settle the dispute between the Franciscan Spirituals—adherents of the doctrine of the absolute poverty of Christ and of the Apostles—and the Conventuals. This Bull (or at least the dispute on which it attempted to adjudicate) was probably at the forefront of Ramon Llull's mind when alluding to this exactly contemporaneous event.

51. Cat. *accidia*; Eng. 'accidie' or 'acedia'. Llull generally defines this term as negligence in doing good or in loving God.

had no wife, nor did he wish to have one, nor were the possessions he owned of benefit to him or to any other. He always sat in the main square, scoffing at all those who passed in front of him. He felt angry whenever he saw good works being done; he felt pleased whenever he heard anyone speak ill of men as well as women. It happened one day that while that slothful man was on his way to eat, he came across Evast and Aloma, who were in the street along which he was passing, even as two women, for whom Evast and Aloma had found husbands for the love of God, were arguing with each other over Evast and Blaquerna, for that day both of them wished to invite the two latter to eat with them.

[2] The slothful man passed on and saw Evast and Aloma's hospice, which was very large and well constructed. There were many paupers therein, as well as many servants who attended to them with great diligence. All the paupers lay on a very fine bed and were provided with the food that they needed. This slothful man began to think about the great good that Evast and Aloma were accomplishing. He tried to evoke in his conscience whether he had ever done anything good for the love of God in return for those goods which God had bestowed upon him, yet he was unable even to ascertain from reflection that all the alms he had given during his lifetime were equal to the food alone that the sick people housed by the hospice were provided that day.

[3] 'Alas, you wretch!', said the man in servitude to sloth, 'how much harm you have caused to the poor of Christ—and for so long! And where are the merits which await you after your death, when they proffer your soul to the Lord of Heaven and Earth and protect you from the mortal enemy who waits to place that soul after such death into perpetual fire? You wretch! You cur![52] Which patient in this hospice is as sick as you are?'

While he was saying such things to himself, he saw two beds consisting of vine branches in the attic, beds on which there was a relatively small amount of straw, and on each bed there was but a single blanket. This man went over to one of those beds, undressed himself, lay down on the bed, and asked for food to be brought to him, for he

---

52. Cat. *caytiu/caitiu* has the equivalent term 'caitiff', now obsolete, in English, meaning 'wretched or despicable person'.

was sick and had come to that hospice so that he might be healed of
the sickness from which he suffered.

[4] The man who was suffering from sloth received an ample
amount of whatever he wished to eat, and he lay in the bed until
nighttime, when Evast and Aloma came to go to sleep. Evast found
the slothful man lying on his bed.

'Brother, friend', said Evast, 'who are you who has lain down in my
bed? Go and lie on one of the other beds, which are better than this
one.'

'My lord', said the sick man, 'it is my intention not to rise from this
bed until I am healed.'

Evast and Aloma asked the sick man what his illness was.

'My lord', said the sick man, 'sloth has imprisoned my soul and
will not allow me to do anything good with the goods with which God
has entrusted me. Yet I have faith and hope in the prayers of Aloma
and yourself, namely, that if you pray to God to release me from the
servitude in which sloth keeps me bound, then He shall grant your
prayers.'

[5] So Evast said:

'Neither sloth nor any other sin is sufficiently strong in man that
it can destroy within him the free will that God has created in such
strength and power that it cannot be defeated or overcome by any
sin. But, since you feel reverence towards our prayers, even though
we are unworthy of being heeded, we shall offer prayers to God so
that He may make you remember so fully His virtue and excellence,
as well as the Holy Passion of Jesus Christ and the baseness and transience of this world, that hereafter you, bodily and in terms of all
your wealth, may be a servant of Our Lord God all the days of your
life.'

[6] With great devotion and contrition of heart, the sick man repented and prayed to God together with Evast and Blaquerna. Once
his prayers were complete, the sick man felt that he had been healed
of his illness and begged Evast and Aloma to take him to the altar.
Evast and Aloma led him before the altar of Saint Andrew, in whose
presence he offered himself bodily and in terms of all his wealth so
that he might be a servant of that hospice in perpetuity.

## 16. ON ENVY

[1] There was a very wealthy man in that city, who had wished to buy Evast's house. That house was of great beauty, and every time that rich man left his own house he could see the other in front of him, and he felt immense envy in its regard. So great was his envy with respect to that house that he wished deadly evil upon the master thereof, and he invariably cogitated upon how he could find a way whereby he might become its owner.

[2] This man felt envy and ill will for a long time. While he remained subject to this sin, it came about by God's decree that the rich man who had bought the house from Evast died. At the gate awaiting alms were many paupers, as is customary when a person is to be buried, and for the sake of the departed's soul people give alms to the poor at the house of the deceased. Among the other paupers awaiting alms were Evast and Aloma, who were hoping that alms might be given to them.

[3] The notables who had escorted the body drew great humility and a very suitable example from Evast and Aloma, whom they observed to be present among the paupers and who were awaiting alms, and they spoke many words about the two of them. While they were speaking about them and were making very favourable comments about the works they performed, the envious man heard their words and remembered and recognised his sin, saying to himself the following words:

[4] 'O senseless fool! And of what use is this house to the man who was its master? And who has the better reputation: the man who has just died or Evast, who has sold the house and with the money received therefrom has built a hospice in which there is such great giving of alms? You envious and sinful man! What wrong had the man who has died ever done to you, that man against whom you have harboured ill will so unjustly and for such a long time? You wretch! When will you be able to make satisfaction for this sin by which envy has held you for so long at the fiery gates of Hell, which fire never ceases to torment all those who die in the sin of envy? Might there be anything you can do to prevent envy ever re-entering your heart?'

[5] While he was cogitating in this manner and reproaching himself for the sin to which he had fallen prey, he decided in his heart that while he still possessed good intentions in this respect he should

perform some act so noteworthy that on account of that act, and by the grace of God, charity and virtue should grow so strong in him that thereafter envy would have no control over him. He said the following words, therefore, while all the notables who had come to pay their respects to the body and who now wished to depart, listened:

[6] 'O lords, you who have come to this place in order to pay your respects to the man who was once master of this house! I beg you for God's sake and for that of Holy Mary to follow me to my house, and for Evast and Aloma to accompany us.'

Evast and Aloma and all the men and women who had gathered in that square followed him to his house. When the man had reached the doors of his house, he had them thrown open and in the street in front of everyone he confessed his sins and placed his house—a very fine one, which he donated to the hospice—under the ownership of Evast and Aloma. And, in front of everyone, he said that he wished to donate his house and, while they were all present, to say the words that he had previously said, so that he might have occasion to become an enemy of envy, to yield to charity, and to be more harshly punished for his sin.

## 17. ON ANGER

[1] In Evast's hospital there was a patient who had a fistulated ulcer on his leg from which he was unable to recover. This ailment caused the sick man very great distress. It happened one day that the man experienced great suffering as a result of the pain that the ailment caused him and he considered the lengthy period of time he had been unwell. Such great anger entered his mind that he desired death, cursing himself and the day he was born, as well as the life he had been leading. So angry was he, that in his mind he cursed both God and all that exists.

[2] While the sick man was struck by anger in this way, Evast, as was his custom, along with the doctor, tended the patient's leg. And when the doctor had applied thereto the powder he was in the habit of using, Evast dressed and bound the wound and kissed the man's feet while kneeling, as he had become regularly accustomed to doing.

[3] On account of the great humility and charity shown by Evast, God enlightened the sick man's conscience as to the flaws in his

thinking. So the sick man cogitated upon Evast's great humility, remembered his own misdeeds and his anger, and said the following words:

'Alas, you wretched thing! How peculiar this all seems. For you are an enemy of God and of all that exists, on account of the anger that you feel! Evast thinks he is serving God, yet, in fact, he serves the Devil!'

Evast was very surprised by these words and asked the sick man to explain to him what these words meant.

[4] 'My lord', said the sick man, 'my mind was filled with such great anger because of the ailment from which I suffer that I would have preferred death to life. And anger has gained such a hold over me that it leads me to curse God, myself and all that exists. Your humility, compassion and charity, however, make me think about my own trespasses and cause me to cogitate upon the immense grace that God has bestowed on me by giving me a man such as yourself as my servant. And since my wrongdoings and ingratitude are so great, it is not right or just that from now on you should have to support or serve in this hospice such a guilty sinner as myself.'

[5] 'My brother and friend', said Evast, 'God wishes that I should gain merit by serving you and that you should gain merit through patience. You can see the lowly and wretched state in which we exist in this world, for you should derive pleasure from that which causes you anger. You have come into this world in order to gain merit whereby God may rightfully call you to His glory. The more God increases your ailments, therefore, the more opportunity He gives you to exercise patience and to remember the acute suffering He underwent while hanging from the Cross for you and for all mankind.'

Evast spoke to the patient with such devotion and counselled him so compassionately to have patience, to repent and to rein in his anger, that the sick man expressed repentance for his sins and said the following words:

[6] 'Ah, patient God! Who could conceive of such great patience, in the One who has overcome my anger so thoroughly thereby that from now on I shall submit to such patience every day of my life! And so, the more suffering You inflict upon me, the more pleasing to me shall be my life and the more evident to me Your dominion and love.'

The sick man said these words and many others while asking God for forgiveness and rejoicing in His mercy.

## 18. ON VAINGLORY

[1] On a great feast day, it came to pass that a monk had preached in a church where a great crowd of people had assembled to celebrate the feast. A large number of notables escorted the brother to his monastery in order to pay honour to him.[53] It pleased the brother that they had escorted him so that the other brothers might see that he was honoured by the notables who were in his train. While they were walking along, he struck up a conversation with them so as to induce them to praise him for his sermon. They gave very full praise to the brother for the sermon he had delivered, so, accordingly, the brother felt great pleasure in his heart.

[2] While the brother entertained vainglorious thoughts at the words he had heard spoken about his sermon, they came across the young lady whom Evast and Aloma had released from enslavement to lust by their worthy example. When the brother saw her, he remembered that for a great length of time he had wrestled with that lady, whose confessor he was, in order to liberate her from sin, yet that neither his preaching nor the confessions he administered were as effective as the worthy example set by Evast and Aloma. While the brother was engaged in such cogitations, he recognised himself to be guilty of vainglory and decided to punish himself by submitting to some form of penance and never to allow vainglory to enter his sermons.

[3] After the aforesaid cogitation, a lay brother, a fellow of the brother who had preached, asked him:

'My lord, which kind of sermon bears the greater fruit: a sermon consisting of words or of good deeds and worthy example?'

The brother replied:

'Given that it is a greater virtue to do good deeds, and that it is harder to do such than merely to tell someone else to do such, the fruit borne from worthy example is greater than that which arises from words being uttered. Only recently, moreover, Evast and Aloma succeeded in converting a lady to chastity by their worthy example, a lady I was unable to convert thereto either via preaching or by words.'

---

53. Monastic preaching, both within and outside the monastery walls, was common in the Middle Ages and was conducted for a variety of purposes by a variety of religious: monks, nuns and hermits.

[4] When the brother had finished speaking, he took his leave of the notables, who wished to escort him all the way to the monastery, at which the brother demurred, however. And by God's power and the worthy example set by Evast and Aloma, the brother formed the intention that his deeds should be akin to the virtuous words he uttered in his sermons.

[5] In the manner you have just heard, Evast and Aloma, by the grace of God, subdued and extinguished the aforesaid sins by their worthy example. It would be a lengthy matter to recount all the benefits that resulted from the lives of Evast and Aloma. While they both did all they possibly could to serve and love God, it pleased Our Lord God to call Evast to His blessed glory, so He removed him from the wretchedness and dangers of this world.

[6] In this world Evast had died, but in glory he lived. Aloma was alone. Daily she prayed to God for the sake of Evast and in order that God might remove her from this world so long as her penance had been fulfilled. She dared not grieve, for she feared being disobedient to God's will, yet she could not draw comfort, because she was unable to see Evast or her son Blaquerna. She had grown old, and her body, by reason of its afflictions and age, brought her pain for as long as she lived. God, Who does not forget his servants, called her to His beatitude, wherein she found the soul of her husband Evast, whom she loved so dearly.

Here ends the First Book, which concerns Evast and Aloma.

## HERE BEGINS THE SECOND BOOK, WHICH CONCERNS THE ORDER OF RELIGION

### 19. ON THE DISPUTE BETWEEN NATANA AND ANASTASIA

[1] Ever since Blaquerna had left her, Natana continued to think deeply about the words he had spoken to her. She cogitated upon the Passion of Jesus Christ and upon the trials and death that Saint Catherine, Saint Eulalia and Saint Mary Magdalen had endured in this world for the love of God.

[2] By the power of God, and since it is the nature of cogitation to convert one's desires into that thing upon which one cogitates a great deal, Natana had a profound desire to withdraw from the world and to enter the order of religion.

[3] Anastasia watched as her daughter spent her whole time deep in thought, and saw that she had completely changed from her customary state of being. It seemed to her that her daughter was in love with Blaquerna, so she said the following words to Natana:

'Beloved daughter, what is the matter? And what are you thinking about? It seems to me that you can't get Blaquerna out of your mind. If you desire Blaquerna to be your husband, you should forget that idea, for he has gone to be a hermit for the rest of his life, as you know. So, if you wish to have a husband, an honourable burgher has a very agreeable young son and you can marry him. Since your dowry is large, you are of honourable descent, attractive in appearance and well bred, you may choose therefore from within the entire city the best and most honourable bachelor therein for your husband.'

[4] Natana asked Anastasia whether she knew a man within this world who was better, more beautiful and more powerful than all the other men who exist in the world, and whether that man was able to or would wish to be her husband. For she felt herself to be so noble

and rich of heart that not only did she wish to choose from within the city the best man there might exist to be her husband, but rather she wished to choose the best man in the entire world and desired him to be her husband and spouse at all costs.

'Daughter', said Anastasia, 'who could choose, or know, the best man in the world? You are not so wealthy or of such honourable descent that the kings and emperors and other princes should wish you to marry any of their sons.'

Natana said:

'If I lack the wealth, honour or good breeding to deserve to be the wife of any king's son, would any king's son that you may know possess sufficient humility and graciousness that he might condescend to be my husband?'

Anastasia replied by saying that she knew of no king's son or prince who might have sufficient humility that he might deign to be her husband.

[5] Natana spoke to Anastasia by asking her if she had ever heard of Jesus Christ, who is the Son of the King of Heaven and Earth and all that exists, which Jesus Christ is better, more beautiful, wiser and more loveable than any man who has ever existed. And He possesses such humility that the divine nature condescended to be a single person with a human nature. This Jesus Christ possesses such humility and graciousness, that compassion and love caused Him to deign to be poor, to be tormented and to be put to death so that sinners, who were incapable of being saved or of receiving God's blessing, might come to everlasting life and escape from the torments of Hell, which are eternal.

'Mother', said Natana, 'I ask for this Jesus Christ as my spouse and husband, and I beg you to give Him to me as soon as you can, since I fervently desire to have Him. Fear Him not, even if He is as highly honoured and powerful as He is, for He has very frequently performed other acts of humility as great or greater than what I ask.'

[6] Anastasia was very displeased when she learned that her daughter desired the order of religion, and she spoke critically thereof, while praising the order of matrimony. So the question arose, therefore, between Natana and Anastasia as to which was of greater merit: the order of religion or the order of matrimony. Anastasia praised the order of matrimony by saying that God established this order in Paradise and that the world is governed by matrimony, for were everyone to be in order of religion, the world would rapidly become unpeopled; as well

as that the order of religion owes its existence to matrimony, yet that matrimony can exist without its religious counterpart. Natana replied by saying that just as God bodily established the order of matrimony in Paradise, so too spiritually by the light of grace does He enable one to conceive of the order of religion within one's mind. And if matrimony is an order designed to enable people to exist in the world, religion is an order designed to enable people to reside in glory. And although the fruit cannot exist without the tree, it nevertheless does not follow from this that the tree is better than the fruit, since the fact is that God created the tree in order that the fruit may exist.

[7] While Natana and Anastasia were in dispute concerning the orders of religion and matrimony, Anastasia said to Natana that she had once entertained the wish to enter the order of religion, but that certain monks and certain nuns had dissuaded her from doing so and had advised her instead to take a husband. She believed, there-fore, that there are certain hardships involved in the order of religion which are very grievous to suffer and that in the order of matrimony there are certain pleasures which are very agreeable.

[8] 'Mother', said Natana, 'the men and women who are in reli-gious orders each differ as to their desires, yet the order of religion is such a noble thing that it does not countenance any wicked soul's being tainted therein by any vain feeling of concupiscence. The greatest trial one can undergo in the order of religion, therefore, oc-curs when that order is not to one's liking and one desires the vanities of this world, yet the greatest pleasure of all that a person can have in this world is found in the religious who loves his or her order, consid-ers that he or she has escaped the vanities and the dangers of this world, and keeps God and His Honours in his or her mind.'

[9] Anastasia said to Natana:

'Daughter, in this city there is a very agreeable and well-bred young nobleman and, from what I have heard his mother and other people say, he would like you to be his wife since he is greatly smitten by you.'

'Mother', said Natana, 'is this nobleman so strong that he can for-give my sins? And if I fall ill, will he be able to cure me? And would he be able to grant me heavenly glory? And if there is famine in the land, will he be able to grant us a liberal abundance of worldly goods?'[54]

---

54. Cf. I Kgs 8:37; 2 Chr 6:28.

While Natana was defeating and overcoming Anastasia by argument, as is revealed above, the latter cut short her own words so that Natana might not become too resolute as to her devotion and so that at a later date Anastasia herself might be able to inspire in her a desire for the order of matrimony. She rose, therefore, from the place where she had been sitting and went to gaze out of the window at the people passing by in the street.

[10] While Anastasia was standing at the window, a maiden came by with a very great crowd of people to offer prayers to God at the church, for the following day she was due to be married. The maid was of great beauty, very nobly dressed, and rode a fine palfrey. Many honourable men were escorting her on foot, while many honourable ladies, tourneyers,[55] minstrels who were singing and playing instruments, as well as dancers, paid honour to her. Anastasia called to Natana and told her to stand by the window alongside her. Natana came to the window.

'Daughter', said Anastasia, 'see how beautiful it is to look upon the maiden and all those who accompany her.'

While Anastasia said these words, a body that was being carried for burial at the church passed by. Who could possibly describe to you how his wife wept and grieved.

'Mother', said Natana, 'do you see what great sorrow this woman who has lost her husband feels?'

Anastasia failed to answer Natana's words and rose from the window so that Natana should do likewise, rather than witness the tears and suffering the lady was undergoing.

[11] When Anastasia and Natana were in the bedroom, a serving girl presented herself to them very tearfully, telling Anastasia to go to pay her respects to a lady who had died during childbirth, and who had been opened up so that her baby might be removed from her womb alive.

'Mother', said Natana, 'did you hear these words?'

Anastasia did not reply to Natana's question, but rather left the house and went to the lady who was due to be buried that day. While Anastasia was out of the house, Natana considered what Anastasia had told her and how she had tempted her so as to induce her into the order of matrimony. Natana feared the Devil and the frailty of a

---

55. One who engages in a knightly tournament or tourney; a jouster.

woman's heart, which so swiftly changes, and she was frightened that her mother might play some kind of trick on her whereby she might rid her of the devotion she felt towards the order of religion. Natana, therefore, dispatched a secret message to the abbess of an acclaimed monastery of ladies, asking her to send two nuns the following day when her lady mother would be attending Mass, for she wished to visit her in order to say a few words.

[12] When Natana had dispatched the message, she turned to the window in order to observe the return of the woman who was weeping over the death of her husband. While she was standing at the window, she heard a public announcement which proclaimed that people should come to watch punishment being meted out to a burgher's son who was being taken to be hanged because he had killed a man. The man who was being taken to be hanged passed in front of Natana. His father, mother and a large number of his relatives were escorting him. Who could possibly describe to you the grief they felt? While Natana was at the window and witnessed all these things, she saw Anastasia approaching. And Anastasia, who happened upon the man who was being taken to be hanged, wept out of compassion for the lady who lamented her son's plight. When Anastasia had entered the house, Natana said to her:

'My lady, it appears to me that your eyes have wept and that your heart has been stirred to devotion. Have you felt contrition of heart and do you feel remorseful at having reproached me for the saintly devotion God has placed within my heart?'

'Daughter', said Anastasia, 'from now on do not speak such words to me and do not conceive of any order other than that of matrimony. For, should you do so, you will be disinherited and beaten by me, and I shall ask your relatives to rain down many blows upon you and deliver countless slaps to your face.'

'Mother', said Natana, 'you wish me to be like the saints who underwent great trials in this world for the sake of their spouse Jesus Christ, a spouse who Himself underwent acute suffering and death in order to give them glory without end. Do not threaten me with what I should already like to have. I beg you, rather, to make me undergo and obtain what my will desires.'

[13] Anastasia remained deep in thought during the entire night as to how she might find her daughter a husband, whom she would consider her son and would adopt, and who would have enjoyment of

the great wealth that her own husband had bequeathed to her daughter Natana, for she lamented the fate of such wealth were her daughter Natana to enter an Order. And Natana, for her part, remained deep in thought during the entire night as to how she might enter a religious order. The following morning, when Anastasia was at Mass, the abbess sent to Natana two nuns who might escort her to the monastery. When Natana left her house, she said to the serving girl that she wanted to go to the monastery of ladies, and that the girl should tell this to Anastasia lest she thought that Natana had gone to a different and dishonourable place.

## 20. ON HOW NATANA ENTERED AN ORDER

[1] Once Natana had reached the monastery, the abbess and all the other nuns gave her a very honourable welcome. Natana was present in the chapter house[56] together with the abbess and the ladies of that monastery, and she said the following words to them all:

'Divine virtue has subdued in me the false temptations offered by the Devil, which made me tempt Blaquerna so that he might be disobedient to the divine inspiration which called him by way of the eremitic life to become both a lover and a contemplator of God. Blaquerna assigned me seven mistresses, whom I wish to serve in this monastery among yourselves. These seven mistresses are the seven virtues whereby people serve Jesus Christ our God, and whereby they proceed towards His beatitude and recoil from the seven demons, who consist in the seven deadly sins that Evast and Aloma mortify ceaselessly within this city. I ask to have bread and water in this monastery every day of my life; I wish to escape the world before it takes hold of me or prevents me from serving and being subject to the seven mistresses, whom I could not serve so well in the world as in a religious order.'

---

56. The term 'chapter house' derives from the Rule of St Benedict, insofar as it was the place where daily community meetings were held in order to discuss the monastery's business and, where necessary, to administer discipline. The term 'chapter', to indicate such a meeting, likewise derives from the same origin. The Rule of St Benedict was relatively late in taking root within the Iberian Peninsula, though was adopted in Catalonia in the early ninth century as the region became incorporated into the Carolingian empire.

[2] Natana uttered her words tearfully and with great devotion of heart. And so devout and noble in spirit were her words that the abbess and all the other sisters drew a worthy example therefrom and were moved thereby to devotion and tears. The abbess replied to Natana by saying that blessed should be the name of Jesus Christ and magnified be His virtue, Who had sent them such a suitable example and mirror whereby they might love their order and despise the vanities of this world.[57]

'My daughter', said the abbess to Natana, 'may you be truly welcome. Divine radiance has enlightened your mind, by which light you enlighten us so that we may persist in good works. I am very grateful to be in your company, but I must ask the convent, as is our custom, if it wishes me to admit you into our company.'

[3] Natana went to the church to pray to the Heavenly Queen that she might obtain her Son's grace for her so that the abbess and the other sisters might invest her into the order. While Natana was tearfully offering her prayer, the abbess asked the sisters' counsel as to whether it was their wish or recommendation that she admit Natana. All the sisters were pleased that Natana might be their sister. And one nun said that Natana was very wealthy and that on account of her wealth great good would come to the monastery.[58] The abbess and the other nuns, however, reproached her, saying that when one admits a person into a religious order one ought not pay attention to worldly wealth, for a wrong is done to the person one admits thereinto when one does so in view of the wealth she leaves behind and scorns rather than admitting her on account of the virtues she brings to that Order.

[4] The sacrist[59] told the abbess that Natana's devotion should be put to the test for a period of time prior to her being invested.[60] The

---

57. I.e. the order of religion.

58. The family of a female postulant customarily paid a dowry on the latter's entry into a convent, though their doing so could not be a condition of the postulant's admission thereto, for such would constitute simony on the part of the receiving institution.

59. A sacrist (or sacristan) is the (here female) religious responsible for the care and maintenance of the vessels, vestments, shrines, altar(s), relics and physical structure of a chapel, church or cathedral. I avoid the translation 'vestry nun' for its anachronism (the term 'vestry' only entering Middle English between 1350-1400) and the particular associations it carries for the Churches of England and Wales.

60. The sacrist thus recommends a novitiate for the postulant.

abbess replied, however, that many people had remained in a religious order out of shame for a very long time before they had developed a sense of devotion whereby they loved being in that Order.
While the abbess was uttering these words, she sent word to Natana to
come, saying that she and all the other sisters would admit her into
their company.

[5] The abbess asked Natana if she would prefer to receive the
habit immediately or to live within the monastery for a period of time
so that she might try out the austere life that the sisters led in order
to inflict suffering upon their bodies, and see whether the conduct
and customs of the monastery might be to her liking. Natana replied
by saying that it was not necessary for her to put her devotion to the
test, for He who had imbued her with the devotion she felt towards
religion was, in view of His grace and compassion, able to preserve it
for as long as He wished. Natana decided to take the habit without
further delay so that, should her mother and her relatives determine
to retrieve her, the monastery could offer her protection therefrom,
as was its prerogative.

[6] While Natana was receiving the nun's habit and was promising
to adhere to the requirements of the Order, and the abbess was con-
ferring her blessing upon her, as was her custom, Anastasia had come
back from the church and was endeavouring to find Natana. The
serving girl told her, however, that Natana had gone away with two
sisters to the female monastery. Anastasia was greatly displeased and
immediately went to the monastery, where she demanded that her
daughter be shown to her. The abbess showed Natana to her mother
in her nun's habit. Anastasia wept and issued forceful threats when
she saw her newly invested daughter, and she returned to her house
and sent messengers to all her relatives, as well as to the relatives of
Natana's father.

[7] All of them assembled at Anastasia's house. They were stirred
to great anger against the monastery. A course of action was decided,
namely, that if the abbess failed to return Natana to them, they would
take her out of there by force and would demolish, destroy and burn
down the entire monastery and kill the sisters.[61] Anastasia and all the
others went to the monastery to ask for Natana. The abbess said that

---

61. The perpetrators would have been carrying out their actions at risk of excom-
munication, given that Natana had already professed her vows.

they could not have her. They all cried out together and said that if she did not return Natana, they would burn the monastery and all its nuns. The abbess and all the sisters were very frightened, so the former replied that she wished to take counsel with the latter to see whether she would return Natana.

[8] The abbess and all of the sisters assembled in the chapter house. Natana wept, and begged and implored the abbess and the sisters under no circumstances to cast her out of the Order or to deliver her to her mother, who wished to subject her to the vanities of this world. The abbess and the sisters remained in great doubt and danger, and they felt great fear, yet deeply lamented that they might have to return Natana. While the abbess and the other sisters were faced with this obstacle, one such said that it would make better sense if they were to return Natana than if they were all to die and the monastery be destroyed. Natana replied by saying the following words to the abbess and the other sisters:

[9] 'You have all heard that our spouse Jesus Christ wished to die and to be a martyr out of love for our redemption. God wished to impart devotion to the Apostles so that it might be made manifest that the Son of God has servants who do not hesitate to die in order to pay honour to His honour and to show love for His love. God imparted devotion to Saint Catherine, Saint Eulalia, Saint Margaret and the other martyrs so that they might desire to suffer death out of love for Him, and to serve as an example to people of how they might seek to die in order to honour God. If you die on my account, you shall die for the sake of honouring God, and you shall be martyrs and shall set a good example. If you allow me to be forcibly removed from this Order, however, you shall thereby set an example and precedent for the people at large, who shall threaten you whenever you take any woman in contrary to their desires.'

Natana asked them very earnestly not to forsake her nor to reveal any lack of devotion in themselves. She reminded them of the Passion of Jesus Christ and evoked in them thoughts of the martyrdom of Saint Catherine, Saint Eulalia, Saint Margaret and of the other virgins who died in order to honour Jesus Christ.

[10] So devout were the words that Natana addressed to the abbess and the sisters and so great was their power that the abbess and all the other sisters decided to suffer and endure death rather than to return Natana, and they put their trust in Natana's words, placing their hope

in God, Who protects His servants whenever it so pleases Him. Neither the abbess nor any of the sisters dared to give their answer to Anastasia and the others concerning the intention that the abbess and all the sisters had conceived through the workings of the Holy Spirit.

[11] The abbess and all the sisters fled, and hid themselves, and felt great fear of death. Natana made the holy sign of the Cross in front of her face and, since she had a noble and stalwart heart, said the following words:

'Hope, fortitude, charity and justice, since you have made me submit to serving you, now is the time for you to come to my aid against your enemies, who because of me wish to destroy this monastery as well as its ladies, who are not to blame for my sins.'

While Natana was saying these words, she went up with the keys to a window which overlooked the main door, and from the window she showed herself to her mother and to all the others, and said the following words:

[12] 'I offer a welcome to my lady mother Anastasia and to you all. I give you all my greeting. Over all of you I make the holy sign of the Cross, whereby we may remember the Passion of the Son of God, Who wished to be man for our sakes, which man He delivered unto death in order to save us. On behalf of the lady abbess and of all the monastery I greet you and let you know that they are minded to suffer death rather than to return me to you. They wish to show you that Jesus Christ has women who desire to die for the love of Him. They put their trust in God and remember His justice and His power. They are women. There is no need for you to bear arms against them, for they have no intention of resisting you. See, here are the keys to the door. Do what you wish!'

Natana threw the keys to Anastasia and prayed that the first woman to die might be she herself, since she was the cause of the death of all of the nuns as of the monastery's destruction.

[13] Hope, charity, justice and fortitude would not have been virtues if they were to have failed Natana. God, Who does not forget those who praise and love Him, placed so much power within Natana's words that Anastasia and all the others wept on account of the devout things she had said. And because of the saintly lives led by the abbess and all the ladies in the monastery, who had chosen death for the love of Jesus Christ, the intentions and ill will of Anastasia and all the others were transformed. And they were filled with devotion, restraint, remorse,

charity and justice. They all repented and praised and blessed God,
Who had afforded such power to Natana and to all the ladies of the
monastery. Everyone wished Natana well and told her to have no fear
of them, and asked her to say prayers to God so that He might forgive
the foolish and wrongful intentions they had conceived.

[14] In the presence of Natana they all turned and left, and Natana went to ring the bell[62] to summon the abbess and the nuns to the
chapter house. On account of the fear they felt, however, they would
not come, so Natana went to look round the monastery for the abbess
and the other sisters, whom she informed of the mercy and compassion of God, Who does not forget those who place their hope in Him.
The abbess and all the sisters felt great joy. The abbess looked out of
the window and saw that everyone had gone away. Anastasia, however,
had remained at the door all by herself. She uttered great laments
and wept very bitterly, saying the following words:

[15] 'Alas, you wretch! Where are the thanks and the gratitude
that you feel towards God, Who has given you such a noble daughter?
And what wrong had the abbess or the ladies of this monastery done
to you, a monastery you sought to have destroyed by your relatives? Is
there any wrong akin or equal to your own? And even if the compassion and mercy of God is greater than your sins, would He still wish to
forgive you? And would the abbess and the ladies of this monastery
wish to forgive you? And would they condescend to admit into their
company a woman as blameworthy as you?'

Anastasia's words were very pleasing and agreeable to the abbess
and all the nuns, and especially to Sister Natana. Anastasia threw the
keys to the abbess at the window so that the latter might open the
door to her and she might enter the monastery to ask forgiveness
from her and from all the sisters.

[16] The abbess and all the nuns received Anastasia with great
courtesy, and together they went to the church to praise and bless the
name of God, and they gave thanks to Him, Who had delivered them
from death. Anastasia was present in the chapter house together with
the abbess and the entire convent. First of all, she asked forgiveness
from the abbess whilst kneeling and kissing the ground, and then she
asked forgiveness from all the nuns in a similar manner. Everyone
forgave her and all the nuns kissed her. When Anastasia came to her

---

62. Cat. *esquella*: a portable bell or handbell.

daughter to ask forgiveness, she knelt down and wept profusely, saying the following words to Natana, who knelt down in front of her
mother and kissed her hands whilst weeping, and amid tears she
kissed the ground while praising God's power and mercy:

[17] 'Beloved daughter', said Anastasia, 'it is normally the custom
among us for a daughter to kneel down before her mother and ask
for her forgiveness. Through sin, however, I am so profoundly at fault
towards you that I am unworthy to ask for your forgiveness or to be in
the presence of yourself, whom I have sought to make the cause of
the death of all the ladies within this monastery. Daughter, if you feel
in your heart any compassion or mercy, might you choose to forgive
me? Might you delight me and console me with your friendship and
company? And on account of your prayers and merits might God
choose to remember me and call me to His glory?'

Anastasia kissed her daughter Natana repeatedly, uttering the
above words and many others which would take too long to recount.
Natana was so overcome by joy, devotion and charity that she was unable to speak, so instead she raised her eyes and her hands to the
heavens and to the crucifix which stood in the chapter house, and
she kissed her mother's hands and feet again and again. Anastasia
and Natana were not alone in weeping, for the abbess and all the
nuns wept as a result of Anastasia's and Natana's words.

[18] 'O daughter', said Anastasia, 'On what does your heart dwell?
Hear my voice. Answer my words. Do not recall my past misdeeds.'

'My lady', said Natana, 'My heart and my own person are yours.
Sin cannot exist within a heart to which God grants as much devotion
as He has granted to yours. Your faults and sins have been forgiven. If
you bear no fault, why do you ask for forgiveness? If you desire anything from me or within my power, you shall have it all.'

[19] On that day the name of God was roundly praised and blessed by all the ladies in the monastery. Anastasia asked for the habit of
religion to be conferred upon her. However, because she was an elderly lady of frail constitution, the abbess, Natana and all the other
sisters counselled Anastasia to build a house outside the monastery
and opposite the church door, so that she could reside there, and eat
and have some pittance for her body, which she could not have within
the monastery.[63] Anastasia abided by the recommendations of the ab-

---

63. A pittance is an additional allowance of food and wine.

bess, her daughter and the other sisters, and she lived there in the manner they had specified, setting a commendable example to all the nuns who saw her. Her clothing was humble and resembled in part the attire worn by the latter.

### 21. ON HOW NATANA BECAME SACRIST

[1] Natana learned how to read very well, learned how to chant and learned the Divine Office within a brief period of time.[64] She continually remained at prayer in the church, and willingly assisted the sacrist. The abbess took note of the office which gave Natana the greatest satisfaction, so that she might perform that office more readily. And because Natana willingly remained in the church and assisted the sacrist, the abbess, therefore, with the recommendation of the entire convent, made Natana sacrist by saying the following words:

[2] 'Natana', said the abbess, 'it is now time for you to hold an office. And since you greatly enjoy seeing the Cross and the altar, which signify Our Lord Jesus Christ, Who is the Spouse of your soul, and because you shall keep the church very clean, as also everything that is required to honour Jesus Christ in the Office of the Church,[65] the entire convent, therefore, wishes and entreats you to become the sacrist.'

[3] Natana offered profuse thanks to the abbess and to the entire convent for the honour they had chosen to confer upon her. Yet she asked them to withhold from her that honour, of which she was unworthy. For she had not entered the monastery in order to be honoured, and reason did not permit the office to be taken away from the sacrist, since the latter had committed no wrong in the performance thereof.

[4] The abbess replied to Natana by saying that the nature of reason demands that the best people should perform each office, so that the Rule of the Order be better preserved; and that when a particular

---

64. In the Middle Ages, the Divine Office consisted in the seven daily canonical hours, also known as the Liturgy of the Hours, an eighth hour of 'Lauds' being added in later centuries. The hours are the following: Vigils (later called Matins, terminating at dawn, and, in time, distinguished from the *Laudate* psalms, which give Lauds their name); Prime; Terce; Sext; None; Vespers; Compline. For the timing of the hours of the Divine Office, see below, Appendix II.

65. I.e. everything required for the administration of the sacraments.

nun has striven hard at her office, then her Order exempts her therefrom:

'And since the sacrist is an elderly lady and has striven hard at her post, we wish her to rest, therefore, and to exercise patience and humility if we assign her office to you; and we wish you to work in this post and to be obedient to our commands.'

[5] Natana was made sacrist and performed her tasks very capably. She was invariably in the church at prayer with Anastasia, her mother, and they would speak about God, and about His power and His honour, as well as about the Passion of Jesus Christ, the glory of Paradise and the torments of Hell.

'Mother', said Natana, 'these words we constantly exchange are much more seemly and pleasing to God and to the saints in glory than were those we used to utter while we were in the world and we spoke of earthly matters.'

Anastasia replied and blessed the name of God, Who had placed her in that estate and had granted her the company and consolation of her daughter Natana:

[6] 'Sacrist and daughter of mine', said Anastasia, 'I am only too aware that I would have in no way enjoyed your company as fully, were you to have lived in the world and got married, as I do now that you are within an Order. I now realise that the eyes of my understanding were blinded when I advised you against entering religion. It might be time that we shared out the worldly goods we possess among the poor of Christ.'

Natana replied by saying that she continually gave consideration to the fact that the worldly goods her father had bequeathed her might profitably be distributed, and in such a way that for a good deal of time thereafter great benefit might come of it.

'So, therefore, given the circumstances of this monastery, I always take note of how we may enhance the latter using our worldly wealth.'


22. ON THE DEATH OF THE ABBESS

[1] God's mercy and justice wished to provide a reward to the abbess, who was a very elderly lady and had striven hard in the service of God. God wished to call her to His glory so as to reveal to her which Lord she had served. He wished to reveal to her that His power is capable

of rewarding His servants, and He wished to bestow Himself upon her in glory in order to constitute her glory, since the abbess had given herself to Him in this world. The messengers God sent to her so that she might come to Him were the hardships she patiently bore during her illness, which hardships God gave her so that she might possess patience and obedience and might cleanse her body of all sin, and so that after this life she might proceed directly to everlasting rest.

[2] While the abbess was unwell, the nuns came to an agreement that they should ask her to counsel them as regards the matter of selecting an abbess once she had died, for she was better informed about the sisters and their obedience than was any other nun. Certain of the finest ladies in the monastery privately implored the abbess to indicate to them which of their number would be best suited to being abbess. The abbess replied by saying that, in her opinion, the nun best suited to being abbess was Sister Natana, for she had always found her to be extremely obedient:

'Being a nun brings her great pleasure; and she has forsaken immense wealth and honour in favour of religion. And since I am nearing death, you can judge in all earnest that I have no reason to lie, so I counsel you, therefore, to appoint Sister Natana as abbess.'

[3] It pleased God that the abbess should pass from this life into everlasting glory. Her body was most honourably tended in its tomb, and the notables and the ladies of the city, as well as the religious orders, showed great honour that day to the abbess. She inspired great grief in all the people and all the ladies of the monastery, and most of all in Sister Natana. On that day, numerous Masses were said for the abbess in the monastery and such was the saintliness of her life that throughout the churches within the city High Mass was celebrated for the abbess's soul. The ladies from the monastery spent that entire day in tearful prayer, having lost what they most loved in this world. A decision was taken by these ladies to the effect that in the chapter house, once the brother had delivered his sermon on the subject of the abbess, one of their number should offer comfort to all the sisters via some words of consolation.

### 23. On consolation

[1] It was the desire of all the nuns in the convent that Natana should utter some words in order to console them for the death of the abbess.

Natana rose to her feet, offered supplications to the Holy Crucifix, and gave thanks to God and to the sisters who had bestowed honour upon her above all the others. Natana said that there were many nuns in the chapter house who were more capable than her of expressing consolation, but that, since it was their pleasure, she would utter her words according to how God bestowed upon her the grace to do so. Natana begun and spoke her words in the following manner:

[2] 'I am inclined to offer comfort and consolation to myself, so that from my own consolation you may draw the method and example whereby to console yourselves. This method is new, and was acquired by a wise monk who preached very nobly by conversing with himself.

[3] 'My superior has died. Charity and justice stir my soul to feelings of loss and sorrow towards my lady abbess. My soul stirs my heart in order to bring tears to my eyes. I wish to weep, for weeping and loving correspond to each other. Justice wishes people to weep for their superior. If I wish to console myself I must weep, for without weeping I should not be able to console myself. I weep since I cannot see that lady who used to love me and to show me the path of salvation. At the joy of her beatitude I must rejoice; yet at that rejoicing I must weep, for, without tears, happiness finds no fulfilment in this world. Among us, lack and want are followed by the fulfilment and repose to which our superior has attained. I must rejoice at her happiness, yet I must grieve at my lack and my want. I must weep, therefore, out of joy and sadness at the same time. If I should weep for two reasons, then I must weep twice over; if I fail to weep, since reason wills it so, then I shall be compelled to weep for this my omission. My soul does not forget itself, in order that it may weep. If justice seeks to deprive me of consolation and to punish me, then may it not let me weep; yet if it seeks to console and reward me, I beg it to let me weep to my heart's content.

[4] 'My will has been created so that it might take pleasure in the will of its Creator. If my will does not desire what its Creator wills, then I should be deprived of consolation. If, for my own requirements, I choose to retain what might merely be imperfection in my superior, then what has happened to charity, which at one time caused me to love her?[66] If I feel sorrow at her bodily death, who causes me to re-

---

66. Imperfection here referring to the abbess's corporeal nature. The clause refers, therefore, to Natana's desire to have the abbess alive in this world and physically present.

joice at the happiness of her soul? My superior has been removed
from danger, yet how is it that you, Natana, still feel anger at the fact
that you cannot behold her in life? If you, my body, a brutish creature
by nature, seek to rid my soul of consolation on account of a creature
akin to you, my soul seeks to console me on account of a creature
akin to her. Weep if you wish to, my body, for from your weeping my
soul shall draw consolation. To you, my body, does it fall to weep, and
to my soul to remember the virginity, perseverance, holiness, good
works, dignity and worthy end of my superior.'

So devoutly and with such natural words befitting consolation did
Natana comfort herself and so piously did she weep, that she stirred
all the sisters to compassion and tears. And she comforted them all
with her devout words and with her own tears. So all the sisters praised
and blessed God and His power by saying that it was time to love, to
weep and to exercise patience by praising God's will, which had chosen to make use of its power. So their weeping and their loving were
the cause and occasion of their drawing consolation.

## 24. ON HOW NATANA WAS ELECTED ABBESS

[1] Natana and all the nuns entitled to vote had assembled in the
chapter house to elect an abbess. Natana told all the sisters that there
was a very great need to have a good superior, since in the goodness
of the superior, God bestows virtue upon the inferior.[67]

'Thus, since our superior has passed from this life into the next, as
nature and reason demand, it is necessary for us to seek among ourselves to discover which of us is greater in terms of the holiness of her
life and her love of God, for she is worthy of being our pastor according to God's will and ordinance.'

[2] All the nuns wished to elect an abbess in accordance with the
method to which they had become accustomed. Natana, however,

---

67. The opposition Llull sets up here operates on two levels, given that the Catalan term *major* has a literal sense of 'greater', though can equally designate the superior of an order or organisation, while the term *menor* typically has the sense of 'lesser',
and in a conventual context can designate a lower or inferior member of an order; so
the phrase also contains the sense of 'in the goodness of the greater, God bestows virtue upon the lesser', particularly in view of the fact that 'Majority, Equality and Minority' are principles of Llull's Art.

said that she had learned a new method of election, one which consists in an art and in figures, which art adheres to the conditions of the *Book of the Gentile and the Three Wise Men*,[68] which itself adheres to the *Art of Finding Truth*.[69]

'By this method', said Natana, 'is the truth discovered, by which truth we shall be able to discover which sister is the best and most suitable person to be abbess'.

[3] Natana was entreated by all the nuns to speak of the method according to which they might discover and elect by means of an art the best sister to be abbess. Natana replied by saying the following words:

'I shall briefly speak to you about the principles of the art of election. This art is divided into two parts: the first part consists in electing the electors who elect their pastor; the second part concerns the method they should use to elect their superior. First of all, therefore, I wish to tell you about the first part, and thereafter about the second.

[4] 'In this chapter house', said Natana, 'we number twenty sisters who are entitled to vote in order to elect a pastor. The method dictates that, from these twenty sisters, we must elect an odd number amounting to either five or seven, for this number is more suitable than any other for an election, and the number seven is more suitable than the number five. First of all, therefore, an oath must be sworn by all the sisters to speak the truth and the first sister should be asked privately which of the nineteen sisters are best suited to being the seven who elect the superior. Afterwards, the second sister should be asked, and following this the third, and so on in sequence as far as the last. And each time let one write down what each of the sisters says. Finally, let it be seen which sisters are those who have received the most votes, and let those who have so received be the seven sisters who should elect the abbess.

[5] 'The second part of the election occurs when the seven electors elect the pastor. It is necessary first of all, therefore, that the seven electors should agree as to the particular number and identity of

---

68. Llull's *Llibre del gentil e dels tres savis* or *Book of the Gentile and the Three Wise Men* (1274-76 (?)) (hereafter *Gentile*) features a cordial exposition of the respective faiths of a Jew, a Christian and a Muslim, who present their beliefs, all expounded according to the 'Trees' and 'Conditions' of this work (i.e. Lullian principles), for the illumination of a Gentile who is charged with adjudicating as to the superior faith.

69. I.e. the *Ars compendiosa inveniendi veritatem* or *Brief Art of Finding Truth* (c.1274). This was the first version of Llull's Art.

the people to be elected, as they see fit, and that they should compare
each person with the other in line with four conditions, namely:
which one knows and loves God more; and which one knows and
loves virtues more; and which one knows and abhors vices more vehemently; and, fourthly, which one has the most suitable disposition.

[6] 'Each of the seven electors can choose a person to be among
the number from which the superior is to be elected, and each of the
seven electors themselves must be among the number from which the
superior may be elected. And so that you may understand the art more
clearly, let us assume that the particular number of persons from whom
our pastor may be chosen and elected should be nine. It is necessary
first of all, therefore, that the seven be divided into two parts, with two
on one side and five on the other; the five must investigate which of the
two should be elected, and the one who acquires the most votes should
be noted down in secret. After this, it is fitting that another of those five
be compared with the one who has received the most votes and should
replace the one who has been defeated as a result of fewer votes received. Let the defeated party then replace the one who is compared
with the first or with the second. And let the same be done with all the
others in sequence. And let the eighth and ninth candidates, who are
not among the electors, be comprised within this number. From this
number, therefore, can be generated thirty-six compartments in which
the votes of each person will appear. So, let the person be elected who
has the most votes in the most compartments.'[70]

[7] When Natana had expounded the art of election, a sister
asked her:

'If it so happens that there are candidates who have an equal number of votes in their compartments, what does the art prescribe in
such a case?'

Natana replied:

'The art prescribes that one examine those two or three or more
candidates via the art alone; and that one should examine which of
them corresponds better to the above four conditions; and the one who
best corresponds to the conditions is the one worthy of being elected.'

---

70. Here Llull is referring to the 'compartments' which make up the tabular half-
matrices seen in the 'Second Figures' of his early Arts, namely, the *Ars compendiosa inveniendi veritatem* (*c*.1274) (hereafter *ACIV*) and the *Ars demonstrativa* (*c*.1283) (hereafter *AD*).

[8] The art and method of election greatly pleased all the nuns, and they all said that one could not err in elections if one conformed to that art. So they all laid down the rule that they should conduct elections in perpetuity according to the art and method that Natana had described. So they set about studying it and learned that art. After a few days they conducted an election in line with the art and discovered by this method that Natana should be abbess.

[9] So Natana was elected abbess, but was greatly displeased by the honour conferred upon her. Nevertheless, she gave thanks to God, Who wished to honour her above all the others. She feared, however, that the sisters had erred in the art, so she wished to see the thirty-six compartments in which the art resides, so that, if they had erred in the art and she should not be abbess, they might elect that person with whom the correct use of the art was in accord. Natana and the other sisters who had not been among the seven who had been electors, checked the method used by the latter in the election according to the art, and discovered that they had adhered to that art in the appropriate manner. Natana began to think deeply about how she might be able and might manage to govern herself and the nuns, and continually cogitated upon how she might direct the monastery towards worthy habits.

## 25. ON THE ORDINANCE THE ABBESS GAVE REGARDING THE FIVE BODILY SENSES. AND, FIRST OF ALL, ON HEARING

[1] The abbess rang the bell so that the sisters might congregate in the chapter house, for she wished to ask their counsel as to how she could bring it pass that their sense of hearing might be employed within that monastery in such a way that they could follow the Rule of their Order better. While the abbess was in the chapter house and the sisters were congregating for the purpose of holding the chapter meeting, a sister who was in the habit of begging in the city for the love of God came to the chapter house and told the ladies that she had seen a very beautiful and nobly dressed bride-to-be, who was being led with great honour to the church. The sister eagerly spoke her words and the ladies eagerly listened to them. The abbess perceived in the sister's words the absence of order which results when sisters who beg speak of worldly pleasures to the other sisters.

[2] The abbess and the other sisters were in the chapter house, so in the presence of all the abbess gave thanks to God and said the following words:

'My soul has cogitated at length, seeking to discover how my lady mother Anastasia and I might render unto God the possessions with which He has entrusted us. Now, by God's power, my soul is enlightened as to how we may bequeath our wealth to this monastery, under the following condition, namely, that from now on no sister should go to beg in the city nor recount any worldly matter concerning what she sees or hears. For, by hearing about worldly pleasures are the vanities of this world remembered and desired, and by reason of such desires are prayer and cogitation upon the Passion of Jesus Christ precluded.'

[3] A statute was laid down to the effect that no nun should leave the monastery without great need to do so. And the wealth that the abbess and her mother bequeathed to the monastery was so plentiful that it was sufficient to provide for the needs on account of which they had been accustomed to begging. These funds were overseen by lay brethren, elderly and worthy men, who had already been put to the test in another Order, from which funds the brethren allocated money to the monastery without setting foot therein. And if the abbess or any lady from the monastery had need with regard to any personal matter which had to be concealed from the brethren, there were discreet widows in the city who were Beguines and were trustworthy women, and who catered to their needs.[71]

[4] A certain number of nuns were enrolled, after which no more were to be admitted. This statute was laid down so that the funds the abbess had bequeathed to the monastery might suffice, and so that they might have reason to refuse to accept too many nuns. And if any lady wished to enter the monastery or place her daughter there, she

---

71. Beguines (female) and beguins (male) were members of lay religious orders who lived according to a set of Rules, though did not take formal vows; they forswore marriage and embraced poverty, among other things. These orders originated in thirteenth-century Northern Europe, often lived in loose communities and gave expression to an increasingly common sense of popular piety. According to one author, however, in fourteenth-century Languedoc, at least, the term *béguin/e* meant not a holy man or woman living in a *béguinage*, as in Northern Europe, but a member of the Third Order of St Francis, and that increasingly the term would have come to mean a devotee of Peter John Olivi (1248-98) and of his ideas on poverty and the Apocalypse; see BURNHAM (2008), 33; cf. also, LEFF (1999), 195-230; and above, Ch. 9, § 1.

would have to make a payment until another lady in the monastery had died, which payment was to cease after the death of that sister, who should be replaced by a further sister.

[5] The abbess went through the monastery regularly to see if she could find anything which called for regulation of the sense of hearing. One day the abbess entered the garden and she saw two nuns spinning, seated apart, and she saw another spinning by herself. She then entered the dormitory and from there she went into the other rooms where the nuns were in the habit of spinning, and she observed that they did not do their spinning all together in the same place.[72] The following morning the abbess called a chapter meeting and she laid down the rule that all the nuns should spin in the same place and that a particular nun should read out to them a certain book which was in the vernacular, so that they might understand it. This book should treat the Passion of Jesus Christ and the lives and martyrdom of the saints, both male and female, as well as the lives of the Holy Fathers now departed. In this book should be included the miracles of Our Lady, Holy Mary, and of the virgins and martyrs and the other saints. And this book should be read both on Feast Days and on other days, as it fell to each nun in turn and in sequence. This book was sought out and the ordinance was enacted within that monastery and in many others which followed its example.

[6] The abbess very fervently wished that this rule be adhered to, so that by hearing this book one's soul should not cogitate upon vanities or disorderly thoughts whereby it might be inclined to sin, as likewise that each nun should become enamoured of the virtuous lives of the saints departed. For just as the soul is stirred to loving at the sight of beauteous things, so too is it stirred to desiring when it hears pleasant words.

26. ON SEEING

[1] The abbess was in the chapter house with all of the ladies of the monastery, and she said the following words:

---

72. In the Middle Ages, the practice of spinning was viewed as an honest and chaste occupation for women, both 'ladies' and 'maidens'. Here the practice also has the further economic role of providing an income for the monastery.

'In keeping with what the divine ordinance has chosen to prescribe for man, it has been ordained that he should employ his sight
in an orderly manner, so that good order as regards his spiritual life
might arise therefrom. Accordingly, it is desirable for us to enact an
ordinance and a rule among ourselves so that we may know how to
employ our bodily sight. Let our eyes thus first be properly ordered
to contemplate the crucifix and the image of Our Lady, Holy Mary, as
well as the other figures which depict for us the lives of the saints who
have departed from this world. Let us do honour to such figures by
petitioning them whenever we behold them, and let us remember in
our souls what they signify to us.

[2] 'Let our attire be humble, and let no trace of artistry or super-
fluity be present in our features, but that alone which nature has
placed there according to the will of God. When worldly ladies come
to see us and to listen to our words, as has been ordained in the chapter concerning the sense of hearing, and when we see their proud
attire and their artfully painted faces, then should we praise and bless
God for having chosen us to be servants of humility and for having
protected us from the vanity of this world. Then should your spiritual
eyes see how Jesus Christ, our spouse, and Our Lady and the saints
wore humble attire. Each of us may earn merit if she is able to recall
this fact when she beholds proud attire. Let us tell the worldly ladies
that they should come among us humbly attired and that embellish-
ment and artistry should be absent from their features so that they do
not tempt our souls to covet the vanities of this world.

[3] 'When we look upon the graveyard, then is the time to cogitate upon death, and spiritually we may see the worms that will gnaw
and devour the eyes with which we see, the ears with which we hear
and the tongue with which we speak. When we are in the privy and we
see the filth that issues from our bodies, then is the time to cogitate
upon the baseness of our nature, so that pride may in us be curbed
and humility thereby exalted. When we enter the garden and we see
the ass drawing the water-wheel,[73] and we look at the trees and the
grass, then is the time to offer thanks to God, Who has fashioned us
in a more noble nature than the beasts, the trees and the grass for,

---

73. Cat. *sènia* or *sínia*, meaning 'noria' (in English and Spanish), the technical
term for a kind of water-wheel, common in Spain, which has buckets attached to its rim
in order to raise water from a stream, etc. Cf. below, Ch. 35, § 6.

had He so wished, He could have created us in a manner similar to theirs.

[4] 'Let us look up at the heavens and see how vast they are, our gaze fixed upon the sun, the moon and the stars. Let us cogitate upon the sea and the land, and upon the birds, the beasts, the plants and the people. Let us praise God, Who is so great; for, if God has created so many creatures so diverse and so beautiful, how much greater is the One who is Creator! And if God has created all creatures for the sake of mankind,[74] how great must be the gratitude we should feel towards God!'

In all these ways and in many others, the abbess entreated the nuns to employ both their bodily and their spiritual eyes so that their hearts might be raised up to a love of God and not tend towards wickedness and wrongdoing.


## 27. ON SMELLING

[1] 'Smelling roses, lilies and flowers in general brings joy and pleasure to one's body, so because of such pleasure there is a danger that the soul might tend to desire some fleshly vanity. It is to be recommended, therefore, that we, who reside within this monastery for the purpose of performing penance and of leading a harsh life, should not have any flowers unless we place them upon the altar so that, thereby, it might more fittingly be decorated. When we smell the perfumes, such as amber and musk, given off by the garments of worldly ladies, then is it only right that we should remember the gall, the soot and the vinegar which our spouse Jesus Christ was given to drink on the day of His Passion.[75] Thus can we remember the stable in which He chose to be born so that He might show us by example that we should not take pleasure in odours which stir one to sin.

[2] 'When worldly ladies sit among us and we smell the odours of certain colourings with which they have carefully painted their faces, then is the time to recollect the baseness of their hearts. And it is right that we should reprimand them, for if, among us, they are not ashamed to indicate their foolish intentions, then we should not feel

---

74. Gen 1:28-30.

75. Matt 27:33-34 and Mark 15:23, though Mark refers to the gall mixed with the vinegar as 'myrrh'.

an ounce of shame in reprimanding them, since it is the case that shame pertains to matters of wickedness and wrongdoing alone.

[3] 'Smelling a foul odour is something to be avoided because such an odour pollutes the air, by virtue of whose pollution illness and death are generated in one's body. Something to be avoided even more, however, is the friendship of a woman who applies perfume to her face or her attire, by which means she signifies the type of wrongdoing she desires. For if polluted air causes the body to tend towards physical death, friendship and intimacy with an immoral woman frequently causes the soul to tend to cogitate upon and desire evil deeds, whereby a sinful will and memory in a man are the occasion of eternal suffering.'

In this way and in many others, the abbess ordained that, within the monastery, no sin proceeding from the sense of smell should occasion the loss of supreme and perpetual beatitude.

### 28. ON TASTING

[1] The abbess said the following words to the nuns:

'The chief reason we are in a religious order is so as to contemplate, worship and serve God. And among the other things which most forcefully preclude prayer and contemplation is a surfeit of eating and drinking. It is a just rule, therefore, that we should eat and drink in moderation, so that there might not exist hypocrisy among us. Such hypocrisy is present in those who join an Order and give the impression of leading an ascetic life as regards eating and drinking, while, in fact, eating and drinking exquisitely and excessively.

[2] 'If meat is forbidden to a religious, it is not fitting that fish or other food should afford similar flavours or pleasure to one's mouth, which flavours or pleasure the mouth encounters when foods are garnished with sauces and other such things. If it is good to fast, it is not lawful to eat as much once a day as you would if you ate twice, for if it were, there would not be great virtue in fasting. If our clothing and our beds indicate the religious life, the bread we eat and the wine we drink must equally indicate the ascetic life.

[3] 'Eating and drinking too much gives rise to boils as well as illnesses of the blood, and it brings on sickness and death. The body, due to an excess of food, occasions the soul to desire carnal pleasure.

Many religious houses are poor and in debt as a result of just such excesses relating to sustenance. If any monks or nuns eat better and more exquisitely than they did when members of the laity, then they performed more penance in their laypeople's habit than they do in that of a religious. Patiently to feel hunger and thirst constitutes the mortification of sin and the health of one's body, since nature consumes within one's body a certain excess of ill humours.

[4] 'Let us eat and drink so that our lives may consist in loving and serving God, rather than living so that we may eat and drink. If we are in servitude to God because we are His creatures and because He has redeemed us in the Incarnation of the Son of God, let us not be in servitude to our bellies, which fail to forgive or offer relief to their slaves. Let us not place greater trust in the foods that sustain the body than in the virtues that sustain the soul.'

The abbess spoke all these words and many more to the nuns so that each of them might impose hardships upon her body through hunger, thirst and meagre nourishment; and so that because of the austerity of their lives God might forgive those members of the laity who are in thrall to the sin of gluttony.

## 29. ON TOUCHING[76]

[1] 'Touch is a sense which applies to the whole body. One's whole body is a creature of God, so one's whole body should feel pain for the love of God. If we are in winter, then it is the season for feeling cold; if we are in summer, then it is the season for feeling hot, for the love of God. If we stave off our sense of heat and cold, then we offend our mouths if we do not likewise stave off our sense of hunger and thirst. As the lord wishes to be served by his vassal, so God wishes to be served by the body, which belongs to Him. If the body fails to endure suffering, then where is the service it renders to God? For just as God has given us eyes to see bodily things and so that by these the soul may see Him spiritually, so too has He also conferred a sense upon the body so that, through this sense, the soul, which constitutes the body's form, may exercise patience.

---

76. Cat. *De sentir*, a verb which has the general meaning of perceiving (i.e. feeling) via any of the senses, though in Old Catalan can refer specifically to the sense of touch.

[2] 'Coarse clothing, a hard bed and the order of religion are in accord with each other. Thus, fine clothes and lying in a soft bed are in accord with life in the world. If we feel fleas and lice in our bed and we are unable to sleep, this signifies to our understanding that our prayers are brief, since we keep vigil for only a short time while praying to God. It is much better to pray to God while keeping vigil, than to desire to sleep while feeling fleas or other types of lice. If we do not wish to feel fleas and lice, may we be pleased to keep long vigils. Lengthy sleep and the order of religion are contraries, for if they were in accord with each other, there would be no difference between the order of religion and that of the laity.

[3] 'If we wish to feel carnal pleasure, our virginity is corrupted when we conceive the thought. A virginal body deserves to feel the fires of Hell if its soul desires its own corruption. To be more aware of the nature of one's body than the virtue of one's soul reveals that one's body is the master of one's soul. If, for our sakes, Jesus Christ suffered[77] grave hardship and an agonising death, then let us, out of love for Him, endure a life of austerity. If we are gathered together in this place so that we may spurn worldly feeling, then let us not occupy this place in the world with a view to desiring its vanities. If you wish to experience[78] vanities whereby you may be sentenced to feel everlasting fire, then place your finger in the fire and test whether you can withstand that fire for an hour.

[4] 'Sickness from fever or pain or anything else causes the body to suffer, by which suffering the soul, if you have patience, may exercise its virtue. If God wishes your body to feel suffering and yet you lack patience, remember within your soul whether your will is in accord with or contradicts that of God. If within your heart you feel longing and desire for your relatives, then also seek within your heart whether you feel God's presence. If you feel temptation or some foolish thought within your soul, then God wishes to make you feel His power, through prayer, via remembrance of His Passion, for through temptation He wishes your soul to awaken by contemplating His blessing.'

---

77. Cat. *sentí*, perfect tense of the verb *sentir*.
78. Cat. *sentir*.

[5] When the abbess had laid down this statute and had given instruction to the sisters as to how they should employ the five bodily senses, she then said the following words to them:

'By God's will and ordinance it came to pass that Blaquerna entrusted me to the grace of, and bound me in slavery to, seven queens, who are virtues of the greatest necessity to us. Therefore, since it pleases you that I be abbess, I beseech and command our entire community that these seven queens be held very dear among us and that in all our deeds we may prove obedient thereto. And if any of you commits any fraud or wrongdoing against any of them, then let her, in the chapter house, in front of all the nuns ask forgiveness and remission for this so that she may feel greater shame concerning her fault, so that a similar situation may not recur in due course, and that the other nuns may draw an example therefrom and accordingly oppose the enemies of the seven queens.'

All the nuns endorsed the abbess's words and they set aside a particular time of the day at which they might assemble in their chapter and each of them might examine her conscience to see whether she had done anything which was contrary to the seven queens or was in accord with the seven deadly sins.[79]

## 30. ON THE SEVEN VIRTUES AND, FIRST OF ALL, ON FAITH

[1] One day it happened that a sister, taking counsel from the Devil, experienced temptation against the faith while she was considering the Holy Trinity of Our Lord God, the Incarnation of the Son of God, the virginity of Our Lady, Holy Mary and the transubstantiated Sacred Host of Our Lord God. While the sister was suffering temptation as regards the aforesaid Articles, she remembered the statute and ordinance which had been laid down by the abbess and by all the ladies in the convent, as has been stated above. When the abbess and the other sisters were in the chapter house, the sister who had expe-

---

79. What the abbess Natana describes is a distinctively Lullian construal of the monastic practice of confession conceived as a 'chapter of faults', namely, the public or private admission to the superior of a religious house of one's personal faults or infractions of the Rule, for which penance may be fulfilled by means of the imposition of disciplinary measures (see next chapter).

rienced the temptation rose to her feet and asked for punishment, using the following words:

'It is God's ordinance that when the soul suffers some temptation, it should have recourse to God and to the virtues He has given us so that these may assist us in our needs. My soul surrendered to frailty and niggardliness, so that through its misdeeds God's power might be known and fortitude and hope be strengthened in my soul. Since my soul, however, was forgetful of God, hope and fortitude, it felt doubt concerning the Trinity of the Most High while cogitating upon how there could exist in God a unity of essence and a plurality of persons, which might be diverse without diversity and composition of essence. Not only was this doubt in my soul, but rather I likewise doubted the Incarnation of the Son of God while cogitating upon how there could be such humility in the divine nature that it wished to unite human nature with itself, with which nature it might be a single person. My soul doubted divine power and virtue while cogitating upon how it could be that Our Lady, Holy Mary might be a virgin both before and after the birth. In all these ways did my soul succumb to doubt, and all the more so on account of the Sacred Host, which has the colour and flavour of bread, beneath which colour and flavour lies the flesh of Our Spouse, Jesus Christ. For such doubts I ask penance and I confess in front of the whole convent the frailty of my faith, so that all the sisters may draw an example therefrom and that they may know how to protect themselves from temptation in a similar situation. I should like an explanation concerning this doubt to be given to me so that it may never recur in my soul again.'

[2] The abbess replied:

'It is not fitting that our soul should understand the very manner of the operation that God enjoys within Himself, wherein the Father generates the Son and the Holy Spirit proceeds from the Father and the Son. For, if our soul fails to understand all that God has created —which is finite and limited—then how much less can we understand all that God performs within Himself! Thus, what we fail to understand in God is that which our intelligence lacks the capacity to understand. By the light of faith, therefore, does God wish that we should believe what we are incapable of understanding as regards His Trinity and the other Articles. God, however, has bestowed strength upon our intellect so that it may acquire knowledge of Him by means of His creation. For, just as the intellect can understand that man is a single person composed of two diverse natures, namely, body and soul, so too—and to an incomparably greater degree—can God consist in a single essence and in three Persons, which three Persons constitute a single essence. And were God not to possess such power, it would follow that He was more capable of uniting a plurality within a creature than within Himself, and to this we should not assent.

[3] 'Everything that God has created in the world He has created so that He may reveal His Virtues to us, in order that He be known and loved by us, through which knowledge and love He has cause to employ justice and mercy towards us, whereby He may grant us everlasting glory. The Son of God assumed our nature, therefore, so that He might exercise humility in us and set us an example of how we might exercise the same. He wished to reveal His power and His charity. For His power and charity are revealed better in His making the Person of the Son incarnate in a human nature than they are in His having created the world from nothing. And we are under a greater obligation to love God for the reason that He wished to become incarnate and to die for our sake, than we are for any other thing He might do on our behalf. Therefore, just as our intellect understands that, in accordance with the course of nature, it seems impossible for the Son of God to have become incarnate, so too does our intellect see spiritually, in accordance with God's great humility, charity and power, that God wished to become incarnate and was capable of so becoming. For had He not wished or had he been unable to unite our nature to Himself, it would have been made manifest that there existed within Him a lack of will and of power whereby He might impose upon us the obligation to know and to love Him. For all these reasons, therefore —and for the further reason that God is capable of uniting soul and body with each other to form a single person, even while the soul is of one nature and the body another—can our soul curb the doubt which it entertained regarding the Incarnation of the Son of God.

[4] 'God created Adam in an earthly paradise, and fashioned Eve, his wife, from a rib which He removed from him. This work was not carried out, therefore, in accordance with the course of nature, but was performed, rather, in accordance with the working of miracles. The conception the Virgin acheived, while still a virgin, of the Son of God, Who came into her as man and God and was born of her as man and God, while she was still a virgin, consisted in the working of a miracle counter to the workings of nature, and one designed to prove

that God has greater power, virtue and will than has nature, insofar as
He can perform a deed which nature cannot. And by so doing He
proves Himself to be the master of nature. So, had God not performed this supernatural deed, He would not have proved that His
power itself was beyond nature.

[5] 'Man cannot be seen with bodily eyes, for man is composed of
soul and body, yet bodily eyes can see only part of man, namely, his
body. Man can be seen, however, using both spiritual and bodily eyes:
the intellect sees one's soul by understanding, even as bodily eyes see
one's body. Thus, with bodily eyes one sees the form and colour of
bread in the Sacred Host, while with spiritual eyes one sees the flesh
of Jesus Christ. For, just as the eyes of the body see bodily things, so
too do the eyes of the soul see spiritual things. And just as one's bodily eyes see the Host by means of light and of colour, so too do one's
spiritual eyes, using God's Virtues, see in the Host the flesh of Our
Spouse, Who wills with an infinite will, almighty power and all-perfect
wisdom, that in that bread's form and colour shall exist the true flesh
and blood of Jesus Christ. And if God were so to have willed, yet it
could not be, it would follow that His will, power and wisdom would
not possess infinitude or perfection. And since our intellect sees that
all perfection and all infinitude exist in God's Virtues, by means of
these latter it sees, therefore, what we cannot see when we use our
bodily eyes.'

[6] In this way as well as others, the abbess suppressed the doubt
against faith to which the sister had succumbed. So the sister in question along with all her fellow nuns felt great joy in their hearts at this,
and in them faith was so sturdily fortified against temptations pertaining
to belief, that the Devil was powerless thereafter to insinuate doubts
in them against the faith and its Articles. So all the nuns praised
and blessed God, Who had bestowed such wisdom upon the abbess, for
having given them such an excellent pastor who, through her knowledge and her saintly life, had given them such robust instruction as to
how to love and know their spouse Jesus Christ and His works.


31. ON HOPE

[1] In the monastery was a lady who had been very sinful while living
in the world and who, since entering the Order, had committed cer-

tain deadly sins. One day she recalled God's great justice and the sins she had committed both in the world and within the Order. So clearly did that sister remember her sins, while forgetting God's mercy, and so guilty did she feel about her sins (and all the more so those she had committed within the monastery) that she succumbed to despair concerning whether God might forgive her, for it seemed to her that whatsoever virtuous acts she performed, she could not win God's blessings.

[2] While the sister was engaged in such cogitations, she formed the intention of reverting to the sins she had been accustomed to practising. Owing to the merits of the penance she had performed for her sins, however, and to the sanctity of the abbess and of her fellow nuns, God decided to look upon her with merciful eyes and caused her to remember what the abbess had prescribed with regard to hope and the other virtues. So, in the chapter house, before the abbess and the entire convent, she confessed the temptation she had suffered against hope, and she asked for forgiveness and counsel to combat the temptation which placed her in such grievous distress.

[3] The abbess replied, saying the following words:

'The error of despair has a way of making one think that God is more just than merciful, so, therefore, many sinners succumb to it . Yet since God is merciful and is greater than His creatures, it necessarily follows that a person, who is a creature, is unable to sin as much as God's mercy is able to forgive. So it is necessary, therefore, that when one cogitates upon one's great trespasses, one should likewise cogitate upon God's great mercy, to which those who consider it to be equal to His great justice pay honour and show their esteem. And it is on account of such honour and esteem that mercy forgives people their mortal trespasses by granting them sorrow and remorse for their sins.

[4] 'To remember the conception and the Passion of the Son of God fosters hope and curbs despair. For if God wished to unite and join our human nature to His nature, and if He wished to put the nature He assumed to grave trials and death so that He might spare us from the Devil, it certainly follows that He should wish to forgive us if we put our trust in His mercy and compassion. It happens, however, that through lack of love, which is absent from one's soul when one is in despair, people fail to remember the holy humility that God exercised when He assumed human nature, as well as during His Passion, so despair, therefore, subdues and overpowers hope. When charity and hope are in accord against despair and sin, however, then

do they oblige God to be forgiving, for the reason that they cause one to love Him and to place one's trust in Him. And readily may all the sins of that person be forgiven, therefore, who with love can bring hope to bear on her memory, intellect and will.'[80]

[5] While the abbess was uttering these words, the cellaress[81] told the abbess that she often sinned against hope when cogitating upon the provision of the monastery and that she frequently doubted that such provision might suffice. The abbess replied that the opposite of that sin which led her to despair would be the opportunity whereby she might remember the wealth and generosity of God, Who provides so many creatures with all that they need. For if God provides sustenance for beasts, birds and fish, which lack reason, and for laypeople who love the world, He would be unjust were He not likewise to provide for them, who have gathered together in this monastery in order to serve Him and to spurn worldly pleasures and who place their trust in Him. So, to cogitate upon such things and to trust in God, therefore, constitutes virtue, which virtue and cogitation one should engage in as soon as one is tempted by the aforesaid sin.

## 32. ON CHARITY

[1] In front of the abbess and all the nuns, a sister spoke of the offence that she had long been committing against charity. For she had loved God more intensely for the reason that He might bestow glory upon her than she had for His own sake, and she had feared Him more for the reason that He might not inflict the torments of Hell upon her than she had by virtue of His goodness. The abbess replied to the sister in the following words:

---

80. The Augustinian triadic powers of the soul, namely, memory, intellect and will are prominent features of Llull's dynamic understanding of human spiritual psychology, appearing as this does in Figure S from the 'quaternary phase' of his Arts (i.e. until 1290) along with the sometimes disjunctive logic of the acts of such powers (i.e. memory remembering/forgetting; intellect understanding/not knowing; will loving/hating).

81. The cellarer or cellaress in a monastery or convent was the individual responsible for the acquisition, storage and distribution of provisions and goods, as well as the overseeing of any estates or granges. The role and conduct expected of the cellarer within a monastic community are specified in Ch. 31 of the Rule of St Benedict, for which see *RSB*, 116-119.

'So well-suited is God to being loved and feared on account of the excellent goodness and virtue that reside within Him, that one should love and fear Him for His own sake rather than for the purpose of attaining glory or avoiding Hell. For in loving glory one loves oneself, and as a result of the love one feels for oneself, one fears the torments of Hell. And since one must love God more than oneself, it runs counter to charity and justice, therefore, that one should fear God for the sake of that which is less noble; rather, one must love and fear Him for the sake of that which is more noble, because He is worthier and nobler than all the other creatures.'

[2] When the abbess had revealed the reason why one should love God, and had also shown how one may love glory and fear eternal suffering, another sister said that she had committed an offence against God, as well as against all the nuns, insofar as the intention she had had in entering a religious order bore no relation to the charity she might have felt towards God and the sisters, but resulted from the fact that, within the world, she was poor. So, having been unable to acquire the wherewithal to live, she entered the Order. The abbess replied by saying that in a single action can one exercise one's intention in either an orderly or a disorderly manner. For if one enters an Order as a consequence of poverty, one may feel love firstly for God and that Order, while secondly one's intentions may be directed towards oneself and one's own needs.[82]

'Since your intention was directed exclusively towards yourself, however, yet you could have intended to enter the Order for the love of God and of the company of nuns, you have caused offence both to God and to such nuns, as a result of which offence you deserve to endure penance.'

[3] 'It is true', said another sister, 'that I wished to become abbess, more for the sake of my own honour than as a result of the charity and love I bore towards God and my fellow nuns.'

The abbess replied:

'To love prelacy for the sake of being honoured constitutes pride and vainglory, and is contrary to the life of Jesus Christ, Who in this

---

82. Here Llull is calling on his doctrine of first and second intentions, i.e. man's primary and secondary objectives, namely, the overriding goal of loving, knowing, praising, honouring and serving God and, subordinately, any means which contributes to the attainment of that goal. For discussion of these concepts, see Bonner (2007), 72-77; Artus (1995) in Bazan et al (1995), 978-990.

world wished to be poor. To love prelacy for the sake of serving God
and so that those who lead disorderly lives are set right upon the path
to salvation, is to love God and one's neighbour, and constitutes charity which is pleasing and agreeable to Him. Such fatuous desires,
namely, the love of prelacy for the sake of being honoured, may be
curbed, however, by remembering the lives of Jesus Christ and the
Saints, who loved poverty. This aim can also be accomplished by remembering the trials the prelate undergoes in ruling over her subordinates and the relation of servitude in which she stands to all of the
latter. So, because of the foolish desires you entertained, you stood
against freedom, for to be a nun within a convent involves submission
to one's superior alone, while to be an abbess involves submission
and servitude to all the nuns. Thus, were it to be pleasing to God as
well as to the nuns, and were your desires to be correctly ordered, I
would willingly exchange my office for yours.'

[4] 'My lady abbess', said another sister, 'I have long desired to be
able to feel love for God and my neighbour. I ask you to instruct me
how how I might feel such a thing.'

The abbess replied:

'Whoever wishes to feel love in the way that one should, must
know how to remember and understand. For if wisdom is not present
in one's memory or intellect, charity cannot be present in one's will.
It is necessary, therefore, frequently to remember and understand
God, together with His power, wisdom and will, His works and His
Virtues. It is necessary also to remember and understand the baseness of this world, the glory of the next and the torments of Hell. It is
necessary further to remember and understand the great love God
has shown us and that we are all of one nature, one flesh and one
blood; which nature, flesh and blood the Son of God decided to assume for our sake, as too for our sake He chose to be hung up and
put to death on the Cross. By such remembrance and understanding,
then, does the will conceive of charity and love. And by forgetting
and ignoring such things, does charity depart from one's will and do
anger, ill will, falsity and evil enter therein.'

[5] When the abbess had spoken these words, she said to all the
sisters that they should strive to entertain charity towards all things,
for it is not prohibited to anyone who may wish to entertain it; and
each person may entertain as much of it as she wishes to have. By
means of charity can one bear any kind of hardship; and what is hard

to bear it enables one readily to endure. And as regards what is pleasant to desire and consider, one is gladdened whenever one is able to remember and understand such things with charity.

'Such a noble and lofty virtue is charity, that it caused God to descend from Heaven to Earth and to be made incarnate, and to weep, suffer, hang and perish. And charity caused Him to create the world and all that exists. And His charity sustains us, for He has given to us every creature upon which we live, and every creature that is in our service He has likewise given to us. And Divine charity has created Paradise for us, to which He calls us and in which we may enjoy everlasting glory and deliver ourselves from infinite torment. Since so many and such great and necessary benefits may redound upon us by virtue of charity, and since charity is granted to whomsoever may desire it, great evil and great sin dwell in the heart that entertains no charity.'

## 33. ON JUSTICE

[1] In the monastery was a nun who was very gravely ill. Each day, as was her custom, the abbess made rounds throughout the monastery to see whether she might be able to improve it in any respect or whether any advantage was to be had from her presence. She entered the infirmary where she discovered the ailing nun, who bore her illness with impatience and uttered words whereby it was signified to the abbess that justice was absent from her soul.

The abbess asked the ailing nun whether she had exercised justice, charity, fortitude and patience. The nun replied:

'So forcefully has the illness seized hold of me, that there is no longer any room in my soul for virtue, but rather I am overcome by such great anger that I would rather be dead than alive.'

[2] 'What a fool you are!', said the abbess, 'I should like you to answer me and to tell me which would cause you greater suffering: that you might be standing on top of a great mountain full of fire and sulphur or the illness you are enduring? If you die lacking justice, your soul shall dwell within the everlasting fires of Hell. Who is it that makes you ill? Since you lack patience, you fail to love God, Who makes you ill in order to punish you for your sins. You are contrary to His justice, since you fail to love His works. Fortitude is absent from

your heart, for your illness casts out charity and justice therefrom, inserting impatience and injustice instead. While God makes you ill, He is asking you to surrender yourself to Him with justice, charity and patience, so that He may confer upon you the eternal blessing of salvation.'

The abbess uttered so many edifying words to the ailing nun, that charity, justice, fortitude and patience retrieved the soul they had lost, and the nun said the following words:

[3] 'I bless and adore you, O divine virtue of justice, since you punish me and yet indulge me insofar as you omit to punish me according to the multiplicity of my sins, though I deserve to suffer such hardships and many more besides. Do with me what pleases Your will. And may my will desire all that You desire. I am not worthy of glory; there are sins within me on whose account I deserve everlasting torment. If You wish to punish me, may it please You to exercise Your great justice. If You wish to forgive me, may it please You to exercise Your great mercy. Whether You punish me or forgive me, I bless and adore Your great justice regardless, and I place my hope in the sweet mercy that the Queen of Heaven requests from You for the sake of us all regardless.'

While the nun was saying these words, she felt within her heart such great fervour and devotion, bestowed upon her by charity, justice, fortitude and patience, that her illness became easy for her to bear.

[4] When the abbess had consoled and instructed the ailing nun, she entered a secret room where a nun who had grievously erred and sinned against her own honour and her own order was confined.[83] When the abbess went in to see this nun for the purpose of consoling the latter in her penance, she found her kneeling and saying amid tears the following words:

'O Holy Justice of God, which has all things in Your power! I bless and adore You, for in the trials I undergo I acquire knowledge both of You and of my own faults. From such knowledge my soul derives pleasure, and causes me to love Your justice and to abhor my sins. The harsher the trials You cause me to endure, therefore, the more You reveal Yourself to my understanding and the more You cause me to remember the great mercy that lies within You. I desire such bod-

---

83. The order here referred to is the order of religion.

ily suffering to continue forever so that my soul may know and love You and that in You I may rejoice.'

So holy and devout were the words that the sister was uttering, that they stirred the abbess to devotion, mercy and forgiveness, and amid tears the abbess spoke the following words:

'No defect should exist in that wherein the Holy Justice of God may be pleased to participate or abide. I am prepared to forgive you and to entreat the convent to do likewise, since Divine Justice forgives all those, men and women, who in their deeds praise and bless it. Your body is thin and worn down by the great suffering it has endured, your clothes are shabby, your meals are few and meagre, your bed consists of vine branches, and for company you have solitude and the shadows of your own making. Your soul as its company, however, has the divine radiance, which causes you to love and have knowledge of God's justice. Ask and it shall be given to you.[84] Repent and you shall be forgiven.[85] Your repentance and devotion render you more noble than I am by my virginity.'

[5] Devoutly and amid tears the abbess stopped speaking and the sister thanked her profusely, saying the following words:

'It is the nature of a worthy lord that he loves the blessing of his subject. My confinement and hard life serve as a lesson to the sisters so that in their hearts they may fear wrongdoing and evil. My happiness lies in chastising my body and in contemplating God in His justice. I ask for forgiveness and repent of my sins. I ask to have the penance I now perform every day of my life, for the more worn down is my body, the more exalted is my soul in God. May God be in my soul and penance and hardship be upon my body.'

[6] The abbess entered the garden, where she saw sitting beneath a tree a nun who was weeping. This nun had lived in the world amid great wealth and honours, and because of the refined conditions she was accustomed to enjoying, she bemoaned the hard life she endured within the monastery. The abbess asked her why she was weeping and in despair, so the nun told her all about the desires of her heart.

'O foolish and unjust soul!', said the abbess, 'Have you never at any time had knowledge of justice, which in a religious order chas-

---

84. Matt 7:7; Lk 11:9.
85. Acts 3:19; 8:22.

tises with coarse foods those who have eaten exquisite meals within the world, and with modest attire humbles those who have worn proud garments, and with a hard bed torments those who have lain in their noble equivalents? What a fool you are! Why do you not go to the church to weep? Raise your eyes to the Cross and behold in what kind of bed lies Our Spouse Jesus Christ, Lord of Heaven and of Earth. Behold likewise His garments, stained crimson[86] with the blood which has issued from His body. See how He has been left hanging, naked and forsaken. He felt thirsty; yet see how He was given salt, soot, gall and vinegar as his drink. See what crown he wore in honour, and how his body was scourged and wounded.'

So forcefully did the abbess reproach the nun that in due course the latter no longer entertained the foolish thoughts she had formerly had.

## 34. ON PRUDENCE

[1] A nun had succumbed to sin, yet did not know for certain whether her sin was mortal or venial, albeit that she felt no desire to ask or inquire whether that sin was in fact mortal or venial. She behaved in this way because she loved succumbing to that sin and feared that she might have to renounce it were she to know that it was mortal. One day it happened that, while the abbess was holding a chapter, the sister came to an awareness of the wrong that she had committed against wisdom, as has been described above. The abbess replied, saying these words:

[2] 'God has granted humanity reason and discretion so that people might exercise reason against sin by loving the virtues. So, when one feels no desire to exercise reason, lest one be made aware of the sin to which one has succumbed, God's justice is correct in chastising that person and in withdrawing the latter's discretion and awareness while she is alive in this world. A great sinner in this world, therefore, is she who has blinded the eyes of her understanding so that thereaf-

---

86. The 'crimson garments' of the Messiah are prophesied by Isaiah (Isa 63:1-3). The colour crimson was associated with sinful humanity, itself redeemed by the (crimson) blood of Christ. The Virgin Mary was also connected with crimson garments in the Middle Ages, as the Mother of the Saviour or Messiah. See Twomey (2013), 104ff.

ter she may not experience awareness of or repentance for her sins. We see many people die, therefore, in circumstances which enable us to have knowledge of their damnation, insofar as, at their life's end, they make no restitution for their wrongs or show any repentance for their sins. So, since friendship and fellowship obtain between justice and wisdom, justice therefore chastises those who fail to love or honour wisdom.'

[3] While the abbess was saying these words, there was a sister in the chapter who had a son who was an eminent lawyer in that city. Before becoming a lawyer, this son of hers had wished to enter a religious order and to study Divine Scripture, but his mother made him study Civil Law so that he might live within the world and have a wife. The sister remembered that she had seen her son put his learning to ill use, and became aware, therefore, of the wrongs she had committed against wisdom, so she said the following words:

[4] 'I have sinned against wisdom and against Holy Scripture, whereby a person gains knowledge of God.'

The sister asked for forgiveness and remission for the aforesaid sin she had committed. The abbess told the sister that she had erred very profoundly against the wisdom and understanding that the Holy Spirit bestows. For the desire which her son had felt to be a religious and to understand God's Scripture was granted to him by the Holy Spirit, Who wished to imbue him with wisdom so that He might be known and loved by him and that He might confer heavenly bliss upon him. So, for that wrong and for all the others that her son would commit by putting the science of Law to ill use the sister bore the blame, on account of which she would enjoy less glory if she won salvation or greater suffering if condemned to damnation. The abbess was deeply stirred against the sister and the penance she gave her was very harsh.

[5] While the abbess was talking about the gifts bestowed by the Holy Spirit, a nun called to mind her own ignorance, which she exhibited insofar as she did not know the fourteen Articles of Faith or the seven gifts bestowed by the Holy Spirit, or the eight beatitudes that Jesus Christ promises in the Gospels, or the seven virtues whereby one proceeds to Paradise; nor was she familiar with the seven deadly sins whereby a person goes to the fires of Hell, or the Ten Commandments which God gave in the Law. Of all these things was the mind of this nun ignorant, things which are very beneficial to

know. So she asked forgiveness for this ignorance and requested that all the above things be taught to her.

[6] The abbess reproached the sister very harshly, saying the following words:

'Whoever does not know the fourteen articles in which our faith resides knows not how to believe or to practise the faith in the appropriate manner. And whoever does not know the seven gifts bestowed by the Holy Spirit, how shall she be able to show gratitude to Him if she fails to understand that which is bestowed upon her? And whoever does not know the eight beatitudes knows not how to desire everlasting glory. And for whomever is ignorant of the seven virtues, where is the light whereby she may see to proceed along the path to salvation? And whoever does not know the seven deadly sins, from what can she protect herself, and how can she repent or confess, and where is the contrition she can feel? And whoever does not know the Ten Commandments, how can she be obedient to God? And if she is disobedient, how can she become aware of it? Whoever wishes to know all the above things, should remember that these and many other things are contained in the book *On the Instruction of Children.*[87]


## 35. ON FORTITUDE

[1] Just as we have called prudence 'wisdom',[88] so too do we call fortitude 'strength', in order that the nuns may have readier knowledge thereof.[89]

Thus, while a nun was worshipping God without pause, praying that He might grant her the seven virtues whereby she might serve Him and that He might protect her against the seven deadly sins, she was tempted very frequently by vainglory. This she felt with respect to her virtuous life and the devout prayers that she offered, wherein charity and contrition for her sins caused her to weep and to remember God's mercy.

---

87. Llull's own *Doctrina pueril* (1274-76), for details of which see above, Ch. 2, § 5 and corresponding note.

88. I.e. in the preceding chapter.

89. Cf. Prov 8:12 and Wis 8:7.

[2] So strongly was she tempted by vainglory, that it seemed to her that God was bound to perform miracles on her behalf and to honour her in His glory above all the other nuns. It came to pass one day that while this nun entertained vainglory with respect to her prayers, she became aware of her wrongdoing and wondered deeply at how such a wicked thought as vainglory could enter her mind while she was engaged in such devout prayer. So, therefore, in the chapter house, and in front of all her fellow sisters, the nun asked the abbess from where the above misdeed had come to her. The abbess replied, saying the following words:

[3] 'Fellowship and brotherliness obtain between one virtue and another so that each virtue is exalted by the others, through their mortification of the vices. So, since charity, justice, faith and hope are raised greatly aloft in prayers for the sake of contemplating God's Virtues, prudence and fortitude wish to be their fellows. So, when one's mind is tempted by vainglory, therefore, and is sufficiently wise to be able to recognise that temptation, yet reason proves resistant to the temptation; and while one's memory is disposed to be aware of the wretchedness in which we exist on account of sin, and one's intellect is heightened for the purpose of understanding God's nobility; then are wisdom and strength lofty in virtue, and fellows of the other virtues. When vainglory prevails, however, and one's mind forgets its misdeeds, fails to apprehend God's Virtues and consents to vainglory, then, through lack of wisdom and strength of resolve, the other virtues succumb to sin.'

[4] When the abbess had explained the way in which vainglory tempts those engaged in virtuous works, another nun told her that she had often felt tempted to leave her order.[90] So the abbess replied that that temptation resulted from a lack of strength of resolve:

'Or the charity required to love the order of religion and to scorn the world is lacking. And because memory remembers the world and forgets about the honourable nature and the saintly lives of the nuns within an Order, fortitude is suppressed within one's will. So for this reason one should forget that which leads temptation to arise, and should remember other things.'

---

90. Again, the order of religion.

[5] A further nun told the abbess that every day she felt the temptation to eat, drink and speak in a manner contrary to the Rule of the Order. So the abbess said:

'God has been pleased to ordain that creatures be many and various so that in many and various ways may they serve people, to whom God has given them so that people in many and various ways may serve God. Your temptation arises, therefore, so that, through abstinence, fortitude may triumph over greed and disorderly words. Such triumph it achieves when charity and justice help it to combat sins. So, thus does temptation give the virtues occasion to exercise the power that God has given them so that the soul may gain greater glory therefrom.'

[6] In the chapter house was a most beautiful nun of very honourable descent who had bequeathed immense wealth to the order. This sister was constantly tempted by pride, so she asked the abbess to offer her counsel against such pride. The abbess answered the sister by saying to her that whenever she was beset by such temptations, she should go into the garden and contemplate an ass which drew the water-wheel, and should consider in exchange for how much money she would willingly become an ass. The price that she would reject to become an ass, therefore, would strengthen her resolve against pride by helping her to cogitate upon God, Who could have created her as an ass if He so pleased. When she had engaged in such cogitation, she should go to the cemetery, should cogitate upon the dead and should remember the rotting that occurs within their flesh. And she should remember the filth within her bowels. Afterwards, she should go to the church and she should look upon the Cross so that she might remember the humility to which God chose to condescend. The abbess said all these things and many more to the sister in order to give her instruction whereby she might strengthen her resolve against pride and in order that she might reject all things rather than commit any sin against God.

## 36. ON TEMPERANCE

[1] When the abbess was in the chapter house with the sisters, she said the following words:

'By God's virtue, we have discussed and given ordinance regarding the six virtues. Now we must discuss temperance, so I wish to know if there is any sister among us who has committed any wrong against temperance.'

One nun replied, saying that she had had no knowledge of temperance, so did not know, therefore, whether she had erred against it. The abbess said to the nun that temperance was a virtue that lay in between 'too much' and 'too little', so that, by 'too much', the human intellect might understand the greatness of God, which is greater than all things, no absence of order being entailed thereby; and that, by 'too little', one might understand that in God there exists nothing which is little.[91] And because excess and paucity find their mid-point in creatures, there is no temperance in God, insofar as there exists in God nothing which constitutes either excess or paucity.

[2] 'God has created temperance between two terms for another reason', said the abbess, 'namely, so that temperance might be the mean whereby people may know how to and be capable of exercising wisdom, justice, fortitude and the other virtues. For in eating, drinking, speaking, sleeping, keeping vigil, travelling, dressing, spending, cogitating, and in all other things, one requires temperance so that one's wisdom may be aware of that which is too much and that which is too little; and so that charity may love that mean, and that justice may derive temperance from the two vices and deliver it up to charity, and that fortitude may reside in a person's mind against excess and paucity in order that it may be in accord with temperance, by which temperance fortitude is likewise in accord with the virtues, which themselves are in accord with temperance.'

[3] When the abbess had revealed the concordance which exists between temperance and the other virtues, the sister remembered the wrongs she had committed against temperance, so she said the following words:

'Alas, O sinful woman! How great is my guilt, for in eating, drinking, speaking and in many other things have I ignorantly erred against justice, charity, wisdom, fortitude and temperance. For justice granted me conscience, while wisdom revealed to me excess and paucity so that charity might love temperance. Yet since my will lacked fortitude, it tended towards excess or paucity and failed to exercise

---

91. The idea that virtue consists in a 'mid-point' or 'mean' lying between two extremes derives from Book 2 of Aristotle's *Nicomachean Ethics*, 1106a26-b28, and was very common in the medieval period.

temperance. And, since God has granted freedom to the soul, which is capable of practising the aforesaid virtues, yet my soul did not choose to practise them but, rather, to practise the vices, I am, therefore, sinful and ask for penance and forgiveness, and surrender myself as a sinner.'

[4] The abbess said to the sisters:

'There are three powers in the soul, namely, memory, intellect and will.[92] Everything the soul does, it does with these three powers. Our soul should be properly ordered as regards these three powers, therefore, so that it may impose proper order upon the five bodily senses, which are apt be set in proper order by the soul, so that, as previously noted, we may be properly ordered with respect to the soul's seven virtues, which we shall be if we order ourselves properly in terms of those three powers. We shall speak first, therefore, about memory.'


## 37. ON MEMORY

[1] 'Memory is granted to our soul so that we may have remembrance of the Supreme Good, whence all goods proceed, which has created us and bestowed grace upon us, who are gathered together in this monastery to remember Him and to forget the vanities of this world. To receive a benefit from another, yet to forget it, is a sin for the soul. Since we have received a benefit from God, therefore, and since for the sake of our salvation He has assumed our nature and has delivered this unto severe hardship and grievous death, it is our great duty to remember these things every day and every hour of the day. I desire and command, therefore, that each of you should remember the goodness, greatness, eternity, power, wisdom, love and perfection of God, and that you should remember His Incarnation, Passion and the other things which pertain to God; and that each sister should remind the other of such things. For by such remembering is temptation put to flight, hardship alleviated and the soul illumined by the light of benediction.

[2] 'It befits us to remember the glory of Paradise so that we may desire it. And let us remember the torments of Hell so that we may

---

92. See above, Ch. 31, § 4 and corresponding note.

fear them. And let us not forget death so that we may be ready for
it, since we do not know when it will come, yet are certain that we
have to die. Let us remember whence we have come so that pride be
not among us. And let us not forget the corruption or the putrefac-
tion of our body, so that we may possess humility. Let us remember
one another in charity and justice so that peace be among us. If we
are able to remember, we shall be able to forget; and if we are able
to forget, we shall be able to remember; and if we are able to remember, as well as to forget, we shall be able to understand and
love.[93] Let us remember our sins so that we may remember God's
justice and mercy; let us remember the virtues so that we may seek
them in God.

[3] 'It is not fitting to remember what we have done in the world,
because by such remembrance the will is stirred to desire that world.
If we suffer temptation, may we profit by remembering God, Our
Lady and the Saints in Paradise and let us ask for their help. May each
of us remember the angel that God has assigned her to protect her
against sin, and may each one render it daily some form of honour.
And may each of us remember some particular saint who may act as
her proxy within the heavenly court. May we remember the lives of
the saints, men and women, so that we may become enamoured of
those lives. May we remember the unbelievers so that we may entreat
God to send them the light of intelligence and of faith, in order that
they may know Him and love Him and may be steered towards the
path of salvation. At night, after Compline,[94] may each of us remember whether, during the day, she has offended her Creator in any respect. In the morning, after Matins, let us remember in what state we
have found ourselves during the night.'

In all these ways and many others did the abbess instruct all the
nuns to remember, so that they might be remembered by the sweet,
compassionate mercy of God. So all the nuns praised and blessed
God, Who had bestowed so much wisdom, charity and saintliness
upon their abbess Natana.

---

93. Here Llull is emphasising the fundamental dependence of the acts of the intellect (i.e. understanding/not knowing) and the will (loving/hating) on those of
memory (remembering/forgetting), cf. above, Ch. 31, § 4 and corresponding note.

94. Under the Rule of St. Benedict, the Divine Office commences with the Night
Office (i.e. Vigils or Matins) and finishes with Compline, the last hour of the Day Office.

## 38. ON INTELLECT[95]

[1] The abbess Sister Natana told the nuns that intellect was a spiritual light which illumined the soul so that the latter might apprehend the truth of its Creator and of His works, and, likewise, so that the will, prior to being stirred to love or hate anything, might receive the light of understanding, lest it err in its operation. For just as blind people, through defect of bodily vision, err as to the paths they take, so too does the soul err in terms of its remembering and willing when it fails to receive light from the understanding.

[2] 'It often occurs that one's intellect becomes disturbed by excessive remembering and willing and, for this reason, it is necessary that whoever wishes to receive spiritual light should be temperate in her remembering and in her understanding. Whoever wishes to understand, therefore, let her be capable of remembering and willing; and whoever wishes to remember and will, let her be capable of understanding. For a high degree of understanding is generated by a high degree of remembering and willing, and a high degree of remembering and willing by a high degree of understanding, when one is able to bring into accord the operation of one's memory, intellect and will.

[3] 'If we wish to understand God, we must first make use of faith and then of understanding, and we must believe that which we are unable to understand.[96] Likewise, we must understand that, in His essence and in His works, God is greater than we are able to understand. For if our intellect does not suffice for us to understand all that we are and all that we do, how much less, beyond all comparison, can our intellect suffice for us to understand God's entirety or His works! And if such were not the case, it would follow that, with respect to our essence and our works, we should be greater than God, which is impossible.

---

95. This chapter reveals a deep Augustinian and Anselmian influence, given, of course, a distinctive Lullian twist.

96. Here we note Llull's characteristic take on the Augustinian/Anselmian principle of *Credo ut intelligam* ('I believe in order that I may understand'), *Proslogion*, 1, insofar as Llull claims that we should also, and in particular, believe that which we cannot understand, in view of the ultimate ineffability and incomprehensibility of the Divine Essence. Llull's inspiration, nevertheless, stays within the boundaries of the Anselmian project, defined as it is by *fides quaerens intellectum* ('faith seeking understanding'), the *Proslogion*'s initial title.

[4] 'There is no defect in the intellect with regard to that which it is able to understand. There is a deficiency, however, in that man or woman who possesses understanding yet does not know how to exercise it with regard to that which it is capable of understanding. And whoever does not wish to exercise her intellect with regard to that which it might be capable of understanding, wishes not to exercise the finest creature that God has been pleased to create, nor to have the supreme pleasure the soul enjoys through understanding, nor is she fearful of the sadness to which the soul succumbs through not knowing. So, the more powerfully the intellect understands, the nobler, greater and loftier it becomes through such understanding. Through excessive remembering, however, the capacity of one's memory can become less in terms of its remembering; and through excessive loving or hating the capacity of the will can become less in terms of its willing. Why, then, is she who does not wish to understand that which she is able to understand still eager to remember and to will?

[5] 'The will should not wish the intellect to understand that which it is not able to understand, but rather it should wish it to be ignorant of that which it is unable to understand. And if the intellect understands truth, the will must love that truth, yet if it understands falsity, the will must hate that falsity. And if the intellect understands the will, the will should love the intellect, for just as the will is created in order to love the intellect, so too is the intellect created in order to understand the will. And if memory frequently remembers without understanding or willing, the imaginative faculty becomes accustomed to operating in such a way that one becomes witless.'

[6] While the abbess was giving instruction to the sisters as to how they should exercise their intellect, one sister asked her how memory could remember without willing or understanding. So the abbess told her that everyone tends to remember first one particular thing and then another, and that this happens so often that one's will is unable to accommodate loving or hating, nor one's intellect understanding; one's memory, therefore, is used haphazardly, as a result of which use one's imaginative faculty becomes disordered, whereby the power of one's memory is destroyed.

## 39. ON WILL

[1] The abbess informed the sisters that God had granted will to man, the beasts, the birds, the fish and to all living things. The will which he had given to man and woman, however, was nobler than that of the beasts and the other creatures which lack reason. And this is because the human will must not desire anything without reason. When, therefore, a man or a woman loves or hates something without reason, then is their will worse than that of any other creature.

[2] 'Will accords with loving what is good and hating what is bad, so when one loves more fondly that which is a lesser good than that which is a greater good, then does one order one's will towards loving what is bad and hating what is good.'

So, while the abbess was uttering these words of great subtlety, a sister told her that it was not lawful for such subtle words to be spoken to a woman.[97] So the abbess replied by saying that since the intellect was capable of understanding them, it was fitting that the will should wish the intellect to be exalted thereby so that it may understand, and that consequently the will might better be able to contemplate and understand God and His works. For, had God not wished to be contemplated through love and understanding, He would not have placed such great power in creatures, nor in remembering, understanding and willing, which power He placed therein so that He might better be understood and so that through better understanding He might more fondly be loved. And if, by wishing to understand a particular subtlety, some kind of doubt is generated, it is therefore necessary for one to have recourse to faith and fortitude, whereby the human mind receives the strength to believe that which it fails to understand.

[3] 'In this world, freedom accords better with will than with memory or understanding. And obedience is more befitting within religious orders than outside them. And this is because freedom is more constrained within religion than it is in the world, since a will which, of its own volition, loves to subject its own freedom to obedi-

---

97. Cat. *subtilesa* is one of Llull's five 'spiritual senses', which exist in addition to the three mental powers of the soul (i.e. memory, intellect and will), the other four of which are: cogitation, apperception, conscience, and courage or fervour. *Subtilesa* assists in sharpening our knowledge of God's divine nature.

ence has risen higher in terms of its possessing merit, charity and
justice than has a will which does not lie under obedience. For if it is
a delight to love one's beloved willingly, greater merit lies in loving
obedience to one's superior against one's will. For one's will is in
thrall to itself insofar as it loves that which it feels more inclined to
hate. So, if you dare not cogitate upon this subtlety, you harbour fears
concerning the exaltation of your faith, which exaltation you should
love so that in you there is greater fortitude and hope. What I have
told you, therefore, conveys to you a certain kind of secret, one which,
given the times in which we live, I dare not explain to you.

[4] 'Each of you possesses will and intellect. May each of you hold
your will in thrall to your intellect. And I desire and command that
the will of each be subject and beholden to my will; and may my intellect
and my will be subject and beholden in general to your intellects. For in
this way may one identify the role of an abbess or abbot in religion.'

## 40. ON PRAYER

[1] The abbess was in the chapter house along with all the ladies of
the convent. And the abbess wished to know the manner in which
they all prayed, for it is very necessary to have good order in one's
prayers, since prayer is the noblest practice that exists in religion and
ill-ordered prayer is highly displeasing to God. While the abbess was
saying these words, a sister asked for forgiveness on the grounds that
she had often sinned against prayer by saying a few words thereof
while her mind, even as she prayed, remained fixed upon other, vain
matters contrary to prayer. The abbess replied by saying that there
are four kinds of prayer. The first is when one's mind contemplates
God though one's mouth utters no words.[98] The second is when, in
prayer, one's mind and one's mouth are in accord and one's soul

---

98. I.e. silent prayer or *oratio mentalis* (lit. 'mental speech'), as William of Ockham
(*c*.1287-1347) would later call it; cf. PANACCIO (1999), esp. 120-49, 153-250. Note that,
in his *Enigma fidei*, 91 (*c*.1142-44), William of Saint-Thierry, a Cistercian and disciple of
St Bernard of Clairvaux, posited the existence of mental language *in interiore cordis*,
stating: 'Est enim in homine in interiore cordis eius verbum aliquod de quaecumque
re conceptio aliqua veritatis, *sine voce, sine syllabis, sine forma aliqua*' ['In the interior of
man's heart there exists some word, *without any sound, syllables or form*, for anything
whatsoever which constitutes a particular conception of the truth' (emphasis added;
my translation); cf. Panaccio (1999), 159; and Davy (1959), 170.

understands that which the words express. The third kind is when a person lives virtuously and without mortal sin, for everything she does constitutes prayer. The fourth kind is when one's mouth utters words of prayer and one's mind cogitates upon other matters. This fourth kind of prayer is displeasing to God, bears no fruit, and is the result of a lack of charity, wisdom and fortitude, through which lack one's soul forgets and ignores what the words signify. In such prayer, therefore, must one have recourse to the aforesaid virtues and, using them, must bring one's soul and one's words into accord, one's soul understanding, remembering and loving the words that one's mouth utters.

[2] 'You have heard how Blaquerna worshipped God in the fourteen articles, and how Evast worshipped God in His Essence and Virtues, as well as how Aloma prayed to Our Lady, Holy Mary, for the sake of her son Blaquerna. The immense affection and love they expressed in their prayers, therefore, were in accord with their words. So, for this reason, we must love God and His works so ardently that our soul and our words are in accord when we pray to Him, in such a way that the water from our heart rises to our eyes so that they run with tears and that in our soul the virtues overcome and subdue our sins, while our soul comforts itself with tears and rejoices with devotion, giving glory and blessings to God.

[3] 'While we are at prayer we should remember, understand and love God's Virtues and His works. And we should lend order to our soul and our body by means of faith, hope, charity, justice, wisdom, fortitude and temperance so that we may cause memory, understanding and will to ascend to contemplate and desire His glory. And afterwards we must remember, understand and abhor our sins and the wretchedness of this world. So, through such deeds, and with the help of the fire of the Holy Spirit, our soul shall be enlightened as to how to pray to God, and our prayers shall be granted by the justice and mercy of God, in Whom resides all perfection and in Whom every perfect prayer finds the power to grant the blessedness of salvation.

[4] 'We should pray for Our Holy Father the Pope and for the cardinals, the prelates, the princes and for all Christians, that God may give them devotion so that their entire life might consist in knowing and loving God, and that in them may return the holy devotion to exalt the faith which once existed in the world at the time Our Spouse Jesus Christ and the Apostles lived on this earth.

[5] 'Let our soul not forget the unbelievers when at prayer, for they share our blood and have a similar form to us. They are ignorant regarding faith and demonstrative knowledge[99] owing to a lack of teachers, which they do not possess, as far as we can see. They do not know, love or believe in God, nor do they give thanks to Him for the goods that He gives them. Many among them consistently blaspheme against Our Spouse Jesus Christ, and many of them think that He was a sinner and a fraud. He would have very great virtue who professed before them God's name and virtue, as well as the honour that resides in Our Spouse. He would be pleasing to God who caused Him to be honoured by those who dishonour Him. Those willing to suffer martyrdom[100] in order to exalt God's name would arrive at the heavenly court on the Day of Judgement clad in garments like those of Jesus Christ.

[6] 'Let us offer thanks to God since He has given us human existence and has placed so many creatures in our service. We cannot sufficiently thank Him for the good we have received and continue to receive from Him. Let us pray to Our Lady, Holy Mary, and all the angels and saints in Paradise that they may thank Him on our behalf. Let us confess our sins and ask forgiveness. Let us not consider ourselves worthy of the good we receive or the glory for which we hope. Let us thank God, Who has removed us from bondage to the world and brought us together in this place, where we may perform penance. Let us ask God for virtues that we may be protected from vices by means of our holy lives. Let us worship Our Saviour with love, tears, contrition and devotion. Let us persevere so that we may not become weary of worshipping, loving and praying to Him Who has given us a heart whereby to love, eyes whereby to weep and a mouth whereby to praise His power and His works.'

In all these ways and many more did the abbess give instruction to the sisters as to how they should contemplate, worship and pray to God.

---

99. But cf. below, Chs. 44, § 2; and 48, § 9. Cat. *ciència*. Aristotle delineates his theory of *epistēmē* (Lat. *scientia*) via the demonstrative syllogism in his *Posterior Analytics*. For the difference between such notions of *scientia* and modern conceptions of knowledge and, especially, scientific knowledge, cf. Jenkins (1997), 38ff.

100. Cat. *penrien passió*; lit. 'undergo suffering'.

## 41. On spying

[1] The abbess spoke the following words in front of all the sisters:

'I am inwardly reminded how, when I used to see our lady abbess, may God forgive her, I feared her presence and concealed certain things so that she might not come to learn of them. In order that our souls may at all times of day fear the justice of our order,[101] therefore, with your counsel I wish to establish a new rule[102] within this monastery, namely, that each week we should secretly elect a sister to act as a spy, who may closely observe the things you do. Likewise, none of you should know which sister is the spy so that you are as fearful of one another as you are of my own presence. Further, this sister should describe all that she has seen you do which may be improper or opposed to our order.

[2] 'I likewise wish to ordain that we place spies within the city, who may remain watchful as to whether certain of our sisters enter therein in pursuit of some need, and may closely observe their behaviour and the places they visit, as well as whether they hear any dishonourable words spoken about such sisters or about us or anything else whereby blame may be imputed to us.

[3] 'Not only do I wish you to be kept under watch, but also I wish to be kept under watch myself, the better to avoid all wrongdoing. So I therefore wish you to elect three sisters weekly and that these sisters may secretly elect a sister who may closely observe the things that I do without my knowing that she is spying on me. And in the chapter house I wish her to denounce me in front of all the sisters if she has seen me do anything unbecoming or opposed to my order. And rightfully, in front of everyone, I should bear penance and beg forgiveness for such things.'

All the sisters considered what the abbess had said to be beneficial, and they all approved of what she sought to ordain.

[4] The abbess lived for a long time within this monastery and complied with all the aforesaid ordinances. And there were many virtuous sisters within the monastery on account of the saintly life and teachings of the abbess Natana. Many ladies from the city followed

---

101. I.e. The order of religion.
102. Lit. 'institute', i.e. a rule or custom.

her commendable example and many other monasteries derived their Rule and method from the one the abbess Natana had ordained.

[5] Through God's grace and assistance, here ends the book concerning the order of nuns. We must now return to Blaquerna, who is in the forest and is going in search of a place where he may worship, contemplate, know and love God.

## 42. ON THE TEN COMMANDMENTS[103]

[1] After he had parted from Evast and Aloma, Blaquerna travelled through the forest for the entire day. At night he arrived at a lovely meadow where there was a beautiful fountain over which hung a fine tree. It was there that Blaquerna slept and rested that night. As was his custom, Blaquerna began his prayers very early in the morning. And because of the solitude and isolation of that place and because he could see the sky and the stars, his soul was greatly uplifted to contemplate God. The wild beasts he heard going about the forest, however, disturbed his prayers owing to the fear such noises aroused in him, though he strengthened his faith in God's supreme aid with hope and fortitude.

[2] Blaquerna remained at prayer until sunrise, after which he set off on his journey and travelled during the entire day until, at dusk, he arrived at a place where there was a great mass of trees, in which place stood a fine and very nobly wrought palace. Blaquerna went up to the palace gates. Inscribed above the doorway in gold and silver lettering were the following words:

'Thou shalt not have false gods. Thou shalt not swear falsely. Thou shalt observe the Sabbath. Thou shalt honour thy father and thy mother. Thou shalt not commit murder. Thou shalt not commit fornication. Thou shalt not steal. Thou shalt not bear false witness. Thou shalt not covet thy neighbour's wife. Though shalt not covet thy neighbour's goods. These are the Ten Commandments, who reside within this palace. They live exiled within this forest; they are scorned, disobeyed and forgotten by

---

103. Llull also treats of the Ten Commandments in *LC*, Book IV, Dist. 37, Chs. 255-264, in ORL VI, 264-339, and the *Doctrina pueril*, Chs. 13-22, in NEORL VII, 47-68, among other places in his oeuvre.

people within the world. In this palace do they weep, despair and lament
the honour they once had in the world so that God might be honoured
and that people might come to everlasting salvation.'

[3] Blaquerna felt great wonder when he had read the words inscribed above the doorway, so he knocked on the door and sought to
enter the palace with a view to seeing the Ten Commandments. A
handsome pageboy opened the door. Blaquerna wished to enter but
the page told him that no one could enter the palace who was disobedient to the Ten Commandments. Blaquerna replied by saying that
he had rid his mind of all things and had devoted his entire soul to
the service of God, Lord and Creator of all good things. Blaquerna
described his circumstances to the page so that he might be able to
enter the palace. The page closed the door and said that before he
could allow him to enter the palace he would have to ask permission
from the Ten Commandments. The page asked permission from the
Ten Commandments, to whom he described Blaquerna's circumstances, regarding which they expressed a certain pleasure, and instructed the page to allow Blaquerna to enter and to bring him into
their presence.

[4] Blaquerna went into a large and very beautiful hall in which
were inscribed the names of those who were disobedient to the Ten
Commandments. In that hall stood ten finely carved chairs of gold
and ivory upon which the Ten Commandments were very honourably
seated. They were dressed very nobly in gold and silk; they had large
beards and long hair, and gave the impression of being aged men.
Each of them had a book on his lap, and each wept and lamented
very bitterly, saying the following words:

[5] 'Alas, how people scorn you!', said the First Commandment,
'Your lovers, by whom you were very respectfully served, are dead.
There are many in this world who believe in idols and make false gods
of the sun, the moon and the stars. To entertain greater love for one's
son, one's castle or one's own person is to make a god of that which
one loves more fervently than the Most High, who is the Supreme
Good above all other goods. Alas! Where are those who love God
above all things? And who is he who, in order to honour God, will
surrender himself to death and will endure every kind of hardship?
The more I remember the great mass of people and the fewer I find
among them who truly love God, the more intense does my suffering

become and the deeper does my sadness grow. Sinners are remembered by the mercy of God, Who sustains them and provides them with these worldly goods. Who, however, remembers or fears God's great justice and who gives thanks to Him, as is fitting?'

When the First Commandment had finished uttering these words, he read from his book. Amid his weeping and lamenting he read, and as he read he grieved and grew sad.

[6] Blaquerna felt great wonder at the sorrow experienced by the First Commandment, and asked him what it was he was reading in that book.

'Beloved son', said the First Commandment, 'in this book is written the great glory that resides in heavenly beatitude and the great suffering that shall be undergone by those who are disobedient to me. In this book are written down all those who are obedient to me, as well as those who are disobedient. And since the number of those who are disobedient to me is much greater than that of those who are obedient to me; and since I have committed no wrong or offence whereby I may deserve to be disobeyed; and since I am disobeyed most unreservedly by those people to whom God grants the greatest honours in this world, my grief and sadness consequently grow, therefore, every time I read from this book.'

[7] While the First Commandment was speaking to Blaquerna, the Second Commandment lamented and wept so bitterly that Blaquerna listened to his words and observed his tears, and was stirred to compassion and contrition of heart.

'You unheeded cur!', said the Second Commandment, 'To swear by God falsely constitutes contempt for your Lord and confers honour upon creatures over the lofty dominion of their Creator. God loves the individual soul more than all the riches of this world, yet a perjurer loves more that by which he falsely swears than God or the everlasting glory he is capable of attaining.'

[8] The Third Commandment lamented and wept in a similar manner, saying these words:

'God commanded the Jews to observe the Sabbath day, while the Son of God became incarnate and ordered Christians to keep Sundays holy. Since the Jews blaspheme against Our Lord Jesus Christ, therefore, and have fallen into error, yet better observe the Sabbath day than Christians do Sundays, who shall comfort my soul for such wrongdoing? And since on holy days people commit more wrongs through eating, drinking and practising vain pursuits than they do on the other days of the week, who is he that remains obedient to me?'

[9] The Fourth Commandment said loudly amid tears:

'God is the father of all creatures by creation and by grace. God's mercy and justice are the mother of all men. I am the Commandment which states that man must honour his father and his mother. Who, by honouring God as Creator, is obedient to me? And who places trust in His mercy? And who fears and loves God's justice?

[10] The Fifth Commandment was unable to refrain from saying the following words:

'Charity is dead in the one who murders his neighbour. Whoever is disobedient to me murders his soul through sin. I am disobeyed more flagrantly in terms of spiritual rather than bodily death. Earthly lords are more greatly feared for their justice than is God in Heaven. I am dishonoured and despised by those who are disobedient to me. My soul, which sees them go down paths that will lead them to everlasting torment, feels sad.'

[11] The Sixth Commandment said:

'I am God's commandment against fornication. I am issued by God in order to put an end to uncleanliness of mind and of body. Hair and eyebrows are dyed, colours are applied to faces and garments are decorated, all with the aim of disobeying and despising me. I have lost my inheritance and my dominion on account of lust in those to whom I am sent. If my enemy, lust, causes me to remain dishonoured, sad and disconsolate, my sister, justice, shall take vengeance against those who make my dishonour endure.'

[12] The Seventh Commandment began to utter, while weeping, the following words:

'Friendship and love obtain between myself, charity and justice. Theft invariably calls forth wickedness and deceit. I am the Commandment against theft so that charity may be present among men. Justice punishes thieves, but does not cause me to be obeyed through charity but rather through fear of itself. The good that God gives to those who disobey me is stolen from Him, for they feel no gratitude towards Him for the good He has given them, and grant and attribute to themselves the good that is within them. If in this world I endure suffering and sorrow on account of the wrong they do, in the next world they shall endure everlasting torment for the dishonour they inflict upon me in this world.'

[13] The Eighth Commandment spoke with a compassionate heart, uttering these words:

'False witness constantly pursues me and causes to be disobedient those by whom I had thought I was honoured. They bear false witness with respect to the honour of their God who love more the honour attaching to their order than that which attaches to Him. To deny the Trinity in God and to deny that the Son of God has been made incarnate constitutes false witness against God's goodness, power, wisdom, love and perfection. Spreading calumnies and denying the truth are contrary to my will. Each day I issue my commandment and each day I am disobeyed. False witness has stripped me of my inheritance and the honours which I once received are now conferred upon him. To love this world more than the other is to bear false witness against God's glory.'

[14] Envy[104] has grown, so the Ninth Commandment complained about the harm that envy and lust had caused him, saying the following words:

'If you, charity, had such great power against envy and if you, justice, were to punish immediately all those who covet their neighbour's wife, I should be honoured and feared by those who persist in dishonouring me and who scorn my power. If lust and envy exercise control over me, where is the help that I should receive from you? May charity and justice not omit to strengthen noble-mindedness so that I may be honoured and obeyed in defiance of envy and lust. Obedience, my friend, do not abandon me for the sake of envy and lust, which render you displeasing to God and to myself each time you defer to lust and envy.'

[15] Blaquerna was in the presence of the Tenth Commandment, who complained in the following manner about hope and fortitude:

'Alas! And who has brought the anger and displeasure of hope and fortitude upon me? For I have never previously practised any fraud or deceit against them. To covet the wealth or possessions of one's neighbour constitutes despair and feeble-mindedness which fails to invest hope or trust in the wealth or the Virtues of God. Charity, justice and prudence take too long to bring my enemies to ruin and to return me to the friendship I once shared with hope and for-

---

104. As in covetousness.

titude. I am forgotten by my guardians, and scorned and dishonoured by my enemies.'

The Ten Commandments uttered these words and many others, and they wept and lamented so bitterly that Blaquerna could not refrain from weeping himself.

[16] For a long time Blaquerna wept in the company of the Ten Commandments. He asked them whether there was anything which might help or assist in fulfilling their desires and putting an end to the sadness they felt. But the Ten Commandments told him that nothing could help their grievous sorrow unless a very great devotion and affection of the heart were to be practised by prelates and princes, as well as religious:

'Who, lovingly and with great fervency, should punish all those who are disobedient to us.'

[17] Blaquerna knelt down in front of the Ten Commandments and requested their leave and permission to be able to continue on his journey, asking them also to bestow upon him the grace and virtue to observe each one of them and to hold them constantly in his heart, so as to obey them in his hermitage. Each of the Ten Commandments blessed Blaquerna, so he parted from them amicably and went to seek the place where he might be a hermit for all the days of his life.


## 43. ON FAITH AND ON TRUTH

[1] Blaquerna departed from the palace in which the Ten Commandments resided and went through the forest from one place to another trying to see if he could find a location where he might build his cell. When the ninth hour had arrived and Blaquerna had said his Hours, he sat down close to a spring and ate one of the seven loaves of bread he was carrying. When he had eaten and had drunk some water from the spring, he gave thanks to God and went on his way. As he was going through the forest he saw lions, wolves, bears, wild boar, snakes and many other harmful beasts. And since he was all alone and was not in the habit of seeing such beasts, he felt fear and dread in his heart. Hope and fortitude, however, reminded him of God's power, while charity and justice strengthened his resolve, so he threw himself into prayer and gave thanks to God, Who gave him such company whereby he remembered His power and Who caused him to trust in His hope.

[2] While Blaquerna was travelling in this manner through the forest, he heard a piercing and doleful voice, on hearing which he felt great wonder. When he had gone on a little further he saw approaching through the forest two unaccompanied ladies, very nobly attired and very pleasing in appearance. One of the ladies, however, was weeping and lamenting bitterly. Blaquerna stepped out into the path of the two ladies and asked the lady who was weeping what had occasioned her tears and sadness. The weeping lady replied by saying the following words:

'I am Faith, and I have travelled with this lady, Truth, to a land of Saracens in order to direct them towards the path of salvation. Yet they did not wish to embrace me, nor Truth either. They are unbelievers and are resistant to myself and to Truth. My soul is sad since God is not honoured, believed in or loved in such lands. I feel sorrow and compassion at the damnation of these ignorant people. I can only weep at the great harm that results from the error in which they abide and only lament the merit that is lost in those who will not reveal to them my brother and my sister.'

[3] Blaquerna asked Faith who her brother and her sister were. Faith replied:

'This lady is my sister and Intellect is my brother, towards which latter I travel in order that he may go to those people whence I come and that by necessary reasons he may demonstrate to them the fourteen articles. For the time has come when they no longer wish to accept the authority of saints; nor are there miracles such as those whereby people unaware of myself or my sister were once enlightened. So, because people require necessary reasons and demonstrations, let my brother go, who, by God's power, is capable of proving the fourteen articles.'[105]

[4] Blaquerna replied by saying that faith would lose its merit if the intellect were to demonstrate the articles by means of which faith

---

105. In this paragraph, Llull has the disconsolate Faith abdicate her position in securing conversions to her brother Intellect on the grounds of the greater efficacy of rational argument ('necessary reasons') and demonstrative proof in this field. Llull's Art, on principle, rejects the traditional (Dominican) methods of missionising, some of which are mentioned here (i.e. arguments from authority, miracles, etc.), methods which often merely result in the dismantling of one's opponents beliefs, in favour of multiple arguments providing 'necessary' proofs of the positions one wishes to defend as well as disproofs of the positions against which one is arguing.

is enlightened to believe, even in defiance of one's understanding.[106]
Faith said to Blaquerna, however, that it was not proper that the principal reason on account of which people desire to convert the unbelievers should be so that thereby faith may be the occasion of greater
merit:

'Faith, rather, should be the second intention while the first intention should be that God is known and loved and that the intellect may
exercise its power so that I may thereby become greater and loftier.
For however much higher the intellect can rise by understanding the
articles, I can rise still higher by believing that which it fails to understand.[107] And insofar as someone asserts that my sister Truth is not
present in necessary reasons, that person speaks against me, as well as
my sister and brother, even if such reasons may be reviled on certain
flimsy grounds when compared to me, my sister and my brother.'

[5] Blaquerna said that monks and other men had often gone to
preach the Roman faith to unbelievers yet that they had not been
able to convert them, for which reason it appeared that God had not
desired their conversion; yet when God *did* desire this, it would then
be a straightforward matter to convert them. Faith replied:

'If God had not desired people's conversion, then why would He
have become incarnate? And why did He wish to endure suffering on
the Cross? And why did He honour so greatly the Apostles and martyrs, who suffered death in order to exalt me within this world? God,
however, always awaits His lovers, whom He wishes to come to Him of
their own free will rather than under constraint, so that they may be
worthy of great glory. Yet people tempt God[108] and think that when
He so wills, He shall grant them the will to suffer martyrdom out of
love for Him. And what stronger assertion can there be that God
wishes people to suffer trials and death out of love for Him than that
which the Cross represents to our eyes, or the words that Jesus Christ
spoke in the Gospel when He said to Saint Peter three times that if he

---

106. Cf. Gregory the Great: 'nec fides habet meritum, cui humana ratio praebet
experimentum' ('faith has no merit if human reason provides proof thereof'), Homily
26.1 in *XL Homiliarium in Evangelia Libri duo*, *PL* 76:1197C.

107. Llull often uses the analogy of oil on water to describe the relation between
faith and reason, 'faith being like oil which floats on the water of understanding: the
higher our understanding, the higher faith can rise on top of it', Bonner (2007), 84.

108. Cf. Deut 6:16; and, in the context of prayer, Sir [Ecclus] 18:23. Cf. above, Ch.
6, § 14 and corresponding note.

loved Him he should feed His sheep?[109] And what error has any power over God, my brother, myself or my sister? But since people do not maintain or persevere in disputations against the unbelievers, it appears to them that error cannot be overcome by us.'

[6] When Faith had reproached Blaquerna very firmly, she returned to her weeping and began to lament and cry out, as she had previously been doing, and continued on her way to her brother, Intellect. Blaquerna followed Faith and Truth, consoling Faith as best he could with the following words:

'God is wise in every respect yet in none is His justice lacking. Since God knows, therefore, that you, Faith, have done all you possibly can to seek to convert the unbelievers, God's justice forgives you. You must, therefore, be comforted according to the wisdom and justice of God. And your merit is as great as if you had converted the unbelievers you so wish to convert.'

Faith replied to Blaquerna amid tears:

'Alas, wretch that I am! Never before had I thought that I should be so roundly scorned by people! Yet how can anyone imagine that I might be comforted when my Creator and my light is despised, ignored, rejected and cursed by people? Were I to be consoled by my merit and by my abilities, where in my will would be charity? Such consolation occurs through lack of love, devotion and compassion, who are my sisters, in conflict with whose virtue my consolation would stand.'

While Faith was reproaching Blaquerna, and Blaquerna was overcome by shame and remorse, they arrived in the area where Intellect had his abode.

## 44. ON INTELLECT

[1] In the shadow of a beautiful tree laden with flowers and fruits, on lush grass, close to a clear spring stood a tall chair very subtly carved and adorned with gold, silver, ivory, ebony and precious stones. On that chair sat a venerable old man, very nobly clad in crimson samite,[110] by which the Passion of the Son of God was signified. This

---

109. Jn 21:15-17.
110. A heavy silk fabric—often interwoven with gold or silver—worn in the Middle Ages.

man was Intellect, who was reading philosophy and theology to a
large number of students. While Intellect was reading to his students,
Faith, Truth and Blaquerna arrived at that place, greeting him and
his students, and they received a gracious welcome from him and all
the others.

[2] Intellect asked Faith and Truth how they fared, and what they
had accomplished in terms of the reason they had gone on their travels. With great compassion and sorrow, Faith replied to her brother,
telling him all about the manner in which she had gone among the
Saracens and how she had found men very learned in philosophy[111]
who did not believe in the articles of the Saracens, yet were not willing to accept the authority of the saints[112] or to hold the Catholic
faith.

'My sister Truth and I have come to you, therefore, to say that you
must go to them to demonstrate the truth by necessary reasons and
to remove them from the error in which they abide, so that God may
be known and loved by them and that my woes may be assuaged.'

[3] Intellect looked at his students and said these words:

'The time has come when our knowledge has reached great heights,
and unbelievers call for necessary arguments and demonstrations,
yet shun faith. It is time we went, and made use of the demonstrative
knowledge we possess. For if we fail to use it as we should in order to
honour the one by Whom we possess it, we act against our conscience
and against that which we know, and prove unwilling to acquire the
merit or the glory we shall be able to attain if we avail ourselves of
that knowledge. Very great is the doubt learned Saracens feel towards their faith; the Jews are doubtful because of the servitude in
which they abide, so wish to acquire knowledge; and there are many
idolaters who have no faith at all: it is time we went! I wish to know
which of you desires to set forth in the company of myself and my
sisters. We have a new method for disputing with unbelievers, namely, by teaching them the *Brief Art of Finding Truth*;[113] and when they

---

111. But cf. above, Ch. 40, § 5; and below, Ch. 44, § 9.

112. Here Llull is referring to 'arguments by authority' and the fact that his Muslim (though also Jewish) interlocutors simply did not acknowledge the applicability of
(all) Christian authorities, the Biblical witness included; hence his own willingness
within his apologetics to use 'necessary reasons' according to his Art.

113. Cf. above, Ch. 24, § 2 and corresponding note.

have learned it, we shall be able to confound them using the Art and its principles.'

[4] When Intellect had finished speaking, the students excused themselves to him, saying these words:

'To die, enduring pain and torment, is a fearful thing! To suffer hunger and thirst, to leave one's country and one's friends behind and to travel to foreign lands amidst people who torture and kill you when you reproach them for their faith, are things best avoided!'

While the students were uttering such words, Truth could not refrain from saying the following:

'If all these things you say are to be feared, how much more fearful it is to be an enemy of myself, my sister and my brother, or likewise of hope, charity, justice and fortitude! If my brother has granted me to you, where is the honour that you pay to me as opposed to falsehood, who continues to dishonour me in front of so many people? And is there any among you who wishes to be similar to Jesus Christ, on the Day of Judgement, in his crimson garments?[114] And were you not to die a natural death, which of you would die to honour his Heavenly Lord?'

Truth wept, Faith once more lamented her grievous sorrows, and Intellect said:

'Alas, where is the gratitude shown to me by those to whom I have taught the truth?' Intellect then said to Faith and Truth: 'Go to your sister Devotion and beg her to come to these students, who lack piety, so that she might inspire love in them and grant them the courage to escort me on the journey you so desire!'

So Faith, Truth and Blaquerna went to Devotion. While Blaquerna was escorting Faith and Truth, he praised and blessed God, Who had brought him to such a place in which he had heard the above words, words he had never heard before.


45. ON DEVOTION

[1] Faith and Truth, along with Blaquerna, arrived at the place where Devotion was to be found, beneath a very beautiful pine tree. She was at prayer, and wept, desiring the honour of Jesus Christ while remem-

---

114. See above, Ch. 33, § 6 and corresponding note.

bering His grievous Passion. Devotion welcomed and greeted Faith
and Truth wearing a cheerful expression, although Faith and Truth
greeted Devotion wearing ones of sadness and distress, from which
expressions Devotion feared that her brother Intellect had experienced some misadventure, so she asked Faith and Truth about their
brother's condition. Faith and Truth answered Devotion by summa-
rising the above words, and they described how their brother Intellect had begged very insistently that she go to inspire love in his
students so that they might follow him in giving praise to the Holy
Trinity and the Incarnation of the Son of God:

'So that, among us, God and His works may have the honour
that befits them, that we may be pleasing to God and that those who
abide in falsehood and error may be enlightened by Faith, Truth and
Intellect.'

[2] 'How can this be?', asked Devotion, 'My brother's students do
not have me in their hearts when my brother reveals my sister Truth to
them? It is contrary to nature', said Devotion, 'to know God and His
works yet not to possess the charity and devotion to honour God and
His works. Contrariety of this sort, therefore, is generated by forgetting Divine virtue and Heavenly glory and the torments of Hell and by
remembering the vanities of this world and fearing death. Alas, you
wretch! Where is hope, charity, justice, prudence and fortitude? Do
they neglect to assist you, as well as the wisdom of my brother?'

Devotion felt great wonder and deep distress as she uttered the
above words.

[3] While Devotion wondered at the ignorance of the aforesaid
students, who feared dying and enduring pain for the purpose of
honouring God and attaining heavenly beatitude more profoundly
than they did living without charity, hope and fortitude, Faith and
Truth begged Devotion to go to the students, since she dallied too
long and it was time for the unbelievers to receive preaching from
devout instructors. For each day souls passed downwards to everlasting fire, just like rivers, which never cease to flow towards the sea.

Devotion replied:

'As well you know, power exerts no influence over the free will of my
brother's disciples. I cannot exist in them, therefore, unless they freely
choose me, for were I to do so my deeds would run counter to charity
and justice which accord with the deserts of glory and of sin. You must
return to my brother and his students, therefore, to tell them that they

may have me in their hearts for as long as they wish, as soon as they
decide to remember and love me. And in order that they may wish to
acquire me is the image portrayed upon the Cross of Jesus Christ, towards Whom they should feel great shame since they do not wish to
acquire me for the purpose of paying respect to His excellence.'

[4] Faith and Truth returned to Intellect very downcast. Blaquerna took his leave of them very courteously and went in search of his
abode. While he was travelling through the forest all alone, he remembered the words that Devotion had spoken to him, so he praised
and blessed God's charity, wisdom and justice, which, through the
Incarnation and the Passion of His Son, had impelled devout Christians not to baulk at suffering any hardship or death in order to honour God and His works.

## 46. ON DILIGENCE

[1] Blaquerna went through the forest from one place to another in
search of the location he so desired. His heart did not cease to love, nor
his soul remember, nor his mouth praise God's name. While Blaquerna was thus travelling through the forest, he saw a man on horseback
come riding towards him at full speed. This man was carrying a large
amount of money. Blaquerna greeted him and asked him the reason
why he was travelling at such speed. The man replied by saying that he
was steward to a king, who had sent him to a city in order to prepare
the latter's lodgings and to purchase those things the king required for
his honour as regards a great court he intended to hold with a large
number of high barons. Blaquerna asked him many things, but that
steward did not wish to stop with him lest he lengthen his journey, so
he did not care to answer every question he asked him.

[2] Blaquerna travelled throughout the entire day until after the
ninth hour, when he ate some bread and some raw herbs close to a
spring. While he was eating, a squire came riding along on his palfrey at
great speed. That squire came from Court and was going to a city wherein a bishop had been elected, and, because the latter had received the
Pope's approval, the squire was making his way to deliver the good news
to the chapter and to the relatives of that bishop. The squire watered his
palfrey at the spring which lay in front of Blaquerna. While his palfrey
was drinking, the squire related the above words to Blaquerna, though

he was in such a hurry that he was scarcely able to convey his words to him or to allow his palfrey to drink sufficiently from the spring.

[3] Once Blaquerna had eaten, he fell to his knees and gave thanks to God. While he was praising God at the ninth hour, as was his custom, he saw a merchant coming on foot, naked, who was weeping and lamenting bitterly in the following terms:

'Alas, you wretch! So long have you toiled in diverse lands and endured such hunger and thirst, such heat and cold, and such fear, in order to earn what you have since lost! You wretched cur! What will you do? And your wife and children, how will they manage? You have been robbed and deprived of all your wares! Should you mount a claim against those who have robbed you? You are in mortal danger lest the robbers kill you, for you have entered and are caught in their clutches!'

'Dear friend', said Blaquerna, 'where are you heading? And who has caused you such great sadness as is signalled by your despair?'

The merchant related to Blaquerna how he had been robbed by a knight who owned a castle near to the place through which he was passing, and how he was preparing to mount a claim against the knight who had robbed him, and how he had lost all that for which he had ever laboured.

[4] A short time after the merchant had left Blaquerna, a man came walking along at great speed. He was laden with geese and hens that he was carrying on his shoulders. Blaquerna asked him if he knew of any place in the entire forest where he might reside, a place situated upon some mountain where there might be a spring and some wild fruit to hand from which one might live the life of a hermit. This man did not reply to Blaquerna's words, however, so absorbed was he by the lawsuit he was conducting, and he thought that Blaquerna had asked him about his circumstances and his journey, so for this reason he said to Blaquerna the following words:

'My lord', said the man, 'I am making my way to a town, near a castle, and in this town I am bringing a lawsuit against my brother, from whom I demand a vineyard that my father left me in his will. And I am carrying this present that you see to the judge and to the lawyers representing both parties; I am also bearing money for them, which I have borrowed at a high rate of interest. If you are knowledgeable about lawsuits, I beg you, for the sake of God, to assist me and give me counsel.'

[5] Blaquerna felt great wonder at the powerful desire the man had to gain the vineyard, and he remembered the words of Faith and Truth, as well as Intellect and Devotion, and the great diligence he had recognised in the aforesaid men. Blaquerna knelt down, his heart stirred to devotion and his eyes to weeping and tears, and he uttered these words:

'O aberrant will, contrary to order as well as nature, in which will there is a lack of courtesy and civility! What have you become, you who so thoroughly cause the honour and knowledge of God to be forgotten and who are unwilling to grant devotion to those who dread suffering trials and death for the sake of honouring God and of guiding the errant along the path of salvation? You are foolish, O will, and scant is the gratitude you feel for your Creator and scant is the fear you have of the torments of Hell, where you shall never attain your desires. Where is the good with which you can be rewarded by the steward, the squire, the merchant or the peasant? You wretch! How can you fail to remember the salvation you can achieve in this world? And why do you not fear to lose in this world that which is irrecuperable in the next?'

The peasant wondered greatly at the words Blaquerna uttered, so he parted from him and returned to the thoughts in which he had previously been engaged.

## 47. ON AUGURIES

[1] The day was bright and the sun lit up the entire forest through which Blaquerna was travelling. On a high peak waited a knight on horseback in full armour. The knight was an augur[115] who had come to watch out for auguries which might signify to him the truth concerning a horse raid he wished to mount against another knight who was his mortal enemy. While the knight was looking to see whether he might catch sight of an eagle, a crow, a sparrowhawk or any other bird from which he might learn what he wished to know, Blaquerna

---

115. Cat. *avuyrer*, Lat. *auspex*: 'an observer of birds', particularly their flight, for the purpose of divination.

climbed that mountain to ask him if he knew of any place which might prove suitable to the life he sought.[116]

[2] When Blaquerna had reached the knight, they both greeted each other amicably. They asked each other about their respective circumstances, and each told the other why he had come to that place. When Blaquerna had heard the reason why the knight was there, he then said to him the following words:

'Sir knight, are you as strong and noble of mind as the beauty and robustness of your body, your horse and your weapons would indicate? You seem to me to be sufficiently well-equipped to be able to defend yourself against another knight.'

'My friend', said the knight, 'my body is strong, I am very well armed and deep within me feel no failings which might incline me towards wickedness or deception. And by the grace of God I have upheld the order of chivalry for a long time. It seems to me, therefore, that there is not a single knight who could overcome or defeat me.'

[3] 'My lord', said Blaquerna, 'everything that exists in this world arises and occurs by virtue of two things, namely, occasion and chance. Occasion is that which has regard to future events according to the knowledge reason and discernment gain thereof via an enlightened intellect or the illumination of faith. Chance, however, consists in an event which occurs in the absence of any occasion or foreknowledge. So I ask you, therefore, which of them is the more powerful: occasion or chance?'[117]

'Dear friend', said the knight, 'occasion, since it accords with reason and intention, is more powerful than chance, which accords with the event itself in the absence of any deliberation of reason, or any discernment or intention.'

Blaquerna replied to the knight by saying that he had answered wisely, but that his deeds were at odds with his words inasmuch as he was watching out for auguries:

'For birds, which go flying through the air, are occasioned to fly so that they might be able to hunt for their food, yet their flight is a matter of chance as regards the direction in which they fly past a person.

---

116. In 1274-76 Ramon Llull wrote the *Book of the Order of Chivalry*, which was subsequently translated into a number of languages, including French and English.

117. Cf. above, Ch. 3, §§ 3ff. for the question concerning 'occasion' and 'ultimate end' (Cat. *final intenció*) posed by Evast to his son Blaquerna.

A knight, therefore, who does battle with another knight after seeking guidance from the chance flight of birds, is not as strong or as wise in terms of the art of warfare as is he who does battle by means of the judgement attaching to the reason and discernment of his understanding, which indicates to him the events which will befall him in accordance with the circumstances of war. By these words, therefore, can you understand that your enemy is stronger against you if he adheres to what reason demonstrates to him than you are against him if you adhere to that which birds perform by chance and which lacks any necessity of reason, which reason is unable to exercise its virtue; and all the more so since such a practice is displeasing to God and is contrary to hope, fortitude and justice. For this reason, then, will you be defeated in your contest.'

[4] The knight cogitated at length upon the words Blaquerna spoke to him, and because of Blaquerna's merits and the nature of reason, he recognised his failings and said these words:

'It has frequently happened to me that reason had showed me how I might carry out certain attacks and perform certain feats of boldness, but since I believed in auguries more than in my intellect, I rejected what reason suggested to me and was guided by auguries, which led me to do what was contrary to reason and intellect. O, blessed be God, Who, through you, has transmitted such knowledge to me. From now on auguries and omens shall never have power over me.

[5] 'My lord', said Blaquerna, 'God has established a further law of warfare, namely, that when reason suggests and shows how one may cause harm to one's enemy, then such reason must take into account whether it is in accord with charity, hope, justice, prudence and fortitude. For all these virtues are reason's sisters, yet reason cannot arise in one's thoughts if it defies its sisters. It is fitting, therefore, that you should bear in mind the concordance which must obtain between reason and the aforesaid virtues.'

The knight found Blaquerna's words very pleasing, so he said to him that he would modify his thoughts accordingly, as he had never done before in his life.

[6] The knight thought at length about whether he had practised charity, justice and hope in warfare. Yet his conscience reminded him of the discourtesy and hostility he had shown towards his enemies, of how he had placed his hopes in auguries and of how pride and vain-

glory had dwelt in his mind under the guise of fortitude. Thus, when the knight had cogitated for a long time upon these matters and many others, matters whereby he became aware of his failings, he then praised and blessed God and repented of his faults. He entrusted himself to the care and service of reason and its sisters, and said these words to Blaquerna:

'Blessed be God, Who has granted me the fortitude with which I have defeated the enemies within my mind! Never before have I won such a beneficial and agreeable battle! Through the enemies I have defeated within my mind, I shall defeat my enemies within the mind of that knight of whom I have long been the mortal foe! Alas! What battle is successfully waged or won if not that which uses charity, justice, patience, humility and fortitude to defeat and overcome discourtesy, ill will, pride, wickedness and deceit?'

While the knight was saying these words, Blaquerna took leave of him and continued on his journey.


## 48. On Worth[118]

[1] Blaquerna travelled onwards, feeling a keen desire to find a suitable place to do penitence. While he was passing through the forest in this fashion, he came across a path along which a minstrel was approaching on foot, very poorly dressed, his appearance and manner indicating his poverty and sadness of heart. Blaquerna asked the minstrel why his face wore such an expression of sadness and misery.

'My lord', said the minstrel, 'I have come from a court where a noble baron from this region has just been dubbed a knight. In this court I had thought to find Worth who might serve to repair my wretched clothing and reward me for the reproaches I have long delivered to those who are enemies of Worth, as well as for the fact that I have praised those who uphold Worth in this world. Yet in that court I was never rewarded by Worth or by any of its admirers. For this reason alone have I begun to think that I should compose a new *sirventes*[119] in which I may censure Worth and its servants.'

---

118. Cat. *De Valor.* lit. 'On value'.

119. Cat. *serventesch.* An Old Occitan and Catalan form of satirical lyric verse practised by the troubadours, in which the poet-lover positioned himself as a servant to-

[2] 'Dear friend', said Blaquerna, 'before you compose the *sirventes* you must have knowledge of Worth and of those who are its servants, so that your words contain the truth.'

'My lord', said the minstrel, 'I have long had knowledge of Worth and have always sought it in various lands, yet it has never assisted with my poverty nor by means thereof have I ever been able to escape the torments inflicted by wicked people.'

'My friend', said Blaquerna, 'if Worth were what you say it is, it would necessarily have to be of worth to you, for were it not so it would not be Worth. It might be the case, however, that what you call Worth is in fact Unworth,[120] wickedness and wrongdoing. If wickedness, censure, ignorance, and Unworth, therefore, lead you to go about in poverty, you are wrong to state that Worth has done you any injustice or iniquity.'

[3] 'My lord', said the minstrel, 'since you make yourself such a staunch upholder of Worth, I should like you to tell me what Worth is.'

Blaquerna replied by saying that that Worth is the value of virtues against vices. And Worth is that thing whereby usefulness and preservation stand opposed to deceit and wrongdoing.

'Underlying such Worth are truth, generosity, civility, humility, circumspection, loyalty, compassion, knowledge and many other virtues which are daughters of faith, hope, charity, justice, prudence, fortitude and temperance, which are themselves Worth's daughters.'

While Blaquerna was explaining Worth to the minstrel, a knight came by on foot, carrying his lance in his hand and his sword over his shoulder. When he was close to the minstrel and to Blaquerna, the minstrel said to Blaquerna that the knight in question was the emperor, for he recognised him and had often seen him. The minstrel and Blaquerna paid honour and respect to the emperor and the emperor greeted them in a friendly manner.

[4] The minstrel asked the emperor what chance circumstance had led him to travel by himself, and on foot, through the forest. The emperor replied by telling Blaquerna and the minstrel how, while hunting, he had pursued a wild boar for so long that he had become separated from his companions, and how in a vast forest he had caught up with the boar and the boar had killed his horse and he had

---

wards his mistress.

120. Cat. *Desvalor*. Llull's use of the term *desvalor* appears to be his own coinage.

mortally wounded the boar. When the emperor had narrated the adventure which had happened to him, he asked the minstrel and Blaquerna if they could give him something to eat, for he was oppressed by a ravenous hunger, as he had neither eaten nor drunk for the past two days.

'My lord', said Blaquerna, 'there is a spring close by where you can drink fine water and you can eat the cool grass that surrounds the spring.'[121]

The emperor replied by saying that he could not drink without eating and that he was not accustomed to consuming grass, so he believed, therefore, that he would shortly be dead if there were nothing he might eat, and which he should be accustomed to eating.

[5] Blaquerna led the emperor to the spring. All three of them sat down on the fresh grass close to the spring. Blaquerna took out three loaves he still had left, and they ate their lunch together. While the emperor was eating, Blaquerna asked him which thing was of greater benefit to him: the bread that he was eating or his empire? The emperor replied by saying that in that place the bread that he was eating was of greater benefit and worth to him than was his empire. Blaquerna replied by saying that the empire which is not as beneficial to its lord as is the bread he was eating is of little worth.

'You, O minstrel, may therefore know', said Blaquerna, 'what Worth is. For all Worth resides in three things: the first is when earthly things serve to nourish the body; the second is when they serve towards the acquisition of virtues and merit; and the third is when all things are worthy inasmuch as God is served, known and loved thereby and chooses to exercise His power in His creatures.'

[6] The emperor asked the minstrel and Blaquerna what conversation they had been having with respect to Worth, and they repeated to him the words they had been exchanging regarding Worth at the moment when they had encountered him. And Blaquerna said to the emperor:

'My lord, on many occasions have you performed many noble deeds whereby you have been Worth's friend. If, therefore, you have done anything untoward against Worth, it cannot be of any assistance to you whatsoever in this forest where you possess as little power as

---

121. Here, and not for the first time, we see Llull's evocation of a bucolic *locus amoenus*, though here for comic effect.

does one of us. However, if there lies within your soul nobility of mind, which is in accord with Worth, the aforesaid virtues, which are Worth's daughters, can help you in this forest to acquire patience and humility and to find consolation in the hope of God, Who can assist you in this and other places.'

[7] All three of them spoke a great deal about Worth and they travelled for so long together that they arrived at a lovely meadow surrounded by many beautiful trees. In the middle of that meadow had been built a fine palace, all carved and enwalled with marble. Above the portal were written these words:

'This palace belongs to the Lady of Worth, wherein no one who is Worth's enemy or persecutor may or ought enter. In this palace resides Worth, who has been banished from the world and from the admirers thereof, who all love Unworth. Worth continually weeps and bewails her loss, desires to recover her honour and awaits guardians who may restore her to the world, so that God's honour may flourish in every country. Worth is downcast, and wickedness and deceit prosper. All people suffer loss at the dishonouring of Worth. If Unworth were Worth, God's honour would be greater within the world. Worth awaits the person who remembers and loves her in his heart, who bewails her loss and who desires her honour.'

[8] When the emperor, Blaquerna and the minstrel had read the above letters, they felt great wonder at what they signified, so they knocked at the palace door in order that they might enter. A lovely maiden came to the window and asked what they wanted and what was the condition and estate of all three. Each of them told the maiden his name and estate, and they said that they wished to enter the palace in order to see Worth. The maiden reported the names and estates of all three to Worth and asked her whether she wished to allow them to enter the palace. Worth, however, did not want the emperor or the minstrel to enter, for the latter were her enemies and were among those who had persecuted her in the world and had caused her to reside in this forest. Since Blaquerna, however, was her servant, she wished him to enter and to be cordially received.

[9] Blaquerna alone entered the palace, where he found Worth, who uttered these words:

'I, Worth, have been created in order to signify and demonstrate the Worth of my Creator and my Lord. God confers Worth upon plants, beasts, birds, the heavens, the stars, the four elements and upon metals, so that mankind may have Worth above all these things. Yet since mankind does not wish to possess you, it is worth less than any other creature, because it loves Unworth, which it wishes to possess since it considers it to be Worth. Many men in whom Unworth abides acquire honours and wealth in the world, while in that same world Worth's admirers are despised and lowly. There are many books in which the truth is written concerning the Incarnation and the Passion of the Son of God, which truth is of worth to Recreation;[122] these books, however, are of no worth to the infidels, who lack teachers.[123] Many men have possession of the property of the Holy Church so that they may rise in worth; but who wishes to exalt the Holy Church in terms of worth or honour against dishonour, error and lack of faith? There are many men who wish God to have Worth so that they may have honour; few, however, are they who love Worth so that God may have honour. If I have never committed an injustice or wrong, why is dishonour rendered to me? And if Unworth has never delivered justice or recompense, why is honour rendered to her?'

While Worth was saying these words and many others, tears entered her eyes and sadness and sorrow her heart, and she sorely lamented her loss.

[10] Blaquerna remained with Worth until the following morning, comforting her and giving her hope with these words:

'God is mighty above all other powers. His wisdom bears no defect, and the world is His creation. It is fitting, therefore, that the world should come to fulfilment, at which it would not arrive were Unworth not to suffer a decline or Worth not to receive praise and to regain its honour. God's mercy does not forget sinners, nor does His justice maintain friendship with the enemies of Worth.'

Blaquerna uttered all these consolations and many others to Worth. With tears and devotion Blaquerna took leave of Worth, to whom he yielded his heart for the rest of his life, while Worth placed him under her care and named him her heir.

[11] Blaquerna left the palace and, while travelling, related to the emperor and the minstrel the tears and despair in which he had found Worth, as well as the words she spoke while she bemoaned her

---

122. I.e. loosely speaking, 'redemption'.
123. Cf. above, Chs. 40, § 5 and 44, § 2.

enemies. For a long time the emperor and the minstrel cogitated and pondered upon the words Blaquerna had said regarding Worth, and their consciences curbed each of the misdeeds they had frequently committed against her. While the emperor was considering his misdeeds, he questioned Blaquerna about his circumstances, so Blaquerna informed him about these, as well as those of Evast and Aloma, and how he had left to become a hermit so that he might have God and God's honour in his heart and might escape the world, which was Worth's enemy.

[12] God's humility stirred pity and patience to pardon, and the emperor was remembered by God's mercy; contrition and repentance for his sins were present in his soul. So he said the following words:

'O foolish, sinful man, who persecutes Worth and pursues wild beasts at the risk of death! You have served Unworth all the days of your life while asuming that it was Worth! Wrongs demand satisfaction and disorder demands proper order. So, in this place, therefore, in the presence of Blaquerna, I promise that my whole empire and my whole person shall subsequently be in servitude to Worth, so that she may recover her ownership thereover in myself and in others, of which ownership she has been stripped for so long now. For the sake of honouring Worth, proper order should prevail in my person and my empire, therefore, so that, by my example, due honour may be rendered to her and that she may happily, rather than sadly, return to us.'

[13] While the emperor was saying these words, they had all three been travelling along a path which had been diverting Blaquerna from his journey. So Blaquerna told the emperor that he was obliged to turn back towards the area in which he had been seeking his hermitage. Beneath a fine tree, Blaquerna very courteously took leave of the emperor and the minstrel, and the emperor uttered the following words to Blaquerna:

'Blaquerna', he said, 'blessed be the hour that I met you on my journey! Sorrowful is my parting from your agreeable person! I must set my household in order, as well as that of my wife the empress, and I intend to impose order upon my whole empire and entrust it to people who love Worth, so that I may give satisfaction to her, as I have promised. Upon such ordering I intend to write a book. And I intend to send this minstrel and many others throughout the world so that they may give an account of Worth in the Courts where she is censured and may persecute and reprehend Unworth in all those places where she is praised. I do not wish them to receive anything from anyone apart from me alone, so that they may praise Worth all the better. I intend to provide for my sons and name them my heirs, and wish to relinquish my empire and to serve God forever alongside you in your hermitage, so that I may have God and Worth in my heart. I beg you to pray to God for my sake, that He may forgive me and grant me your company!'

## 49. ON CONSOLATION

[1] On the way to the region towards which Blaquerna was heading, stood a shepherd who was tending a large flock of sheep. This shepherd had a son who was seven years old. Owing to the great love the shepherd bore towards his son, he one day took him with him. It so happened that the shepherd fell asleep, as was his habit, and his young child moved away from the place where his father was sleeping. A wolf approached the flock, found the child and snatched him away. The shepherd awoke at the cries the young boy let out when the wolf snatched him, and saw that that the wolf was carrying his son away. The shepherd pursued the wolf with his dogs, but, before he had caught up with it, the wolf had devoured and killed his son and had consumed the innards of his belly.[124] When the shepherd reached the place where he found his son dead, he was cast into despair and said these words:

'Alas, you wretch! You have lost what you loved most! Your son is dead. You are the occasion of his death, since you brought him to this forest against his mother's wishes. You have plunged your wife into sadness and sorrow for the rest of her life! Your despair shall be unparalleled and your tears unsurpassed! Your sadness shall be so profound that you will never be able to enjoy consolation or delight. In front of your wife you shall stand shamed and guilty.

---

124. Cf. Chs. 1-6 and the Prologue to Book 8 of *Felix* (1287-89). The incident recounted in this chapter, which inspires a consolatory oration or *consolatio* on the part of Blaquerna, recalls the myth of the infant Archemoros (or Opheltes of Nemea), who, left alone within a forest for a time by his nursemaid Hypsiple, was killed by a snake. Llull's direct source for this episode may, in fact, have been a common repertory of exempla. Cf. Curtius (1990), 81.

While the shepherd was uttering these words, he hugged and kissed his son, saying:

'Son, the fair expression your face once wore, where is it now? And the great delight my heart felt thereat, where has it gone? Son, your death makes me want to die! You alone occupied my mind! From now on, who shall be present within my thoughts? I am alive yet I wish to die! I suffer grievous distress since I do not feel myself expire! My life consists in death at your death! I have no hope of comfort or of forgiveness for the wrong I have incurred in your death.'[125]

[3] So loud were the cries, laments and tears emitted by the shepherd that, as a result thereof, as well as of the barking of the dogs which were fighting with the wolf, Blaquerna headed towards the sound of the voices, at which he felt very great wonder. Blaquerna arrived at the place where the shepherd was weeping and lamenting, and repeatedly hugging and kissing his son. Blaquerna wished to console him, but the shepherd seemed not to see him or to hear his words, so greatly was he constrained by the grief and anguish he was suffering.

[4] Blaquerna saw the wolf, which had killed one dog and was holding the other to the ground, and he thought that he might help the dog and might kill the wolf, so that from its death the shepherd might draw some consolation. Blaquerna took hold of a club which the shepherd carried, and vigorously set about the wolf in the manner of a man stirred to compassion by the death of the young child. The wolf attempted to flee, but the dog held onto it until Blaquerna had finally killed it. Blaquerna then said to the shepherd:

'Your enemy is dead, as a result of whose death your sadness should be transformed into consolation!'

[5] Blaquerna uttered many devout words bearing great consolation to the shepherd, yet whatever Blaquerna said or did, the shepherd would not reply to him nor cease to grieve in earnest. Blaquerna felt great wonder at the shepherd's grieving, as well as great pity thereat, and he concluded that, as a result of excessive anger and sadness, the shepherd had lost his memory, and was oblivious both to him and his words. So, in order to make the shepherd aware of such,

---

125. The Catalan original here consists of two rhyming prose sentences: *Ma vida es mort en ta mort! No he sperança de conort ni que·me sia perdonat lo tort que he de ta mort.* Unfortunately, this aspect cannot be conveyed in English.

by which awareness he might lead him towards consolation, Blaquerna began to try a new method, in accordance with natural reason, and said the following words to him:

[6] 'O foolish cur, who art the occasion of your son's death! Why do you not lament and why do you not weep at the loss you have suffered? You are oblivious, yet with ease have you consoled yourself in regard to that which you loved so fondly! Your son is dead, and the wolf has slain your wife and slaughtered your dogs!'

The shepherd loved his wife very dearly and believed that Blaquerna was telling the truth, so he thought that he could not have wept or undertaken to mourn, as he had in fact done. While the shepherd was entertaining such thoughts, he said the following words:

'Is it true that my wife is dead? And what am I currently engaged in: weeping or drawing consolation?'

Blaquerna replied:

'Come, and you shall see your wife, whom the wolf has slain.'

The shepherd followed Blaquerna to the place where the dead wolf lay.

'This is your wife!', said Blaquerna.

The shepherd felt great wonder at Blaquerna's words, and thought that he had lost his wits or that the wolf was indeed his wife.

[7] When Blaquerna saw that the shepherd's memory was beginning to return and to regain its natural function, and that his intellect had begun to recover its powers, he led the shepherd back to the place where his son lay dead, and he took hold of the child and started to hug and kiss him, and he wept and grieved in the same way as the child's father had done. The shepherd felt great wonder at Blaquerna's grieving. And the more wonder he felt the more noticeably did he recover the power of his intellect, which he had lost. When the shepherd had come to his senses, he went to the place in question and recognised that it was a wolf; he felt delighted that it was not his wife, and by virtue of such delight he partly checked and assuaged his sadness. He then went to Blaquerna, who was holding his son and was weeping over him.

'My lord', said the shepherd, 'why do *you* weep for *my* son? Give me back my son and let me resume the tears I was shedding earlier.'

Blaquerna replied to the shepherd:

'In the country from which I have come, it is customary for a person to join in the weeping and lamentation at the loss suffered by another. For this reason, I wish to join you in weeping and lamentation so that the lament you offer for the death of your son may be great, since you have a very good reason to utter a deep lament. And if you wish to follow the custom of my country I shall reveal to you the art and method whereby you shall be able to weep and lament for the death of your son in a fitting manner, bearing, as you do, the blame for his death.

'My lord', said the shepherd, 'your words are pleasing to me and I beg you to tell me the method and custom of your country, whereby I may bitterly weep and lament while death still keeps me alive, so that such life may thereby afford me greater torment.'

[8] Blaquerna said to the shepherd:

'Before you can learn of the method whereby you may grieve unreservedly, it is necessary for you to be acquainted with charity, justice, prudence, fortitude and hope, and it is necessary for you to tell me the truth concerning the things I shall ask you.'

'My lord', said the shepherd, 'I shall learn all such things and shall tell you everything I know, provided that you teach me the method whereby I may feel so much sadness and so much sorrow that death may strike me down at the peak of the despair I must needs feel concerning my son!'

Blaquerna told the shepherd to tell him the truth as to whether he had loved God or his son more greatly. The shepherd replied by saying that he had felt greater love for his son than for God. Blaquerna said that charity was lacking in anybody who loved anything more than God.

'And justice is that thing which punishes those who love God less than they do anything else. And since you entertained greater love for your son than you did for God, justice has, therefore, punished you through the death of your son. And God's wisdom wishes you in due course to love God above all things so that prudence may dwell within you, prudence whereby you may have fortitude against the anger that you harbour, may blunt your anger and entertain the hope of seeing your son, who resides in God's glory.'

[9] The shepherd began to remember and understand the words that Blaquerna was saying. And the more that he thought about them, the more he felt his sadness assuaged, even though he had presumed that his sorrows were bound to increase! He felt great wonder, therefore, and said the following words to Blaquerna:

'The more vividly I remember your words, the lesser the sadness I feel within me and the greater the consolation I draw! Where is the sadness that you, by your words, seek to foster in me?'

Blaquerna replied, asking the shepherd to tell him the truth as to whether, before his son had died, he had loved joy or sadness more. The shepherd replied by saying that he had loved joy more. So Blaquerna said:

'If, now that your son is dead, you love sadness more than joy, then, depending on the way you love, death is mistress of both joy and sadness! So, since death has caused you such hurt, you should not grant it so much authority that it makes you desire sadness rather than patience and happiness; it is necessary, rather, for you more resolutely to oppose death now that it has taken your son than you did previously, when your son was alive.'

[10] 'Blaquerna', said the shepherd 'and how might I oppose death, who has taken my son and now refuses to end my life?'

Blaquerna replied:

'With patience and consolation, by taking pleasure in all that God's justice performs and by feeling gladness of heart, wherein lies the fortitude to resist sadness; and, likewise, by delighting in the exercise of prudence and utility in the face of losses one incurs from such earthly affairs, does one oppose both bodily and spiritual death, and accord with life in Heaven, which life is everlasting.'[126]

[11] It would take a long time to recount the words Blaquerna spoke to the shepherd with a view to consoling him; yet, by means of the art and method that Blaquerna adopted, he drew the shepherd out of his sadness and lead him to consolation and joy, which joy the shepherd revealed by saying these words:

'From now on, my soul rejoices in the knowledge of its Creator and in possessing the virtues it used not to possess and did not even know how to exercise! My son has been removed from grave danger and resides with his Lord in glory! May my will always be subject to obeying that of my Lord God.'

---

126. Appeals to prudence and utility are characteristic of deliberative rhetoric— urging action or forebearance and thus seeking to influence the future—according to the Aristotelian division thereof (the other two genres being forensic, i.e. judicial, and epideictic, i.e. demonstrative). Cf. Aristotle, *Rhetoric*, I, 3, 1358b6ff.

When the shepherd had said these words and many others, he took hold of his son, kissed him and placed him over his shoulders. He then blessed and praised God, saying that greater was the gain he had derived as a result of his son's death, by exercising the aforesaid virtues on account of that death, than was the loss he had received from that same death. Blaquerna and the shepherd courteously took leave of each other, and Blaquerna begged the shepherd always to keep God in his memory, as well as consolation and patience in his will, for the rest of his life. The shepherd promised Blaquerna that he would draw consolation and exercise patience, but that he was wondering how he might console his wife for the death of their son, whom she loved above all else.[127]

[12] Blaquerna counselled the shepherd as to how he might console his wife according to the method he had himself used to console him. And he said to the shepherd that when he informed his wife about the death of their son, he should tell her at the same time about the death of one of her brothers whom she loved very dearly. Afterwards, her brother should come to console his sister, from the life of which brother she would draw consolation, just as the shepherd had himself when he realised that the wolf was not his wife.

## 50. ON FORTITUDE AND CHARITY

[1] In the forest through which Blaquerna was travelling stood a very sturdy castle, which belonged to a knight who, on account of that castle's sturdiness and the fact that he enjoyed bodily strength and was highly skilled in feats of arms, was very proud and committed many offences against those who lived in neighbouring areas. It so happened that one day, when all alone on his horse, the knight, equipped with those weapons he was in the habit of bearing, mounted an attack on a castle belonging to a lady who had a very beautiful daughter. Chance would have it that the knight found the maiden far from the castle gates in the company of other maidens, and he seized her. He put the maiden across the shoulders of his horse, against her will and that of all the other maidens, and made off with her into the

---

127. For the exercise of patience in the Bible and the consolations resulting therefrom, see Ps 9:19 and Jas 5:11.

vast forest. There was a loud uproar and the knight was vigorously pursued in order to retrieve the maiden from him. While the knight bore her away, the maiden wept and cried out very stridently. A squire who was following the knight caught up with him and fought against him, but the knight wounded and unseated the squire and killed his horse, and then continued on his way towards his castle with the maiden.

[2] It so happened that, as chance led Blaquerna from one place to another through the forest, the knight and Blaquerna came across one another. The maiden was weeping and letting out cries, and she begged Blaquerna to assist her. Blaquerna, however, considered that his bodily strength was feeble in comparison with that of the knight, and he therefore mused upon how he might assist the maiden with fortitude and charity, which are spiritual strengths. So, for this reason, he told the knight the following exemplary tale:[128]

[3] 'As the story has it, a man very learned in philosophy, theology and other sciences felt the urge to go to the Saracens to preach the truth of the Holy Catholic Faith so that he might eliminate the error of the Saracens and that the name of God might be worshipped and blessed amongst them as it is amongst us. The holy man went to the land of the Saracens and preached and demonstrated the truth of our Law, eliminating that of Muhammad as much as he could. News spread throughout that country concerning what he had been doing. The Saracen king had a command issued to that holy Christian requiring him to leave his entire country, and that if he failed to comply, he would be put to death. The holy man refused to obey the bodily commandment, for charity and strength were in his heart, causing him to disdain bodily death.[129] The king felt very indignant towards him, so he summoned the man to appear before him and addressed these words to him:

[4] '"O foolish Christian, who has disdained my commandment and the strength of my dominion! Do you not realise that I possess so

---

128. Cat: *exempli*: a short narrative or anecdote often used for moralistic purposes. As Mark D. Johnston points out, however, the term *exempli*, as used by Llull, comprises not only exemplary anecdotes, but also 'any sort of illustrative device, including allegories, analogies, metaphors, and proverbs', in Llull (2003), 5, n. 5. In 1295-96 Llull devoted a distinct 'Tree' of his *Tree of Science* (*Arbre de ciència*), namely, the 'Tree of Examples' ('Arbre exemplifical'), to the examination of how 'science' (or demonstrative knowledge) could be 'translated' into forms of exemplary literature.

129. A 'bodily commandment' is a carnal or physical commandment as opposed to a spiritual one; cf. Heb 7:16-17ff.

much power that I can torture you and put you to death? Where is your power, whereby you have disdained my strength and my dominion?"

"'My lord", said the Christian, "it is true that your bodily power can defeat and overcome my body, but the strength of my mind[130] cannot be overcome by the strength of your mind or by the strength which lies in all the minds of the people of your country. And since strength of mind is nobler and greater than bodily strength, therefore the charity which dwells in my mind loves the strength of my mind so ardently that it causes me to disdain all the bodily strength you have in your person and in your kingdom. The strength and charity in my mind, therefore, stand ready to fight against all the powers of your soul and of those souls which fall under your dominion."

[5] 'The king felt great wonder at the words he had heard, so he asked the Christian what had lent him the courage to attack the full strength and charity that lay in the souls of the people of his country.

"'My lord", said the Christian, "so momentous is the Incarnation of the Son of God and the Passion he underwent in order to save us, and so powerful is truth against falsehood, that I possess so much charity and fortitude in my mind, therefore, that there does not exist, within your country or among all the people at your disposal, any charity or fortitude which might, by means of argumentation, resist mine. And the reason for this is that all of you abide in error and lack devotion to the Incarnation and Passion of Our Lord God, Jesus Christ."

[6] 'The Saracen king was very angry at the Christian and issued a commandment throughout his country to the effect that all the wisest men and those who possessed the greatest charity should come and should overcome the Christian's fortitude and charity of mind, and then that they should cause his body to suffer a most violent death. They all assembled together to combat the Christian, yet the Christian defeated and overcame them all with spiritual strength and charity. And he told the king that he would commit an offence against the body if he were to detach it from the soul which enjoys greater power in terms of fortitude and charity than do all the souls of his people,

---

130. Lit. 'strength of my heart'; the Catalan word *coratge* can be translated as 'heart', 'mind', 'resolve', 'intention' or 'courage', depending on the context.

and that he would commit an offence against the soul if he failed to reward it for its merits.'

[7] When Blaquerna had narrated the above example to the knight, he put the following question to him:

'My lord', said Blaquerna, 'which to you seems to be the stronger and nobler power: the strength of mind which defeated and overcame so many other minds or the greater bodily strength the Saracen king enjoyed in comparison to the Christian?'

The knight replied by saying that strength of mind is the greatest strength to exist in man.

'My lord', said Blaquerna, 'the greater and nobler the strength is, the more it should be loved by charity. You are well aware that my bodily strength and that of the maiden you are carrying have no power against the strength of your horse, your weapons and your person. May you be aware, therefore, where greater strength resides: whether in your mind or in your horse, your weapons and your person. For, if your mind more strongly opposes wickedness, wrongdoing and lust than do your person, your weapons and your horse, then you will return the maiden to the place from which you seized her and you will not dispose your mind towards wickedness or wrongdoing. And just as God has given strength to your body, by God's virtue shall you possess strength in terms of nobility of mind, whereby you shall bear charity towards all good deeds wherein loyalty, courtesy, civility and humility reside.'

[8] The knight gave deep consideration to the words Blaquerna had spoken, and did not wish any incivility or discourtesy to master or overcome his mind, whereby he had frequently mastered and overcome many knights during attacks and battles. The knight said the following words to Blaquerna, therefore:

'Never have I been bettered or overcome by any man. So, were I not to obey your words, baseness and discourtesy would overcome my mind, which mind is most beloved by me, for by its strength I have always been mightier than my enemies. My mind is not defeated by your words, but rather it defeats and overcomes in me the wickedness and discourtesy that once were there. This maiden you behold, I beg you to return her to her mother's castle. I have mortally wounded a squire from her castle and, therefore, doubtless could not return the maiden to that locality.'

With these words, the knight parted courteously from the maiden and Blaquerna.

## 51. ON TEMPTATION

[1] Blaquerna was greatly displeased that he had to go out of his way by accompanying the maiden whom the knight had entrusted to him. Charity and fortitude, however, led him to go with the maiden towards the place where the castle lay. While Blaquerna was travelling with her, Blaquerna felt his resolve being tested by carnal pleasure owing to the maiden's great beauty and the solitude in which they found themselves within the forest. As soon as Blaquerna felt the temptation, however, he recalled the remedy whereby one suppresses all temptation, namely, God and His Passion, and heavenly glory and the torments of Hell. So he began fervently to pray, asking for assistance from the seven virtues, which kept company with him, and he recalled the baseness and filthiness wherein the deed of lust consists, and wished to enjoy a noble deed wherein the virtues consist when these assist one against the vices.

[2] Blaquerna frequently felt the temptation of lust while he was travelling with the maiden, so he would devote himself to prayer, as is mentioned above, and he would suppress his temptation. It so happened, however, that on account of the Devil, the maiden was likewise tempted to sin with Blaquerna, yet since she did not possess Blaquerna's method of combatting temptation, she said these words:

'My lord', said the maiden, 'your words have delivered me from the hands of the knight, and I am under your authority. No other reward can I give you than that, as far as you can, you may derive pleasure from me to your complete satisfaction.'

[3] Blaquerna felt the temptation within him increase at the words the maiden had uttered, so once more he remembered God and the virtues, as he had become accustomed to doing. While he was meditating upon fortitude and nobility of mind, he remembered and understood, by the light and inspiration of divine wisdom, how God would forsake many sinners so that they might be the occasion for just people to be able thereby to increase their virtues. Blaquerna, therefore, discerned that the maiden had been forsaken by God's grace in order that he might have greater occasion for virtue and might more staunchly resist temptation and lust, so that through greater fortitude he might acquire greater merit. For this reason, Blaquerna knelt down and blessed and adored God, Who had given him so many methods whereby he might greatly exalt his own virtues.

While Blaquerna was blessing and adoring God, by divine power he formed the intention of giving instruction to the maiden as to how to resist temptation whenever she might be tempted by lust or some other sin.

[4] 'O maiden', said Blaquerna, 'it is in the nature of one's intellect to cause one deeply to love or hate that which is greatly remembered.[131] Whenever one feels tempted to commit any sin, therefore, one must greatly remember the baseness and filthiness of sin as well as the harm caused thereby. For the more one greatly remembers in this way, the more robustly does one's intellect lead one's will to hate sin. There exists another method of suppressing temptation, namely, that one should remember God and His goodness, greatness, power, wisdom, love, perfection and justice; and likewise remember how He has shown great love for man and has prepared great glory for him, as well as how it is noble to exercise faith, hope, charity, justice, prudence, fortitude and temperance. The third method is that, when one is tempted, one ought to forget the sin and all its surrounding circumstances. For by forgetting the sin is the desire to love that sin curbed, for which reason one ought to remember other things. By means of these three aforesaid methods can one suppress every temptation.'

The maiden realised that Blaquerna had spoken these words to her because he had recognised that by which she was tempted, so she blessed and praised God, Who had given so much virtue to Blaquerna with which to resist temptation. So, whenever she experienced temptation in his regard, she availed herself of the teachings that he had imparted to her, with which teachings she suppressed temptation and accustomed her soul to exercise virtues.

[5] Blaquerna and the maiden travelled through the forest for a long time. They had travelled for so long, in fact, that that the maiden had become fatigued thereby and wished to rest under a tree, in whose shade she fell asleep. While the maiden was sleeping, Blaquerna remained at prayer, contemplating God's blessings. While he was at prayer, he heard a voice weeping, lamenting and conveying a sense of great sadness and distress. Blaquerna moved towards that voice

---

131. Here Llull is referring to the acts of the intellective soul, specifically the combined acts of memory remembering, the intellect understanding and will loving or hating, enshrined as these are in Figure S of his Art.

and found the squire whom the knight had wounded, which squire was returning in grave distress.

[6] 'My dear friend', said Blaquerna, 'what ails you? And what could relieve your injury so that you might draw consolation?'

'My lord', said the squire, 'I am distressed and angry because I am unable to accomplish the mission on which I have been sent.'

The squire told Blaquerna how he had followed the knight so that he might seize the maiden from him and how the knight had wounded him and made off with that maiden.

'My dear friend', said Blaquerna, 'reason would have you take comfort, since you have done the best you could; for you should feel as pleased by that as if you had recovered the maiden.'[132]

'My lord', said the squire, 'it is the nature of charity that no one should take comfort from having done his best if, in the event, he fails to achieve what he desires. And since I desire to serve the lady who has always provided for me, yet I have not fulfilled her wishes, it is fitting, therefore, that I should feel distressed by her own distress even though I may have done my best.'

[7] Blaquerna gave deep consideration to the squire's words, which indicated great perfection of charity and fortitude. And by virtue of such consideration, he remembered that, through lack of charity, certain men who had sought to spread the Catholic faith considered themselves to be exonerated, insofar as they had done all they could, yet had failed to achieve what they so keenly desired; as a result of which failure they ought to have felt distressed at the dishonour God receives from those who do not know Him or who fail to honour Him as they know Him. While Blaquerna was entertaining such thoughts, he said to the young squire:

'My dear friend, here beneath this tree is the maiden for whom you ask. And since you possess perfect charity, God wishes your aim to be achieved and that you should receive the merit for that for which you have striven.'

The squire went to the tree, and he found the maiden, who was asleep; so he woke her and returned with her to the castle, after they had both very courteously taken their leave of Blaquerna.

---

132. The argument used by Blaquerna here recalls one he previously used in order to console Faith in Ch. 43, § 6 above.

[8] Blaquerna resumed his journey, travelling with great concern as to how he might find a location in which he could serve God as he desired. For two days he went through the forest, finding nothing he might eat. On the third day, he was very greatly troubled by hunger. And the more greatly troubled he was thereby, the more firmly he placed his hope and trust in God, that He might help him resist his hunger, as well as the temptation he felt whereby the Devil sought to make him sin against hope and patience by means of despair and impatience. While Blaquerna was struggling as best he could against his hunger and temptation with the aid of the virtues, prudence sought to assist its servant, and enlightened the eyes of his mind, whereby he gave consideration to the fact that great affection and exaltation in prayer strengthen the body via the influence of devotion. When Blaquerna had thus considered, he endeavoured with all his might to contemplate and pray to God, as well as to exercise his virtues, so as to delight in Him. And by virtue of God's power and of the nature of the intellect, which understood God, and of the will, which loved Him, Blaquerna's eyes were filled with tears and his heart with devotion and love. And so loftily transported was Blaquerna by his prayers that he did not feel hunger, thirst or suffering, but rather his body enjoyed very great bliss, and drew power and strength from prayer. Thus engaged in worship, Blaquerna travelled through that forest without eating or drinking. And whenever he felt hunger, he worshipped God in the manner described above, and God transmitted to him power and vigour, whereby his soul remained in devotion and his body drew sustenance and strength.

## 52. ON PENANCE

[1] Blaquerna was travelling through the forest while remembering and loving his Creator and his God, and he was singing the *Gloria in excelsis Deo*. While he was going along in this manner, he came upon a road along which he walked until the ninth hour, at which point he encountered a squire who was approaching very tearfully along a different path, and whose face showed signs of great sadness. Blaquerna asked the squire why he was weeping, and the squire replied:

'My lord, I am weeping because a master I used to serve, named Narpan, has robbed me of my wages. So I have left him since I cannot serve him as he would wish, for he is so vexing and disorderly in his customs that no one can tolerate his wicked ways.'

[2] 'My dear friend', said Blaquerna, 'where is this Lord Narpan you mention?'

'My lord', said the squire, 'he lives close to here within an abbey. He has made his lodgings in that monastery and has come there to do penance. The penance he performs, however, is like that of the wolf.'

Blaquerna asked the squire what the wolf's penance was.

'My lord', said the squire, 'once upon a time, it came to pass that a wolf entered an enclosure in which there were many sheep, and he killed and devoured them. The following morning when the owner of the sheep entered the enclosure and found the sheep dead, he felt very great anger against the shepherd, who had failed to watch over the enclosure that night, so he killed him. And when he had killed him, he grieved at the death of the shepherd and the sheep. The wolf, who witnessed the shepherd's death and heard the sounds of the farmer's mourning, felt contrition of heart and said that it was fitting that he should perform penance for the loss he had caused to the farmer as also for the fact that he had occasioned the death of the shepherd. So, in a vineyard in which there were many grapes and which belonged to the farmer whose sheep he had killed, the wolf went to do penance while each day eating his fill of the grapes. In similar fashion, therefore, does the lord with whom I remained for a long time perform his penance, for within the world he has been a sinful person, has killed men and has committed many transgressions, yet he has come to that monastery in which he eats, drinks and lies with women to his complete satisfaction and lives in great luxury, by which all the monks of that monastery, many of whom are envious of him, are set a dire example.'

[3] 'My friend', said Blaquerna, 'do you believe that, if I were to go to the monastery and were to stay a while with Narpan, I might be able to convert him to the virtuous life?'

The squire replied:

'If you stay with him, what happened to the parrot will likewise happen to you.'

Blaquerna asked him to recount to him the tale of the parrot.

'My lord', said the squire, 'in a certain country it came to pass that two monkeys placed wood upon a glowworm, thinking that it was fire, and they blew upon the wood so that the fire would ignite. A parrot was sitting in a tree and said to the monkeys that the glowworm was not fire, but the monkeys paid no heed to his words. A crow told the parrot that he should not strive to correct those who refuse to learn. The parrot flew down from the tree and positioned himself between the monkeys so that they might hear him, but one of them seized and killed him. The same will happen to you if you attempt to correct a person who refuses to be corrected, for you shall be corrupted by his vices, in spite of any good upbringing you may have received.'

[4] Blaquerna said:

'I trust in the counsel that the fox gave to the boar.'

The squire asked Blaquerna to recount to him this particular tale, so Blaquerna said:

'A fox was travelling through a forest when he came upon a boar who was awaiting a lion against whom he wished to fight. The fox asked the boar whom he was awaiting, so the boar informed him of his intention. The fox told the boar that he had but two teeth with which he might fight the lion, yet that the lion had many teeth and many claws to use against the boar, so it seemed, therefore, that the lion would have the better of the battle. The lion arrived and fought against the boar, killing and devouring him since he possessed superior weapons. Likewise, therefore, do I possess superior weapons against Narpan, for I shall fight him with the assistance of the Divine Virtues and the created virtues, and he shall not be able to fight me other than with vices alone, which vices have no power against God or the virtues.'

[5] When the squire had heard the exemplary tale, he left Blaquerna and went on his way. Blaquerna considered the dangers which might arise in the monastery on account of the dire example set by Narpan, who falsely did his penance there. So charity and hope led him to go to the monastery, where he found Narpan, about whom the squire had spoken to him.

'My friend', said Narpan, 'from where have you come? And would you like to be in the service of a master for a year, or longer?'

'My lord', said Blaquerna, 'I have emerged from this forest and go in pursuit of my gain, yet would serve a master with whom I might find improvement and who might himself derive improvement from me. And since you have asked me about my estate, I beg you to tell me the estate according to which which you reside at this monastery.'

[6] Narpan replied to Blaquerna:

'I reside at this monastery in order to perform penance for the sins I have committed within the world, from which I have retreated. A squire has left my service and, therefore, I need another squire. So, if you wish to serve me, I shall remunerate your labour in such a way that you will be satisfied thereby.'

'My lord', said Blaquerna, 'if you are performing penance and I am serving you, it follows that I too should perform penance, and therefore I shall serve you for a year under such form and contract, namely, that you should perform penance.'

Narpan and Blaquerna agreed upon their undertaking, and, for the period of a week Blaquerna served Narpan in accordance with the latter's wishes, so that Narpan might conceive love for him in his heart and might gain greater faith in him and, furthermore, so that Blaquerna might learn about Narpan's habits.

[7] On the last day of the week, Narpan told Blaquerna that he should kill a goose from amongst those he had been fattening, and should prepare it for lunch. Blaquerna entered the shed in which the geese lived, along with a large number of hens and capons, and he discovered a fox, which had entered that shed. So Blaquerna killed the fox and skinned it, leaving the tail, and placed it on the spit. And when Narpan was ready to eat, Blaquerna brought the fox in to him on a platter. Narpan felt great wonder and asked Blaquerna why he had not brought the goose but had brought the fox instead, which was a horrible thing to eat and to behold.

'My lord', said Blaquerna, 'geese and hens have no enemy as deadly as the fox, and since you love geese and hens you must eat their enemy.'

Narpan was greatly displeased with Blaquerna and uttered many coarse words to him because the latter had advised him to eat the fox and had failed to prepare the goose.

'My lord', said Blaquerna, 'just as foxes are contrary to geese and hens, so too are geese, hens, capons and rich foods[133] contrary to penance. And since I am obliged to serve you according to the proper form of penance, if you eat the fox you shall perform penance by resisting the delights and exquisite dishes you desire to eat.'

[8] Narpan spent the entire day without eating meat, and felt great anger towards Blaquerna. At night-time when Narpan sought to get

---

133. Cat. *grasses scudelles*; lit. 'greasy bowlfuls'.

into his bed, Blaquerna had placed the quilt beneath the feather mattress and the feather mattress beneath the straw mattress, and the blankets beneath the sheets and the bedspread. Narpan asked Blaquerna why he had not made the bed in the manner he had been accustomed to doing. Blaquerna replied that the bed was made according to the work of penance, and that he would not know how to make a penitential bed in any other way. Narpan was a slothful man and did not wish to make the bed in the way it was usually made. Narpan waited for Blaquerna to kneel down and to remove his shoes for him in the manner he had been accustomed to doing, but Blaquerna told him that humility was the friend of all those who performed penance. That night Narpan lay in the bed which Blaquerna had mismade, yet he could not sleep, and dwelt upon the wrongs he had committed within the world and upon the words Blaquerna had said to him.

[9] At midnight, when the monks rose for Matins and Blaquerna heard the bell, he called out to Narpan and told him that he should rise for prayer, since it was time to do so. Narpan told him that he was not in the habit of rising at such an hour. Blaquerna wanted him to rise at all costs, so he removed the bedcovers from on top of him. And first of all he gave him a scapular[134] made of coarse and rough cloth, which Narpan normally wore over his tunic.[135] Since Narpan had thought deeply during the night and since contrition had begun to enter his heart, he obeyed Blaquerna and wore that habit, which was of goatskin, against his flesh. Afterwards, Blaquerna gave him the tunic, made of white Narbonne cloth, and then he gave him his shirt, made of fine linen, which he placed on top of the tunic.

[10] When Narpan had risen and dressed, Blaquerna went with him to the church in order to remain in contemplation and prayer. Narpan, however, told Blaquerna that he felt very great shame at the fact that the abbot and the monks might see him dressed in this way. Blaquerna replied that shame and fortitude were in accord with penance, and that God had already blessed those who would exercise patience and humility while being mocked and berated for performing works of penance.

---

134. Scapular or scapulary: a sleeveless ankle-length monastic cloak, open at the sides, hanging from the shoulders and worn on top of the habit of certain religious Orders, particularly when their members are working outdoors.

135. Cat. *gonella*: a long tunic worn by both men and women; also, a surcoat worn by knights.

[11] Narpan and Blaquerna remained in the church all the way through to daybreak, when the monks would feel the desire to enter into chapter and, after making their satisfaction[136] and performing their disciplines, would say Mass, which is celebrated all the more deservedly once satisfaction has been made in the chapter. Once the monks had entered the chapter house and the Lord Abbot had asked Narpan why he was so peculiarly dressed and why he had risen so early, Narpan replied that his squire had dressed him thus and had awoken him, and that from that point on he wished to be obedient to Blaquerna in all that the latter counselled him. Blaquerna told the abbot that he wished to say a few words about Narpan in the chapter house, in the presence of the entire convent. So the abbot, Narpan and Blaquerna entered the chapter house, and all the monks marvelled at Narpan's attire.

[12] Once they were all in the chapter house, Blaquerna rose to his feet and said these words:

'Three things accord with penance: contrition of heart, confession of mouth and satisfaction for the wrongs one has done.[137] In contrition, it is appropriate to weep, to repent and to remember and hate the sins one has committed; and one must place one's trust in God's mercy and must fear and love God's justice. In confession, it is appropriate for one to confess one's sins and never wish to revert to them. In satisfaction, it is appropriate for one to return that which one unjustly possesses and to inflict suffering upon one's body through vigils, prayer, coarse food, a coarse bed, coarse and humble clothing, and other things similar to this. So, since the three above things accord with penance, and a deed[138] and undertaking exists between Narpan and myself to the effect that I may serve him according to penance, I therefore ask Narpan, in the presence of all, that the contract which obtains between us both should be preserved.'

[13] When Blaquerna had finished speaking, Narpan said, in the presence of all, that he had long been blind and had ignored the terms which correspond to penance, that God had sent Blaquerna to him, who had enlightened the eyes of his soul, and that subsequently

---

136. Cat. *satisfació*: in this case, the performance of penance by a repentant sinner.

137. Cf. Hugh of Saint Victor, *De sacramentis* II, XIV; English version available as Hugh of St Victor (2007), 405, 417.

138. Cat. *carta*. Here, in the sense of written document or legal contract.

he wished to serve God for the rest of his life and to perform penance in all those ways which might be pleasing and agreeable to Blaquerna. The abbot and all the monks praised and blessed God since He revealed His power in the words of Narpan and of Blaquerna.

[14] Narpan and Blaquerna were all alone in Narpan's room. Blaquerna had not forgotten his journey and wished to go in search of his hermitage. He told Narpan his intention, therefore, and asked him to release him from the promise to which he was bound, namely, that of remaining with him for a year. And he said that, since Narpan had recognised his own wrongdoings, he should return his deed to him and release him from their agreement. Narpan was greatly displeased when he learned that Blaquerna wished to leave him, and with devotion and contrition of heart he said these words to Blaquerna, while weeping:

[15] 'I am enlightened by divine inspiration; I am stirred to the devotion of contrition, confession and satisfaction. If my wicked ways seek to regain control over me, who shall help me? If I remain without a master, who shall teach me to love, serve and honour God, Who is worthy of such great honour and against whom I have sinned so gravely? I demand of justice that the pact which has been promised to me should be preserved. If I obey my teacher, how can my teacher show me hostility by leaving me? I wish to be Blaquerna's companion and servant rather than his master, as we had previously agreed. I would go with my lord and teacher Blaquerna to his hermitage;[139] however, I must live within this monastery in order to make satisfaction to the Lord Abbot and to all the monks, who have served me for a long time. I must set a commendable example and this monastery must derive some benefit from my improvement.'

[16] Narpan's words were so devout and reasonable and he uttered them with such piety that Blaquerna was moved to devotion and tears, and he became sorrowful and pensive. So he reflected, therefore, upon how he might live for the entire year with Narpan, with a view to preserving him in his virtuous condition and so that both of them might provide a virtuous example to the monks of that convent. That day Blaquerna reaffirmed the promise he had made to Narpan, and they both decided that they should wear a hairshirt against their skin and that they should be companions throughout

---

139. Cf. Jn 13:14.

the entire year in that monastery, giving glory and praise to God by performing penance. Narpan, the abbot and the entire convent were greatly pleased that Blaquerna had reversed his decision to leave.

## 53. ON PERSEVERANCE

[1] Throughout that entire year Blaquerna and Narpan persevered and accompanied one another in doing penance. And, in church with the monks, Blaquerna sang antiphons, sequences,[140] hymns and responses and explicated the Scriptures for them. The abbot and all the monks greatly desired that Blaquerna should become a monk and that he should teach them Latin and theology and all the other sciences he knew. Blaquerna, however, shrank from becoming a monk since he wished to persevere with the intention he had previously entertained of leading the life of a hermit.

[2] It so happened on a feast day that the abbot wished to preach. However, he hesitated to preach since he did not know how to speak Latin or to explicate the Scriptures, and he felt ashamed with regard to Blaquerna because he knew that the latter would be aware of all the mistakes he made in speaking. The abbot and all the monks were in the chapter house, however, and Blaquerna and Narpan entered therein for the purpose of listening to the abbot, who was due to preach. But before the abbot had uttered any words, the hospitaller[141] came into the chapter and told the abbot that a vast number of knights and other men had come to honour the feast day, and intended to eat that day within the monastery.[142] The abbot gave instruction that a fine meal should be prepared for them, that oats should be given to their animals and that they should have everything they might need, for such was the

---

140. Cat. *proses*. Probably originating in the ninth century, the 'prose', or 'Sequence at Mass', which consisted in unrhymed chants, was an extension of the Alleluia verse and was intended for meditative purposes. The use of sequences, however, went beyond the Mass proper, as they were included extensively in the Divine Office. Later forms thereof were developed as rhyming verse. The term may also refer to a processional hymn having a refrain.

141. The monk in charge of making arrangements for guests in a monastery.

142. Prescriptions regarding the reception of guests at a monastery are found in Ch. 53 of the Rule of St Benedict, in *RSB*, 172-75. It was generally the responsibility of a monastery to feed and lodge guests, particularly eminent ones, guesthouses being constructed within the monastery precincts for this purpose.

custom of that monastery. When the abbot had uttered these words, he said the following to Blaquerna:

'It was my intention to preach, but since I am ignorant of learning, I find that my soul is not equipped to be able to preach in accordance with the honour of the saint whose feast we celebrate today. I have a very great desire, therefore, that you, Blaquerna, should become a monk and that you should preach to us and to all those who come to this monastery on feast days. For, if we are in the habit of satisfying our bodies with bodily foods via alms, we do offence to our souls if we fail to satisfy them with spiritual foods via sermons and God's word.'

[3] Blaquerna replied to the abbot by saying that perseverance was a virtue wherein the perfection of the other virtues was made manifest, for without the perfection of the virtues perseverance itself cannot be a virtue.

'And since I am constrained to be the servant of virtues, I must therefore serve perseverance, wherein the virtues make manifest their operation. So, were I to abandon the purpose for which I left my country and adopt a different aim, I should do offence to charity, fortitude and the other virtues. I, therefore, beg the Lord Abbot and all the monks to grant me dispensation.'

[4] 'Blaquerna', said the abbot, 'once upon a time, it came to pass that a hermit entered a city. The king of that city had died, and custom had it that the first stranger to enter therein three days after the king's death should become king. By God's ordinance, it so happened that this hermit entered that city and was made king. The hermit, however, opposed his election because he wished to persevere with his eremitical life. The electors who had chosen him to be king discussed the question of whether he could persevere in the devotion he had previously practised. The judgement and opinion favoured the electors, and stated that, by accepting the office of king, the hermit could more easily be excused from his intention and desire, than he could were he to remain isolated from people in a rural setting in which he led the life of a hermit; it stated likewise that, as king, he would be able to make readier use of fortitude, hope, justice and the other virtues, and, therefore, would be better able to serve perseverance. We have likewise held discussions to the effect that you should remain[143] with us, who are hermits and wish to be your companions.'

---

143. Lit. 'persevere'.

[5] Blaquerna replied, saying these words:

'My lords, you may remember that Saint John the Baptist was a hermit who lived all alone in the forest, ate locusts and wild honey, and wore garments made of camel's hair;[144] and that Jesus stated that a better man was not born of woman than Saint John the Baptist.[145] So because Saint John remained alone in his hermitage and underwent great suffering, God honoured him in His glory in accordance with how He spoke of him.'

[6] When Blaquerna had uttered these words, the prior said to him that Jesus Christ, who is a better man than Saint John, travelled and lived in the company of the Apostles in order to convey that perseverance is a nobler virtue in people when they are together, inasmuch as it does not perish as a result of the company of others, than it is when it exists merely in a person who lives all by himself. In his view, therefore, it was fitting that, in accordance with justice and hope, Blaquerna should obey by deferring to the request of the abbot and the entire monastery.

## 54. ON OBEDIENCE

[1] The cellarer told Blaquerna that there was no more meritorious virtue in the whole world than obedience. So, since obedience would be stronger in a person who subjects himself to another than it would in one who lives all by himself in a hermitage, Blaquerna, therefore, would be contrary to obedience if he were to forsake it as regards that in which it enjoys greater virtue and is more pleasing to God.

[2] Blaquerna replied:

'Once upon a time, it came to pass that a blind man had a son who would lead him from door to door begging alms for the love of God. The blind man's son had been rearing a dog. The young child died, so the blind man put the dog on a lead, and the dog led him from door to door, just as his child had been in the habit of doing. An occasion arose on which the blind man left a particular city and travelled towards another such. A hare ran across the path along which they were walking and the dog wanted to chase the hare, so it left the

---

144. Matt 3:4.
145. Matt 11:11; Lk. 7:28.

path, and the blind man followed the dog. The dog went in pursuit of the hare and arrived at a steep slope, and it sought to go down after the hare, which had already descended the slope. The blind man followed the dog and tumbled down the hill, breaking his leg. So he said the following words:

[3] '"God bestows great grace upon man when he grants him bodily sight so that the eyes of his mind may comprehend[146] the fact that, in all creatures capable of seeing, bodily sight signifies the nobility of the Creator. God bestows greater grace, however, upon the will which obeys the eyes of the intellect, which latter understands those things towards which the will ought to be more obedient. For a will which is obedient to him who has no understanding is in a similar situation to me. And if one's intellect were to be obedient to one's will, intellect would not be so greatly honoured thereby, unless one's will were to show stricter obedience thereto."'

[4] When Blaquerna had said these words and many others, the sacrist replied:

'We know and understand perfectly the analogy in accordance with which you speak, signifying that the will is in danger when it obeys an intellect wherein there is a lack of understanding. As a result of your words, therefore, we wish charity and justice to issue judgement thereupon.'

While the sacrist was saying these words, a messenger came to him and asked him to go to give communion to a lay brother who was mortally ill. The sacrist, the abbot and all the others followed the Body of Jesus Christ and comforted the sick man. When the sacrist said to the sick man that he should believe this Host to be the Body of Jesus Christ, the former replied by saying that he did not believe this Host he saw under the form of bread to be the flesh of Jesus Christ.

[5] The abbot and all the others were greatly displeased when they realised that the brother did not believe and had fallen into error. So they summoned Blaquerna and asked him to reply to the sick man and to free him from the error into which he had fallen. So Blaquerna asked the sick man whether the human intellect enjoys a nobler power than do man's bodily eyes. The sick man conceded to Blaquerna that intelligence was nobler in one's intellect than sight

---

146. Cat. *obeesquen*, from the verb *obeir*: lit. 'to obey', but figuratively, 'to embrace, grasp or comprehend'.

was in one's bodily eyes. Blaquerna said to the sick man that because intelligence was nobler than bodily sight, one was obliged to be more obedient to intelligence than to bodily sight in order to preserve the honour owed to intelligence, which intelligence understands a miracle to be performed by divine power in the Host, just as it understands that the world has been created from nothing.

[6] 'The four elements exist by nature under the form of man, and these elements are invisible to one's bodily eyes, which see but the form of the man in which they stand combined, while the prime form lies concealed therein.[147] So, if nature is capable of such a task, how much more capable are the power, wisdom and will[148] of God of causing flesh to exist under the form of bread! And if such were not the case, God would not reveal that His power was above that possessed by nature.'

Blaquerna said these and many other words to the sick man, who received the body of Jesus Christ as a devout Christian while praising, blessing and adoring God, Who had drawn him away from the error into which he had fallen. The sick man died and God received his soul, so the abbot and the monks returned to the discussion in which they had previously been engaged with Blaquerna.

[7] 'Blaquerna', said the abbot, 'this event which has just happened to us is an example which signifies to you that God wishes you to be His servant within our community. For, had you not been with us, God would have lost this soul which today has passed from this world, and we should have felt great remorse at his damnation on account of the ignorance that defines us, inasmuch as we ourselves were not able to say to the dead man the words that you have spoken to him. It often happens that God brings about events such as these so that one may thereby perceive His will. You have not been of benefit to the soul of the dead man alone, for you have given instruction to us all as to how we might resist temptation were we to be faced by it in a similar instance.'

[8] Blaquerna replied:

---

147. 'Prime form' and 'prime matter' are the joint and fundamental constituents of 'Chaos', according to Lullian cosmology and elemental theory.

148. 'Power, Wisdom and Will' are three of the sixteen 'Dignities' (or attributes of God) used in Figure A of the Arts of the *ACIV* (*c.*1274) and *AD* (*c.*1283) cycles (the two cycles of Llull's 'quaternary phase').

'Another method whereby one can free from error a person who experiences temptation regarding the Body of Christ, consists in faith. For God desires one to be obedient to faith by curbing one's imagination, which seeks falsely to present to the intellect a similitude[149] which contradicts the operation of Divine power. And you can employ this method even if you suffer from ignorance through lack of knowledge.'

The abbot replied to Blaquerna:

'It is more certain and secure to combat error by means of understanding and faith than by means of faith alone. Justice, therefore, accuses your conscience of contradicting your words, which release you from our community.'[150]

## 55. ON COUNSEL

[1] Blaquerna gave a great deal of consideration to the words which had been spoken to him, as well as to the event which had occurred regarding the temptation of the deceased man. While Blaquerna was engaged in such consideration, the abbot and all the monks begged him to submit to becoming a monk himself. Narpan, tearfully, said the following words to him:

'My beloved friend Blaquerna, what can you mean by this? Will you not obey the requests of our Lord Abbot and all the monks? And will you not defer all the more to your intellect, which will cause you to feel remorse if you fail to provide these servants of God with the understanding whereby they may have better knowledge of God? For the more exalted the intellect becomes on acquiring knowledge of God, the more pronounced becomes the readiness the will possesses on raising itself up to love God and His servants dearly. So, if you submit to becoming a monk, I shall submit thereto alongside you, and wish to be your companion and your servant. So you shall bring advantage upon yourself and on all the others, yet, if you remain all by yourself in a hermitage, you shall bring advantage upon yourself alone.'

[2] Blaquerna replied to him:

---

149. Cat. *semblança*; i.e. a resemblance.
150. This, then, is the judgement of Justice, for which see above, § 4 of this chapter.

'Wrong would be done to the contemplative man, who lives all by himself for the love of God, were his prayers to be of advantage to himself alone but not to others. I have, therefore, begun to think about things differently, namely, by means of my conscience which causes me to remember that diverse wills should be sheep and should remain in the charge of an enlightened and exalted intellect which is their shepherd. And conscience has caused me to remember the chapter "On Devotion"[151] as well as the loss borne by the students of Intellect when they lack devotion.'

So, on account of all these things, Blaquerna told the Lord Abbot and all the others that one should enter into consultation and take counsel concerning all matters before one passes from one resolution to another, and that he would take counsel from the seven virtues, which had frequently counselled him well. The abbot and all the others prayed to God that as regards the counsel and decision which Blaquerna had so far withheld from them,[152] their own rights and needs should be preserved.'

[3] During that entire day and night, Blaquerna's thoughts were upon other matters, because one should think about certain other things for an interval prior to taking counsel. For one's intellect begins to recover its power once again regarding the matter one has decided to pursue, and understands it more clearly, since it returns to it a second time. The following day, after Mass, Blaquerna was engaged in prayer and, once his prayers were finished, he began to think, and he remembered each of the virtues one at a time, continuing in such thought until the ninth hour. After he had eaten, Blaquerna went to take recreation in the garden in order to revive his spirit. And when he had done this, he slept, so that the food might be digested better and that during the night he might be more able to keep vigil for the purpose of meditation. At dusk he did not wish to remain awake, so he went to sleep in order that he might be able to resume his thoughts once again in the early morning, and he did this all the more so since at that early hour one's imaginative faculty is in greater accord with one's intellect.

[4] At the hour of Matins, Blaquerna rose and went to the garden to look upon the sky and the stars, so that he might acquire greater

---

151. See Ch. 45 above.
152. Cat. *retenir l'acord*: 'to keep one's decision to oneself'.

devotion. He knelt down on the ground, made the sign of the Cross, raised his hands and eyes heavenward with a loving will, and prayed God that He might be pleased to remember His servant and to enlighten him as to the course of action which might best please Him. By God's will it came about that Blaquerna decided to become a monk since he considered that he could be of greater service to God within a monastery than he could in a hermitage. Blaquerna strengthened his resolve and remembered that, whenever he had given consideration to this subject, he had reached the very same conclusion and that none of the virtues had been in conflict therewith. And hope comforted and reassured him that the time would arrive when he would be a hermit and would lead the life he so desired. And prudence showed him that the life he would live in the monastery would cause justice to increase the holiness of his life as a hermit.

[5] Once Blaquerna had conceived such devotion, he went to the chapter house where he found the Lord Abbot and all the monks, who were discussing with Narpan the holiness of Blaquerna's life. Blaquerna knelt before the abbot and all the monks and agreed to submit to the Order and to their every command without reservation, at which the abbot and all the others felt great joy. So Blaquerna and Narpan received the habit and the benediction with great honour and made the pledges which correspond to that Order.[153]

## 56. On the ordering of studies

[1] The abbot and the entire convent were in the chapter house with Blaquerna for the purpose of issuing an ordinance in relation to the monks' studies. It was ordained by all that they should create a school or area for study in a separate part of the monastery whose location might prove conducive to such. When they had selected an isolated location suitable for study, they made stipulations regarding time, for without the organisation of time there exists no profitable study. After they had made their stipulations regarding time, they ordained

---

153. Patrick Gifreu plausibly suggests that in this context Llull is referring to the Cistercian Order, here associated with the monastery of La Real, which lay outside present-day Palma de Mallorca and with which Llull is known to have had contact. See Llull (2007a), 222, n. 15.

which people should receive instruction, according to their age, propensities, natural understanding and good customs. After all these regulations had been drawn up, they established a rule regarding the sciences, namely, as to which of these they ought to study.[154]

[2] While they were seeking to ordain which of the sciences they should study, a man brought a letter into the chapter house from two monks who were asking for money to cover their expenses as well as for the purchase of books on Law. The abbot read this letter in the presence of the entire chapter. The abbot told Blaquerna about how they had two monks in Montpellier who were studying Law with a view to being able to assist the monastery in its worldly affairs.[155] While the abbot was recounting such matters, a squire appeared before him, and said that, at a grange[156] belonging to that monastery, a lay brother was very gravely ill and that the abbot should send him a physician who might tend him. The abbot sent to a city for a physician, who was unwilling to go to the grange without considerable recompense and refused to remain with the sick man for more than a single day. The brother died on account of the deficiencies of a physician who would not pay him frequent visits, and the abbot and all the others felt remorse at his death.

[3] As chance would have it, a bishop happened to come to this monastery while the abbot was in chapter with all the monks. The bishop entered the chapter house and the abbot and the entire convent gave him a very honourable reception. The bishop was a great scholar knowledgeable in many sciences and he asked numerous questions and made great inquiry concerning a range thereof. There was no one within that monastery, however, who was able to answer

---

154. Cathedral and monastic schools were forerunners of the University or *studium generale*. Graduates of these *studia* were entitled, in theory, to teach at any school within the bounds of Christendom, possessing as graduates the *ius ubique docendi*, a universal licence created by the papacy in the thirteenth century in order to supersede the *licencia docendi* until that point issued by the scholaster (master of a cathedral or monastic school) as a local monopoly applicable solely within a diocese, for which latter information, see Verger (2007), 24.

155. The city of Montpellier constituted one of the regions forming the Kingdom of Majorca (the others being the island of Majorca itself, the remaining Balearic Islands and Roussillon). *Blaquerna* itself was at least completed, if not composed in its entirety, within that city.

156. A 'grange' is a farm which forms part of a monastery's estates though is situated at some distance from the main house, and is overseen by a monk and worked by lay brothers (*conversi*).

the questions the bishop posed apart from Blaquerna alone, who resolved and explained all the questions the bishop asked. The abbot
and the monks spent the entire day in the company of the bishop.
The following morning, after Mass, the abbot and the monks returned to the chapter house for the purpose of ordaining which sciences Blaquerna should teach.

[4] 'Blaquerna', said the abbot, 'which sciences does it seem to
you that you ought to teach?'

'My lord', said Blaquerna, 'once upon a time it came to pass that
a man was mortally wounded, and had received a wound to his face.
The physician first tended the wound which he first of all saw, yet the
wounded man had a deadly wound to his abdomen, from which he
lost so much blood while the physician was healing the wound to his
face, that he died on account of that wound. Another time, it occurred that a fox asked an eagle why it had wings, feathers, a beak and
claws. The eagle replied to the fox by telling it the reason why nature
had given it all these things, which were necessary to it. By means of
this analogy and by many others can you understand which science is
most necessary and which sciences your monks ought to learn.'

[5] The abbot and all the others asked Blaquerna to explain the
words he uttered by means of analogies. Blaquerna explained the exemplary tale of the wounded man by means of another such, saying:

'Once upon a time, it came to pass that an abbot sent a monk to the
Schools. This monk was of good customs when he left the monastery;
when he was in the Schools and was among worldly people, however,
he learned their customs and forgot his own. When the monk returned
to the monastery he was riddled with vices, so through his deeds he
gave instruction in vices and through his teaching he gave instruction
in the sciences. By his vices he corrupted all the monks to wicked ways
and the monks made poor use of the knowledge they learned.'

After Blaquerna had explained the first exemplary tale, he explained the second by means of a further such, saying that:

'Once upon a time, it came to pass that a nightingale was in a tree
upon which grew and blossomed many leaves and flowers. This nightingale asked the tree why it had so many flowers and so many leaves.
The tree replied that nature ordained that there should be leaves and
flowers so that there might be fruit. So, according to these words, it is
signified that, in keeping with the reason why we are in this place and
have left the world, it is fitting that we should acquire various sciences

so that we may acquire the science of theology, which is the end and perfection of all the other sciences.'

[6] When Blaquerna had explained the aforesaid examples, the monks ordained that Blaquerna should teach Latin grammar first of all, to facilitate an understanding of the other sciences. After this, he should teach logic in order to help the monks understand and learn about the natural sciences,[157] as well as philosophy so that they might better be able to understand theology. And once they had learned theology, he should teach them medicine and, after this, the science of law. While this ordinance was being enacted, a monk said that it was impossible for the students to be able to learn all those sciences. Blaquerna, however, replied by saying that they could learn a suitable amount about each science and, within a year, could ultimately learn the principles and the art pertaining to the four general sciences which are the most necessary, namely, theology, natural philosophy, medicine and law. By means of such principles, indicated by these arts, the monks could practise the sciences according to their needs, for by applying the principles prescribed and indicated by such arts is one also able to draw upon other principles.[158]

## 57. ON VAINGLORY

[1] Blaquerna taught the sciences and the art in accordance with the aforesaid ordinance. One day, the abbot, the prior and the cellarer were in the abbot's bedchamber and were discussing Blaquerna and his students. The cellarer said to the abbot and the prior that he feared a time might come when they should be despised by Blaquerna's students, since knowledge occasions pride and vainglory, whereby those who lack knowledge are disdained. The cellarer counselled the abbot and the prior, therefore, to dissolve the school—all the more so, because of the great expense it incurred.

[2] The abbot and the prior reflected deeply upon the cellarer's words; the abbot, however, was a very saintly and devout man and,

---

157. I.e. natural philosophy.

158. In this pedagogical programme of advanced studies, Llull draws on arguments relating to the subordination of the sciences in order to recommend the unifying and foundational 'meta-science' of his own Art, from whose principles those of all the other sciences can be derived.

despite his not being highly educated, possessed natural sense mixed with devotion. So he said the following words, therefore, to the cellarer:

'In natural science there is a book which discusses the moral virtues, and Blaquerna gives instruction in theology on the three theological virtues. These virtues, therefore, shall provide the foundation and instruction whereby the students may possess humility and justice and pay honour to us, who provide and procure for them the knowledge they may acquire. I am confident, therefore, that vainglory and pride will not dispose their intentions in our regard towards anything which is villainous or wicked.'

[3] On many occasions the prior had imagined, considered and desired that he might become abbot after the latter's demise. And he cogitated on the fact that, because he had little learning, when the abbot died, it would follow that Blaquerna or one of his students would become abbot. The prior constantly felt great sadness, therefore, and he wished that the school should be dissolved. The abbot was wise and intelligent, and was attentive to the monks and to their situation, so he noticed that the prior remained continually in a state of great sadness. The abbot wished to know what had occasioned the prior to fall prey to such great despondency. For sadness is a bad sign in a monk or religious, unless he is stirred to this by remembrance of his sins or by the wrongs that exist in the world, whereby that honour is not rendered to God which befits Him.

[4] The abbot commanded the prior in virtue of obedience to tell him his innermost thoughts. The prior replied, saying that the object of such thoughts was secret and that it was not suited to being known except by way of confession. The abbot understood that the sadness to which the prior had fallen prey was not virtuous and he remembered that day on which the cellarer had said the above words, so the abbot, therefore, recounted to the prior the following exemplary tale:

'Once upon a time, it came to pass in this monastery that the son of a highly acclaimed burgher decided to become a monk. So his father, along with a large number of the latter's friends, came to this monastery and forcibly removed him therefrom, saying that they would not consent to his becoming a monk for the reason that we were lacking in education. They did consent, however, to his joining a different order wherein there were highly educated men.'

[5] While the abbot was talking to the prior and speaking to him at length in order to console him and to draw him out of his sadness, two religious, who were noted scholars, came to the monastery with the aim of seeing the Lord Abbot, who was with the prior. All four spent a long time together speaking about God, and the two brothers posed questions regarding Holy Scripture to the abbot and the prior, who were unable to answer. In the midst of these discussions, the abbot remembered a monk, one of Blaquerna's students, who was always very joyful and gave signs of immense happiness. The abbot sent a messenger to that monk asking him to answer the questions that the two visiting brothers had posed. The monk came and settled their questions, and asked them many others, which the two brothers were unable to answer. In the midst of these discussions, the hospitaller called the two brothers to come and eat. After the brothers had left, the abbot asked the monk why he was always so joyful.

'My lord', said the monk, 'so great is the delight I receive from the science I am learning, whereby philosophy affords me the opportunity to have knowledge of God, and so fortunate do I consider myself to be in religion and to have escaped from the world, that I am joyful and delighted day and night, and all the more so since my knowledge causes me so deeply to scorn the world and vainglory and to love humility and God.'

[6] The monk returned to hear the lesson Blaquerna was giving, in which lesson he was demonstrating by natural reasons from philosophy how creatures signify the Creator and His works. The abbot stayed with the prior, and recounted the following exemplary tale to him:

'Once upon a time, it came to pass that there was a great dispute between the pine, the date and the fig tree, in which each one asserted the greater nobility that nature had given it over the others. The pine tree claimed that within it lay the pine cone and the pine nut shell in order to preserve the nut, which itself preserved the lineage of the species, and that, therefore, it was nobler. The date tree invoked its own right to be so considered since the flesh of the date was sweet while the pit within preserved its own species. The fig tree said that it was better than the others because the fruit of the entire fig was edible and was wholly good. So, likewise may your soul be comforted', said the abbot to the prior, 'for we are the shell, while the nut and the pit are Blaquerna and his students; and we are the outer part of the date which one eats, while the pit consists in the preservation of knowledge. After our deaths, therefore, the time shall come when this entire monastery will resemble the fruit of the fig tree, and there shall be many great scholars, including abbots, officials[159] and students within our Order.'

[7] When the abbot had said these words, the prior recognised his error and how pride had made him desire honour and vainglory, so he confessed his fault to the abbot, which relieved his soul of the anguish that sorrow had imposed upon it for so long now, and uttered, therefore, the following words:

'Once upon a time, it came to pass that a very wealthy man was ill, and he vehemently bemoaned death since he would leave behind his wealth, his wife and his children. And because of the sadness of his soul and his fear of death, he was tormented doubly, for his illness tormented him in one way and the sadness of his soul in another.'

By means of the aforesaid analogy, therefore, the prior had revealed to the abbot the thoughts he had been entertaining, so he asked for pardon and forgiveness from the Lord Abbot and emerged from his servitude to sorrow and returned to the gladness he customarily felt.

[8] In that country it came to pass that the king held a great court and requested counsel from his barons. So he sent a messenger to the abbot asking him to come to his court and to bring with him the wisest monks there were within his convent. The abbot and the prior came to the court with Blaquerna, along with some other monks. And Blaquerna's counsel was chosen and selected, above all other such given to the king. Blaquerna preached that day to the king and to all the people, as well as to many religious who had been summoned to that court. And his sermon greatly pleased the king and all the others. While the abbot and the prior were returning to the monastery with Blaquerna, the two former began to converse with Blaquerna about what he had said within his counsel and within his sermon. Blaquerna, however, changed the subject so that he might suppress vainglory. The abbot said to the prior that Blaquerna possessed great virtue and had thus succeeded in conducting himself well, and that on that day he had thereby brought honour upon all

---

159. Llull may be referring here to either the local or the provincial superiors of the Order who operated under the supervision of the superior general.

the monks of that monastery, and that also, on account of the pleasure and satisfaction he had gained from Blaquerna, the king had chosen to be buried within that monastery.


## 58. ON ACCUSATION

[1] At Easter, Blaquerna had finished his lectures, and because of the efforts he had invested in his studies, the abbot and the cellarer took him round the monastery's granges so that he might have some bodily relaxation. The abbot and the cellarer had obtained salted fish, sauces and other things to bring with them. Blaquerna reproached them by saying that it was contrary to hope and poverty to bring such things on one's journey and that it was fitting, therefore, that they should take virtues with them on their journey and that they should leave behind those things which were contrary to an austere life and consistent with the active life. Blaquerna made the abbot and the cellarer leave behind many things they wished to bring. The cellarer, however, argued with great vigour against Blaquerna, and particularly as regards the quilts, cushions, drinking vessels and jugs that Blaquerna had unloaded from the mule.

[2] While Blaquerna was travelling along with the abbot and the cellarer, they came across a bishop, who was out taking recreation, and riding in his company was a nephew of his whom he loved dearly, which nephew was among a large group of companions who were hunting and had brought with them goshawks, sparrowhawks and falcons, along with dogs of different breeds. This bishop invited the abbot and his companions to dine with him, so together they entered the city that day and ate with the bishop. On the table were various kinds of food variously prepared, and upon it also stood gilded goblets, silver bowls and jugs. And a great multitude of people ate in the palace every day. After grace, and when everyone had risen from the table, minstrels appeared playing various instruments, and they sang and danced, uttering words which were at variance with the prayers that had been said at table.

'My lord', said Blaquerna to the bishop, 'there are minstrels here who think themselves obliged to do your pleasure, since you have fed them. I too have dined with you, and if it were your pleasure, I should like to be your minstrel and should like to say a few words.'

It pleased the bishop and all the others that Blaquerna should speak and should say his words.

[3] Blaquerna rose to his feet and harshly rebuked the bishop for the excessive amounts of food on offer, for his attire, for his vast suite of followers and for the table decorations. He rebuked the bishop above all for the fact that he listened to minstrels hostile to the honour of Jesus Christ, by virtue of Whom he was himself so highly honoured and Who had created for him so many creatures whereby He afforded pleasure to the bishop's person. Blaquerna was wearing a crucifix depicting Jesus Christ, which he showed to the bishop and all the others while saying these words:

'Jesus Christ died, yet devotion too has perished. Prelacies, canonries and prebends[160] are conferred for the sake of honouring Jesus Christ. But who pays due honour to Him?'

Blaquerna wept. The bishop and all the others felt deeply ashamed; but the abbot and the cellarer were very displeased with Blaquerna for having so harshly rebuked the bishop.

[4] The abbot and his companions went to stay at a monastery where there was an accomplished preacher who ruled and governed over that entire monastery. And all the people in the surrounding areas honoured and loved that monastery on account of that brother. That night the abbot, Blaquerna and the cellarer received a very warm welcome. And the same night the cellarer spoke with the brother who preached so well and counselled him to leave that particular Order and to come to their monastery to join theirs. When the abbot and Blaquerna had left that monastery, the cellarer recounted how he had done his best to persuade that brother to come to take their habit. Blaquerna rebuked the cellarer very harshly by saying these words.

'Envy, lack of charity, pride, greed and injustice are in our midst! Those brothers with whom we lodged last night took very good care of us and gave us a courteous welcome, yet we have stolen and lured away from them a brother who is their perfection. Against such wrongdoing an accusation must be made in chapter so that it may be punished.'

---

160. A prebend is a benefice, usually in the form of part of a cathedral's (or a collegiate church's) estate assigned by such to a canon or a member of the cathedral chapter (i.e. a prebendary), in order to provide him with a stipend.

[5] In the evening, the abbot, Blaquerna and the cellarer went to stay at an acclaimed monastery. While the abbot and Blaquerna were talking to the brothers, who were showing them around the monastery, the cellarer was arguing with a brother from that monastery, and told him that the chapel, the chapter house, the dormitory and the other buildings in his own monastery were bigger and more beautiful than the chapel and the other buildings in that monastery. When they had quarrelled over the buildings and the offices, they argued about their Orders, and each of them praised his Order so highly that he maligned the other Order. Blaquerna committed the cellarer's words to memory so that he might accuse him of them in chapter.

[6] As they travelled along, the abbot, Blaquerna and the cellarer passed in front of a noble place abounding in streams, fields, vineyards, trees and pastures. This place belonged to a wealthy burgher. The cellarer said to the abbot that whenever he passed by this place he yearned for it to belong to their abbey, for it would make a very noble grange. The abbot asked the cellarer if the treasurer held funds sufficient to enable them to purchase that place. The cellarer replied that the funds held by the treasurer were needed to pay the debts they owed on account of a castle they had bought, but that when they had repaid those debts, they should gather together the funds to buy that place and should be more frugal with food so that they might be able to purchase it more easily, a frugality they had practised when they bought the castle. Blaquerna noted these words in his heart and said that envy, injustice and greed were still in their midst, so he uttered the following words:

'Alas! How great is the error of this world! For the religious is not guarded against sin by the habit he wears but by justice and charity. Eating beans, drinking old, sour wine, wearing long habits and double cowls, using wooden stirrups and rising for Matins: why do such things not help justice and charity to be in our midst?'

Blaquerna asked the abbot if they might return to the monastery, for his soul was very troubled and he wished to revive it by following the rules of monastic life, and to have fellowship and diversion with his companions while conversing about God.

[7] When the abbot, Blaquerna and the cellarer had returned to the monastery and were in the chapter house, Blaquerna accused them both of having taken a large amount of provisions with them when they left the monastery. And he said that a monk should be

pleased when on his travels there is a lack or scarcity of certain things, for scarcity is the occasion in him of hope, patience, penitence, poverty and humility, and sets a good example to the grangers and the other people whom one meets on one's journey.

[8] The abbot and the cellarer accused Blaquerna of having harshly rebuked the bishop who had invited them to dine; Blaquerna, however, justified himself with these words:

'Love, truth, justice and fortitude caused me to censure the bishop, and this cannot cause me any harm as regards either my bodily or my spiritual life. If I had felt ashamed to censure him, where would the aforesaid virtues be? If I felt ashamed or was afraid to speak, I should have been pleased to remain silent concerning the dishonour and the offence caused to my Lord, Creator and Saviour. To love and to die remembering Christ and His works stand together in their opposition to eating and living in obliviousness to the honour and gratitude which warrant being paid to God.'

[9] Blaquerna justified himself thus, having good reason to do so, and he reproached the cellarer, who had sought to lure the accomplished preacher away from the brothers who had so warmly welcomed them. Blaquerna presented many true and compelling arguments in order to prove that injustice, falsity, villainy and covetousness dwell in those who lure one group of brothers away from another. And any brother who lures another brother away from his Order acts against the interests of community, and can be reproached and punished for the vice of private ownership.'[161]

[10] To praise a religious Order is permissible when that Order faces a challenge to its Rule.[162] To praise one's own Order over another such, however, is to speak ill of order and runs counter to com-

---

161. I.e. the vice opposed to the virtue of voluntary poverty, which latter formed one of the vows (along with chastity and obedience) professed by members of Catholic religious communities, particularly the Mendicant Orders, in the medieval period and beyond. The Benedictine Order notably shunned private ownership, for which see Chs. 33 and 55 of the Rule of St Benedict, in *RSB*, 122-23 and 178-81, respectively. Following the death of St Bonaventure (1274) and his period as Minister General of the Franciscan Order, a schism arose between the so-called 'Spiritual' members thereof (adherents of absolute poverty) and their 'Conventual' counterparts (adherents of a more relaxed observance).

162. Cat. *Loar orde es leguda laor contra inregularitat de orde*. As the reader can see, the Catalan here is much more synthetic than the equivalent English. My translation is guided by the editors' note in the Catalan critical edition.

munity, charity, justice, brotherliness and God's unity. To covet towns, castles and granges constitutes greed and the desire for private ownership. To incur debt and to borrow money in order to acquire wealth and many granges constitutes fellowship and association between the orders of religion and laity, as well as the enslavement of the former to the latter. It also squanders a monastery's pittance[163] and the alms distributed therefrom to the poor. It is permissible, however, to bring a monastery into debt on account of the scarcity of food, the lack of which has been brought about by pestilence, drought or other natural causes.

Blaquerna said that he accused the cellarer of all the above things and that he desired that, in his presence, he should be given a lashing.

[11] The cellarer was sentenced to receive lashes. A monk brought a large bundle of twigs, tied together, and sought to administer lashes to the cellarer. Blaquerna, however, untied the twigs and said words to the following effect, namely, that a bundle of such twigs aimed at administering lashes signified vainglory, and caused injury to a body insofar as it bruised it, yet failed to impart a sense of suffering as intense as that left by a single switch. The cellarer, therefore, was beaten with a single switch, from which he received greater suffering than he would have from all the twigs at once. A statute was laid down, therefore, to the effect that lashes should always be administered using a single switch against bare flesh.

[12] The cellarer felt deeply perturbed and extremely ashamed, so he exonerated himself of certain things, by saying the following words:

'The reason why I stand accused of envy and covetousness is contrary to justice and charity, which cause me to desire that our monastery might possess many towns, castles and granges so that a large number of monks might reside within this monastery and that therein plentiful alms might be given.'

Blaquerna replied:

---

163. An endowment established to finance a series of Masses for the soul of a departed person is known as a chantry. The Mass itself is known as an *obiit* (obit). Often such endowments also made allowance for the provision of a 'pittance' (or extra portion of food or wine) to each monk or nun in the monastery on the occasion of the anniversary of the deceased person's death.

'Jesus Christ could have kept company in this world with many princes, had He elected to. However, in order to signify humility and poverty he decided to choose the company of only a few people in order to eliminate pride and vainglory. It is better, therefore, to desire the saintliness of few people than a multitude of people in whom there is wrongdoing and sin. Saint Sophia[164] gave greater alms towards the building of the church in Constantinople than did the emperor, for God was better pleased by the penn'orth she gave every day towards the work than by all the remainder that the emperor himself gave, whereby the church was built and completed. And since you have exonerated yourself in defiance of justice, repentance and contrition, you must make satisfaction once again by receiving lashes.'

The cellarer was beaten once more because his exoneration was not valid according to law.

### 59. ON HOW BLAQUERNA BECAME SACRIST

[1] Blaquerna continued to teach his students for so long that there were many of them who learned wonderfully well and who became noble preachers and masters.[165] Word spread throughout the entire region as to the estimable teaching he had imparted, so many other monasteries sent monks there in order to learn those particular teachings while, in turn, the abbot sent numerous students to various monasteries in order to be masters. And many men from that region founded chaplaincies[166] in perpetuity within that monastery for the salvation of their souls. And great good accrued to that monastery from the knowledge that Blaquerna taught. While Blaquerna was a master, it came to pass that the sacrist passed from this world to the next.

[2] Blaquerna wished to remain continually in contemplation, which activity he was unable to pursue on account of the impediment posed by his studies, to which he applied himself very assiduously.

---

164. Saint Sophia the Martyr (d. 137 CE), to whom the Hagia Sophia in Istanbul (Constantinople) was dedicated.

165. I.e. teachers.

166. An ecclesiastical benefice (or chantry), the income from which formed the salary of a chaplain, established by a private individual ('the founder') for whom the chaplain would periodically offer Masses. For the meaning of 'chantry', see above, Ch. 58, § 10 and corresponding note.

The abbot and all the monks wanted Blaquerna to become sacrist and wished another monk, who had become a master by virtue of the knowledge Blaquerna had imparted to him, to hold the classes instead of Blaquerna. Blaquerna had recently been ordained a priest and had assumed that office with great trepidation since he did not consider himself to be worthy thereof, so he celebrated his first Mass humbly, in secret and in the absence of all vanity. Blaquerna was elected to become sacrist. He kept the church and all that pertained to his office very clean, he said Mass daily and spent almost the entire day at prayer. In the evening he prostrated himself in front of the altar of Our Lady, Holy Mary. Who could possibly describe to you the tears Blaquerna shed and the prayers he offered up? And who could recount to you the lofty manner in which he engaged in contemplation? And who could know the art he employed to elevate his soul to God?

[3] One evening, after Compline, it came to pass that Blaquerna was at prayer. He had been weeping from an abundance of devotion, and had cogitated upon the fact that while the priest is celebrating Mass, angels pay honour and reverence to the holy sacrifice of Jesus Christ, their Lord. This thought formed very clearly in his mind. But while he was engaged in such thoughts, he fell asleep and dreamt about what he had conceived while he was still awake. For, under the influence of the powerful imaginings he had entertained while still awake during the aforesaid ministry,[167] it seemed to him, while sleeping, that he was saying Mass and that Saint Michael and Saint Gabriel were his altar servers. Blaquerna awoke two or three times during that night, yet each time he returned to that very same dream. At midnight, Blaquerna rose in order to ring the bell, and he said Matins with the monks. Afterwards, he remained at prayer and recalled what he had dreamt that night. While Blaquerna was recollecting in this manner, he put on his vestments in order to celebrate Mass. When he was before the altar, it seemed to him that on each side thereof he saw an angel with wings, and that each of them held a Cross in one hand and a book in the other. He felt great wonder at this vision, and believed that things were precisely as they appeared to him to be. Blaquerna, however, did not wish to proceed with saying Mass until he had ceased to feel such doubts. So he began to remem-

---

167. I.e. the ministry of prayer.

ber once more the virtues with which he always tended to his needs. Justice led him to be reminded of his unworthiness to look upon angels. Prudence provided him with an understanding of how, under the influence of his thoughts and as a result of a weakness of the brain enfeebled by abstinence, vigils and fasting, as well as of a great lack of sleep, fantasy represents certain vanities as if they are the truth.[168] Fortitude strengthened his mind against the imaginative faculty which, at times, imagines things in a disorderly manner, on account of which disorderliness bodily sight receives certain vain similitudes which are in conflict with the truth. Blaquerna was assisted by all these virtues and ceased to feel the doubts to which he had succumbed, and afterwards celebrated Mass very devoutly, as was his custom.

[4] One night it occurred that Blaquerna was in the church all by himself and was cogitating upon demons and the horrific shape they assume when they seek to frighten a person. While Blaquerna was engaged in such meditation, he felt fear and dread enter his mind, so he was terrified of remaining alone in the church and felt the urge to go off to the dormitory that night to sleep. He remembered, however, that such temptation was directed at fortitude and prudence so that he might cause them to be exalted, an exaltation they received when Blaquerna remembered God's perfect power, which could protect him just as easily in the church while he was all alone as it could in the dormitory while he was among his fellows. Blaquerna, therefore, was fortified against the temptation and the fear to which he had succumbed, so he began to pray and remembered God's great power, which wished him to be tempted, as mentioned above, so that he might conceive that power to be as mightily effective in one place as in another.

---

168. For Ramon Llull, the imagination is a process which retains past images and creates further images for future use; it also summarises what is received from the five bodily senses and is presented to the imagination via 'fantasy', prior to any intellectual activity on the part of the human soul. The imaginative faculty thus represents the point of contact between material reality and the rational soul. Much of the medieval theory of knowledge constituted a response to the reception in the Latin West of Aristotle's treatise On the Soul (De anima) and its Graeco-Arabic commentary tradition, yet was obliged to orientate itself as regards the pre-existing—and in the case of Franciscan thinkers, prevailing—tradition surrounding St Augustine's theory of (immediate) illumination.

[5] Blaquerna was tempted in many ways, both day and night. And as soon as he was tempted, he remembered the seven virtues and, depending on which virtue was best suited to suppressing the temptation, he worshipped God in those uncreated virtues which were presented to him by his remembrance of the seven created virtues. And the more he was tempted and the more he struggled against the temptation, the more exalted became his merits, so he praised and blessed God, Who caused his merits to be great so that His justice might bestow great glory upon him. And thus did Blaquerna live and serve God all the days of his life. And God showed great virtue to lie within Him as regards Blaquerna, who was a radiant light and a perfect example to the monks and all the people in that country of how they might lead holy lives. And on account of Blaquerna's saintly conduct, God blessed all the people and all the countries of that region with health, peace, and an abundance of spiritual and earthly fruits. Everybody blessed and adored God, Who had granted so much virtue to a single man that, through him, by the grace of God, a great number of people possessed so many virtues.

## 60. On how Blaquerna was elected abbot

[1] The Lord Abbot grew aged and was no longer bodily capable of meeting the requirements of the monastery. He was in the chapter house with all the monks, and he asked for their mercy, saying these words:

'You, sirs, have long done me great honour by considering me as your superior. I have been unworthy to receive such great honour. I have reached a point at which my bodily strength fails me, and because of this loss of vigour I am even more unworthy of being your pastor. I am at the end of my days, and should like to submit myself to some person among you, so that I might become more obedient. I beg you to elect another abbot and to show compassion towards me.'

[2] Counsel and decision were taken by Blaquerna and the entire chapter that favour should be shown to the Lord Abbot for the purpose of signifying charity and justice, which desired that a reward should be given to the Lord Abbot for the efforts in which he had long persisted in the interests of protecting and serving his flock. Charity wished the Lord Abbot to be given a suitable place at a grange where he might remain and abide, and that a monk should serve him

and that his body should enjoy a certain pittance so that it might survive longer. The abbot thanked the entire chapter for the mercy they had shown him, and handed back the seal and relinquished the abbacy, so the monks made arrangements as to how they might elect an abbot.

[3] It was undertaken that an abbot should be elected according to the art of election whereby Natana was elected abbess. So, when the electors asked Blaquerna whom he thought should be abbot, Blaquerna said the following words:

'Our common brotherhood consists in the charity which obtains between us. So, in order to signify that charity is a common virtue and to set a good example, it would be appropriate for us to elect as our pastor some bishop from this region who might be more saintly in his life than the other bishops.'

The electors replied by saying that it was not the custom of their Order to elect as abbot a man who did not belong to that Order and that, besides this, they did not believe that any bishop would abandon his bishopric and that he would submit to their Order with a view to becoming abbot, since a bishop follows a more lenient rule than does an abbot.

[4] Blaquerna told the electors that it very often happened that an abbot was elected bishop and that it was only just, therefore, that a bishop might be elected an abbot, since the role of an abbot is in greater accord with the contemplative life than is that of a bishop, whose role accords more closely with the active life than does that of an abbot.

'So, since the contemplative life is far superior and closer to God than is its active equivalent, if abbots pass from the former to the latter, how much more should bishops leave the former behind in order to become abbots engaged in the latter! And thus, for it to become customary for a bishop to be elected abbot and for the contemplative life to be loved and exalted above the active, it is, in my opinion and in accordance with my desires, advisable for us to elect a bishop as our abbot.'

[5] One of the seven electors was the cellarer, who said to Blaquerna that, were they to elect as abbot a bishop or other person who did not belong to their Order or monastery, it would seem as if there were a lack of suitable people within this monastery of theirs, none of whom proved worthy of being elected abbot thereof. It was, there-

fore, not appropriate for them to elect a bishop as their abbot, and all the less so because he believed that they would not be able to find a bishop who was willing to relinquish his bishopric to become an abbot. Blaquerna replied:

'The cellarer's words signify pride and vainglory, despair and the vice of private ownership, and stand opposed to justice, charity and hope. And since prudence wishes the best person to be elected, charity forges community from a variety of Orders. Justice, on the other hand, condemns ownership over that which is rightly the province of common charity and brotherliness, while hope causes one to remember that if Our Lord and Shepherd Jesus Christ suffered death in order to save those men who hold bishoprics, it therefore follows that we shall find some bishop who wishes to relinquish his bishopric for an abbacy in order to honour Christ.'

[6] The cellarer abandoned the line of argument he had employed against Blaquerna and took up another, saying these words:

'An abbot has to be accustomed to eating our food and to following the rules and customs of our monastery, so that he may be a light and example to us that we should persist in these customs of ours. So another man who does not belong to our Order is, therefore, not as suitable to be abbot as is a man who belongs to our Order and who, for many years, has adhered in an orderly fashion to the Rule of our Order.'

'Cellarer', said Blaquerna, 'your will continues along the trail and path of despair, for God, Who has caused you to submit to the Rule of your Order, can also cause and accustom another religious from a different Order, should he enter our own, to submit to such a Rule.'

While Blaquerna and the cellarer were arguing in this manner, the bishop whom Blaquerna had rebuked, as has been recounted above, arrived at the monastery. So the discussion between Blaquerna and the cellarer came to an end, and all the monks went to welcome the bishop in order to pay honour to him and his companions.

[7] The bishop himself wished to pay honour to the monk who had relinquished the abbacy, in accordance with the honour that befits an abbot. That monk told the bishop, however, about the favour the chapter had shown him, and how he had relinquished his post as abbot and had been assigned a very delightful place outside the monastery in which he was to live and there provide for his body a certain pittance greater than he could receive within the monastery. The

bishop and that monk then went off to live at the grange in question. The bishop sent away his entire retinue, keeping back for himself a single squire alone. The bishop and the monk performed penance for a long time, and every day they would speak about God and His glory and would scorn the vanities of this world.

[8] The cellarer and the other electors resumed the discussion they had previously been having, and sought to discover, by means of both art and necessity, which person out of all the monks in that monastery was the most capable of being abbot. It was clear to all the electors that Blaquerna should be abbot, according to all the conditions which accord with being an abbot, apart from one condition alone, namely, that Blaquerna loved the contemplative life more fervently than he did the active. And the active life befits the role of abbot so that he might better provide for the needs of the monastery. A debate arose among the electors as to whether, if on account of the aforesaid condition, Blaquerna would be prohibited from becoming abbot. One of the electors, however, said to the others that:

'Just as Blaquerna, our teacher, has taught us how with the virtues we may tend to our needs, in this instance we must have recourse to hope and justice, and must place our trust in the saintly life of Blaquerna, who, by contemplative living, shall justify our choice as electors as much as or more than if he led an active rather than a contemplative life. Let us not hesitate, therefore, to make Blaquerna our abbot, and let him be our pastor, since he has been our teacher.'[169]

[9] Blaquerna was elected abbot, yet he was greatly displeased at his election and put forward many arguments whereby he might be exempted from that office. The monks, however, refused to accept any of them and wished him to become abbot at all costs. So Blaquerna became abbot and each day he duly persevered in his post, according to which he was obliged to call to mind and deal with worldly affairs, which prevented him from considering heavenly matters. Blaquerna wept at the slavery into which he had fallen. He desired the freedom to contemplate God and to cogitate upon the Passion of his Redeemer, so he, therefore, said these words:

---

169. The last two clauses could also be translated: 'and let him be our shepherd, since he has been our master'. The rhyme 'pastor'/'master', is to be avoided, not least because no such rhyme appears in the Catalan original.

[10] 'O virtues, my friends, who once used to assist me and would deliver and protect me from the slavery into which Evast and Aloma wished to place me! Where have you gone? And why have you not helped me to combat the slavery into which I have fallen?'

While Blaquerna was saying these words, within his thoughts he discovered Fortitude and Prudence, which inwardly spoke the following words to him: 'The mind is strong which does not grow proud at the honour of being an abbot or at exercising dominion over many men. An abbot is obedient through strength of mind when he adheres to what his intellect teaches him, so that he may abide by the Rule of his Order and only rarely admit himself to the infirmary.' While Fortitude was speaking in this manner, Prudence replied to Blaquerna, saying that a share in the merits of all the monks accrues to the abbot who keeps his will ordered towards being a servant and subject of those same monks. 'I am great', said Prudence, 'when I hold sway over one person; I am much greater, however, when I hold sway over many people. Justice and merit, therefore, are in greater accord with me now than they once were.'

[11] Blaquerna felt the desire to rejoice at the fact that Prudence indicated to him an increase in his glory, but charity caused him to remember that he could not contemplate God as easily as he had done before. And since he loved God more than he did the merit of glory, charity and longing, therefore, caused him to weep at length. And Blaquerna lived in this manner, and remained abbot for a long time. Out of the desire for consolation and contemplation, he would go at times to the grange where the bishop and the monk who was formerly abbot lived, and with them he would have bodily recreation and would comfort his soul by contemplating Our Lord God.


61. On how Abbot Blaquerna wrote the book Ave Maria[170]

[1] Blaquerna was abbot of a highly acclaimed abbey in which there was a great multitude of monks and which yielded considerable revenues. Blaquerna constantly cogitated upon how he might honour

---

170. Rather than transcribing a book written by Blaquerna about the Virgin Mary, this chapter provides an account of how he built within the monastery a particular room devoted to her praise.

Our Lady in some new way. One day, Blaquerna was considering Our
Lady's honour and, by divine power, he formed the intention of
building a chamber, set apart within the monastery, in which should
live a monk who, there, might continually salute Our Lady. And he
should eat and sleep in that building, and should not have to follow
the Rule of the Order and should be free as regards all those things
whereby he might better salute and contemplate Our Lady. Abbot
Blaquerna had that building constructed and gave it this name: 'Ave
Maria'. The abbot was in the chapter house with all the monks and he
said these words:

'In the womb of Our Lady was accomplished every greatest honour
that a creature has been capable of receiving from his Creator, when
the Son of God took human nature therein. And it is fitting, therefore,
that our Order, which has made Our Lady its head, should honour her
as best it can.[171] So, therefore, which of you wishes continually to salute
Our Lady and to live in the room called "Ave Maria"?'

There were many monks who felt the desire to stay in that building and to hold that office. The abbot, however, said that the monk
who would fulfil that role had to be a great scholar in the various sciences so that by these he might know how to elevate his understanding in order to contemplate and salute Our Lady; and that, likewise, he
had to be devout and a man of saintly life. That monk was elected from
amongst the others, therefore, who best met the aforesaid conditions.

[2] That monk lodged in the 'Ave Maria' chamber, wherein he
had his books, his cell and an image of Our Lady. Every day a lay
brother brought him a portion of food from the monastery. That
monk said Mass in the church and could walk throughout the monastery and talk with whomsoever he wished, and enjoyed many other
privileges. One day it occurred that the abbot entered the monk's
chamber and wished to know in what way the monk saluted Our Lady,
Holy Mary. The monk knelt down before the image of Our Lady and
said the following words and many others, as had become his custom:

[3] 'Ave Maria, your servant salutes[172] you on behalf of the angels,
the patriarchs, the prophets, the martyrs, the confessors and the vir-

---

171. The reader should note that all Cistercian monasteries were dedicated to
Mary as Mother of God; cf. below, for instance, Ch. 64, § 8.

172. As in 'hails'. The reader should note that in Ibero-Romance languages, as
well as Romance languages more broadly and Latin itself, the term *salut* (and its vari-

gins, male and female. He likewise salutes you through all the saints in glory! Ave Maria, he brings you greetings from all Christians, the righteous as well as the sinners! The righteous salute you because you are worthy of salutation and because you are the hope of their salvation. The sinners salute you because they ask for your forgiveness and they entertain the hope that your merciful eyes may look upon your Son in order that He may take pity and have mercy on their faults, while calling to mind the acute suffering He underwent in order to grant salvation and to forgive faults and sins.

[4] 'Ave Maria, your servant brings you greetings from the Saracens, Jews, Greeks, Mongols, Tartars, Bulgars, Hungarians from Lesser Hungary, Cumans, Nestorians, Russians, Guineans![173] All these and many other unbelievers salute you through me, who am their proctor. I include them in your salutation so that your Son may wish to remember them and that you may beg Him to send them messengers who may lead them to know and to love yourself and your Son, in such a way that they may be saved and in this world may know how and wish to serve and honour you and your Son with all their might.

[5] 'Ave Maria! These unbelievers on whose behalf I salute you are ignorant of your salutation and of the honour God has granted you. They are men, alike in nature and kind to your Son, whom you love so much and by whom you are loved and honoured so greatly. Through ignorance they proceed towards everlasting fire; they forfeit the everlasting glory of your Son since nobody preaches to them or demonstrates to them the truth of the Holy Catholic Faith. They have lips with which they would be able to praise you if they only knew you; they have hearts with which they could love you; they have hands with which they could serve you; and they have feet with which they could walk along your pathways. You are worthy of being known, served, loved and praised by all people, in all countries. They salute you! And through me do they ask you for aid, grace and blessings!

---

ants) along with its verbal form *saludar* denote not only health, but also greetings/salutations and salvation as well (the ultimate bodily and spiritual 'health').

173. This list comprises three main groups: unbelievers or 'infidels', namely, the Saracens and the Jews; schismatics, namely, Greeks, Bulgars, Nestorians and Russians; and, third, pagans, namely, Mongols, Tartars, Eastern Hungarians, Cumans and Guineans. The Cumans were Turkic nomads, many of whom had settled in Hungary and Bulgaria both prior to and following the Mongol invasion of 1237, though they originated from 'Cumania', situated on the western Eurasian steppe north of the Black Sea. 'Guineans' is largely conjectural, from Cat. *guinovins*.

[6] 'Ave Maria! I must weep and offer penance; I must endure a life of austerity; I must praise, love, know and serve you, so that my salutations may be more pleasing to you!'

While he was saluting Our Lady, the monk wept very bitterly. Blaquerna wept likewise at the monk's great devotion and at the devout salutations he offered to Our Lady. Who can recount to you the sweetness and virtue that dwelt within the abbot and the monk while they wept and saluted Our Lady?

[7] 'Beloved son', said the abbot, 'give salutations to Our Lady, who is our salvation and blessing. In her salvation are saved those who, in the absence of her salvation, would be damned. In our mother Eve lay our damnation and in Our Lady lies our salvation. Mary is light and radiance, both illuminated and illumining. "Ave" means to be without evil and without defect, so let us salute and love her! We have a Lady through whom we shall acquire virtues and overcome vice. Remember, my son, that many are those who salute Our Lady and that blessed are those who are loved and remembered by her, who has such a noble memory and such a merciful will. See how vast the heavens are, and how they are strikingly illumined by the sun, the moon and the stars. The sea, the land, men, birds, beasts, fish, plants, herbs and all living things, indeed all things that exist, are in the service of Our Lady and all pertain to her Son, Who has created them. Salute and weep, for Our Lady delights in such salutations. Salute and remember Our Lady, who does not cease to love, remember and succour all those who salute her with an elevated understanding and an affectionate will. Son, muster all the powers of your soul and see if you can invest them all in giving salutations to Our Lady.'

[8] While the abbot coaxed and encouraged the monk who resided in the 'Ave Maria' chamber as much as he could, the latter said the following words to him:

'My power is conquered, and the honour of Our Lady exalted. I am unable to love or to give consideration any more loftily. I must remain here below amid all my failings. Were it possible, I should like to weep, love and remember more resolutely when I salute the Queen of Heaven and of all the Earth and the Sea. Our Lady gives me solace and joy whenever I salute her. Her salutation is my company, my consolation and my comfort!'[174]

---

174. The alliteration is present in the original Catalan text.

[9] To his great wonder, the abbot was highly pleased that the monk in the 'Ave Maria' chamber was so well able to salute and contemplate Our Lady. So, many times each week, he would go to salute Our Lady with the monk, so as to pay her honour and so that each of them might assist the other in weeping; and also, so that each might more fervently exalt the other's soul to contemplate Our Lady. The monk in the 'Ave Maria' chamber was a man of such virtuous life that there were many monks in that monastery who served Our Lady in a more orderly fashion as a result of him. And when they felt temptation or discontentment regarding anything, they would go to the monk so that they might be consoled and instructed by his words in the service of Our Lady.

## 62. 'GRATIA PLENA'

[1] Once upon a time, it came to pass that there was a great dearth of wheat in that land, brought on by lack of rain. The alms the abbot gave to all the poor who came to the monastery were very great. The almsgiving that was undertaken in that monastery lasted a long time. And because word had spread throughout that land, and because in that monastery they were in the habit of giving alms consisting of bread and vegetables to all those who came there, the poor who came to receive alms increased very greatly in number. One day it occurred that the cellarer entered the granaries situated within the monastery and travelled around the granges, and he discovered that the alms the abbot was distributing could not last long and that the monastery did not have further wheat to dispense until the next harvest. The cellarer was deeply displeased and told the abbot to cease giving out alms since he had found so little wheat at the granges and in the granaries that in only a little time the monastery would run short of it.

[2] The abbot was greatly dissatisfied at what the cellarer had told him, so he went round the granges and the granaries in order to learn the truth as to whether the quantities of wheat were as paltry as the cellarer had said. While the abbot and the cellarer were returning to the monastery, the abbot passed by a grange whose granger was a lay brother who loved and honoured Our Lady above all things. In that entire grange there was but a single

granary pit[175] containing wheat. The abbot was greatly displeased at there being so little wheat and deeply regretted having to cease giving out alms, as a result of which regret his soul grew sad and his eyes flowed with tears. The brother-granger asked the abbot why he was weeping.

'My fair son', said the abbot, 'I feel bound to weep for the death of the poor who shall die if the almsgiving to which the monastery is accustomed should cease, as cease it must on account of a lack of wheat.'

'My lord', said the granger, 'give alms for the honour of Our Lady, for I shall provide you with sufficient wheat to last the entire year. So, do not doubt this, and turn to Our Lady, who is full of grace, for surety.'

The abbot replied:

'So proper and sufficient is her surety, that we should be guilty were we to refuse it or our almsgiving to cease!'

[3] The abbot returned to the monastery very joyously and gave instruction that alms be handed out daily, as had been the custom. He gave out alms for so long and to so many people that all the wheat in the granaries and in all the granges was exhausted, apart from the wheat in the granary below ground which was situated at the grange whose granger had invoked Our Lady as surety. The abbot sent a messenger to the granger asking him to provide him with sufficient wheat, as he had promised. The granger opened up the underground store and sent half of the wheat that lay within to the monastery. The next time the granger opened the pit he found it half-full, as he had left it, and sent all the wheat to the abbot. When the granger had closed the pit and the animals which carried the wheat had departed from the grange, he said Hail Marys, as was his custom. As he was saying 'full of grace', he felt great wonder at the fact that he had left the pit empty of wheat and that Holy Mary had not kept it full given that he had invoked her as surety to the abbot.

[4] While the granger was engaged in such thoughts, he doubted that Holy Mary was full of grace, for it seemed to him that, if she were full of grace, the pit should at all times be full of wheat. Once more the abbot sent word to the granger to convey wheat to him, for that which he had previously sent him had run out. The granger placed his trust in Our Lady and opened up the pit once again, and found it to be full

---

175. Cat. *çija*: lit. 'silo': 'a pit or underground chamber used for storing grain, roots, etc.', *SOED*.

of wheat, so he remembered how she was indeed full of grace. Throughout the entire year, the granger found the underground granary to be full whenever he opened it. So that pit provided sufficient wheat for the entire convent as well as for all the alms dispensed, until the arrival of the next harvest. The abbot and the monks praised and blessed Our Lady, who had chosen to remember their needs.

[5] It occurred one feast day that the granger was at the monastery in order to attend the festival. The abbot asked him how it had come about that the wheat had been sufficient to last them the entire year. The granger told the abbot that, among the other words that are in the *Ave Maria*, he felt great devotion towards 'full of grace', and therefore trusted that Our Lady would keep the pit of wheat full while there was a dearth of food in their country. The abbot cogitated at length upon the words that the brother-granger had spoken to him about Our Lady and on how he felt devotion towards the phrase 'full of grace'. So he therefore had a room built in part of the monastery, calling that room 'Gratia plena', and he determined that the brother should abide within that chamber all the days of his life, while adoring and contemplating Our Lady full of grace.

[6] The brother of 'Gratia plena' was a very devout and saintly man, and each day he adored Our Lady with all his might while considering the grace of which she was so full. And because of that brother's great age and saintly life, the monks would come to pass a number of hours with him and would listen to his devout words, which edified them and stirred them to devotion and charity, and by which they were comforted and gladdened. The entire monastery was enlightened by that brother and by the brother of 'Ave Maria', and on many occasions the monk from 'Ave Maria' and the brother from 'Gratia plena' visited each other, and the monk spoke about 'Ave Maria' while the brother spoke about 'Gratia plena'. Who could describe to you the delight and the brotherly fellowship between them both? And who could tell you of the worthy example they set to all the monks and all the brothers?

[7] The abbot Blaquerna felt a desire to weep and to contemplate Our Lady, for the great worldly affairs, with which he was obliged to deal on the monastery's behalf, had very strongly inclined his thoughts towards such worldly matters. One day, therefore, the abbot went all alone to the brother of 'Gratia plena', for the purpose of learning how he contemplated Our Lady. As the abbot was entering

the room in which the brother lived, he found him kneeling in tears before the image of Our Lady and saying these words:

[8] 'You are full, O Mary, of a fullness which is your Son, Who is the fullness and plenitude of all that exists. In you, who art full, lies the fullness of my soul's memory, intellect and will. The whole world cannot be as full as the fullness you have within you. And do you know why? Because, by virtue of your Son, you are able to be fuller than the whole world, since the whole world is not as worthy as you are. You are full of grace so that we may regain the grace that we had lost. In you lies the fullness of our faith, hope, charity, justice, prudence, fortitude and temperance. And our fullness stems from yours. Whoever remembers and loves you is full of grace; whoever is remembered and loved by you lacks for nothing.

[9] 'Full of grace! Full of God and man were you when the angel Gabriel saluted you. That God and man of Whom you are the mother is full of infinite and eternal goodness and of infinite and eternal power, wisdom and will. Thus, if your fullness is infinite and eternal in goodness, greatness, power, wisdom and will,[176] that fullness cannot be voided, or reduced or increased. So, since you, in your great fullness, Mary, art "full of grace", fill my soul with charity whereby it may fully know and love you, and fill my eyes with weeping and tears so that I may pay honour to Your Honours[177] and lament my faults and my sins.'

[10] The brother was adoring and contemplating Our Lady using these and many other words when the abbot came to visit him. The abbot felt great wonder that such subtle and devout words could issue from a layman's mouth, but concluded that, by reason of the plenitude of Our Lady, his words were full of infused knowledge and devotion.[178]

'O fair son and brother', said the abbot, 'may God save you, Who has filled you with the fullness of Our Lady's grace!'

The brother replied to the abbot:

---

176. Goodness, greatness, eternity, power, wisdom and will are the first six of the divine 'Dignities' or attributes in Llull's Art.

177. For the term 'Honours', see above, Ch. 3, § 8 and corresponding note.

178. In the Roman Catholic tradition there are three types of knowledge: acquired, infused and beatific. Infused knowledge does not come into being via the abstraction of intelligible species from the intelligible object; instead, the intelligible species is 'infused', i.e. is imparted directly by God.

'My lord, were you to know any means whereby I might greatly love and honour Our Lady, I beg you to teach them to me. For she is full of great grace and virtue, and for that reason I am in need of the fullness of intelligence, whereby I might know her fully, so that, through the fullness of my knowledge, my will might acquire the fullness greatly to love and praise her who is "full of grace".'

[11] When the abbot saw the great abundance of grace, devotion and charity that resided in the brother's soul and recalled that, in his own soul, there was not as much devotion as there was in that of the brother, he said these words:

'Ah! Why did I become abbot rather than a brother hermit, so that I might have a fullness of devotion as great as this brother has?'

The abbot Blaquerna knelt down before the brother of 'Full of Grace' and begged him to instruct and teach him how he might revert to the devotion he had formerly entertained, and which he had forfeited by reason of the affairs of the abbey. The brother wept, and Blaquerna likewise, and each looked at the other in a loving manner. Neither of them could speak to the other, so overcome were they by love, but each indicated to the other by signs the image of Our Lady, the Passion of her Son and the suffering she endured while her Son had been tormented and put to death on the Cross, from which He hung so that all might see Him and deride Him.[179]

[12] They stayed together for a long time, weeping profusely, before they were able to speak. The abbot remained kneeling until the brother said the following words:

'Our Lady was full of grace when her Son died. That grace signifies the grace with which the sons of God[180] in this world are filled when they endure trials and death in order to honour the Son of Our Lady, which Son, Who is in glory, is the fullness of Our Lady's grace. In this world there is a lack of fullness of grace, so Abbot Blaquerna laments the sins of those who do not allow that fullness of grace to dwell in this world!'

Blaquerna wept and said these words:

---

179. Cf. above, Ch. 8, § 3 for an earlier example of shared mutism occurring between two closely linked characters overcome by emotion. It was common for members of monastic Orders, either during periods of obligatory silence or vows taken to that effect, to communicate with each other using sign language.

180. For 'sons of God', cf. Ps 81 [82]: 1-8; John 1:12; and Rom 8:14.

[13] 'O tears, knowledge and love—might you possess sufficient power to cause Our Lady, who is full of grace, to remember how deficient we are in this present life? Would she, on your account, be inclined to pray to her Son that He might fill us with the requisite grace to lead us to go to preach about His honour to the unbelievers, and that the Holy Church might regain the Holy Land which the Saracens control to our great dishonour? For in such dishonour is signified ingratitude, as well as a lack of charity and of remembrance towards the Holy Blood which was shed for our sake.'

'Is there anything which might assist you in such matters?'

'Brother', said Blaquerna, 'assist me in weeping and praying! And let us weep so bitterly and at such length until the queen you love so fervently should see fit to come to our aid, and should bestow so much of her grace upon this world that she should cause it to be disposed in its entirety towards honouring her Son.'

The abbot and the brother wept for a long time, and after they had wept they parted courteously from each other. And Abbot Blaquerna felt in his soul that the devotion he had previously entertained had reverted to its former state. The abbot, therefore, proposed to come back frequently to the 'Full of Grace' chamber to weep and to contemplate Our Lady.

## 63. 'DOMINUS TECUM'

[1] One day it came to pass that Abbot Blaquerna was holding chapter, when a granger came to the chapter house and stated that a peasant farmer had entered a vineyard on the grange with a view to hoeing the soil. This peasant said that the vineyard belonged to him and fiercely threatened the brother, who wished to eject him therefrom. The abbot requested the monks' counsel as regards this man about whom the granger had told them. An elderly monk said the following words to the Lord Abbot:

'There has long been dispute between the peasant and us over that vineyard, and great loss has been suffered both by the monastery and the peasant, who has spread great calumnies in our regard throughout the country. It is fitting, therefore, that we should go to the grange and that we eject him from the vineyard or that we place ourselves under the protection and governance of some knight who may safeguard the vineyard from the peasant on our behalf.'

[2] The abbot cogitated at length upon the words the monk had spoken and, in the presence of all, said these words:

'It is unsuitable for a religious to place himself in mortal danger or to kill any man for the sake of property. Yet it is contrary to justice that a religious should allow himself to be dispossessed. So in accordance with charity and hope, therefore, it is fitting that in such a case one should have recourse to God and to the virtues, and thus combat the vices by means of those virtues. For every man—and the religious in particular—should employ such weapons in the first instance when doing battle.'

When the abbot had said these words, he mounted his horse, taking the cellarer with him, and went to that place where the peasant was hoeing the vineyard. The abbot greeted the peasant by saying 'Dominus tecum'. The peasant failed to return a greeting to the abbot, but rather continued to hoe, keeping his weapons alongside him so that he might be able to defend himself. Each time the peasant struck the ground with his hoe, the abbot said 'Dominus tecum', but the peasant pretended not to hear or see him, and instead continued to hoe the vineyard.

[3] The abbot felt great wonder at the fact that the peasant failed to reply to him and even greater wonder at the fact that the power of his greeting was to no avail. The abbot, however, cogitated upon the fact that he ought to dismount and that he should kneel before the peasant and greet him with devotion and humility in order to introduce virtue into his salutation. The abbot dismounted and knelt before the peasant. He raised his eyes, his thoughts and his hands, and said these words:

'Queen of Heaven and Earth, God became both man and God in you. And the Lord is in you in glory, as God and Son. In this world, our Order belongs to you and is in your care. By that power whereby the Lord was in you, I beseech you to stand between us and this man, so that through you we may receive power, whereby we may be servants of the power you possessed by virtue of the Lord's being in you.'

[4] The cellarer harshly rebuked the abbot, saying that the entire monastery was demeaned by the honour he paid to the peasant. The abbot replied to the cellarer, however, by saying that the Son of God, in choosing to exist fully, as both man and God, in the Holy Virgin Mary, practised great humility:

'And on the Cross He chose to be tormented, brought low and put to death. And the weapons of a monk are humility, charity, patience and prayer.'

So devoutly and humbly did the abbot pray and utter the phrase 'Dominus tecum' that God imparted such great power to the words he spoke and the devotion he showed that the peasant felt remorse at the wrong he had been doing to the abbey. And on account of his remorse, he came to contrition, charity and justice, and said these words, therefore:

[5] 'Lord Abbot, what is it that has led my mind to turn towards contrition, charity and justice? And who has expelled greed, anger and injustice therefrom?'

The abbot replied:

'By God's will, it came to pass that the angel Gabriel saluted Our Lady, Holy Mary, and, among the other words he uttered, he said to her "Dominus tecum". And by virtue of the power of this phrase, hope has given me confidence that "Dominus tecum" may bestow upon you the virtue whereby the Lord of Heaven and Earth and of all that exists may abide within you and with you, so that the virtues may dwell in your heart, on account of which virtues the vices may prove displeasing to you.'

[6] When the abbot had said these words, the peasant stated that 'Dominus tecum' had defeated and overcome him. He resolved, therefore, to be the constant servant of 'Dominus tecum', and he begged the abbot to provide him with food from the monastery whereby he might live the life of a hermit on a tall hill close to the abbey. The abbot granted the peasant's request and made a cell for him on that high peak where he wished to live, so that he might contemplate Our Lord and Our Lady in the phrase 'Dominus tecum'. The abbot named that place 'Dominus tecum' and decided to build a chapel at that hermitage. The peasant did not wish this to be done, however, so that nobody should come there by reason of pilgrimages or vigils who might hinder his prayers or curb his devotion.

[7] When the peasant was in 'Dominus tecum', the abbot gave him a Rule and method as to how, by means of 'Dominus tecum', he might contemplate God and Our Lady in accordance with the form of the following words:

'The Lord of angels and of all that exists performed in Our Lady the greatest work that a creature can receive, when He chose to assume human nature in her, and no nobler work can He perform in a creature! God is Lord of Nature in Our Lady and in all things wherein Nature natured exists,[181] but in her He exalted Nature more highly than in any other creature. So, for this reason, Our Lord abided more fully within Our Lady and with Our Lady when the angel said to her "Dominus tecum" than He did with any other creature. We should all pay reverence and honour, therefore, to "Dominus tecum".'

By these words and many others the abbot provided the hermit with a rule and instruction as to how he might contemplate God and Our Lady by means of 'Dominus tecum'.

[8] The hermit lived in that place for a long time in penance and austerity, while contemplating God and Our Lady. And an abundance of fervent devotion exalted his understanding to greater intelligence through infused knowledge than the understanding of many monks who possess acquired knowledge, which through lack of devotion cannot achieve knowledge of the Divine Essence or of its operation. So great was the hermit's devotion that many monks came to that place to stimulate their own devotion and knowledge, on account of the saintly life he led and the holy and lofty words he spoke about 'Dominus tecum'.

## 64. 'BENEDICTA TU IN MULIERIBUS'

[1] It was Abbot Blaquerna's custom to go frequently to visit the monk who had formerly been abbot, as well as the bishop who lived on that grange where the aforesaid monk resided. One day it occurred that the abbot was passing through a large forest while he was

---

181. *Natura naturans* (lit. 'nature naturing') and *natura naturata* (lit. 'nature natured') formed the two sides of a medieval dichotomy expressing the generative, dynamic and active aspect of nature and the inert, passive side thereof, respectively, this latter being conceived as nature in the sense of already completed creation. In scholastic philosophy, however, this binary had a broader compass, one in which *natura naturans* designated God and *natura naturata* the created world in general. It has been suggested that the term *natura naturans* has its origins in Michael Scot's (1175-1232 (?)) translations of certain Aristotelian commentaries by Averroes. For Scot, however, *natura naturata*, as one side of the distinction between divine and human nature, does not denote simply the created world in general, but rather, more specifically, 'the motion-producing power within the four elements, which in turn causes generation', Pick (2004), 95-96. Llull may well be calling on Scot's reading of these terms here.

travelling to the grange on which the monk and the bishop lived. Along the route there was a lovely spring beneath a fine tree, in the shade of which lay an armed knight who was going in search of adventure out of love for his lady. This knight had removed his helmet from his head on account of the great heat. His horse grazed upon the cool grass close to the spring. The knight was singing a new song,[182] in which he reproached the troubadours who had maligned love or had failed to praise above all other women that lady whom the knight loved.

[2] The abbot Blaquerna heard the song, understood its words and arrived at the place where the knight was singing. The abbot dismounted and sat down close to the knight, saying these words to him:

'It is the nature of love to cause a person to love that thing which is pleasing and agreeable to him. From what your song indicates, it seems to me that you are in love with a certain lady, since you praise her above all others. I beg you to tell me whether, were there to exist a better, nobler and fairer lady than yours, you would love her more than the one you now love.'

The knight stopped his song and replied to the abbot, saying these words:

[3] 'Should chance have it that another lady were nobler and fairer than the one to whom love has enslaved me, then love would be unjust if it failed to make me love the better lady above all the others. For the lover who does not love the better lady fails in his love, while love itself fails the better lady if it does not cause her to be loved more fervently—and by a better lover—than any other lady who lacks her worth or perfections.'

When the knight had said these words, the abbot posed the following questions to him:

[4] 'Sir knight, I beg you to tell me why you bear arms.'

The knight replied:

'So that I may thereby defend my body against those who seek to attack me.'

The abbot asked the knight whether he had any weapons with which he might defend his lady against the lady whom the abbot loved. The knight replied:

---

182. Cat. *cançó*, 'love song'. The *canso* was the most popular form of song used by the troubadours until at least the mid-thirteenth century.

'Love, beauty and worth help me to prove that my lady is better and worthy of greater praise than is any other lady.'

'My lord', said the abbot, 'my lady can and should be praised in a nobler manner than yours, because in her are love, beauty and worth of greater succour. So, therefore, my lady is worthier of praise than yours, and for this reason I am a nobler lover, servant and praiser of my lady than you are of yours.'

[5] The knight was greatly displeased by what the abbot had said, so he replied that if the abbot were a knight he would have put him to death or taken him captive on account of the words he had spoken, and that he would have made him concede by force of arms that his lady was better and fairer than any other lady.

'My lord', said the abbot, 'knowledge and reason are spiritual weapons whereby one conquers wickedness and error. So, if you wish to do battle with me using such weapons, so that we may see which lady is better, fairer and worthy of greater honour, your arguments cause me no fear, but rather I feel the courage and strength to make you concede that my lady is better than yours.'

[6] There was a great dispute between the abbot and the knight over which lady was better. They both agreed that each of them should praise his lady in order to see which could speak greater praise thereof. The abbot wished the knight to praise the lady whom he loved first of all. So the knight praised his lady, saying the following words:

'So fair and kind is my lady, that love has caused me to defeat and overcome many knights. And many times have I placed myself in mortal danger for the sake of honouring my lady; and for her have I suffered great hunger and thirst, and heat and cold. And many hardships has my body suffered in order that I may serve her. So, since all these things are greater and more toilsome than that which you do for your lady, therefore, sir monk', said the knight, 'is it signified that if your lady were better and fairer than mine, you would do and would have done greater things and would have undergone greater effort in order to praise and serve your lady than those things which I have done and undergone in order to praise mine.'

The knight spoke many other words to the abbot in praise of his lady which would take a long time to recount.

[7] 'Sir knight', said the abbot, 'I could indeed speak many praises of my lady, but since one alone suffices to laud her and to prove

that she is better and fairer than yours, I simply wish to counter your praises, therefore, by means of one such expression alone, namely, "Benedicta tu in mulieribus".'

The knight wished the abbot to explain to him the aforesaid expression of praise, so the abbot explained the words that the angel Gabriel spoke to Our Lady in the following manner:

[8] 'It was the will of the Son of God that He wished to choose Our Lady, Holy Mary, above all other women and wished to bestow greater grace upon her than any other grace that abides in all other women. For God accepted human flesh from the Holy Virgin Mary when He became incarnate within her and when, through the grace of the Holy Spirit, she conceived God and man within her womb, while remaining a virgin. This lady is the Mother both of God and of man. The God of whom she is the Mother is better than all the creatures, and the Son of Man of whom she is the Mother is better than all creatures because He is a single Person with the Son of God, Who is the Creator of all creatures. This Lady is my lady and she is the head of our Order. And such praise suffices to conquer any other praise which may be spoken about any other woman.'

[9] The knight carefully considered the praise the abbot had spoken about Our Lady, Holy Mary. And through the light of grace and the merits of the abbot, the knight considered likewise the vain and foolish love he had entertained for the lady whom he loved; and upon how, because of that love, he was in mortal sin; and how he was at risk of damnation; and how his lady did not possess the power whereby she might protect him from the fires of Hell, nor give him heavenly glory as a reward, nor prolong his life. While the knight was engaged in such cogitation, he sighed and wept, and uttered these words:

[10] 'O Love, long have you delayed in making this guilty sinner love the most perfect of ladies. Were I, O Love, to have known and loved you, every day of my life should I have been the servant and subject of the most perfect of ladies, whose servant is this monk who has done honour to his Lady insofar as he has made known to me that she is the most perfect of all women. If in you, O Love, there were pity or pardon, or gifts,[183] or patience, or charity and humility,

---

183. Cat. *ni perdó ni do*; the equivalent play on words here in English, though now obsolete, might be (reversing the order): 'don [as in 'gift'] or pardon'. This pairing

might you be able to make me the servant of this most perfect of ladies? And would I be willing to suffer death until I had accomplished many things for the sake of love?'

The knight uttered these and many other words with such great contrition and devotion that the abbot was moved thereby to tears and devotion himself.

[11] 'Sir monk', said the knight, 'would it be possible that the lady whom you love might wish to let me love her and that, in order to love her, I might exert myself to the fullest of my ability every day of my life in battles and wars wherein I should continually oppose those who cause her dishonour and deny her worth?'

The abbot said to the knight:

'The greater the worth of this most perfect of ladies, the more pleasing to her is a sinful man who repents and becomes her servant and lover! She is worthy, therefore, of enjoying honour above all other women!'

The knight felt very great delight and wept for a long time, saying these words:

[12] 'I am not well-educated and I do not know the languages whereby I might be able to speak praise of Our Lady to the unbelievers, but with arms do I wish to go to honour the lady whom God has honoured above all women. I wish to adopt a new method of honouring Our Lady. This method consists in my going to do combat in the land of the Saracens with a knight who is not Our Lady's servant, and when I have defeated that one, I shall defeat another.'

When the knight had said these words, he took his leave of the abbot, and the abbot gave him his blessing and assigned to that new Rule which the knight had adopted the name of 'Benedicta tu in mulieribus'.

[13] By God's will, it came to pass that the knight who served 'Benedicta tu' went to the country of a Saracen king. When he had arrived there, he went fully armed upon his horse to the king's palace and said that he wished to speak to the king. It was the king's wish that the knight should be admitted into his company. When the knight stood before the king, he said the following words to him:

'I am the servant and lover of a lady who is better than all women, and who is the Mother of God and man by the grace of the Holy

recurs in Ch. 100, *Lover*, v. 311; and Chs. 104, § 8 and 105, § 6.

Spirit. And within your court I shall do combat with anyone who refuses this honour to Our Lady in order to make him concede the
honour which should be paid to Our Lady the Holy Virgin Mary,
whose knight I have recently become!'

[14] The Saracen king told the knight that he did not believe Our
Lady to be the Mother of God, but rather a saintly and virginal woman, and the mother of a man who was a prophet; yet that he did not
wish the knight to engage in combat on this account but to respond
to him by means of arguments, given that he, the king, refused that
honour to Our Lady which the knight attributed to her. The knight
replied to the king by saying that the greatest honour Our Lady enjoys is that of being Mother of God, and that he would do combat
with any man, for such honour should be attributed to Our Lady. But
since he was unlettered and did not know the Scriptures, he did not
wish to respond to the king by means of arguments, therefore, but
rather by force of arms would do battle with all the knights of his
court, one after another.

[15] The king felt great anger towards the knight who accosted
his entire court and he gave orders that he should be put to violent
death. One Saracen knight, however, said to the king that if the
knight were to die without battle, it would seem as if there were a lack
of chivalry in his court, so he begged the king to allow him to do combat with the knight. It pleased the king and all the others that there
should be a battle between the two knights. When the knights were
on the field, the Christian knight remembered his lady and said 'Benedicta tu in mulieribus', made the sign of the Cross in front of his
face, dug his spurs into his steed, attacked the knight and, by force of
arms, defeated and killed his Saracen opponent.

[16] The king was assailed by great anger, as were all the others.
The king commanded that, one by one, a sufficient number of
knights should engage the Christian knight in combat until they had
defeated him. A further knight entered the field and they both did
battle with each other all day long, neither one of them being able to
overcome the other. That night both of the knights rested and the
king made sure that justice was observed in the battle so that the rumour did not spread that, by force of the king's will, the Christian
knight had been unjustly treated in the battle. When the following
morning came, both knights returned to the field to do combat. And
when the Christian knight sought to wound the Saracen knight with

his sword, the Saracen accepted defeat and conceded that Our Lady was worthy of being praised according to the manner in which the Christian praised her. He uttered these words in the presence of all, and said that he wished to conform to the Rule and belong to the Order of 'Benedicta tu', and that he was ready to do battle with any other Saracen knight who might refuse to pay due honour to Our Lady. The king felt great anger and commanded that both knights should be seized and killed. These knights were martyrs for the sake of Our Lady, who honoured them in the glory of her Son because they had accepted martyrdom in order to honour her. And she is ready to honour all those who in like manner seek to honour her.

## 65. 'Benedictus fructus ventris tui'

[1] When the abbot had arrived at the grange where the bishop and the monk were in contemplation, the abbot described the adventure which had happened to him regarding the knight whom he had found singing about love by the spring, and he recounted the words that the knight had spoken and the Rule to which the latter had bound himself. The bishop cogitated at length upon the account the abbot had given concerning the knight and recalled the words in the *Ave Maria* which follow 'Benedicta tu in mulieribus'. And when the bishop had cogitated at length, he said the following words to the abbot:

[2] 'I bless the divine light of compassion and grace which has enlightened this sinful man, who every day of his life commits himself to being the servant of the blessed fruit which was in the womb of Our Lady. I worship that fruit and commit myself to praising it with all the corporeal powers of my body as well as all the powers of my soul.'

The bishop, courteously and with great devotion, took his leave of the abbot and the monk in whose fellowship he had honoured Our Lady, and left for his bishopric. The canons, the entire chapter and all the people within that city felt very great joy at the fact that they had regained their bishop, whom they thought they had lost.

[3] The bishop constantly cogitated upon how he might find a certain method whereby greatly to honour the fruit that Our Lady had in her womb through the grace of the Holy Spirit. One day it

came about that the bishop held a synod and was preaching to the clergy, from whom he requested counsel as to how he might greatly honour the blessed fruit of Our Lady. In that synod there was, by chance and fortune, a clerk who came from an island overseas named Majorca, and he told the bishop, in the presence of all, that that island belonged to a noble and learned king, called King James of Majorca.

'That king is of good habits and is eager for Jesus Christ to be honoured by means of preaching among the unbelievers. So he has ordained, therefore, that thirteen Friars Minor should study Arabic in a monastery called Miramar, set apart and established in a suitable place, and has himself provided for their needs.[184] And when they have learned Arabic, with the permission of their Minister General, they should go to honour the fruit of Our Lady, and in order to achieve this they should endure hunger, thirst, heat, cold, fear, torment and death.[185] And this enactment has been made in perpetuity.

[4] This enactment greatly pleased the bishop and all the others, and the devotion of the king and of the friars who desired to be martyrs for the sake of God received high praise. After a few days the bishop ordained and built a very fine monastery in a suitable location, far from any inhabited places. And by will of the Pope and of the chapter of that bishopric, this monastery was endowed in such a manner that thirteen people might live and study there, and might learn various sciences and various languages, so that the Holy Church might settle its debt by honouring the blessed fruit of Our Lady. The bishop assigned the name 'Benedictus fructus' to this monastery and relinquished his bishopric, and together with a number of canons and religious, as well as laymen, he moved into this monastery so as to honour the fruit of Our Lady according to the Rule and method of the monastery of Miramar, which is on the island of Majorca.

---

184. The foundation of the Franciscan monastery at Miramar, situated on the north coast of the island of Majorca between Deià and Valldemosa, was confirmed by Pope John XXI (Petrus Hispanus, author of the *Summulae logicales*) in 1276 at the request of James II of Majorca (1243-1311), himself acting at the behest of Ramon Llull. The monastery's remit was to educate its brethren in Arabic and other languages for the purpose of mission. After 1295 the monastery is believed to have become inactive, to judge by Llull's own testimony, and by 1300 had come under the wing of the monastery of La Real.

185. I.e. They should follow not only an ascetic but also a martyrial model.

## 66. 'SANTA MARIA, ORA PRO NOBIS'

[1] The monk who had formerly been abbot deeply regretted the absence of the bishop who had once been his companion. The monk remembered the words 'Santa Maria, ora pro nobis' in the *Ave Maria*, and wished throughout his entire life to be a preacher of those words, in honour of Our Lady. He considered the fact that there were many preachers who preached the word of God in towns and in churches, but that preachers were not assigned to the shepherds who passed through forests and across mountains. So the monk said these words, therefore, to Abbot Blaquerna:

[2] 'As far as I know, people who live or stay in the mountains or forests, and who do not go to church, are in great need of preachers. I request, therefore, a Rule and an Office whereby every day of my life I might be a preacher to the shepherds, to whom I shall preach 'Santa Maria, ora pro nobis'. For shepherds have the opportunity to think and to cogitate, since they are all alone and there is no one to prevent them from cogitating upon that which can be communicated to them concerning the honour owed to Our Lady. And the greater their cogitation, the more can love and devotion increase in them with regard to loving Our Lady.'

[3] The devotion and the new method which the monk wished to practise when honouring Our Lady greatly pleased the abbot. So he went to the monastery to enact and ensure that, with the agreement of the entire chapter, it should, in perpetuity, be the custom for a monk from that monastery to be a preacher to the shepherds, and that this Office should bear the name of 'Ora pro nobis'. This enactment pleased the entire monastery, and the monk who was formerly abbot assumed that office and requested from the abbot a rule and instruction as to how he might preach the phrase 'Santa Maria, ora pro nobis' to the shepherds. So, using the following words, the abbot made known the rule and instruction the monk had requested:

[4] 'It is quite natural', said the abbot, 'that there should be great concordance between the intellect and the will when the intellect understands that which the will loves and the will loves that which the intellect understands. A sermon is beneficial, therefore, when proofs concerning the arguments which are demonstrable according to the nature of the intellect are, in fact, provided therein. So, since shepherds are people more apt to gain an understanding from arguments

than authorities, they will love more readily the qualities attributable to Our Lady, therefore, if they understand these by means of demonstrable necessary reasons than they would if they were obliged to believe them by means of authorities.

[5] 'When the intellect has understood an argument from among those which the preacher is preaching, it entrusts it to memory, and then understands the following argument that the preacher preaches. And when the sermon is lengthy or contains overly subtle arguments, memory cannot retrieve everything the intellect entrusts to it. And, for this reason, ignorance and a lack of devotion abound in those who listen to sermons. And, since this is the case, it is a good rule, therefore, for one to deliver short sermons.

[6] 'It is will's nature to love that which is more pleasing to it. So, the better the subject matter in which the arguments consist, the more one should delay using these until the end, so that the will remains eager for such, from which eagerness springs devotion to the words, and from which devotion action itself emerges. It is fitting, therefore, that in a sermon one should keep the best words until the end.'

The abbot mentioned many things which were essential for preaching: virtuous deeds and devout words, in particular.

[7] When the abbot had taught the aforesaid methods, as well as many others, to the monk of 'Ora pro nobis', by which methods the latter might be able to preach, he contemplated Our Lady in front of the monk so that the latter might derive therefrom a rule and instruction as to how to preach the phrase 'Ora pro nobis'. So the abbot, therefore, said these words:

'Holy Mary, I worship and bless your glorious Son, to whom you pray for the sake of us sinners. If you are more devoted to praying for us sinners than we are ourselves, then we need not pray to you that you may pray for us. But since we would not be worthy of being included in your prayers were we not to pray to you and to trust in your prayers, we are obliged, therefore, to pray to, as well as to contemplate, you and your qualities, so that we may pay reverence and honour to you, and so that you may remember us with your compassionate remembrance and may look upon us with your merciful eyes during these dark times in which we live as a result of a lack of devotion and of charity. This lack causes us to forget the Passion of your Son, insofar as we fail to remember it in the way we ought, and when honouring you and your Son we fail to do what we ought or what we might, yet you do not cease to pray for us, using your full capacities. So, since this is the case, then, you, Queen of both kings and queens, help us to honour you by honouring your Son in those places where He is despised, rejected, disbelieved and reviled by those people whom your Son hopes will honour Him and forgive Him the sins which are falsely attributed to Him by those who abide in error and who proceed towards everlasting fire.

[8] 'O Queen, as soon as you became filled with the Holy Spirit and with the Son of God Whom you conceived, you were obliged to pray for us sinners. For the greater was your honour, the more was it fitting that both the righteous and sinners should have trusted more firmly in you. And the more firmly we trust in you, the more does your justice make you attentive to healing our languor and forgiving our sins.

[9] 'Look here below among us, O Queen, and see how many people pray to you and beseech you by singing, remembering and adoring. Where is your justice, compassion, charity and nobility if you fail to pray for us? And if you pray to your glorious Son for our sake and if your Son fails to grant your prayers,[186] where is the love that He once bore for you when He became incarnate in you, and when, hanging from the Cross, nearing death, He remembered you and entrusted you to Saint John?

[10] 'Beloved son', said the abbot to the monk, 'you may go to the shepherds to contemplate Our Lady and to preach about her in accordance with the method you have heard, and may live among them, and on certain feast days during the year you may return to us. May you be commended to God and Our Lady and may you enjoy their grace and blessing. You have humbled yourself in order to honour Our Lady, and you shall be raised up if you cause her to be remembered, besought and loved, for her prayers shall cause you to ascend to everlasting glory.'

The monk took leave of the abbot and of his companions and departed to those places where the shepherds lived.

[11] The monk of 'Ora pro nobis' travelled over mountains, across plains and through forests preaching to the shepherds about the qualities[187] of Our Lady, who prays both for the righteous and for

---

186. Cat. *exoeix tos prechs*. The verb *exoir* fuses the senses of 'to hear or heed' and 'to respond to', and can, therefore, be rendered as 'to grant'.
187. Lit. 'Honours'.

sinners. It came to pass one day that the monk arrived at a great valley where there was a large flock of sheep. In that valley was a cave in which a shepherd was keeping a woman concealed, a woman whom he had stolen from her husband and with whom he was sinning. The monk came by chance to that cave, wherein the shepherd and the woman were eating. The monk was received with courtesy by the shepherd and the woman, and was invited to eat with them.

'My lord', said the shepherd, 'our food is bread and water, and a small amount of cheese and of onion. May it please you to eat what God has given us.'

The monk ate and drank water with the shepherd, as he had become accustomed to doing when he ate with the other shepherds to whom he had preached.

[12] While they were eating, the shepherd was obliged to go to drive out the sheep from a wheat field into which they had entered, so the monk stayed behind with the woman, about whose circumstances he inquired. The woman described to him how she had been the wife of another shepherd, how she was living in sin with the present shepherd and how she felt repentant for the sin she had committed against her husband. Out of fear, however, she dared not return to her husband, and the shepherd with whom she was living would not let her do so on account of the great love he bore her. The shepherd returned and they ate together, and when they had finished eating the monk made the sign of the Cross, blessed the table and said these words:

[13] 'Once upon a time, it came to pass that a shepherd was living in sin with a woman on a high peak. Every day this woman prayed to Our Lady, Holy Mary, to draw her away from sin. One night the shepherd was sleeping, and it seemed to him that he could see Our Lady, who was writing down the names of all those for whom she prayed to her Son. And in that book she wrote the name of the woman whom the shepherd kept, and the shepherd entreated Holy Mary to write his name in that book. Holy Mary replied, saying that because he failed to pray to her daily, he was not worthy to have his name written in that book.'

[14] 'My lord', said the shepherd to the monk, 'do you know if Our Lady would be willing to pray for me if I were to pray to her every day?'

The monk replied that he would stand as his guarantor that Our Lady would pray for him so long as he did not do any dishonour to her Son, to whom all those who live in sin do dishonour and all those who renounce sin do honour. As the monk was saying these words, the shepherd felt remorse for the sin to which he had given way and said to the monk the following words:

[15] 'I have given way to the sin of lust and should like to renounce it so that I might honour Our Lady's Son and that Our Lady might pray for me. But since this woman would lack counsel if I were to abandon her and she would not dare to return to her husband, it is therefore necessary for me to remain in sin.'

The monk asked the woman if she had sufficient confidence in the prayers of Our Lady that she wished to go with him to her husband. The woman replied to him, saying that she would return to her husband and that she would confess to her wrongdoings so that her husband might exact vengeance upon her, and that she would trust in Our Lady to help her as regards the penance her husband would make her endure by reason of his vengeance.

[16] The monk and the woman went on their way to the house of the husband whose wife the woman was. The shepherd, who stayed behind, performed continual penance, and entreated and besought Our Lady every day. In the course of their journey, the monk and the woman found, sleeping in the shade of a tree, her husband, a shepherd, who had gone in search of his wife and was bearing weapons so that he might kill the shepherd who had carried her off. The monk and the woman knelt down in front of the sleeping shepherd, and the monk said these words:

[17] '"Santa Maria, hora pro nobis"! Holy Mary, your prayers are answered in this sinful woman who repents of her sin, for had you not prayed for her she would not have repented thereof. It befits you to ensure that this shepherd should receive grace from your Son whereby he may forgive his wife. It befits you to reward our hope, which we have placed in you so that you may help us.'

When the monk had uttered these words, the woman, while weeping with great contrition of heart, said the following:

'I am guilty and have sinned against my husband and master, who may exercise justice or forgiveness towards me. I am content with whatever he may do in that regard. Should my husband choose to forgive me, I should be eager to live the life of a hermitess and to live alone and do penance for the wrong I have committed against him. If he hits me, tortures me or imprisons me, my husband shall implement justice, and I shall patiently endure my trials. I shall give thanks to the Queen of Heaven, and shall bless her Son, who wills that in this world I should endure suffering for the sins of which I am so guilty.'

As the woman was saying these words, she repeatedly uttered the phrase 'Santa Maria, ora pro nobis!', since it seemed to her that these words might aid her in her needs.

[18] While the monk and the woman were kneeling before the sleeping shepherd, the shepherd dreamt that he was being hanged on account of a man whom he had killed. And when his soul was due to leave his body, a demon very horrible to behold sought to take that soul. Our Lady, however, kept his soul in his body so that the demon might not take it, and she entreated her Son to forgive the shepherd for the death of the man, whom he had very unjustly killed. When the shepherd's dream was finished, yet while he was still drowsy,[188] he heard the words that the monk and his wife were saying. The shepherd was awoken by these words and saw his wife and the monk, who were kneeling in front of him and were tearfully entreating and offering prayers to Our Lady using the aforesaid words.

[19] The shepherd felt very great wonder at the sight of the monk and his wife. And because of the power of the words they had spoken and because of the dream he had undergone, the shepherd was moved to forgiveness and tears, and together with them he praised and adored Our Lady. They remained for a long time with each other in prayer and tears, and after such prayer the shepherd said these words:

'If lust stirs the body to sin, how much more ought remembrance of Christ's Passion and of Our Lady's nobility stir one's will to pity and forgiveness! And whoever repents and judges herself should not be punished twice. If I do not grant forgiveness, I have no right to ask for forgiveness. I do not simply forgive, but rather would I grant all that I possibly could to whomever asked for my forgiveness. If Our Lady asks that I be forgiven, it is only right that I should grant forgiveness!'

---

188. Cat. *en gravit* (deriving from the past participle of the verb *engravir*: 'to burden/oppress/weigh down/overwhelm', f. Lat. *gravare/ingravare*, to which the late-Latin *gravedo, -inis*: 'head cold, catarrh' is related) has elicited a range of differing interpretations, spanning, in the latter case: 'unconsciously/while sleeping'; 'half asleep'; 'breathing heavily'; and 'while suffering nightmares'. Beatrice Schmid provisionally concludes that the most plausible senses of this term are: 'drowsiness'; 'the state between wakefulness and sleep, in which the subject has not completely lost the use of his/her senses or consciousness'; and 'disturbed sleep characterised by the presence of dreams' [my translations], in Schmid (2004) in Colón, Martínez and Perea (2004), 459-69, here 467.

[20] The woman knelt down before her husband and kissed his hands and his feet, and her husband forgave her and told her to return to his house, in which she might live in the peace which she had long enjoyed.

'My lord', said the woman, 'I am not worthy to be in your company. It is not forgiveness alone which you must grant, but rather also a gift whereby I may live alone and, in poverty, lead the life of a hermit, eating raw herbs and doing penance for the wrongs and misdeeds I have committed against you.'

An arrangement was reached between all three of them whereby the righteous woman should do penance in a cave situated on a high peak close to a spring, her husband should occasionally bring her a certain pittance with which she might provide sustenance for her body, and whereby subsequently the two of them should not know each other in carnal delight and should each remain in chastity. Very great were the devotion shown and the saintly lives led by each of them, and when her husband came to see her very great were the blessings they expressed to each other, as well as the instruction they imparted to each other so that they might honour God and Our Lady.

[21] In a meadow close to a beautiful spring there was a great number of shepherds who were watching over their flocks. The monk of 'Ora pro nobis' arrived at that meadow, greeted them, and said that he was a preacher to shepherds and asked them courteously to listen to the sermon he wished to deliver to them. The monk preached to them by means of exemplary tales so that he might more easily prompt them to devotion. So pleasing were the sermons the monk delivered to the shepherds that the latter cogitated all day long upon what the monk had preached to them, and because they cogitated thereupon, they grew to love honouring God and praying to Our Lady. The monk remained in that place with them for seven days, and on the eighth day he took his leave of them and went to preach to other shepherds who lived in other areas. Who could possibly describe to you the righteousness and the praise whereby God was honoured by these shepherds to whom the monk had preached? And who could convey to you the good reputation that the monk achieved in every country? And who could count the number of shepherds who came to listen to him?

Here ends the Book of Religion.

## HERE BEGINS THE THIRD BOOK, WHICH CONCERNS PRELACY

### 67. ON HOW ABBOT BLAQUERNA WAS ELECTED BISHOP

[1] After the bishop had relinquished his bishopric and was attending the school for the study of Arabic, the canons assembled in the chapter house in order to make arrangements as to how they might elect a pastor. One of the canons said that they ought to ask the bishop which of them all he believed should be bishop since, because he had been bishop and had relinquished his bishopric and now wished to die in order to honour Jesus Christ, it was fitting that he be asked and that he have a vote in the chapter. All the canons approved of what the canon had said. So the former bishop came to the chapter and in the presence of everyone stated that they should elect Blaquerna as bishop, for he did not know any man as worthy of being bishop. He did not believe, however, that Blaquerna wished to be bishop, so were the latter to refuse the post, he gave counsel that they should elect a bishop according to the art and method of election.

[2] The archdeacon was highly displeased by what the former bishop had said, as were some of the canons, for they were canons secular and feared that if Abbot Blaquerna were bishop he would he cause them to become canons regular.[189] The majority of the canons thought it good that Abbot Blaquerna should become bishop, though

---

189. Canons were clerics who initially lived a communal life under an ecclesiastical rule in clergy houses and subsequently within premises in the vicinity of a cathedral or church, forming thereby a chapter. From the eleventh century onwards, a distinction was instituted between 'canons regular' (who lived in monasteries) and 'canons secular', this distinction being based upon the fact that the former were subject to the particular ecclesiastical (in this case, monastic) rule, amongst others, of renouncing worldly goods, as had originally been prescribed by St Augustine, while the latter were not so subject. The latter, in effect, were not bound by any vows of poverty, obedience or chastity beyond the rule to which they conformed, and constituted part of the diocesan clergy.

they wished to hold the election according to the specified art. The archdeacon, along with certain canons, however, objected to the election's being held according to this art, as was intended; so, therefore, the remaining canons, who wished Blaquerna to be bishop, elected him to that post without recourse to such art, although certain other canons demurred and elected the archdeacon as bishop.

[3] There was great discord among the canons by reason of the election they had held amid such disagreement. Two canons went to Abbot Blaquerna and told him that he had been elected bishop and that he had gained more votes than the archdeacon, and, therefore, they begged him on behalf of all their fellow canons to accept the bishopric and to go to Rome in order to be confirmed. Abbot Blaquerna exonerated himself by saying that it did not befit the contemplative life to forsake the monastic order in order to become a bishop, and he stated that under no circumstances would he be bishop. It greatly displeased the two canons that the abbot did not wish to become bishop, as it likewise did all the others who had elected him to that position. The archdeacon went to Rome to request his bishopric and to receive his confirmation; however, the majority of the canons sent a proctor[190] to oppose him, and they begged the Lord Pope to command Abbot Blaquerna to become bishop.

[4] After he had listened to both sides, the Lord Pope said these words:

'Every semblance of simony is to be shunned in elections, while its contrary therein is to be recommended.[191] It seems, therefore, that Abbot Blaquerna, who does not wish to be bishop nor to pass from a strict life to one that is lenient, is worthy of being bishop.'

The pope, therefore, wanted Blaquerna to be bishop no matter what, so he sent him a command to that effect. The pope's command greatly displeased the abbot and the entire convent, so the abbot sent two monks to the pope in order to exempt himself and to assert the rights which he currently enjoyed: for if the former bishop could forgo his bishopric with a view to choosing a stricter life, it was conceivable that he likewise might be able to forgo his election so that he could wear the monastic habit and lead a more contemplative life.

---

190. For the legalistic sense of the term proctor, see above Ch. 9, § 4.

191. Simony is the buying or selling of spiritual things: ecclesiastical offices, benefices or pardons (i.e. indulgences).

[5] The monks went to Rome and begged the Lord Pope not to deprive them of their abbot Blaquerna, for they would feel his absence very keenly, and he had greatly improved the monastery, and they begged this all the more so since he had exempted himself on account of the aforesaid rights. The pope wanted Abbot Blaquerna to be bishop no matter what, so that he might improve the bishopric in the same way he had improved the monastery, and he wanted him to show obedience, so that he might become bishop. The abbot was obliged to forsake his role as abbot and to take on that of bishop. All the monks were greatly displeased, yet the canons who had elected him felt great joy.

68. ON HOW BLAQUERNA LENT ORDER TO HIS BISHOPRIC

[1] The bishop was in the chapter house with all his canons and said these words:

'It is your will, good sirs, that I should be your pastor. When I was abbot, I was already in servitude, but now my servitude is greater, for the shepherd watches over his fat sheep more zealously and in the face of greater danger than he does the lean.[192] Since you wish me to be bishop, I ask for your help and counsel that you may assist me in being a pastor and in watching over my sheep. I wish to know, first of all, how much is the church's income and how many canons and beneficed clergymen there are within the See, as well as how the church's income is divided.[193] All these matters should be put in writing so that I may seek to discover within my soul whether, as far as this church is concerned, anything might be improved or ordered towards the honour of God and towards setting a suitable example to laypeople, who often sin on account of the unsuitable example they have drawn from their pastor and his companions.'

[2] The document that the bishop had requested was made out in his presence and in that of all the canons, and within this document the bishop discovered that in his See there were twenty-four canons,

---

192. Cf. Ezek 34:20. Ezek 34:1-31, which deals with the practices of good and bad shepherds and, hence, pastors, is of great relevance to Blaquerna's first pastoral words as bishop.

193. A benefice was the (permanent) gift of land and the right to receive attendant ecclesiastical revenues therefrom as bestowed upon a cleric in return for his spiritual and pastoral services.

apart from the sacrist and the archdeacon, the provost and the cantor.[194] There were likewise thirteen chaplaincies, and there were further posts, as befits a cathedral church. The church had a large income and the bishop's share had a value of three thousand pounds a year.[195] The bishop cogitated at length upon the state of his bishopric and upon how he might improve it.

[3] It came to pass one day that, at Mass, the gospel was recited in which Jesus Christ promises eight Beatitudes.[196] After Mass, the bishop held chapter, in accordance with the custom he had established of holding such once a week. When the bishop was in the chapter house along with all the monks, he said these words:

'Good sirs, you have heard how our Lord God, Jesus Christ, promises eight Beatitudes in the Gospel. If it is your counsel and desire, I should like to organise this bishopric according to such a rule and ordinance that we might be able to enjoy the eight Beatitudes. I begin, first, with my income and divide it into three parts. Let the first part be given in alms, the next be given to make peace between those who are in strife, and let the last cover the expenses that both I and those who belong to my household need to undertake.'

[4] The archdeacon replied to the bishop, saying that it would be a great dishonour to him and to all the clergy within his See if he failed to maintain in his house a sizeable retinue, so that he might better be attended and more greatly be honoured thereby, which retinue he could not maintain with a third of his income alone. The bishop replied that honours should not be desired other than for the purpose of serving God and that to give alms affords God greater honour than does maintaining a superfluous entourage with the aim of deriving vainglory therefrom. For a prelate's palace is more greatly honoured when it has at its gates many paupers to whom alms are given than it is when it has on its table many silver goblets and many guests seated therearound, and in its stables many animals, and on its clothes racks many garments, and in its coffers large sums of money.

[5] The bishop wanted the income of the canons to be divided into three parts, and he asked the first part to be put aside for the

---

194. The provost is the head of a cathedral chapter while the cantor/precentor directs choral services (i.e. liturgical chant) within a church, monastery or cathedral.

195. Cat. *liures/lliures*: a currency unit, once used in Catalonia and Majorca, consisting of twenty shillings.

196. Matt 5: 3-12; otherwise known as the Sermon on the Mount.

service of the eight Beatitudes, the second for the study of theology and canon law, and the third for the service of the church. And he wanted all of these twenty-four canons, as well as himself and all the others, to be subject to a Rule. After this, he desired that the priests who celebrated Mass and served the chaplaincies should, after Mass and the Hours, study theology and law; and that they should eat in a refectory and sleep in a dormitory, so that they might be made into canons once the others had died; and likewise that the parish church-es should be given into their care. And he wished this ordinance to be made in perpetuity and to be confirmed by the pope and by the en-tire chapter.

[6] There was a fierce argument between the bishop and the arch-deacon, along with some of the canons who were supporters of the latter. The bishop said, however, that he would not be bishop unless they confirmed that ordinance, and that he would send someone to the Lord Pope so that the latter might confirm said ordinance. And if the pope did not wish to confirm it, he should consider him to be excused from being bishop, since he did not wish to be the pastor of sheep which he could not protect from wolves.[197] Using holy and de-vout canons, the bishop sent a report to the pope of all the proceed-ings related to the matter. The pope immediately wrote a reply to the bishop, desiring that the latter's will be carried out in full, and ex-pressed great gladness at having confirmed him as bishop since he had placed his trust in the good the bishop would bring about. When the messengers had returned from the court, Bishop Blaquerna lent order to his bishopric in the abovementioned manner and, first of all, made arrangements with respect to study and, subsequently, to the eight Beatitudes.


## 69. ON POVERTY

[1] When the bishop was in the chapter house with the canons, he said that Jesus Christ promised the kingdom of heaven to the poor.[198] He therefore wished a canon to be assigned to the office of poverty, a

---

197. Cf. Matt 7:15; Matt 10:16.
198. Matt 5:3; Lk 6:20. The first of the eight (in Mark, four) Beatitudes from the Sermon on the Mount.

canon who should preach poverty and be the leader of the poor of
that city. He should likewise donate the income from his canonry for
the love of God, should beg for his livelihood, should be humbly
dressed, and should rebuke the rich in spirit.[199] While the bishop was
explaining the conduct required of this office, a canon who was a
man of saintly life rose to his feet and requested the office of poverty,
and promised to fulfil to the best of his ability all the aforesaid conditions, as were appropriate to the office.

[2] The office was granted to that canon, and the bishop made
sure that throughout the churches it was preached that this canon
would be the leader of the poor and that he would beg on their behalf; and he likewise granted full forgiveness to any person who would
make a donation to the canon. The canon gave away his costly garments for the love of God, as well as all the animals he owned and all
his household trappings; and humbly dressed he begged on behalf of
the shamefaced poor and the helpless poor,[200] as also of maidens yet
to be married and of impoverished orphan children, to whom he
taught some trade from which they might live.

[3] It came about one day that the Canon of Poverty went to eat at
the archdeacon's house. While the archdeacon was eating exquisite
dishes of many kinds, the Canon of Poverty cried out in a loud voice:

'To the streets! To the streets![201] The archdeacon is devouring and
consuming what belongs to the poor of Jesus Christ!'

So, crying out in this manner, the canon left the archdeacon's
house and, still shouting, went through the town and to the houses of
the canons, while many paupers went along with him, calling out and
uttering the same words the canon was saying. The archdeacon felt
very great shame, and by reproaching him the canon aroused remorse in many other people.

---

199. The 'rich in spirit', therefore, are those neither blessed nor possessing the
kingdom of heaven.

200. See Ch. 2, § 1 above and corresponding note. The 'helpless poor' constituted
a distinct social group, representing 'a very small proportion of the population [who]
depended on poor relief at all times [...] and included invalids, the young, the aged
and the mentally ill. Their numbers grew in times of famine as refugees from the coun-
tryside came to the cities and towns in search of food or alms', in Grendler (2004), 208.

201. Cat. *Via fora! Via fora!*: the call to arms, accompanied by the pealing of bells,
let out in order to muster an army of free citizens against any threat, external or internal.

[4] On another day it came to pass that the Canon of Poverty was eating with the cantor. While they were eating, a large group of animals laden with wheat belonging to the cantor entered his premises, a cantor who was a miserly man and had amassed money so that he might enrich a nephew of his, whom he dearly loved. As soon as he saw the animals entering the premises, the canon got up from the table and went into the streets, gathering together the poor. And when he had gathered a large number thereof, he went to the bishop's palace and cried out 'Justice! Justice!', and all the paupers called out in unison with him. The bishop felt great wonder at such cries, as did all the others. The bishop and his canons came out to the gate, where they found the paupers who, with the canon, their proctor, were calling out 'Justice! Justice!' The bishop asked the canon why he was calling out and the canon said to the bishop the following words:

[5] 'My lord, it is written that whatever the clergy possesses in excess of its needs should belong to the poor of Christ. The cantor has amassed a great deal of wheat, and he wishes to sell it so that he may buy a castle for his nephew. I demand to be given the money he shall earn from the wheat, for it ought to belong to these paupers whom you have entrusted to me. For his nephew is not a clerk, nor does the cantor have a mouth or a stomach which requires all that wheat. I demand, therefore, that justice be done unto me!'

The bishop sent for the cantor and learned the truth of the matter, discovering that the situation was just as the Canon of Poverty had described. The cantor felt ashamed and perplexed, and the bishop gave judgement that all of that wheat should be given to the poor, and that if the cantor's nephew wished to be judged a pauper, then he might acquire a share thereof just like any other poor person.

[6] The Canon of Poverty preached poverty and reproached wealth in the town squares. One day it came to pass that a very rich and highly acclaimed burgher of that city had invited him to dine. Before they ate, the canon begged the burgher to show him his entire property. He led him through all the buildings thereof and the canon saw that throughout the entire property there was no chamber or building which lacked anything, for the property was very beautiful and finely wrought. Each building possessed everything that pertained to its function, for in the bedchambers there were many beds and many expensive counterpanes, while in the palace there were

many weapons and many tables, in the stables there were many animals, and in the kitchen many utensils. In the courtyard there were
many hens and geese, and plenty of firewood, while in the garden
there were many trees. In the granaries there was plenty of wheat and
in the larder plenty of bread and flour, and in the cupboard many
silver cups, and on the clothes racks plenty of garments, and in the
coffers large sums of money. The burgher, his wife, and all of his children, as well as all of his entourage, had an abundance of garments,
as of everything that they needed. When the canon had seen all these
things, he said that he had not looked around sufficiently to be able
to detect the presence of poverty in any building. Therefore, he did
not wish to eat with him, since he was clearly a servant of wealth,
which was contrary to his lady, poverty.

[7] When the canon sought to leave the burgher's residence with
a view to eating in a different place, the burgher told him that there
was a secret room therewithin, which the canon had not viewed, yet
which he wished him to see. The burgher led the canon to this room,
which was sparsely furnished. That day, within this room, the canon
ate in private with the burgher and his wife, and they ate meagrely.
And the burgher showed him the humble bed on which he and his
wife lay, and the hairshirts[202] they would wear, and a book within
which were written the payments of alms he had secretly made. In
another secret room was the crucifix, and here the burgher and his
wife would remain in prayer and contemplation while invoking God
and speaking about Him. The canon felt very great wonder at the
lives of the burgher and his wife, so he asked him why he maintained
his entourage and his household in such opulence of food and clothing, and how he kept it so well-provided with all things. The burgher
replied, saying that he kept his residence amply supplied with all
things so that he might thereby be poorer in spirit, for the greater
wealth and opulence other people enjoyed and the more frequently
he saw such things and scorned them, the poorer he became in spirit.
The lives of the burgher and his wife greatly pleased the canon, so he
praised and blessed God, Who had granted him such a worthy companion in the service of poverty.

---

202. Cat. *çilici*: the technical term for which, in English, is 'cilice'.

### 70. ON MEEKNESS

[1] Bishop Blaquerna conferred the office of meekness upon a canon, who was obliged to preach meekness, as well as to be meek so that his sermons might thereby be more truthful. He divided up the other offices among the other canons who were assigned to serve the Beatitudes, while he retained the office of peace for himself.

It so happened one day that the archdeacon's steward had purchased meat, hens and partridges, and the Canon of Poverty was walking with a great crowd of paupers along the street when he met this steward, who was accompanied by two men laden with meat. The canon and the paupers cried out: 'Thief! Thief! The archdeacon has stolen meat from the poor of Jesus Christ!' The steward felt great outrage and anger, and the archdeacon, whom the steward informed of the event, felt even greater anger as a result. So angry did the archdeacon feel that he made to strike the Canon of Poverty, but the Canon of Meekness reminded him that Our Lord Jesus Christ was meek when on the Cross, upon which He allowed himself to be nailed, hanged, wounded and put to death, though He was without sin. So, since the archdeacon had committed a sin, how very patient he should have been, then, if the Canon of Poverty reproached him with good reason, reprimanding him for the wrong he inflicted upon the poor, who had been entrusted to the Canon of Poverty by the will of the bishop and of the entire chapter! The Canon of Meekness addressed his words to the archdeacon with such devotion and such expressions of humility that the latter felt remorse and exercised patience, curbing his anger and his ill will, and asking for forgiveness from the Canon of Poverty.

[2] In that city there was a lady who dearly loved her husband, who was lustful. And as a result of the sin he had committed against her, the lady became impatient at the wrongs he had been doing. On a particular occasion, it happened that she was going to church with other ladies and the Canon of Meekness was preaching patience and meekness in the street, using the following words:

'The meek and simple person is stronger than the one who is angry, impatient and proud. For the meek person fights with charity, justice, prudence and fortitude, while the impatient and angry person fights with things that are contrary to the above virtues.'

The lady cogitated at length upon the words the canon preached and thought that she should test whether she could chastise her husband for the vice of lust using simple, humble words, and meekness and patience. The lady, therefore, uttered meek and humble words to her husband and made an outward show of contentment. And the more gravely her husband sinned, the more vigorously a sense of remorse grew within him. And through the growth of his remorse came chastity, justice and shame, which are in accord with remorse, and, in combination with fortitude, they defeated lust in the will of her husband.

[3] In the town square, the canon was preaching meekness when a man accused another of theft, and the latter angrily and threateningly vindicated himself, and he did so in such a manner that it seemed, from his words, as if he were God and that he could not err or commit any wrong. And the more vigorously he vindicated himself, the more the anger grew and increased in the man who had accused him and now felt greater suspicion towards him, for anger and suspicion accord with each other, and people who are guilty vindicate themselves more vigorously in their words than do those who are not so. While both men were arguing in this manner, the canon who was preaching said these words:

'They falsely accused Jesus Christ when they said that He was drunk[203] and possessed by the Devil;[204] yet Christ answered humbly, devoutly and succinctly, saying that He was not possessed or drunk.[205] So, whoever vindicates himself more vigorously than did Jesus Christ, makes it seem by his words that he could not possibly err or commit a sin.'

[4] While the canon was saying these words, a tile fell from a roof and injured him on the head, inflicting upon him a large wound, yet he exercised patience and calmly put up with the wound, uttering humble and devout words. While they were taking the canon to the physician, two men were having a fight, and one of them decided to stab the other with a knife, yet he injured the Canon of Meekness on the arm instead, inflicting upon him a large wound. So the canon meekly said that God would forgive him for that, and praised and blessed God, Who wished him to exercise patience and utter words of meekness. The canon's words greatly edified all those who were with

---

203. Matt 11:19.
204. Jn 7:20; 8:48; 10:20.
205. Matt 11:25-30; Jn 7:21-24; 8:49-51; 10:25-30.

him and, in particular, the man who had so forcefully exonerated himself from the theft.

[5] After some time, the canon recovered from his wounds. The sovereign of that country had disendowed the Church and had done great wrongs thereto, for this prince was not a good Christian and did not wish to obey Bishop Blaquerna regarding what the latter had told him, as his office demanded. The wrongs that this prince had committed against the Church came to the pope's attention, so he sent a message to the bishop telling him to interdict and to excommunicate the prince.[206] Everyone was afraid of placing the prince under interdict for they knew him to be wicked and cruel, and they feared death and hesitated, therefore, to place him under such. One day, the bishop was with the canons in the chapter house, and with him were those canons who exercised the offices of the eight Beatitudes. Their discussion concerned which, out of all eight of them, should, as his office demanded, go to lay the interdict upon the prince, and it was decided by the bishop that the Canon of Meekness should fulfil that office on the grounds that Jesus Christ—Who is their shepherd, and of whom the pastors of this world are proxies—was Himself meek. And since an interdict ought to be imposed by means of meek words and contrition of heart, it was resolved, therefore, that the Canon of Meekness should go to lay interdict upon the prince.

[6] When the canon stood before the prince, he said these words:

'Our Lord Jesus Christ said that the meek would possess the earth.[207] Since I am meek, I was chosen to be sent to you so that I may lay interdict upon you in virtue of the wrongs you commit against the Church. Meekness has conquered me and causes me to be in mortal danger. If within you there is fortitude, justice, humility and patience, meekness shall render my words pleasing to you; if within you, however, there is anger, disobedience and injustice, I intend to combat your proud words with humble ones of my own.'

[7] The prince was highly displeased by the interdict, and commanded that the canon should be stripped, bound and scourged before him, and that afterwards he should be violently put to death. While the canon was being bound and scourged, he offered prayers

---

206. Under Roman Catholic canon law, an interdict is an official ecclesiastical sanction upon an individual's or a group's freedom to participate in certain rites.

207. Matt 5:4.

to God for the sake of the prince, as well as of the men who were scourging him, and praised God, Who caused him to receive penance for the sins he had committed in this world. So, the more fiercely they scourged and tortured him, the more pious his expression became and the more devoutly he uttered these words:

'Jesus Christ, my Lord! You have created me after your likeness and You have taken on a human nature like my very own. In the same way that You chose to be tortured, You cause me to be tortured so that I may be more perfectly like You. I would be incapable of rewarding You for the gifts You wish to grant me. I bless You, Lord, since You have desired to honour me! I should not be meek nor like You were I to abhor those who torture me.'

[8] The prince felt great wonder at the words the canon spoke and gave order, therefore, that he should not be scourged or caused any further harm, and he said these words:

'There was once a time when clerks were proud and spoke impiously! How has it come about that you speak such humble and devout words? Might the time have arrived when humility and devotion have achieved concordance within you clerks, and when we laymen might draw our example therefrom? By God, I beg and beseech you to describe to me the estate of your bishop and of your fellow canons, for in those who have sent to me a man such as yourself in a situation such as this resides some new kind of virtue!'

[9] The canon described to him the estate of Bishop Blaquerna, how he was formerly abbot, how they had elected him bishop, how the bishop had set his bishopric in order, and how he, the canon, was one of the eight companions who by their lives gave indication of the eight Beatitudes that Jesus Christ promised to his Apostles and to their successors. A divine light kindled heavenly love in the prince's heart, and he said the following words:

'It is not fitting that such a bishop or his companions should be disobeyed in any matter!'

The prince and the Canon of Meekness travelled to see the bishop, and the prince asked for forgiveness, made satisfaction and entrusted himself to the grace and blessings of the bishop and the entire chapter.[208]

---

208. Cat. *comená·s en gracia e en benedicçio de*: this phrase means to place oneself under the protection of or to request kindness of treatment from somebody.

## 71. ON WEEPING

[1] Bishop Blaquerna gave a rule to the Canon of Weeping as to how, in general, he might weep for the sake of all those things to which tears are suited. And he gave him an art and a rule as to how he might stir his heart to love God so fervently that his heart might cause water to rise to his eyes, so that they might weep. One day, it came about that this canon was passing by a butcher's shop, when he saw the Canon of Meekness inside. This canon was watching how the butchers bound and slaughtered the lambs in such a way that they suffered no distress and calmly accepted their death. The Canon of Weeping asked the Canon of Meekness why he was in that place, and the latter replied to him, saying that he was there so that, by seeing the lambs slaughtered, he might remember his Lord, Jesus Christ, who let himself be bound and slaughtered just as calmly as the lambs, in order to save sinners. When the Canon of Weeping heard these words, he said that it was his duty to weep over the death of his Lord, Jesus Christ. Both of the canons spent a long time in tears and devotion, and they came to that place very often to weep together on account of the pleasure they found in doing so and of the effect they thereby produced on many people in that place, who felt contrition for their sins and wept for the Passion of Jesus Christ.

[2] The Canon of Weeping passed in front of the synagogue belonging to the Jews and he saw, entering that synagogue, many Jews who had come to pray to God. He sat down at the door to the synagogue. The canon recalled how the Jews had brought about the Passion of Jesus Christ, how they had dishonoured Him in this world and how they consistently refused to believe in Him and reviled Him. While the canon was cogitating upon such matters, as well as upon the damnation towards which the Jews, in their ignorance, were proceeding, the canon wept very bitterly, saying these words:

'Ah, charity and devotion! Why do you not come to honour Our Lord among these people who think that they honour Him, yet do Him dishonour? Ah, compassion! Why do you not have mercy upon these people who, in their ignorance, proceed daily towards everlasting fire?'

The canon said many other words and shed many tears in that place, which he regularly frequented for the purpose of weeping, in order that divine grace might enlighten those in error and impart devotion to Christians so that, by God's virtue, the latter might acquire greater diligence than they actually have in enlightening unbelievers.

[3] A virtuous lady had a husband whom she loved dearly, which husband was a prisoner and could be ransomed for a large sum of money. The lady sold all her possessions, as well as those of her husband, in order to pay the ransom, and what she lacked in this respect, she acquired by begging in the town's squares. One day, the Canon of Weeping found himself in the company of this lady, in the square. The lady wept as she begged, and informed a large number of notables about the captivity in which her husband was held and the torment he underwent in the prison. She was leading four small children with her. All the notables felt pity for the lady, gave her money and comforted her in her trials. When the lady had said her words, and had received the alms, the Canon of Weeping said the following things, while weeping:

'The lady weeps for her husband and pities the torments he endures in prison. Her children live in poverty, and for that reason she goes begging with them. The lady does all she possibly can to retrieve her husband. Who, though, does all he possibly can to honour his creator, redeemer, benefactor and Lord of all that exists? This Lord is more loveable than is the lady's husband, yet the place in which He was conceived, born and crucified is in captivity, for the Saracens have possession of it. Which of you will assist me in weeping at the ingratitude of the people, who fail to do all they possibly can to honour their Lord?'

The canon wept, yet the people in the square busied themselves with the counting of their money and discussions about their merchandise, so for this reason the canon's weeping began to increase.

[4] Brothel women would gather at the entrance to the city. One day, it happened that the Canon of Weeping was passing through this place when he saw a large number of such women, so he sat down beside them and said these words:

'I wish to weep for the sins of these women, who sell themselves to devils for money. The entire world does not enjoy the same value as a single soul, yet each of them gives her soul for money to the Devil! It is my duty to weep since the prince does not forbid these women, who cause men to sin, to remain in this place. My eyes weep since there is nobody in this city who makes sure that these penniless women do not have such an occupation.'

While the canon was weeping in this manner, the brothel women wept together with him and exonerated themselves on account of their poverty. The canon was in tears with the women, and the people who passed along the street felt pity for them. While they were weeping like this, a wealthy, childless burgher entered the city riding his palfrey, as his wife and other retinue followed in his train, and he heard the words that the canon and the women were saying. Because of the canon's merits, God wished to inspire the burgher and his wife with divine grace, and so they received these women as their daughters and took them back with them to their house. And the burgher established a hospice in which all those women who wished to forsake the sin of lust might stay. And he and his wife commissioned them to become servants or introduced them to some trade from which they might earn their living. And the burgher spoke with the prince and with the city council to ensure that brothel women would never again be able to position themselves along the roads at the entrance to the city, so that men and women who enter and leave the city should not be set an unsuitable example.

[5] At Easter time, on Easter Sunday, when the Canon of Weeping wished to have some respite from the weeping to which he had devoted himself on account of the Holy Passion of Our Lord, he went to the church in which Bishop Blaquerna was due to preach. And when he was at the portal thereof, he saw many ladies entering therein, these ladies all being dressed in very noble attire. Their eyebrows and their hair had been dyed; and their faces had been coloured with white and rouge, so that they might be noticed by men and coveted for the pleasures of lust. Young men, in fine clothes, wearing garlands on their heads, entered the church and gazed at the ladies before they did the altar or the Cross in which the Passion of the Son of God is represented. When the canon had seen all these things, he sat down at the church door and wept at these people's sins and at the forgetfulness they showed towards the Passion of the Son of God.

[6] While the canon was weeping, Bishop Blaquerna arrived at the church, where he found that canon in tears, so he asked him why this was. So the canon said the following words to him:

'The Son of God remembered the people He had lost, and came to take on human flesh and to undergo His Passion in order to redeem His people. His Passion is forgotten and there is no one who rejoices in His Resurrection; lust alone is remembered. The women and men who bear the signs of lust come to this church so that they may see us weep.[209] So, I shall console myself through my tears, for these are my consolation, while the cogitation I devote to their sins deprive me of any such comfort.'

[7] The bishop was greatly pleased by how the canon wept, and he sat down alongside him and they both wept for a long time together, and all the people within the church learned of the reason why they wept. And, as a result, the men and women who bore the signs of lust felt very ashamed and perplexed. So the bishop delivered a sermon in which he said that in due course he did not wish men or women to be in a church unless within that church there was some means whereby the men and the women were prevented from seeing each other. And he cited the Saracens and the Jews as an example of this, for if they follow such a rule even though they abide in error, how much more should Christians follow the same, who abide in truth and should avoid there being any dishonour which might fall upon the holy sacrifice of the altar, since this sacrifice is worthy of such great honour!

[8] The canon went to the church daily in order to weep for the sake of sinners, and he went through the streets and wept whenever he saw that he had reason to do so. For he endeavoured to weep in response to anything which enabled him to perceive that God was not known, loved or obeyed, so that people might thereby feel contrition and remorse, and might ask God for forgiveness and beg Him for devotion. Who could possibly describe to you the good that he did and the evil that ceased as a result of what he did? And if they really wish to be like him, how is it that those who laugh so heartily manage to get to sleep?

72. ON AFFLICTION

[1] Every day the Canon of Affliction preached fasting, vigils and affliction, by saying that Jesus Christ promises satiety to all those who suffer hunger or thirst out of love for Him. It came to pass one day that a mule driver was eating bread and onion while his mule was eat-

---

209. The 'us' here is taken by the editors of the Catalan critical edition to be an anticipatory reference to the weeping pair consisting of the bishop and the canon in the following paragraph.

ing oats. This mule driver was thin and pale, yet his mule was fat. The canon asked him why he was more attentive to his mule than he was to himself, and the mule driver said that his mule could not carry its load without an abundance of oats, yet that he could make do with bread and onions. When the mule driver had said these words, the canon, in the presence of many people, said the following:

'Fasting or eating only frugally on account of miserliness do not give rise to the Beatitudes which God promises in the Gospels! Nor does sating one's donkey, yet starving oneself on account of miserliness, accord with justice!'

[2] It came to pass one day that the Canon of Affliction was preaching in the square when the archdeacon passed through on horseback on his way to take recreation at a castle which belonged to him. And the mule he was leading was laden with barrels of wine and hens which had already been slaughtered so that they might thereby be more tender on eating, as well as white bread, sauces and sweetmeats. This archdeacon was immensely fat and was a heavy eater. In front of everyone, the canon asked the archdeacon which type of satiety was of greater value to the body and the soul: either the satiety of worldly foods or that of grace, which God promises to all those who out of love for Him suffer hunger, thirst and affliction. The archdeacon could offer no justification, so he departed without giving him any answer.

[3] The canon left that city and went to preach affliction in a different one. At a fork in the road he met two religious who were having an argument, for one of them wished to go one way and the other the other way. The one who wished to take the first route was keen to go to preach at a castle while the other exempted himself since the castle was far away and he would have become hungry and thirsty along the way, so in order to avoid hunger and thirst he wished to take the other route. When the Canon of Affliction had learned of the reason for their argument, he reproached very harshly that brother who was fearful of suffering hunger and thirst in order to preach the word of God. For if Jesus Christ did not fear hunger, thirst or death so that He might save His people, how much less was any man excused from suffering hunger and thirst in order to honour and to preach the word of God.

[4] When the canon had travelled so far that he had arrived at the entrance to the city towards which he was heading, he met a man who

was giving a coin to a pauper in order that he might exonerate himself from having violated Lent on a particular day.[210] The canon and this man disputed at length over whether that coin exonerated him or not from his fasting. The man employed the following argument, by stating that since a greater good resulted from the coin than from his fasting, the gift of alms he had made exonerated him from the latter. The canon said that, in this instance, the giving of alms was not in accordance with justice, for if the man had sinned through an excess of gluttony it was fitting that he be punished for this by hunger, hunger which he did not suffer by donating the coin. The canon reproached him very harshly and defeated his arguments.

[5] When the canon had entered the city he came across a large number of paupers who roamed the streets in search of alms for the love of God. All the paupers made the canon their leader, so the canon accompanied them to the houses of the wealthy, crying out 'Hunger! Hunger!' One day, it came to pass that a rich merchant ordered as much food to be given to the canon and the paupers as might leave them sated. When the canon and the paupers had eaten, they cried out even louder than they had before 'Hunger! Hunger!' The merchant felt great wonder, and thought that they had not sufficiently eaten, so he ordered more food to be given to them.

'My lord', said the canon, 'we have eaten and drunk a great deal, through God's grace and your kindness. The hunger which we proclaim, however, consists in the fact that you and the others should feel hunger and thirst for the love of God, so that you may be sated by the blessings of salvation.'

[6] The canon endeavoured to the best of his ability to feel hunger and thirst in order to punish himself for his sins and to give instruction to the people as to how they might undergo afflictions, and how they might remember the hunger Jesus Christ experienced in the wilderness and the thirst He suffered on the Cross. The canon did not only have the role of preaching about bodily hunger, but rather also about spiritual hunger, so that the people might hunger for justice, charity and the other virtues, and that they might be sated thereby while leading virtuous lives.

---

210. I.e. by breaking the fast.

## 73. ON MERCY

[1] Every day the Canon of Mercy preached mercy. It came to pass one day that, in accordance with justice, a man was due to be put to death. That man had a wife and five children, who lived from the hard work he undertook in plying his trade. While the king was commanding that justice be done to that man, his dutiful wife sought out the canon who was in the service of Mercy, and she asked him to beg the king on behalf of her and her children to show mercy to her husband, so that she and her children might have something on which to subsist. The canon went to the king and said these words to him:

[2] 'My lord, mercy and justice are sisters. So, if you have been chosen as king in order to serve justice, yet have ever felt an inclination towards sin, it is your duty to be in the service of mercy, so that she may forgive you and that in you may be fulfilled the words that Jesus Christ speaks in the Gospel to those who show mercy, namely, that they shall obtain mercy.[211] So, if you are not sometimes merciful, you shall not be forgiven. And since I am Mercy's agent, in the presence of justice I demand you, therefore, to have mercy on this woman and to return her husband to her.'

The king considered deeply the words that the Canon of Mercy had spoken to him, yet was fearful of acting against justice if he were to obey the canon's words, so he therefore said the following:

[3] 'It is my duty to honour justice and, if I forgive, I am fearful that I may cause dishonour to justice; yet, if I do not forgive, I fear that justice may be aggrieved because I fail to obey mercy, her sister. So I am in great deliberation, therefore, and do not know how to choose the better of the two.'

The canon replied, saying that the more like unto God man was in his deeds, the better and nobler he was, and the more exemplary his conduct. So, since God sometimes forgives and sometimes condemns, and since princes were put on this earth to represent God and to perform His offices, it was permissible for an earthly lord sometimes to forgive and sometimes to condemn. The canon presented so many worthy arguments to the king and asked for his mercy with such piety that the king returned to him the man who had been condemned to

---

211. Matt 5:7.

death, telling the canon that anyone who was so truly the servant of Mercy and had asked for it as piously as he, should not be disobeyed.

[4] The canon fulfilled his office with such diligence that he frequently went to the square where the court was held, to plead cases and to assist without receiving any fee for so doing. And he acted as lawyer to the poor, the orphans and the widows who had no one to support them. The canon was a worthy clerk who was learned in law, and he reproached the lawyers who falsely pursued cases, all of whom were afraid of him, and, because of their fear in his regard, refrained from many duplicitous and deceptive practices in the cases they were bringing.

One day, it came to pass that a peasant farmer had suffered a wrong arising from a field that one of his neighbours had usurped from him. This peasant had attended the court on many occasions, yet the magistrate would not listen to him. The peasant went to the king's palace in order to demonstrate the wrong which had been inflicted upon him, yet he was unable to arrive at the right time or occasion whereby he might speak with the king, for sometimes the latter had gone hunting, and at others he was in his private chambers, while at still others he was eating, sleeping or taking recreation. The peasant sought out the Canon of Mercy, and he asked for his assistance and notified the canon of his requirements and of how he could not speak with the king. The canon, who was in the square and was pleading the case of a poor woman, cried out loudly, in such a way that all those who were in the square heard him, and he said:

'Is there in this square anyone who has hope in Mercy?'

Many men and women answered, saying that they had hope in Mercy. The canon asked and begged them to help him honour Mercy, and he went off with them all to the gates of the king's palace, and in loud voices they all cried out in unison, 'Mercy! Mercy!'

[5] The king felt great wonder at these cries, as did all the others, so he went out to the gates and asked the canon why he and his companions were calling out.

'My lord', said the canon, 'Our Lord Jesus Christ surrendered himself to death in order to show mercy, yet you have completely surrendered yourself to hunting, eating, sleeping and taking recreation, instead of showing mercy. For this reason, people who are in need of justice are not able to see you or to speak with you.'

The king was put to great shame by the words the canon spoke to him. So he laid down a statute that a man should remain at the palace gates to listen to those who sought out his help as a consequence of the failings of the court, and that this man should represent their grievances to the king, so that the magistrate and the other officials might be punished for having failed properly to exercise in such matters the office which pertained to them.

[6] It came to pass one day in the presence of the canon that, at the beginning of winter when one ought to sow the fields, a peasant farmer lost an ox and was left with only one other. So he gathered together as much money as he could and went to the market to buy an ox. The draper, to whom the peasant owed money, was at the market, and he brought a court case against the latter, and the court compelled the peasant to pay the money. The peasant asked the Canon of Mercy to assist him, and asked likewise that he be given a period of time in which he might pay, and that the ox might still be purchased so that his seed might not go to waste, and that his wife and children might have something upon which to subsist that year. For all that he begged the Canon of Mercy to act in his favour with respect to the judge and the draper, the latter would not grant the peasant an extension on his debt. The Canon of Mercy did not have the means whereby to help the peasant, for he had given away the entire income deriving from his canonry for the love of God, so he told the peasant to bring the ox that still remained to him. The peasant brought the ox, and the canon and he led the ox through the market and through the whole town, crying out to ask whether there was anyone within that town who would give himself in exchange for that ox. For all their walking around and crying out, they were unable to find a single man willing to give himself in exchange for the ox. While the canon and the peasant were leading the ox through the town, they came across the king, who was returning from Mass, so the canon asked the king whether he was willing to give himself to the peasant in exchange for the ox. The king felt great wonder at these words which the Canon of Mercy had addressed to him, so he asked the canon to explain to him what his words signified.

[7] 'My lord', said the canon, 'God gives Himself to those who give themselves to Him. And since God is of greater worth than those to whom He gives Himself, He exercises mercy with the surplus. So, greater is the mercy that God exercises in His own regard when He gives Himself to those whom He forgives and who give themselves to Him than would be the mercy that you exercise in your regard to-

wards the peasant were he to give you the ox and were you to give him yourself!'

The words which the canon spoke about God's mercy greatly pleased the king and all the others, and put them in great hope of mercy. So the king commanded that the money which the court had forcibly taken from the peasant be returned to him, and he paid the draper on the peasant's behalf. And he caused it to be written down against the draper's entry in the protocol book[212] that were the occasion to arise when he might ask the king for mercy, the king would exercise justice upon him. After this, the king laid down a rule that nobody, on account of any debt, should be dispossessed of the oxen he required to carry out his occupation.

[8] Every day, the canon walked through the city and took notice of those who caused offence or insult to mercy, writing down their names. And then he went to see the Canon of Cleanliness in order that the latter might inspire remorse in them, and he communicated their names to the Canon of Weeping so that he, in turn, might weep for their sins and so that the Canon of Affliction might fast and pray on their behalf. The canon strove day and night in this way to serve Mercy. All eight of the canons who performed the offices of the eight Beatitudes, moreover, assembled in one place and helped each other to honour the Beatitudes wherein God might be honoured. Who could possibly describe to you the benefits and good order which arose from their deeds within that city? And who could convey to you the worthy example other cities derived from these canons?

## 74. On cleanliness

[1] Every day the Canon of Cleanliness preached cleanness of heart, so that in the world to come all those who had a clean conscience might see God, as Jesus Christ had promised in the Gospel.[213] This

---

212. Cat. *capbreu*: a document signed in front of a notary, which gathers together all the formal agreements between a lord and his vassals, and includes an acknowledgement of the seigneurial rights and usages, under the terms of the lease on a property enjoyed by a leaseholder (e.g. a tenant farmer or a draper) and the corresponding obligations owed (e.g. the rent due, etc.); as such it can be construed as a seigneurial register of tenancy holders and their holdings, and can be defined as a notarial protocol book.

213. Matt 5:8. Cf. also Prov 22:11.

canon went about the city and closely observed who was in sin and who was in penance,[214] and he would preach to those who were in sin, recounting many analogies whereby he caused them to feel remorse. It came to pass one day that he made the following comparison before a large crowd of people by saying these words:

[2] 'In a certain country, there was a man who had a large serpent within his belly which was gnawing and devouring his insides. And he held in his hand a jewel that was a great pleasure to behold, the sight of which brought him a degree of relief from the concerns he felt regarding the serpent, which was torturing and killing him without his being able to protect himself against it. While the man was in this condition, a physician came to him and said that he would remove the serpent from his belly if he were to give him that jewel. This man loved the jewel so much that he did not wish to give it to the physician. But the serpent killed this man in the presence of the physician, and the physician carried off the jewel. The serpent signifies remorse, which torments one's soul because of the sins to which one has succumbed; while the jewel signifies worldly wealth, which is ill earned yet pleasant to possess; and the man's death signifies the way in which wealth remains with the living and the soul which undeservedly possesses it loses it and proceeds to everlasting fire. So, since this is the case, then, he who dies in sin while suffering remorse is more foolish than the man who did not wish to give the jewel to the physician.'

[3] While the canon was uttering these words, a man wept very bitterly in front of him, and said the following:

'The serpent is in my belly, and is gnawing my heart; the jewel is in my hands, and the physician is asking me for it. And death has come, accompanied by the Devil, who wishes to take the jewel away from me and to carry off my soul!'

The canon privately begged the man to tell him what his words signified. This man told him that he was in sin and that he felt remorse at the fact that he had not made his confession and had not renounced his sin, for he had lived in such sin for twenty years but had never confessed it. The canon strongly rebuked the man since he

---

214. The distinction being made here is between those who have sinned and have failed to make their confession and those who have sinned and have made their confession and, hence, are 'in penance'.

had not renounced sin and, in particular, because he had not made his confession.

'My lord', said the man, 'I am so very fearful that confession will take the jewel away from me, that I have no desire to confess! And when I desire to confess, yet consider that I shall not cast off the sin, I show contempt for confession, which confession is worthless if one fails to confess with the aim of renouncing one's sin.'

It was a matter of great debate between the canon and the man as to whether someone who did not intend to abandon his sin should make confession. While they were both arguing, the Canon of Mercy arrived, whom they chose as their arbiter, and his ruling was that mercy was closer to people who confessed their sin even if they did not wish to forsake it, than it was to those who made no confession. And this was because mercy, remorse and confession are in accord against obstinacy, cruelty and despair.'

[4] Before them all there passed a very nobly attired lady who had applied various colours to her face so that she might be seen to be amenable to the pleasures of lust. The Canon of Cleanliness asked in front of them all, and in such a way that the lady might hear him, which of these two things could possibly be the greater: the cleanliness of one's body or the uncleanliness of one's soul. A wise man who was standing before the canon replied, saying that insofar as the soul was a cleanlier and purer creature than was the body, it could all the more be soiled by dint of an unruly will and an unclean memory which might remember uncleanliness so that the soul might love it. The canon was very pleased by the wise man's truthful words, and he begged him to be his companion in the service of cleanliness. So, while they were both talking to each other, a pig which had wallowed in a pool of mud passed before them, so the canon said in front of everyone that that pig was less unclean than was the lady who had applied colour to her face. In that square was a foolish man, who was one of the lady's relatives and who, with menaces, reproached the canon very severely. The canon replied by saying that to remain silent about the truth was just as contrary to cleanness of heart as it was to utter words against one's conscience, and he therefore asked for a ruling as to which of the two of them had erred.

[5] Every day the canon called round at the clerks' houses so that he might know which of them led virtuous lives. And he noted their names and informed the bishop and the canons about them so that,

in the event of an election or the award of a benefice, it might be known to whom these should be given. And among the laity, he sought out and closely observed their sins and trespasses, as well as their wicked conduct and wrongful customs, putting it all in writing. And he asked for assistance in abolishing evil habits and in promoting virtuous ones. And, at night, he went through the streets calling out and blowing through a horn so that people might hear him. And he uttered these words:

'Day has passed, night has come! Before anyone goes to sleep, let him search within his conscience to see whether he has done anything today which is contrary to cleanness of heart or is against his conscience. And tomorrow ask forgiveness and make confession for such things. For if it is shameful to look upon a rotting corpse or upon the unclean places of the body, which nature commands us to conceal, how much more shameful is it to remember, understand and love sins and trespasses whereby one's soul forfeits the vision of God and sees itself forevermore in Hell amid devils, which are horrible things to behold!'

## 75. ON PEACE

[1] Bishop Blaquerna wished to perform the office of peacemaking, for those who perform it shall be called children of God.[215] The bishop, therefore, wished to take up this office and to spend a third of his income on peacemaking and on bringing peace between those who are at war or in strife.

It came to pass one day that the bishop was returning from vespers, which he attended daily in the cathedral church, where each day he celebrated Mass so that the See might thereby be more greatly honoured. While he was returning from vespers, a large number of Jews came to him to register complaints against Christians, who on Easter Eve[216] had stoned and struck two of their number. The bishop cogitated at length upon the complaints the Jews had lodged against the Christians, and considered that if Christians and Jews had a single faith, then the ill will and strife would cease. Every Saturday, there-

---

215. Matt 5:9.
216. I.e. Holy Saturday.

fore, the bishop went to pray and to dispute with the Jews in the synagogue so that they might become Christians and might praise and bless Jesus Christ, and might likewise be at peace with Christians.[217] Many Jews were baptised and came to the Holy Roman faith. And, from the third of his income, which he donated for the love of God, the bishop made generous gifts of alms to them. And he appointed a proctor for them who might provide for all those who became Christians until they had found an occupation and a means whereby they might live from their labours.

[2] In the city environs were two knights who owned a castle,[218] which had been left to them by their father, yet they were in disagreement over how it had been divided up and were in dispute over a vineyard. There was a great conflict, therefore, between both knights, and they felt implacable hatred towards each other, yet nobody was able to bring peace between them. One day, Bishop Blaquerna invited one of the knights to dine with him, and he gave him a horse and begged him to sell him his share of the vineyard, which the latter sold to him for one thousand Morabatins.[219] The following day he invited the other knight to dine with him, and he gave him a horse and bought his share of the vineyard for a further thousand Morabatins. That vineyard was only worth a thousand Morabatins, yet the bishop had purchased it twice, and each knight had intended to sell the entire vineyard, for each of them considered it to be his own. When the bishop had come into ownership of the vineyard, he went there, and begged the two brothers to assist him in dividing the vineyard into two equal shares. When both of the knights, along with the bishop, had divided the vineyard, the latter gave one part thereof to one knight and the other part to the other knight, and brought agreement and peace between them both.

---

217. On 30th October 1299, Llull himself would be granted permission by James II of Aragon to preach in all the synagogues and mosques within the latter's domains.

218. The term 'castle' frequently indicates not just the structure itself but also the entire demesne attaching thereto.

219. Also known in Castilian Spanish as the *maravedí*, a unit of currency in use between the eleventh and fourteenth centuries, which initially took the form of a gold coin, the Almoravid *dinar*, whose gold content was reduced under James I of Aragon (1213-76) and eliminated entirely under Alfonso X of Castile (1252-84), such that it ultimately became a form of silver coin. In 1247, according to the equivalency table of James I the Conqueror, the Morabatin was worth twelve Valencian sous or shillings, there being twenty sous to a pound.

[3] In that city of which Blaquerna was bishop, there was a burgher who was honoured for his lineage and wealth, though held in dishonour because he was subject to the sin of lust. This burgher was in great strife with his wife and her relatives because he had abandoned her for a prostitute, whom he dearly loved. Try as he might, the bishop could not succeed in making the burgher leave the prostitute he kept. So one day, in secret, the bishop sent a messenger to the woman, begging her to leave the burgher, and he commanded her to do so by reason of his office. But the woman replied to him that she was poor and that unless the burgher or someone else were to assist her by means of his wealth, she would not have anything upon which to subsist. The bishop begged her with such devout and humble words that she promised him she would take a husband and would not live with the burgher. The bishop donated five hundred Morabatins in dowry to the woman and endowed her with a husband. So, on account of the worthy example the bishop had set him and the fact that the woman did not wish to revert to sin, the burgher returned to loving his wife, peace was achieved between him and her relatives, and the ill will that was formerly between them ceased.

[4] One day, the Devil exerted his power and brought it to pass that in that city a draper killed a merchant to whom he owed a large sum of money for cloth he had purchased from him. That merchant had two sons, one of whom was an adult and who raised an outcry about the death of his father, so there were great divisions within the city between both sides. Nobody was able to make peace between them, so the notables of the city went to beg Bishop Blaquerna, whose office was that of peacemaking, to do whatever was necessary for there to be peace between both parties. The bishop went to the house of the man who had raised an outcry about his father, and begged him to place his brother, who was currently at school, under his control, since he wished to make him into a canon once the latter was old enough. The man gladly handed his brother over to him. Many times each week, therefore, the bishop invited him to his house so that he might grow in friendship with him; and he made him his bailiff.[220] And whenever the brother who was at school was in his presence, the bishop showed signs of great love towards this brother, the student, so that he might himself be more beloved by his bailiff. When the bish-

---

220. In the sense of steward.

op had done what was required to ensure that his bailiff loved and feared him, since love and fear are in accord with each other, he held a great banquet at which both factions in the city were in attendance. When they had feasted and made great celebration, the bishop, in the presence of everyone, endowed the younger brother with a generous benefice, and knelt in front of his bailiff, holding a Cross in his hands, and begged him, for the honour of that Cross, to forgive the draper, who had repented very bitterly for the murder he had committed. All the notables, canons and other people who were in that place knelt down when they saw that the bishop had knelt. The draper was forgiven, and concord and friendship were established between both factions, expressly via a marriage in which the bishop gave out jewels and coins from the income which had been assigned to bringing peace between people.

[5] Every day, and in many different ways, the bishop made peace between people. And he held banquets for and made gifts to each and every notable within the city. And he paid great honour to them so that they might all love him and, through their love, obey him. And when any trouble arose within the city, the bishop immediately brought peace thereto on account of the love and gratitude the people felt towards him. This bishop preached peace every day, and was in the habit of saying that war and strife were the occasion of all evil and that peace was the occasion of all good. And for this reason, Jesus Christ constantly preached peace while He was among us. And the bishop accomplished great good, and all the people praised and blessed God, Who had given them such a worthy pastor. And on account of the merits of this bishop, God blessed that city.

## 76. ON PERSECUTION

[1] The Canon of Persecution considered the great responsibility that had been placed upon him by reason of his office in order that he might exercise justice.[221] It came about one day that he was passing in front of a tavern where a large number of gamblers, goliards[222] and

---

221. Matt 5:10.
222. In the sense of gluttonous, dissolute and licentious young men. Strictly speaking, goliards were twelfth- and thirteenth-century groups of itinerant students, given to wild living and the composition and recitation of satirical Latin verse (or songs).

scoundrels had assembled, and in that place were drinking, singing, dancing and playing instruments. The canon entered the tavern and bought some wine, and he danced with the gamblers and recited these verses concerning Our Lady:

[2]  'To you, O Virgin Lady, Holy Mary,
     I give my will, which wishes to fall in love
     With you so ardently that, in your absence, it would not seek
     To desire or love any other thing.
       For every will is superior
       To every other which fails to direct
     Its willing towards you, who are the Mother of Love:
     Whoever fails to desire you can find no other love!

[3]  Since my will desires Your Dominion,[223]
     I wish to give to you my memory and intellect;
     For without my will, O Lady, to what end would they serve?
     And you, O Lady, I pray you cause the clergy
       To remember, understand and love,
       So that they may go to Syria
     To preach to and convert the unbelievers,
     And to make peace between Christians.

[4]  Many a man boasts that he would die
     For your Son, if he went to that place;
     Though few are those who go to preach Him
     To the unbelievers, for death makes them fearful.'

[5] When he had recited these verses, he asked them to be seated, to drink and to recount certain agreeable tales. While the canon was among these people, the people who passed along the road derided him and reproached him for being in the company of such worthless men. Yet the canon did all he could to ensure that he was loved by those with whom he was keeping company, and they all took pleasure in his companionship, and made him their leader, and listened to his words, which he uttered in relation to Jesus Christ and the Apostles and to disdain for this world. He regaled them with such soothing

223. Cat. *senyoria*: here, lit., 'Mistressship' (obs.).

words and placed himself in the company of such men so many times
a week that he thereby converted many of them to virtuous habits and
worthy conduct, and was not discouraged from so doing by reason of
public censure.

[6] The canon walked daily through the streets of the city, taking
special note of the tradesmen at work therein, such as drapers, cobblers, furriers, blacksmiths, butchers, and those engaged in other
pursuits. And when he learned that anyone had committed any dis-
honesty in his trade, he immediately reproached that person and
censured him in such a way that he let it be known to all those who
were in the street. All the tradesmen in that city lived in fear and
dread of him, and many of them bore him ill will, yet, because of such
fear, within their occupations, they all ceased performing a multitude
of dishonest and guileful deeds.

[7] It happened one day that the canon arrived at the drapery,
while the drapers themselves had gone out to eat, and he was accompanied by a large number of gamblers and scoundrels, and they
climbed onto the canopies that drapers fashion so that shadows are
cast in the shop and one cannot properly discern the colour of the
cloth. And they broke, tore to shreds and damaged all those canopies
and all those curtains which prevent the proper display of the cloth.
When the drapers returned from lunch, they found the canon and
his companions destroying all the wares in the shop. Heavy blows and
foul language were exchanged on both sides, and the canon and his
companions cried out 'Justice! Justice!' So the drapers went to the
court and lodged a complaint against the canon and his companions.
The bailiff and the chief magistrate of the city reproached and in-
sulted the canon and his companions very harshly, and they censured
the canon for keeping company with such worthless men.

[8] In that square was the Canon of Mercy, who had come to defend the case of his companion, and he said these words:

'The Canon of Persecution toils on behalf of justice, which desires
and commands that sunlight, which God gives to our eyes, with which
eyes He desires that we see, should not be shut out of the shops by the
dishonest drapers who deceive the people that buy cloth from them.
The gamblers and scoundrels do not conceal their vices, but rather
display them to all. The drapers conceal that which justice commands
that they reveal, and therefore the drapers are people of even lesser
worth than the gamblers insofar as they are more contrary to justice.'

When the Canon of Mercy had said these words, the Canon of Persecution and the gamblers cried out in a loud voice:

'Injustice! Injustice prevails in the king, who does not have a bailiff or a magistrate who are lovers and servants of justice!'

While crying out 'Injustice! Injustice!', the canon and his companions went to see the king, to whom they made their complaints about the magistrate, the bailiff and the drapers. And the king issued a statute to the effect that, in due course, nothing should be in front of any drapers' shop which might hinder the view of those who wish to purchase cloth from such places.

[9] In that city a knight died. And when they carried him to be buried, his wife and his relatives accompanied his corpse. They were dressed in black, wept very bitterly, and performed great mourning by pulling out their hair and tearing at their faces and their clothing. On a large and fully harnessed horse rode a squire in armour who cried out and lamented at the death of his lord, and he carried his weapons back to front. The Canon of Persecution encountered the corpse and saw, among those who wept, that the will of Our Lord God, Who desired that the knight should have passed from this world, had been dishonoured. It was the canon's duty to toil on behalf of justice, so he sought assistance from the Canon of Poverty and the Canon of Weeping, and he begged them to help him save the honour which should be rendered to the will of God. All three canons went to the prince and the bishop, and they pronounced these words before them both:

[10] 'My lords, in the two of you is represented divine authority', said the Canon of Persecution. 'I request you to judge for me whether those who weep for the knight whom God has chosen to kill do dishonour to His will. If it is judged according to law that they cause offence to God, I request the following satisfaction for this, namely, that in due course no person who weeps or who gives the impression of sadness at what the divine will has desired, should accompany a corpse, and that no obstacle to the Divine Office of the Mass should arise as a result of their weeping.'

The Canon of Weeping then spoke to say that one weeps for the purpose of feeling contrition and devotion:

'So, when those who escort the corpse weep from vainglory or from hypocrisy, and their tears are contrary to God's will, I therefore make complaint against them, who do dishonour to the office which has been entrusted to me, insofar as they do not weep for the reasons one should weep.'

The Canon of Poverty spoke next, saying that the money which had been spent on black attire had been stolen from the poor and from the soul of the deceased, and for that reason he wished to retrieve it. He added that, henceforth, what they were due to spend on black attire should be given to the poor, and that nobody should, on account of anyone else's death, be dressed in black. The prince and the bishop held counsel with the city notables as to the words which had been addressed to them by the three canons, and they decided that, within that city and in perpetuity, a law should be established in accordance with the will of the canons regarding the aforesaid matters.

[11] At that time, after the celebration of the Nativity of Our Lord Jesus Christ, it occurred that the archdeacon wished to say his first Mass. There was great congress and assembly of numerous people who had come from distant lands to do honour to the archdeacon. When the latter had entered the church with great pomp and circumstance and wished to start the Mass, the Canon of Persecution cried out in a loud voice, saying:

'So Jesus Christ was foolish, then, Who with such great humility wished to be born in such great poverty! Is not an archdeacon, who agrees to add such great solemnities to his Mass, seeking in effect to resemble Jesus Christ by way of pride and vainglory!'

[12] While the canon was crying out in this fashion, the people were threatening and rebuking him; yet, for all that, he did not cease to proclaim to the best of his ability the misdeeds the archdeacon had committed; and he declared that it was unseemly that any man who carried the devil of vainglory deep within him should say Holy Mass. The Canon of Weeping, therefore, lamented the dishonour that had been done to the Mass, and the bishop preached so that he might make peace between humility and the archdeacon. But the Canon of Cleanliness reproached the bishop, who had given the archdeacon permission to begin to practise with pride the most noble, holy and humble office there can be. And he rebuked the king, who had come to a Mass which was dishonoured by all those who were in attendance.

[13] During the month of April, there was a very severe drought in that country to which the Canon of Persecution had gone to

preach. So the bishop along with many clerks and many religious had held a procession in God's honour so that He might provide rain to the wheat, which was starting to spoil. As had become his habit, the canon went about the town in the guise of a fool, uttering certain foolish phrases so that by means thereof he might lead people towards good deeds. While the canon was going about in this manner, and everybody thought that he was a fool, he introduced himself into the very midst of the procession and loudly proclaimed these words, so that everyone might hear them:

'God is honoured by many clerks and many religious in order that He may provide rain to the wheat, though few are the clerks and religious who go to honour God among the Saracens, the Jews and the unbelievers, by whom the name of God is dishonoured and ignored. So, if in this place there are so many religious and clerks whose aim is to petition God for rain, why are there not as many such men in the entire world who go to the unbelievers to preach the Trinity, and the Incarnation and Passion of the Son of God?'

The canon cried out these words in a very loud voice and would not fall silent on anyone's behalf. So two clerks violently beat and struck him for the words he had been saying; and the harder they beat him, the harder he prayed to justice that she might assist him on the grounds that he was in her service.

[14] After the procession, it happened that a thief was being taken to be hanged. The canon asked those who were escorting him why they were going to hang him, and they replied to him by saying that this man was a great gambler and a great thief. So he asked the man whether what they had said was true, and the man answered that he was a thief so that he might be able to play dice.[224] The canon said, therefore, that the king should be hanged sooner than the thief, and on higher gallows than him. It greatly displeased all those who belonged to the king's household that the fool had said such discourteous words about the king, so they hanged the thief and then led the fool, with his hands bound, before the king, to whom they repeated the words that he had said. The king wished to know the reason why he had said them, so the canon replied that he had said them on account of justice, in whose service he was. For, since the king had failed

---

224. Cat. *jugar a la graesca* (also written: *graescha* or *gresca*): this was to play, in medieval Latin, *ad ludum de graescha*, and involved gambling with dice.

to prohibit the game of dice within his domains, this man—who would have been righteous and true were it not for that game—had become a thief.

'So, when a prince who is the occasion of evildoing hangs those who do his very will, he should either hang himself or those who do not commit evil deeds!'

The king cogitated at length upon the words the fool had spoken, and said that the latter was dissembling, and was pretending to be a fool so that he might thereby be able to make other people wise. So he commanded that honour should be paid to him and that subsequently it should be a statute and custom that in that country there should be no dice playing.

[15] It came to pass one day that the canon was leaving the city and was travelling to another such, when he encountered a large number of men on his journey who were returning from Santiago[225] and were dressed in the manner of the Apostles. The canon asked them to which Order they belonged, and they replied by saying that they were members of the Order of the Apostles.[226] The canon replied by saying that his office and the name of their Order were in accordance. The brothers who called themselves the Order of the Apostles asked him to explain the concordance he had mentioned, so the canon told them that an Apostle must be persecuted by injustice. So, therefore, if they wished to belong to the Order of the Apostles, it was necessary that in the cities, towns and castles through which they passed they should preach the Word of God and that they should rebuke people for the sins they saw them commit, and that they should not fear hardship or death, and that they should go to preach the Catholic faith to the unbelievers, in order more closely to resemble the Apostles.

The canon travelled in this manner throughout every country, and he rebuked those who failed to perform the duties of their office,

---

225. Santiago de Compostela.

226. I.e. the Apostolic Brethren (Lat. *Apostolici*) founded in Parma, northern Italy, in the second half of the thirteenth century by Gerard Segarelli (*c.*1240-1300). His was a Mendicant Order based on an apostolic model, though was prohibited in line with the decrees of the Second Council of Lyon (1274), which suppressed all Mendicant Orders founded after the Fourth Lateran Council (1215). Pope Honorius IV severely reprimanded the Brethren in 1286, and this reprimand was reiterated some four years later by Pope Nicholas IV. The Order was branded heretical specifically because it ignored the prohibition which had been issued against it.

and he was frequently persecuted and tortured by those whom he reproached. And, on account of his merits, God accomplished great good within all the countries wherein the canon travelled and had dealings, for by increasing the pain and persecution suffered by the canon, God likewise, through the merits of that canon, increased His power and grace in His people.

## 77. ON QUOLIBET[227]

[1] As had become his habit, Bishop Blaquerna ordered there to be a quodlibetal disputation so that, if any clerk or layman were to see anything which needed improving or adopting as a custom, this should be declared to him according to the method of questions,[228] in order that he might set matters right. One day, it happened that, while the Bishop was in the chapter house and had ordered such a disputation to be held, a layman raised the following question:

[2] 'Whether a bishop, in the morning, after he has risen, should go to take recreation before he attends Mass.' There were many arguments on either side; the bishop, however, resolved the question by saying that, if laymen observe the custom and rule of going to Mass before they take recreation or perform any other tasks, how much more should clerks, who subsist on the patrimony of the Holy Church, attend or celebrate Mass prior to performing other tasks or going to take recreation. And if they fail to do this, they are setting an unsuitable example to the laity.

---

227. *Quodlibeta* were formal public oral disputations in which a university Master, particularly a Master in Theology, was expected to give a determination on difficult questions relating to any topic within his field. The practice was introduced into the Theology Faculty at the University of Paris in the early part of the thirteenth century. Such disputes were not obligatory, and occasions for such only arose twice a year, namely, in the periods leading up to Christmas and Easter. The Master in question had no advance warning as to the topic or topics to be considered. The quodlibetal session would be reconvened for a second day, at which the Master in question would be expected to make his final determination on the matter or matters, this final determination often forming the substance of a published text.

228. Here Llull is referring to the dialectical method adopted by the scholastics, that is to say, the method of resolving *dubia* (dialectical problems) or *quaestiones disputatae* (disputed questions).

[3] Many questions were posed to the bishop, and he resolved and put an end to them all. These ten questions, however, were also posed to him:

[4] Question: 'Whether Christians are to blame for the ignorance of unbelievers who do not know about the Holy Catholic Faith.'[229]

[5] Question: 'Do Catholics, who are in possession of the the truth, enjoy greater power and opportunity to convert unbelievers to the true path, than unbelievers do to cause Catholics to abandon truth and embrace error?'

[6] Question: 'Whether Christians are to blame for the fact that the Saracens are in control of the Holy Land of Outremer,[230] where Jesus Christ was conceived, born and crucified.'

[7] Question: 'Whether the Christian Articles can be understood by means of necessary reasons.'[231]

[8] Question: 'Whether faith has either more or less merit if the Articles can be understood.'[232]

[9] Question: 'What is the principal reason why man was created?'

[10] Question: 'Whether visitations should be paid to bishops and archbishops for the sake of deposing them if they abuse their office.'

[11] Question: 'Which is the greater sin: either for a bishop to give the possessions of the Holy Church to his relatives or for a Christian who was previously a Jew to retain ownership of his property?'[233]

[12] Question: 'Whether one should make use of the Holy Church's possessions in order to make peace between Christian kings and princes.'[234]

[13] Question: 'Which is the noblest deed one can seek to accomplish in order to honour God?'

---

229. 'Whether' [Lat. *utrum*; Cat. *si*] is the first of the ten 'Questions' or 'Rules' introduced into Llull's later Arts. The other questions are: *quid* (what?), *de quo* (of what?), *quare* (why?), *quantum* (how much?), *quale* (which?/of what kind?). *quando* (when?), *ubi* (where?), *quomodo* (how?)/*cum quo* (with what?).

230. Lit. 'overseas'. 'Outremer' was the term by which the Crusader States in the Levant were known in the Latin West after the First Crusade (1096-99). There were three such states: the principalities of Edessa and Antioch and the kingdom of Jerusalem.

231. See above Ch. 43, § 3 and corresponding note.

232. Cf. Ch. 43, § 4 and corresponding note.

233. It should be noted that during this period and beyond, Iberian Jews and *conversos* (Jews who had converted to Christianity) were frequently subject to the confiscation of their goods, among other instances of mistreatment.

234. Cf. above, Ch. 75, §§ 2-4.

[14] The bishop felt wonder and astonishment at the aforesaid ten questions, for they indicate a very great depth of thought and much had been said on one side and the other. The bishop did not wish to determine the ten questions, so he departed for the Roman Court in order to raise them in the presence of the pope and his cardinals, so that they might resolve and determine them, and might perform the deeds befitting their resolutions and determinations. And were they to fail to do so, he would rebuke and censure them for such omission in front of everyone, without fear of suffering hardship or death.

[15] When Bishop Blaquerna was in Rome, at the Consistory[235] in the presence of the pope and his cardinals, he raised the aforesaid ten questions and said these words:

'Error prevails in the world, charity and devotion are absent and Worth has abandoned us, as has been narrated in 'The Book of Religion'.[236] I therefore ask that the ten questions be resolved and determined for me and that satisfaction be made to the rightful solution and determination so that truth may drive out error from the world and may cause charity and devotion to flourish.'

The questions greatly pleased Our Holy Father the Pope and his cardinals, as well as everyone else in the Court, so they inquired about the saintly life of the bishop, of whom they had heard many good words spoken. While the pope and his cardinals were discussing how they might answer and determine the questions, it was God's will that the pope should die, which prevented there being a resolution.[237]

Here ends the Third Book.

---

235. An assembly of cardinals presided over by the pope for the solemn promulgation of papal acts.

236. I.e. Book Two of our text, especially Ch. 48: 'On Worth'.

237. Llull recounts in his biography, the *Vita coaetanea* (1311), the fruitless journey he made to Rome to see the then pope, Honorius IV, who died on 3rd April 1287. Llull's own journey, therefore, must have occurred after this date. The Holy See remained vacant until the election of Nicholas IV on 22nd February 1288, by which time Llull had left Rome for Paris. Honorius IV was the first pope whom Llull had petitioned to set up monasteries in which languages could be taught to prospective missionaries.

# HERE BEGINS THE FOURTH BOOK, WHICH CONCERNS THE PAPAL ESTATE

## 78. ON HOW BISHOP BLAQUERNA BECAME POPE

[1] Bishop Blaquerna was greatly displeased by the death of the pope for many reasons, but, in particular, because of the questions he had raised. While the cardinals were discussing the election of a new pope, the bishop went to a cardinal and begged him to ensure that, were the election to be drawn out, he might receive a reply to the ten questions he had raised, for he ardently desired to know the intentions the cardinals entertained as regards the determination of those questions. The cardinal replied to the bishop by saying that he believed they would shortly have a pope, since it was improper for the papacy to remain vacant for any length of time. He, however, answered one of the ten questions according to his own beliefs, though without determining the matter, saying that if the Articles could be comprehended by necessary reasons, faith would thereby be of lesser worth for the reason that one would not have such great merit.[238]

[2] The bishop replied by saying that there are two kinds of demonstration. The first is when a thing is proved incontestably, as occurs with a quadrangle, where there are more angles than in a triangle.[239] The second is when a proof may be contested, as occurs when one proves the cause by the effect.[240] A demonstration, therefore, con-

---

238. See § 8 of the previous chapter.

239. I.e. a self-evident truth. Euclidean geometry is a logico-deductive method based upon axioms (or postulates) and theorems. Axioms are intuitive and self-evident statements about reality which are acceptable without controversy, and from which the theorems are derived.

240. The technical term for this form of proof, namely, from effect to cause, is *demonstratio quia*. Another form of proof is demonstration *propter quid*, from cause to effect, more potent than the former—though not mentioned by Llull here. Llull, in fact, devised a third and—in his view—superior form of demonstration, *demonstratio per aequiparantiam*, based upon the equality of the Dignities from his Art.

cerning the substance of faith may be contested. So, he did not mean to say that the Articles might thus be demonstrated incontestably, as occurs with the first kind of demonstration. For were they to be demonstrable by the first such kind, it would be impossible for the Articles to retain their status as faith. He was asking, however, whether, according to the second kind of demonstration, the Articles could be understood or not. And he conceived demonstration to be that which could not be refuted by necessary reasons, yet whose opposite could be so refuted. And he said that if the Articles could be understood by necessary reasons, then he intended to prove by such reasons that faith would thereby be nobler, greater and worthier, and that understanding and charity would thereby have a nobler disposition, as is signified in the first book of the *Demonstration of the Articles*.[241] And if such were not the case, it would follow that faith and understanding would each consist in the refutation of the other, and that is impossible according to the conditions of the Trees in the book called *On the Gentile and the Three Wise Men*.'[242]

[3] The bishop's answer greatly pleased the cardinal. So, when he was in the Consistory with his fellow cardinals, he gave high praise to the bishop's knowledge as shown by the answer the latter had given him. While the cardinal was thus praising Bishop Blaquerna, it came to pass that the clerk who used to be bishop in the bishopric where Blaquerna now held that office, arrived at Court with two friars and a layman. And all four of them had learned Arabic very well and had come to Court to ask for blessing and for letters whereby they might be sent to some country to preach and to convert that country and to receive martyrdom for the sake of praising God. While they were in the Consistory with the cardinals and were making their request, Bishop Blaquerna came into their company, and they welcomed him with the greatest of warmth. The cardinals asked about Blaquerna, so they told them many good things about him and described the benefits he had brought to the abbacy and to the bishopric, as we have previously narrated.

---

241. I.e. Llull's own *Llibre de demostracions* (*Liber mirandarum demonstrationum*), dating from 1274-76. This work applied the fundamental principles of his first Art, namely, the *ACIV* (*c*.1274), to the demonstration of the Articles of Faith. Llull's overriding purpose in this text was to show how the human intellect has the capacity to demonstrate God's existence, as well as the Trinity and the Incarnation.

242. See above Ch. 24, § 2 and corresponding note.

[4] It happened one day that while a cardinal was eating, a very finely dressed and well-arrayed minstrel arrived at his court, a man of pleasing words and handsome body, who sang and played instruments very capably. This minstrel was called the Minstrel of Worth, and was the same minstrel that Blaquerna had met in the forest before encountering Worth and the emperor, as has been related in the chapter 'On Worth'. When the cardinal had eaten, the minstrel sang songs and verse[243] which the emperor had composed about Our Lady, Holy Mary, and Worth, and he played instruments on which he performed the verse set to music[244] that the emperor had composed in honour of Our Lady. The minstrel and his instruments made for very agreeable listening, so the cardinal asked him for details regarding his estate.

[5] 'My lord', said the minstrel, 'by God's command it occurred that my lord emperor and I met a saintly man named Blaquerna, who was travelling through a great forest in search of a place where he might make his hermitage, wherein every day of his life he might worship and contemplate God. In that forest lived Worth, who complained about those who have changed her name and who persecute her within the world. So the emperor, therefore, has appointed various minstrels to travel throughout the world and to act as advocates of Worth, and he chose me from among the others to come to court to give praise to Worth and to censure all those who oppose her and who praise Unworth instead of Worth.'[245]

The words and arguments of the minstrel were pleasing to the cardinal and to all those at his court, so the cardinal ordered him to be given the fine silver goblet from which he was drinking, but the minstrel did not wish to receive it, and said these words:

---

243. Cat. *cançons e cobles*: i.e. in a general sense, 'songs and verse'; for the *cançó* in a more particular sense, see Ch. 64, § 1 and corresponding note; the *cobla* is a verse form very closely related to the classic octave, though can occasionally occur, as it does in *Blaquerna*'s final poem (cf. below, Ch. 115, § 4) in a nine-line form. The form itself entered medieval Catalan metrics from troubadour verse.

244. Cat. *fahia los bals e les notes*: *bals* (or *balls*) here indicating a type of poetic composition.

245. Both Llull and Dante adopted the medieval commonplace according to which poetry was valued on account of its capacity to praise and to blame or censure. Llull considered that it was poetry's role to praise God and to censure the vices and, therefore, that the courtly poetry of the troubadours had reversed this function, insofar as the latter praised what should be censured and censured what should be praised.

[6] 'I have been commanded by my lord, the emperor, and have bodily sworn on the Holy Gospels not to receive anything from any person other than my lord, the emperor, alone, who every year pays me an income which is more than enough for me. So, for this reason, I am exonerated from receiving your gift. For, since it is by the receipt of gifts that minstrels are corrupted into praising those who warrant blame and blaming those who warrant praise, and since by such false praise and blame Worth is dishonoured, my lord emperor, therefore, does not wish me to receive a gift from you, or any other minstrel who belongs to his court to dare to receive a gift either.'

[7] 'My fair friend', said the cardinal, 'were you to see him, then, would you recognise the man whom you call Blaquerna?'

'My lord', said the minstrel, 'were I to see him, I think that I should recognise him very easily, but I don't think I shall see him in such a place, because I believe he has made his home in an inhospitable and uninhabited location, in which place my lord, the emperor, offered to be his companion once he had set his empire in order and his son had reached a sufficient age that he might be able and know how to govern.'

The cardinal sent word to Bishop Blaquerna to come to him, and the Minstrel of Worth saw and recognised him, and felt great joy at seeing him. He felt great wonder, however, at the fact that he saw him so nobly attired and that he was wearing a gold ring upon his finger. The bishop inquired about the emperor, and recounted to the minstrel his changes of estate, about which the latter wished to learn so that he might scold Blaquerna if the devotion he had once felt towards being a hermit had since cooled.

[8] Each of them felt great delight at the other's company, and the minstrel begged the bishop to assist him in preserving Worth within that court while he was there, and the bishop promised him that he would. The following morning after Mass, the minstrel entered the Consistory where the cardinals were waiting for one another so that they might discuss the election, and the minstrel said these words:

'Worth entertains greater hope in those who are most eminent and most honoured in this world than she does in all the others; yet those who by virtue of her receive the greatest honour do her the most dishonour, and, consequently, greater fault and blame attaches to them! Through such greater fault, then, they shall have greater suffering in the next world on account of the greater dishonour that they do to Worth in this, than will those who do not hold Worth in such honour in this world.'

[9] Each of the cardinals considered at length the words the minstrel had uttered. And the said cardinal recounted to his fellows what the minstrel had told him about Blaquerna. As a result of the words the cardinal told them about Blaquerna and of others they had already heard in his regard, the cardinals desired that Bishop Blaquerna should be made pope. And they all declared and resolved that he should be pope, and they sang the *Veni Creator Spiritus*[246] and the *Te Deum Laudamus*,[247] and wanted Blaquerna to sit upon the Papal Chair, but Blaquerna refused to do so, and said these words:

[10] 'Throughout the world it is well known that the pope, together with his fellow cardinals, could bring order to almost the whole of our world, if he so wished. And since the world is in such great discord and disorder, it is a fearful thing to be pope. And great fault would be revealed in a pope, were he not to make use of his authority to bring order to the world by conforming his will to all of the authority that God has invested in the papacy for the purpose of so ordering it. So, since I am unworthy of exercising such great authority by virtue of my lack of wisdom and will, such noble and such great papal authority, therefore, should not be entrusted to one whose wisdom and will are as feeble as mine. I renounce papal authority, therefore, and request that answers be given to the questions I have raised in this Court.'

[11] The more readily Bishop Blaquerna renounced and exempted himself from the papacy, the more readily was the ardour of the cardinals kindled and stirred to make him pope. For it was a condition of the election that those who more readily renounced it and exempted themselves therefrom should sooner be elected, so long as they met the other conditions which befit a man worthy of being elected. While they remained in this predicament, and Blaquerna wished on no account to be pope, a cardinal who had the desire to be

---

246. A hymn reputedly written by Rabanus Maurus (*c.*780-856) in the ninth century. It is sung in the form of a Gregorian chant, and customarily accompanies the procession of cardinals into the Sistine Chapel at the election of a new pope.

247. The *Te Deum* is a hymn of early-Christian origin in regular use within the Catholic Church, and is included in the Liturgy of Hours, as well as being sung in celebration of the election of a new pope.

pope said that he wished to speak privately with his fellow cardinals, to whom he said the following words:

'It often happens', he said, 'that, by reason of guile, people allow themselves to be begged and forced into receiving that which they desire to possess. It seems, therefore, that Bishop Blaquerna is allowing himself to be begged to accept the papacy, so that we thereby feel a greater urge to elect him pope. If he indeed has such a desire, then, for that very reason, he is unworthy of being pope.'

[12] All the cardinals cogitated at length upon what the cardinal had said. But because no guile was indicated by Blaquerna's words, and since he enjoyed a good reputation; and, also, because they were aware, as a result of certain suspicions, that the cardinal himself wished to be pope, they knew, therefore, that what the cardinal had said was itself guileful, and they wished Blaquerna to be pope, no matter what. Yet Blaquerna would not concede to this, until a cardinal assured him that, were he to be pope, he could ordain that which he desired to achieve in terms of the resolution of the aforesaid questions. With great dread, and with the hope that God might aid him, as also with the aim of rendering the adjustments indicated by the questions more productive and useful, Bishop Blaquerna, therefore, consented, and accepted the papal office, saying these words:

[13] 'I lack the wisdom and will to be equal to papal authority! If I am elected pope by you, I ask for your assistance, so that by means of an equal will and equal wisdom we may avail ourselves of the authority invested in me to ensure that God is known and loved, and that his people are blessed by Him. If you fail to do so, you do me wrong and sin against me.'

All the cardinals promised with good grace that they would assist him in his every wish, as far as the power and wisdom that God had granted them permitted, and in accordance with the burden to which God had harnessed their will to serve Him. Following this, Blaquerna was elected pope.

## 79. ON THE ORDER POPE BLAQUERNA BROUGHT TO HIS COURT

[1] As we have recounted, Blaquerna was elected pope, for which may God be blessed! Before he decided to bring order to his Court in any respect, Pope Blaquerna devoted some time to finding out the

precise conditions obtaining therein, and each day he wrote down on some tablets he carried those things which needed to be improved within his Court.

It happened one day that the pope was at his window, and he saw a cardinal arriving with a large retinue consisting of members of his household, who were all very nobly attired and mounted. And among that retinue was a large number of people who were the cardinal's relatives. Immediately afterwards, the pope saw another cardinal arriving with a small retinue, which was less well attired and arrayed. The pope cogitated at length upon what he had seen as regards the two cardinals, so when he was in the Consistory he said these words to the cardinal who had arrived with a small retinue and in humble attire:

[2] 'I wish to know from you why you did not come to my Court with as great a retinue and in as noble attire as did the other cardinal who arrived just before you, since you are obliged to honour my Court as much as the other cardinal, and since you receive as much income as he does.'

'My lord', replied the cardinal, 'I spend on my retinue and on almsgiving all the income I receive from my cardinalate, yet have forsworn receiving any gratuities from anyone. And since my income does not allow for more, I have, therefore, been unable to bring greater retinue with me.'

The pope asked the other cardinal why he had come with such a large and well-arrayed retinue, and the cardinal replied that it was so that he might honour the Papal Court. The pope made discreet inquiries regarding the cardinal's estate,[248] and discovered that he was receiving gratuities and had violated the sacrament and broken the promise he had made when he was elected cardinal. And the people who gave him those gratuities, so that he might cause their business affairs to prosper through prayer, accompanied him whenever he came to Court, and for this reason he brought with him a greater retinue than did the others.

[3] It happened one day that the pope invited all the cardinals to dine, and held a grand court that day. When they had eaten at the court, a man dressed as a fool arrived, shaven-headed and bearing in one hand a sparrowhawk and in the other a leash to which was at-

---

248. I.e. circumstances.

tached a dog he was leading. He greeted his lord the pope and his cardinals and the entire court on behalf of his lord the emperor, and he said these words:

'I am Ramon the Fool, who has come to this court by command of the emperor in order to practise my craft and to seek my companions.'

When he had said these words, he gave a morsel of food to his sparrowhawk and then made it fly back to his fist two or three times. After this, he beat and struck the sparrowhawk with the leash to which his dog was attached, and once more summoned the bird to return to his fist, yet, because the fool had frightened it and struck it, the sparrowhawk flew off and escaped from the palace in which the pope lived and returned to the wild. When Ramon the Fool had lost his sparrowhawk, he struck his dog with two or three very heavy blows, yet whenever he called it, the dog would willingly come back to him.

[4] 'Ramon the Fool', said the pope, 'what is your estate? And why do you say that you have come to this court to seek your companions? And what is signified by that which you have done to your sparrowhawk and your dog in our very presence?'

'My lord', said Ramon the Fool, 'I was a cousin[249] at the emperor's Court and I pretended to be a fool in order to gain money. Yet the emperor told me so much about the Passion of Jesus Christ and about the nobility of God that I wish to be a fool so that I may give Him honour and acclaim. And I wish my words to transcend method, on account of my great love.[250] And since your Court enjoys greater honour than does any other by reason of the Incarnation and Passion of my Beloved, I thought I might find many companions in your Court who practise my craft.[251] The sparrowhawk signifies those people who do not help others or assist in upholding the honour and proper order of your Court without money and favours. And when one implores them

---

249. 'Cousin' is a form of address used between monarchs or between a monarch and a member of the high nobility from within his own kingdom. As an extension of this usage, the term also designates a noble child who receives at the court of a prince the education which pertains to a future knight. The reader should bear in mind that Ramon Llull's youth was spent in just such circumstances at the court of James I of Aragon (and of Majorca, from 1229 onwards) and in the service of his second son, the future James II of Majorca.

250. Here we have an anticipatory reference to the *Lover* (for which, see below, Ch. 100). The method without—or beyond—method to which Ramon the Fool refers here represents an *excessus mentis* or state of rapture.

251. I.e. other 'Holy Fools'.

yet omits to give them anything, their hearts are struck by sloth and affliction, on account of which they behave oddly and wildly towards others. The dog signifies those people who are, by love, so kindled and coupled to the honouring and proper ordering of the Court, for the purpose of honouring God therein, that, despite not being compensated for their efforts, they nevertheless endure pain and suffering for the sake of a person obliged to attend to certain things at court, and behave amiably and courteously towards people.'

[5] Once Ramon the Fool had practised his craft and had replied to the pope, the Minstrel of Worth sang and played instruments very sweetly in honour of Worth. Afterwards, he said these words:

'To honour a lord, one pays honour to his horse by providing it with a fine saddle and harness. And if the lord carries in his heart a love of virtue and a hatred of vice, then Worth is honoured in his heart as well as in his harness. And if honour is paid to the lord who loves vice and hates virtue, then Worth is dishonoured by the honour given to her enemy, who loves the dishonour into which Worth falls.'

'Minstrel of Worth', said the pope, 'what do your words signify?'

'They signify the questions you asked of the two cardinals, one of whom honoured Worth with injustice, false witness and vainglory, and the other of whom honoured her with justice, truth, humility and fortitude.'

[6] When the minstrel had uttered the above words, the pope wept, and said:

'Ah, Canon of Weeping! I wish that you were in this Court, so that you might assist me in weeping at the dishonour Worth receives herein, as a result of which dishonour ceases the honour which befits my Lord!'

The pope wept profusely, saying that if the dishonour that Worth received in his Court were not banished therefrom and Worth were not honoured therein, then all the cardinals should have committed a sin against Worth, as should most of all their lord, the pope, whom they had promised to assist, using all their wisdom and will, in maintaining the power at their disposal to honour Worth. Apart from the chamberlain, all the cardinals told the pope that they were fully prepared to give their consent and to arrange everything so that Worth might be restored to the honour she once enjoyed.

[7] Tearfully, and with great devotion, while recalling the great responsibility which had been placed upon him to honour the Passion of the Son of God, the pope said the following words:

'Fifteen cardinals have been granted to me as companions so that I may be sustained and assisted in being, on earth, the chief representative of Jesus Christ. Let us divide the *Gloria in excelsis Deo*[252] into fifteen parts, and let the first part be given to me, since I am the first by dignity of office. May a part thereof be given to each cardinal in line with his seniority as regards dignity of office and with the sequence of each successive part. And may each part constitute an office whereby each cardinal should consider himself bound to honour and preserve the Court, so that therein may Jesus Christ Himself be honoured and that by virtue of the Court He be honoured throughout all the countries of the world.'

All the cardinals approved of what the pope had said, so the pope took upon himself the phrase 'Gloria in excelsis Deo', and the cardinal who was the most senior within the Court took 'Et in terra pax hominibus bonae voluntatis', and the cardinals went on to assume the other parts, each in sequence. And to each part they assigned a particular office, and each cardinal was named according to the part which fell to him in sequence from the *Gloria in excelsis Deo*.

[8] When the pope and his cardinals had made the above arrangements, both he and they ordained that all the cardinals should enjoy an equal income, which they should spend upon their needs, and that they should keep a certain number of people and of animals in accordance with what befitted justice, temperance and humility. And in addition to their expenses, they should enjoy equally some perquisite to cover extraordinary expenditure which might be so completely sufficient as to obviate their need to receive any gratuities, unless it were in the form of foodstuffs. And were any cardinal to receive such gratuities from any person, he should relinquish his post. And if he failed to do so, the pope and his cardinals would fast upon bread and water every Friday until he had so done.

This statute was ratified by the pope and his cardinals, and a promise and oath was sworn. So, officials and spies were chosen who might detect whether any cardinal happened to contravene the aforesaid statute. And further spies were assigned to the spies themselves in order to ensure that the latter were performing their tasks

---

252. This hymn, also known as the Greater Doxology, probably dates from the second to third centuries after Christ. It was a hymn of praise to God, and a type of prayer composed by early Christians in imitation of the Psalms.

properly; and, if they were not doing so, then they should relinquish their posts and at no time might they be in receipt of a prebend.[253] The aforesaid statute was very sensibly laid down, for it is very necessary that it be adhered to, lest the cardinals, on account of their great power, engage in dissension or pride against each other. And the people who attend Court should not return therefrom having been robbed and impoverished, or set a poor example; nor should they speak ill of the pope or of his companions, but, rather, on account of the saintly lives, brotherliness and charity of both of the latter, they should acquire greater devotion to praise and serve God.

[9] After the aforesaid decrees and statutes, it was ordained that the offices the cardinals had assumed from the *Gloria in excelsis Deo* should be endowed from the coffers of the Holy Church and from the surplus which the bishops, archbishops and other prelates enjoyed following their distribution of such wealth. It was likewise ordained that one of the cardinals should be obliged to take responsibility for the expenditure all the offices would incur, and that all the bishops, archbishops, prelates and their subordinates should make sufficient contributions to the cardinal so that he might be able to endow the said offices.

[10] It was ordained by the pope and his cardinals that once a week the former should hold chapter with the latter alone, and that they should report each other's faults as do the religious, and likewise that each cardinal should receive forgiveness for his trespasses in the presence of the others.[254] This very statute was laid down by them with a view to each cardinal's holding a chapter once a week with his officials. After this, it was ordained that one cardinal should hold chapter with the Court scribes once a week, and another the following week, and likewise with the judges and the Court lawyers in sequence.

[11] The pope and his cardinals laid down a further, and highly necessary, statute, namely, that throughout the world they should have agents who might keep them informed, by letter or messenger, about the circumstances which prevailed in the various countries, so that, if anything peculiar or any change were to occur or if there were

---

253. Cf. above, Ch. 58, § 3 and corresponding note. Here it is a question of a prebend's being payable, or not, as the case may be, to an official or 'spy' from the Cathedral of Rome, that is to say, the Archbasilica of St John Lateran (here unnamed).

254. For a similar practice among the monastic orders, see above, Ch. 29, § 5 and corresponding note.

need of any improvement, they might immediately be able to discuss what might benefit or enhance the countries in question.

Pope Blaquerna disposed and brought order to his court in the above manner. Yet the benefits and adjustments he introduced therein defy description! And the merit he shall derive therefrom is impossible to relate!


## 80. 'GLORIA IN EXCELSIS DEO'

[1] Pope Blaquerna was in the Consistory with his cardinals so that by their good works glory might be given to God in Heaven. In entreaty to the cardinals, therefore, the pope asked them to assist him in exercising his office for the glory of God, in such a way that they might cause people to revert to the purpose for which the various offices and sciences were intended, namely, to give glory to God. For so flawed has the world become, that there scarcely exists anyone who directs his intention towards the very reason he has been created and the reason he performs the office he does.

While the pope was entreating the cardinals, and in the presence of both the former and the latter, a Saracen envoy delivered a letter to him from the Sultan of Babylonia.[255] Many words were written in that letter; among such, the sultan told the pope that he felt great wonder at how, when they conquered the Holy Land of Outremer, he and all the Christian kings and princes had adopted the methods of their prophet Muhammad, who occupied by force of arms the countries he had conquered, since they had not chosen to adopt those of Jesus Christ and the Apostles, who by preaching and martyrdom converted the world. And because the pope and the Christians did not adopt the methods of their forefathers when conquering countries, God did not wish them, therefore, to have possession of the Holy Land of Outremer. The Saracen brought these letters to Our Holy Father the Pope, and brought similar letters to the Christian kings and princes. The pope and his cardinals cogitated very deeply upon the words that the sultan had written to him, and Ramon the Fool said the following words:

---

255. I.e. Egypt.

'Faith asked Contrition and Hope to send her Devotion and Forgiveness, so that these might honour her in those places in which her Beloved is dishonoured.'

The Minstrel of Worth said that Worth receives great dishonour in those places where the Son of God and the Apostles did her greater favour and honour than in any other place in this world.

After these words, a messenger entered the Court bearing the news that two Assassins[256] had killed a Christian king, and that they had been violently put to death. After the messenger had spoken these words, the Minstrel of Worth said:

'Of what worth to Jesus Christ was His humility or the charity with which He offered Himself to His people and wished to undergo His Passion on their behalf if, through error, the Assassins are more devoted to dying for the sake of their master than are Christians to honouring their superior?'

The Fool saw two cardinals talking, and thought that they were discussing his Beloved, yet they were conversing about the election of two bishops who had been elected *in discordia.*[257] So the Fool, therefore, told the cardinals that the most pleasant words that exist are the words exchanged between the Lover and his Beloved.

[2] The pope was moved by great wonder to ordain that the faith of the Holy Church might yield readily to being expanded and that, likewise, the devotion towards honouring God which once prevailed might yield readily to being restored. So he sent messengers across various countries to the superiors of religious orders and to the Masters of the Temple and the Hospital instructing them to come to speak with him in order to arrange how they might give glory to God. When all of the latter had arrived and were gathered before the pope and his cardinals, Ramon the Fool said:

'The Lover and the Beloved met, and they closed[258] their mouths and their eyes, with which they had been exchanging signs of love. They wept and their loves spoke to each other.'

---

256. Members of an eastern Shia sect originating in eleventh-century Persia, now identified with the medieval Nizari Ismailis, whose presence extended to both Persia and Syria.

257. I.e. the election was disputed: that is to say, the bishops were elected by a majority vote rather than unanimously.

258. Cat. *callaren*: lit. 'silenced'.

'This exemplary tale', said the Minstrel of Worth, 'signifies that
which has been brought to the attention of the pope and his cardinals by the sultan and the Assassins. So, if no advantage follows therefrom, Worth shall have suffered an affront, while those most honoured
of creatures who die for the sake of love shall themselves remain un-
loved, albeit that loves which converse with each other are far worthier than mouths which eat.'

The Fool said:

'A scribe was writing down the names of lovers and beloveds in a
book. So a man who was a lover asked him whether he had written
the name of his beloved therein. And the scribe said to him: 'Have
you eaten food which was cooked by the fire of love? And have you
washed your hands with tears from your eyes? And have you been
made wild and intoxicated by the love you have drunk? Have you ever
been in danger for the sake of honouring your beloved? Do you possess the medicine of love whereby I may make ink with which to write
the name of your beloved? Without all these things, your beloved is
not worthy of being written in this book.'

[3] After these words, the pope, the cardinals and the religious
ordained that, in order to honour God's glory, brethren from among
all the members of the latter group who had acquired learning should
be assigned to study various languages; that houses for this purpose
should be set up throughout the world; and that they should be fittingly administered and provided for as regards their expenses, in the
manner of the Monastery of Miramar, which is on the island of Majorca. The pope and all the others were pleased by this ordinance, so
the former sent envoys throughout the nations of the unbelievers to
bring back a number thereof in order that the latter might learn the
language of the Christians and that these might learn theirs, and likewise so that Christians might accompany them to preach to the others within their countries. Moreover, those who had learned Latin
and had acquired knowledge of the Holy Catholic Faith should be
given money, clothing and palfreys, so that they might express praise
towards Christians, and so that when they had returned to their own
countries, they might assist and support them.

[4] The pope divided the whole world into twelve parts, and he
chose twelve representatives to each travel through his part and to be
informed about the circumstances prevailing in that country, so that
the pope himself might have knowledge of the condition of the

world. It came to pass that those who travelled to the unbelievers brought back Christian religious from Alexandria, Georgia, India and Greece, so that they might live among us and that their wills might be united with those of our own religious, through which union and participation they might be corrected regarding certain matters in which they erred against the faith, and might themselves go to correct those who lived in their own countries. The pope, therefore, sent some of our religious to their aforesaid counterparts, and ordained that each year they should send him a certain number of their brethren so that, while among us, they might take part in our lives and learn our language.[259]

[5] 'Beloved sons', said the pope to the religious, 'there are Jews and Saracens who believe error and who disbelieve and disdain the Holy Faith whereby we are all obliged to honour the glory of God. I ask and desire that some of those Jews and Saracens who dwell in Christian lands be assigned to learning Latin and to understanding the Scriptures; and that by a certain time they should have learned to do so, and that if they fail to have so done, they should suffer accordingly some form of punishment. And while they are learning, they should receive provision from the coffers of the Holy Church. And after they have learned, they should be made free and should be held in honour above the others. And these shall be able to convert the others, and they shall be better suited to understanding the truth and to undergoing conversion than will these others.'

[6] When the pope had uttered these words, the chamberlain said that if the pope were to lay down such a statute, the Jews and Saracens who lived among Christians would flee to other countries and the income of the Holy Church would be lessened thereby. So Ramon the Fool said to the chamberlain that a man loved a woman, which woman he informed that he loved her more than any other.

'And the woman asked him why he loved her more than any other such, and he replied that it was because she was the most beautiful. The woman pointed with her hand in a certain direction and said that there was a woman more beautiful than her over there. And because the man turned around and looked in that direction, the wom-

---

259. As well as the emphasis upon language learning, the reader should note the importance Llull attaches to the desideratum of intra-Christian unity, a theme of critical significance to the Mendicant Orders.

an said that if there were to have been another woman more beautiful than her, he would have loved that woman more. And, by this, she indicated that he did not love her perfectly.'

The Minstrel of Worth said that if anything better than God were to exist, the chamberlain would love it more than God. So he posed the question as to what was more contrary to the glory of God and to Worth, either the lessening of income or the dishonour that Jews and Saracens do to the glory of God and to Worth.

[7] The matter was ordained precisely as the pope desired. Afterwards, he asked the Masters of the Temple and of the Hospital what part they would play in honouring the glory of God, and both of the Masters replied by saying that they were already present in the Holy Land of Outremer to defend the territory and to expand the Catholic faith. The Minstrel asked Ramon the Fool whether the love he felt for his Beloved grew the more the latter afforded him joy, and the Fool replied:

'If the joy He affords me were to lessen, it would follow that I should love Him less, were I able to love Him any more.'

And since he could not refrain from loving Him, he was likewise unable to increase the love he felt in loving his Beloved. The hardships he daily underwent grew, however; and the greater these were, the more joy he felt in loving his Beloved.

Our Holy Father the Pope told the two Masters that, from what the above words signified, it followed that if they wished to honour the glory of God they should both make preparations to become a single Order, so that the Minstrel of Worth might not complain about the dishonour they cause to Worth when they are in dispute over that in whose regard they shall reach agreement if they are a single Order. He likewise said that within their own communities and dominions,[260] they should found houses and places of study wherein their knights might learn certain concise arguments from the *Brief Art of Finding Truth*[261] in order to prove the articles of the Holy Faith and to give counsel and to be counsellors to their Masters, princes and prelates, using the aforesaid Art. They should likewise learn various languages and should travel to the kings and princes of the unbelievers so as to

---

260. Cat. *maestrats*. The territories or domains under the jurisdiction of the Master of a Military Order.

261. See Ch. 24, § 2 and corresponding note.

challenge other knights to do battle either by feats of arms or learning, in order to uphold the honour and truth befitting the value
which resides in the Holy Catholic Faith. The aforesaid ordinance
was granted to the pope by the two Masters and by all the brethren of
their Order. So Ramon the Fool said the following words:

'Humility conquered Pride, and the Lover said to his Beloved, "If
You, O Beloved, were to die, I should go to weep at Your tomb." And
the Beloved replied: "Weep before the Cross, which is my sepulchre."
The Lover wept bitterly and said that excessive weeping had dimmed
his eyesight while shedding the light of knowledge upon the eyes of
his intellect.

So, therefore, the Order did everything in its power to honour the
glory of God.

[8] As has already been mentioned, Our Holy Father the Pope
ordained that the glory of God should be made law. And he selected
officials, administrators and proctors in order to achieve what he had
ordained, and he constantly strove to ensure to the best of his ability
that benefit should arise from the aforesaid ordinance. One day, it
came to pass that Ramon the Fool and the Minstrel of Worth brought
ink and paper before the pope. And they said that they wished to
send the aforesaid ordinance in writing to the sultan and to the Caliph of Baghdad,[262] in order to see whether the latter possessed as
noble subjects as the pope did, subjects in whose regard they might
fashion an ordinance as fine as the pope had done for the purpose of
honouring the glory of God in Heaven and of restoring Worth to this
world.

[9] One day, it happened that the cardinal of 'Domine Deus Agnus Dei Filius Patris' sent a spy to a certain country in order closely to
observe the conduct of the bishop and the prince of that land. While
the spy was residing there, a command was issued to the bishop on
the part of the pope to the effect that, every year, he should provide
for fifty Tatars[263] and ten friars whom the pope had sent to that bish-

---

262. The Sultan of Babylonia at the time of *Blaquerna*'s composition was al-Manṣūr
Qalūwūn, seventh Mamluk Sultan of Egypt (*c.*1222-1290). The Caliph of Baghdad was
al-Hakim I, whose reign stretched from 1262 to 1302. Al-Hakim was thirty-ninth Caliph
of the Abbasid Caliphate, and ruled, as had his predecessor al-Mustansir, from Cairo,
as a result of the sacking of Baghdad at the hands of the Mongols in 1258.

263. The Tatars were a tribe from the Mongolian plateau who became subjects of
Genghis Khan (*c.*1162-1227), the founder of the Mongol Empire. As used by Europe-

opric so that the Tatars might teach them their language and the friars teach theirs to the Tatars, as had been ordained in the Papal
Court. He likewise instructed the bishop to build a monastery outside
the city where they might live and ordered them to be granted a certain income in perpetuity. The bishop was highly displeased by the
command the pope had given to him, for he wished to spare the expense, and spoke ill of the pope and his cardinals in the presence of
that country's prince, who harshly rebuked him. The prince said that
he had never heard before of any pope or cardinals who had put
their power to such good use in ordaining that the glory of God be
honoured to such a degree. He went on to say that, in order to honour the glory of God and in response to the perfect example thereof
that the pope and his cardinals had set him, he wished to pay a
share of the expenses for which the students would be liable and
to fund half the cost of the monastery himself. The king highly
praised the ordinance of the pope and his cardinals, and said that it
seemed as if the time had come when God desired that his servants
should render great honour to Him and that those in error should
arrive at conversion.

[10] As soon as the spy had heard the words that the prince and
the bishop had spoken, he wrote those very words to his lord, the
cardinal, and he likewise wrote that the bishop had purchased a castle for one of his nephews at a cost of twenty thousand pounds, as he
had learned through close observation. These letters were read out
in the Consistory before the pope and his cardinals, and the cardinal
to whom the letter had been sent wrote down the name of the king so
that, were a crusade[264] to arise, or any favour the Church ought to
show a monarch, she should show it to him. The pope sent his envoy
to the king and, thanking him, commanded that the castle now be
his, and that he should pay ten thousand pounds towards the construction of the monastery. And he gave instruction to the chapter of

---

ans, however, the term 'Tatar' could denote Mongols as well as Turkic peoples who had
fallen under Mongol dominion.

264. Cat. *passatge*; Lat. *passagium*. There were two types of *passagium*, the 'traditional', grand-scale or 'massed crusade' of the *passagium generale*, associated in particular with Pope Gregory X (*c.*1210-76), and the later, smaller-scale *passagium particulare*.
The former was still in force at the time of the Second Council of Lyon (1274), though
had been replaced by the time of the Hospitallers' Crusade, under Pope
Clement V (*c.*1264-1314), which occurred in 1309/10. For further information, see
Jotischky (2013), 246-48.

that bishopric that, if the bishop did not wish to be bishop and to incur the expenditure which he ordered him to undertake, they should elect another bishop instead of him, and that the bishop who had spoken ill of him should receive the income of a simple canon alone.

'The Fool said to his Beloved: "Pay me, and reimburse me for the time I have served You." The Beloved increased the Lover's love and the languor he felt on account of love, and said to him: "Here are the pope and his cardinals, who honour the glory of their Lord".'

So, out of devotion, the Minstrel sent letters to console Worth, who lamented the dishonour that her enemies had long done to her Lord.

[11] The news of the pope's great goodness and his saintly life spread throughout the world, and, each day, Worth grew and Dishonour abated. The good which resulted from the ordinance the pope had decreed cast light upon the whole world and inspired devotion in all those who had heard it recounted. And a written account of the process leading up to his ordinance was sent throughout the world. It so happened one day that the pope had dispatched a knight-priest, belonging to the Order of Knowledge and Chivalry, to a Saracen king. By force of arms, this knight defeated ten other knights, one after another, on ten different days; and afterwards, by arguments, he defeated all the learned men in that land, and to all of them he proved the Holy Catholic Faith to be true. The aforesaid ordinance which Our Holy Father had decreed cast light upon the world by means of such blessed errands, among many others.

[12] Once, it came to pass that of the fifty Tatars who learned our language and understood our faith, thirty became converts. So the pope sent them, along with five friars, to the Great Khan.[265] These thirty, together with the five friars, who had learned the Tatar language, were admitted to the presence of the Great Khan, and they preached the Christian faith, converting many people within his Court. And they caused the Great Khan to set aside the error in which he had persisted and introduced doubt into his mind, as a result of which doubt, after some time, he arrived at the path to salvation.[266]

---

265. Kublai Khan was Mongol emperor between 1260-94. During that period, the Mongol empire stretched from the Pacific Ocean to the Black Sea.

266. Kublai Khan's mother was a Christian. The Khan himself had made expressions of benevolence towards Christians in communications with the papacy. Following the travels of the Venetian merchants, Niccolò and Marco Polo, father and son, to the

[13] In a certain country, ten Jews and ten Saracens were studying alongside ten friars. And when they had learned our Law and our alphabet, half of them converted to that Law, and they preached it to the other Jews and likewise preached the Holy Christian Faith to the Saracens, in front of those who had not been converted. And they did this daily and without fail. So, because the Papal Court had done everything in its power, and because the disputations were sustained over time, God, for the reason that truth prevails over falsehood, bestowed His grace upon all the Jews and Saracens of that land so that they were converted and baptised, and preached the Holy Faith to others. This being the case, then, the good and the honour that resulted to the Christian faith by reason of Pope Blaquerna lies beyond description.

## 81. 'Et in terra pax hominibus bone voluntatis'

[1] The cardinal who performed the office of 'In terra pax hominibus bone voluntatis' sent out his spies around the entire city of Rome in order to detect whether any man was in conflict with another, and he did likewise across a range of countries and, to the best of his ability, made peace his concern.

It happened one day that a spy whom he sent out around the city of Rome told him that, within this city, there was a Christian and a Jew who were in constant dispute concerning their Laws, and that there was great strife between them. Their disputes set them against one another, and each of them, therefore, bore ill will towards the other. The cardinal went to that place where they held their disputes, and spoke to them in the following terms:

[2] 'It is the nature of the intellect that it understands better when a person is happy and contented than when that person is angry, for anger disturbs the intellect and, therefore, the latter is unable to understand what it would be able to understand were that same person not to be angry. The intellect, however, has another nature whereby

Khan's capital in (the then) Peking, and further indications of his sympathy towards and interest in Christianity, the rumour spread that he had been baptised. A mission to the Khan organised by Pope Nicholas III (whose papacy spanned 1277-80), hoping to capitalise upon his conversion, met with failure, however, as the Khan had, in fact, embraced the Buddhist faith. For the above information, see Lawrence (2013), 213-14.

it may understand, namely, when one affirms as being possible that thing which the will wishes the intellect to understand. For if, prior to the intellect's understanding that thing, it affirms it to be impossible, the intellect shall not be disposed to being able to understand the possibility or impossibility which lends itself to being understood therein. The intellect has yet another nature whereby it may be enhanced for the purpose of understanding something, namely, when the will loves equally that which it affirms or denies prior to the intellect's understanding. For, when the will tends towards one side prior to the intellect's understanding it, the intellect is prevented from understanding.[267] All of these methods, and more besides, are essential to the intellect in order that it may understand. And in the event that it is still unable to understand, despite using all such methods, recourse should be had to the *Brief Art of Finding Truth*, which is an art whereby the intellect may be enhanced for the purpose of understanding, as is one's voice for the purpose of singing when trained by the art of music.'

The cardinal gave instruction in the above manner to the two wise men who had been engaged in dispute, and as a result of the humility he showed in coming to them, they befriended each other. So they disputed amicably with one another, reached an understanding, and each conceded the truth to the other. As the cardinal was leaving them, he gave them his blessing, and told them that they should send each other jewels so that these might occasion friendship between them, by which friendship they might more readily come to an understanding.

[3] It happened that, at that time, there was an intense war and great conflict between two very noble and very powerful Christian kings, who had challenged each other to combat. The cardinal, bearing letters from the pope, went to visit the two kings in order to make peace between them, taking with him a large number of jewels and a large amount of money, so that he might give the jewels he bore to each of them, and he gave plentiful gifts to their counsellors. The cardinal endeavoured to the best of his ability to reconcile the two kings. But since they had long persisted in their ill will and had never

---

267. Here Llull is referring to the functions of Figure S from his Art, and specifically to the act of 'will loving', though here combined with the principle of 'equality' from Figure T.

negotiated peace, each king felt such great ire towards the other that the cardinal was unable to bring such peace or achieve a truce between them. So the cardinal wrote these words, therefore, to the pope:

[4] 'War broke out between God and the human race once Adam had sinned and all people had been diverted from peace and from God's blessing. And because the war was very intense, it was fitting that God should come, in person, to bring peace and concord between God and His creatures. The person of the Son of God, therefore, came to assume flesh within Our Lady, Holy Mary, and, once grown, to suffer death on the Cross insofar as He was man.'

These letters were read out in the presence of the pope and his cardinals, and Ramon the Fool recounted the following exemplary tale:

'A lady was experiencing great strife with her husband. It came to pass that they had a fair son, and that, on account of their son, whom they both loved, they achieved peace and concord all the days of their lives.'

The Minstrel of Worth said that humility, charity and peace were sisters of Worth.

[5] The pope considered deeply what the above words signified and, because of the desire he felt to achieve all that was good, he understood their signification. The pope, together with three cardinals, went to visit the two kings, who lived far from Rome, and he gave gifts and jewels to both of them, and he held a great court consisting of prelates, princes and barons, and went to great expense within that court. Before the pope spoke about peace between the two kings, he said in the presence of everyone that he had come to that country in order to ensure that a crusade took place against the enemies of the Cross, and that he desired and prayed that both of the kings might take charge of that crusade. Moreover, he wished that one king should direct his forces against the Saracens who lived in the east, and the other against the Saracens who lived in the west. And, once they had defeated these, each should make his way towards the other so that, together, they might defeat the Saracens who lived in the south.[268] The pope granted full remission of sins and ordered a cru-

---

268. The Almohad and Marinid dynasties account for the western Saracens mentioned here. The Sultanates of Egypt and Tunis, under the Mamluk and Hafsid dynas-

sade, and from the coffers of the Holy Church he made great gifts to the two kings and to other barons, and took the territories of the two kings into his care and under his command. The two kings were so greatly pleased by this ordinance and each of them felt such a great desire to do combat, that they both agreed that they should place their dispute in the hands of the pope. So they took up the crusade and suspended the argument over which they were in disagreement, so that the crusade might not be disrupted thereby.

[6] The two kings set off on a very great crusade, accompanied by a large number of friars who had learned Arabic in order to be envoys to the Saracens, so that the latter might be converted rather than being killed by the two kings and their souls' going into everlasting fire. The pope returned to Rome and ensured as best he could that the crusade might have everything it required.

The cardinal who held the office of peace-maker lived for a long time in the land of the two kings so that he might reconcile their two peoples. It happened one day that he was out riding, and he passed through a town square in which two drapers were arguing because each envied the other as regards what they earned, for it seemed to each of them that the other was eroding his profit. The cardinal purchased both of their workshops, which belonged to a burgher of that city, and had two more shops built, each a long way from the other, and gave one to the first draper and the other to the second draper. And from the two workshops he had purchased, he had two houses fashioned. In each of these, he placed a man in order that both might live as recluses and subsist on alms, and might preach peace and edifying words to the people gathered in that square or who passed along the street.

[7] It came to pass that one of the cardinal's spies passed through the square and saw that both of the recluses were having a dispute and were exchanging foul language on account of the fact that each was envious of the other. When the cardinal learned of this, he evicted one of the recluses from that place and moved him to another location distant from the one from which he had evicted him. And out of the house from which he had ejected him, he made a square in

---

ties respectively, account for the eastern and southern areas identified by Llull. Modern-day Libya and Algeria also fell under the Hafsid dynasty during this period, i.e. after 1229 when the Hafsids split from the Almohads.

which might stand the people to whom the recluse could speak about peace and about God, and he made a similar square for the other recluse. Both of the recluses accomplished great good within that city, and the enactment to the effect that in town squares, where so many ills occur, there should be people who curb such ills through their example of virtuous living, their devout words, and their reading of books of prayer and devotion, was highly commendable.

[8] The cardinal went to another city which fell within the domains of both an archbishop and a king, who were in dispute concerning the boundaries of that city, and there was, therefore, great conflict between them both. The cardinal was unable to reconcile them since he could not dislodge the greed which had taken root in each of their souls. The cardinal went to Rome and begged the pope to come in order to bring peace between the archbishop and the king. The pope immediately went to that city in which the dispute was occurring. The pope summoned the king and the archbishop and held a great banquet and reception. That day, the pope preached about peace and about how Jesus Christ had always preached peace. Before they went to eat, the pope wanted the king to reveal to him the matter of his dispute with the archbishop. The king showed the pope the boundaries up to which he claimed his dominions extended, and the pope told the king that he had understood the latter's dominions to extend further than that. So he wanted the king to accept the land belonging to the Church, for the peace which would result from this was of greater worth than was the income that the archbishop earned therefrom. When the king realised that the pope wished to grant him more of the city than that to which he had laid claim, he said to the latter:

'My lord, come and take your share of the part that belongs to me, of which I have long divested[269] the Church.'

So the king wished to transfer to the Church more than that to which the bishop had himself laid claim. There was great toil and strife before the pope and the king could be made to reach an accord, for each wished to grant the other his right. The dispute was, therefore, placed in the hands of two men who were familiar with the truth concerning the city's boundaries, and their decision was fol-

---

269. The technical term for this in English, i.e. 'to disseise': 'to wrongly dispossess of a freehold interest in land', may be applicable here.

lowed, and peace and friendship were established between the king and the archbishop.

[9] In a city in which the cardinal who was going in search of peace found himself, there was an elderly man who had a young wife. He loved her so ardently that he felt great jealousy in her regard, which jealousy caused him very great turmoil. And he was so intensely jealous, that his wife and all his entourage were thereby also caused great turmoil. It came to pass one day, that the jealous man was in the town square when the cardinal passed through, and everyone said 'Here is the cardinal who goes in search of peace!' This man considered whether the cardinal could bring him peace and rid him of the turmoil which jealousy had brought to him.

When the cardinal was at his lodgings, the jealous man told him in private about his situation, and begged him to give him counsel as to how he might attain peace. The cardinal uttered many admirable words to this man, and told him that he should come to speak with him once every day. So the cardinal spoke to the man's wife in private, advising her not to adorn her clothing, apply colour to her face or betray upon her body any indications of lust. He advised her, moreover, to render full honour to her husband and to exercise patience, were the latter to speak in anger. When the cardinal had instructed the lady, completely unbeknown to her husband, he preached daily about God and about saintly living, censuring lust and praising chastity. And wherever he preached, he always took with him the man afflicted by jealousy. And when he was at his lodgings, the cardinal invited the jealous man to dine with him and they both read from Holy Scripture. And the cardinal stayed so long in that city with a view to bringing peace to that man, that the jealousy the latter once harboured completely vanished, for the words the cardinal had spoken to him concerning God, and the virtuous life of his wife, had rid him of the habit of dwelling upon those thoughts whereby a man becomes jealous.

[10] The cardinal went to another city in order to find out whether there was any strife therein. It happened one day that, as was his habit, the cardinal sent four of the city's notables to ascertain for him whether there was need within that city for him to make peace between any man and another. Among those four notables was a man who was of noble descent and had been extremely wealthy, and he was in great turmoil night and day when he considered the fact that he could maintain no more the lofty status with which he had begun

and which he had long retained. This nobleman, therefore, asked for the cardinal's counsel, recounting to him the turmoil into which his thoughts had cast him. He had no wife, though he had five sons. The cardinal counselled him to join a religious order so that he might not dread being reduced to shamefaced poverty, and entrusted one of his sons to the prince of that country and another to a bishop so that he might become a clerk; another, he adopted for the purpose of raising him and providing him with a benefice. The remaining two received handsome bequests from the father's possessions, while the father himself, taking flight from the world and from the vainglory to which he had been in the habit of succumbing, entered a religious order and lived in peace all the days of his life.

[11] While the cardinal was staying in that city, a messenger sent by one of the spies he maintained came to him from Rome, requesting him to go there to make peace between two proxies in the service of two princes who were in great conflict with each other. The cardinal went to Rome and secretly sent a message to one of the proxies, and made him swear to keep what he would tell him secret. After the cardinal had made him swear to do so, he told him that he would send jewels and gifts in his stead to the other proxy with whom he was in dispute, and that since the latter was a greedy man and would think that it was the first proxy who had sent him the jewels, his anger would be curbed. And if his adversary were to thank him for anything, he should make it seem as if he had, in fact, sent them to him. And the cardinal spoke likewise to the other proxy. So the cardinal would often send jewels to each of them in like manner, so that each thought that one was sending them to the other. On account of the jewels that the cardinal had sent, the two of them exchanged thanks and greetings. And without the cardinal's having to say anything more, they both became friends and behaved amicably towards one another. The cardinal brought peace between people in this way and in many others, so that they might feel goodwill towards each other and that peace might prevail on earth, in order that such peace might lead to the path of salvation. The cardinal achieved great good, and as soon as there was any conflict on earth men had recourse to him so that he might negotiate peace between people.

[12] The cardinal had proctors in the courts where the disputes and lawsuits were heard in order to reconcile those who were pleading their cases, and he frequently came to court to make peace be-

tween such people. There were likewise Beguines of his close acquaintance, as well as virtuous women, to whom he imparted a Rule and instruction as to how to bring peace to women who were in strife with each other. The great good the cardinal accomplished through reconciliation was so pleasing to God and to all the people that, on account of the cardinal's merit, He granted peace and blessings within the territories through which the cardinal travelled and in which he lived.

## 82. 'Laudamus te'

[1] The cardinal of 'Laudamus te' assumed the office of praising. And he sent out his proctors to the Roman Court and across Christian territories for the purpose of praising God. And he himself frequently travelled through these territories in order to give praise to God and to the activity He enjoys in respect of Himself, namely, as regards His divine Persons, as well as to the activity He exercises by way of His creatures.

Once, it occurred that the cardinal was praising God within a city in which there was a lady who had two sons, one of whom was a clerk, the other a layman. And the lady and her sons praised God; so, in that city, a debate arose as to which of all three of them praised God most fervently. Each side had its advocates, who described in the following manner the praise that each of them offered to God:

[2] The upstanding lady who was the mother of the aforesaid two sons had raised them to praise God, and it had been her habit, since her husband died, to call on women in order to reproach them as regards those matters in which they committed wrong and to praise God to them as best she could. And on account of the reproaches the lady offered to the other women as far as their attire, their ablutions or the wickedness of their conduct were concerned, there were many women of exemplary customs in that city, and they all feared her on account of how keenly she discovered, ascertained and reproached their secrets and their wrongdoing.

[3] The clerk was a priest, and he loved poverty and celebrated Mass every day. And when it was mealtime, he would go to someone's house and beg to eat that day, offering to say Mass the next day for that person's soul. Often the clerk would go to eat and to receive alms

with the paupers at the gates of monasteries or of the bishop's palace. And he would call on other clerks, whom he reproached for the wrongs he saw them commit, and he did not hesitate to tell the truth to any clerk whom he witnessed holding honesty and saintly living in contempt. So, in reproaching them he praised God and in praising God he reproached them. It was the habit of this clerk to go daily through the city streets and, when, as he went along, he encountered clerks whom he saw doing wrong, he would reproach them. After this, he would go to the churches, in which he would remain in prayer and contemplation while praising God, and he would reproach the clerks in the church when he saw them commit any wrong; and he did likewise in the other churches.

[4] The other brother, who was a layman, would go through the streets of the city and, when he found any other layman who erred as to his attire, his bearing or his speech, or in whichever house he might be, he would immediately reproach him without fear of censure or harm thereby to his person. And when he had reproached them, he praised and blessed God in front of those same people. And on account of his boldness in reproving those who committed wrong and in praising God, all the people of that city feared him, especially those who committed wrong.

[5] This man accomplished great good within that city, as did the lady and the clerk. A debate arose, therefore, among the women, the clerks and the laymen as to which of all three of them praised God the most. And each side supported the person who, among its number, was the praiser of God. Each of the sides went before the cardinal and raised the question. This question greatly pleased the cardinal; so he took it to Rome in order that the pope might resolve it, and that in the city of Rome there might be another lady, another clerk and another layman who might praise God in a similar fashion, and that the pope might decree that in that city these three offices should exist in perpetuity.

[6] When the cardinal was in Rome and had raised the question before the pope and his cardinals, Ramon the Fool came into their presence bearing fire and firewood, a sieve, flour and water, and he said that he wanted to make a loaf of hope, charity, justice, chastity and humility so that with it he might be able to feed those in whom there was despair, cruelty, injustice, lust and pride. After these words, the Minstrel of Worth said to the cardinal who had raised the ques-

tion that he begged him to ensure that attention be paid to Ramon the Fool on this matter, since it was precisely in order to praise God and to reproach the vices of the Roman Court that Ramon the Wise had assumed the office of Fool. The cardinal and all the others were greatly pleased to pay attention to Ramon the Fool on this matter.

[7] While the pope and his cardinals were discussing how they might resolve the question, one of the emperor's couriers brought a letter to the Minstrel of Worth stating that he should ask the pope and his cardinals on his behalf to judge which of the four praise-givers, who praised Him in the manner described by the following words, did so most fervently,:

[8] 'In a monastery there was a brother who was a man of saintly life and was a very great scholar. This brother was devoted to praising God for those activities which He enjoys in respect of Himself, namely, as regards the Father's generation of the Son and the Holy's Spirit's procession from the Father and the Son.[270] This brother gave himself over completely to praising the Trinity by saying that the praise which should be given to the noblest activity there is must be above all things. And since the greatest activity is to generate God and to give Him procession, in which generation and procession resides an infinity and eternity of goodness, power, wisdom, love and perfection, the brother, therefore, had no intention of praising God unless it were in respect of His Holy Trinity and Unity. This brother praised God in word and in thought, as is mentioned above, and, by means of His creatures and the activities God achieves in those creatures, he strove as best he could to prove to Christians that in virtue of which he praised God. And, on account of the praise he both uttered and proved, devotion and charity arose in those to whom the brother praised God; and, on account of such devotion and charity, many good works ensued and many evils ceased.

[9] 'There was a bishop who was devoted to praising God in terms of His Incarnation. For the greatest activity that the Creator can accomplish in a creature is for that Creator to unite a creature to Himself, with which creature He is but a single person. So, on account of

---

270. Roman Catholic Trinitarian theology specifies that the Son is 'begotten' of the Father and that the Holy Spirit 'proceeds' from The Father and the Son, jointly. These intra-Trinitarian relationships are also termed 'generation' and 'spiration', respectively. Latin Christians and their Eastern Orthodox counterparts have long been in dispute over this double procession, known as the *Filioque* clause.

the great devotion the bishop felt towards praising God in respect of
the greatest activity He can accomplish in a creature, he became likewise devoted to going to praise Him among the unbelievers, so that
by such praise he might be able to convert them and might also be
able to suffer martyrdom. This bishop went to the land of the Saracens to praise the Holy Incarnation and Passion of the Son of God,
and he accomplished great good within those lands and suffered
martyrdom for having praised God.

[10] 'In that city wherein the bishop had suffered martyrdom was
a philosopher who was a very great master of that subject. And on account of the words he heard the bishop say about the Incarnation of
God, he became a Christian and devoted himself to praising God in
those territories wherein God is not known and all of the people who
inhabit them worship and believe in idols. This philosopher travelled
to those lands to praise God, to prove that He exists and that He is
One, Who is the First Cause and the Supreme Good. And he praised
God for the good He performed in His creatures, which according to
their goodness signified the goodness of their Creator. While the philosopher was proving, by means of His creatures, that God exists and
is wholly good, the people of that city put him to death and he became a martyr for having praised God, Whom he had praised as being Lord of all the creatures.

[11] 'After the death of the philosopher, a Christian knight went
to that city where that philosopher had become a martyr for having
praised God. And in that city God had performed many miracles as a
result of the philosopher's death, on account of which miracles many
people had become converts. The knight went to that city to challenge to hand-to-hand combat any man who might say that God did
not exist or that God was the sun, the moon or the other creatures
which idolaters venerate as a likeness of God. The knight did combat
with a great number of knights from that land, and defeated many
thereof. Yet, in the end, an archer fired an arrow at him which split
his heart in two, so the knight became a martyr for having praised
God through the exercise of arms.'

[12] After the letters had been read, the pope and his cardinals
praised and blessed God for the praise the four said praise-givers had
given to Him. And in the Court many arguments were advanced for
the purpose of pleading on behalf of one side or the other. And the
more resolutely the sides disagreed with each other when it came to

deciding which of all those four had given greater praise to God, the more fully devotion flourished in the people who were listening to the dispute between the sides. The cardinal of 'Laudamus te', therefore, said to the pope that he should defer resolving the aforesaid questions for a long time, and that in his Court advocates should be introduced who might continually plead on behalf of each of the sides, and that all their arguments should be set in writing. For if, within his Court, a suit between two kings, who were in dispute over the empire, had lasted for twenty years, how much longer ought the determination of the aforesaid questions be delayed, so that thereby, within his Court, devotion and a fitting example might flourish more fully, by which devotion and example many similar praise-givers and martyrs might be brought into being!

[13] That which the cardinal had requested was granted by the pope and the other cardinals, so advocates who might plead on behalf of the various sides were endowed from the coffers of the Holy Church. It came about one day that the advocate who was pleading on behalf of the bishop who perished for having praised the Incarnation of God, put forward two arguments as part of his suit, namely, that God can be more greatly praised for His justice and mercy with regard to a sinful clerk than he can with regard to any other man, since, because a clerk performs the office of Jesus Christ, he is more sinful when he sins than is any other man, and for that reason God can thereby manifest greater justice if He punishes him or greater mercy if He forgives his sins. And since this greater demonstration of praise is yielded by the Incarnation of the Son of God, by the sacrifice of the altar and by the Passion of Jesus Christ, the advocate intended to prove, therefore, that the bishop had more roundly praised God than had all the others. The other advocates availed themselves of similar arguments, and many sound arguments and questions were articulated in the above case, from which there arose great good within the Court.

[14] While the above case was being conducted daily in the Court, Ramon the Fool posed a question to the pope and his cardinals as to how it could be and why it was that the Apostles, who were poor in terms of worldly goods, receive greater praise than their successors, who have become richer since they have been in possession of the empire of Rome. The pope replied to Ramon the Fool that it was easy to resolve this question.

## 83. 'Benedicimus te'

[1] The cardinal of 'Benedicimus te' came into the presence of the
pope and his cardinals accompanied by a great number of men to
whom he had entrusted a range of offices for the purpose of blessing
God, which men might travel through various countries in order to
bless God, so that God Himself might bless those countries for the
reason that His name had been blessed therein.

It was the duty of these men to go through the streets proclaiming:
'Blessed be God, Who has created trees, animals, birds, men, metals,
elements, heavens, stars, angels and all the other creatures! And blessed be God, Who lends order to the world inasmuch as He has created
diverse offices therein: clerks, knights, monks, prelates, princes, farm-
ers, merchants, blacksmiths, carpenters, drapers, cobblers, furriers,
butchers, fishermen, and all the other offices!' These men have promised to proclaim and bless God for the fact that He chose to become
incarnate, to be put to death and to perform miracles; and that He has
created Paradise and Hell; and, likewise, that He shall resurrect the
virtuous and the wicked, assigning the former to everlasting glory and
the latter to eternal torment. It is the duty of such men, moreover, to
proclaim and bless God as regards His Essence, His Trinity, His Virtues,
and all things which may signify His nobility.

[2] When the cardinal had informed the pope and the other cardinals about the ordinance he had issued as regards blessing the name of
God, he begged the pope to grant forgiveness to all those who would
hold this office and to ensure that the clergy gave them food while they
were in the territories in which they would bless God's name. The pope
and his cardinals were very pleased by what the cardinal had ordained,
and the pope issued a command to all the bishops to the effect that they
should each take care of such men while the latter were within their
bishoprics, and he granted the men full remission of sins and sent them
out in pairs, enjoying his privilege, across various bishoprics.[271] They
praised and blessed God in wondrous fashion, proclaiming His name
and His virtue day and night. As a result of the blessings they pronounced concerning God, God Himself blessed them and their words,
and imparted devotion to people whereby they lived saintly lives.

---

271. A papal privilege or indult exempts its holder from the normal operation of
Canon law. Privileges were customarily issued to accompany military campaigns.

[3] The cardinal would go through the city of Rome carrying a great number of coins which he would donate to the poor so that they might bless God. And as he was going through the streets, he would implore people to bless God. It came about one day that a crier who used to cry the wine[272] considered the cardinal's great devotion and, by divine will, earnestly desired to become a crier of God's name, so he went to the cardinal and, with the latter's permission, assumed the office of proclaiming that God's name is blessed. And the cardinal gave him five shillings of income every day from which he might live, and with which he might buy hazelnuts and fruit to give to the children who followed him while proclaiming that the name of God is praised and blessed, by calling out: 'Blessed be God! Praise be to God! May God be worshipped! May God be obeyed! May the operation and virtue of God ever be praised and served!' This crier, without fail, went through Rome surrounded by children, and together with these he proclaimed and blessed God and His virtue. While the crier and the children did as described, many sinful people remembered, understood and loved God, by curbing vices and fostering virtues within their hearts. And righteous people heightened their devotion through loving and serving God.

[4] It so happened that, in a city to which two men who proclaimed and blessed God had travelled, a wise merchant had lost his wife, so he conceived the desire to bless God in that manner whereby he could do so most effectively. So he converted everything he owned into money, with which he bought a palfrey and a golden goblet. And he rode the palfrey while carrying his goblet, and he proclaimed throughout the town that he would give that palfrey and that goblet to the man who could best instruct him to bless God. While the merchant went about throughout the city proclaiming in this manner, many men within that city felt a strong desire to own the palfrey and the golden goblet, which were worth a great deal of money, so they conceived of many different ways to bless God. A dispute arose, therefore, as to which of these was the best way to do so.[273]

---

272. Criers of wine were evidently common in the Catalan territories. A wine crier would cite the prices of the wines he had on offer and present samples for tasting.

273. §§ 5-12 below detail some of the questions or dilemmas presented to the merchant so that he might decide on whom he wished to confer his palfrey and the goblet.

[5] In an election, a canon received many votes to become bishop, yet he blessed God for the fact that he was not such. And the bishop who carried the election blessed God for having charged him with such a great and hazardous responsibility and such an honoured and useful office. And so the question arises as to which of them gave a greater blessing to God.

[6] The question is, who gives greater blessing to God: a person to whom God has brought an increase of wealth and given health and honour in this world, and who blesses God accordingly; or a sick and dishonoured person whom God deprives of his worldly goods, yet who nonetheless blesses Him?

[7] A man mortally wounded another, who had done him no wrong. And the wounded man blessed God and exercised patience, while the man who had wounded him likewise exercised patience, and he praised and blessed God and judged himself to be guilty while he was being hanged.

[8] There was a man who praised and blessed God when he saw lepers and animals and sinful people, on the grounds that He had not made him a leper or an animal, but a man. Another man blessed Him for having given him the grace to live without mortal sin. The question arises, therefore, as to who blessed Him more perfectly.

[9] The question arose between a man and a woman as to who should more greatly bless God: the man, because He had not made him a woman; or the woman, because she was not a man and was more downtrodden in this world than was man?

[10] A different question arose between a Christian and a Saracen, namely, which of them, according to their Laws, should more greatly bless God?

[11] A question arose between a lady and her son, since the son blessed God for having given him a good mother, while the mother blessed God for having given her a good son.

[12] A king blessed God for having given him good subjects, while his subjects blessed God for having given them a good prince. The question arose, therefore, as to who blessed God more perfectly.

These questions and many others were handed in writing to the merchant, so that he might confer the palfrey and the goblet upon the person who had brought him the question that most clearly signified in all likelihood which of them blessed God in the most commendable manner.

[13] When the merchant was in possession of the aforesaid questions, he went to Rome, riding on his palfrey and bearing the questions and the golden goblet, in order to see the cardinal assigned to blessing God. And he begged him to have the aforesaid questions settled for him, so that he might adopt the most suitable manner in which to bless God and might give his goblet and his palfrey to the person who had brought him the best question. The cardinal, accompanied by the merchant, went into the Consistory to stand before the pope and his cardinals for the purpose of resolving the questions. A decision was reached by the pope and his cardinals, however, that lengthy discussions should be held at court concerning the questions, lest these be forgotten, and so that by remembering them many people might be afforded an example and the necessary devotion by which to praise and bless God, in the hope of fostering the custom and practice of blessing Him, whereby the office of cardinal might be of greater benefit. A statute was laid down, therefore, to the effect that at the gates to the church of Rome should be fashioned a marble palfrey being ridden by a man bearing a goblet, and that in the inscription should be written the above-mentioned questions and the reason why the merchant came to Rome.

[14] One day it occurred that the cardinal was riding through the city to see if he could hear any man blessing God, and he passed in front of a tavern where there were many rogues and scoundrels who were playing dice. And one of them cursed and blasphemed God, uttering many foul and filthy words about Jesus Christ and Our Lady, Holy Mary, on account of a game of dice he had just lost. The cardinal descended from his palfrey and gave it to the rogue who had been blaspheming God so that he might bless Him and never again blaspheme Him. And he went to the pope and his cardinals, and said the following words to them:

'One day, a friar was at Mass, which was being celebrated by a Master of Theology, and this friar considered the master, who, through his words, had long been explaining how God should be blessed by his students. So, I am stirred to very great anger', said the cardinal 'when I cogitate upon the fact that there are so many rogues and scoundrels who curse and blaspheme God, Our Lady, and the saints in glory, over a game of dice. I demand that satisfaction be made to me for the wrongs and injustices that dice-playing has done to me in abolishing the office which has been entrusted to me. If satisfaction regarding my office is not made to me by those who have the power to do so, they shall be in conflict with God's blessing and in accord with receiving His curse.'

The cardinal spoke such forceful words to the pope and his companions that he cast their hearts into contrition and deep thought, and they became aware of the power they held, which power exceeded their will. So the Minstrel of Worth said:

'Of what use is a Lover if he fails to prevent the dishonour of his Beloved?'

And Ramon the Fool said that the Lover was once tormented by his Beloved, and his tormentors asked him whether it was the right time for him to take a rest even as they tormented him. So he replied by saying that as long as his Beloved knew about it, it was the right time for him to take a rest from the trials he had endured for the sake of Him.

[15] While they were engaged in such talk, a legate entered who told the pope that he had fulfilled the latter's command by excommunicating a prince who had divested the Church of its property. So the cardinal of 'Benedicimus te' asked the pope which of the following should be prohibited more forcefully: that in virtue of which people blaspheme and dishonour God or the prince who had dispossessed a single bishopric alone?

[16] One day, Pope Blaquerna was riding through the city of Rome and he saw a large group of rogues who were at a tavern, and were calling out and proclaiming 'Blessed be God's name!' The pope asked how it could be that rogues were blessing God in such a place and that He was being blessed by such people.

'My lord', said a knight who came from the city of Rome, 'a rogue to whom the cardinal of 'Benedicimus te' gave a palfrey has acquired the habit, when in the company of other rogues, of uttering words to them concerning God. And he utters such devout words that he often causes them to weep, on account of the words he speaks to them about God and His Passion. And he consoles them in their poverty and leads them to exercise patience. And when he has imparted such devotion to them, he causes them to bless and proclaim the name of God. So all the rogues and scoundrels in this city have made that rogue their lord and leader, and that rogue practises such good customs that he imparts intense devotion to people through his words and his good works.'

The pope was very pleased to hear these words spoken about the rogue, and he said that even if the latter's reputation was shameful, his life was saintly and glorious. The pope summoned the rogue and asked him how he had been able to make such shameful people as rogues and scoundrels bless God, and in a tavern, of all places.

'My lord', said the rogue, 'in such places as God's name is most often dishonoured and by such people as bless Him the least, must one endeavour all the more to ensure that His name is praised and blessed.'

The pope cogitated at length upon the words the rogue had addressed to him, and said that it was highly necessary for God's name to be blessed by those people who are unbelievers, who pay no honour whatsoever to His name.

[17] When the pope had said these words, a knight came to him and spoke as follows:

'My lord, I have been a man-at-arms and have devoted my entire life to killing and slaughtering men so that I might gain glory and a good reputation[274] at arms among people. Were it to please you, I should wish to perform every day of my life the office of going among people who are nearing death, either as a result of justice or of sickness, and of speaking to them about God, so that I might make satisfaction to Him for my wrongdoings. I should perform this office to the people who are dying, so that thereby they may be more confirmed in their faith and in the mercy of God, and that, in death, they may praise and bless His name; and that, afterwards, I may act as consoler to the relatives of the deceased.'

The pope conferred the office upon the knight, and when he had returned to his palace, he wrote a book in which he set down the teachings he wished to impart to the knight, including the words the latter ought to say to the people as they lay dying and to those who were in need of consolation. The knight committed to memory the book in which were written the words corresponding to that office, and he went through the city of Rome in the hope of detecting those who were nearing death. And he uttered such devout words to them that they were thereby confirmed in their faith. And he led them to

---

274. Cat. *nom.* Llull is setting up a contrast in these sections between the 'name' or reputation attributable to human beings and the 'name' or reputation of God, which must be praised and blessed.

feel such remorse, that he caused them to make amends for any wrongs or injustices they had committed. And he led them to despise this world and desire the world to come; and as they died, they blessed and praised God. And the knight uttered so many wholesome words that the dying people's relatives were thereby consoled and granted patience, and they praised and blessed the justice and mercy of God accordingly. The knight accomplished such great good within that city that when any person was nearing death or when anyone was in need of consolation, they always sent a messenger to the knight, who brought with him his book, and read and spoke the teachings Pope Blaquerna had imparted to him.

## 84. 'ADORAMUS TE'

[1] The cardinal of 'Adoramus te' was deep in thought as to how he should adopt a method whereby God might be fervently worshipped by His people. And he considered that he should go away to live all alone for a certain period in the company of a saintly hermit who resided on a high peak, and that in that place he should likewise consider the method whereby he might ensure that God was worshipped and contemplated as befitted Him and as He has charged us to do. While the cardinal was on his way to see the hermit and was considering that which he so ardently desired, on the road along which he was passing stood a church, in which an impoverished man served as its lamplighter[275] and ensured that Mass was celebrated, by begging for the alms that people would give him. In that church was a very large and very nobly carved and inlaid crucifix. But a pilgrim had entered that church and, by throwing stones, was breaking and shattering the crucifix, while the man who served the church was doing all he could to prevent him. While the two men were struggling with each other, the cardinal arrived and entered the church. He felt very great wonder at the pilgrim who had cast stones at the crucifix, so he asked him why he had dishonoured the form[276] which represents the image of Jesus Christ.

'My lord', said the pilgrim, 'in times gone by, it was the custom for people to worship idols, yet, in our own times, there are still many

---

275. Cat. *lumenaria*.
276. Cat. *figura*: 'form, shape, figure'.

people who do so. And the Saracens and Jews reproach us Christians for worshipping images. For a carved and inlaid image is closer in form[277] to an idol than is a simple one, and so, to indicate that simple images are more suitable than ones that are inlaid, I have made it my custom to destroy all the carved images upon the altar that resemble idols.'[278]

[2] While the cardinal and the pilgrim were having this discussion, a man who had come from far off lands entered the church and knelt before the altar, worshipping and praying to God very intently. The cardinal thought that God had placed some special power in that man whereby he worshipped Him so devoutly, and he wished to learn from him the method according to which he worshipped God.

'My lord', said the man, 'it is little short of customary for all the other people in this world to worship God so that He may give them glory rather than punishment, and they very often worship Him so that He may give them the worldly goods they desire. So, since it is an offence to worship God more with regard to the needs man has than to the goodness that resides in Him, I am travelling to see the pope, therefore, in order that he may grant me his blessing, and I wish to proclaim throughout the squares and streets of towns and cities that people ought to worship God principally and primarily because He is good and deserves, on account of His goodness and perfection themselves, to be worshipped and loved, and paid reverence and honour.'

[3] The cardinal was struck by great wonder and great joy, so, together with the pilgrim and the man who wished to act as crier for the best method one can adopt in worshipping God, he returned to the city of Rome so that he might present the two said men to the pope. While all three of them were travelling along and discussing the method according to which one should worship God, they came across an elderly Jew who was making his way to the Court and was

---

277. Cat. *pus prop en figura*.

278. A 'carved and inlaid crucifix' would necessarily be construed as a 'graven image' by a Christian pilgrim averse to 'idols'. The obvious reference point for such attitudes are the controversies associated with the two periods of iconoclasm within the Byzantine Empire, namely, 726-87 CE and 814-42 CE. A further reference point might be the Cistercian Order's reputed aversion to decorative sculpture; however, in an early statute defining artistic legislation within this Order, figured crucifixes were, in fact, permitted, even if sculptures and pictures were forbidden, in the church or other rooms within the monastery, Reilly (2013) in Birkedal Bruun (2013), 125-39, here 129 and n. 10.

extremely fatigued by the long journey he had undertaken. His countenance and bearing were indicative of great discontentment and sorrow. The cardinal asked the Jew why he was so sorrowful and meditative.

'My lord', said the Jew, 'I have long entertained grave concerns, of which I am unable to rid myself. And these concerns torment my soul so cruelly that I scarcely feel any joy at anything I hear or see.'

The cardinal wished to know at all costs what these concerns were, so the Jew revealed his considerations to him in the following words:

'My lord', said the Jew, 'in the beginning, when it pleased God (Blessed be He!) to honour the Jewish people above all other peoples, we twice lived in captivity; the first of these periods lasting four hundred years, the second, seventy. We underwent such captivity twice because we had committed certain sins. However, after the punishment of the captivity we bore, we regained the freedom we once enjoyed. Yet now that we don't kill prophets or worship idols and we lead the life of this world under great hardship, we have endured more than one thousand two hundred years of captivity, and we don't know why. I am very fearful, therefore, that we may bear the guilt for the death of Christ, for which reason we are in captivity. And therefore I travel like a wanderer across countries to seek to discover if anyone could show or reveal to me whether we are in captivity because we fail to worship Jesus Christ, whom we have crucified.

[4] When the Jew had finished speaking, the cardinal posed the following question to him:

'A debate arose between three wise men as to which of the three of them worshipped God in the most perfect manner. It was the duty of one of them to travel across mountains and plains, and to worship God in the grasses, plants, beasts, birds, men and all the other creatures. The other wise man worshipped God in terms of what He accomplished beyond nature, such as in the miracles He performed, in creating the world from nothing, in raising the dead and in all the other things that nature is unable to perform. The third wise man worshipped God in terms of those things which He is, and of those things which He performs in Himself, through Himself and of Himself, and of that which He performed within Himself as regards creatures. The question arises as to which of the three of them worshipped God in the most perfect manner. And if there exists someone else who worships God in accordance with all three said methods, the question arises of whether he worships Him more fervently than do any of the three aforesaid wise men.'

'My lord', said the Jew, 'the person who worships God on account of that which He performs in Himself rather than that which He performs in another's regard, worships God more perfectly. And the person who worships Him in accordance with the three said methods worships God more fervently than does the person who worships Him by means of one method alone.'

The cardinal replied by saying that the Jew had judged soundly.

'The philosophers of yore were those who would praise God for the works He revealed in natural things. And the Jews were those who worshipped God in terms of the miracles and works they believed that God had accomplished beyond nature. The time has now come when Jews have ceased to believe in miracles and ceased to worship God, inasmuch as they fail to believe what He accomplishes beyond nature in order to demonstrate His power. Christians, on the other hand, believe that God performs a better work in Himself than nature would be capable of accomplishing or receiving. For the Father, who is God, generates the Son, who is God, while the Holy Spirit, who is God, proceeds from both, albeit that together they are but one God. And, likewise, God the Son unites to Himself the human nature of Christ, with whom He is but a single Person. And since Christ was crucified and put to death by you, the Jews, having come among you to take on human nature and having suffered death to save you, and since you fail to worship Him, He has punished you, therefore, by placing you in the captivity of Christians and, what's more, of Saracens, in order to signify that you are in every respect unworthy of being free, for which reason He has enslaved you to both believers and unbelievers.'

The Jew gravely considered the words the cardinal had spoken to him, and by virtue of the questions and arguments the latter had addressed to him, he grasped the truth and became a Christian. And he undertook the office of visiting synagogues to worship God in the presence of everyone and in accordance with the three above methods, and the pope granted him a privilege for this office.

[5] While the cardinal was standing before the pope, appointing the officials who might help him to attend to his office, a very elderly and aged Saracen was presented to the pope and handed a letter to him on behalf of a Saracen king. In this letter, the king begged the

pope to send word to him as to whether that which a Christian had informed him about the Holy Catholic Faith was, in fact, true, which Christian had caused him to renounce the faith of Muhammad he had previously held. Yet, since the Christian had told him that the Catholic faith could not be proved by argument, he therefore did not desire to become a Christian, for he did not wish to give up one faith for another.[279] He said, however, that, in the hope of understanding, he would abandon the faith of Muhammad and embrace that of the Catholics, provided that the pope sent word to him as to whether the latter was susceptible of proof. For, were it to be so, he would become a Christian and would worship Jesus Christ as God and would turn his entire country over to the Church of Rome, so that all the inhabitants of that country might worship Jesus Christ.[280]

[6] When the letters had been read in the presence of the pope and his cardinals, there entered a gentile who came from a country to the south, located amidst the desert, beyond the city called Ghana.[281] In that country there were a vast number of kings and princes who worshipped idols, as well as the sun and the stars, and the birds and the beasts. The people of that country are many, and are black, and they have no Law. And it happened one day that a man from that country considered that a particular thing alone should be worshipped, and it should be nobler than any of those they had previously worshipped. So in honour of that thing, of whose identity he was unaware, he travelled across countries proclaiming that one should seek to discover and ask what that thing was which alone

---

279. The Christian (Dominican) missionary (associated with Ramon Martí) mentioned here is a leitmotif which occurs a further six times in Llull's oeuvre, for which see Hames (2012) in Ripoll and Tortella (2012), 51-74; here 52-53.

280. The principle of appealing to and, in the best instance, converting the highest representatives of Islamic culture, whether monarchs or men of learning, within certain non-Christian countries, forms the basis of much of Llull's apologetic missionary strategy. Note also the expressed wish of the Muslim king only to renounce his own faith for the sake of a rational understanding of a different faith which must necessarily be rationally demonstrable.

281. Llull is probably referring to the capital city of the Ghana Empire, which empire was located some 800 kilometres (500 miles) north-west of the modern-day Republic of Ghana and was the dominant power across West Africa. It was instrumental in trans-Saharan trade and cultural exchange between the Sahel/Gold Coast regions and Europe, not to mention the Middle East. The main items of trade, from the perspective of the Ghana Empire, were gold (exported) and salt, fabrics and copper (imported).

ought to be worshipped. This man held that office for so long and performed it with such diligence that he stirred the people of that country to devotion, and they felt a desire to become acquainted with that thing which alone should be worshipped above all others. They held a court, therefore, and assembled themselves, ordaining that they should send envoys out across various countries in order to seek to discover what that thing could be which was worthy of being worshipped above all things. And one of the envoys was the very one who had come to see the pope. So the pope immediately sent the Articles of Faith and the books whereby they are proved to be demonstrable, along with the friars who had learned Arabic, which friars went to see the Saracen king who had sent the letter to the pope. And, by the grace of God, these friars converted the Saracen king and a vast number of his people. And, together with the pope's envoys, this king travelled to those countries from which the gentile had come, and together they proclaimed and, by necessary reasons, proved God to be sovereign over all things, which God all the people of that country should worship, and they destroyed the idols in which these people used to believe. And agreement and friendship was forged between such people and the Catholics. And, before long, through the friendship and participation the Catholics enjoyed with them, many of these people had received baptism.

[7] On a certain feast day, the pope held a procession which included a large number of prelates, religious and other clerks. The chants and praises these men offered to Our Lord God were great indeed. The cardinal of 'Adoramus te' took part in that procession, and he cogitated upon the fact that there were many countries in the world, containing many people, countries wherein God was neither praised nor worshipped, and he desired very fervently that God should be worshipped throughout all these countries. While the cardinal was engaged in such consideration, it so happened that he was proceeding in the direction of a large number of silversmiths and shopkeepers, who kept in their shops a vast number of goblets, bowls, jugs, dishes, gold and silver basins, and other items of jewelry, namely, rings, bags, belts and precious stones. The cardinal instructed four squires to cast and scatter all these goblets and jewels onto the street and to let it be known that he had commanded them to do so. The squires fulfilled his command, and the men to whom the jewels belonged expressed deep outrage. And that which the cardinal had in-

structed his squires to do very nearly disrupted the entire procession, given the quarrel that was on the verge of breaking out between his men and those to whom the jewels belonged.

[8] After this unusual event came another such, namely, that the cardinal of 'Adoramus te' saw a lady who was following the procession, which lady was completely adorned with gold and silver, as well as precious stones, and, as a result of the way she had painted her face, it shone as do those images to which one has applied varnish. The cardinal knelt down before the lady and pretended that he wished to worship her, saying that she resembled an idol and that it was for this reason that he knelt before her. Great was the shame felt by this lady and all the others who were with her.

When the pope had completed the procession and had celebrated Mass, he wished to know the reason why the cardinal had disturbed the procession, and why he had knelt down in front of the lady. So the cardinal recounted to him the devotion he had felt when he reflected upon the fact that there existed many countries in which God was not worshipped, and upon how gold and silver goblets and other jewels with which prelates adorn their tables and fill their coffers hinder such worship, for which reason he had instructed that these items of jewelry should be destroyed. The pope, therefore, laid down a statute that, thereafter, no such jewels should be in any city or place where he might stay, lest they occasion any dishonest desire in a prelate. Afterwards, he laid down the statute that no woman who was clothed and adorned in the manner of an idol should come to his procession or attend any church in which he might celebrate Mass.


## 85. 'Glorificamus te'

[1] The cardinal to whom the pope had entrusted the office of 'Glorificamus te' said to the latter that he wished to assume the office of honouring the will of God in this world to combat those who do Him dishonour, so he, therefore, recounted the following exemplary tale:

'There was once a king who had gone with a large number of his intimates to a beautiful forest in order to take recreation, and, while dining and revelling, remained within that forest. It came to pass, however, that the weather turned, bringing cold, snow and rain to that place where the king had settled. But the king was in his tent, and had sauces, strong wines and heavy garments at his disposal, so neither the cold nor the harsh weather there could cause him any harm. His retinue and his intimates, however, who were unable to protect themselves against the harshness of the weather, met with death and destruction.'

Once the cardinal had recounted the tale, he explained it using the following words:

'The king is the pope, the cardinals and the prelates of Our Holy Mother Church, who fail to dispatch to their frontiers friars and worthy men who might learn various languages so as to communicate with the people living there, to understand them and to preach to them without the need for other interpreters. And since this custom would be agreeable to God's will, all those who might and should, yet fail to, do that whereby His will is served in this world, defy that very will. Those who perish are the Christians who live among the Saracens and the Tatars, to whom they are subject and who are ignorant of the faith and of preachers. And, because of the captivity in which they live against their will, great harm is done to the persons of such Christians, as well as to their wives and daughters. Very often they cease to believe in and renounce the Holy Catholic Faith, therefore, and adopt the belief amidst which they live, against the will of God.'

[2] When the pope had listened to these words, he ordained, by means of the Orders[282] in which learning prevails, that just as a prince who wages war against another such establishes frontier posts at the outer limits of his realms, so too should monasteries be built across the territories occupied by Christians who are in communication with unbelievers. And, depending upon the language spoken by such people, the religious in question should learn their language, communicate with them and preach to them. The pope ordained such things so that he might do everything within his power to satisfy the will of God.

[3] The cardinal felt a great desire to honour the will of God so that by honouring His will he might glorify Him, thus he appointed his officers, who through their various offices, assisted him in honouring that will. It happened one day that the cardinal was travelling around the city of Rome when he passed through a square in which there were many people. So he asked the people who were moving back and forth across that square what urge it was that led them to

---

282. I.e. religious orders.

move about with such diligence. Each of them replied that the urge
they felt with respect to worldly affairs caused them to move about
with such diligence. So the cardinal, therefore, ordained that a man
should be stationed within that square, who might proclaim to the
people that they should direct their intentions towards serving God
while they sought to attend to the affairs of this world, and that they
should attend thereto solely by virtue of their intention to serve God,
so that in such attendance the will of God might be honoured rather
than that will which loves worldly affairs. This man was stationed in
the square and issued proclamations just as the cardinal had ordained, and as a result of what those people heard him say, many of
them directed their intentions towards serving that of God.

[4] The cardinal appointed another officer to go through the
streets proclaiming that people should obey the will of God by believing the fourteen Articles and by doing what they are enjoined to do
by the Ten Commandments; and likewise proclaiming that they
should glorify the will of God since He has chosen to create the world,
to be made incarnate and to give the world to man. And it fell to this
man to tell each person to glorify the will of God, Who had made
them men and Christians; for, had God so chosen, His will would not
have created the world, nor would He have taken our nature or given
the world to man, while those whom He has made men He could
have made beasts. When the cardinal had given instruction to a man
who might perform the aforesaid office, this man asked the cardinal
on what he was to subsist. So the cardinal told him that if a minstrel
were able to subsist on that which people gave to him, even though
he was incapable of saying anything other than that he was attempt-
ing to identify the good wine on their behalf, how much more ought
he be able to earn his living if he were to serve the will of God by uttering the above words!

[5] The cardinal gave ordinance for a further office which is very
necessary to the purpose of honouring God's will, namely, that a man
should go among clerks and religious and, in the streets or churches
or wherever he might find them, should remind them that they ought
to obey the will of God, Who commands them in the Gospels to travel
throughout the world in order to preach to all creatures. This officer
was appointed by the cardinal. It happened one day that this officer
came across two clerks in the street, to whom he said that which the
cardinal had instructed him to say. So they replied that, when God

wished people to go to preach to the unbelievers, He would impart to them the desire to do so. That man was utterly outraged by their reply, so, in turn, he said that God had already commanded them when He spoke in person to the Apostles about the Holy Church. And because God, since He had chosen to become man and to die for all those who belong to the Holy Church, had charged each one of us to to do as much out of love for Him, nobody should expect Him to force one's free will accordingly, without which will one would not be worthy to preach the will of God. There was great dispute between the proctor and the two clerks, so they went to the Papal Court to obtain judgement thereon.

[6] The cardinal asked one of his squires who had long been in his service whether he wished to serve the will of God by going from door to door begging for the will of God, and told him that he should glorify that will when he was given alms for the love of God. And were people to refuse him when he begged for the love of God, he should feel aggrieved thereby in his soul and should weep at the fact that those who refuse to give alms for the sake of God's will, yet so give for the sake of their own, are not loved by the will of God. This squire assumed the office and, accompanied by the poor, went out begging for the love of God, so that he might become familiar with those who honour the will of God and those who prize it less than the alms one requests from them, which alms they refuse to those who request such for the love of God. This squire performed his office very ably each day and, after he had begged from door to door for that particular day's sustenance, he spent the remainder thereof in church contemplating the will of God.

[7] A philosopher came to see the cardinal and said the following words to him:

'My lord, it is the custom among us to deny that which is against the course of nature. Though I too have observed this custom, I now wish to change such and to assume the office of going among philosophers and great masters, and stating that, if a miraculous work is incompatible with nature, how much less compatible with the Lord of Nature is it that He be unable to do that which pertains to His will and lies beyond the workings of nature!'

This office brought the cardinal considerable pleasure, and the philosopher thereby accomplished a great deal of good by demonstrating many things which are against the course of nature, so that

God Himself might not be contrary to His will as regards perfection of justice, goodness, infinity, power, wisdom, mercy and humility.

The cardinal appointed these officers and many others, so that, by honouring God's will, He might be glorified by people, who might themselves be glorified by His will in glory.

## 86. 'GRACIAS AGIMUS TIBI PROPTER MAGNAM GLORIAM TUAM'

[1] The cardinal of 'Gracias agimus tibi', who had assumed his office so that he might honour the wisdom of God, stood before the pope and his companions one day and said these words:

'It is natural that the more effectively the human intellect addresses itself to understanding God, the more prepared one's will is to love God and to abhor sin. I request an office, therefore, whereby I may ensure that the human intellect is raised up to understand God, so that God may be known and loved by His people, who may give Him thanks and bless His glory.'

So the pope and his cardinals granted him the office he requested:

[2] While they were engaged in this discussion, an Artist[283] presented himself before the pope and told him that on account of the proliferation of the sciences of theology, nature,[284] law and medicine various opinions had likewise come to proliferate in each of the said sciences. The reason for this was that the authors and masters had written works concerning the sciences in which some did not share the opinion of the others. The Artist said to the pope and his cardinals, therefore, that one should bring all the said sciences into accord with certain concise and necessary principles, which form the basis of an Art, so that, were any error or false opinion to arise, one could, using such an Art, direct oneself towards the principles of each science and put an end to all the false opinions which are contrary to the said sciences.

[3] The cardinal of 'Gracias agimus tibi' was greatly pleased by what the Artist had said, so he urged and counselled that his petition be adopted. After such discussion, a master of decretals,[285] acts and laws

---

283. Given the petition the Artist goes on to make, this term most probably indicates a practitioner of Llull's own Art, rather than a member of a university Arts faculty.

284. Here 'nature' comes under the heading of philosophy.

285. Decretals are papal letters giving decisions on points of canon law. A master of decretals, therefore, was a master of canon, as opposed to civil, law.

presented himself to the pope, and said that there were so many gloss-
es and writings within the science of law that the human intellect would
thereby end in confusion, and, therefore, that he could not judge the
facts clearly nor could students who learned that science receive a
grounding therein. He thus counselled that this science should be expressed as an Art, which rested on concise principles conforming to
necessity and reason, towards which principles every science of law
should address itself. On different occasions, a master of theology, a
master of philosophy and a master of medicine likewise made their
petitions to the pope and his cardinals requesting that concise and
necessary principles be provided to each science by means of an Art, so
that no science might be in confusion as a result of the proliferation of
writings, and that during the time of the Antichrist one might be better
prepared to put an end to his false opinions.[286]

[4] When the aforesaid masters had spoken, the cardinal said that
he was very happy at their words, and that this matter bore reference
to his office, which he had assumed in order to honour God's wisdom, and that, therefore, he wished his office to concern itself with
this particular matter. After these words, a wise religious rose to his
feet and said, in front of everyone, that he requested the office of
travelling to the Saracens, Jews, Tatars and all the unbelievers in order to expound to them the Articles of the Holy Catholic Faith. For
many unbelievers hesitated to embrace the Roman faith since they
failed to understand the way in which Christians believed its articles,
for they thought that Christians held beliefs other than they did and,
therefore, themselves hesitated to become Christian.

[5] Before the pope and his cardinals had replied to the masters
who had requested the said offices, two wise men presented themselves to the pope. The first was a Latin and the second a Greek, and
they addressed the following words to the pope and his cardinals:

'My lord, in the *Book of the Holy Spirit*[287] a disputation is held between a Latin and a Greek in the presence of a wise Saracen who had
asked them what the truth was concerning the Person of the Holy

---

286. Llull, in fact, had already written a *Llibre contra Anticrist* in 1274-76. In this text,
it is the falseness and defeat of the Antichrist which will bring ruin to the world; only
the logical, argumentative methods of Llull's Art can prevent this happening.

287. I.e. Llull's own *Liber de Sancto Spiritu* (1278-81). This text contains a dialogue
between a Greek, a Latin and a Muslim concerning the doctrinal differences between
the two former parties (i.e. between Greek Orthodoxy and Roman Catholicism). The

Spirit, namely, whether it proceeds from the Father and the Son or from the Father alone. Each of the two wise men proved his opinion to the best of his ability, using ten arguments, but the Saracen withheld his decision as to which of the beliefs he would incline towards. We have travelled through Greece, therefore, and have covered a large part of the territory which belongs to the Latins. And, wherever we go, we put forward such questions to wise men, so that they may seek the truth and discover which faith it seems likely that the Saracen would have adopted.'

The pope and his cardinals were greatly pleased by what the two wise men had said, and the pope entrusted the answer to the cardinal who had assumed the office of honouring the wisdom of God. In the company of these wise men was a Christian who had gone among the Saracens and the Jews in order to ask a Gentile which of the three Laws he had adopted, as is narrated in the *Book of the Gentile and the Three Wise Men.*

[6] The cardinal had many men who helped him perform his office, and he sent them throughout the world to make inquiries regarding the manner in which masters practised the sciences they taught. And when he discovered that any master practised poorly the science he taught, he punished him and deprived him of that office. A great deal of good came from this, therefore, since all the masters feared him, on account of which fear their students much sooner received a grounding in the sciences they learned, for the reason that their masters taught them with greater diligence, and spoke to them more succinctly. It once happened that the cardinal was travelling to a city in which there was a great university for the various sciences. At the entrance to the city, he came across two sons of the Lord King of that city, who was having his sons taught how to bear arms and to practise swordsmanship. The cardinal asked the instructors of the two princes whether the king was having his sons educated in the science of letters,[288] but the wise men replied that he was not, yet that he was having them taught how to ride and to bear arms.

'Foolish is the king', said the cardinal, 'who sooner teaches how to kill men than to know whether one ought to kill men.'

---

debate focuses in particular upon the *Filioque* clause, and shows how discussion between these parties can be conducted under conditions defined by Llull's Art.

288. I.e. The seven liberal arts.

After having spoken these words, the cardinal went to the king and harshly rebuked him for not teaching his sons the arts and sciences, as had long since been the custom of kings and princes, who ensured that their sons were taught the sciences, so that they might know how to govern their peoples. The king was greatly pleased by what the cardinal said and was obedient to his counsel.

[7] The cardinal felt such a great desire to foster and lend order to wisdom, that he went to the General Chapter of the religious who were trained in the sciences and, together with them, he disposed and ordained that, to honour the wisdom of God, scientific knowledge should be fostered in all men so that they might know and love God. On a certain occasion, it occurred that a Count's son was travelling to Bologna to study law, and the cardinal, who was likewise travelling to Bologna, where a General Chapter of the Preachers was due to be held,[289] met that Count's son, and spoke so many edifying words to him along the way that he inspired in him a love of the science of theology, which is more necessary to a clerk than is the science of law. This Count's son, therefore, returned to Paris and learned theology, of which he became a Master.

[8] One day the cardinal went to the school of the Preachers to listen to a lecture on theology, and on his way he came across a great school of law in which there were many students wearing ecclesiastical attire. He continued his journey and came across another school full of decretalists who likewise wore ecclesiastical attire. So the cardinal issued a command to the students of law stating that, as civil law was a worldly science, so should they learn about that science dressed in worldly attire, in order that they might not cause dishonour to the honour that the science of canon law should enjoy over civil law. And he issued that command, in particular, so that simony might not take root among jurists who, having learned the science of law, become decretalists so that they might ascend to some prelacy.

[9] After he had issued this decree, the cardinal entered the school of the Preachers, where a master of theology was lecturing, and in that whole school there was hardly any student who was not a

---

289. The Dominican Order's first general chapter was held in Bologna in 1220, and from that date onwards until 1244 the location of the chapter alternated between there and Paris. After 1244 the *acta* of each chapter were to specify the location for the subsequent one. The most likely candidate for the chapter referred to here within the text is that of 1285; see above, Introduction, § 2.

religious. And for this reason the cardinal cried out in a loud voice that wisdom received great dishonour from those who loved lucrative rather than meritorious knowledge which revealed divine wisdom. The cardinal issued a command, therefore, stating that, once every week, Friars Preacher and Friars Minor should preach in each of the law schools, and that they should inform those in attendance of the great loss theology suffers in terms of those who are beneficed from the wealth of the Holy Church, yet who learn the science of law or learn more law than they do theology.

In these ways and many others did the cardinal strive to honour wisdom, so that through wisdom people might be aware of how each of them is obliged to give thanks to God for the goods He grants them, with which thanks ignorance is inconsistent.

## 87. 'Domine Deus, rex celestis, Deus pater omnipotens'

[1] The cardinal of 'Domine Deus' was in the Consistory, and in front of the pope and his cardinals, he said that he wished to assume the office of honouring the power of God, which received dishonour in this world from many people who in various ways dishonoured it. It came to pass one day that the pope wished to send his envoys to a country called Georgia, of which a Christian king is lord. So the pope sent word to that king asking him to send him some religious from his country so that they might teach their language and their arts to Latin friars, and that they might learn Latin and might return, along with the Latin friars, to their country in order to preach the holy faith and doctrine of Rome. While Pope Blaquerna was ordaining these things, the chamberlain said that it would take great effort to send word to these people, to learn their language and to teach our Latin tongue to them, and that, moreover, it would require a great deal of time and expense.

[2] The cardinal was greatly displeased by what the chamberlain had said, so he narrated the following exemplary tale:

'It came to pass one day that a certain Japheth[290] was travelling along a road when he came to a river along whose bank stood a large

---

290. Shem, Ham and Japheth were Noah's sons, Japheth being the third thereof, from whom, according to both the Bible and the Quran, European, as well as certain Asian, peoples descend; cf. Gen. 10:1-5.

crowd of people, who were gazing at a man who had drowned therein. Japheth asked these people why this man had not gone to the head of the river, where he might have been able to cross to the other side. A man replied: 'But that would have taken him forever, seeing that it's five days' journey to get up there!' So Japheth replied : 'And how long will it take him to get up from here?'

So the cardinal, therefore, rebuked the chamberlain very harshly, saying that, through its prolonged exercise, power can bring order and conclusion to that which the pope wishes to ordain as regards the religious of Georgia, but that it cannot return those damned in Hell to the state of salvation, since they have passed from this present life.

[3] The cardinal had a squire who had long been in his service so that he might thereby gain advancement. It came to pass one day that the squire fell very gravely ill with a continuous fever. His illness greatly saddened the cardinal, so the squire asked him to cure him and rid him of the fever which tormented him so acutely. The cardinal replied that he did not have the power to relieve the fever, for such lay in God alone, whose power was capable of accomplishing whatever it pleased as regards that possessed by nature. The squire recovered, and assumed the office of honouring God's power throughout the world by affirming and proclaiming that God's power is above that of nature:

'So God, therefore, was able to create and resurrect the first man, and, by divine power, was likewise able to cause a virgin woman to conceive and bear child. And the power of the stars and of the heavenly bodies is defeated and overcome, as well as countenanced by, the supreme power.'

The office the squire had assumed was of great value, for very often, in exercising it, he confirmed Catholics in their faith, and defeated and overcame unbelievers, who did not believe that a virgin might conceive or bear child, or that a man might be resurrected, for in such matters is God's power as potent as it was when it created the world from nothing, which creation was beyond nature's power.

[4] 'My lord', said the cardinal to the pope, 'I ask you, which has greater power: truth or falsehood?'

The pope replied by saying that truth had greater power than falsehood since truth enjoyed God's aid and was in accord with being, while falsehood did not enjoy such aid and was in accord with nonbeing. So, after the pope had spoken, the cardinal asked him how falsehood could enjoy such power within the world, whereby there

are more people who are idolaters and believe in idols than there are
who believe in God. So the pope replied that such error did not come
into being so that falsehood might prevail over truth, but rather because of a lack of devotion and charity, which chooses not to reveal
the truth:

'So, therefore, just as a lack of light yields shadows, so too does a
lack in those who dare not speak or preach the truth yield error and
falsehood.'

[5] In a certain province it came to pass that the devout and blessed men who went to preach the word of God to the unbelievers were
not listened to and were expelled from the country. So the cardinal
turned to the secular arm and held discussions with Christian princes, as well as the pope, to the effect that all those who failed to allow
into their country the holy Christians who wished to preach the word
of God therein might, by force of arms, have war waged upon them
and suffer defeat; and that the Church should not conclude a truce
with any unbelievers who failed to permit Christians to demonstrate
the truth of the Catholic faith within their realm. So great was the
power of the Christians that the unbelievers of that country permitted these men to preach to them and, likewise, that a state of truce
might exist between them for as long as they allowed such Christians
to preach to and convert unbelievers within their territories.

[6] It came to pass that a very powerful Saracen king refused to
allow Christian religious to enter his country in order to preach. So
two friars, whom the Saracens had expelled from their country, came
to see the cardinal of 'Domine Deus', and told him that they could
not remain in that country because the Saracens were not willing to
let them do so. The cardinal, however, said that they had dishonoured the power of the will, which is stronger and nobler than that of
the body, so he complained to the pope in the following words:

'My lord pope', said the cardinal, 'the power of the will leads people to fast, weep and strive in the hope of praising and honouring the
power of God. And God has bound and subjected bodily power to its
spiritual counterpart. So, if the king defends himself by means of
bodily power against the power of our souls, his power must be defeated and overcome by the great love and honour we bear towards
the Passion of God and by the shedding of tears and blood, as well as
by the holy men who both secretly and openly go among unbelievers.
So, by persistent effort, bodily power must be defeated by its spiritual

counterpart, in order to signify that the power of God spiritually defeats the sensual and intellectual powers which reside in creatures, as
is made manifest in the sacred Host.'

[7] So fervent and devout was the cardinal in honouring the power of God, that he established various offices for that precise purpose.
For, to one man, he granted the office of going to preach throughout
the world proclaiming that one should not trust the power of wealth,
friends, wisdom, youth, auguries, sortilege, omens or any other powers whereby man forfeits the grace of God's own power. The cardinal
appointed a further officer, who proclaimed the power of God to be
so great that it could accomplish all things, so long as sin should not
arise therefrom. Another officer proclaimed that God was unable to
commit sin because sin and powerlessness are in accord, and are contrary to power and to virtue, which themselves are in accord. Another
officer proclaimed that God did not exhaust His power in creatures,
since He could accomplish more things than He actually did. Another proclaimed that in His Trinity God accomplished everything
He could. There were many other officers who honoured God's power, and they all adhered to rules and instructions whereby they might
honour and bless that power. Among the other officers was one whose
task was to demonstrate by nature how one could curb one's vices and
fortify one's virtues, as well as how one could lament one's sins. A
further office was performed by a man who carried a branch and a
bird, while leading a dog and proclaiming that there was nobody who
could create a leaf on a branch or the feather of a bird or the hair on
a dog's back or the nail on his finger.

[8] So greatly renowned were the cardinal and his officers for
honouring the power of God, that when anybody felt a lack of power,
he was immediately assisted and given counsel by the cardinal and his
disciples. And it occurred likewise in the cases of the cardinal who
served the will of God and the cardinal who served divine wisdom. So,
therefore, whoever felt a lack of will, wisdom or power immediately
sought out the aforesaid cardinals.

## 88. 'DOMINE, FILI UNIGENITE, JHESU CHRISTE'

[1] There was a cardinal who exercised great devotion towards the
Person of the Son of God, Who united to Himself human nature. So,

on account of such devotion, he said the following words to the pope
and his cardinals:

'It is evident that you, O Holy Father the Pope, and we, the cardinals, have received an honour above all other Christians within this
world from the Son of God. It is a commendable thing for us, therefore, and we are deeply obliged, to send out envoys throughout the
world who may tell us about the state of affairs obtaining in the various countries as regards how the Son of God is honoured within the
world by certain peoples and dishonoured and forgotten by others.
So, in order to accomplish this task, I request this office and ask for
the provision of money to my envoys. These men I wish to send
throughout the world so that they may tell me about the overall state
thereof and that I may tell you about such, so that you may ordain
how the Son of God should be loved and praised throughout the
world, and so that people may be told about His virtue, as well as what
He did within this world out of love for us.'

The pope and all the cardinals were greatly pleased by this office
of telling that the cardinal of 'Domine fili' had requested, and everything for which he had asked was granted him. And thus was the
prefiguration provided by the Emperors of Rome fulfilled—which
emperors were lords of the entire world and had envoys who informed them about the overall state thereof—inasmuch as they pre-
figured the fact that the pope would be God's lieutenant and Lord of
Rome, and would himself be informed about the state of all the countries, so that these might be made subject to the Holy Catholic Faith.

[2] The cardinal divided the world into twelve provinces and appointed twelve envoys to travel its length and breadth in order to learn
what state it was in. It so happened that one of the cardinal's envoys
travelled southwards and encountered a caravan consisting of six thousand camels, laden with salt, which had set forth from a town called
Tibalbert[291] and was heading towards the country in which the River

---

291. Most probably Tabelbala (in Béchar province, in modern-day south-western
Algeria), a settlement which had served as a staging-post on the caravan routes between southern Morocco (particularly Sijilmasa) and the Sahel region (particularly
Sudan) since the thirteenth century at least. According to the celebrated *Atles català*
(Catalan Atlas) of 1375, Tibalbert was identified as being al-Tebelbelt, a settlement located in the former country of Biledulgerid (Bheladal Dsherid), approximately 230
km (142 miles) south east of the medieval city of Sijilmasa.

Damietta[292] has its source. This envoy encountered so many people that, within a fortnight, all the salt had been sold. And those people are, without exception, black, and they worship idols. And, although they are cheerful, they exercise very harsh justice and put to death anyone caught in a lie. And all they possess, they hold in common.

In that country, there is an island in the midst of a great lake. And on that island lives a dragon to whom the people of that country offer sacrifices and which they worship as God. This envoy travelled through that country in order to learn about the customs of its people and to estimate the great number of its inhabitants. And these people felt great wonder at the fact that this envoy was white and was a Christian, since never before had they heard of a Christian's having come to their country. By means of one of his squires, this envoy sent written reports to the cardinal detailing all of the aforesaid matters, as well as many others, about which matters the cardinal told the pope and his companions. The pope and his cardinals felt great dissatisfaction when they heard that the dragon was worshipped as a god, so they discussed how they might be able to eradicate the error into which these people had fallen.

[3] Another envoy travelled northwards, where he heard and saw Latins who told him that in those parts there were many people who held diverse beliefs, and that the devil kept them in error by means of certain illusions and deceptions. For there was a certain country, named Girland,[293] in which, every five years, a white bear would appear as a sign that that year they would have a great abundance of fish, on which those people live. There is also another country in which, by casting a spell, they induce the trees to talk. And there is yet another country, near Bochnia,[294] in which a hoopoe enters a forest and, if anybody cuts any branches therein, thunder and lightning immediately fall from the sky and place everyone who is within that forest in mortal danger. There is another country in which each man

---

292. I.e. The River Nile.

293. From the description which Llull goes on to give, most probably Iceland or Greenland.

294. Cat. *Boçinia*. I make the suggestion here that the location to which Llull is referring is Bochnia in southern Poland, 37 km (23 miles) east of Kraków. Bochnia is indeed significantly 'northwards' of the Catalan-Aragonese kingdoms; it is an ancient city, and is famous for its salt mine. The fact that Llull has already referred to the transportation of salt two paragraphs earlier in this chapter, would seem to support my conjecture.

considers himself to have a god in his field, and another in his live-stock, and another in his kitchen garden. In another country, near Dacia,[295] there are people who live from hunting alone and who pursue the beasts that they slaughter, and once they have killed one, they remain in that place until they have eaten it, and then go in search of another such.

The northern envoy sent written reports to the cardinal containing all such information and much besides. So the pope and his cardinals ordained that holy and devout men should be dispatched to these people, men who might know these people's languages and might preach to them by means of exemplary and moral tales, as well as by metaphors and analogies, until their sensory faculties were sufficiently well-ordered as to cause the analogies to ascend to the powers of the soul, as a result of which their intellectual faculties might be enlightened by the Holy Catholic Faith.

[4] One of the cardinal's envoys went to Barbary,[296] where he found many frauds and scoundrels who were preaching the *Quran* and the beatitude of Paradise to the Saracens. And they preached such devout words that almost all those who listened to them fell to weeping. The envoy felt great wonder at the devotion the people expressed towards such words, since the fact was that what was being preached constituted error. And he discovered that the people wept because of the fine way in which these men spoke and because such men narrated the lives of many a person who had died on account of his devotion. He likewise discovered a *Book of the Lover and the Beloved*,[297] in which it was recounted how devout men composed songs about God and love, and how, on account of their love of God, they left the world and travelled around it enduring poverty. The envoy likewise discovered that in the courts where lawsuits were heard the disputes and arguments that one party maintained against another were brought to a close voluntarily.

---

295. I.e. The former Roman province whose territories correspond approximately to modern-day Romania.

296. Historically, those parts of North Africa which included the states of Morocco, Algiers, Tunis and Tripoli.

297. Llull is referring to a possibly fictional precedent of and model for his own *Llibre d'amic e amat*, namely. Book V, Ch. 100 of *Blaquerna*. The reader should note, however, that the work Llull goes on to describe in the following lines bears only a slight resemblance to the opuscule he is, in fact, advertising.

The envoy sent word of all these things and more besides to the cardinal. And the *Book of the Lover and the Beloved* was translated and a method adopted whereby through the devoutness of their words sermons might be made more agreeable to people; and through the good order manifested by the Saracens, the lawsuits and disputes that exist among us might be reduced in length.

[5] An envoy went to Turkey, where he discovered four friars who had learned the Turkish language, but whom the Turks would not allow to preach within their land. So the envoy wrote about this matter to the cardinal, and envoys were elected whom the pope sent bearing great jewels to the Lord of the Tatars, who had subjected Turkey to his authority. By means of his envoys, the pope begged the Tatar to allow the four friars to be able to preach about the honour of the Son of God throughout Turkey. So, on account of the pope's entreaties and of the jewels he had sent him, the Tatar allowed them to do so, from which time onwards the Turks dared not forbid the friars to preach.

[6] A teller of tales[298] went to Outremer, and he wrote to tell the cardinal that two Assassins had murdered a prince, and that they had been put to death. So the cardinal went to preach to the religious who were learning various languages, and he urged them to desire death for the sake of Jesus Christ on the grounds that there were people who, even in error, wished to die in order that their relatives might enjoy freedom. A statute was laid down, therefore, whereby these religious might be preached to once a week, so that they might both learn and desire to die more willingly.

[7] It was ordained in the above manner that the envoys should travel throughout the world. And there were many men who, in a different manner, assumed the office of telling exemplary tales and speaking edifying words to people, so that these might frequently remember the Son of God and the Passion He suffered for our sake.

---

298. Cat. *recomptador*: a 'storyteller'/'narrator'; also 'informant', as in 'one who supplies information'. I have translated this term as 'teller' or 'teller of tales' (though on three occasions, for which see below, § 9, as 'news teller', and once as 'news telling', phrases in which the qualification 'news' or Cat. *de noves/noves* is specified by Llull himself) and its cognate verb (*recomptar*) as 'to tell' (though on one occasion as 'to recount') throughout this chapter. It is to be noted that the discourse transmitted by such a 'teller' is fundamentally oral.

Such tellers travelled through towns, cities and castles, and visited those who held office, to whom they told profitable exemplary tales.

It came to pass one day that one of these men went to see a carpenter who was planing a piece of wood, and he told him that he had heard it said that a particular piece of wood had been so strong that it had withstood a weight heavier than the entire world. The carpenter felt great wonder at these words, and on account of his wonder he conceived a desire for the teller to explain his words to him; to wit, the Cross on which hung the Son of God, Who has placed on His people a burden to serve Him weightier than the entire world. So, on account of the desire the carpenter conceived, he became a man of virtuous living and was delivered from the state of deadly sin in which he had been.

[8] It came to pass one day that one of the tellers left a town and travelled to a castle. On his way, he encountered a large number of pilgrims who were going to Santiago, so he joined their company and went with them as far as that city. And while they were travelling along the road, he told exemplary tales and spoke edifying and devout words to them. He likewise related to them stories from the Old and the New Testaments, and he narrated to them the events which had occurred to the Apostles and emperors as they are written down in the chronicles. So great was the pleasure the pilgrims derived from his edifying words that, accordingly, they exercised greater devotion towards their pilgrimage and suffered less hardship in terms of their travel and their toils. There were many men, therefore, who assumed this office so that they might make the journeying of pilgrims more bearable and might maintain the latter's devotion.

[9] Great good arose from the office of the cardinal, which cardinal kept the pope and his cardinals very satisfied with the news and information which came to him daily from various parts of the world. It came to pass one day that, in order that he might earn money, a certain man pretended to be a news teller in the cardinal's service, and he travelled alongside the pilgrims, who gave generously to him and treated him very well. This man, however, was not well-trained in news telling and, so, came to the cardinal's attention, which cardinal ordered him to be seized and placed in prison, since this man had assumed the office without his permission. So the cardinal laid down a statute whereby no news teller should receive anything from any pilgrim; and if he had need of anything, he should be given assistance

by the bishop of that region; and each news teller should carry with him the cardinal's seal.

## 89. 'Domine Deus, Agnus Dei, Filius Patris'

[1] One day, the pope was in the Consistory with his cardinals, and he said these words:

'The Orders of religion which exist among us are, without exception, ruled and governed by chapters, in which they make annual arrangements as to how the Order should be properly preserved as regards religion and saintly living.[299] It is necessary for us, the secular clergy, therefore, likewise to organise chapters, in such a way that our life be pleasing to God and to mankind. For unless we convene both general and special chapters, we cannot live in a perfectly ordered manner within this world. So, this being the case, I thus beg each of my companions to help me discuss how general and provincial chapters are to be organised among us.'

All the cardinals were very pleased by what the pope had said, so, together with him, they organised their chapters in the following manner.

[2] First it was ordained that every bishop should hold a chapter meeting once a year, and that he should have inquisitors[300] within his bishopric, and that it should be reported at the chapter whether any clerk was worthy of being punished for any misdeeds he may have committed during that year. Following this, it was decreed that once every year each archbishop should hold a chapter with his bishops, and that he should appoint inquisitors over them who should indict them at the chapters, and that their archbishop should punish them. Next, the pope and his cardinals ordained that they should divide the world into four parts, and that the archbishops from one quarter should convene in one place, while the others from the other quarter

---

299. Chapters of monastic Orders can be conventual (i.e. local), provincial or general. General chapters customarily involve representatives of the entire Order, and can take place annually, though often they occur only every four years. For dates of Dominican chapters, see above Ch. 86, § 7; Franciscan general chapters had been held since at least 1219; the first Benedictine chapter was held in 1132.

300. As in 'investigators'; i.e. those who seek evidence either in support of an accusation or independently thereof.

should convene in another, and so on for the others. Moreover, four cardinals should hold annual chapter meetings with them, with one cardinal travelling to each corner, and the cardinals should make inquiries concerning the archbishops. Following this decree, it was ordained that the pope should hold an annual chapter with the four cardinals, and that he should appoint inquisitors over them, and should punish them if they had committed any breach of their rule. Following this, it was decreed that inquisitors should be appointed over the pope, and that there should be an annual chapter thereof, and that if he had committed any wrong during the entire year, he should be punished for it. After this, they ordained that every five years a general chapter should be held, which archbishops should attend while accompanied by two discretes[301] in the service of the bishops of their archbishopric. Following this, they ordained that every ten years they should hold a council which all the bishops, archbishops and abbots should attend.

[3] After they had organised the manner in which they should hold chapter meetings, the pope said to the cardinals:

'Which of you wishes to assume the office of being chief inquisitor, with responsibility for the other inquisitors, and for organising the chapter?'

When the pope had spoken these words, a cardinal said that he desired and requested that office of serving 'Domine Deus, Agnus Dei, Filius Patris'. So the pope granted him that office in perpetuity, so long as he exercised it properly. Without further delay, they wrote a book in which were set down the rules and methods according to which the cardinal might perform his office and chapter meetings might be held.

[4] Once more without further delay, the pope commanded the presence of his prelates from all over the world, and he held a council at which said ordinance was enacted. So the cardinal decreed and appointed spies who, in secret, might investigate and detect whether the prelates would adhere to the aforesaid ordinance; and whether matters had come to the knowledge of the chapter in precisely the

---

301. In an ecclesiastical context, a 'discrete' or 'discreet' (literally 'a person of discernment') is a confidential advisor to a Superior in a religious community and an assessor thereof. In a more general social context, the term connotes a respectable and trustworthy citizen.

manner that the cardinal had caused them to be detected; and likewise whether the spies acting on behalf of the clerks against the prelates or those acting on behalf of the prelates against the clerks, or those acting on one cardinal's behalf against another, or on one prelate's behalf against another, would have the same things to report as the cardinal's own spies. Great benefit and good order arose from the aforesaid ordinance, and the princes and barons drew such a profitable example therefrom that, within their courts, they appointed inquisitors and enacted ordinances whereby justice and peace might be preserved.

[5] There were certain matters in whose regard inquiries had to be conducted, namely, vainglory, pride, greed, simony, lust, injustice, infidelity, gluttony, and so on for other matters similar to these.

It came to pass one day that a bishop had conducted an inquiry within his bishopric, from which money had been taken, yet he failed to indict or punish those responsible. So the archbishop's inquisitors discovered that the bishop had forgiven the misdeeds in question in return for money he received for so doing. When the archbishop convened a chapter, these inquisitors indicted the bishop, but the bishop secretly gave money to the archbishop, for which reason the latter failed to punish the former. The cardinal's inquisitors, however, learned of this matter, and they indicted the archbishop when he attended the chapter. So the cardinal who had convened that chapter punished the archbishop, as well as the bishop, and deprived them both of their office.

### 90. 'Qui tollis peccata mundi, miserere nobis'

[1] A cardinal long considered how he might assume a certain office in order to serve Jesus Christ, Who took away the sins of the world. While he was riding through the city of Rome and was seeking to discover which office he could fulfil, he saw two proctors who were in the service of two princes and were arguing furiously and exchanging foul language. The cardinal realised, therefore, that in the Roman Court a proctor was required who might have authority over all the other proctors, so that they, in turn, might all fear him. He went to see the pope, therefore, and said these words:

[2] 'My lord pope, you know that within your Court there are many proctors from different countries and that they are in conflict

with each other, as a result of which disputes and strife arise between them. So, were it to please you, I would assume the office of procuracy and would ensure that proctors observed proper order in their affairs. And were they not to do so, I should be able to punish them on such grounds, as justice demands.'

The pope was very glad to bestow this office upon the cardinal, so he made him master of all the proctors. The cardinal had other proctors under him who, within the Court, might act as such in a general capacity, namely, towards all those who lacked proctors within that Court. And such proctors should be remunerated from the coffers of the Holy Church, and should not receive gratuities from anybody else.

[3] One day, it occurred that a case which was being conducted between a bishop and one of his canons was due to be settled, yet, before judgement had been passed, one of the two proctors died, and so the case was held up. The other proctor, therefore, sought out the cardinal, who appointed a proctor who, in his turn, might continue the case previously pleaded by the deceased. Judgement was passed, yet a debate arose in the Court as to whether it was valid under law. The Court decided that the judgement must be valid, because the pope had issued a decree to the effect that the cardinal might appoint a proctor who should be capable and should not receive any gratuities.

[4] On a different occasion, it came about that a proctor in the service of an archbishop brought a case against the canons within his chapter, who did not have any proctors at Court. So the cardinal assigned one of his proctors to fulfil that role on the chapter's behalf, and he sent word to the chapter informing them of the charges the archbishop's proctor had levelled against the canons in that archbishop's service. And, at the Court, that proctor acted on the canons' behalf until they had sent their own proctor there.

[5] The cardinal appointed one proctor among the others to remain at the gates to the papal palace, having instructed him to act as such on behalf of those who lacked money to give to the gatekeepers, and to inform the pope of what it was they required. It occurred one day that the proctor was at the palace gates, and a poor clerk, who had been wrongly evicted from a church by his bishop, wished to have an audience with the pope, but the gatekeepers would not let him enter, although they allowed the bishop who had evicted him

from said church to do so. So the proctor for the poor, therefore, represented the clerk before the cardinal, and the cardinal pleaded his cause,[302] against that of the bishop, to the pope.

[6] 'My Holy Father the Pope', said the cardinal, 'the dead have been forgotten, yet they lack proctors who may ensure that their wishes are fulfilled as regards the Wills they leave. I, therefore, desire to have your permission to be their proctor.'

The pope decided that the cardinal should be the proctor for the dead, so the cardinal appointed his own proctors, whom he sent to different parts of the world in order to discover whether there existed anyone in such parts who might have complaint against living people who had failed to fulfil the wishes of the dead. Each of the cardinal's proctors, therefore, conducted an investigation into the bishop or archbishop of that territory to see whether he had, in fact, obliged the executors to execute the Wills. And if any bishop or archbishop had been negligent or biased in doing so, he was denounced for such to the cardinal and the cardinal punished him as he saw fit.

[7] In a town called Montpellier, in which this *Book of Evast and Blaquerna* was written, there was a very important General Chapter of the Preachers.[303] At the chapter were bishops and other prelates, as well as friars from all the Christian territories. And they read out letters at the chapter concerning various matters and reported the deaths of the friars who had died during that year. At these words, a layman—a proctor to the unbelievers, so that these might come to the Holy Catholic Faith—stood up and said in front of everyone that, if mention were made of the deaths of the friars, whose souls are alive in Paradise, how much more should remembrance be given to the souls of the unbelievers, who die in the sin of ignorance, forfeit the life of salvation and perish in everlasting fire. And these unbelievers should be given instruction whereby there might arise in them the belief that Jesus Christ has taken away the sins of the world by His Incarnation and Passion. The cardinal who was proctor of the dead came to learn about what the layman had said in the chapter meeting, as is stated above. And he, therefore, laid down a statute to the

---

302. Cat. *tench sa rahó*; in Old Catalan, the phrase *tenir la raó* (*d'algú*) means to maintain that someone is speaking or acting truthfully or in conformity with justice.

303. The Dominican Order held a number of general chapters in Montpellier during Llull's lifetime, namely, in 1247, 1265, 1271, 1283 and 1294. Llull is here referring to the 1283 chapter.

effect that at all the general chapters of the mendicant friars remembrance should be given to the unbelievers, who have died in the sin of ignorance. And to each of these chapters, the cardinal sent his proctors and his letters, so that throughout the world the Holy Catholic Faith might be preached.

### 91. 'QUI TOLLIS PECCATA MUNDI, SUSCIPE DEPRECACIONEM NOSTRAM'

[1] The pope and all his cardinals, apart from five, had assumed various offices, which were named after the *Gloria in excelsis Deo*. So the pope told these five cardinals, therefore, that, in accordance with the state of affairs which prevailed at the Court of Rome, they should seek offices wherein the number of rubrics found in the *Gloria in excelsis Deo* might be completed. So a cardinal, therefore, rode through the city of Rome to try to find out which office he could assume that might be called 'Qui tollis peccata mundi'. While he was riding through that city and was passing by the Court, he saw a man who was tearfully uttering these words:

'Alas, you wretch! What great dishonour is done to the Catholic Church, for a Jew, who repudiates, disbelieves and blasphemes against Our Lord Jesus Christ, the Son of God, Who is the foundation of our Church, has advocates and lawyers pleading his case against you! Yet you have nobody to safeguard or uphold your right against him! And, therefore, you must needs become poor, and go with your wife and your children begging from door to door for the love of God.'

[2] The cardinal felt great wonder at the words this man spoke, so he asked him why he wept and why he uttered such words:

'My lord', said the man, 'a Jew, on account of his great wealth, wrongs me and demands more money from me than I could possibly acquire! And for a long time have we both pleaded our cases, yet since I am not as well equipped as he to give a large salary to the judge or to my lawyer, I cannot, therefore, obtain justice in the Court. So I thereby feel great shame, since, through lack of money, my just cause comes to nothing at the Court of Rome, to which, judging by their beliefs and their ill will, the Jews are more hostile than other people!'

[3] Astonished at this, the cardinal felt great displeasure in his heart when he heard the words that this man spoke to him, and he

entered into deep thought. While the cardinal was thinking, a bishop who enjoyed twenty thousand silver Marks[304] of income entered Rome and passed through the square in which the cardinal was standing, so the people who were in that square said:

'This is the bishop who enjoys twenty thousand silver Marks of income and who has purchased an annuity for his brother at a cost of thirty thousand silver Marks!'

When the cardinal heard these words, he let out a great sigh and said deep within his conscience:

'Alas! A man lacking in sense, devotion and charity, to whom God has entrusted His place on earth! And how poorly are the possessions of the holy Church divided up!'

[4] When the cardinal had considered at length, he presented himself to the pope and his cardinals and, while standing before them, put forward the following question, using these words:

'Once upon a time, Intellect was called upon to give a judgement. Intellect had two sisters, the first being Memory, the second Will. There was an argument between them both as to which of the two ought to accompany Intellect. Will laid a charge against Memory, stating that it was on account of her own efforts that Intellect was diligent in seeking the truth and in desiring to judge in accordance with justice; and that very often Intellect is prevented from understanding on account of excessive remembrance. It was right and proper, therefore, that Will should accompany Intellect in making that judgement. Memory, for its part, laid charges against Will, stating that Intellect is corrupted and tends towards ignorance on account of excessive willing; and that it is fitting, therefore, that Memory and Intellect be sooner in accord than Intellect and Will. For this reason, then, according to natural justice, it was right and proper that Memory should sooner accompany Intellect than should Will.'

When the cardinal had put forward the arguments for each side, he begged the pope and his cardinals to give him judgement on this question.

---

304. The Mark had its origins as a Danish unit of account. The silver Mark, was a measure of silver in medieval western Europe, and was generally equivalent to eight ounces thereof (gold Marks likewise), though was subject to variation both geographically and across time. Evidence that the Mark also existed in the form of coinage, at least in medieval France, can be found in Kibler and Zinn (1995), 535-6.

[5] The dispute was fierce, and consultation and counsel were required, therefore, in order to reach the proper solution. When they had examined the arguments on each side and had sought the correct answer, the pope and his cardinals decided that Memory should accompany Intellect in the first instance, so that Will should not incline Intellect to take sides from the very beginning, and that, accordingly, there should be equality between both sides. They decided likewise that Will should go afterwards, so that it might thereby gain equality by virtue of the prior equality which exists between Memory and Intellect. The judgement which the pope and his cardinals had given pleased the cardinal greatly, so he spoke these words:

[6] 'According to the nature of the three powers of the soul it is ordained in law that a judge should be appointed who possesses intellect and memory first and foremost; and that the two lawyers who conduct the case against each other should likewise possess memory and will first and foremost. Through gifts and favours,[305] however, memory is replaced by will in the judge, while lawyers, through similar favours, foster will and neglect memory, through which neglect their intellect deviates from understanding. Cases, therefore, become drawn out and on many occasions are assigned false judgements, and accordingly the number of disputes, conflicts, wars, deaths and sins increases. So, in order to put an end to the aforesaid evils, it would be more appropriate to provide an adequate income from the coffers of the Holy Church to ten judges and twenty lawyers who might attend the Court of Rome and might refrain from accepting favours from anybody, than it is to provide this bishop with an income of twenty thousand silver Marks, which bishop has purchased an annuity for his brother at a cost of thirty thousand silver Marks, which thirty thousand silver Marks are aliened[306] from the work of the Holy Church.'

The pope and his cardinals were greatly pleased by what the cardinal had said, so a statute and ordinance was issued whereby ten judges and twenty lawyers might frequent the Court and the pope might remunerate them adequately from the coffers of the Holy Church and in such a way that they might refrain from accepting favours from anybody. And were they to do so, they should forfeit their

---

305. 'Favours' in the sense of gratuities.
306. To 'alien' or 'alienate' is a term in law meaning 'to transfer ownership (of property, etc.) to somebody else'.

living. So by this ordinance were court cases shortened and many constitutions laid down in order to expedite such cases.

[7] The aforesaid ordinance gained renown in every country, and many people came to plead their cases at the Court so that these might sooner be expedited. So great was the press upon the ten judges and twenty lawyers that they were unable to cope with all the cases that came to the Court, so they turned to the cardinal under whose authority the office of judges and lawyers fell, and they said that they could not endure such toil. The cardinal, therefore, presented their petition to the pope and his cardinals and pointed out that they were kept excessively busy by the vast number of cases. So, for this reason, the pope and his cardinals ordained that in each bishopric there should be judges and lawyers who judged and represented the poor in their disputes, and that both of the former should be endowed from the coffers of the Holy Church and that they should refrain from accepting favours from anybody whom they might judge or represent in court.

### 92. 'QUI SEDES AD DEXTERAM PATRIS, MISERERE NOBIS'

[1] On a very great feast day, it came to pass that, in the city of Rome, a deacon had recited the Gospel in which Jesus Christ said that it was better to enter Paradise with one eye and one foot than Hell with two eyes and two feet.[307] The deacon carefully considered this comparison and, by the grace of the Holy Spirit, he formed the intention of travelling around the world making comparisons to people, so that he might lead them to the path of salvation. The deacon went to see the pope and his cardinals, and he requested the office of comparisons. The pope said that he would assign this office to a cardinal, who should have under him many officers who might travel around the world making comparisons, and that this office should be called 'Qui sedes ad dexteram Patris, Miserere nobis'. When the pope had uttered his words, a cardinal rose to his feet and assumed the aforesaid office. This cardinal commanded a book to be written in which might be included the comparisons his disciples should convey to people.

It came to pass one day that a king came to Court and made a complaint to the pope concerning a king who had divested him and

_____

307. Matt 18:8-9.

had expelled him from his kingdom, even though he had done him no wrong. When he had made all his complaints, the king wept and gave the appearance of great sorrow, while saying these words:

'Long have I been honoured in this world. Now I have become poor and am despised by people, on account of a proud and unjust king who, by reason of his great power and his greed, has taken my territory away from me.'

While the king despaired and wept, the cardinal holding the aforesaid office asked him what was more agreeable to him: either justice or injustice. 'Justice', the king answered. The cardinal told him that it was better to be divested yet to be just and patient than to be an unjust, greedy and proud king; and that, therefore, he acted against justice, insofar as he wept for that at which one should rejoice, for the one who had divested him should weep instead, at his own injustice and pride. Following this comparison, he offered him another, namely, that it is more beneficial for someone who exercises patience and humility to be loved by God, than it is harmful to be censured by people. The king carefully considered the words the cardinal had spoken to him, and then said the following:

'If, in this world, my body has possessed the kingdom which has been taken from me, from this moment forward my soul shall possess patience, hope, humility, justice and charity, while praising and accepting the will of God.'

The pope and his cardinals were greatly pleased by what the king had said, and they made honourable provision for him from the coffers of the Holy Church, and they discussed how that of which he had been divested might be returned to him.

[2] A bishop against whom an accusation had been made by his chapter came to that Court. This bishop was a just man of saintly life. And because he exercised justice towards his clergy, they, in turn, wished to depose him and to have as their master someone who might consent to their wrongdoings. This bishop went to see the cardinal, and asked his counsel as to what would serve him better: either to let himself be accused without speaking in his own defence, and to exercise patience, humility and poverty; or to defend himself and to accuse his chapter and to conduct the accusation at the Court, as the law itself permitted him to do. The cardinal and the bishop spoke at length regarding the above-mentioned matter, seeking to discover according to which of the two aforesaid alternatives the bishop could

exercise greater perfection and more numerous virtues. And they found that, as far as the bishop was concerned, it would be better for him not to defend himself, since greater patience, fortitude and humility would arise accordingly; but that, as far as justice and charity were concerned, it would be advisable for him to mount a defence and for the truth to be made evident, so that justice might not lose its prerogative within his chapter. So the cardinal, therefore, answered the bishop that he could make whichever choice he wished, given that he could avail himself virtuously of either of the alternatives, and in such a manner as might thereby be agreeable to God.

[3] A man who made comparisons arrived in a city and went through the streets asking in a loud voice which of the following two things was more necessary: either to raise one's son to good customs or to bequeath to him great wealth. And he likewise asked which was better: either to return ill-gotten gains and to leave one's children impoverished, but to enter Paradise; or to leave one's children wealthy and not make amends for one's wrongs, but to enter Hell. While this man was going through the streets crying out in such a manner, he passed by the house of a usurer who cogitated at length upon the words this man had said. And so often did he hear those words cried out that remorse overcame his sensual nature, strengthened his charity, reversed his wrongs and made him raise his children to exercise good conduct.

[4] Death, which spares neither young nor old, struck down the son of an honoured burgher of Rome. This burgher had no other son and had no hope of ever having another such, so his son's death caused him very great sadness and rage. The cardinal came to learn that this burgher was profoundly grief-stricken, so he went to see him and offered him the following comparison, using these words:

'Beloved son', said the cardinal, 'what benefits a person more greatly: either praising God for the goods He has given one in this world or doing likewise for those He has taken away?'

'My lord', said the burgher 'the first kind of praise concerns gratitude, the second patience. And since patience yields suffering, in the absence of sin, greater virtue corresponds thereto than to gratitude, which yields pleasure, in the absence of suffering.'

'Blessed son', said the cardinal, 'you have judged correctly, and, therefore, you yourself have judged that you must exercise patience. God has put you to the test in two ways: the first was by means of gratitude, which you showed in praising God once he had given you your son; the second had regard to patience, when he called your son from this life to the next. So, had your son not died, you would, being tested in the first way alone, have forfeited the merit that was prepared for you so as to be the occasion of great happiness.'[308]

[5] A man was going through the main square in Rome asking in a loud voice which was better: to sell something cheaply and to tell the truth, or to lie and to sell at too high a price. While he was proclaiming these words, a large number of ladies passed through the square. Among all the others, there was one who was dressed in very ornate attire and who had greatly embellished her features with colourings and other things. This man cried out, asking what was better: a beautiful lady who revealed herself to be overly fond of lust or a hideous one who gave the impression of being chaste. This man went to stand in front of these ladies, crying out the aforesaid words. In her retinue were squires who accompanied this lady, so she commanded that this man be beaten and put to shame for the words he had spoken. These squires beat the crier of comparisons, at which he was unable to exercise patience and, so, made complaint to the cardinal concerning the wrong which had been done to him. The cardinal, however, harshly rebuked him, dismissed him from his post and replaced him with someone else, who might show a fondness for patience.

[6] A crier went to a city and called out in a loud voice, asking who was better: 'What-Will-People-Say?' or 'Little-Do-I-Care'. As he passed through the main square crying out like this, the people therein asked him to explain to them those words he was calling out. So he said that 'What-Will-People-Say?' was the censure people fear when they carry out anything which is at variance with the vanities of this world; and that 'Little-Do-I-Care' was the censure one despises since it is at variance with virtue, God's honour and contempt for this world. So a wise man replied to this crier by saying that Sir 'What-Will-People-Say?' had more supporters, but that Sir 'Little-Do-I-Care' had better ones.

[7] Once upon a time it came to pass that two friars who had learned Arabic travelled to the land of the Saracens in order to preach the Incarnation and Passion of the Son of God. But in one of

---

308. The happiness here referred to, of course, is that of Heavenly beatitude.

them devotion and charity cooled, so he made his way back and abandoned his companion, for he feared death and he longed for the good food he used to eat and the respect he used to enjoy amongst people. While he was making his way back, he encountered at the entrance to a city a crier who was calling out to ask which death was better: death which occurred through illness; or death which occurred through martyrdom.

'And which death accords better with the seven virtues and is more contrary to the seven deadly sins? And by which death does one resemble more closely the crimson garments that the Son of God received from human nature?'

While this man was crying out in this manner, the friar, who was fatigued from his journey, sat down beside a beautiful woman and felt the temptation of carnal pleasure. So the crier made a comparison by asking which of the following was more worthy of merit: to go among the unbelievers at the risk of death while suppressing one's fear through strength of resolve, or to live among Christian believers while resisting worldly pleasures? The religious cogitated at length upon the words that the crier had called out, and he returned to his companion and felt contrition for the weakness of resolve to which his lack of devotion had led him to succumb.

[8] On another occasion it came to pass that, at the king's palace, this crier called out to ask which was better: to be king or to be a simple knight of one shield?[309] Following this, he went off to the bishop's palace and called out to ask which was better: to be a bishop or to be a simple parish priest? After this, he went to an abbey and called out to ask which was better: to be an abbot or to be a claustral monk? Next, he went before the pope, calling out to ask which was better: that the tithe of the Holy Church should always be assigned to setting the world aright or that bishops spend it on trifling and superfluous things?

In all these ways and many besides did the officers of comparisons cry out. And they accomplished great good, for they continually

---

309. Cat. *cavaller simple de un scut*: the 'estate' of *cavallers de un escut* reappears in Llull's *Arbre de ciència* (*Tree of Science*) (1295-96) in the 'Imperial Tree', ORL XI, 307, between those of 'barons' and 'burghers'. According to Noel Fallows, such knights are 'the lowest rank [thereof] in the chivalric hierarchy', see Llull (2013), 45 and 88, n. 5.

awakened devotion, remorse, charity, diligence and the other virtues in people's hearts.


## 93. 'QUONIAM TO SOLUS SANCTUS'

[1] One day, Pope Blaquerna was with his cardinals and they were reflecting upon whether they could do anything from which benefit might arise for the exaltation of the Catholic faith. While they were all together, a cardinal entered who had preached to a large crowd of people, so the pope asked him whether he had seen anybody weeping in response to his sermon; the cardinal replied that he had not, but that he had seen many people sleeping while he preached. The pope told the cardinals that it was a great wonder that the people exercised such scant devotion towards sermons, given that the Saracens themselves, who abide in error, weep in response thereto. One of the pope's scribes, versed in Arabic, who had been born and raised in the land of Outremer, and who belonged to the Christians of the Girdle,[310] said that the Saracens preached on the subject of devotion and the contemplation of the glory of Paradise and the torments of Hell, and that therefore their audiences felt devotion towards their sermons and wept on account of that very devotion.

[2] After these words, a cardinal, very learned in natural philosophy, said that in order to preach it was of use to prove by means of natural reasons the manner in which virtues and vices are contrary to each other, and how one virtue is in accord with another, and one vice, similarly, with another.

'And likewise', he continued, 'how one can curb a vice using a given virtue or even two, and how one can foster a given virtue using another such. And this method exists in the *Brief Art of Finding Truth*. Preaching, therefore, has need of a natural art, along with devotion,

---

310. 'Christians of the Girdle' or 'of the Belt', were so called because of the wide belts or sashes they wore. It has been said that 'Christians of the Girdle [...] followed the primitive Syrian rite of the Church of Antioch', in Chareyron (2005), 247-8, n. 29. It has also been said that the purpose of their girdle, instituted by the secular authorities, was to distinguish Christians living in Muslim lands from the Muslim population at large, and was regarded as 'a mark of ignominy' by the laity, in Butler (1884), 103-104. For the lack of clarity surrounding the term, even among fourteenth-century writers, see Jotischky (2004), in Allen (2004), 88-106, here 93 and n. 40.

contemplation and short sermons, so that people retain their devotion without lapsing into boredom.'

[3] When the cardinal had said these words, the pope and his cardinals ordained that as many sermons should be delivered as there were days in a year, and that contained therein should be all the best subject matter which might be suitable for preaching. They likewise ordained that these sermons should be of a suitable quantity and should be comprehensible to people, since their minds most often lack devotion by reason of ignorance. These three hundred and sixty-five sermons should be general and should be preached sequentially each year, one after the other. Next, the pope ordained that devout men of saintly lives should proceed daily through the streets of the cities and towns giving voice to their contemplation of the torments of Hell and the glory of Heaven, so that people might daily call to mind such torments and such glory. Once all these things had been ordained, the pope entrusted this office to a cardinal, who might serve as the officer of 'Quoniam tu solus sanctus' via the activities of preaching and contemplation.

[4] The cardinal who was endowed with the aforementioned office appointed his proxies and officials who might travel through countries proclaiming the torments of Hell, the glory of Paradise and death in this world, as is recounted in the *Book of Instruction for Children*,[311] which a man wrote for his beloved son. After this, and in consultation with the religious and with those who held the office of preaching, he ordained how they ought to preach; and how, were any excess to occur in the exercise of that office, it might be corrected; as well as how one might so elevate one's will by preaching that God might thereby be loved and served with fervour via the reinforcement and exaltation presented by great devotion.

## 94. 'Tu solus Dominus'

[1] It came to pass that an envoy from the cardinal of 'Quoniam tu solus sanctus' sent a message to the latter stating that, because of the diversity of languages, preaching was being hindered and the criers of contemplation could not in all clarity impart to people devotion

---

311. Llull's own *Doctrina pueril,* written in 1274-76. For details, see above Ch. 2, § 5.

towards Paradise or fear of the suffering and torments of Hell. When the cardinal had received the message, he presented it to the pope so that an ordinance might be issued whereby the preachers and contemplators might have greater freedom in exercising their office.

[2] While the cardinal was presenting to the pope the letters his envoy had sent him, it came to pass that an envoy from the Cardinal of Telling[312] was presented to the pope, to whom he reported that he had encountered great strife in the world between people on account of the fact that they belonged to various nations which used a range of different languages. And because of this diversity of languages, these people waged wars against each other, on account of which wars and languages they divided themselves into different beliefs and sects, which were in conflict with each other. The pope cogitated at length upon the two aforesaid messages and assembled all the cardinals, and he asked them what counsel could be taken in order to eliminate the diversity of languages, and to which language it would be preferable to make all people in general conform, so that they might understand and love each other, and might agree to serve God.

[3] A cardinal replied:

'My lord pope, in order to achieve what you ask, it is necessary for you and your Court to be on pleasant and amicable terms with Christian princes, and to reconcile them and their subjects in the matter of customs, by selecting the best thereof. And in each province there should be a city wherein Latin is spoken by all parties, for Latin is the most prevalent language and other languages contain many words in Latin, and our books are written in Latin. Once this has been achieved, it is necessary that women and men should be assigned to go to this city in order to learn Latin and that, when they return to their countries, they should teach it to their children as soon as these start learning to talk. Thus, through lengthy persistence, you will be able to ensure that there is but a single language, a single belief and a single faith in the entire world, for which reason each pope in succession must be devoted to the above task, as is necessary if one wishes to attend to as important an enterprise as you have undertaken.'

[4] When the cardinal had finished speaking, the chamberlain told him that what he had said would be too difficult to achieve and that too great an expense would be incurred in carrying out such a

312. Cf. above, Ch. 88.

task. While the chamberlain was saying these words, a recently elected bishop, who had come to Court to be confirmed, presented himself to the pope. The bishopric to which he had been elected possessed an income of approximately fifteen thousand silver Marks. Accompanying this bishop was a messenger in the service of the cardinal of 'Domine Filii' who reported that in the places where he had been, he had heard it said that all the evil and error that was in the world derived from the faults and failings of the pope and his cardinals, who could have taken counsel as to how to set the world in order, yet had not taken care or diligence to do so; and that because of the unsuitable example that they and their officers had set to the people, the world was in conflict and error.

[5] After the messenger had conveyed these words, the pope asked the chamberlain which was better: to attend to the aforesaid enterprise and to endow it with five thousand Marks of income from the aforesaid bishopric or to confirm the bishop and for the pope and his cardinals to retain the ignominious reputations they had acquired. The chamberlain replied by saying that it would be better to attend to the aforesaid task, provided that one could be certain it might be achieved. The pope asked the chamberlain if it was possible, given the power of God and that of the Holy Church, that this undertaking might be accomplished, either in part or in full, so the chamberlain, ashamed and perplexed, was obliged to concede to the pope's aims.

[6] 'My lords and companions, friends, beloved sons', said the pope to the cardinals, 'in order to honour the Passion of Jesus Christ, I require you to assist me in ensuring that we may convert all the languages which exist into one alone. For, if there exists but one language, people will be able to understand each other and, through such understanding, will love each other and more readily adopt similar customs, in regard to which they shall be in accord. And, using such methods, will our preachers go among the unbelievers with greater boldness and secrecy, and these latter will sooner understand the truth of the path to salvation. And through such an enterprise can the whole world attain a wholesome condition wherein those in error can be led to conversion.'

The cardinals were very pleased by what the pope had requested of them, and each of them volunteered to attend to the task with all of the powers of his intellect and will. So, on the basis of this ordinance, the pope and his cardinals issued a decree, and entrusted that post to a cardinal who might fulfil the office and possess sufficient funds to maintain its existence.

## 95. 'TU SOLUS ALTISSIMUS, JHESU CHRISTE, CUM SANCTO SPIRITU IN GLORIA DEI PATRIS. AMEN'

[1] Pope Blaquerna was thinking about how he might secure peace and accord between communities who are in profound discord because they have failed to reach agreement in terms of showing obedience to one prince alone, who might maintain peace and justice. While the pope was engaged in such considerations, two friars conversant in Arabic who had been unable to get to a city in which they had wished to preach the Gospels, sent a letter to him stating that they were hindered by the fact that they could not travel safely along the roads. So they begged him to write to the prince of that country, so that the latter might send them envoys through whose agency they might be able to proceed to that city they desired to visit. When the pope had received their letter, he summoned the cardinals and said these words:

[2] 'Between us, we reached an agreement whereby, for as long as the *Gloria in excelsis Deo*, which is sung in the Holy Church, might last, a cardinal ought to be assigned to each part of the hymn in order to fulfil that office. So, it is necessary to organise envoys who might travel throughout the world to visit princes, and might ensure that our friars may travel its length and breadth to preach the word of God. These princes should receive from us letters, entreaties and thanks, so that out of love for us they may show favour to the friars. It is likewise necessary for us continually to send envoys to the Communes so that we may negotiate peace with Lombardy, Tuscany and Venice,[313] as also for us to ensure that justice and charity obtain between one

---

313. City communes were self-governing republics answerable to no lords below the level of king or emperor. The Lombard League was established in 1167 to act as a bulwark against Imperial pretensions regarding influence over Italy, and ended in 1250 following the death of Frederick II, the last of the Hohenstaufen emperors. The Republics of Venice, Pisa and Genoa were wealthy and powerful in the area of overseas trade, and all had significant merchant and naval fleets.

commune and another. So I entrust this office, therefore, to the cardinal who is yet to assume one.'

[3] The cardinal was greatly pleased by the office of envoys which the pope had conferred upon him, so he sent his envoys across his provinces and sought to discover which territories were suitable for his friars and to the other men who had learned various languages, so that they might be able to travel along those routes between one country and another. Once the cardinal had organised all these matters, the pope sent his envoys and jewels to those princes so that they might keep the roads safe for those who would be sent by the pope.

[4] The cardinal built hospices, bridges, churches and bastions along the routes so that one might be able to travel along them in greater safety, and that on account of the communication of one group of people with another there might be love and accord, as well as that the Holy Roman Faith might be preached in the countries which belonged to pagans and to unbelievers. The chamberlain provided the cardinal with large amounts of money, so that the latter might accomplish the aforesaid task. And he asked the pope, therefore, to gather treasure from the coffers of the Holy Church so that it might suffice for the officers of *Gloria in excelsis Deo*, so the pope commanded that the aforesaid officers should have what they required. And on account of the expansion the Holy Church underwent by dint of their activities, that Church acquired income over and above the money that was spent upon the offices.

[5] 'Holy Father', said the cardinal, 'how can we dispose our envoys to negotiate peace between the Communes?'

The pope replied by saying that the envoys should travel through the Communes closely observing which one had committed wrongs against another. So the pope ensured that each Podesta[314] might annually go to a safe place where all the Podestas could meet. He likewise said that mutual friendship and correction should be discussed, following the form of a chapter meeting, and that monetary punishments should be exacted upon those who were unwilling to abide by

---

314. Cat. *potestat*; It. *podestà*: the podesta (or podest) was, in Lombard cities, a governor appointed by the Holy Roman Emperor, at least until the formation of the Lombard League, that is, or a chief magistrate in the Italian medieval city states, such as Florence. Often his role was perceived to be in conflict with or aginst the interest of the communes. Many of the doctors of civil or canon law were recruited by the Italian Communes for the role of podesta.

the decisions of the definitors[315] of the chapter. So, on account of the ordinance the pope issued in the abovementioned form, the communes attained peace and accord.

[6] One day, it occurred that two of the King of India's envoys came to visit the pope so that he might provide them with students who would learn their language. So, the pope immediately sent word to the cardinal of 'Tu solus sanctus altissimus', commanding him to perform what the King of India had requested, for such performance befitted his office. The cardinal carried out and performed the above task.

The benefits and the virtuous example which arose from the cardinal's office were inestimable. And since the pope and his cardinals did all they could to fulfil the offices they had undertaken to fulfil, God, therefore, granted them blessings and success in their works, and caused them to be pleasing to people.

Here ends the book of *Gloria in excelsis Deo*.

---

315. A 'definitor' or 'diffinitor' is itself defined by the *DCVB* as follows: 'each of the religious who, together with the minister general or provincial, defines points relating to the discipline and rules of an Order'. It was a term for an office which originated within the structures and constitutions of the nascent Cistercian Order and was interpreted differently by the Cistercians themselves, the Dominicans and the Franciscans.

96. ON HOW BLAQUERNA RELINQUISHED THE PAPACY

[1] Pope Blaquerna grew old, and he remembered the desire he had once entertained to live the life of a hermit, so when he was in the Consistory, in private with all his cardinals, he said the following words:

'By divine blessings, the papacy and the Court of Rome are in a very good condition, and from such good order arises great expansion to the Catholic faith. So, on account of the grace that God has bestowed upon the Court, so that He may preserve it in the good order in which it exists, it would be profitable for us to appoint an officer who might daily offer prayers and lead a contemplative life, a life in which he might pray that God preserve order within the Court so that the latter might be to His honour and might itself receive benefit.'

Each of the cardinals considered the above to be advisable. So they sought to discover a saintly and devout man of great perfection in order that his prayers might thereby be more pleasing to God.

[2] When the pope had heeded the cardinals' intentions, he knelt down before them all, begging them to allow him to relinquish the papacy and to be granted this office of prayer. All the cardinals knelt before the pope and remonstrated with him, saying that it was not appropriate for him to relinquish the office of pope, and in particular because, were he to do so, there would accordingly be a risk that the Court might not exist in such a well-ordered state as it had by virtue of God and of the saintly life of Blaquerna. Pope Blaquerna replied that the cardinals had achieved such a great degree of perfection on account of the offices of *Gloria in excelsis Deo*, that henceforth such a state of good order could not be destroyed, and still less so by the governance of a different pope elected according to the art by which the abbess Natana herself was elected. For so long did the pope remain kneeling, and so profusely did he weep before the cardinals

and with such great insistence did he ask for mercy, that they all obeyed his command.

[3] Who could describe to you the joy and happiness Blaquerna experienced when he was released from the papacy and felt free to go to serve God by leading the life of a hermit? So, while he was engaged in such considerations and delight, he said the following words to the cardinals:

'My lords, I have long desired to be the servant and contemplator of God by leading the life of a hermit so that there might not be anything else in my heart but God alone. Tomorrow after Mass, I must go to seek my hermitage and must, begging your grace and blessing, take my leave of you, sirs, you who shall be in my memory and in my prayers all the days of my life. And I give great thanks to God and to you for having so admirably assisted me in upholding the papacy for so very long.'

[4] The cardinals were greatly displeased when they heard that he wished to go to the forests and to become a hermit, so they begged him to live and remain in the city of Rome or in another city he might prefer, in which city he could remain in contemplation and prayer. The blessed Blaquerna, however, did not yield to their entreaties, so kindled was he by divine inspiration! So the following day, after Mass, he decided to go to his hermitage and to take leave of his companions.

[5] 'My lord Blaquerna', said the cardinals, 'we have all long been obedient to you and have fulfilled your commands. You are old and thin and require such food and such a place that you may enjoy bodily sustenance, so that you might better be able to labour at the spiritual and contemplative life. We beg you, therefore, to remain among us for as long as it takes us to find a suitable hermitage for you and have prepared it in such a way that you may inhabit it, and sing and celebrate the Divine Office. And in the meantime, with your counsel, we shall have elected a pope who will give you grace and blessings when you take your leave of us, who shall remain greatly saddened by your departure.'

The cardinals entreated Blaquerna with such devotion and such reasonable words that he felt obliged to obey their entreaties.

[6] While Blaquerna was with the cardinals in the city of Rome, the latter sent out envoys through the woods and across the high peaks in order to seek a suitable place in which Blaquerna might live.

So, on a high peak where there was a hermit's church, next to a spring, they made preparations for Blaquerna to be able to live there. And they ordained that a monastery which stood at the foot of the mountain should provide him with all his needs to the end of his days. And, during this period in which the cardinals had sought a location for Blaquerna, they elected the cardinal of 'Laudamus te' to be pope, who became such in the manner whereby the art thereof had shown them to elect him. Thus, the office of *Gloria in excelsis Deo*, which Blaquerna had previously held, was entrusted to this pope, while the cardinal's own office was entrusted to a newly elected cardinal who replaced that of 'Laudamus te'.

### 97. ON THE LEAVE THAT BLAQUERNA TOOK OF THE POPE AND HIS CARDINALS

[1] Blaquerna rose early and celebrated the Mass of the Holy Spirit in private.[316] Afterwards, the pope sang solemn Mass and prayed. And he recounted all the benefits and good order that Blaquerna had achieved within the Court, and how he had relinquished the papacy and had gone to perform penance in the high peaks, as well as how he had wished to live in the company of trees, birds and beasts and to contemplate the God of glory. The pope had at his disposal such worthy subject matter whereby to speak about Blaquerna the hermit, and he uttered it with such devotion, that the cardinals and the people of Rome who were present at the sermon were unable to refrain from weeping. And everyone lamented the fact that Blaquerna was leaving them; all the more so since he was an elderly man and had decided to torment his body with solitude and a life of austerity.

[2] While the pope was preaching and the people were weeping, a hermit who lived in the walls of Rome, said the following words to him:

'My lord father the Pope, there are a vast number of hermits within the city of Rome who live in the walls and are recluses. And many a time it happens that we face temptation, yet know neither how to

---

316. Masses of the Holy Spirit were traditionally celebrated in the first medieval universities at the start of the academic year, thus indicating the beginning of a new period; they were also frequently celebrated prior to battle, thus indicating the beginning of a new ordeal.

contemplate nor to lament our sins. So, since Blaquerna has appointed many officers to serve God and to set the world in order, I beg him,
on behalf of all the hermits of Rome, to live alongside us within this
city and to be our teacher and our visitor, and that this may be his office. So, through this office, he shall be of benefit to us and to himself, and shall be able to persist in leading the life of a hermit.'

[3] The pope and his cardinals begged Blaquerna to remain and
to accept the office the hermit had mentioned, for great good would
come of it, and all the more so from the worthy example he would set
people. Blaquerna exempted himself, however, and said that on no
account would he dwell among people. So he took leave of everybody, begging, imploring and beseeching their pardon; and he said
that if he had done any wrong to them, he asked them to forgive him
and to pray for his sake to the God of glory. Once Blaquerna had
finished speaking, the hermit requested the office which he had
asked Blaquerna to accept, and the pope granted it to him with his
grace and blessings.

[4] Blaquerna adopted the humble clothing consistent with the life
of a hermit, made the sign whereby our redemption is signified and
kissed the pope's feet and hands, tearfully commending him to God.
The pope, in turn, kissed him and commanded that two cardinals
should escort him as far as the hermitage in which he was to live and
that, if anything were to need mending in that place, the two cardinals
should carry it out at once. The cardinals escorted Blaquerna, and the
entire populace did likewise as far as the city gates. Blaquerna begged
the cardinals to turn back and to stay behind, along with the entire
populace, but the cardinals did not wish to stay, so they went with him
as far as the cell in which they had prepared his dwelling place.

[5] In that place was a very beautiful spring and an ancient chapel, as well as a very fine cell. Close by, at a distance of a mile from that
chapel, was a house in which lived a man who might serve Blaquerna
and prepare food for him, so that the latter might better be able to
contemplate. This man was a deacon whom Blaquerna dearly loved
and who did not wish to be parted from him, a man in whose company Blaquerna chose to live, so that the former might assist him
daily in the Divine Office. Once Blaquerna was in his hermitage and
had the trappings which befit a hermit, the cardinals took their leave
of Blaquerna very courteously, commended themselves to his prayers
and returned to Rome.

## 98. On the life that Blaquerna led in his hermitage

[1] Blaquerna would rise at midnight and open the windows of his cell so that he might see the sky and the stars, and he would begin his prayers as devoutly as he could, so that his entire soul might be with God and that his eyes might shed tears and weep. When Blaquerna had contemplated and wept right up until Matins, he would enter the church and ring the Matins bell, and the deacon would come to assist him in saying them. After dawn, he would celebrate Mass. Once he had done this, Blaquerna would say a few words to the deacon concerning God in order to make him enamoured of Him, and they would both converse about God and His works, and together they would weep on account of the great devotion which was present in the words they had uttered. After they had finished talking, the deacon would go into the kitchen garden and work on certain tasks, while Blaquerna would leave the church and give diversion to his soul from the hardships his body had endured, and he would gaze upon the mountains and the plains in order that he might have some recreation.

[2] As soon as Blaquerna felt refreshed, he would commence his prayers and contemplation, and he would read from the books of Divine Scripture or from the *Book of Contemplation*,[317] and he would remain like this until Terce. After this, they would say Terce, Sext and None; and after Terce, the deacon would return to the garden and prepare certain grasses and legumes for Blaquerna. Blaquerna would work in the garden or on certain tasks so as not to remain idle and so that his body might thereby attain greater health and, between Sext and None, would go to eat. After he had eaten, he would return to the church all by himself, where he would give thanks to God. When he had completed his prayers, he would remain there for an hour, and he would then go to take recreation in the garden and at the spring, and would frequent those places where he might best uplift his soul. Following this, he would sleep, so that by doing so he might better endure the hardships of the night. When he had slept, he would wash his hands and face and would remain there until the moment he rang Vespers, at which the deacon would join him. And when they had said Vespers, they would say Compline,[318] and the dea-

---

317. I.e. Llull's own *LC* (1273-74 (?)).
318. For all the Canonical Hours here mentioned, see below, Appendix II.

con would then go back. So Blaquerna would start to consider those
things which best pleased him or which might best be able to prepare
him to begin his prayers.

[3] After the sun had set, Blaquerna would climb up onto the flat
roof which lay above his cell, and would remain there in prayer until
the early hours of the night, gazing at the sky and the stars with tearful eyes and a devout heart, while considering God's Honours and
the wrongs that people commit in this world against Him. Blaquerna
remained so very steadfastly and fervently in contemplation from
sunset until the early hours of the night that, when he had gone to
bed and was asleep, it seemed to him as if he were with God according to the manner in which he had performed his prayer.

[4] Blaquerna remained living like this, in a state of happiness,
until the people of that region developed a great devotion to the virtues of the altar of the Holy Trinity, which stood in that chapel. And
on account of the devotion they entertained towards that place, men
and women came there, and they disturbed Blaquerna's prayer and
contemplation. However, in order that the people should not lose
the devotion they felt towards that place, he hesitated to tell them not
to come there. Blaquerna, therefore, transferred his cell to a mountain which lay a mile away from the church and a mile further away
from where the deacon lived. And he lived and slept in that place,
refusing to go to the church at any time when people were there or
to allow any man or woman to visit the cell to which he had transferred himself in order to live.

[5] So Blaquerna the hermit lived and dwelt thus, believing that
he had never led as agreeable a life nor ever been as well equipped to
greatly raise his soul to God. So saintly was the life he led, that God
accordingly blessed and gave guidance to all those who felt devotion
towards the virtues of that place in which the chapel stood. So the
pope, his cardinals and their officers lived more fully in the grace of
God on account of Blaquerna's saintly life.

99. ON HOW BLAQUERNA THE HERMIT WROTE THE *BOOK OF THE LOVER
AND THE BELOVED*

[1] One day it happened that the hermit who lived in Rome, as we
mentioned earlier, went to visit the hermits and recluses who also

lived there. And he discovered that they underwent many temptations in certain regards because they did not know how to adopt a method best suited to their lives. So he thought that he should go to see Blaquerna the hermit in order to ask him to write a book concerning the eremitic life, so that by using this book he might gain the ability and wisdom whereby to maintain the other hermits in contemplation and devotion. One day, while Blaquerna was at prayer, this hermit came to his cell and requested the said book from him. Blaquerna cogitated at length upon the method and subject matter according to which he would write the book.

[2] While Blaquerna was engaged in such thoughts, he decided fervently to devote himself to the worship and contemplation of God, so that in his prayer God might reveal to him the method and subject matter concerning which he might write this book. While Blaquerna wept and worshipped, and when God had raised his soul to the furthest limits of its ability to contemplate Him, he felt that he had transcended method[319] as a result of the great fervour and devotion he experienced. So he cogitated upon the fact that the power of love adheres to no method when the Lover very fervently loves his Beloved. So Blaquerna, therefore, decided to write the *Book of the Lover and the Beloved*, in which the Lover would be a faithful and devout Christian while the Beloved would be God.

[3] While Blaquerna was meditating in this way, he remembered how, once, when he was pope, a Saracen had told him that, amidst all the others, the Saracens had certain pious men, among whom those held in highest esteem were certain people called 'Sufis'. And these people use words of love and brief exemplary tales which inspire great devotion in a person. These words need to be explained, and such explanations cause the intellect to ascend, and on account of such an ascent the will rises and grows in devotion. So, having entertained such thoughts, Blaquerna set out to write the book in the above manner. So he told the hermit to return to Rome and that, after a short time, he would send the deacon to him with the *Book of the Lover and the Beloved*,

---

319. Cat. *se sentí exit de manera*: the expression 'eixir de manera' means literally 'to exceed (or go beyond) method (or reason)'. In this expression we see an example of *excessus mentis* or ecstasy/rapture, terms used since the time of St Ambrose (*c*.340-397) and also present in Richard of St Victor's description of the sixth and final stage of contemplation in *The Mystical Ark* (or *Benjamin major*).

by means of which he might increase the fervour and devotion of the hermits, in whom he wished to inspire the love of God.

## 100. ON THE *BOOK OF THE LOVER AND THE BELOVED*

### PROLOGUE

[1] Blaquerna was at prayer, so he considered the manner in which he was contemplating God and His virtues. And when he had finished praying, he wrote down that very manner whereby he had done so. And this he did every day, incorporating new reasonings into his prayers, so that in many and various ways he might compose the *Book of the Lover and the Beloved*, and that those ways might be concise and might enable the soul to go over a great number of them in a short time.

So, with God's blessing, Blaquerna began his book, which he divided into as many versicles as there are days in a year. And each versicle is sufficient for contemplating God throughout the whole day, in accordance with the art of the *Book of Contemplation*.

### HERE BEGIN THE MORAL METAPHORS

#### [1]
The Lover asked his Beloved whether there remained anything else to love within Him. And the Beloved replied that whatever could increase the Lover's love was to be loved.

#### [2]
The paths along which the Lover seeks his Beloved are long and dangerous, peopled with cares, sighs and tears, and enlightened by love.

#### [3]
Many lovers gathered to love a Beloved, who lavished love upon them all. And, for his fortune, each of them had his Beloved and his agreeable thoughts, whereby they each felt pleasurable tribulation.

#### [4]
The Lover was weeping and said: 'How long will it be until the shadows in this world disappear, so that the paths to Hell might do like-

wise? And when will the time come when water, which normally flows downwards, is apt to flow upwards? And the innocent, when will they outnumber the guilty?'

## [5]

'Ah! When shall the Lover boast that he will die for his Beloved?[320] And the Beloved, when shall He see His Lover languish for the love of Him?'

## [6]

The Lover said to the Beloved: 'You who fill the sun with radiance, fill my heart with love.'

The Beloved replied: 'Without the fullness of love your eyes would not be in tears, nor would you have come to this place to look upon your Beloved.'

## [7]

The Beloved tested His Lover as to whether he loved perfectly, and asked him what the difference was between the presence and absence of a Beloved.

The Lover replied: 'Between ignorance and forgetting, and knowledge and remembrance.'

## [8]

The Beloved asked the Lover: 'Do you recall anything whereby I have rewarded you for having chosen to love Me?'

He replied: 'Yes indeed, the fact that, in my regard, You make no distinction between the pains and the pleasures You afford me.'

## [9]

'Tell me, Lover', said the Beloved, 'Will you still exercise patience if I increase your languor?'[321]

'Yes, so long as You increase my love.'

---

320. A familiar theme of the courtly lyric, here transposed to a religious context; cf. also above, Ch. 76, § 4.

321. Here, the theme of languor is carried over by Llull from the Song of Songs, 2:5 and 5:8: 'quia amore langueo' ('because I languish with love'), and, plausibly suggestive of a state prior to ecstasy, permeates the *Lover*.

[10]

The Beloved said to the Lover: 'Do you know yet what love is?'

He replied: 'If I did not know what love is, would I know what pain, sadness and sorrow are?'

[11]

They asked the Lover: 'Why do you not reply to your Beloved, Who is calling you?'

He replied: 'I venture into grave danger so that I may reach Him, and I speak to Him already by desiring His Honours.'[322]

[12]

'Foolish Lover, why do you bring ruin upon yourself, spend all your money, forsake the pleasures of this world and go scorned among people?'

He replied: 'In order to do honour to the Honours of my Beloved, who is rejected and dishonoured by more people than he is honoured and loved.'

[13]

'Tell us, Fool of Love, which is more visible: the Beloved in the Lover or the Lover in the Beloved?'

The Lover replied by saying that the Beloved is seen by Love, and the Lover by sighs, tears, anguish and sorrow.

[14]

The Lover sought someone who might inform his Beloved that he, for the sake of his love, was undergoing grave hardship, and was dying. And he found his Beloved, Who was reading from a book in which were written all the languors that love had given him on account of his Beloved, as well as all the pleasures he had gained therefrom.

[15]

Our Lady brought her Son to the Lover so that the latter might kiss His feet, and might write down in his book the virtues of Our Lady.

---

322. For 'Honours', see above, Ch. 3, § 8 and corresponding note.

### [16]

'O bird who sings, tell me, did you place yourself in the care of my Beloved so that He might protect you from love's absence and cause love to grow in you?'

The bird replied: 'Who makes me sing, if not the Lord of Love alone, Who considers love's absence to be a dishonour?'

### [17]

Between fear and hope has Love made its abode, where it lives upon its cares, yet dies in oblivion when its foundations rest upon the pleasures of this world.

### [18]

A debate arose between the Lover's eyes and his memory. For his eyes said that it was preferable to see the Beloved rather than to remember Him.[323] But his memory said that, through remembering, one's eyes well up with tears and love is kindled in one's heart.

### [19]

The Lover asked Intellect and Will which was closer to the Beloved. So they both began to run, but the Intellect reached its Beloved sooner than did Will.

### [20]

The Lover and the Beloved were arguing and were seen doing so by another lover, who wept for as long as it took peace and accord to be achieved between the Beloved and the Lover.

### [21]

Sighs and tears came for judgement to the Beloved and asked Him by which of them He felt most ardently loved.

The Beloved judged that sighs are closer to love, and tears to eyes.

---

323. The *visio Dei* mentioned in Matt 5:8, is reserved for the 'clean of heart', among whom the Lover is clearly numbered. For cleanliness of heart in Ramon Llull's programme of ecclesiastical and moral reform, see above, Ch. 74; for the 'spiritual senses' in Llull's thought, see above, Ch. 39, § 2 and corresponding note. The *visio Dei* was generally associated with the Beatific vision, though was often held to be accessible to mystical experience via mystical union.

[22]

The Lover went to drink at the spring from which he who does not love shall, on drinking, feel love, but his languor underwent increase.

So the Beloved went to drink from the spring so that He might increase beyond increase His Lover's love, wherein He might likewise increase his languor.

[23]

The Lover fell ill and his Beloved tended to him. He fed him with merit and gave him love to drink, making him lie down in patience, clothing him in humility and prescribing him truth.

[24]

They asked the Lover where his Beloved was.

He replied: 'He is here, in a house nobler than all the other noble things in creation. He is here, in my love, in my languor and in my tears.'

[25]

They asked the Lover: 'Where are you going?'
    'I come from my Beloved.'
    'From where have you come?'
    'I go to my Beloved.'
    'When will you return?'
    'I shall remain with my Beloved.'
    'How long will you remain with your Beloved?'
    'For as long as my thoughts are upon Him.'

[26]

The birds were singing the dawn,[324] and the Lover awoke, who is dawn. The birds finished their song and the Lover died for his Beloved at dawn.

---

324. Readers should note that the Catalan word for dawn, namely, 'alba' is also used to designate the dawn song (or aubade) common in Old Occitan lyric poetry, which is a genre conventionally depicting the separation of lovers after a night spent together, their tryst now at risk of discovery by their spouses in the early morning light of sunrise.

### [27]

The bird was singing in the Beloved's garden. The Lover arrived, and said to the bird: 'If we do not understand each other through language, let us understand each other through love, for your song represents my Beloved to my eyes.'

### [28]

The Lover was sleepy because he had toiled hard while seeking his Beloved, yet he was fearful lest he might forget that Beloved. He wept lest he might fall asleep and lest his Beloved might become absent from his memory.

### [29]

The Lover and the Beloved met, and the Lover said: 'You need not speak to me, though make me a sign with Your eyes, which are as words to my heart, whenever I give You what You ask of me.'

### [30]

The Lover disobeyed his Beloved. The Lover cried. So the Beloved came to die, wearing His Lover's gown so that the Lover might retrieve what he had lost. And He gave him a greater gift than the one he had lost.

### [31]

The Beloved inspires love in the Lover yet shows no pity towards his languor, so that He may more fervently be loved and that in that languor's increase the Lover may find pleasure and refreshment.

### [32]

The Lover said: 'The secrets of my Beloved torment me when my deeds reveal them, since my mouth keeps them secret and does not disclose them to people.'

### [33]

The conditions governing love are that the Lover be long-suffering, patient, humble, fearful, diligent and trusting, and that he venture into great danger in order to honour his Beloved.

And the conditions governing the Beloved are that He be true, bountiful, compassionate and just to His Lover.

### [34]

The Lover sought devotion in the mountains and plains in order to see whether his Beloved was well-served, but in each of these places he found such devotion to be wanting.

So he dug down into the ground, therefore, to see if he would find a plentiful supply, since above ground it was completely wanting.[325]

### [35]

'Tell me, O bird who sings of love to my Beloved, why am I tormented with love by the one who has taken me into His service?'

The bird replied: 'Were you not to undergo hardship for the sake of love, with what would you love your Beloved?'

### [36]

Deep in thought the Lover walked the paths of his Beloved, and he stumbled and fell among thorns,[326] yet to him it seemed as if they were flowers and that he lay upon a bed of love.

### [37]

They asked the Lover whether he would exchange his Beloved for another.

He replied by saying: 'And which other is better or nobler than the Supreme Good, Who is eternal, and infinite in greatness, power, wisdom, love and perfection?'

### [38]

The Lover was tearfully singing songs about his Beloved. And he said that love strikes a lover's heart more swiftly than one sees a flash of lightning or hears the sound of thunder; and the water in one's tears flows more rapidly than do the waves in the sea; and sighs are closer to love than snow is to whiteness.

### [39]

They asked the Lover why his Beloved was glorious.

He replied: 'Because He is glory.'

---

325. Here the phrases 'into the ground' and 'above ground' also carry the senses of 'into the earth' and 'on earth', respectively.

326. Cf. Matt 13:7; Mk 4:7; and Lk 8:7 and 8:14.

They asked him why He was powerful.
He replied: 'Because He is power.'
'And why is He wise?'
'Because He is wisdom.'
'And why is He loveable?'
'Because He is love.'

### [40]

The Lover rose early and went in search of his Beloved. And he came across people who were travelling along the same path, so he asked them whether they had seen his Beloved. They replied by asking him at what point his Beloved had disappeared from the eyes of his mind? The Lover replied by saying: 'For as long as I have seen my Beloved in my thoughts, He has never been absent from my bodily eyes, since all things visible portray my Beloved to me.'

### [41]

With eyes full of yearning, languor, sorrow and tears the Lover gazed at his Beloved. And with eyes full of grace, justice, compassion, mercy and generosity the Beloved gazed at His Lover.

And the bird sang of the sweetness of their gazes.

### [42]

The keys to the gates of love are gilded with cares, sighs and tears. The cord holding the keys is made of remorse, contrition, devotion and satisfaction. And the gatekeeper is defined by his justice and mercy.

### [43]

The Lover knocked at the gates of his Beloved with blows of love and hope. The Beloved heard the knocking of His Lover with humility, compassion, patience and charity.

Deity and humanity opened the gates, and the Lover went in to see his Beloved.

### [44]

The private and the communal met and mingled, so that there might be friendship and kindness between the Lover and the Beloved.

[45]

There are two fires which lend ardour to the Lover's love: one is built from desires, pleasures and cogitation; the other consists of fear, languor, tears and weeping.

[46]

The Lover desired solitude and went to live all alone, so that he might enjoy the company of his Beloved, with Whom he remains all alone when among people.

[47]

The Lover was all alone, under the shade of a beautiful tree. People passed by that place and asked him why he was alone. So the Lover replied that he was alone once he had seen and heard them, and that beforehand he had been in the company of his Beloved.

[48]

The Lover and the Beloved spoke to each other using love's signs. And with fear, concern, tears and weeping the Lover described his languor to the Beloved.

[49]

The Lover feared that his Beloved might not meet his greatest need. The Lover withheld his love from his Beloved. The Lover felt contrition and remorse in his heart. So the Beloved rendered hope and charity to the Lover's heart, and tears and weeping to his eyes, so that love might return to the Lover.

[50]

Between the Lover and the Beloved proximity and distance are equivalent. For the loves of the Lover and the Beloved mingle like water and wine; their loves are connected like heat and light; and they are in accord and unity, like essence and existence.

[51]

The Lover said to his Beloved: 'In You lies my healing and my languor. And the more You heal me, the greater is my languor. And the more languor You cause me, the greater the health You bestow upon me.'

The Beloved replied: 'Your love is a seal and imprint whereby you reveal My Honours to people.'

[52]

The Lover found that he had been captured, bound, beaten and put to death because of his love for his Beloved. Those who tortured him asked: 'Where is your Beloved?'

He replied: 'He is here, in my love's increase and in how it leads me to endure my tortures.'

[53]

The Lover said to the Beloved: 'Ever since I have known You, I have never retreated or withdrawn from loving You, for wherever I might have been I was in You, by You and with You.'

The Beloved replied: 'And, ever since you began to know and love Me, I have not forgotten you, nor have I ever committed any deceit or fraud.'

[54]

The Lover went around a city singing about his Beloved like a fool, so the people asked him if he had lost his wits. He replied that his Beloved had taken hold of his will and that he had given him his intellect. All that remained to him, therefore, was his memory, with which he remembered his Beloved.

[55]

The Beloved said: 'It is a miracle contrary to Love when a lover falls asleep and forgets his Beloved.'

The Lover replied: 'And it is a miracle contrary to Love when the Beloved fails to rouse him, given that His Lover has desired Him.'

[56]

The Lover's heart climbed to the high peaks of the Beloved, lest it be prevented from loving in the abyss of this world. And when it had reached its Beloved, it contemplated Him with gentleness and delight.

And the Beloved lowered it back down to this world so that it might contemplate Him with tribulation and languor.

## [57]

They asked the Lover: 'In what does your wealth consist?'
He replied: 'The poverty I endure for the sake of my Beloved.'
'And in what does your repose consist?'
'The languor that love affords me.'
'And who is your physician?'
'The trust I have in my Beloved.'
'And who is your teacher?'
He replied by saying: 'The significations that creatures provide of their Beloved.'

## [58]

The bird was singing on a branch bearing leaves and flowers, and the wind stirred the leaves and carried the fragrance of the flowers.

The Lover asked the bird what the leaves' movements and the flowers' fragrance signified. The bird replied:

'Through their movement the leaves signify obedience, while their fragrance signifies suffering and unhappiness.'

## [59]

The Lover went walking, filled with desire for his Beloved, and he came across two lovers who greeted, hugged and kissed each other amidst love and tears.

The Lover fainted, for the two lovers reminded him so strongly of his Beloved.

## [60]

The Lover cogitated upon death and felt afraid, until he remembered his Beloved. So he cried out to the people who stood before him.

'Ah, dear people, act lovingly, so as not to fear death or danger when honouring my Beloved!'

## [61]

They asked the Lover where his love first began. He replied that it began in the lofty attributes of his Beloved, and that from this beginning it gladly came to love himself and his neighbour, and to reject deceit and fraud.

## [62]

'Tell us, Fool, if your Beloved were to reject you, what would you do?'

The Lover replied by saying that he would love so that he might not die, since love's absence constitutes death and its presence, life.

## [63]

They asked the Lover what perseverance was. He said that perseverance was happiness and unhappiness in a Lover who perseveres in loving, honouring and serving his Beloved with fortitude, patience and hope.

## [64]

The Lover asked his Beloved to pay him for the time he had served Him. The Beloved counted the concerns, desires, tears, dangers and hardships that His Lover had endured because of his love for Him. And the Beloved added eternal beatitude to that calculation, and gave Himself as payment to His Lover.[327]

## [65]

They asked the Lover what happiness was. He replied that it was unhappiness borne for the sake of love.

'Tell us, Fool, what is unhappiness?'

'Recollection of the dishonour done to my Beloved, Who is worthy of all honour.'

## [66]

The Lover gazed at a place in which he had previously seen his Beloved, and said: 'O place which portrays to me the fair customs of my Beloved! Will you tell Him that I endure hardship and unhappiness because of my love for Him?'

The place replied: 'When your Beloved lived here, He suffered, because of His love for you, greater hardship and unhappiness than any other hardship or unhappiness that love can bring upon its servants.'

---

327. See below, v. 167.

[67]

The Lover said to his Beloved: 'You are all, and are through all, and in all and with all. I desire all of You so that I may have and be all of myself.'

The Beloved replied: 'You cannot have all of Me unless all of you belongs to Me.'

So the Lover said: 'Have all of me, then, that I may have all of You.'

The Beloved replied: 'What shall your son or your brother or your father have?'

The Lover said: 'You are such an all that you more than suffice to be the all of each person who gives all of himself to You.'

[68]

The Lover waited, prolonging his thoughts upon the greatness and the enduring nature[328] of his Beloved, and he found therein no beginning, middle or end.[329]

So the Beloved asked: 'What are you appraising, Fool?'

The Lover replied: 'I am appraising the lesser by means of the greater, deficiency by means of perfection and beginning by means of infinity and eternity, so that humility, patience, charity and hope may thereby be more strongly lodged in my memory.'

[69]

The paths of love are long yet short, because love is clear, pure, clean, true, subtle, simple, strong, diligent, bright, and abounding in new thoughts and old memories.

[70]

They asked the Lover what the fruits of love were.

He replied: 'Delights, cogitations, desires, sighs, longings, hardships, dangers, torments and languor. Without such fruits, love will not permit itself to act upon its servants.'

---

328. Cat. *durabletat*. 'Goodness, Greatness and Eternity (or Duration)' constitute the first three of the Dignities from the principal Figure of Llull's Arts; 'Eternity' applies to the divine realm; 'Duration' to the created. Here Llull is referring to God's eternity.

329. An assertion of the absence of beginning, middle or end amounts to an assertion of infinitude.

## [71]

A large number of people were standing in front of the Lover, who was complaining that his Beloved had not increased his love, and likewise that Love had afforded him hardships and sorrow.

The Beloved vindicated Himself by saying that the hardships with which Love was charged were love's very increase.

## [72]

'Tell us, Fool, why do you not speak? And what is it that keeps you so dumbfounded and pensive?

He replied: 'The beauty of my Beloved and the resemblance between the happiness and the sorrow that love gives and affords me.'

## [73]

'Tell us, Fool, what came first: your heart or love?'

The Lover replied by saying that his heart and love came into being all at once; for, had they not, the heart would not have been created for loving nor love created for cogitating.

## [74]

They asked the Fool where his love first began: in the secrets of his Beloved or in revealing these to people? He replied by saying that love, when it has attained its fullness, makes no such distinction; for through secrecy the Lover keeps the secrets of his Beloved secret, and through secrecy he discloses them, yet in disclosing them he keeps them secret.

## [75]

A secret love that remains undisclosed brings suffering and languor; yet a love disclosed brings fear resulting from fervour.

The Lover, therefore, feels languor come what may.

## [76]

Love summoned its lovers and told them to ask it for the gifts which were the most desirable and gratifying. So they asked Love to clothe and adorn them in its own finery so that they might thereby be more pleasing to the Beloved.

### [77]

The Lover called loudly to the people, saying that Love commanded
them to love when either walking or sitting, when waking or sleeping,
when speaking or when silent, when buying or selling, when crying or
laughing, when enjoying or languishing,[330] and when winning or losing. And in whatever things they might do, they should love, for they
had been commanded to do so by Love.

### [78]

'Tell us, Fool, when did Love first come to you?'

He replied: 'When it enriched and filled my heart with concerns,
desires, sighs and languor, and lavished tears and weeping upon my
eyes.'

'What did Love bring you?'

'My Beloved's fair countenance, Honours and worth.'

'How did these reach you?'

'Through my memory and intellect.'

'How did you receive them?'

'With charity and hope.'

'How do you retain them?'

'With justice, prudence, fortitude and temperance.'

### [79]

The Beloved was singing, and said that the Lover knew little about
love if he felt ashamed of praising his Beloved, or if he feared honouring Him in those places where He was most gravely dishonoured.

And he who grows infuriated at unhappiness knows little about
love. And he who despairs of his Beloved fails to bring love and hope
into accord.

### [80]

The Lover sent letters to his Beloved, in which he asked Him whether
He had another lover who might help him to bear and withstand the
grave trials he endured for the sake of his love.

The Beloved wrote back to His Lover, saying that He lacked any
means whereby to do him harm or wrong.

---

330. Note here that languor is construed as the contrary of enjoyment.

[81]

They asked the Beloved about His Lover's love, and he replied that His Lover's love was a mixture of joy and unhappiness, as of fear and courage.

They asked the Lover about the Beloved's love, and he replied that his Beloved's love was the influence of infinite goodness, eternity, power, wisdom, charity and perfection, which influence the Beloved exerts upon the Lover.[331]

[82]

'Tell us, Fool, what is wonder?'

He replied: 'Preferring absent things to present ones, and preferring visible and corruptible things to invisible and incorruptible ones.'

[83]

The Lover was searching for his Beloved and he found a man who was dying without love, and he said that it was a great shame for a man to die any kind of death without love.

The Lover said to the dying man, therefore: 'Tell me, why are you dying without love?'

The man replied: 'Because it was without love that I lived.'[332]

[84]

The Lover asked his Beloved which was greater, either love or loving? The Beloved replied by saying that, in creatures, love is the tree and loving is the fruit, while hardship and languor are the flowers and leaves. Yet, in God, love and loving are one and the same thing, free from any hardship or languor.

[85]

The Lover felt languid and sad, being overburdened with cares, so he dispatched pleas to his Beloved to send him a book describing His countenance in order to provide him with some form of remedy.

---

331. Goodness, eternity, power, etc., are some of the Lullian Dignities. 'Influence' (Cat. *influència*) should be interpreted in the light of (Christianised) Neoplatonic doctrines of primary and secondary causality deriving from the writings of Proclus and the pseudo-Dionysius, among others.

332. Cf. below, v. 202.

The Beloved sent that book to His Lover, whose hardship and languor underwent increase.

[86]

The Lover fell ill from love.[333] So a physician came to see him, and increased his languor and his cares. And at that moment the Lover was healed.

[87]

The Lover and Love grew estranged, yet they drew solace from the Beloved, Who appeared before them. The Lover wept, and Love vanished as the Lover fainted.

The Beloved revived His Lover by reminding him of His countenance.

[88]

The Lover told the Beloved: 'The paths are many along which You enter my heart and appear before my eyes, as are the names with which my words name You; but the love whereby You both give me life and withdraw it from me is but one alone.'

[89]

The Beloved identifies Himself[334] to His Lover by His new, crimson garments. And He opens His arms to embrace him, and lowers His head to give him a kiss. And He exists on high so that He may be found.

[90]

The Beloved departed from His Lover. The Lover sought his Beloved in his memory and intellect, so that he might love Him.

---

333. Cf. once more, Song of Songs 2:5 and 5:8: 'quia amore langueo' ('because I languish with love'). See above, v. 9 and corresponding note.

334. Cat. *entresenya·s*: an *entresenya* is a pre-agreed, secret signal between two people, often one given in response to another sign: between lovers, for instance; hence, a lover's token. An archaic English translation of this verb, therefore, might read: 'The Beloved betokened himself to his Lover [...]'. The term *entresenya* can therefore variously mean 'token, countersign or password/codeword', and can thus mean in its verbal form 'to give evidence of' or 'to identify' oneself. For communications via sign language, cf. above Ch. 62, § 11 and corresponding note.

The Lover found his Beloved and asked Him where He had been. The Beloved replied: 'Within the absence of your memory and the ignorance of your intellect.'

## [91]

'Tell us, Fool, are you ashamed when people see you weeping for your Beloved?'

He replied: 'Shame without sin stems from a lack of love, in not knowing how to love.'

## [92]

The Beloved sowed desires, sighs, virtues and love in the Lover's heart. The Lover watered the seeds with tears and weeping.

The Beloved sowed hardships, trials and languor in the Lover's body. The Lover healed his body with hope, devotion, patience and consolation.

## [93]

On a great feast day the Beloved held a grand court for many acclaimed barons, and He provided a lavish banquet and lavish gifts. The Lover came to that court.

The Beloved asked him: 'Who summoned you to appear at My court?'

The Lover replied: 'Necessity and love bade me come to look upon Your features and Your countenance.'

## [94]

They asked the Lover to whom he belonged.

He replied: 'To Love.'

'Of what do you consist?'

'Of Love.'

'Who conceived you?'

'Love.'

'Where were you born?'

'In Love.'

'Who raised you?'

'Love.'

'On what do you live?'

'On Love.'

'What is your name?'

'Love.'

"From where do you come?'

'From Love.'

'Where are you going?'

'To Love.'

'Where are you now?'

'In Love.'

'Do you possess anything apart from Love?'

He replied: 'Yes: sins and trespasses against my Beloved.'

'Is there forgiveness within your Beloved?'

The Lover said that there was mercy and justice within his Beloved, and that, therefore, he dwelt between fear and hope.

### [95]

The Beloved departed from His Lover, so the Lover sought Him in his thoughts, and asked people about Him using the language of love.

The Lover found his Beloved, who was scorned among people, so he told his Beloved that a great wrong was being committed against His honour. The Beloved replied by saying that He received dishonour on account of a lack of fervent and devoted lovers. The Lover wept and his sorrows grew.

The Beloved comforted him by revealing to him His countenance.

### [96]

The light from the room of the Beloved lit up the room of the Lover, so that it might drive out shadows therefrom and fill it with pleasures, languor and cares.

So the Lover emptied everything from his room so that it might accommodate his Beloved.

### [97]

They asked the Lover what device his Beloved displayed upon His standard. He replied: 'A dead man'. They asked him why He made use of such a device. The Lover replied: 'Because He was a man put to death on the Cross. And so that those who boast of being His Lovers might follow His trail.'

## [98]

The Beloved came to stay at His Lover's abode, and the steward asked Him to pay His lodging.[335] The Lover, however, said that his Beloved should be accommodated free of charge.[336]

## [99]

Memory and Will went walking together, and they climbed the mountain of the Beloved so that Intellect might become heightened and Love might increase through loving the Beloved.

## [100]

Sighs and weeping are unfailing envoys between the Lover and the Beloved, so that there may be solace, companionship, friendship and kindness between them both.

## [101]

The Lover longed for his Beloved. He sent Him his thoughts so that they might retrieve for him from his Beloved the happy state in which the latter had maintained him for so long.

## [102]

The Beloved gave His Lover an endowment of tears, sighs, languor, concerns and sorrows, and by means of this endowment the Lover served his Beloved.

## [103]

The Lover begged his Beloved to give him bounty, peace and honour in this world. And the Beloved revealed His countenance to the Lover's memory and intellect, and gave Himself as an object to his will.

## [104]

They asked the Lover: 'In what does honour consist?' He replied: 'In understanding and loving my Beloved'. So they asked him: 'In what

---

335. Lit. 'hostelage': a bed or a night's lodging as a guest. Cf. below, v. 224.

336. The phrase *en perdó*, translated in this instance as 'free of charge', contains a second sense of 'in forgiveness', here also carrying the implication that the Lover, as if excusing his steward's lack of recognition and tactlessness, insists that full courtesies should be extended to his noble guest.

does dishonour consist?' He replied: 'In forgetting and failing to love my Beloved.'

## [105]

'Love tormented me until I had told it that you were present in my torments, so love reduced my languor. And in recompense you increased Love, which intensified my torments.'

## [106]

'I met on the path of love a lover who did not speak. With tears, a gaunt face and languor, he reproached and censured Love. Love vindicated itself with loyalty, hope, patience, devotion, fortitude, temperance and happiness. So I censured the lover, therefore, who complained about Love, since Love had given him such noble gifts.'

## [107]

The Lover was singing and said: 'Oh, in what great unhappiness love consists! Ah, what great happiness it is to love my Beloved, Who loves all His lovers with infinite and eternal love, the fulfilment of every perfection!'

## [108]

The Lover was travelling in a foreign land where he thought he might find his Beloved, and on his way he was attacked by two lions. The Lover feared for his life, because he wished to live, for the sake of serving his Beloved. So he sent his memory to his Beloved so that love might be present at his demise, by means of which love he might be more easily able to endure death.

While the Lover was remembering his Beloved, the lions humbly approached the former, whose tears they licked from his eyes, which wept, and whose hands and feet they kissed.[337] So the Lover set off in peace to search for his Beloved.

## [109]

The Lover walked across mountains and plains, but he could find no doorway through which to escape the prison of Love, in which his

---

337. The lions, that is, demonstrated traditional signs of chivalric obeisance.

body and his thoughts, and all his desires and his joys, had long been held captive.

While the Lover was walking along in such torment, he came across a hermit who was sleeping close to a beautiful spring. The Lover roused the hermit, and asked him if he had seen his Beloved in his dreams. The hermit replied by saying that one's thoughts were equally held captive within the prison of love whether one was awake or asleep. It greatly pleased the Lover that he had found a companion in prison. So they both wept, for the Beloved did not have many lovers of that kind.

### [110]

There is nothing in the Beloved from which the Lover does not draw anguish and tribulation. Nor is there anything in the Lover from which the Beloved does not draw enjoyment and dominion. The Beloved's love, therefore, consists in action while that of the Lover consists in languor and passion.[338]

### [111]

A bird was singing on a branch and it said that it would give a new concern to a lover who gave it two such concerns.

The bird gave the new concern to the Lover, who, in order to ease his torment, gave two such to the bird. But the Lover felt that his sorrows had grown.

### [112]

The Lover and the Beloved met, and greetings, embraces, kisses, tears and weeping were witnesses to their meeting. And the Beloved inquired about the Lover's estate, but the Lover became dumbfounded in the presence of his Beloved.

---

338. Passion in the sense of 'affection', understood as the reception of change from some other object. Action (Gk. *poiein*: 'to make or do'), i.e. the production of change in some other object, and passion (Gk. *paschein*: 'to suffer, undergo or be affected') are the twin poles in any causal relation. Quite apart from the contrast here set up between action and passion, Cat. *passió* has the literal meaning of 'suffering', as well as calling to mind Christ's own Passion.

### [113]

The Lover and the Beloved had an argument, but their love for each other reconciled them.

So the question arose as to which of their loves had contributed greater friendship.

### [114]

The Lover loved all those who feared his Beloved, yet feared all those who did not fear his Beloved.

So the question arose, therefore, as to which was greater in the Lover: love or fear?

### [115]

The Lover hastened to follow his Beloved, and he passed along a road on which there was a fierce lion that killed anyone who passed by sluggishly and without devotion.

### [116]

The Lover said: 'Whoever does not fear my Beloved must fear all things. But whoever fears my Beloved will require boldness and courage in all things .'

### [117]

They asked the Lover about occasion,[339] and he said that occasion consists in enjoyment drawn from penance, understanding from conscience, hope from patience, health from abstinence, comfort from remembrance, love from diligence, loyalty from shame, wealth from poverty, peace from obedience, and conflict from ill will.

### [118]

Love lit up the cloud which came between the Lover and the Beloved, making it as bright and resplendent as the moon at night, the star at dawn, the sun by day or the intellect in the will.

And it is through this so very radiant cloud that the Lover and the Beloved converse.

---

339. See above, Ch. 3, § 3 and corresponding note.

### [119]

They asked the Lover: 'What is the greatest darkness?' And he replied: 'The absence of my Beloved.' They asked him: 'What is the brightest light?' And he said: 'The presence of my Beloved.'

### [120]

The Beloved's sign marks the Lover, who, for the sake of love, suffers tribulation, sighs and tears, concern, and the scorn of people.

### [121]

The Lover wrote down the following words: 'May my Beloved rejoice, for I send my cares to him, and my eyes weep for him, and without this languor I can neither live, nor feel, nor see, nor hear, nor smell.'

### [122]

'O Intellect and Will! Bark and awaken the great dogs who sleep, forgetful of my Beloved! O eyes, weep! O heart, sigh! O Memory, remember the dishonour of my Beloved, which is done to Him by those He has honoured so greatly!'

### [123]

The enmity between people and my Beloved grows. My Beloved promises gifts and rewards, and threatens with justice and wisdom. Yet Memory and Will scorn His threats and His promises.

### [124]

The Beloved drew near to the Lover so that He might comfort and console him for the languor he endured and the tears he shed. And the closer the Beloved came to His Lover, the more the Lover wept and languished over the dishonours which, he regretted, had been done to his Beloved.

### [125]

Using a quill of love and the water of tears on paper of suffering, the Lover wrote some letters to his Beloved, wherein he told Him that devotion was late in arriving, love was dying and that deceit and error were increasing the number of His enemies.

[126]

The loves of the Lover and the Beloved were fastened together with memory, intellect and will, so that the Lover and the Beloved might not be separated. And the cord by which the two loves were fastened consisted of cares, languor, sighs and weeping.

[127]

The Lover was lying on a bed of love. Its sheets were of joy, its quilt was of languor, and its pillow was of tears.

So the question arose as to whether the cloth of the pillow was the same as that of the sheets or the quilt.

[128]

The Beloved clothed His Lover. From love he made him a cloak, a coat, a gown and a hat; from cares, a shirt; from trials, stockings; and from tears, a garland.

[129]

The Beloved begged His Lover not to forget Him. The Lover said that he could not forget Him, since he could not ignore Him.[340]

The Beloved said that He should be praised and championed in those places where to do so is most greatly feared. The Lover asked Him to grant him sufficient love. The Beloved replied that, because of His love for him, He had been made incarnate and had been hung up to die.

[130]

The Lover asked his dear Beloved to show him a way whereby he might be able to make Him known, loved and praised by people.

The Beloved filled His Lover with devotion, patience, charity, tribulations, cares, sighs and weeping. So the Lover's heart was emboldened to praise his Beloved, and his mouth uttered those praises, and his will felt contempt towards the censure of people who judge falsely.

---

340. Forgetting and ignoring (as in 'not knowing') feature in Figure S of Llull's earlier Arts.

[131]

The Lover said the following words to the people: 'Whoever truly remembers my Beloved, through the circumstances of his remembrance, forgets all things. And whoever forgets all things in order to
remember his Beloved is protected from all things and given a share
in all things by my Beloved.'

[132]

They asked the Lover from what was love born, on what did it live and
why did it died. The Lover replied that love was born of remembrance, lived on understanding and died as a result of forgetfulness.[341]

[133]

The Lover forgot everything which lay below the highest heaven,[342] so
that his intellect might be able to rise higher in order to know the
Beloved, Whom his will wishes to commend and contemplate.

[134]

The Lover went off to do battle in order to honour his Beloved, taking with him in his company faith, hope, charity, justice, prudence,
fortitude and temperance, with which he might defeat his Beloved's
enemies. But the Lover would have been defeated had his Beloved
not assisted him by indicating His noble attributes to His Lover.

[135]

The Lover wished to pass to the ultimate end[343] for the sake of which
he loved his Beloved, yet the other ends obstructed his passage. Sustained desire and longing, therefore, brought the Lover sadness and
languor.

---

341. See previous note. Again, remembering, understanding and forgetting are
three of the possible acts of memory and intellect.

342. Llull is here referring to the Empyrean (or firmament), the dwelling place of
God, the angels and the blessed, and the unmoved outermost region of the heavens,
home to the element of Fire.

343. I have translated this expression as 'ultimate end' rather than in a more col-
loquial manner, since it is clearly a technical term in common use among scholastics,
albeit that Llull himself was writing in the vernacular and for a lay as well as clerical
readership. Cf. above Ch. 3, § 3 and corresponding note.

### [136]

The Lover took pride and rejoiced in his Beloved's noble attributes. The Lover languished in profound cogitation and concern.

So the question arose as to which he felt more intensely: the pleasures or the torments.

### [137]

The Lover was an envoy to Christian princes and unbelievers on his Beloved's behalf, so that he might teach them the art and the principles whereby to know and love his Beloved.

### [138]

'If you see a lover honoured with noble attire, honoured for his vainglory, and grown fat through eating and sleeping, know that in him you see damnation and torment. And if you see a lover in wretched clothing,[344] scorned by people, and grown pale and thin through fasting and keeping vigil, know that in him you see salvation and everlasting blessings.'

### [139]

The Lover laments and his heart bemoans the heat of love. The Lover is dying, so the Beloved sheds tears for him and affords him the comforts of patience, hope and rewards.

### [140]

The Lover wept for what he had lost, yet there was no one who might comfort him, because his losses were irrecuperable.

### [141]

God has created night so that the Lover may remain wakeful and cogitate upon the noble attributes of his Beloved. Yet the Lover thought that He had created it so that those who are tormented by love might rest and sleep.

---

344. Cf. above, Chs. 8, § 8 and 48, § 1; and below, v. 149.

[142]

People mocked and rebuked the Lover because he went about like a fool on account of his love. Yet the Lover scorned their mockery and rebuked them because they failed to love his Beloved.

[143]

The Lover said: 'I am clad in coarse cloth. But Love clothes my heart in pleasant thoughts, and my body in tears, languor and suffering.'

[144]

The Beloved sang, and said: 'I have directed My praise-givers to praise My worth, yet the enemies of My virtue torment them and show them contempt. So I have sent My Lover, therefore, to lament and to weep for My dishonour. And his laments and his weeping are born from My love.'

[145]

The Lover swore to his Beloved that he loved and endured pain and suffering for the sake of His love; so he begged his Beloved, therefore, to love him, and to show compassion for his suffering.

The Beloved swore that it was the nature and property of His love that it should love all those who loved Him and that it should take pity upon those who endure suffering for its sake.

The Lover rejoiced and drew consolation from the essential nature and property of his Beloved.

[146]

The Beloved forbade His Lover to speak, so the Lover consoled himself by gazing upon his Beloved.[345]

[147]

The Lover wept and cried out to his Beloved so much that the Beloved descended from the supreme heights of Heaven and came to Earth in order to weep, lament and die for the sake of love, as well as to teach people to love, know and praise His Honours.

---

345. See above, Chs. 8, § 3 and 62, § 11 for two instances of a reciprocal access of mutism brought on by profound love and devotion.

### [148]

The Lover censured Christians for failing to place the name of his Beloved, Jesus Christ, at the start of their letters, so that they might do Him the honour which the Saracens afford to Muhammad, who was a charlatan, to whom they give honour when they name him at the start of their letters.

### [149]

The Lover met a squire who was walking pensively; he was thin, pale and wore wretched clothing. The squire greeted the Lover by wishing that God might guide him in the discovery of his Beloved. So the Lover asked him how he had recognised him, and the squire told him that some of love's secrets reveal others, and that because of this, lovers recognise each other.

### [150]

The nobility, honour and good works of the Beloved constitute the Lover's treasure and wealth.

And the Beloved's treasure consists in the concerns, desires, torments, weeping and languor the Lover endures for the sake of honouring and loving his Beloved.

### [151]

Great hosts and great companies of loving spirits have assembled, and they bear Love's ensign, on which stands the image[346] and sign of their Beloved. Yet they refuse to admit to their company any person who is lacking in love, lest their Beloved be thereby dishonoured.

### [152]

Men who pretend to be fools in order to gain money move the Lover to become a fool for the sake of Love. And the shame the Lover feels towards people when going about like a fool provides him with a way in which he may win their love and respect.

So the question therefore arises as to which impulse is the greater occasion for love.

---

346. Cat. *figura.*

[153]

Love brought the Lover sadness from profound cogitation. So the Beloved sang, and the Lover rejoiced upon hearing Him.

So the question arose as to which of these two was a greater occasion for the growth of love in the Lover.

[154]

In the secrets of the Lover are the secrets of the Beloved disclosed, and in the secrets of the Beloved are the secrets of the Lover disclosed.

So the question arises as to which of the two secrets is a greater occasion for disclosure.

[155]

They asked the Fool by which signs his Beloved was known. So he replied that it was by mercy and compassion, existing in His will essentially and inalterably.

[156]

On account of the special love the Lover felt towards his Beloved, he loved the common good over the special good, so that his Beloved might commonly be known, praised and desired.

[157]

Love and Hate met in a garden where the Lover and the Beloved were talking in private. And Love asked Hate with what aim it had come to that place. So Hate replied that it had come to deprive the Lover of his love and to dishonour the Beloved. The Beloved and the Lover were greatly displeased by what Hate had said, so they fostered Love in order that it might defeat and destroy Hate.

[158]

'Tell us, Fool, towards which do you feel a greater desire: loving or hating?'

He replied: 'Towards loving, for I have felt hatred merely for the purpose of loving.'

[159]

'Tell us, lover,[347] which brings you greater understanding: that which you have of truth or of falsehood?'

He replied: 'That which I have of truth.'

'Why?'

'Because I understand falsehood for the purpose of better understanding truth.'

[160]

The Lover noticed that he was loved by his Beloved, so he asked Him whether, in Him, His love and mercy were the same thing. The Beloved conceded that in His essence there was no difference between His love and His mercy.

So the Lover asked Him, therefore, why His love tormented him and why His mercy failed to cure his languor. So the Beloved replied that His mercy gave him that languor so that therewith he might more perfectly honour His love.

[161]

The Lover decided to go to a foreign land in order to honour his Beloved, so he resolved to disguise himself in order to avoid being captured along the way. Yet he was never able to disguise the tears in his eyes, the gaunt features and pallid hue of his face, or the laments, concerns, sighs, sadness and languor in his heart. So, for this reason, during his journey he was seized by his Beloved's enemies and delivered into torment.

[162]

The Lover was held captive in the prison of love. Thoughts, desires and memories[348] guarded and shackled him to prevent him escaping from his Beloved. Languor tormented him; patience and hope consoled him.

The Lover would have died, but the Beloved revealed His condition[349] to him and, so, the Lover revived.

---

347. The Catalan here is *amador* rather than the customary *amich*, for which reason I have not capitalised the initial letter.

348. I.e. the activities associated with the three powers of the human intellective soul, namely, the intellect, will and memory respectively.

349. Cat. *son estament*: lit. 'his estate' or condition.

### [163]

The Lover met his Beloved, and, recognising Him, wept. The Beloved rebuked His Lover for not having wept before he had recognised Him; so He asked him how he had done so given that he had not been weeping. The Lover replied: 'Through my memory, intellect and will, in which there was an increase as soon as You became present to my bodily eyes.'

### [164]

The Beloved asked the Lover what love was. 'Love', he replied, 'is the presence of the words and countenance of the Beloved in the sighing heart of a lover, and the languor brought on by desire and weeping in that lover's heart. Love is boldness and fear aroused by fervour. Love is the ultimate reason to desire one's Beloved. Love is what killed the Lover when he heard someone singing about the beauty of his Beloved. Love is that in which my death consists and in which ever my will resides.'

### [165]

Devotion and longing sent concerns, by envoy, to the Lover's heart, so that tears might rise to his eyes, which wished to cease the weeping in which they had long been engaged.

### [166]

The Lover said: 'If you, O lovers, desire fire, come to my heart and light your lamps. And if you desire water, come to my eyes, which stream with tears. And if you desire love's cares, come to draw them from my cogitations.'

### [167]

One day it came to pass that the Lover was reflecting upon the great love he bore towards his Beloved and upon the great hardships and dangers he had long endured for the sake of his love, and he considered that his rewards should be great. While the Lover was reflecting in this way, he remembered that his Beloved had paid him already[350] because He had caused him to love His countenance and had given him languor on account of his very love.

---

350. Cf. above, v. 64.

[168]

The Lover wiped from his face and eyes the tears he endured for the sake of love so as not to reveal the languor his Beloved had caused him. So the Beloved asked him why he concealed these signs of love from other lovers, signs He had conferred upon him so that in these others He might inspire a love of honouring His worth.

[169]

'Tell us, you who go about like a fool for the sake of Love: how long will you be a slave, prone to weeping and enduring hardship and languor?'[351]

He replied: 'Until the moment my Beloved separates my soul from my body.'

[170]

'Tell us, Fool, do you have money?'

He replied: 'I have my Beloved.'

'Do you possess towns, castles or cities, counties or duchies?'

He replied: 'I have love, cares, tears, desires, hardships and languor, which surpass empires or kingdoms.'

[171]

They asked the Lover how he recognised his Beloved's sentence. He replied: 'In the equivalence between enjoyment and suffering,[352] to which my Beloved has condemned His lovers.'

[172]

'Tell us, Fool, who knows more about love: the one who derives enjoyment therefrom or the one who derives pain and suffering?'

The Lover replied that one can have no knowledge of love from the one without the other.

[173]

They asked the Lover why he had not exonerated himself from the offences and false crimes with which people had charged him. He

---

351. Cf. below, v. 213.

352. Cat. *languiments*, a term I have typically translated as 'languor'; here and in the next versicle I have preferred 'suffering'.

replied that it was his Beloved, Whom people had wrongly accused, that he was bound to exonerate, and that Man, in whom fraud and error can occur, is far from worthy of any such exoneration.

### [174]

'Tell us, Fool, why do you exonerate Love, given that it brings pain and torment to your body and your heart?'

He replied: 'Because it increases my merit and my happiness.'

### [175]

The Lover complained about his Beloved for having caused him to be so severely tormented by Love. So the Beloved exonerated Himself by increasing His Lover's hardships, dangers, worries, weeping and tears.

### [176]

'Tell us, Fool, why do you exonerate[353] the guilty?'

He replied: 'So that I bear no resemblance to those who accuse both the innocent and the guilty.'

### [177]

The Beloved raised up the intellect to understand His lofty attributes,[354] so that the Lover might dispose his memory to remember his sins, and that his will might disdain them and might itself rise up to love the Beloved's perfections.

### [178]

The Lover was singing about his Beloved, and he said that he bore Him such goodwill that all the things he used to hate because of his love for Him gave him greater pleasure and enjoyment than did the things he loved in the absence of his Beloved's love.

### [179]

The Lover was walking through a great city, so he asked whether he could find anyone with whom he might speak to his heart's content

---

353. Note that the repeated use of this verb *s'escusar* ('to exonerate oneself') refers back, directly or indirectly, to the notion of the 'Beloved's sentence' in v. 171, above.

354. Cat. *altees*: lit. 'heights'.

about his Beloved. So they pointed out to him a pauper who was weeping on account of love and who sought a companion with whom he might speak about love.

### [180]
The Lover was pensive and perplexed as to how his hardships could have their origins in the noble attributes of his Beloved, Who enjoys within Himself such beatitude.

### [181]
The Lover's thoughts swung between forgetting his torments and re-membering his pleasures; for the pleasures he derives from love cause him to forget his unhappiness, while the torments he endures for the sake of love remind him of the happiness that love affords.

### [182]
They asked the Lover whether it was possible that his Beloved might deprive him of his love. He replied that it was not, as long as his memory remembered and his intellect understood the noble attrib-utes of his Beloved.

### [183]
'Tell us, Fool, between what is the greatest comparison or analogy forged?'

He replied: 'Between the Lover and the Beloved.'

They asked him why.

He replied: 'Because of the love that lies between them.'

### [184]
They asked the Beloved whether He had ever felt compassion. He replied that, had He not felt compassion, He would not have evoked the Lover's love, nor would He have tormented him with sighs, weep-ing, hardships or languor.

### [185]
Within a great forest, the Lover went walking in search of his Beloved. And he came across Truth and Falsehood, who were arguing about his Beloved, for Truth praised Him and Falsehood censured Him. So the Lover summoned Love in order that it might assist Truth.

[186]

The temptation arose in the Lover to send his Beloved away, so that his memory might awaken and retrieve His presence, by remembering Him more vividly than he ever had, in order that his intellect might be raised further aloft to understand his Beloved and his will to love Him.

[187]

One day, the Lover forgot his Beloved, yet the next day he remembered that he had forgotten Him. So, on the day the Lover remembered that he had forgotten Him, he felt sadness and sorrow, as well as glory and happiness, on account of forgetfulness and remembrance.

[188]

So strongly did the Lover desire praise and honour for his Beloved, that he feared he might not remember them. And so strongly did he hate the dishonour done to his Beloved, that he feared he might fail to hate it.

The Lover, therefore, stood perplexed between love and fear towards his Beloved.

[189]

The Lover was dying from pleasure and living on languor. His pleasures and his torments became joined and united into a single thing in the Lover's will.

And for this reason the Lover lived and died both at once.

[190]

The Lover wished to forget and ignore his Beloved for but an hour, so that he might have some respite from his languor. But since forgetting and ignoring would have caused him suffering, he exercised patience and raised his intellect and his memory up to contemplate his Beloved.

[191]

The Lover loved his Beloved so much that he believed everything the latter told him. And he desired to understand Him so much that everything he heard said about Him he wished to understand by necessary reasons.

So, for this reason, the Lover's love stood between belief and understanding.

### [192]

They asked the Lover which thing was furthest from his heart, and he replied: 'Hate.' So they asked him why, and he replied: 'Because what lies closest to my heart is Love, which is the contrary of Hate.'

### [193]

'Tell us, Fool, do you ever feel envious?'

He replied: 'Yes, whenever I forget the wealth and bounty of my Beloved'

### [194]

'Tell us, lover, do you enjoy wealth?'

The lover replied: 'Yes, of love.'

'Do you suffer from poverty?'

'Yes, of love.'

'Why?'

'Because my love is not greater, and fails to inspire in a large number of lovers a desire to honour my Beloved's Honours.'[355]

### [195]

'Tell us, Lover, where does your power lie?'

He replied: 'In the power of my Beloved.'

'With what do you oppose your enemies?'

'With the strength of my Beloved.'

'With what do you console yourself?'

'With the eternal treasures of my Beloved.'

### [196]

'Tell me, Fool, which do you love more: the mercy or the justice of your Beloved?'

The Lover replied that he was so obliged to love and fear justice that his will should not entertain any greater desire to love anything in preference to the justice of his Beloved.

---

355. Cf. below, vv. 206 and 293 for expressions of this same sentiment.

[197]

Sin and merit wrestled with each other within the Lover's conscience and will. So justice and memory increased his sense of remorse, and mercy and hope increased happiness in the Beloved's will. And for this reason, through his repentance, the Lover's merits overcame his sins and trespasses.

[198]

The Lover affirmed that in his Beloved there lay full perfection, and he denied that in Him there was any imperfection.

The question arose, therefore, as to which was greater: the affirmation or the negation.

[199]

There was an eclipse in the heavens and darkness upon the earth. The Lover, therefore, remembered that sin had long caused his Beloved to be absent from his will, on account of which absence darkness had banished from his intellect the light whereby the Beloved represents Himself to His lovers.

[200]

Love arose in the Lover, and the Lover asked it what it desired. So Love said that it had arisen in him in order to teach and train him in such a way that, at his death, he might be able to overcome his mortal enemies.

[201]

Love fell ill when the Lover forgot his Beloved. The Lover likewise falls ill since, via an excess of remembering, his Beloved gives him hardship, anguish and languor.

[202]

The Lover encountered a man who was dying without love. The Lover lamented the dishonour his Beloved received from the death of this man who was dying without love, so he asked the latter why he was doing so.[356] The man replied that it was because nobody had ever acquainted him with love or taught him how to become a lover. The

---

356. Cf. above, v. 83.

Lover sighed tearfully, therefore, and said: 'Ah, devotion! When will you be greater, so that sin may be lesser and my Beloved may have many fervent and ardent praise-givers and lovers who do not hesitate to honour His Honours!'

### [203]

The Lover tested Love as to whether it would remain in his heart even if he failed to remember his Beloved. So his heart ceased to think and his eyes to weep, and Love was made to disappear.

So the Lover remained perplexed, and asked people whether they had seen Love.

### [204]

Love, loving, the Lover and the Beloved[357] are in such perfect harmony within the Beloved that, in terms of their essence, they constitute but a single act. Yet the Lover and the Beloved are different things, concordant without any contrariety or difference in terms of essence. So the Beloved, therefore, is loveable beyond all one's other loves.

### [205]

'Tell us, Fool, why is your love so great?'

He replied: 'Because the journey on which I go in search of my Beloved is long and dangerous. Bearing a heavy load must I seek Him out and and at great speed must I travel. And I could not accomplish all these things without great love.'

### [206]

The Lover kept vigil, fasted, wept, gave alms, and travelled in foreign lands, so that he might stir his Beloved's will to inspire in His subjects a desire to honour His Honours.[358]

---

357. The triad of *amans, amatus* and *amor* ('loving, beloved and love') can be traced to St Augustine's *De trinitate*, VIII, 10, 14: 'amans, et quod amatur, et amor' ('the one that loves, that which is loved, and love'). As Augustine's text makes clear, love is nothing other than 'a certain life which couples or seeks to couple together some two things, namely, the one that loves and that which is loved', i.e. the lover desires to be joined with the beloved, a desire which serves as the structural dynamic and guiding theme of the entire *Lover*; English translations (here slightly adapted) from, Schaff and West Haddan (2009).

358. Cf. above, v. 194 and below, v. 293 for expressions of this same sentiment.

### [207]

If the Lover's love does not suffice to stir his Beloved to pity and pardon, the Beloved's love suffices to bestow upon His creatures grace and blessings.

### [208]

'Tell us, Fool, how can you become more akin to your Beloved?'

He replied: 'By understanding and loving my Beloved's countenance with all my might.'

### [209]

They asked the Lover if his Beloved lacked anything.

The Lover replied: 'Yes. Lovers and praise-givers to honour His worth.'

### [210]

The Beloved struck His Lover's heart using branches of Love, so that He might make him love the Tree from which He had gathered the branches whereby to strike His lovers. On this Tree He suffered death, languor and dishonour in order to give back to Love the lovers He had lost.

### [211]

The Lover met his Beloved and saw that He was very noble, powerful and worthy of every honour. So he told Him that he felt great wonder at the people, who loved, knew and honoured Him so little, considering how much He deserved their so doing. And the Beloved replied to him by saying that He had been sorely betrayed insofar as He had created man so that He might thereby be loved, known and honoured. Yet, of a thousand men, only a hundred feared and loved Him; and of those hundred, ninety feared Him lest He were to punish them, while ten loved Him so that He might grant them glory. Yet there was almost nobody who loved Him for His goodness and nobility.

When the Lover heard these words, he wept bitterly at his Beloved's dishonour, and said: 'O Beloved, Who have given so much to man and have honoured him so greatly, why has man forgotten You so?'

### [212]

The Lover was praising his Beloved, and said that He had transcended whereness, for He existed there where whereness could not reach.[359]

So, therefore, when they asked the Lover where his Beloved was, he replied: 'He is, although it is not known where.'[360] The Lover nevertheless knew that his Beloved was in his memory.

### [213]

For the sake of His honour, the Beloved purchased a slave, prone to anguish, languor, sighs and weeping.[361] So He asked him what he would like to eat and drink. The slave replied: 'Whatever You wish.' He asked him what he would like to wear. The slave replied: 'Whatever You wish.'

So the Beloved asked him: 'Do you have no desires of your own?'

The slave replied that a serf and a subject has no other desire than to obey his lord and Beloved.

### [214]

The Beloved asked the Lover whether he possessed patience. The Lover replied that all things pleased him, so, therefore, he had no reason to exercise patience, for whoever did not enjoy mastery over his own will could not be impatient.

### [215]

Love bestowed itself upon whomsoever it wished. And since it failed to bestow itself upon a large number of people or inspire ardent love in lovers, as was its prerogative, the Lover, therefore, accused and made complaint against Love to his Beloved. Love, however, justified itself by saying that it did not contradict free will, since it desired great merit and glory for its lovers.

---

359. Cat. *on*: 'where' (or place), translated into Latin as *situs* and Catalan as *on*, is the fifth of Aristotle's ten Categories, none of which, in Christian thought, at the very least, are held to apply to God.

360. Unsurprisingly, the Lover's answer here bears a clear resemblance to the Tetragrammaton (or Hebrew name for God) *YHWH*, translated in the Vulgate, Ex 3:14, as: 'dixit Deus ad Mosen *ego sum qui sum* ait sic dices filiis Israhel qui est misit me ad vos'; DRVCR: 'God said to Moses: *I am who am*. He said: Thus shalt thou say to the children of Israel: *He who is*, hath sent me to you' (italics added in both cases).

361. Cf. above, v. 169.

## [216]

There was great dispute and disagreement between the Lover and Love because the Lover had grown weary of the hardships he endured for the sake of love. So the question arose as to whether this was due to a failing on the part of Love or of the Lover. So they went to the Beloved for his judgement thereon, and the Beloved punished the Lover with languor and rewarded him with an increase of love.

## [217]

The question arose as to whether Love was closer to longing or to patience.

The Lover solved the question, saying that Love originates in longing and is sustained by patience.

## [218]

The Lover's neighbours are his Beloved's beautiful countenance.

And the Beloved's neighbours are His Lover's longings, and the hardship and tears he undergoes for the sake of Love.

## [219]

The Lover's will wished to rise very high so that it might greatly love his Beloved. So it commanded his intellect to rise as high as it was able, and his intellect commanded his memory to do likewise. So all three rose up to contemplate the Beloved in His Honours.

## [220]

The Lover's will departed and surrendered itself to the Beloved. So the Beloved imprisoned that will within the Lover, so that He might be loved and served by him.

## [221]

The Lover said: 'My Beloved should not think that I have gone off to love another Beloved, for Love has bound me wholly to love but a single Beloved.'

The Beloved replied: 'My Lover should not think that I am loved and served by him alone, for I have, rather, many lovers by whom I am loved more intensely and for longer than by his love.'

[222]

The Lover said to his Beloved: 'My dearest Beloved, You have taught and trained my eyes to see, and my ears to hear of, Your Honours. My heart, therefore, is well-trained in longing, and, by means of such longing, You have trained my eyes to weep and my body to languish.'

The Beloved replied to His Lover, saying that without such training and instruction his name would not be written in that book wherein are written all those who proceed to eternal beatitude, and whose names are deleted from the book in which are written those who proceed to eternal damnation.

[223]

The Beloved's noble countenance takes shape in the Lover's heart and increases his longing and his hardship. And the Lover would expire and die were the Beloved any further to increase the presence of His Honours within His lover's longings.

[224]

The Beloved came to lodge at His Lover's abode, so His Lover made for Him a bed of cares, and served Him sighs and tears.

And the Beloved paid for His lodging with memories.[362]

[225]

Love mixed pain and pleasure within the Lover's thoughts. Yet the pleasures made complaint about this mixture and denounced Love to the Beloved.

But the pleasures ceased and vanished when the Beloved had separated them from the torments Love inflicts upon its lovers.

[226]

The signs of the love that the Lover bears his Beloved are, at the beginning, tears, in the middle, trials, and at the end, death.

And by such signs, the Lover preaches to the other lovers about his Beloved.

---

362. Cf. above, v. 98.

[227]

The Lover withdrew into solitude, yet longing accompanied his heart, tears and weeping his eyes, and fasting and affliction his body.[363]

And when the Lover returned to the companionship of people, they rid him of all the aforesaid things, so he remained all alone among them.

[228]

Love is an ocean churned by wind and waves, in which there is no port or shore.

The Lover perishes in the ocean, yet, through his peril, his torments perish and his ultimate fulfilment is born.

[229]

'Tell us, Fool, what is love?'

He replied: 'Love is the concordance of the theoretical and the practical in achieving a certain goal, towards which the fulfilment of the Lover's will aims so that it may cause people to honour and serve his Beloved.'

So the question arises as to whether this goal is in fuller accord with the will of a lover who desires to be with his Beloved.

[230]

They asked the Lover who his Beloved was. He replied that it was He who caused him to love, desire, languish, sigh, weep, be mocked, and die.

[231]

They asked the Beloved who His Lover was. He replied that he was the one who feared nothing for the sake of honouring and praising His Honours and who relinquished everything for the sake of obeying His Commandments and counsel.

[232]

'Tell us, Fool, which is the heavier and weightier burden: pain born of Love or pain born of Hate?'

---

363. Cf. Mk 1:35; and Lk 4:42; 5:16; and 9:10.

He replied that the question should be addressed to those who perform penance either out of love for his Beloved or out of fear for the torments of Hell.

### [233]

The Lover fell asleep and Love died, because it lacked anything on which to live.

The Lover awoke and Love revived in the thoughts the Lover transmitted to his Beloved.

### [234]

The Lover said that infused knowledge derived from will, devotion and prayer; and that acquired knowledge derived from study and the intellect.[364]

The question arises, therefore, as to which knowledge reaches the Lover first, which is more pleasing to him and which prevails in him.

### [235]

'Tell us, Fool, from what do your needs arise?'

He replied: 'From thoughts and from desires, adoration, hardships and perseverance.'

'And from what do all these things arise?'

He replied: 'From love.'

'And from what does your love arise?'

'From my Beloved.'

'And from what does your Beloved arise?'

'From Himself alone.'

### [236]

'Tell us, Fool, do you wish to be free from all things?'

'Yes', he replied, 'except from my Beloved.'

'Do you wish to be a prisoner?'

'Yes', he replied, 'of sighs and concerns, hardship, danger and exile, as well as of tears, in order to serve my Beloved, by Whom I have been created to praise His worth.'

---

364. See above, Ch. 62, § 10 and corresponding note.

[237]

Love tormented the Lover, and this torment caused him to weep and lament. His Beloved called out to him to come closer so that He might heal him. The nearer the Lover drew to his Beloved, the more intensely Love tormented him, because he felt his love increase. And since he felt greater joy as his love increased, the Beloved healed his languor all the more successfully.

[238]

Love fell ill. The Lover tended it with patience, perseverance, obedience and hope. Love recovered, but the Lover himself fell ill. The Beloved cured him by causing him to remember His Virtues and Honours.

[239]

'Tell us, Fool, what is solitude?'

He replied: 'The solace and companionship of the Lover and the Beloved.'

'And what is solace and companionship?'

'It is', he replied, 'the solitude that abides in the heart of the Lover who remembers nothing but his Beloved.'

[240]

The question was put to the Lover as to where greater danger lay: in undergoing hardship or happiness for Love's sake? The Lover concurred with his Beloved and said that the dangers attaching to unhappiness are the result of impatience while those attaching to happiness are the result of ingratitude.

[241]

The Beloved set Love free and gave people permission to take as much of it as they wished, but Love found hardly anyone to place it in his heart.

The Lover wept, therefore, and felt sadness at the dishonour that Love receives here below, among us, from false lovers and ingrates.

[242]

Love killed everything within the heart of his true Lover so that it might find room to abide there. And the Lover would have died had he not remembered his Beloved.

[243]

There were two thoughts within the Lover: the first cogitated steadily upon his Beloved's Essence and Virtues; the second upon his Beloved's works.

The question arose, therefore, as to which thought was more resplendent and more pleasing to the Beloved and the Lover.

[244]

The Lover died as a result of his great love. The Beloved buried him within His domains, where the Lover rose again.

So the question arises: From whom did the Lover receive a greater gift?[365]

[245]

Calamity, danger, languor, dishonour and estrangement lay in the Beloved's prison, lest they prevent His Lover from praising His Honours and inspiring love in people who hold Him in disdain.

[246]

One day, the Lover was in the company of many people upon whom his Beloved had conferred too great an honour in this world, since in their thoughts they now dishonoured Him. These people scorned his Beloved and mocked the latter's servants.

The Lover wept, tore out his hair, struck his face and ripped his clothes. And he cried out in a loud voice:

'Has ever as great a sin been committed as to scorn my Beloved?'

[247]

'Tell us, Fool, do you wish to die?'

'Yes', he replied, 'With respect to the pleasures of this world, as well as the thoughts of the wretches who forget and dishonour my

---

365. I.e. from Love or from the Beloved?

Beloved, for I wish to be neither understood nor desired by such
thoughts, since my Beloved is absent therefrom.'

[248]

'If you, Fool, speak the truth, you shall be struck, mocked, rebuked,
tortured and killed by the people.'

He replied: 'It follows from your words that if I were to tell lies, I
should be praised, loved, served and honoured by the people, yet
spurned by the lovers of my Beloved.'

[249]

One day, givers of false praise censured the Lover in the presence of
his Beloved. The Lover exercised patience and the Beloved justice,
wisdom and power. And the Lover preferred being censured and reproached than being any of the false praisers themselves.

[250]

The Beloved sowed a variety of seeds in the Beloved's heart, from
which was born, came into leaf, flowered and ripened but a single
fruit.

So the question arises as to whether this fruit can give birth to a
variety of seeds.

[251]

The Beloved stands very far above Love, while the Lover stands very
far below Love. So Love, which stands in the middle, lowers the Beloved down to His Lover and raises the Lover up to his Beloved.

And from this lowering and raising does Love, whereby the Lover
languishes and the Beloved is served, derive its life and origin.

[252]

The Beloved stands to the right of Love, while the Lover stands to its
left. So unless the Lover passes through Love, therefore, he cannot
attain his Beloved.

And the Beloved stands in front of Love and behind the Beloved
stands His Lover. The Lover, therefore, cannot attain Love until his
thoughts and desires have passed through the Beloved.

### [253]

The Beloved makes for His Lover two Beloveds like Himself in terms of honour and worth. And the Lover falls in love with all three in equal measure, although his Love is but one, as a sign of the essential unity of one in three Beloveds.

### [254]

The Beloved dressed Himself in the cloth worn by His Lover, so as to be his eternal companion in glory.

So the Lover, therefore, unfailingly desired crimson garments so that their cloth might be more like the garments of his Beloved.

### [255]

'Tell us, Fool, what was your Beloved doing before the world existed?'

He replied: 'It suited Him to exist as distinct infinite, personal and eternal properties, wherein lie the Lover and the Beloved.'

### [256]

The Lover wept and felt sad when he saw how, through ignorance, unbelievers were deprived of his Beloved. But he rejoiced at the justice of his Beloved, who tormented those who knew Him, yet were disobedient to Him.

So the question was put to him, therefore, as to which was greater: his sadness or his joy; and as to whether he felt greater happiness when he saw his Beloved honoured, or greater unhappiness when he saw Him dishonoured.

### [257]

The Lover discerned his Beloved in the greatest difference and concordance between virtues and the greatest contrariety between virtues and vices, as well as in being and perfection, which achieve closer accord, without imperfection or non-being, than they do with imperfection and non-being.[366]

---

366. 'Difference, Concordance and Contrariety' are principles from Figure T in Llull's Art. It is worth noting that being and perfection are in accord with truth, while non-being and imperfection are in accord with falsity.

[258]

The Lover beheld the secrets of his Beloved by means of difference and concordance, which revealed to him plurality and unity within his Beloved by virtue of the greatest concordance of essence without contrariety.

[259]

The Lover was told that if corruption — which is contrary to being insofar as it is contrary to generation, which is itself contrary to non-being — were both eternally corrupting and corrupted,[367] it would be impossible for non-being and end to be in accord with either corruption or the corrupted.

So, on account of these words, the Lover beheld eternal generation within his Beloved.

[260]

If that were false whereby the Lover could love his Beloved with greater ardour, that would be true whereby the Lover could not love his Beloved with such ardour. And if this were the case, it would follow that imperfection would be greater and true in the Beloved, and that in Him there would be concordance between falsity and minority.[368]

[261]

The Lover was praising his Beloved, and said that if his Beloved possessed the greatest possibility for perfection and the greatest impossibility for imperfection, then He must be simple and pure act as regards His essence and operation.

So, while the Lover was praising his Beloved in this manner, the Trinity of his Beloved was revealed to him.

[262]

The Lover saw greater concordance between the numbers one and three than between any other numbers, for the reason that every bodily form came from non-being into being by means of the aforesaid

---

367. I.e. the active and passive elements (i.e. correlatives) of the verb and action 'to corrupt'.

368. 'Majority, Equality and Minority' are three of the principles from Figure T of Llull's Art.

numbers.[369] The Lover, therefore, looked upon the Unity and Trinity of his Beloved by virtue of this greatest concordance in number.

### [263]

The Lover was praising his Beloved's power, wisdom and will, which had created all things but sin. Sin would not exist in the absence of his Beloved's power, wisdom and will, though such power, wisdom and will are not the occasion thereof.

### [264]

The Lover praised and worshipped his Beloved for having created him and given him all things. And he praised and worshipped Him for having been pleased to assume his likeness and his nature.

And in this regard the question must be posed as to which praise and which worship[370] should enjoy the greatest perfection?

### [265]

Love put the Lover's wisdom to the test by asking him whether the Beloved loved him more by assuming his nature or by redeeming him? But the Lover was dumbfounded, until he replied that Redemption accords with the prevention of unhappiness and Incarnation with the provision of happiness.

But another question was posed with regard to his reply, namely, which constituted the greater love?

### [266]

The Lover went begging alms from door to door so that he might remind the Beloved's servants of His love, and might exercise humility, poverty and patience, which are things pleasing to his Beloved.

### [267]

They asked for the Lover's forgiveness out of love for his Beloved. So the Lover not only forgave, but also gave them himself and his possessions.

---

369. Here presumably Llull is referring to the triad of 'matter-form-conjunction' indissociable from the type of hylomorphism he espouses.

370. Cat. *amor.* i.e. 'adoration'.

[268]

With tears in his eyes, the Lover described the suffering and sorrow his Beloved had endured for the sake of His love. And with sadness and concern he wrote down the words that he uttered; and with mercy and hope he consoled himself.

[269]

The Beloved and Love came to see the Lover, who was asleep. The Beloved called out to His Lover and Love awakened him. So the Lover obeyed Love and replied to his Beloved.

[270]

The Beloved trained His Lover to love while Love taught him to expose himself to danger. And patience instructed him how to undergo hardship out of love for Him to Whom he had given himself as servant.

[271]

The Beloved asked people whether they had seen His Lover. So they demonstrated to Him that Lover's qualities. And the Beloved said that His Lover was bold yet fearful, rich yet poor, happy yet sad and pensive, and that he continually languished for the sake of his love.

[272]

So they asked the Lover whether he would sell his desire. And he replied that he had already sold it to his Beloved for such a high price that the entire world could be bought with it.

[273]

'Preach, Fool, and speak words about your Beloved.'

The Lover wept, fasted and forsook the world, and he went in search of his Beloved with love. And he praised Him in those places where He was dishonoured.

[274]

The Lover designed and built a fine city wherein his Beloved might reside. He fashioned it from love, cares, laments, tears and languor. He decorated it with joy, hope and devotion. And he furnished it with faith, justice, prudence, fortitude and temperance.

[275]

The Lover drank Love from the spring of his Beloved, wherein the Beloved washed the feet of His Lover, who has frequently forgotten and scorned His Honours, for which reason the world is in a state of imperfection.

[276]

'Tell us, Fool, what is sin?'

He replied: 'Intention turned and inverted against the final cause and purpose for which my Beloved has created all things.'

[277]

The Lover saw that the world was created, since eternity is in fuller accord with his Beloved — who constitutes an essence infinite in greatness and in every perfection — than it is with the world, which possesses finite quantity.

In his Beloved's justice, therefore, the Lover saw that his Beloved's eternity must have existed prior to time and to finite quantity.

[278]

The Lover vindicated his Beloved towards those who said that the world was eternal, by stating that his Beloved would not possess perfect justice if He failed to restore to each soul its body (for which there would not be sufficient room or primordial matter), and the world would not be directed towards a single goal alone, were it to be eternal. And if it were not so directed, perfection of will and wisdom would be lacking in his Beloved.[371]

[279]

'Tell us, Fool, how do you know that the Catholic faith is true and that the beliefs of the Jews and the Saracens consist in falsehood and error?'

---

371. The argument in this versicle is fleshed out in the *Gentile* (1274-6 (?)), II, 2, 4, where the Jew states: 'For if the world were eternal, God would eternally have to create primordial matter out of which the bodies of rational creatures would be composed; for the primordial matter of this world would not suffice for so many resuscitated bodies with souls, deserving reward or punishment, for which they should be resuscitated, according to God's perfect justice'; English quotation from *SWI*, 161.

He replied: 'From the ten conditions of the *Book of the Gentile and the Three Wise Men.*'[372]

### [280]

'Tell us, Fool, where do wisdom's origins lie?'

He replied: 'In faith and devotion, which constitute a ladder whereby one's intellect raises itself up to understand the secrets of my Beloved.'

'And from what do faith and devotion derive their origin?'

He replied: 'From my Beloved, Who enlightens faith and kindles devotion.'

### [281]

They asked the Lover which was greater: possibility or impossibility? He replied that possibility was greater in creatures and impossibility greater in his Beloved, since possibility and potency are in accord, as are impossibility and act.[373]

### [282]

'Tell us, Fool, which is greater: difference or concordance?'

He replied that, outside his Beloved, difference was greater as regards plurality and concordance as regards unity, but that, within Him, they were equal as regards plurality and unity.[374]

---

372. For the ten (plus two) conditions governing the five Trees explained to the wise men by Lady Intelligence in this work, see *SW* I, 114-115. The two additional conditions state that: 'all [the other] conditions be directed towards a single goal; the other is that they not be contrary to this goal. And this goal is to love, know, fear, and serve God'; English quotation from *SW* I, 115.

373. Aristotelian conceptions of causality involve the eduction of act from potency, i.e. actuality is the realisation of potentiality. God, in scholastic-Aristotelian metaphysical theology was considered to be 'pure act', as an indication of His perfection, given that His essence is identical with His existence. Created beings have potentiality, but not perfect and complete actuality, since they contain imperfections as well as perfections.

374. 'Difference', 'Concordance' and 'Equality' are three of the principles from Figure T of Llull's Arts. Here Llull is making a distinction between the application of these principles *ad intra* (i.e. in God), where they are equal, convertible, and possess unity in plurality, and their application *ad extra* (i.e. to the created realm), where they are not and do not.

### [283]

'Tell us, lover, what is Worth?'

He replied that it was the opposite of worth as found in this world, which worth is desired by false and vainglorious lovers, who wish to be worthy, though being unworthy, become persecutors of Worth.[375]

### [284]

'Tell us, Fool, have you ever seen a man who is witless?'

He replied by saying that he had seen a bishop who had many cups, bowls and silver platters on his table, many garments and a large bed in his bedchamber and many coins in his coffers, but that there were few paupers at the gates to his palace.[376]

### [285]

'Fool, do you know what baseness is?'

He replied: 'Base thoughts.'

'And what is loyalty?'

'The fear of my Beloved, born from love and modesty, which dreads people's censure.'

'And what is honour?'

He replied: 'To cogitate upon my Beloved and to desire and praise His Honours.'

### [286]

The trials and tribulations which the Lover underwent for the sake of love unsettled him and inclined him towards impatience. So the Beloved reproached him by means of His Honours and His promises, saying that whoever was unsettled by strenuous effort or happiness knew little about love.

The Lover felt contrition and wept, begging his Beloved to restore his love.

### [287]

'Tell us, Fool, what is love?'

He replied that love is that which enslaves the free and frees the slaves.

---

375. Cf. above, Ch. 48.
376. Cf. above, Ch. 58, §§ 2-3.

So the question is: to which of these is love closer, freedom or enslavement?

[288]

The Beloved called out to His Lover, who replied to Him by saying:

'What is your wish, O Beloved, who art the eyes of my eyes, the thoughts of my thoughts, the fulfilment of my fulfilment, the love of my love, and even the beginning of my beginnings?'[377]

[289]

'Beloved', said the Lover, 'towards You do I go and in You do I go, for You have called me. I go in order to contemplate contemplation in contemplation, by means of the contemplation of Your contemplation. I exist in Your virtue and make my approach by means of Your virtue, from which I derive virtue. I salute You by means of Your salutation, which is my salutation, as well as in Your salutation, from which I hope for an everlasting salutation in the blessing of Your blessings, wherein I am blessed in my blessings.'[378]

[290]

'You, O Beloved, are lofty in Your heights, to which You exalt my will, exalted as this is in Your exaltation by Your heights, which, within my memory, exalt my intellect, exalted as this likewise is in Your exaltation so that it may have knowledge of Your Honours, and that my will may thereby enjoy exalted loving and my memory lofty remembrance.'[379]

[291]

'You, O Beloved, are the glory of my glory. And by Your glory and in Your glory You bestow glory upon my glory, which gains glory from

---

377. Vv. 288-293 give further abundant examples of Llull's use of the figure of polyptoton or 'transplacement'.

378. In this versicle Llull engages in further dense repetition and word play, the Catalan word *salut*, with which *salutació* (lit. 'greeting') is cognate, denoting health or, in this instance, salvation. Furthermore, the words *benedicció* ('blessing') and *beneit* ('blessed'), carry the further meanings of beatification and the Blessed pertaining to those who have been admitted to Heaven. Note also Llull's use of 'blessing' and 'blessed', the active and passive aspects of the verb 'to bless' in its downward motion, here partially and inversely reflective of the reciprocal relation between the Lover and the Beloved.

379. Cf. Ps 56 (57):6 and 12.

Your glory. And through Your glory, the pains and languor I receive from honouring Your glory constitute my glory, as do the pleasures and thoughts I receive from Your glory.'

### [292]

'O Beloved, in the prison of love You hold me enamoured by means of Your love, which has made me enamoured of Your love, through Your love and in Your love. For You are nothing but love, in which You cause me to remain alone yet in the company of Your love and Your Honours. For You alone are in myself alone, who am alone with my thoughts, so that Your solitude, alone in its Honours, may have myself alone to praise and honour its worth, without fear of the ingrates who fail to have You alone in their love.'

### [293]

'You, O Beloved, are the solace of every solace; for in You my thoughts draw solace from Your solace, which offers solace and comfort to my languor and tribulations, brought on by Your solace when You fail by means of such solace to give solace to the ignorant and when You fail to inspire in those acquainted with Your solace a more ardent desire to honour Your Honours.'[380]

### [294]

The Lover complained to his Lord about his Beloved, and to his Beloved about his Lord.

His Lord and his Beloved both said: 'Who is it that introduces a division between Us, Who are but a single thing?'

The Lover answered, and said that it was the Lord's compassion and the tribulations brought on by the Beloved.

### [295]

The Lover was in peril in Love's great ocean, yet he trusted in his Beloved, Who came to his aid with tribulations, cares, tears and weeping, sighs and languor, because the ocean consisted in love and paying honour to his Beloved's Honours.

---

380. Cf. above, vv. 194 and 206.

[296]

The Lover rejoiced at his Beloved's existence. For by His existence has every other being come into existence and been sustained therein, and is it bound and obliged to honour and serve the existence of his Beloved, Who cannot be destroyed or condemned, or reduced or increased by any being.

[297]

'Beloved, because of Your greatness, You cause my desires, my cares and my pains to be great. For You are so great that everything is great which derives remembrance, understanding and enjoyment from You. And Your greatness causes all things contrary to Your Honours and Commandments to be small.'[381]

[298]

'My Beloved eternally begins and has begun and shall begin; and eternally does He not begin nor has He begun nor shall He begin. Yet within my Beloved such precepts[382] are not in contradiction, because He is eternal and possesses Unity and Trinity within Him.'

[299]

'My Beloved is One, and in His Unity my thoughts and my love are united in a single will. And my Beloved's Unity suffices for all unities and all pluralities. And the plurality which resides in my Beloved suffices for all unities and pluralities.'[383]

[300]

'The good of my Beloved is the Supreme Good, and He is the good of my good, [since] there is no other good but He. For, were He not so, my good would derive from another Supreme Good. But since it

---

381. 'Greatness' is the second of Llull's divine Dignities or attributes.

382. Cat. *començaments*: lit. 'beginnings' (also 'principles', hence 'precepts').

383. The emanation of the Many from the One and their return to Unity, was a favoured theme of Neoplatonic thought, epitomised for the Latin West by the *exitus a Deo* and the *reditus ad Deum* (or egress from and return to God), conceived in terms of the Neoplatonic axiom put to great use by the Scholastics, namely, *Bonum est diffusivum sui* ('the good is diffusive of itself').

does not, let all my good be invested during this life in honouring the Supreme Good, as should be the case.'[384]

### [301]

'Though You know me to be a sinner, O Beloved, You show me compassion and forgiveness.[385] And because what You know there to be in Yourself is superior to what is in me, I therefore know that in You there is forgiveness and love, since You cause me to know contrition and sorrow, as well as the desire to suffer death in order to praise Your worth.'

### [302]

'Your power, O Beloved, is able to save me by reason of kindness, compassion and forgiveness, and able to damn me by reason of justice and the guilt I bear for my sins. May Your power fulfil Your will in my regard, for, whether You grant me salvation or damnation, all is fulfilment.'

### [303]

'O Beloved, whenever my will loves truth, truth visits my contrite heart and brings tears to my eyes. And since Your truth is supreme, it raises up my will so that it may honour Your perfections, and it lowers it so that it may abhor my imperfections.'

### [304]

'That wherein my Beloved did not obtain was never true, that wherein my Beloved does not obtain is false, and that wherein my Beloved shall not obtain will be false. So whatever was, is, or shall exist, therefore, is necessarily true if my Beloved obtains therein. So, therefore, whoever holds a truth wherein my Beloved does not obtain is in error, and no contradiction follows from this.'

### [305]

The Beloved created and the Lover destroyed. The Beloved judged and the Lover wept. The Beloved redeemed and glorified the Lover.

---

384. In Neoplatonism, the One and the Good are identical.

385. The Catalan text here contains both rhyme and aliteration: *Si tu, amat, sabs mi peccador, si·t fas tu piadós e perdonador.*

The Beloved completed His activities and the Lover remained eternally in his Beloved's company.

### [306]

The Lover went in search of his Beloved along the paths of vegetation, sensation, imagination, intellect and will.[386] And along such paths the Lover met with dangers and languor for the sake of his Beloved, so that he might raise his intellect and his will up to his Beloved, who desires His lovers to understand and love Him in an exalted manner.

### [307]

The Lover moves towards being by virtue of his Beloved's perfection, and moves towards non-being by virtue of his own imperfection.

The question arises, therefore, as to which of the two movements has greater natural control over the Lover.

### [308]

'You have placed me, O Beloved, between my evil and Your good. On Your part, let there be compassion, mercy, patience, humility, forgiveness, aid and salvation; on my part, let there be contrition, perseverance and remembrance, accompanied by sighs, tears and weeping for Your holy Passion.'

### [309]

'O Beloved Who leads me to love, if You do not come to my aid, then why did You decide to create me? And why did You bear such great languor and endure such severe suffering on my behalf? Since You have assisted so much in raising me aloft, then help me descend, O Beloved, so as to remember and detest my faults and my trespasses, so that my thoughts may ascend more readily to desire, honour and praise Your worth.'

---

386. 'Vegetation...will': the levels of created, material reality macrocosmically which correspond to humankind and, in part, to animals (the elemental level being here omitted) microcosmically.

## [310]

'You have created my will free to love Your Honours or to scorn Your worth, so that You may increase Your love therein. By such freedom, O Beloved, You have placed my will in danger.[387]

'O Beloved, in such danger must You remember Your lover, who of his own free will incurs servitude in order to praise Your Honours and increase the languor and tears of his body.'

## [311]

'O Beloved, in Your Lover neither fault nor sin ever originated from You; nor in him was there perfection other than through Your gift and forgiveness.[388] Thus, since the Lover has such possession of You, do not forget him in his tribulations or his dangers.'

## [312]

'O Beloved, Who with a single name are called man and God! In this name, Jesus Christ,[389] does my will desire You as both man and God. And if You, O Beloved, have so honoured Your Lover, who lacks all merit in naming You such or in desiring You be so named, why do You fail to honour those many ignorant people who have not knowingly been as guilty towards Your name, Jesus Christ, as has been Your Lover?'

## [313]

The Lover wept, and said the following words to his Beloved:

'O Beloved, You have never been miserly or begrudging towards Your Lover as regards bestowing being upon him, redeeming him or providing him with the many creatures in his service. So, how could it be, O Beloved, that You, Who are supreme generosity, might be miserly towards Your Lover as regards tears, concerns, languor, wisdom and love, whereby to honour Your Honours? Your Lover, therefore, asks from You, O Beloved, a long life so that he may receive from You many of the aforesaid gifts.'

---

387. The Catalan text here contains a triple internal rhyme, which lends the sentence a distinctive rhythm: *En aquesta libertat has, amat, perillada ma volentat.*

388. See above, Ch. 64, § 10 and corresponding note, and below, Chs. 104, § 8 and 105, § 6.

389. Note that in Old Catalan this name forms a single word: *Jesucrist.*

[314]

'O Beloved, if You assist righteous people against their mortal ene-mies, assist in increasing my concern to desire Your Honours. And if You assist unrighteous people to obtain justice[390] anew, assist Your Lover to make of his will a sacrifice to Your praise, and of his body a testimony to love by way of martyrdom.'

[315]

'There is no difference in my Beloved between humility, humble and humbled, for He is wholly humility in pure act.' So, therefore, the Lover repudiates pride, which seeks to raise up to his Beloved those whom the latter's humility has so greatly honoured in this world, and whom pride has clothed in hypocrisy, vainglory and vanity.

[316]

Humility has humbled the Beloved before the Lover through contri-tion, and likewise through devotion.

So the question arises as to by which of these two things the Be-loved was more deeply humbled before His Lover.

[317]

The Beloved felt mercy towards His Lover because of His perfection, and likewise because of His Lover's needs.

So the question arose: for which of these two reasons does the Beloved more fully forgive the faults of His Lover?

[318]

'Our Lady and the angels and saints in glory offered prayers to my Beloved. And when I recalled the error into which the world has fall-en through ingratitude, I likewise recalled how great is the justice of my Beloved and how great the ingratitude of His enemies.'

[319]

Using the ladder of humanity, the Lover raised the powers of his soul in order to glorify the divine nature. And, using the divine nature, he

---

390. The reader should note the presence of cognate terms in this versicle, name-ly, in Catalan, *homens justs* (here 'righteous people'), *homens injusts* ('unrighteous peo-ple') and *justicia* ('justice'), which cannot be preserved in English.

lowered the powers of his soul in order to glorify the human nature of his Beloved.[391]

### [320]

The narrower the paths along which the Lover proceeds towards his Beloved, the broader is his love. And the narrower his love, the broader are the paths.

So, whatever the circumstances, therefore, the Beloved affords love, pain, languor, pleasure and consolation to His Lover.

### [321]

Love emerges from love, concern from languor, and tears likewise from languor. And love enters love, concern tears, and languor sighs.

So the Beloved looks upon His Lover, who bears all such tribulations for the sake of his love.

### [322]

The Lover's memories and desires went on excursions and pilgrimages to the noble attributes of his Beloved, and there kept vigil. And they conveyed His countenance to him and filled his intellect with a radiance whereby his will increased his love.

### [323]

The Lover used his imagination to paint and form his Beloved's countenance in bodily things, and his intellect to burnish them in spiritual things, and his will to worship them in all creatures.

### [324]

The Lover purchased one day of tears for another of concern, and he sold one day of love for another of tribulation. And his love and concern found increase.

---

391. Here the Lover describes his contemplative ascent and corresponding descent via the humanity and divinity of Christ, whose hypostatic union is thus conceived as central to the mystic's enterprise, the ultimate aim of which is the glorification of both aspects (or natures) thereof.

## [325]

The Lover was in a foreign land and he forgot his Beloved. Yet he missed his Lord, his wife and his children, and his friends.

But he remembered his Beloved once more, so that he might be comforted and that his estrangement might not make him homesick or sad.

## [326]

The Lover heard words uttered by his Beloved through which his intellect beheld Him, for his will derived pleasure from hearing such and his memory remembered his Beloved's Virtues and promises.

## [327]

The Lover heard people censure his Beloved, and through such censure his intellect beheld his Beloved's justice and patience, for His justice punished the censurers and His patience awaited their contrition and repentance.

The question arises, therefore, as to which of the two the Lover believed in more strongly.[392]

## [328]

The Lover fell ill and, with his Beloved's counsel, wrote a Will. He left his sins and trespasses to repentance and regret, and left worldly pleasures to disdain. To his eyes he left tears, and to his heart sighs and love. To his intellect he left his Beloved's countenance, and to his memory the suffering his Beloved had undergone for the sake of His love. And to his concerns he left the task of correcting the unbelievers who unknowingly go towards perdition

## [329]

The Lover smelled some flowers, yet recalled the stench of the wealthy miser, the lecher and the proud ingrate. The Lover tasted sweetness, yet understood the bitterness of worldly possessions and of entry into and departure from this life. The Lover felt worldly joys, yet his intellect understood the brief transience of this world, and the everlasting torment occasioned by the pleasures which afford enjoyment here below.

---

392. Cf. below, v. 338.

[330]

The Lover underwent hunger, thirst, cold and heat, poverty, nakedness, sickness and tribulation. He would have died had he not remembered his Beloved, Who cured him with hope, remembrance,
the rejection of this world and scorn towards the censure of other
people.

[331]

The Lover's bed lay between pain and pleasure. It pleased him to fall
asleep, yet pained him to awake.

So the questions arises: to which of these two does the Lover's bed
lie closer?

[332]

The Lover fell asleep in anger for he feared the censure of other
people, yet he awoke with patience when he remembered his Beloved's praise.

So the question arises: towards whom did the Lover feel greater
shame, his Beloved or other people?

[333]

The Lover cogitated upon death and was fearful, until he remembered the city of his Beloved, whose gates and entrance consist in
Death and Love.

[334]

The Lover complained to his Beloved about temptations, which regularly disturbed his thoughts. So his Beloved replied to him by saying
that temptations are occasions whereby one may use one's memory to
remember God and to love His honourable countenance.

[335]

The Lover lost a jewel he dearly loved, and would have been inconsol-
able had his Beloved not asked him which was of greater benefit to
him: the jewel he once possessed or the patience he exercised as regards the works of his Beloved?

## [336]

The Lover went to sleep while considering the hardships and obstacles he faced in serving his Beloved, and he was afraid that his deeds might come to nothing on account of such obstacles. The Beloved sent him conscience, which roused his merits and the powers of his Beloved within him.

## [337]

The Lover had to walk long, hard and rocky paths, and the time came for him to walk such paths and to carry the heavy burden that Love makes its lovers bear. So the Lover relieved his soul, therefore, of worldly cares and joys, so that his body might bear the load more easily, and his soul might walk those paths in the company of his Beloved.

## [338]

One day, in front of the Lover, people spoke ill of his Beloved, yet the Lover made no reply nor did he exonerate the latter.

So the question arises as to who is more blameworthy: the people who censured his Beloved or the Lover who remained silent and failed to exonerate his Beloved?[393]

## [339]

The Lover contemplated his Beloved; his intellect grew keener,[394] and the love in his will did likewise.

So the question arises as to which of the two made his memory keener when remembering his Beloved.

## [340]

The Lover set out on his journey to honour his Beloved with fervour and fear. Fervour led him, and fear preserved him. While the Lover was walking along in this manner, he came upon sighs and tears, who brought him greetings from his Beloved.

---

393. Cf. above, v. 327.

394. Cat. *s'asubtillava en son enteniment* lit. 'his intellect gained in subtlety or acuity'. For the Lullian significance of the term *subtilesa*, cf. above, Ch. 39, § 2 and corresponding note.

So the question arises as to which of these four gave the Lover greater solace as regards his Beloved.

### [341]

The Lover looked at himself so that he might be a mirror in which to behold his Beloved. And he looked at his Beloved so that He might be a mirror for him wherein to gain knowledge of himself.

So the question arises: to which of these two mirrors was his intellect closer?

### [342]

Theology and Philosophy, Medicine and Law met the Lover, who inquired of them whether they had seen his Beloved. Theology wept and Philosophy hesitated, while Medicine and Law rejoiced.

So the question arises as to what each of the four things signified signifies to the Lover, who goes in search of his Beloved.

### [343]

Tearful and distressed, the Lover went in search of his Beloved along the trails of the senses and the paths of the intellect.

So the question arises: on which of the two routes did he first embark while he was seeking his Beloved, and along which of these did the Beloved reveal Himself to the Lover more clearly?

### [344]

On Judgement Day, the Beloved will say that people should place on one side what they have given to Him in this world, while on the other should be placed what they have given to the world, so that it may be seen how deeply He has been loved and which of the two gifts is nobler and of greater quantity.

### [345]

The Lover's will loved itself, so his intellect asked it if it was more akin to the Beloved when it loved itself than it was when it loved Him, since the Beloved loves Himself more than He does any other thing.

So the question arises, therefore: in accordance with which answer could Will reply to Intellect more truthfully?

[346]

'Tell us, Fool, what is the greatest and noblest love that exists in a creature?'

He replied: 'That which is one with the Creator.'

'Why?'

'Because the Creator does not have anything in which He can make a nobler creature.'

[347]

One day, the Lover was at prayer and he noticed that he was not weeping. So, in order that he might weep, he directed his thoughts towards money, women, children, food and vainglory. And within his intellect, he discovered that each of the aforesaid things had more people as servants than did his Beloved. So, for this reason, his eyes filled with tears and his soul with sadness and sorrow.

[348]

The Lover was walking along, thinking deeply about his Beloved, while on his way he encountered great crowds and throngs of people, who asked him for news. But, since he was rejoicing in his Beloved, the Lover failed to reply to what they had asked him, and said that he did not wish to reply to their words lest he be separated from his Beloved.

[349]

Covered with love, inside and out, the Lover went in search of his Beloved.

Love asked him: 'Lover, where are you going?'

He replied: 'I am going to my Beloved so that you may become greater.'

[350]

'Tell us, Fool, what is religion?'

He replied: 'Cleanliness of thought, and a desire to die for the sake of honouring my Beloved, while forsaking the world so that there are no obstacles to contemplating Him or to speaking the truth about His Honours.'

[351]

'Tell us, Fool, what do hardships, laments, sighs, tears, trials and dangers mean to the Lover?'

He replied: 'My Beloved's pleasure.'

'Why?'

'So that He may thereby be more greatly loved and the Lover receive a greater reward.'

[352]

They asked the Lover whether love was greater in the Lover who lived or the Lover who died. He replied that it was greater in the Lover who died.

'Why?'

'Because it cannot be greater in a Lover who dies for love, though it can be so in one who lives for love.'

[353]

Two Lovers met. One of them made his Beloved known, while the other understood him.

So the question arose as to which of the two was closer to his Beloved. And by its solution, the Lover learned how to prove the Trinity.

[354]

'Tell us, Fool, why do you speak with such subtlety?'

He replied: 'So that I may be the occasion of raising up the intellect to my Beloved's noble attributes, and so that He may be honoured, loved and served by a larger number of people.'

[355]

The Lover became inebriated on wine which remembered, understood and loved his Beloved. The Beloved diluted this wine with the tears and weeping of His Lover.

[356]

Love heated and inflamed the Lover with the memory of his Beloved. But the Beloved cooled him down by means of tears and weeping, the forgetting of earthly delights and the rejection of vain honours.[395] So

---

395. Memory forgetting and will hating (which latter I have translated as 'rejection') are components of Figure S from Llull's earlier Arts.

the Lover's love grew when he remembered on Whose account he endured languor and tribulation, and on whose account worldly people endured hardship and persecution.

[357]

'Tell us, Fool, what is this world?'

He replied: 'A prison for the lovers and servants of my Beloved.'

'So who puts them in prison?'

He replied: 'Conscience, love, fear, renunciation, contrition, and the company of wicked people. This world, then, is hardship lacking in reward, wherein lies punishment.'

Since Blaquerna had to compose a book concerning the 'Art of Contemplation', he therefore decided to finish the *Book of the Lover and the Beloved*, which is here concluded to the glory and praise of Our Lord God.

## 101. HERE BEGINS THE 'ART OF CONTEMPLATION'

### PROLOGUE

[1] So lofty and excellent is the Supreme Good, and so base is man through fault and sin, that it often occurs that hermits and holy men have great difficulty in raising their soul to contemplate God. And since an art and method is helpful in such matters, Blaquerna, therefore, considered how he might fashion an art of contemplation so as to help him acquire devotion in his heart and tears and weeping in his eyes, and so that his intellect and will might rise aloft to contemplate God in terms of His Honours and His countenance.

[2] When Blaquerna the hermit had considered thus, he wrote a book about contemplation by way of an art, which book he divided into twelve parts, consisting of the following: Divine Virtues; Essence; Unity; Trinity; Incarnation; *Pater noster*; *Ave Maria*; Commandments; *Miserere mei Deus*;[396] Sacraments; Virtues; and Vices.

[3] The art of this book consists in the fact that, first of all, each of the Divine Virtues should be contemplated by means of the others

---

396. Ps 51 (50).

and, subsequently, by means of the other parts of the book, while the soul of the person contemplating has as its object the Divine Virtues within his memory, intellect and will. In his soul, he should likewise be able to bring into accord the Divine Virtues and the other parts of the book, in such a way that honour and perfection be afforded to the Divine Virtues, which Virtues are the following: Goodness, Greatness, Eternity, Power, Wisdom, Will, Virtue, Truth, Glory, Perfection, Justice, Generosity, Mercy, Humility, Dominion and Patience.[397]

[4] These Virtues can be contemplated in a variety of ways, for one way consists in contemplating one virtue by means of another, or by means of two, three or more. Another way is achieved when a person contemplates the Virtues by means of God's Essence, Unity, Trinity or Incarnation, and likewise as regards the other parts of the book. A still further way is had when, by means of the Virtues, a person contemplates God's Essence, Unity, Trinity or Incarnation. Again, another way consists in the words of the *Pater noster* and the *Ave Maria*, and so on. One can contemplate God and His works using all sixteen of His Virtues or only a few, according to whether one wishes to extend or curtail one's contemplation, and according to whether the subject matter of one's contemplation is better suited to certain Virtues rather than others.

[5] The conditions of this art consist in the fact that one should be suitably disposed to contemplate and in an appropriate location to do so, for contemplation can be hindered by overeating, by very great affliction, by a place in which there is a great press and clamour of people or where it is too hot or too cold. But the overriding condition which applies to this art is that one should not encounter any hindrance from worldly matters in one's memory, intellect or will when one begins one's contemplation.

[6] Since we are busy composing other books, we shall briefly describe, therefore, the manner and method whereby Blaquerna contemplated by way of an art. So, first of all, we shall begin with the first part of the book.

---

397. These constitute the sixteen Dignities from Figure A of Llull's *Ars compendiosa inveniendi veritatem* (*c.*1274) cycle. 'Power, Wisdom [and] Will' (Cat. *poder, saviea, amor*) form a well-known triad in Llull's Arts; I have translate *amor* as 'Will', since this latter is the term which most commonly occurs in Llull's lists of Dignities, *volentat* or 'Will', of course, being the faculty associated with *amor*.

## 102. ON HOW BLAQUERNA CONTEMPLATED GOD'S VIRTUES

[1] Blaquerna rose at midnight, gazed up at the heavens and the stars, emptied his thoughts and began to think about God's Virtues. He wished to contemplate God's goodness by means of all the fifteen Virtues, and he wished to contemplate the fifteen Virtues by means of God's goodness. So, therefore, he uttered the following words using his mouth, and cogitated upon them in his soul with all the powers of his memory, intellect and will, while kneeling down, raising his hands to Heaven and his thoughts towards God:

[2] 'O Supreme Good, Who art infinitely great in eternity, power, wisdom, will, virtue, truth, glory, perfection, justice, generosity, mercy, humility, dominion, and patience! I worship You by remembering, understanding and loving You, and by speaking of You and all the aforesaid Virtues, which form with You and You with them a single thing, one same essence, without any difference.[398]

[3] 'Supreme Good, Who art great; Supreme Greatness, Who art good! Were You not eternal, You would not be such a great good that my soul might succeed in making my memory remember You, my intellect understand You and my will love You. But since You are infinite and eternal good, by infused grace and blessing can You succeed in making the entire soul, as well as every soul, remember, understand and love the infinite and eternal Supreme Good.'

[4] By virtue of the power that Blaquerna remembered in the Supreme Good, he was afforded the strength and ability to transmit his thoughts beyond the firmament. And he considered a greatness so great that infinite motion, such as a bolt of lightning obtaining in all six directions at once, namely, up and down, left and right, forwards and backwards, would not be able to discover any limit, beginning or end thereto.[399] Blaquerna felt great wonder at such a consideration, and all the more so when he expanded upon it by remembering there to exist within said Good such great eternity without beginning or end. While Blaquerna remained wholly perplexed by such considerations, he remembered in how great a good the Divine Good con-

---

398. Blaquerna's manner and terms of address and contemplation in this chapter echo the formula of his father Evast's paean of praise to God in Ch. 8, § 1 above.

399. Llull's arguments here recall St Anselm's own Ontological Argument for the existence of God.

sists, since it is a power capable of being so great and so eternal. It is likewise capable of knowing and willing infinitely and eternally, as well as of possessing infinite and eternal virtue, truth, glory, perfection, justice, generosity, mercy, humility, dominion and patience.

[5] While Blaquerna was contemplating in this manner, his heart began to grow hot and his eyes began to weep on account of the great pleasure he had been deriving from remembering, understanding and loving such noble Virtues within the Supreme Good. But before Blaquerna could altogether weep, his intellect lowered itself down to his imaginative faculty, and, using this, it began to think about and to doubt how it could be that before the world even existed, God might have possessed justice, generosity, mercy, humility and dominion.[400] And because of the participation between his intellect and his imaginative faculty, his doubt cooled down the heat of his heart, and reduced the tears in his eyes. So Blaquerna unbound his intellect from his imaginative faculty, and caused the former to rise above the latter by remembering the Supreme Good to be infinite in every perfection. So, therefore, on account of Its power and Its glory, It is able and knows how to possess all of the aforesaid Virtues just as perfectly, even before the world existed, as It does now that the world exists. But because at one time the world did not exist, there was nobody in existence to receive the grace or influence of the above Virtues from the Supreme Good.

[6] Blaquerna's will was greatly pleased by what his intellect had accomplished. Beneath itself it had left the imaginative faculty, which had hindered its understanding, and in the absence of that faculty, it had heightened its understanding of the infinite power of God, which ought to have primacy within the world with respect to justice, generosity, and so on. For, were this not so, it would follow that a lack of power, greatness, eternity and virtue might exist in the Supreme Good. Yet since it is impossible for lack to exist in God, his will, therefore, heated Blaquerna's heart so intensely that his eyes wept at great length.

---

400. In Llull's thought, and in that of scholastic psychology as a whole, the imaginative faculty lies below those of the rational soul (namely, memory, intellect and will), and is restricted by its relation to the sensitive faculties, lying below it in turn. For Llull's hierarchy of the human faculties, see above, notes corresponding to Chs. 2, § 4 and 59, § 3; for the faculties of the human intellective soul, see above, note corresponding to Ch. 31, § 4.

[7] While Blaquerna was contemplating and weeping, his memory, intellect and will conversed mentally within his soul, and they gained solace from God's Virtues, as the following words reveal:

'Memory', asked his Intellect, 'what do you remember about God's goodness, wisdom and love? And you, O Will, what do you love therein?'

Memory replied by saying:

'When I introduce into my memory the thought of how great it is to know oneself to have superior and nobler knowledge and will than does any other thing, I do not feel as great or as lofty as I do when I remember the Supreme Good, a Good infinite in knowledge and will; and when I introduce therein the thought of eternity, power, virtue, truth, and so on, I feel myself become greater and more exalted by remembering such things.'

By these words and many others did Memory reply to Intellect, and Will replied to it in a similar fashion, saying that it did not feel as lofty or as great when loving the Supreme Good by reason of itself being wiser and more loving than any other thing, as it did when it loved the Supreme Good by reason of the latter's possessing infinite and eternal wisdom and will, and so on. After these words had been spoken, Intellect informed Memory and Will about its similar situation to their own as regards contemplating the Supreme Good.

[8] Memory, Intellect and Will agreed to contemplate the Supreme Good in terms of Its virtue, truth and glory. Memory remembered the virtue pertaining to the Infinite Good, which infinite virtue consists in truth and glory; Intellect understood what Memory remembered; and Will loved what Memory rembered and Intellect understood. Memory set out to remember once more, and it remembered the infinite truth pertaining to the Supreme Good, which consists in virtue, truth and glory; Intellect understood infinite glory, which consists in virtue and truth, which latter constitute the glorious Supreme Good; and Will loved it all together in one and the same actuality and perfection.

[9] Blaquerna asked Intellect:

'If the Supreme Good grants me salvation, what will you understand?'

Intellect replied:

'I shall understand God's mercy, humility and generosity.'

'And you, O Memory, if the Supreme Good damns me, what will you remember?'

It replied:

'I shall remember God's justice, dominion, perfection and power.'

'And you, O Will, what will you love?'

It replied:

'I shall love what Memory remembers, so long as I am in a place where I may do so, for the Virtues which exist in the Supreme Good are in themselves loveable.'

[10] These words having been said, Blaquerna remembered his sins and understood how great a good it is for there to obtain patience in God, for were patience not to obtain in Him, then as soon as man had sinned he would be punished and deprived of this world. So he asked his will, therefore, what thanks he ought to pay to God's patience, which had shown tolerance towards him. His will replied by saying that he ought to love justice in the Supreme Good, even if it were possible that his intellect might know that such justice would punish him with damnation for his sins. Blaquerna was greatly pleased by his will's reply, so his mouth, along with all three powers of his soul, gave praise and blessing to the patience of the Supreme Good by means of all the divine Virtues.

[11] Blaquerna contemplated the divine Virtues in this manner from midnight until the time when he was due to sound Matins, and he gave thanks to God for having condescended towards him insofar as He had guided him in his contemplation. So when he decided to cease contemplating and to sound Matins, he began to remember that he had failed to contemplate God's patience in as exalted a manner as he had His other Virtues since he had contemplated it with respect to himself, as is stated above. It was necessary, therefore, to resume his contemplation once more, so he said that he worshipped and contemplated God's patience for being one and the same thing as the Supreme Goodness and all the other Virtues, without any difference. His intellect, therefore, felt great wonder at the fact that patience could be one and the same thing in essence as the other Virtues. His memory, however, remembered that, in God, there existed no difference between each of the Virtues, but that since the works they perform in creatures are diverse, for that reason they seem to be diverse, just as what one sees appears differently when one looks in two mirrors, one of which is curved, the other flat, yet what one sees is a single thing in each mirror, without any difference.

### 103. ON HOW BLAQUERNA CONTEMPLATED GOD'S VIRTUES IN THREES

[1] 'O Divine Goodness', said Blaquerna, 'Who art infinitely great in eternity. You are the good from which all other good comes, and from Your great good comes all good, whether great or small, and from Your eternity comes all other duration. So I worship, invoke and love You beyond my intellect and my memory with respect to all that in which You consist, namely, goodness, greatness and eternity. I ask You, therefore, to make the good that You have granted me great and durable as regards my honouring, praising and serving You in terms of that which pertains to Your Honour.

[2] 'O Eternal Greatness, Your power is greater than I am able to remember, understand or love. My power ascends to You so that You may make it great and durable as regards amply remembering, understanding and loving Your power, whose capacity is infinite and eternal, and from whose influence, here below, we hope for grace and blessing so that we may eternally be great and durable.

[3] 'O Eternity, Who possess the power of wisdom without end or beginning, You have brought about my beginning and have created me so that I might endure without end. You possess the power either to save or to damn me. Your wisdom knows eternally and Your power is likewise capable of that which You will do to me and to others, for in Your eternity there is no change or alteration. I have not the power to know that to which You will sentence me, for my power and wisdom have a beginning. However You judge me, therefore, may it please You to allow my power, wisdom and duration to be to Your honour, and to praise Your Honours.

[4] 'O Power, You Who know and love Yourself in Your entirety; O Wisdom, You Who are able to produce and to love Yourself in Your entirety; O Will, You Who are able to produce and to know Yourself in Your entirety: take all my power and wisdom, since You have already taken all of my will, so that they may praise and serve You. You, O Power, are able to know and to will in the same degree that You are without addition, reduction or any alteration. And You, O Wisdom, know in the same degree that You will. And You, O Will, will in the same degree that You will through power, wisdom and will. So, this being the case, and since nothing can change or alter it, from such a great influence may there come upon my power the grace whereby it may always be able to produce, know and love itself by honouring

Your power, and upon my wisdom by honouring Your wisdom, and upon my will by honouring Your will.

[5] 'O Divine Wisdom, love and power lies within You. You know Yourself to be love beyond all other love and power beyond all other power, and You know Yourself to be beyond all other wisdom. So, therefore, if, when loving Your will, my wisdom knows my will to be less powerful, Your wisdom must know Your will to be greater when loving me than mine is when it loves You. And, were You not to know the above in this manner, Your wisdom would not know there to be greater power in Your will when it loves than there is in mine, nor would my wisdom or will possess the power whereby they might contemplate God perfectly.'

While Blaquerna was contemplating in this manner, he remembered that were God to know that His will loved sin, He would lack the power whereby to love Himself; so Blaquerna understood, therefore, that, were he to abhor God, he would lack the power whereby to abhor sin. So, for this reason, Blaquerna wept at great length when he remembered himself to have been guilty and sinful during the time he had sinned.

[6] 'O Divine Love, Your power is truer than that of any other love and Your truth is truer than all other truths. For if the power the sun has when it illuminates and that fire has when it heats are true, much truer still is the power that You have when You love. For there is a difference between the sun and its radiance and between fire and its heat, yet between Your love, power and truth there is no room for essential difference. And everything Your love establishes as being true, it accomplishes by means of a power infinite in love and in truth, while everything that other things accomplish, they do so by means of a power that is finite as regards time and quantity. So, this being the case, I, therefore, bind and subject myself to You, O Love, Power and Truth, for all the days of my life, that I may honour Your Honours and declare to unbelievers and undevout Christians the truth of Your power, Your truth and Your love.'

[7] Virtue, Truth and Glory met within the thoughts of Blaquerna, while he was contemplating his Beloved. Blaquerna considered to which of all three he would pay greater honour in his thoughts and in his will. Since he could comprehend no difference between them, however, he paid them equal honour, therefore, by remembering, understanding and loving his Beloved. He said:

'I worship You, O Power who have created me. I worship You, O Truth who must judge me. I worship You, O Glory in whom I entertain the hope of being glorified in power and truth, and who shall never cease to grant perpetual glory.'

[8] Blaquerna asked his Beloved's truth:

'Were the glory and perfection in which You consist not to abide within You, what would You be?'

Intellect replied to him:

'It would be falsehood or a truth akin to yours, or it would be nothing, or it would be something wherein would lie eternal and perpetual punishment.'

[9] Blaquerna asked:

'And were it not truth, what would glory be?'

Memory replied:

'It would be imperfection.'

'And were it not perfection, what would glory be?'

Will replied:

'It would be everything that is nothing, or it would be everything that is imperfection.'

[10] Blaquerna cogitated upon colour, and he understood the difference between white and red, and the contrariety between black and white. He considered the glory, perfection and justice of his Beloved, yet he could not detect difference or contrariety therein.[401] He considered glory, and he understood perfection and justice. He considered perfection, and he understood glory and justice. He contemplated justice, and he understood perfection and glory. Blaquerna felt great wonder at such considerations, considerations by means of which he greatly elevated his memory, intellect and will in order to contemplate his Beloved. He desired his own glory, yet his eyes filled with tears and he wept, fearing his Beloved's justice.

[11] Blaquerna's memory, intellect and will mustered themselves in order to ascend towards his Beloved. His memory wished to ascend in order to remember perfection, his intellect likewise in order to understand justice, as did his will in order to love generosity. Yet none of his three powers was able to ascend above the others, for the rea-

---

401. The reader is reminded that 'Difference, Concordance and Contrariety' are three of the principles of Llull's Art.

son that each of them required his Beloved's three Virtues, in order
to signify that, in Him, such Virtues were one and the same thing.

[12] 'Justice', asked Blaquerna, 'what do You seek from my will?'
Memory replied on behalf of Justice:

'From your will I seek contrition and fear, while from your eyes I
seek tears; from your heart, sighs; and from your body, affliction.'

'And You, Generosity, what do You seek from my will?'
Intellect replied on behalf of Generosity:

'I seek to possess it fully for the purposes of love, repentance and
disdain for the vanities of this world.'

'And You, Mercy, what do You seek from my memory and my intellect?'

Will replied on behalf of Mercy:

'I seek memory in its entirety so that it may remember, and intellect in its entirety so that it may understand, Mercy's gift and Mercy's
forgiveness,[402] and, further still, that they may contemplate Mercy itself.'

Blaquerna devoted himself entirely to that which his Beloved's
Virtues sought to acquire from him.

[13] Blaquerna worshipped and contemplated generosity, mercy
and humility in his Beloved, and he found them to be greater and
nobler than when he contemplated them in himself. He said to his
intellect, therefore, that he was unable to understand all the generosity, mercy and humility within his Beloved, and he told his will that his
Beloved's mercy was possessed of such great generosity that he might
receive therefrom as much humility as he wished, and might acquire therefrom as much generosity and mercy as was required for his salvation.

[14] Blaquerna was in danger, since he was on the point of considering that his Beloved's dominion was greater than His mercy or humility by virtue of the fact that His dominion extends itself over all
people, yet his humility and mercy fail to enlighten the unbelievers
with respect to the Catholic faith. Blaquerna's Beloved, however,
roused his memory, leading it to recall that His mercy had humbled
the Son of God to be made flesh, and to die on the Cross insofar as
he was man, so that His dominion might be made manifest, and
preached throughout the world by those for whom God humbled

---

402. Cat. *son do e son perdó*. See above, Ch. 64, § 10 and corresponding note; cf.
above also, Ch. 100, *Lover*, v. 311.

Himself in His Holy Sacrifice and for whom God has performed so
many honours, as well as to recall that His mercy expects them to
make satisfaction for so many and such grave mortal sins, displeasing
to both God and people.

[15] Blaquerna said that in this world it does not befit a prince to
enjoy dominion without humility or patience, in order to signify that
it would ill befit God to enjoy dominion without humility and patience. So Blaquerna, therefore, who was prince and lord of his memory, intellect and will,[403] humbled his princedom to patience, so that
he might rise to contemplate within his Beloved humility, dominion
and patience, from which he holds his princedom in fief and in which
regard he must render an account to his Beloved.

[16] Blaquerna ended his prayer, yet the following day returned
thereto using a different method, namely, by setting patience to one
side and taking up dominion, and he attended to the Virtues in
threes so that he might be in possession of a different method. The
next day, he attended to the Virtues in fours, in fives, or in pairs, or
he considered them all by means of greatness and eternity, and so on
for the other Virtues. But he always had new arguments and different
subjects and methods whereby to contemplate his Beloved at his disposal, for he exchanged one virtue for another in his contemplation.
For this reason, Blaquerna was so profuse in his contemplation of his
Beloved, for he adhered to an art therein, that in consequence his
eyes were continually filled with tears and his soul with devotion, contrition and love.

### 104. ON ESSENCE

[1] Blaquerna began to contemplate the Divine Essence using the
Divine Virtues, and while remembering, understanding and loving
these, he said the following words:

[2] 'O Divine Essence, so great are You in goodness and eternity
that between You and Your goodness, greatness and eternity there
exists no difference. You are Essence and You are God, for between
Godhead and God there exists no difference. I worship You in one

---

403. The reader should note that the 'Virtue' of *senyoria* (here translated as 'dominion') has the word *senyor* or 'lord/master' as its root.

and the same thing, Godhead and God, and essence and existence.[404] For if, in terms of Godhead and God, and essence and existence, You are not one and the same thing without difference, Your greatness would be finite and limited, and would lie between Your goodness and Your good, and Your eternity and Your eternal existence. So, it would follow that Your Godhead would be one thing and God would be another, and the same would follow for Your existence and Your essence. But since Your greatness is infinite in goodness and eternity, I therefore worship and bless You, O Supreme Essence, with all Your Virtues, as a simple and pure act.[405]

[3] 'O Glorious Essence, my soul remembers and understands about Your goodness and Your good what it cannot remember or understand about any other thing, for goodness and good, greatness and great, duration and durable are not one and the same thing in a creature. For, were they so, there would be no difference between the essence and the existence of a creature, and were there not to be such, Your goodness would not be as supreme in greatness as befits it. So, in order that that the nobility of Your existence and essence be signified, You are greater, insofar as Your essence and Your existence are one and the same thing, than is created essence and created existence, wherein greatness is lacking. From such a lack we gain knowledge of Your great and infinite greatness, to which I raise and hold aloft all the greatness of my will by worshipping, contemplating and serving Your Glorious Essence.

[4] 'In a creature, essence is distinct from its created power, wisdom and will, for power is one thing, wisdom another, and will yet another. Essence, therefore, cannot be one and the same thing as power, wisdom and will. But, since You, O Glorious Essence, do not differ from Your power, wisdom or will, nor is there difference between Your power, wisdom or will, You are, therefore, a single essence without differing in any respect from the existence of Your power, wisdom and will. And since this is the case, You are the Supreme Good, for all other good lacks the power, wisdom and will to be one and the same thing as its essence, and by its nature tends towards cor-

---

404. According to St Thomas Aquinas, God's essence is identical with his existence and, unlike in the case of created beings, in no way limits it, God being necessary and self-sufficient. For his arguments in this respect, see *ST*, I, 3, 4.

405. See above, Ch. 100, *Lover*, v. 281 and corresponding note.

ruption, to which tendency its nature would be opposed if there were to exist no difference between its existence and its essence.

[5] 'O Glorious Essence, Your power is incapable of causing any imperfection in Your existence, though my power is indeed capable of causing imperfection in my existence, and that is because my existence is one thing, my essence another, and my power yet another. And since my power is distinct from my existence and my essence, it is capable of conflicting with such existence and essence. But since Your power constitutes Your essence and Your existence, in the absence of any difference, You are incapable, therefore, of doing anything which conflicts with Your essence or existence. You, O Essence, possess a power, therefore, that is consummate, infinite and eternal in terms of virtue, truth, glory and perfection.

[6] 'One speaks of "humanity", which is man's essence, with respect to man; one speaks of "knighthood" with respect to a knight; one speaks of "justice" with respect to the just person; and "wisdom", with respect to the one who is wise. Yet, as regards Your Godhead and Yourself, O God, whoever speaks of Your Godhead speaks of You, and whoever says "God" utters Your essence, for Your power suffices to be Your essence and Your existence as regards truth, glory and perfection. So, by being one and the same thing, Your existence and essence constitutes a greater truth than does the essence of a creature's being one thing and its existence another, and a just person's being one thing and justice another. Many just people, therefore, and many knights, can be diverse in certain respects while still falling under the heading of justice, humanity and knighthood. The same cannot be said of Your existence and essence, however, for Your glory and Your perfection possess power and truth wherein there exists no difference between existence and essence.

[7] 'If justice did not exist in creatures, it would be impossible for the just person to have been created, as it would likewise be for man to exist were humanity not to do so. Thus, when man, humanity and all creatures were but nothing, the just and justice existed within Your justice, neither the former existing within Your Essence nor the latter within You, Who are just, in consequence of creatures, for You, rather, are the just and justice in consequence of Yourself. For, as man could not exist without his essence, namely, human nature, so, conversely, the just and justice are capable of existing within You in the absence of any creature. As man is not capable of existing in the ab-

sence of something else which is not man, namely, the elements, matter and form, accident, nature and cause, so within Your Essence neither the just nor justice would be able to exist were there to be room for accident, quality or difference between existence and essence, nor, if Your justice were to require something which was not God or the Divine Essence, could it be eternal, infinite, virtuous and perfect.

[8] 'O Divine Essence, generosity dwelt within You before he to whom You give existed, for if You are generosity and generosity is You, in Your eternity and infinity Your generosity does not come into being after Your essence. And this applies likewise to Your mercy and Your other Virtues. Yet now that there exist creatures to whom You give and whom You forgive, Your generosity and mercy are not thereby greater. And were there to have existed a difference between Your generosity and mercy and Your Essence, You would not have been generous or merciful until You had created creatures; but it would be impossible for You to have created anything without having possessed generosity and mercy prior to Creation.'

[9] Blaquerna considered the fact that humility, dominion and patience constitute qualities in creatures, but essence in God. And since qualities differ greatly from essence, when compared with the humility, dominion and patience which constitute essence, Blaquerna therefore worshipped humility, dominion and patience as Divine Essence and Existence, and he uttered the following words:

'Humility without the act of humbling, dominion without the act of dominioning and patience without the act of patiencing are not suited to being an essence supreme in eternal goodness and greatness with respect to all creatures. And in God's essence it is not fitting for the great to humble itself before the lesser, nor for there to be a lord and a vassal, nor for there to be agent and patient wherein the greater and the lesser obtain.'[406]

So, while Blaquerna was contemplating in this manner, he became perplexed and grew fearful of a contradiction. On account of the lofty understanding he employed in contemplation, however, he knew that his imagination had sinned by making a false comparison, so his memory remembered that all things which are good in crea-

---

406. The terms *major* ('the greater') and *menor* ('the lesser') here refer to the principles of 'Majority' and 'Minority' of Llull's Art.

tures should be attributed to God, insofar as all these are suited to existing within the Divine Essence, provided that no imperfection in God follows therefrom. And since humility, dominion and patience are good things in creatures, they must exist within the Divine Essence. But since in creatures they do not exist in such great perfection as they do in God, we must understand humility, dominion and patience to do so within that Essence in a different, nobler manner than that in which they exist in creatures, where they are accidental qualities having a beginning and an end.

[10] While he was contemplating, Blaquerna said that his Beloved's essence was immovable because it understood, yet itself was not understood; that it was unchangeable because it was eternal; and that it was incorruptible because its power, wisdom and will, and its virtue, perfection and justice were eternal. So, therefore, such a Glorious Essence should be present more frequently and loftily in his memory, understanding and will than should any other essence or essences.

[11] A king is no closer, by virtue of his dominion, strength, beauty, wisdom, power, justice and so on, to human essence than is a person whose face is ugly, and who is his vassal, and is poor and has negligible power or wisdom. And this situation obtains because the king can be deprived of all the aforesaid things. But such is not the case with God's Essence and Virtues, since, because His Essence and Virtues are one and the same thing in terms of goodness, greatness, eternity and so on, it is not fitting for any other thing to possess God's Virtues nor to be His Essence. So the Divine Essence, therefore, consists in virtue, in presence, in wisdom and in power, and in all that pertains to its essence everywhere, as well as beyond everywhere, and always, as well as beyond always, and such a thing befits the will of God alone.

[12] Blaquerna contemplated God's Essence in this and many other ways, by mixing certain Virtues with others so that he might acquire further new arguments and more extensive subject matter whereby to contemplate that Essence. So, when he had completed his prayer, he wrote down what he had contemplated, and then read what he had written down; yet he did not feel as much devotion while he was reading it as he had while he was contemplating the same. Contemplation, therefore, is not so devout when one is reading a book as it is when one is actually contemplating the arguments written down in that book. The reason for this is that, during contempla-

tion, the soul rises higher in order to remember, understand and love the Divine Essence than it does when it reads about what it has already contemplated, for devotion better befits contemplation than it does the written word.

## 105. ON UNITY

[1] Blaquerna dispatched his thoughts, cogitations and loves to contemplate God's Unity, and he said these words:

'O Supreme Good, Your goodness alone consists in infinite greatness, eternity and power, for no other goodness possesses that whereby it may be infinite, eternal and infinitely powerful. I worship You alone, therefore, O Supreme Good, in a God Who is supreme in every perfection. You are the sole good, from which all other goods descend and derive. Your good alone sustains all goods. Your good alone is the origin of my good, so I give and submit my entire good, therefore, for the sake of honouring, praising and serving Your good alone.

[2] 'Beloved Lord, greatness which exists without beginning or end in a virtuous essence, consummate in every perfection, befits a single God alone rather than many, because eternity, which, in terms of duration, exists without beginning or end, befits greatness which, in terms of essence and virtue, possesses neither beginning or end, but is itself, rather, consummate beginning and end. And if such were not the case, it would follow, Lord, that justice and perfection would be contrary as far as eternity is concerned, if eternity, which, in terms of duration, has neither beginning or end, were to befit essence and greatness which possess a finite and limited quantity just as well as it did infinite and unlimited essence. And since You, my God, consist in Your justice and Your perfection themselves, it is therefore signified to my intellect that You are one eternal God alone.'

[3] Blaquerna's memory remembered God's goodness, greatness, eternity, wisdom, will and power. Through goodness he understood a better power than any other; through greatness he understood a greater power; through eternity he understood a more lasting power; through wisdom he understood a wiser power; and through will he understood a more benevolent power than any other. So, once his intellect had understood divine power, his memory remembered but a single power that was supreme over all others. So his intellect, there-

fore, understood there to be but a single God, for if there were multiple gods, it would be impossible for the intellect to understand one power which was greater and nobler than all others.

[4] Blaquerna considered the power which resides in plants and in the things which nature orders towards an end, and his intellect understood that all natural things possess a power which exercises dominion over all the other powers present in that body. So, therefore, in each elemented body, nature has a greater natural appetite towards one end than another, because such an end, namely, such a perfection, has every other perfection beneath it.[407] So, while Blaquerna was considering these matters, his memory dispatched his intellect to understand the end for which all people are fashioned and created, and how beasts, birds, plants, metals, elements, the heavens and the stars are ordered towards the end of serving man. So, in accordance with the perfection of power, justice, wisdom and will, it is signified, therefore, that all people must honour and serve a single God alone; for if there were multiple gods, in accordance with the perfection, justice, power, wisdom and will of each of them, they would each have fashioned and created creatures and people to multiple ends. While Blaquerna was contemplating God's Unity in the aforesaid manner, he felt his memory, intellect and will to be greatly exalted.

[5] Will is given to man such that he wishes his castle, his city, his kingdom, his hand, his wife, his son, his memory, his intellect or his will, and so on, to be his alone. And when he wrongfully partakes of such things, he accordingly undergoes suffering that is contrary to glory and dominion. So, when Blaquerna had remembered these matters, he recalled God's glory and dominion, and understood that were multiple gods to be masters of this world, their glory and dominion could not be as great as it is when there exists but a single God. And since it is necessary to acknowledge the greatest glory and dominion in God, it was demonstrated to Blaquerna's intellect, therefore, that there exists but one God. And in order that his intellect might understand the foregoing more loftily, his will was further exalted to fervour and the contemplation of his Beloved, the Spouse of his will, and he uttered the following words:

---

407. Here Llull is outlining a theory of natural law governed by a hierarchy of ends. In this telic order, everything tends towards its perfection, that is to say, towards the final cause for which it was created (*synderesis*).

[6] 'It is true, Lord God, that there is no God but You. To You alone do I give and offer myself in order to serve You. From You alone do I await forgiveness, for there is no other generosity which gives and no other mercy which forgives but Yours alone. I am humble if I am humble towards You. I am lord if I belong solely to You. I achieve victory over my enemies if I am patient for Your sake alone. Wherever I may be or am, and with whatever I have, I give myself to You alone. Towards You alone am I sinful and guilty, so from You alone do I ask forgiveness. In You do I trust and for Your sake do I put myself in danger. So may all that shall become of me be directed towards an end wherein You are praised, worshipped and invoked. Of but You alone am I fearful, from You alone do I draw strength, for You do I weep and feel love, and for no other Lord do I wish.'[408]


## 106. ON TRINITY

[1] Blaquerna wished to contemplate the Holy Trinity of Our Lord God. So, therefore, at the beginning of his prayer he begged God to exalt the powers of his soul so that they might rise to contemplate His Virtues, with a view to his thereby being able to contemplate His Glorious Trinity. So he said, therefore, the following words:

'Holy, Glorious Divine Essence, wherein resides a Trinity of Divine Persons, I request a gift from You, namely, that You might be pleased to humble Yourself so that my soul may be able to ascend to Your Trinity in order to contemplate Your three essential and personal properties by means of Your proper, essential and common Virtues.[409] I am not worthy to request nor to receive the gift I ask from You. But since You are capable of giving it and thereby shall I be better able to love, know and praise You, I therefore request it of You, since my soul desires to know and love all these things so that I may better be able

---

408. Llull ends this heavily rhythmic, and at times internally rhyming, paragraph with consummate poetic artistry, unfortunately unreproducible in English: *De vos tot sol e temor, de vos sol e vigor, per vos plor e m'enamor, e no vull altre senyor.*

409. In this sentence Llull defines the relationship he perceives to exist between God's Virtues or attributes (i.e. His common properties) and God's personal properties (i.e. His existence as a Trinity), and the role the former can play in contemplation of the latter. The technical term for the above relationship is 'circumincession'.

to love and know, praise and serve, and cause to be loved and known, Your honour and Your Honours.'[410]

[2] Blaquerna placed his trust in God's assistance, and said the following words:

'Never has a creature existed, nor does it nor shall it exist which may infinitely and eternally be generated or afforded procession, since it is the case that every created good is limited and finite in greatness and eternity.[411] Were there to exist in a creature, however, a good which was infinitely great in eternity, power, wisdom and will, it would be possible for an infinite good to generate another infinite good; for, were that not to be possible, it would be impossible for an infinite good to exist in a creature, as we have assumed above.'

So, once Blaquerna had remembered, understood and loved the foregoing, he remembered and understood that if the Supreme Good is superior in greatness, eternity, power, wisdom and will than created good, it must necessarily have a loftier and nobler operation and act than does the latter. For were it not to have such, it would be impossible for it to be superior in terms of its infinity of goodness, greatness, eternity, power and wisdom.

[3] Once Blaquerna, with God's assistance, had raised up the powers of his soul to the highest level he could have achieved, he strove to raise them still higher by other means, so he began to consider what a great good it is to generate a God Who is good, infinite, eternal, powerful, wise, loving, virtuous, true, glorious, perfect, just, generous, merciful, humble, lordly and patient. When Blaquerna had thus considered at great length, he cogitated once more upon the great good it is to give procession to a God in Whom all the aforesaid common Virtues reside. And yet again he considered what a great good is that good from which God is generated and God proceeds, eternally and infinitely. When he had considered all these matters, he likewise considered, through negation, that the good he had already considered did not exist within the Supreme Good, and, consequently, he found his soul to be bereft of devotion and understanding. So he resumed his consideration of God, adopting the manner he had used through affirmation, and, consequently, he found his soul to be filled with remembrance, understanding and love of the Supreme

---

410. For the term 'Honours', see above, Ch. 3, § 8 and corresponding note.
411. Cf. above, Ch. 82, § 8 and corresponding note.

Good. So he started to weep and to praise God, Whom the latter three acts of his will had caused him to contemplate in such a lofty manner.

[4] Within his soul Blaquerna remembered created power, which he wished to heighten with the aid of uncreated power by remembering the following words: philosophers have said that the world is eternal, and they meant this in honour of uncreated power, which must be in operation eternally and infinitely. But since they were ignorant of God's Trinity and eternal operation, they attributed to Him eternal and infinite operation within the world and within those things of which the world is composed. Since it befits God's power much better, however, to perform an operation that is eternal and infinite in power, wisdom, will, perfection and glory, within Himself rather than in something else which is not God, His perfect justice, wisdom, glory and truth, therefore, signified to Blaquerna that the world had a beginning and that the operation which the Divine Essence performs within Itself when the Father generates the Son, and the Holy Spirit proceeds from the Father and the Son, is eternal and infinite in every perfection. And were this not the case, it would follow that the world had as much infinite power to receive eternity as Divine Power had to bestow power in respect of eternity, yet this is impossible.[412] This impossibility as signified to Blaquerna caused his intellect to become so exalted that his will was heightened thereby to love the Trinity, and that love gave languor to his body, tears to his eyes, sighs and devotion to his heart, and praise and prayers to his glorious God to his mouth.

[5] With apprehension, Blaquerna uttered the following words mentally and bodily to the Holy Trinity:

'O Excellent and Supreme Trinity, by means of Your common Virtues does my intellect rise up to contemplate and love You, yet my intellect fails to acquire knowledge of You as regards Your proper and personal Virtues; my will, however, rises up to love and understand You by the light of faith illumined by Your blessing. I am able to con-

---

412. The eternity of the world was a theme endorsed in the thirteenth century by the so-called 'Latin Averroists' in response to the reception of the newly rediscovered Aristotelian corpus. In 1277, the Bishop of Paris, Etienne Tempier condemned 219 theses suspected by the Parisian theologians of being excessively in thrall to the influence of Peripateticism, at the behest of the then-pope, John XXI; Proposition 87 of which related to the thesis of the eternity of the world.

template You, therefore, through faith and intellect, without any contradiction following therefrom.'

[6] While Blaquerna was contemplating the Supreme Trinity in this manner, error and ignorance decided to incline Him towards disbelieving the Trinity in God, since he considered that every trinity involved composition. But once again he remembered greatness, infinite in power, perfection and eternity, and therefore he understood it to be impossible that, just because created plurality and eternity cannot exist without composition, it should follow therefrom that the Supreme Trinity had to be composite. For just as the Supreme Trinity and Plurality is superior to created trinity and plurality as regards goodness, greatness, eternity, power, and so on, so too must it be superior to it as regards simplicity. For if God's Unity is supreme in simplicity over every created unity, it must also be the case that the Supreme Good possesses a plurality whereby it is superior in simplicity to created plurality.

[7] 'O Holy Trinity, insofar as I fail to understand You, Your greatness is greater and my intellect lesser; and insofar as I believe in You without understanding, my faith is greater than my intellect and Your greatness greater than my faith. Such is the case, because Your greatness is infinite in every perfection, while my faith and my intellect are contained and limited by Your greatness. So, if, insofar as I believe in You, I am greater by faith than by understanding, then, were I to understand You, I would be greater by loving than by believing. And if such were not the case, it would follow that love would accord better with ignorance than with understanding. And if this were so, it would follow that love was lesser at the heights of understanding and greater as regards the latter's failings. Yet this is impossible without a contradiction's following therefrom with respect to merit and to understanding through faith, which thereby preserves its condition in accordance with the diversity of objects attaching to faith and understanding, which diversity we have indicated above as obtaining between the Divine Virtues which are common to all three of the Divine Persons and the personal divine properties.'

[8] In order to avail himself of his art of contemplation, Blaquerna, within his soul, considered generation in terms of infinity and eternity, lest he think that divine generation resembled the generation that occurs in creatures, which latter he could not introduce into his soul in terms of infinity and eternity. He understood there to be

in supreme generation, therefore, simplicity without composition or corruption.[413] Yet he could not believe there to be neither corruption nor composition in lesser generation because his intellect had knowledge thereof, insofar as he could not introduce created generation into his intellect or memory in terms of eternity, infinity or perfection.

[9] 'Were You not to exist, O Holy Trinity, in what respect would God resemble man?[414] And what significance would the True Word have when it says "Let us make man in our image and after our likeness"?[415] And if Your Trinity does not resemble our own, this is because You are a being Who is infinite and eternal in power, wisdom and perfection.'

Blaquerna contemplated the Trinity in the above manner, and, as far as he was able, raised up to It the powers of his soul, so that he might be obedient to God's commandment, which enjoins man to love God with all his might, with all his mind and with all his soul, wherein lie memory, intellect and will.[416]


107. ON INCARNATION

[1] Blaquerna remembered the Holy Trinity of Our Lord God so that his intellect might understand how, due to the influence of the Glorious Trinity's great goodness of eternity, power, wisdom and will, God was bound to perform a work within a creature who might consist in great benevolence, duration, power, wisdom and charity. His intellect understood, therefore, that, in accordance with the operation that occurs in the Divine Persons, it was fitting for God to assume a human nature wherein and whereby might be signified the Divine Virtues and works He has within such Persons, as a result of which signification Blaquerna's will and those of other people might love God and His works. So Blaquerna, therefore, uttered these words:

---

413. In the created realm, generation always involves the latter two features, the first as a precondition, the second as an ongoing process and end term thereof.

414. Man, at least, resembles the Trinity in terms of the three Augustinian powers of his soul (memory, intellect and will), used by Llull in Figure S of his Art, the figure compiling the combined acts of the human intellective soul.

415. Gen 1:26.

416. Cf. Mk 12:28-31 and Matt 26:36-39.

[2] 'O Virtue Divine', said Blaquerna, 'You are infinite in goodness, greatness, eternity, power, wisdom and will, and in every perfection. Were there to exist anything else which was infinite in greatness,
eternity and patience, therefore, You would be able to operate infinitely therein by means of greatness, eternity and action,[417] because
You are capable of so doing and because that thing could receive
Your agency. But, since every other virtue apart from Your own is finite, no thing is able to be affected by Your operation, in terms of
eternity and infinite greatness, therefore, without having an origin in
terms of time and quantity. So, in order to demonstrate all these matters, Your wisdom chose to create a creature who was better and
greater in virtue than all other creatures and created virtues, and the
Son of God chose to become one person with that creature so as to
signify that, just as Your goodness had been able to bestow upon the
latter greater virtue than upon all creatures, so too was it able to make
it greater than a creature and than all other creatures.

[3] 'O Lord, Your human nature enjoys greater glory than do all
other created glories. The reason for this is that it enjoys greater perfection than does any other perfection. And since Your justice, Lord,
enjoys greater goodness, power, wisdom and will than does any other
such, it wished, therefore, to bestow greater glory and perfection
upon Your humanity than upon any other created nature. So, since
this is the case, it is fitting, therefore, that all the angels and all the
souls of the saints, and, moreover, all the bodies of the latter after
their resurrection, should enjoy glory in Your human nature, and
thereby be able to ascend to enjoy greater glory in Your divine nature.'

[4] When Blaquerna had considered the above matters at length,
he felt that his memory, his intellect and his will had become lofty in
contemplation, though, even so, his heart had not afforded water to
his eyes whereby they might weep and run with tears. Blaquerna, therefore, proposed to raise the powers of his soul higher in order to foster
devotion so markedly within his heart that his eyes might thereby weep
and run with tears, for it is unbecoming to contemplate loftily without
weeping. Blaquerna, therefore, lowered his memory so as to remem-

---

417. For the terms 'action' and 'passion' (viz. 'patience' or 'affection', as in the
state of being affected by something), cf. above, Ch. 100, *Lover*, v. 110 and corresponding note.

ber the baseness and wretchedness of this world and the sins residing therein; as well as the great wickedness that our father Adam committed against his Creator when he disobeyed Him; not to mention God's great mercy, generosity, humility and patience when it pleased Him to take on human flesh, and when He wished to surrender that flesh to poverty, contempt, torment, hardship and an agonising and ignoble death, even though it bore neither blame nor guilt for our trespasses. While Blaquerna's memory was down below remembering such matters, he raised up his intellect in order to understand, and his memory followed it, so they contemplated the lofty Divine Virtues, namely, goodness, infinity, eternity, and so on. His will, therefore, felt such devotion amid the perfections of the Virtues and the Passion and death of Jesus Christ's human nature, that it afforded sighs and contrition to his heart, and his heart afforded tears and weeping to his eyes, as well as confession and divine praise to his mouth.

[5] Blaquerna wept for a long time while contemplating the Incarnation of the Son of God in the aforesaid manner. While he was weeping, however, his imagination wished to imagine the way in which the Son of God and His human nature were conjoined, but since he was unable to imagine this, his intellect began to cease knowing and Blaquerna to doubt,[418] so his sighs, tears and weeping ceased as a result of the lack generated by such doubt, which puts an end to devotion. When Blaquerna realised what had happened to his thoughts, he once more raised up his memory and intellect to the greatness of God's goodness, power, wisdom, will and perfection, and in the greatness of these Virtues his intellect understood that God was able to conjoin human nature with Himself, albeit that his imagination failed to know this and was unable to imagine it, for God is greater in goodness, power, wisdom and will than the imaginative faculty is in imagining. Blaquerna, therefore, by remembering and understanding, eradicated the doubt to which he had succumbed regarding the Incarnation, so he restored devotion and contrition within his heart,

---

418. 'Intellect not knowing' and 'doubt' are components of Figure S of Llull's early Arts, the latter (along with 'affirmation' and 'negation') also featuring in Figure T. As this paragraph goes on to show, and why, the imaginative faculty is incapable of conceiving of the nature of the hypostatic union in Christ. The implication here is that those (Muslims and Jews, etc.) who have not accepted the truth of the Incarnation might only be availing themselves of the powers of their imagination, rather than correctly putting to use those of their intellective souls.

and weeping and tears to his eyes, and engaged in loftier and more fervent contemplation than he had been undertaking at the start.

[6] Blaquerna contemplated a great deal upon the Incarnation of the Son of God in the manner described earlier. Yet when he felt that his soul had grown weary of that subject matter, he adopted another such, so that by refreshing the matters under consideration his soul might recover its strength and power of contemplation. So Blaquerna, therefore, remembered how the Holy Incarnation and Passion of the Son of God is honoured by God's goodness, greatness, eternity, power, and so on, and how, in this world, and through His own honour, He has honoured many men, who themselves fail to render to Him the honour that they could. Following this, he remembered how there are many people in this world who are unbelievers and who fail to honour the human nature of Jesus Christ which God has so greatly honoured in Himself, but rather refuse to believe in and utter blasphemies against it. Yet they have possession of the Holy Land where He assumed that nature and where—in order to do us honour and to restore us to the Supreme Lord Who had lost us—that human nature underwent its Passion and death. So, when Blaquerna had concentrated the powers of his soul upon such matters, devotion, sighs, tears and contrition resumed within him, and his soul was raised greatly aloft in contemplation of the Holy Incarnation of the Son of God. So he said these words, therefore:

'Ah, Lord God, Who, by Your Divine Virtues, have so greatly honoured and exalted our nature! When will the time come that You shall honour highly our memories, intellects and wills by Your Holy Incarnation and Passion?'

[7] So lofty was Blaquerna's contemplation that the powers of his soul conversed mentally with each other. His memory said that great goodness had performed a great work and that great power had produced great power. His intellect replied that great mercy, will, generosity and humility conjoined lesser with greater power. And his will said that it was its duty to love its Lord, Jesus Christ, above all other creatures. One thing, however, caused it wonder, namely, how it could be that Jesus Christ so loved His people and wished to undergo such suffering on their behalf, and that God so wished to humble Himself for their sakes,[419] yet that within the world there are so many people

---

419. Cf. Phil 2:8.

who are unbelievers and idolaters, all of whom are ignorant of His honour. Blaquerna's intellect replied by saying that this circumstance was subject matter for will, so that it might feel such devotion as to cause it to desire martyrdom in order to honour the Incarnation; and that it was subject matter for memory, so that it might remember God's Virtues so loftily as thereby to be able to become exalted by such necessary proofs that it could signify the Holy Incarnation and Passion of its Lord, Jesus Christ, to unbelievers.

[8] Blaquerna's spirit, enlightened and inflamed by the divine light, said the following words:

'O Incarnation, you are the greatest truth ever to have flowed from uncreated to created truth! Why do more people scorn you, remain ignorant of you and fail to believe in you than pay you honour and believe in you? O Justice, which art so great in power, wisdom and perfection! What will you do? Will you punish such great and mortal trespasses? O Mercy, wherein lie such benevolence, love, patience and humility! Will you forgive them?'

Blaquerna was weeping and, between fear and hope, he grew sad yet rejoiced while contemplating the Holy Incarnation of the Son of God.


## 108. ON THE 'PATER NOSTER'

[1] Blaquerna remembered the Divine Virtues and by means thereof wished to contemplate God in the *Our Father*. And he sought to introduce these Virtues and the *Pater noster* into his memory, intellect and will. So he, therefore, said the following words to God:

'You, Lord, are our Father. In other words, God the Father is the Father of God the Son infinitely and eternally with respect to goodness, power, wisdom, will, perfection, and so on. And Your Divine Esssence is the Father of the human nature of Jesus Christ through creation and through benevolence, generosity, mercy, humility and charity. So, when He prayed the *Pater noster*, Jesus Christ said, therefore, that the Father, or in other words, the Father of the Son of God, exists in person within You, and that You are the Esssence which art Father of His humanity, and, moreover, of all other creatures. And because the Apostles were creatures and believed in His Trinity and Incarnation, Our Lord Jesus Christ told them that we should say the *Pater noster*.

[2] 'You, Lord, are God the Father of God the Son in Heaven, which Heaven consists in Your infinite greatness, goodness, eternity, power, wisdom, will, and so on, which constitute Your Essence wherein God the Father generates God the Son. And since infinite perfection lies within Your Essence with respect to goodness, greatness, eternity, and so on, comparisons are drawn, therefore, between Heaven, which is lofty, and Your Virtues, which are so lofty that no other virtues but Yours alone attain such great heights. By such heights and excellence do You signify in the *Pater noster* that You are the Father, because You are loftier than creatures and Your works are in Heaven, works whereby Jesus Christ calls You His own and our Father. So, if Jesus Christ—Who is God and man, and Who is in Heaven and Your equal insofar as He is God and on Earth insofar as He is man—bears witness to Your being His and our Father and Your being in Heaven, it is rightful that we, who are here below on Earth, should believe in His testimony and pray the *Pater noster*.

[3] 'Hallowed be, Lord God, Thy glorious holy name with respect to Thy goodness, greatness, eternity, power, and so on, wherein lies the name of the Father, Son and Holy Spirit through generation and procession, without which generation and procession diverse proper names could not exist within Your Essence eternally or infinitely in terms of goodness, virtue, truth and perfection. But since You are the eternal Father, eternal Son and eternal Holy Spirit, and each of these Persons is infinite in perfection, there exist names infinite and eternal in perfection within Your Essence, therefore, and for this reason it is worthy that Your personal names be hallowed within Your eternal, infinite and perfect Divine Esssence.

[4] 'Not only does justice require, Lord, that Your name be hallowed with respect to Your Virtues, but rather, in accordance with reason, it is worthy that it be hallowed here below among us, throughout the world. And for this reason have You founded the Holy Roman Church on Earth, so that it may ensure that Your name be invoked and known throughout the world, in order that there it may be hallowed within the souls of men and in the Holy Sacrament of the altar. And so that the pope or the cardinals, his colleagues, or the other prelates are not negligent in this regard nor do they cease, on account of other matters of business, to ensure that Your name is hallowed, have You issued a commandment, therefore, from Your own mouth in the *Pater noster*, at the time of Your death, which command-

ment You instructed Your lieutenant Apostles to carry out after You
had died.[420]

[5] 'Your kingdom, Lord, is Your very Essence and Your personal
properties, wherein lie goodness, greatness, eternity, and so on. May
this kingdom come to our souls, Lord, through our remembrance,
understanding and love of Your common properties and Your own
personal properties in order that Your kingdom may be honoured
here below among us and that we may ascend to Your kingdom to
enjoy everlasting glory.

[6] 'Your will is done, Lord, in Heaven as it is on Earth. It is done
in Heaven because goodness constitutes Your Essence, wherein
goodness is possessed of will which proceeds from the Father and
the Son, these being infinite in terms of goodness, greatness, eternity, and so on. Your will, Lord, is likewise fulfilled in the Son, Who
is eternally and infinitely generated as to every perfection. And justice, perfection, power and truth, therefore, desire Your will to be
done on Earth, namely, by the human nature You assumed, wherein
dwells bodily and elemental earth, which desire was fulfilled through
the working of the Holy Spirit when You were made flesh in the
glorious Virgin.

[7] 'O Lord, Your will is so lofty and so wondrous that it must be
obeyed throughout the world on account of Your goodnesss, Your
power, Your perfection and Your justice. It is obeyed, O Lord, on account of Your goodness, humility, patience and mercy by those who
desire to serve You and who hold their memories, intellects and wills
aloft from the Earth in order to contemplate and serve You. And Your
will is obeyed, O Lord, on account of Your justice, dominion, power
and truth in punishing by the torments of Hell those who are unable
to escape from Your sentence or Your control and who fix their memories, intellects and wills upon earthly vanities, while scorning the
blessings of Heaven.

[8] 'Our daily bread, O Lord, consists in Your glorious Holy Body
sacrificed upon the altar. This Your body is in Heaven, yet is constantly here below among us through this sacrifice, which we perceive
in our minds through the operation of Your great benevolence, power, wisdom, will, humility and mercy. For just as our bodily eyes and

---

420. Mk 16:15-18 and Matt 28:18-20, in which latter verse Christ's commandment
is specifically mentioned; cf. also Lk 24:44-49; and Jn 20:19-23.

other senses fail to discern our bread, that is to say, Your flesh and blood, so too, O Lord, with Your assistance, the powers of our soul are capable of perceiving our bread through the working of Your essential Virtues. For, if Your power is great in infinity, it follows that, in order to signify this, flesh and blood, under the form of bread, may constitute a single body sacrificed in various places. And if Your benevolence, will, humility and generosity are infinitely great, it is signified, in accordance with the infinity of Your perfect justice, that You should give us our daily bread in this world which currently exists, for today is the day to choose between damnation or salvation, which day passes by for each of us.

[9] 'Discharge for us, O Lord, the debt we owe You, for we should not be able to pay You, because we were all sinners through our father Adam. And You have placed us under such a heavy obligation when creating us, and out of love for us have chosen to become a man tortured, crucified and put to death, that we should likewise not be able to pay You. And since Your perfection is infinite as regards Your goodness, greatness, eternity, and so on, You do not need us to pay You, therefore, O Lord, for were You to do so, there would be a lack of perfection within You. And since we discharge the debts we owe to our sensitive faculty, which we mortify by means of fasting, affliction and prayer, and of the mortification itself of our intellects by believing in the wonders Your Virtues work, if You, O Lord, were not to forgive us or to discharge our debts, given that out of love for You we discharge our own, greater justice in terms of perfection would obtain in us than in You. And since this is not fitting, it is, therefore, likewise fitting for You to refrain from asking for our debts, which we should not be able to pay.

[10] 'Well do we know, O Lord, that Your great goodness, love, generosity and mercy cause You to desire that we should possess great merit, so that Your justice might have a reason whereby to grant us great glory and perfection. And for this reason You allow us to be tempted by the devil, by the world and by flesh. And since we are lacking as regards memory, intellect and will, it often happens that we are conquered and overcome when faced with temptations. So, since You, O Lord, are so great in benevolence, mercy, generosity and humility, grant us that which we do not deserve, in spite of the temptations we face and conquer, for it is sufficient for us to be in Your kingdom and to enjoy glory in You, regardless of our merits.

[11] 'Deliver us, O Lord, from evil, which we encounter whenever we forget You, fail to know You and abhor You, for from such evil do all other evils draw their origin. And such deliverance must be achieved, O Lord, if we are to remember, understand and love Your goodness, greatness, eternity, power, and so on. And if You do not protect and deliver us from evil, given that You have created us and are able to help us, Your mercy and humility will be without love, and we shall be creatures without a lord who loves his subjects. But this is impossible, O Lord, and for this reason my memory entertains hope in Your assistance.'

In this way, and much better than can be either spoken or written, did Blaquerna contemplate God's Virtues within his soul by means of the *Pater noster.*[421]

## 109. ON THE 'AVE MARIA'

[1] Blaquerna wished to contemplate the Queen of Heaven, Earth, the sea and all that exists, by means of the Virtues of her Glorious Son, Our Lord God. So he said, therefore, the following words:

'Ave Maria! The goodness of your Son, Who is infinitely great in eternity, power, wisdom, will, and so on, saluted you so that the Son of God might assume your nature, whereby He might become a single person, which is equal in goodness, greatness, eternity, and so on, to the Father and the Holy Spirit, and to God's entire essence as regards goodness and power.

[2] 'Full of grace: power, wisdom and will, which, in terms of essence, are a single power, wisdom and will, and which, in terms of filiation, are a single power, wisdom and will, were incarnated in the flesh of your flesh and the blood of your blood.[422] Such power, wisdom and will constitute but a single Son of the Supreme Father. By this Son is created in you a son of man, conjoined so as to be a single person with the Son of God. And for this reason, Queen, are you full of grace through the Son of God and through your son of man, and

---

421. I translate the verb *recomptar's* ('to be recounted/narrated') here as 'to be spoken', since I believe the contrast Llull is making is between oral discourse, written discourse and the internal discourse characteristic of thought, here in its highest, contemplative form.

422. Cf. Gen 2:23.

your son is God the Son insofar as he is one person with God the Son. So, this being the case, through the influence of the fullness of grace with which your son is filled, you are the greatest queen full of grace that we can remember, understand and love. And from the fullness of your grace upon our memory, intellect and will, we receive an influence, which contemplates us in the fulfilment of your grace. So, blessed be your grace, queen, which is so full that it fulfils all those who, on account of your grace, are destined to attain everlasting fulfilment.

[3] 'The Lord is with you, O queen, and is virtue, truth and glory, which are the Son of God. This virtue, truth and glory possess an infinitude of power, wisdom and will; this infinitude is a supreme good in terms of its eternity. This Lord is in you, God and man: He is God through God the Father, and he is man because he has taken flesh and blood from you. The existence in you, O queen, of such a lord causes you to enjoy great virtue and truth, for, after your son, you outdo all other creatures in virtue, truth and glory. And this is because, with the exception of your son, the Lord is not present in any other creature as virtuously, truly and gloriously as He is in you, for He has not given to any other creature as great a capacity to receive His virtue as to you. And since, by reason of His virtue, you are thereby capable of receiving greater virtue than any other creature, His glory dwells more truly in you than it does in any other such.

[4] 'Blessed art thou, O queen, among women, for greater perfection, greater justice and greater generosity have been given to you than to all women; greater, moreover, than to all men, all angels and all other creatures.[423] For the perfection, justice and generosity that have been given to you consist in Christ, your son, who is the perfection of all other perfections, the justice of all other justices and the generosity of all other generosities, and without your son there would exist nothing which possessed being or any perfection. By means of such perfection, which is your son, O queen, justice causes you to be blessed above all women, because you have more perfection than them all. So, since within you lies such great perfection, the perfection of justice and generosity thus wish you to grant perfection to the memory of every soul if it remembers you, to its intellect if it under-

---

423. Llull here exceeds the claim of the *Ave Maria* to the effect that Mary is 'blessed [..] among women', by asserting that she is blessed not only among all women, but among all men and the entirety of creation.

stands you and to its will if it loves you. And, were this not the case, there would be a lack of justice and generosity in your son, as well as in yourself, and this is unbefitting and impossible.

[5] 'Thy fruit, O queen, is blessed with mercy and humility, which have conjoined the fruit of thy womb with the Divine nature, which union is greater than any other such union that can exist between God and creature. O queen, the Divine nature, therefore, has not conferred as much mercy or humility upon any creature or upon all creatures together as it has upon the fruit of thy womb. For this your son, glorious man, is man in the glorious Son of God, Who causes him to be man by permitting him to form with Himself a single person who is God and man. And this person, who is God and consists in infinite mercy and humility in goodness, eternity, power, wisdom, will, and so on, has thereby blessed your son by allowing him to be one with infinity of mercy, humility, goodness, eternity, power, and so on. So, this being the case, O queen, then which fruit can be as greatly or more greatly blessed than the fruit of thy womb?

[6] 'O queen, so great is the splendour of the sun, which imparts light to the moon, the stars and the air. And since mercy and humility are in your son greater than the sun's splendour itself, there comes from the fruit of thy womb, therefore, O queen, an influence of blessings upon the angels and upon ourselves greater than the sun's splendour or that of other creatures. And since, O queen, mercy and humility have so exalted your fruit within you and have placed within you such lofty excellence, it is rightful that you should remember us, in accordance with the greatness you possess through mercy and humility. And if mercy has chosen to honour you, may you wish through your mercy to remember us. And if humility has chosen to bow down to you in order to exalt you, may you humble your thoughts to us so that through them we may be able to ascend in order to receive blessings from your womb.

[7] 'The Holy Spirit has come into you, O queen, and has cast the shade of the Most High's virtue over you. This Holy Spirit, O queen, has come into you bearing the Lord of all this world and, likewise, of the next. It has shaded you with virtue which consists in Virtues, and with Virtues which constitute a single virtue. It has shaded the nature it took in you with infinite goodness, greatness, eternity, power, and so on, and it has shaded you with that nature it took in you, and whereby you are the mother of each and every created virtue, while

within your shadow they all receive splendour and by your shadow are directed towards your Son's own splendour. And, shaded by your shadow of divine and human shade, the saints in glory reside in eternal shade, delivered from everlasting fire, wherein lies no shadow of relief or forgiveness.[424]

[8] 'O heavenly queen, your son is Lord of all creatures for two reasons: the first is because he is God, and the second is because he is man conjoined and united with God. So, since your son is Lord of all the world for two reasons, it is fitting that you be Lady of all the world for two reasons: the first is because you are the Mother of God; the second is because you are the mother of a man who is united with God in person. And since this is the case, may you remember, therefore, O Lady, the grounds whereon you are Lady, so that you may be pleasing to Him Who has made you such, and that we may be exalted by the nobility of His Lordliness.'

[9] Blaquerna contemplated Our Lady in the *Ave Maria* using the Virtues of her Son in this manner. And while he was contemplating, his memory, intellect and will reached such heights that he could not tell whether he was weeping or not. And when he had finished his contemplation, he remembered and knew that his heart had not provided water to his eyes whereby they might have been in tears and weeping while he was contemplating. So, since it was unbecoming to contemplate Our Lady without weeping, Blaquerna therefore began again to contemplate her and to remember the patience her Glorious Son showed on the day He was stripped, spat upon, scourged, crowned, nailed, wounded and put to death. And he remembered how Our Lady had loved Him with very great love, and how, while He was being tortured, He and Our Lady held each other in a compassionate and gracious gaze. Our Lady pitied her son, whom she saw dying; she grieved for Him, since she found herself being separated from Him by death. She knew that He had done no wrong, and she knew the He was Lord and God. While Blaquerna was contemplating in this manner and, by means of the powers of his soul, was examining the virtues of God and Our Lady, his heart was overcome by such deep devotion that his eyes were thereby filled with an abundance of water and tears.

---

424. The Catalan word *refrigeri*, which I have translated here simply as 'relief', also, unsurprisingly, has the sense of 'being alleviated through coolness'.

110. ON THE COMMANDMENTS

[1] Blaquerna remembered the reply Jesus Christ had given in the Gospels with regard to the Commandments,[425] so he decided to contemplate these latter by means of God's Divine Virtues, so he spoke the following words to his will:

'You shall love your Lord God, for you have received a commandment to do so from His goodness, greatness and eternity. So, if you, O will, were so great that you could love God eternally, without beginning or end, you should be obliged to obey the commandment, since it is issued to you by an infinitely and eternally good lord. Since you have a beginning, however, you were therefore unable to love before you existed. But given that you exist, you are obliged to love, and if you fail to do so you are disobedient to eternal and infinite goodness, as a result of which disobedience you shall be called to a punishment eternal and infinite in torment.'

[2] The intellect told Blaquerna that God's power, wisdom and will had commanded his own will to love God with all its heart.[426] But since it understood that his entire will was able to love God only by dint of God's own power, wisdom and will, the power his will exercised when it failed to love God with its full entirety was not attributable to God's own power, wisdom and will, but rather to faults, trespasses and sins tending towards the absence of power, which latter does not wish to be power in respect of God's own power, wisdom and will, wherein created power is sustained, preserved and protected against errant power, if the entirety of created will devotes itself to loving and obeying God's commandment.

[3] While Blaquerna's intellect, thus engaged in cogitation, uttered the above words mentally to his will, his will replied by asking whether it was lawful for it to love anything other than God alone. His intellect replied that the will was able to love all creatures, provided that it did so in relation to God or, in other words, that it loved them in order that it might love God.

[4] While intellect and will were conversing thus, memory remembered how the commandment contained the fact that man

---

425. Matt 19:17-19; Mk 12:28-34.

426. Cf. Deut 6:5; 10:12. In Mk 12:29-30, Jesus, citing Deut 6:5, describes this, following an assertion of the unicity of God, as 'the first commandment' (*primum mandatum*); cf. also Matt 26:36-39 and Lk 10:27.

should love God with all his soul, and because it was one of the three powers of the soul, it considered itself obliged to remember with all its might Divine virtue, truth and glory. So it said to the intellect that it remembered that the latter, which is one of three powers of the soul, was fully obliged to understand God's virtue, truth and glory.

[5] When the intellect had understood the reason that memory remembering had explained to it, it then became aware that it had very often avoided understanding God's virtue, truth and glory so that, through faith, will might thereby gain greater merit.[427] And since as powerful a commandment is issued to intellect in its entirety as is issued likewise to will, it therefore raised its power aloft in order to understand God's virtue, truth and glory, and asked forgiveness for the fact that it had erred through ignorance so that faith might thereby be greater in the will.

[6] Blaquerna said to God that His justice was perfect, and that, therefore, the commandment He had issued to his thoughts as a whole must be just and perfect, which commandment would not enjoy perfection if it were to command human thought to do other than to love wholly His justice and perfection, since the fact is that such thought is wholly created and endowed by such justice and perfection.

[7] While Blaquerna was conversing in this manner with his thoughts and with God's justice and perfection, his will told his intellect that it had loved more ardently when the latter's understanding had been in majority and had understood with all its might.[428] It therefore rebuked the intellect for the fact that it had long erred, since, in order to attain greater glory, it had failed to raise itself aloft in order to understand, given that a commandment to such effect was issued to thought as a whole, meaning the full might of the intellect. While will was saying these words to the intellect, contrition and remorse arose within will, which had not commanded the intellect to understand God with all its might, even though it had itself been commanded to so do. Thus, because of that regarding which will felt contrition, memory remembered that many people are disobedient who believe themselves to be obedient to God's commandment by

---

427. Cf. above, Ch. 43, § 4 and corresponding note.
428. 'Majority, Equality and Minority' are principles from Llull's Art.

exalting faith and suppressing their intellect, from which suppression arise error, wrongdoing and ignorance.

[8] Blaquerna returned once more to the commandment God issues to will when He commands that we should love God with all our heart, and then tells us to love Him with all our soul, and again tells us to love Him with all our thought. So, the three occasions on which this commandment is issued make one aware of the generosity of God, Who shows mercy to Blaquerna's intellect when He understands there to be diverse operations within the three powers of the soul in accordance with the diversity of the three aforesaid commandments. For insofar as God commands us to love with all our heart is signified faith, whereby our will loves more than our intellect is able to understand. And since He commands us to love with all our soul, it is signified that all three powers of the soul are equal with respect to an object that is equally remembered, understood and loved. And when He commands us to love Him with all our thought, it is signified that God commands us to elevate our entire intellect so that thereby we may have, when remembering God, greater remembrance, and, when loving Him, greater will, which bring memory to bear upon the elevation of the intellect whereby God loves greatly to be known.

[9] Blaquerna told his soul that loving God with all his heart, his soul and his thought is the First Commandment. His intellect, therefore, understood the Second Commandment, related as this is to the first, in which Second Commandment was signified an equality of love between Blaquerna and his neighbour insofar as God commands our will to love our neighbour as much as ourselves. And since He does not say 'with all one's soul, thought or even heart', a distinction is drawn between the First and the Second Commandment. By this difference it is signified that the first has dominion over the second, and that the second has been humbled and must be patient with regard to the first, so that, by loving, understanding and remembering God more than oneself or one's neighbour, one may show obedience and reverence in honouring God's humility and dominion.

[10] To love, remember and understand God more than anything else, and one's neighbour as much as oneself are two commandments which constitute the origins of the others. And whoever follows these two commandments is obedient, and obeys God with respect to all the others. And whoever is disobedient to God as regards any of the others, disobeys God with respect to the first two. And whoever loves

himself or his neighbour equally with God, is disobedient to the First Commandment and to all the others.

## 111. ON THE 'MISERERE MEI DEUS SECUNDUM MAGNAM MISERICORDIAM TUAM'[429]

[1] By means of Our Lord God's Virtues, Blaquerna contemplated His Essence, Trinity and Incarnation in the sayings of the holy prophets, as is exemplified by the following words. Blaquerna asked for God's forgiveness according to His mercy, so to begin with he combined greatness and mercy with goodness and eternity, for God's goodness is greater than any other goodness and His eternity is greater than any other duration. And since goodness and eternity are in accord with greatness, and God's mercy is greater than any other mercy, David,[430] therefore, asked goodness for the great good of compassion, forgiveness and gifts, and he asked eternity for such gifts and forgiveness to be everlasting. This request was made on the grounds that, within the Divine Persons, there is concordance between their personal properties which, in God's Essence, consist in goodness, greatness, eternity and mercy.

[2] It was not necessary for David to draw a distinction within God's Essence between greatness, mercy and justice, for they are but one and the same thing. And since he asked God to forgive him according to His great mercy, he signified His great justice, for it befits great mercy to give and forgive according to great justice, in order to signify that it constitutes greater justice for greater, rather than lesser, mercy to give great gifts and forgive great sins. And if such were not the case, it would follow that great mercy and great justice would lack anything wherein they might find concord and agreement.

[3] While Blaquerna was considering the aforesaid words, his soul rejoiced greatly in the hope of God's mercy and justice, as likewise of their greatness. He understood great and everlasting good, therefore, to have been prepared for anyone who requests mercy from God's greatness and justice. When Blaquerna had contemplated goodness, greatness, eternity, mercy and justice within the Divine Essence, he be-

---

429. Ps 51 (50).
430. King David, the second king of Israel, the speaking subject of Ps 51 (50).

gan to consider other matters. So he contemplated the previously mentioned Virtues within the three Divine Persons, uttering these words:

[4] 'Lord God, Who art the Father, and whose power, wisdom and will are great, by virtue of goodness, eternity, mercy and justice! So, on behalf of the Roman Church, David asked You for Your Son, Who is great in power, wisdom and in will pertaining to virtue, as well as in goodness, eternity, justice and mercy. For, insofar as he asked You to show mercy according to Your greatness, it is fitting that You should show such with as great a greatness as You possess, which mercy we should not be able to receive in the absence of something equal to Your greatness, which thing consists in Your glorious Son, Whom You gave us through Incarnation for the sake of our redemption. Your glorious Trinity and Incarnation are signified to us by Your Son, for were there not to exist a distinction of Persons within Your divine nature, You would not be able to grant gifts to us or forgive us according to Your great mercy, for we would lack the capacity whereby to receive it. Since You chose to make Your Son incarnate, however, through Him was our nature able receive it, because insofar as Your Son is God, He is equal in power to Your greatness. So You were able to give, forgive and to judge as much through Him and with Him as by Your own endeavours.

[5] Blaquerna remembered truth, glory and perfection within God, and through David's words he understood that greatness is in accord with truth, glory and perfection. Such greatness must be infinite, for were it to be finite it would not be in accord with truth, glory and perfection, which are infinite Virtues in God. So, since greatness and mercy are infinite Virtues and since David asked for mercy according to God's greatness, it is signified, therefore, that he asked the Father for a son in whom truth, glory and perfection lay, so that gift and forgiveness might be equal to the infinite greatness which the Father enjoys with respect to truth, glory and perfection. And so, the case being thus, it is signified, therefore, that David asked for gifts and forgiveness through the person of Jesus Christ's humanity, to which humanity these things could not be granted unless a union were forged therefrom with a particular person of equal truth, glory and perfection, with a particular person, that is, who might exist within the Divine Essence.

[6] 'Generosity, humility, dominion and patience, O Lord God', said Blaquerna, 'are infinitely great Virtues within You. For, were they

not so, they would be contrary to Your mercy, which is infinite, and it would follow that David had asked for gifts and forgiveness from You which You would have been unable to grant on account of the deficiency of Your Virtues. Yet since it is impossible that there should be any deficiency within You, Your generosity must possess within it gifts equal to itself, Your humility must possess a humbleness wherein it may be completely humbled, and Your dominion must have its equal within itself so that Your mercy, also equal to itself, has a Lord who may grant gifts, and Your mercy likewise must have the patience to bestow patience equal to itself. And if such were not the case, David could ask for greater mercy from You than You could possess or grant, yet that is highly unbefitting.

[7] Blaquerna contemplated God's Essence, Trinity and Incarnation in the aforesaid manner, according to an art, expounding David's words by means of the Divine Virtues. In using this art, one can reveal the secrets and obscurities with which the prophets invested their words, for the purpose of raising one's intellect aloft in search of God's secrets, so that it might understand in a loftier manner, and that through the loftiness of one's intellect, one's will might likewise be raised aloft greatly to love God as regards His Essence, Trinity, and Incarnation, as well as all His works.

112. ON THE SEVEN SACRAMENTS OF THE HOLY CHURCH

[1] Blaquerna wished to contemplate God's Virtues in the sacraments of the Holy Church, so he said to God the following words:

'Lord God, in the holy sacrament of baptism You seek to manifest the greatness of Your power, wisdom, will and virtue. For by great virtue, You reveal to our human intellect Your power, wisdom and will in the very strange and wondrous work that is baptism when, by means of water, the words of the priest and the faith of the godparents, the infant, which does not have the use of intellect or will, is cleansed and purified of original sin through the sacrament. This work, O Lord, so great and wondrous, lies beyond nature, in order that it may signify Your virtue to be so great in power, wisdom and will that You are able, know how to and desire to accomplish beyond nature all that You please.

[2] 'Just as in a city, O Lord, there rightfully exist a variety of oc-cupations, so too in the city of Our Holy Mother Church there right-fully exist seven sacraments. For just as all the occupations pertain to a city's nobility, so too the seven sacraments pertain to demonstrating the noble use Your glorious Virtues enjoy in creatures, which use is revealed and made manifest in the seven sacraments. The goodness and greatness of Your dominion, O Lord, demonstrates, therefore, how all creatures are obedient to Your power, wisdom and will through the seven sacraments.

[3] 'Glorious Lord, since an infant does not possess the eyes of reason until it has grown older, it was necessary that the godparents should possess the virtue that Your virtue imparts and delivers to the child when it is old enough to be confirmed and to consent to that which its godparents have promised on its behalf. So, the fact that the godparents possess such virtue and are freed from that obligation once the child has been confirmed and has acquired that virtue through confirmation by the bishop, signifies the great virtue, truth, perfection and dominion, which accomplish through the sacrament of confirmation all that Your will desires, unopposed by any power, which cannot contend against Your own power.'

[4] Blaquerna wished to start contemplating the holy sacrifice of the altar by means of the Divine Virtues. So, to begin with, therefore, he directed the powers of his soul towards such contemplation, so that when he was engaged therein he might not be hindered by an unruly memory or will, nor be disobedient on account of his bodily senses to the meanings offered by the Divine Virtues. So he said the following words, therefore, to his soul:

[5] 'O soul, my friend, you know that God's humility is great and that His power is equally great. And since His humility and His power are one and the same thing in terms of virtue as are His wisdom, will, truth and perfection, our bodily eyes, which see bread under the form of flesh in the sacrifice of the altar, do not seek to incline to-wards disobedience as regards the aforesaid Divine Virtues, which are so great that they possess the power, will and knowledge to ensure that under the form of bread lies the true flesh and true blood of the body of Christ. And were this not able to be so, it would follow that our eyes could more truly take bodily things as their objects than You could Your Divine Virtues and their operations. And it would likewise follow that greatness would be lacking in God's Virtues and that truth

would be in greater accord with bodily than with spiritual things. And such a thing is unbefitting, since God is a spiritual essence and His virtues are spiritual, while one's body and its bodily, or sensual, senses are corporeal and corruptible.'

[6] Blaquerna mentally spoke with the three powers of his soul for a long time. And his intellect replied to him by saying that it understood there to be such great greatness in God's virtue and power that such greatness could cause true flesh and true blood to exist under the form of bread, although it did not understand why God should wish to perform this sacrament nor why he should be obliged to do so. Blaquerna replied by telling his intellect to draw together within itself God's great goodness, wisdom, will, humility, generosity, mercy and patience, and to understand what great power God revealed in bringing into being both accidents without substance and substance without accidents.[431] And since such a work cannot be performed according to the course of nature, if it is accomplished by God's power, more tellingly is God's power thereby considered to be beyond nature. And since His will desires it, so that His power may thereby be considered greater and nobler, that will shows itself to be more greatly beloved by power. And if power were not capable or will did not desire it, they would not be in such full accord with wisdom nor, accordingly, would humility be so great between us, nor would mercy, generosity or patience be in such full accord with goodness and greatness. So by the fact that we may know that the nobility of the Divine Virtues is in fuller accord with greatness, virtue and truth, is signified the reason, therefore, why God has chosen to create and ordain the holy sacrament of the altar.

[7] 'O intellect, my friend', said Blaquerna, 'strive for virtue so that you may possess it more fully when understanding than do one's bodily eyes when seeing, one's sense of taste when tasting or one's sense of touch when touching, for in many matters do you see them invariably commit wrongs and sins. Do not allow yourself to be defeated by your bodily senses, and protect yourself therefrom by means

---

431. The first canon of the Fourth Lateran Council (1215) defined the five principal sacraments, specifying with regard to the Eucharist that: '[...] the body and blood of Jesus Christ in the sacrament of the altar are truly contained under the species of the bread and the wine, the bread being transubstantiated into the body and the wine into the blood by divine power [...]', and thereby (in the Latin text) using the term *transubstantiatis* for the very first time; see Baldwin (1997), 99-124; here, 110-111.

of the Divine Virtues. Understand that the Trinity constitutes an extraordinary operation in God and that the Incarnation of the Son of God is beyond nature. God decided to establish the holy sacrifice in order to signify the extraordinary character of this operation, so that through such sacrifice we might constantly be reminded of the extraordinary operation the Divine Virtues perform beyond nature. For just as, sensually and bodily, we make the sign representing the figure of Our Lord God Jesus Christ on the Cross, so too during the sacrifice of the altar is a sign issued of the miraculous intellectual operation performed by the Divine Virtues.'

[8] The intellect gave great consideration to the words Blaquerna had spoken to it. And by those words, it understood that the imaginative faculty had long prevented it from comprehending the sacrament of the altar, because it had led it to imagine the sacrament more vividly in terms of natural and bodily operations than in those of the Virtues and agency of its glorious God, to which Virtues and agency imagination is unable to ascend. So the intellect, therefore, conceded Blaquerna's words to him and by means of God's Virtues rose to contemplate and adore the Holy Sacrament of the altar.

[9] A debate arose between Blaquerna's memory and his intellect as to which sacrament, namely, that of the altar or that of penance, was more contrary to one's bodily senses. For memory remembered that man had sinned against God, and that Our Holy Father the Pope and his lieutenants, who grant absolution and forgiveness and impose penance upon their fellow men, are men themselves. Yet his intellect said that the sacrament of the altar reveals itself in sensible and bodily form even though it is a bodily form invisible to one's bodily senses. Memory and intellect argued at length about this matter, so they sought a decision from Blaquerna. He determined that the sacraments were equally contrary to one's senses, because, by means of the Divine Virtues, which are incorporeal, the two sacraments, as well as the others, were created and established beyond the power of nature so that they might manifest the supremacy of their own power over that of their created, natural counterpart. So, while Blaquerna was making his determination, he said the following words:

[10] 'As Divine Virtue makes the virtue of flesh and blood exist under the form of bread, so too it makes the virtue of forgiveness exist under the form of a man who is a priest. And as the virtue belong-

ing to flesh and blood under the form of the Host pertains not to the Host, but rather to God, so too the virtue the priest exercises in forgiving pertains not to the priest himself, but consists, rather, in God's Virtue under the form of the priest.'

[11] 'Blaquerna', said Memory, 'since you speak so subtly,[432] would you be able to prove to me that inasmuch as God has the power to perform the sacrament of penance, He must also entertain the wish that the sacrament should exist? For it is a fact that God is capable of performing many things that His will does not wish to put into practice.'[433]

Blaquerna replied by saying that just as it is signified by God's great goodness, mercy, humility, virtue and so on, that He wills and must will, according to the greatness of justice, which wills that His Virtues be signified in great greatness in the sacrament of the altar, so too by that very ordinance He wills and must will, according to great justice, that the sacrament of penance should exist, in order that His Virtues be made manifest and that people be reformed by contrition, penitence, restitution, counsel, affliction, repentance, hope and other things like these, which could not exist without the sacrament of penance.

[12] 'For the purpose of signifying the order which resides in the three Divine Persons, as well as the fact that the Person of the Son came to take on human nature in an orderly manner, and since disorder fails to accord with baptism, confirmation, the Eucharist, penance, matrimony, unction, it was imperative that the priestly order, wherein all the above sacraments might themselves be set in order, should exist.[434] And this fact is signified by the Divine Virtues and by the greatness according to which they can be signified and made known to us.'

[13] In the aforesaid Virtues Blaquerna perceived the order of matrimony, just as he had perceived the other sacraments therein. And in the same way that justice signified that in temporal matters a range of men should possess different characteristics, so too is it fit-

---

432. For the concept of *subtilesa* (subtlety), cf. above, Ch. 39, § 2.

433. Following the Fourth Lateran Council of 1215, the sacrament of penance, including an act of contrition on the part of the penitent, was to be performed annually at least once, though the canon in question (no. 21) of this council may have merely served to formalise already existing Roman Catholic practice.

434. The priestly order to which Llull refers represents, in fact, the sacrament additional to the six he lists, namely, Holy Orders. In terms of rhetoric, of course, we note Ramon Llull's further use of polyptoton or transplacement.

ting that man and woman should possess different characteristics,[435] so that there may exist chastity and virginity in opposition to lust, and that by means of sensual things the powers of the soul may be set in order so as to obey the commandments of the Lord our God.

[14] 'God created matrimony in the earthly paradise', said Memory to Will. 'And in order to signify this matrimony, God wishes there to exist in this world the sacrament of matrimony. For, were it not so, God's wisdom and will would not accord so well with perfection in manifesting His great glory, which itself accords with justice, with which the disorderly union of man and woman conflicts. As a result of such disorder, one is unworthy of attaining God's glory, which would be contrary to greatness and perfection were one to achieve God's truth and glory by means of the disorderly union of man and woman. And divine wisdom and virtue would have placed greater power bodily within the elements, which unite and mingle in an orderly manner so as to generate a body in a likewise orderly manner, than it would in the desire of man and woman to generate children so that the human species might be preserved in this world.'

[15] Blaquerna remembered that, in this world, people have a beginning, a middle and an end.[436] So, therefore, in order to signify God's eternity and dominion, divine wisdom has ordained that when one enters the world, baptism should be the first sacrament, while extreme unction should be the last, so that the servitude under which one has been obedient within the world to the first such, as well as to the others which lie between the first and the last, might likewise be signified. And since, in virtue of those sacraments which precede the last, justice has greater reason to grant rewards to a person, and mercy to forgive by means of confession, contrition and confirmation, God's great justice and dominion have decided, therefore, that extreme unction should be a sacrament, so that confirmation may be given to all other such, and that the sacrament which the body of Our Lord God, Who was anointed with the blood from His own body, the tears from His own eyes, and His own sweat, performed upon the Cross for the purpose of distraining death, may be signified.[437]

---

435. Cf. Gen 1:27.

436. For these terms and their Lullian connotations, see above, note accompanying the opening invocation to *Blaquerna*.

437. 'Distraint' is a legal term indicating the seizure of a person's chattels for the purpose of causing him or her to carry out an obligation or the sale of those chattels

113. ON VIRTUES

[1] Blaquerna remembered the seven virtues which had frequently assisted him against the Devil, so by means of these he wished to contemplate the Divine Virtues which had given him those seven such virtues. So he, therefore, said the following words:

'Beloved Faith, you are great because you believe great things of God, and you are good because, through you, man attains eternal beatitude. You are enlightened by divine wisdom through the light of grace. You love true things, for the love of the Heavenly King makes you love His virtue, truth, glory and perfection.

[2] 'Faith, O friend, you believe in the Unity of Essence and Trinity of Persons within God. It is a great thing to believe in things that are invisible, namely, to believe that there is an infinite good which is infinitely and eternally generated from infinite and eternal good; and to believe that from both of these there proceeds an infinite and eternal good is a very great and very wondrous belief, and is illumined by great radiance from the light of grace. So, therefore, beloved Faith, since you are great, it is my soul's duty to feel very thankful and very loving towards the great and eternal greatness and goodness which have created you so great, and which have, through your greatness, made me so great.

[3] 'On account of you, Faith, do I believe that from great charity, power, wisdom, mercy and humility, the Son of God took flesh from Our Lady, Holy Mary, which flesh he conjoined to Himself, becoming therewith a single person possessing a divine and a human nature, without corruption, alteration, composition or accident pertaining to the Divine Person, and without change to the human nature which He took.[438] So, by believing that such great and wondrous things as these exist through the great greatness and virtue, instruction, mercy and benevolence of the Supreme Good, my soul is deeply obliged,

---

in reparation for a debt. The idea here is that death itself is put under an obligation to the crucified Christ, who through the exercise of such distraint obliges death to waive any rights it may have over humanity in favour of the universal salvation secured for humanity by Christ's own Passion and death.

438. The reader may wish to recall the formula articulated at the Council of Chalcedon (451 CE), which states: 'in two natures which undergo no confusion, no change, no division, no separation'; English translation in Tanner (1990), 86. For Llull's own meditations on the theme of the Incarnation, cf. above, Ch. 107.

therefore, to remember, understand and love, and to honour and serve the Divine Virtues which you, Faith, cause to exist within me in such great quality,[439] such great quantity and such great radiance.

[4] Within his soul Blaquerna spoke with Hope, saying that one ought to entertain great hope as far as great things were concerned. For from such great goodness, greatness, eternity, power, wisdom, will, virtue, truth, glory, perfection, justice and generosity, wherein is generated as great a good as that in which the aforesaid Virtues consist, and wherefrom likewise proceeds as great a good as that in which said Virtues consist, must great beatitude be hoped for and desired, since it is impossible for there not to proceed from such noble and such great things as those in which the aforesaid consist, a very great influence of such great beatitude to those enamoured of the Divine Virtues.

[5] 'Consider, O Hope, how great a thing it is for the Son of God, who is so great in Virtues, to have conjoined to Himself a human nature, which is a creature, and to have surrendered that creature to death and torment for the sake of us sinners, so that you may become greater by placing your trust in the Virtues of the Supreme Good. Take note, O Hope, how God has created great things, many and various, as well as beautiful and virtuous goods, such as the angels, the heavens, the sun, the moon, the earth, the sea, men, beasts, birds, fish, plants, metals and other creatures. And since these aforesaid things are so numerous, so noble and so great, you, O Hope, are therefore obliged to place your hope and trust in great graces and great blessings from goodness, greatness, eternity, power, and so on.

[6] 'O Hope, were the Trinity or the Incarnation not to exist you would not be able to hope for such great gifts and blessings from God as you can in virtue of the fact that the Trinity and the Incarnation exist indeed. For God's Virtues would not reveal themselves to be as great to you as they do in virtue of the fact that the Trinity and the Incarnation exist. And were the resurrection not to exist, you would be less than you are, because we should not perceive charity, power, mercy, humility, dominion and patience to be as great in God as we do in virtue of the fact that we believe the resurrection to exist. So you, O Hope, and we alike, therefore, perceive the resurrection by means of the Divine Virtues, and by means of the resurrection we perceive the greatness of

---

439. Cat. *honrament.*

the Divine Virtues. So Faith and yourself, therefore, are in accord by each being greater in the other, and consequently we are greater in you, and thereby achieve greater accord with faith.

[7] 'O Divine Love, Who possess within You a Lover infinite and eternal in His loving. From You, Who, in Your heights, are so great in every perfection, shall thereby come love. For, if in Your Essence there are three Beloveds and Lovers infinite and eternal in power, wisdom, will, virtue, perfection and glory, from this influence of love so great which dwells within You, so much thereof shall reach us here below that we shall not love to honour or serve any other thing but You alone.

[8] 'It is the nature of the good to generate another good, and the nature of power to generate another power, and the same also applies to virtue, glory and perfection. So, since You are such a great and noble love, and are infinite in goodness, eternity, power, wisdom, and so on, how can it be that we, who are Your creatures and Your recreated, who are Your servants and Your redeemed, are not more ardent in our love for You? Where, O Love, is the concordance You enjoy with generosity, mercy, humility and patience? For by virtue of such concordance, compassion must dwell within You, and hope, happiness and love within us.

[9] 'O Divine Justice, among us "justice" is spoken of the just, while in You just and justice are one and the same thing. So, since You are just, as well as infinite justice, by being an essence without difference, and because that which within You is just and justice, as well as being and essence, consists in goodness, eternity, power, wisdom, will, virtue, truth, glory, perfection, mercy, generosity, humility, dominion and patience,[440] in accordance with such common Virtues and properties, then, You must needs be just, as well as justice, with regard to us, by means of mercy, humility, charity and patience, while we must needs receive from You justice, whereby we may live justly by praising, honouring and serving You. But if in us there is no justice deriving from the justice that lies within You, where is the influence which thereby comes to us? And where is the concordance that exists between Your justice and Your benevolence, charity, mercy, humility, patience and generosity?

[10] 'Divine Essence, the great justice that lies within You causes the just which, likewise within You, is infinite and eternal in goodness,

---

440. For this list of Virtues, see Ch. 101, § 3 and corresponding note.

power, wisdom and charity, to generate a just which is infinite and eternal in goodness, power, wisdom and love. And from both of the aforesaid justs, it causes yet another to proceed which is infinite and eternal in goodness, power, wisdom and love. So, this being the case, such a great influence proceeded from Your justice, therefore, that it caused one of us to become a single person with one of the three of You. So, some of the very great influence of justice which fell upon one of us by means of charity, mercy and humility, shall likewise fall upon all of us, so that You may make us just by loving, knowing, honouring and serving You. And if You fail to do so, where is the influence of humility, patience, charity and generosity that lies within You? And which is that lord to whom we belong, since it is reasonable that a lord should love, assist and bestow gifts upon his subjects?

[11] 'I ask for prudence, Lord God, from Your power, wisdom and will, for in virtue of the benevolence which lies within You, You ought to grant it to me in accordance with justice and mercy, while in virtue of Your power and wisdom, You are able to grant it to me. And since I ask for the prudence to love You, truth and justice should make You love prudence in me, therefore, so that I may know You in order to be able to love You and, through my knowledge and love, know how and desire to praise, honour, obey and serve You.

[12] 'Lord God, if You wish to exercise greatness of justice when punishing us sinners, You can make greater use thereof if You punish us for being aware of Your Trinity and Incarnation yet failing to honour, love and serve You, than You can towards those who are unaware of the Trinity within You and who, unawares, fail to believe in Your Incarnation. And if You wish to exercise mercy, humility and kindness towards us, You can show these to us more effectively if we know You and love You than if, unawares, we are disobedient towards You. Such being the case, for all these and many other reasons, therefore, You should grant us devout Christians, as well as unbelievers, prudence whereby we may know You and love You, since it is a fact that Your generosity is in accord with Your will, which has created us to know and love You more than for anything else.

[13] 'Temperance, O friend, I have constant need of you against my enemies, who prevent me from contemplating the Virtues of my Lord, for which reason I have come to this hermitage. I ask for you from the Virtues of the Lord Who has created you, for I have need of you in order to serve them. I have abandoned father and mother, wealth and relatives

so that I may reside in your company within this hermitage. Without you, one cannot combat gluttony or overeating, whether one lives in a hermitage, in a religious order, or wears sombre attire. I cannot exercise you without the goodness, greatness, power, wisdom, will, virtue, humility, mercy and generosity of the Lord in Whom dwell all these Virtues.

[14] 'O Temperance, one can neither remember, understand nor love God too much. However, by remembering, understanding, loving, weeping, fasting, suffering and keeping vigil too much can one's body languish, sicken and die, so one's soul cannot contemplate God's Virtues either at such length or with such fervour. I have need of you, therefore, O temperance, both bodily and spiritually. Grant yourself to me so that you may possess me and be your own mistress, and may emerge from servitude to gluttony and to my stomach.'

[15] In this manner, and in many others, Blaquerna asked for created virtues from their uncreated counterparts, so that by exercising virtue he might be a servant of God.


## 114. ON VICES

[1] Blaquerna remembered seven deadly sins which cause the world to remain disordered, a world which God's Virtues have created. Blaquerna asked divine goodness, therefore, from where the aforesaid demons, which are the seven deadly sins that destroy the world, had come. So he said the following words, therefore:

'Supreme goodness, you who are so great in virtue and perfection and are superior to every creature in terms of eternity and nobility, from where have gluttony, lust, greed, sloth, pride, envy, anger come? For these seven beasts destroy, ruin and corrupt the goods which are yours through creation and dominion. So, since you are such powerful, beloved and virtuous wisdom, why do you allow there to exist within the world such wickedness, deceit, error, difficulty and ignorance as a result of the seven aforesaid demons?

[2] 'If you, O goodness, were evil or imperfection, the seven deadly sins could have come from you. However, since you are the consummation of every consummation, and since perfection is contrary to imperfection, and since all sin and all evil necessarily have a beginning, may your eternity, which existed before there was a beginning, tell me from where sin and imperfection have come.'

[3] While Blaquerna was contemplating the Supreme Good in terms of its greatness, eternity, power, wisdom, will, and so on, in the aforesaid manner, he heard Memory and Intellect conversing with each other within his soul, and Memory said to Intellect that it remembered Will which harboured greed and lust, and so on, within its desires. So Intellect replied, therefore, by understanding that the desire which wishes for greed and lust or another vice is begotten by one's will, which will is at fault because the desire which loves sin proceeds therefrom. So, as a result of that desire, the intellect which understands both the sin and the desire is similarly at fault, and, by means of that very desire, one's free will becomes inclined to wish for sin, so one's memory, therefore, which remembers all these sins, likewise falls under censure. And since one's memory, intellect and will are created by the Supreme Good yet give rise to the remembrance, understanding and love of sin, Blaquerna's intellect, therefore, said to his memory, while exonerating God's own goodness, that the seven demons derive their origin from those workings of one's memory, intellect and will which concern themselves with matters repugnant to the goodness of God.

[4] 'Divine wisdom, you who are the light of all lights, show me the art and method whereby I may curb the seven vices in my memory, intellect and will.'

Memory remembered the Divine Virtues, and Intellect understood the short life of this world and the torments of Hell, while Will loved God and all His Virtues and hated the sins, asked for forgiveness and scorned the vanity of this world. And Blaquerna felt within his soul that the vices and sins had been curbed by the workings of his memory, intellect and will. So he said, therefore, the following words to divine wisdom:

[5] 'Supreme erudition, from you comes virtue, and from your power comes power, and from your will comes love to the soul which wishes to remember, understand and love you. Yet when memory does not wish to remember you, nor intellect to understand, nor will to love, sins and trespasses arise from that which the will does not wish to love, as well as from that which it wishes to love in terms of its remembering, understanding, loving or hating. So, therefore, supreme erudition, may my remembering, understanding and loving be yours, so that by means of my memory, intellect and will I may contemplate, remember, understand and love your Virtues and hate

vices, sins and trespasses, for the purpose of constantly entertaining your praise, honour, dominion and virtue within my memory, intellect and will.

[6] 'Supreme generosity and mercy, you have given me memory so that I may remember, intellect that I may understand, and will that I may love your Virtues. Yet these things do not suffice for me, unless you give me the memory whereby to remember, and the intellect whereby to understand, and the will whereby to love your Virtues and the seven virtues which are contrary to the seven deadly sins. I ask you, still further, to give me memory so that I may remember, and intellect that I may understand, and will that I may hate gluttony, lust and the other vices. So, since your power is capable of giving me all these things, and since they are necessary to me, and since you have created me for the sake of all these things, I ask you, therefore, to grant me gifts whereby all my powers may be devoted to honouring your Honours.[441]

[7] 'O Glory and perfection, to grant us the power to sin is to provide us occasion for having faith, hope, charity and the other virtues. To grant us the power to have faith, hope, charity and so on, constitutes a gift against gluttony, lust and so on. I, therefore, ask from you the gift of virtues and the freedom to sin, provided that you have granted me the ability to remember, understand and love your Honours, and to remember, understand and hate my sins and the vain pleasures of this world.

Blaquerna wept and sighed while he was asking for these gifts, and God granted to him what he wished, so Blaquerna tearfully gave thanks to Him. Nobody could relate or convey to you the contemplation and devotion that Blaquerna performed or the art and method he used, but God.

Here ends the book concerning the 'Art of Contemplation'.

---

441. Cat. *honrar vostres honraments*. For this phrase, as also for its sense and significance, see above, Ch. 3, § 8 and corresponding note.

## 115. THE END OF THIS BOOK

[1] One day, Blaquerna was contemplating God, while holding the *Book of Contemplation*.[442] A minstrel came up to him, very tearfully, indicating by his features that the sadness of his soul was very great. The minstrel said the following words to Blaquerna:

'Blaquerna, my lord, your saintly life is renowned throughout the world, and as a consequence remorse torments my soul with contrition for the wrongs I have committed by means of my office, so I have come to you, therefore, in order that you may give me penance.'

Blaquerna asked the minstrel what his office was, so the latter told him that he was a minstrel.

'Fair friend', said Blaquerna, 'the office of minstrelsy was discovered for a worthy purpose, namely, in order to praise God and to give solace and consolation to those who are oppressed and tormented when serving Him. We have come to a time, however, when hardly anybody puts into practice the ultimate purpose for which the various offices were initially accorded their principles.[443] For the principles applicable to the clergy were originally founded upon a worthy purpose, as likewise applies in the case of knights, jurists, artists,[444] physicians, merchants, religious, hermits and all the other offices. We have now reached a time, however, when, since people fail to put into practice as fully as they should the purpose for which the various offices and sciences exist, the world has fallen, therefore, into error and difficulty, and God is ignored, abhorred and disobeyed by those who are obliged to love, know, obey and serve Him. So, thus, fair friend, for your penance I instruct you to go throughout the world proclaiming and singing on behalf of one office or another, stating the purpose for which minstrelsy and the other offices were initially brought into being. So carry with you this *Romance of Evast and Blaquerna*, wherein are indicated the reasons why the aforesaid principles were discov-

---

442. *LC* (1273-74 (?)).

443. Cat. *foren començats al començament* lit. 'were begun at the beginning'. Here Llull is considering the principles of 'Beginning' and 'End' from his Arts, the former both in its temporal and its axiomatic sense (i.e. as 'principle'), and the latter largely in its causal sense (as 'final cause', here translated as 'ultimate purpose').

444. This term is also used, though differently, in Ch. 86, § 2 (see corresponding note), though here probably indicates the following professions: surgeons, apothecaries, grocers, barbers and notaries, if not also members of the Arts faculties.

ered. And challenge and catch unawares all those who practise their offices incorrectly, as your abilities and the time, location and opportunity permit, yet do not fear censure, hardship or death in order to be pleasing to God.

The minstrel received his penance from Blaquerna and accepted the office the latter had conferred upon him. So he went throughout the world narrating the purposes underlying the existence of theology, the clergy, the orders of religion and chivalry, the prelacy, the seignory, the merchantry, medicine, law, philosophy and all other things like these; and he rebuked those who failed to maintain the ultimate purpose for which the aforesaid things had been discovered. And he read out the *Romance of Evast and Blaquerna* in the town squares, the courts and the monasteries so that he might foster devotion for it and that he might derive greater courage and fortitude therefrom for the purpose of fulfilling the penance that Blaquerna had given him.

[2] We have now narrated the *Romance of Evast and Blaquerna.* So the tale returns to the emperor whom Blaquerna encountered in the forest, which emperor had brought order to his empire so that Worth might be restored therein, and had bequeathed his empire to his son, for whom he had composed a book of instruction for princes regarding the governance of his household, his person and his realm.[445] And once he had done all these things, he left the world and went in search of Blaquerna, so that together, living as hermits, they might contemplate Our Lord God.

[3] While the emperor was searching for Blaquerna, he came across a bishop who was travelling to court for the purpose of teaching the *Brief Art of Finding Truth*.[446] This bishop planned to petition Our Lord Pope to ensure that this Art be read and taught throughout all the universities, so that as a result of the elevation of the intellect there might be greater devotion within the world towards loving, honouring and serving God, as well as towards imparting knowledge of Him to the unbelievers who, unawares, proceed towards everlasting torment. So, in order to accomplish this enterprise, the bishop planned to devote all of his time and all of the income from his bishopric thereto. When the emperor and the bishop met, they both rec-

---

445. For the emperor's first appearance in *Blaquerna*, see above, Ch. 48.
446. See above, Ch. 24, § 2 and corresponding note.

ognised each other, so they greeted and welcomed each other
cordially. Both of them inquired about the other's circumstances and
plans, of which each informed the other. The emperor was greatly
pleased by the bishop's devotion, as was the bishop by that of the
emperor, who begged the bishop to be Worth's proctor at the Court
of Rome, where Worth has been wronged by so many people and
prevented from rendering praise and honour to God.

'And tell the Minstrel of Worth to sing these verses[447] at the Court,
so that the pope and his cardinals may better remember the life of
the Apostles, in whose time thrived sanctity of life, devotion and
worth:

[4]   Lord true God, glorious king,
      Who wished to unite man to Yourself,
      Remember Your servants
      Who wish to suffer death for You
      And make them ardent in their praise
      By honouring and obeying You
          With all their might,
      For You are the soft, sweet desire
          Of their hope.

      A new fervour is born
      And there arises once more the desire
      Of the Apostles, who in praising You
      Underwent a death that was sweet.
      So then, may whoever is truthful and good
      Step forward and proclaim
          The great power
      Of God, Who, in His wisdom,
          Let Himself be made man.

      The Friars Minor have remembered
      Our Saviour, who wished to dress

---

447. Cat. *cobles*. In Ch. 78, § 4 above (see corresponding note), the Minstrel of
Worth had already sung *cançons e cobles*, composed by the emperor, to a cardinal. As
noted there, the *cobla* is a verse form very closely related to the classic octave, though
can occasionally occur, as it does here, in a nine-line form. The rhyme scheme in this
particular instance (abababcbc in the longer stanzas, at least) is atypical, however.

In the style of the holy monks,
And they have caused Miramar to be built
By the loving King of Majorca.
They will go to convert the Saracens
    So as to please
God, Who wished to die
    In order to save us.

So then, what do the Preachers do,
Since they love to take such delight in God?
And what is done by abbots or priors,
Bishops and prelates, who so love to increase
Their possessions?
And what do kings do, who, by sleeping
    And hoarding,
Think that they have found Paradise
    And can see God?

The small, the middling and the great
Take pleasure in ridiculing me.
Love, tears and weeping,
And sighs cause my body to languish.
Yet my soul increases its joyous
Remembrance, its free choice
    And its love
Of God, Who daily causes me to rejoice
    In its duty.

I wish to serve the sweet Virgin
    With all my might,
For I know that she has sent me sweet desire
    And worthy hope.

Blaquerna, who can tell me
    Where to find your cell,
In which I desire
    To be with God alone?'

[5] 'What was that, my lord?' said the bishop to the emperor. 'Are you acquainted with Blaquerna?'

The emperor told him in reply that he had met Blaquerna one day when he was travelling all alone through the forest in which Blaquerna himself was seeking his hermitage, and that he had promised him that he would give Worth satisfaction for the wrong he had caused her. The bishop recounted the saintly life of Blaquerna to the emperor, and made known to him the environs wherein he could find the place in which Blaquerna was living as a hermit. The emperor was greatly pleased by what the bishop had informed him regarding Blaquerna, as well as by the fact that he had indicated to him the route whereby he might find the latter. The bishop accepted the verses, very graciously took his leave of the emperor and commended him to God's blessing.

[6] Here ends the *Romance of Evast and Blaquerna*, which treats of married life and the order of the clergy in order to provide instruction as to how one should live in this world, so that, in the next, one may dwell eternally in the glory of God.

# Appendix I

## ON THE PASSION OF JESUS CHRIST

[1] Blaquerna said to his memory that he wished to contemplate the Passion of Our Lord Jesus Christ by means of the act of the sixteen Dignities of Our Lord God, so that using this the three powers of his soul might acquire the art and doctrine whereby greatly to remember, understand and love his Lord Jesus Christ as well as that which must needs be remembered, understood and loved for the sake of His love. So he said the following words, therefore, to God's goodness:

[2] 'Divine goodness, which art an act infinite in bonifying, magnifying, eternifying, possifying, knowing and loving, and so on: Your act and Your being are equal in infinity to bonifying well by means of all the infinite Dignities wherein resides an infinite and eternal act of unified good and unity, which is infinite and eternal good and essence in all Your Dignities. And since You, goodness, are bonifying and good in an act of paternal, filial and processional good, You wished that the Holy Passion of the Son of Man, Who is one Person with Your infinite and eternal good, might be, to the entire human race, a highly useful and profitable good whereby to recover the good that we had lost on account of our father Adam and our mother Eve, and that by reason of Your Passion our souls might strive to acquire virtues, which are good, and to shun vices, which are evil.'

[3] 'Blaquerna', said his intellect, 'God is great in essence and in essentifying, as well as in unity and unifying, and in Dignities and Dignifying, for infinity and infinifying and eternity and eternifying pertain to goodness, power, wisdom, and so on.'

Blaquerna replied by saying:

'By reason of that greatness so great, wherein there is no minority pertaining to the Divine Being, was the cruel Passion of my Lord Jesus Christ very great; great was it as regards His being betrayed, mocked, sold, scourged, scorned, forsaken, denied, crucified and put to death. Who could imagine in all its greatness the very great pain and suffering that my Lord endured? For inasmuch as the human

nature of Christ is greater than any greatness which exists in creatures, so was its Passion greater, which Passion had to be so great that
it might suffice to recreate the human race, which had been lost.'

Blaquerna spoke many words about the greatness which resided
in the Passion of his Redeemer. And his intellect considered how
great was the dishonour done to that Passion by those who on its very
account enjoy such great happiness, wealth and honour, yet who fail
to honour it or cause it to be honoured as they might and ought. And
because of what his intellect considered, Blaquerna wept, and said
the following words:

[4] 'O Will, my friend, do you love in God the act of eternifying
which is equal in duration to His eternity itself? If by negation you fail
to love an eternification equal to the act of eternal duration, you love
in God the act of beginning, minority of duration and eternal imperfection.'

Before his will had replied to Blaquerna, it caused his eyes to weep
and his heart to sigh from contrition, and it made his memory remember for a very long while, until the latter had recalled the eternal
act, without beginning or end, of eternity, which act united distinct
personal, eternal and essential properties, and within which act the
latter are eternally distinct bringing infinitely into concordance, without any contradiction, a single divine being.[1] Based on what his
memory had remembered, his will answered the question which
Blaquerna had posed to it, he having asked it whether it loved the
cruel Passion of his Lord, which Passion He had endured by reason
of His love. So his will replied by saying that if it were deeply to love
the great Passion of Jesus Christ, it would make its body go to die for
the sake of His love in order to honour His Honours[2] and to imitate
the torture He endured so that He might grant salvation to all.

[5] Blaquerna felt ashamed at what his will had said to him, so he
began to consider the act of divine power, as a result of which consideration his intellect spoke the following words inwardly:

'If power is infinite without possifying while being infinite in terms
of infinite causes, it consists in an infinite potency, yet its act is finite,

---

1. Difference (as in distinctness), Concordance and Contrariety are a triad of
principles from Llull's Art, the latter of which does not apply to the divine being.
2. For this phrase, cf. above Ch. 3, § 8 and corresponding note and *Lover*, vv.
194, 202, 206 and 293.

by which finitude and infinitude power and its act are composed of minority and majority. So my sister, Memory, cannot remember in God such great power or actuality,[3] as a result of which absence of power her sister, Will, cannot lament so fully the agonising Passion of Christ, nor love so fondly God and the virtues nor hate so bitterly the vices; nor can I consider that infinite power may more suitably possess an infinite rather than a finite act, nor that a finite act befits a finite power.'

[6] Blaquerna's intellect considered God's wisdom at length, and it said that knowing is the act pertaining to God's wisdom, as is the act of bonifying, magnifying, eternifying, and so on. For, were wisdom not to have such an act as regards its knowing, it would have willing, or it would have suffering and imperfection, insofar as it would not know in terms of its actuality the perfection of the act of willing or of the other Divine Dignities. While his intellect was considering in this manner, his memory remembered that the Passion of Our Lord Jesus Christ is not known by unbelievers, who are ignorant thereof and in whose willing it is not loved or honoured. So memory, therefore, posed a question to his intellect as to who, within God's wisdom, are known to be more guilty: the unbelievers who ignorantly fail to honour the Holy Passion of Christ or those Catholics who are aware of it, yet fail to honour it or to cause it to be honoured by those who lack such awareness, whom they could induce to love and become acquainted with it?

[7] Blaquerna asked his willing, which is the act of his will, in what respect it resembled the act of the divine will. And his willing replied by saying that it resembled the willing of God's will insofar as it wished to be equal to the act of his memory and of his intellect, so that it might be able to acquire all that can be remembered and understood perfectly and without defect. After posing this question, Blaquerna asked the act of his will in what respect it failed to resemble the act of his God's will. Willing replied that [it differed] inasmuch as it was an act distinct from the will, which is a potency,[4] for God's willing and will are one and the same thing, and God's will is equal to the act of goodness, greatness, eternity, power, wisdom, and so on. So God can achieve, therefore, all that He chooses to will or that resides in His

---

3. Cf. above, *Lover*, v. 281 and corresponding note.
4. See previous note.

wisdom according to the infinite act of power, justice, perfection and glory.

Blaquerna was greatly pleased by that which the act of his will had replied to him, so he asked it what it willed as regards the Passion of Christ. His will replied by saying that it wished and desired that this Passion might be preached and known throughout the world, since it had taken place for the sake of the entire human race; and he desired that it might gain more imitators by way of martyrdom than of natural death, so that it might more markedly constitute an object of the act of people's wills.

[8] Blaquerna's intellect understood that virtue within a substance in the absence of an act is a habit composed of mater and form, and that the act of a virtue is the activity which was in potency before the activity itself existed. And since the intellect enjoys a nobler and more virtuous act when contemplating the act of divine virtue than the act of created virtue, it understood, therefore, that there is no distinction between the act of God's virtue and His essence and substance; for, were there to be so, the intellect would possess equal virtue when contemplating created and uncreated acts, and in God there would exist habit and virtue and these would be in potency without act, yet this is impossible. As a result of the foregoing, his intellect switched to understanding that, in the act of divine virtue, paternity is essence, act and substance without distinction, as likewise applies to the filial and processional acts, and that all three acts, different, concordant and equal[5] as regards His personal properties and His personal proper Dignities, constitute a single virtuous act within a single essence which consists in virtue and the act of virtue, wherein lie the Dignities common to the three Divine Persons.

While his intellect was thus considering the act of divine virtue, which it understood to be distinct as regards Persons and single in essence without diversity, his memory remembered what great virtue and act of virtue it is to desire to die for the sake of honouring the Passion of Christ, and it remembered that, within men's wills, the act of will is lacking in virtue when they fear more greatly bodily death than they do losing the aforesaid virtuous act. So, because of what his

---

5. For Difference, Concordance, Contrariety, cf. above, § 4 and corresponding note. Majority, Equality and Minority are principles from Llull's Art, only the second of which, as noted earlier, is strictly applicable to God.

memory remembered and his intellect had understood, an act of contrition arose in Blaquerna whereby his will wept at and lamented the dishonour which is done to Christ and to His Holy Passion.

[9] Blaquerna remembered that in the case of truth wherein the verifying of the true obtains in terms of an act which is infinite in bonifying, magnifying, eternifying, and so on, there arises a supreme majority concerning truth, verifying and the true wherein no difference obtains between a majority distinct in terms of truth from its act and its true. So, because of what his memory remembered, his intellect understood that in God it is necessary that one true thing should verify another such, for were it not to do so, there would ensue in the act of divine truth a minority of the infinite act of goodness, greatness, eternity, power, and so on, and the infinite and the finite would be one and the same thing within the act of truth, yet this is impossible. Blaquerna's will, therefore, said the following words:

'The act of death is to die, and to die for the sake of honouring, praising, making known, loving and serving the Passion of my Lord Jesus Christ, is the act of truth. And to weep for the cruel death of my Lord, yet to be afraid of dying for the love of Him is an act composed of the false and the true, which composition is displeasing to my Lord.'

[10] While inwardly understanding and loving, Blaquerna glorified the act of God's glory, by saying:

'To glorify infinite bonifying, magnifying, eternifying, possifying, and so on, constitutes an act of glory which, by the act of glory's infinity, is remote from suffering; so, were there not to exist difference, concordance and equality between equal personal properties within the act of glory wherein lies the act of infinity, there would abide within the act of glory and of infinity a confused glory as regards bonifying, magnifying, and so on, as a result of which confusion the act of infinite glory would have greater concordance with finifying rather than infinifying, yet this is impossible.'

Blaquerna inwardly spoke these and many other words concerning God's glory and its act. His memory, however, altered the subject matter of his words, insofar as he remembered the cruel Passion of Jesus Christ, whose Passion, in order to bestow great joy, God wished to be greater than all other passions, the greatness of which Passion is apt to provide many tears, laments, sighs and sorrows, as well as contrition and love, to the people who on its account are on the road to everlasting glory. Yet because those people fail to love, lament or weep as they ought, justice and its act, which is to judge, are greatly to be feared.

[11] Blaquerna asked all three acts of the three powers of his soul if they could perfectly contemplate the Holy Passion of Our Lord God, Jesus Christ. His intellect replied by saying that it was first necessary for them to contemplate the act of God's perfection, so that therefrom they might receive grace, blessings and influence, whereby they might attain perfection when contemplating the perfection of Christ's Passion. After these words, Blaquerna strove with all the powers of his soul to contemplate the perfection of God, by saying:

'O supreme perfection, fulfilment of all perfections, your infinite act is to perfect perfection in terms of an act which consists in bonifying, magnifying, eternifying, and so on. And if such were not the case, it would be impossible for you to enjoy a perfect act, and were you not to have such, you would be potency without act, yet this is impossible. It is signified by reason of this that within you abides perfecting and perfect in an act of perfection and of goodness, greatness, eternity, and so on.

[12] While Blaquerna was contemplating God's perfection thus, his intellect ascended by saying that it behoves perfection infinite in goodness, greatness, eternity, and so on, to bestow perfection upon a thing infinite in goodness, greatness, eternity, and so on. For, when it bestows perfection upon another, perfection accords as strongly with perfecting as it does when it enjoys perfection in itself; for, were it not to do so, the act of perfection would be a habit or potency wherein abides the act of imperfecting. His will wished to ascend still higher in order to contemplate God's perfection, but Blaquerna said that it was time for them to descend in order to contemplate Christ's Passion, so he uttered the following words:

'Memory, my friend, what do you remember about the Passion of your Lord?'

Memory replied by saying:

'I recall my wonder regarding God's perfection as to how it can be that, here below in the world, it fails to grant perfection to people that they may honour the perfection of Jesus Christ's Passion, for, on account of the imperfection of their understanding, loving and remembering, people are ignorant of Jesus Christ, and devotion perishes as a result of the demise of the preaching which formerly obtained when the Apostles rendered honours throughout the world for the purpose of honouring Jesus Christ.'

Blaquerna wept, and within his soul memory, intellect and will conversed with each other, saying:

'Ah, when will that time come when the honour which befits it is rendered to the Passion of Christ?'

[13] The act of justice is to justify, which, in God, must needs be the act of bonifying, magnifying and eternifying; for in the absence of justifying, bonifying could not achieve concordance with generating an infinite good and would accord with the act of injustice, which is to fail to justify,[6] were it not to magnify and eternify that which it is able to magnify and eternify, and so on, within its own good. Blaquerna considered at length the aforesaid act of supreme justice, and he said that perfection and justice could not achieve concordance with an infinity of possifying, knowing, willing, glorifying, and so on, without justifying by means of infinite things, namely, that justice should justify in terms of each of the acts of the common Divine Dignities so that such acts may obtain in distinct personal properties which themselves have distinct acts wherein justice abides by justifying, and that each act may constitute goodness, greatness and eternity, and so on, without which distinct acts justice could not perfectly achieve its act within the Divine Dignities.

So loftily did Blaquerna contemplate the act of justice within God's Trinity that he could scarcely descend in order to remember the supreme act of justifying that God accomplished in the Incarnation of the Son of God and in the Passion. So he wondered greatly at how the Passion of Jesus Christ is caused such offence[7] and dishonour by so many people given that God has placed such great justice and honour therein.

[14] 'Were there not to exist, within Our Lord God's being, personal properties possessing different, equal and concordant acts in an act of infinite generosity, such generosity in God would be potency without act, for there would not exist anything which might infinitely receive therefrom a gift in terms of bonifying, magnifying, eternify-

---

6. Occ. *iniuriar* the primary senses of this term are 'to insult or offend; to injure or harm; and to wrong or illtreat'. The noun *iniuria*, however, also carries the sense of 'wrong' or 'injustice'.

7. Occ. *iniuria*. See previous note.

ing, possifying, and so on; generosity would infinitely exist by infinitely constituting imperfection in itself, as well as in the act of each Divine Dignity, wherein would infinitely exist avarice and its act, yet this is impossible.

While Blaquerna was thus considering, his memory remembered that from such a great act of generosity as he had understood within the Divine Being, generosity must needs influence the Son of God and bestow Him upon human nature by means of the Incarnation and Passion, so that the act of bestowal might be the greatest a creature could receive, in order to signify that, just as generosity could enjoy an infinite act within the divine essence, it could also enjoy such in a creature as regards the latter's being, albeit that a creature is not capable of receiving it all because it possesses a being limited and finite in terms of time and quantity, wherein it cannot contain the entirety of infinite generosifying, which is the act of infinite divine generosity.

When his memory had remembered, his will caused Blaquerna to weep, sigh and lament by saying that, were it to please supreme generosity, it might be the time and hour for it to provide many brave, fervent and devout men with a view to their honouring, praising, serving, blessing and making known the Holy Passion of Jesus Christ to those unbelievers who were ignorant thereof. And his intellect replied to Blaquerna that God's generosity had provided the greatest opportunity one can receive to honour and preach Christ's Holy Passion in the very fact that the Son of God had been made incarnate and had delivered that humanity to poverty, torture and cruel death in order to save man, so that he may lack any reason to avoid or fear honouring His Honours[8] and obeying God's commandments.

[15] God is mercy, and the act of mercy is to mercify; and because to forgive and to mercify are in accord, in Blaquerna's fantasy[9] his imagination sought to imagine that forgiveness obtained eternally in God. So, therefore, by means of fantasy his intellect sought to become disposed to considering that the world existed without beginning or end. His memory, however, detached his imagination from his intellect by remembering that God consists in mercy and the act

---

8. Cf. above, § 4 and corresponding note.

9. For the role of 'fantasy' in relation to the imagination, cf. above Ch. 59, § 3 and corresponding note.

thereof, insofar as these latter accord with the exercise of forgiveness at a creature's origin—inasmuch as a creature cannot consist in an origin—and would lack the exercise of eternal forgiveness were eternifying apt to be accommodated within a creature. So, on account of what his memory had remembered, Blaquerna's intellect detached itself from his imagination and understood the difference between mercy and its act in relation to man in accordance with how the former received him as an object; according to the being of divine mercy and the act thereof, however, these latter were, in terms of essence, one and the same thing as regards goodness, greatness, eternity, and so on.

Blaquerna's will was greatly pleased by what his intellect had understood, so it said:

'O Divine Mercy, Who, through your infinite and eternal Son, have shown mercy to the human race by means of a miraculous Incarnation and agonising death. In order that the act of Your mercy may thereby be greater in terms of our honouring and serving You, may Your eyes turn towards us and mercify in us great holiness and perfection, so that we may go to honour and teach to the unbelievers the great exercise of mercy You performed on that occasion when You caused Our Redeemer Jesus Christ—who with His entire being had mercy upon us—to be put to death, scorned and mocked on the Cross.

[16] On account of what his will had been saying with regard to God's mercy, Blaquerna remembered God's great humility, wherein he was unable to understand an act which pertained to humbling in terms of bonifying, magnifying, eternifying, and so on, since the fact is that humbling cannot obtain in the absence of the lesser and the greater.[10] So it was necessary for him, therefore, to understand the act of divine humility, which it exercises in creatures, an act which he could not understand to be in greater majority than that the infinite might have humbled itself in terms of goodness, greatness and eternity to become a single person with the finite and limited as regards time and quantity, and have delivered that person to the humility of death, torture, scorn and poverty, as well as the oblivion of the people.

---

10. I.e. without reference to the principles of 'Minority' and 'Majority' from Llull's Art, principles both which do not obtain in God, hence the impossibility of conceiving of an act of humbling within those of God's Dignities (i.e. bonifying, magnifying, etc.).

When Blaquerna had remembered the aforesaid great humility, he understood that had God not been humbled to take on human flesh or had He failed to humble such flesh to a cruel death and accidental suffering,[11] He would not have been so contrary to the act of pride. And since, by means of the greater contrariety, the act of God's humility accords more strongly with majority, it was therefore necessary that the Son of God should have been a man who was poor, betrayed, scourged, tortured, crucified and put to death, as well as forgotten, forsaken and killed.

[17] Blaquerna considered at length the act of God's dominion, by saying:

'O Supreme Dominion, which exercises dominion over that which exists and that which does not exist (for that which exists has been created from nothing, which nothing cannot oppose the act of Your Dignities which has created therefrom that which exists, which latter the act of Your Dignities maintains in being, while under Your dominion lie all things which have a beginning), in order to signify Your eternity do many creatures enjoy endless duration, for the purpose of showing that You are without end and that, when Your dominion has possession of the righteous and the sinners, Your justice shall judge them in perpetuity according to their merits.'

After Blaquerna had spoken these words, his intellect said that, were the world to have had no beginning, it could not itself so manifestly know God's dominion to exercise such dominion over that which exists and that which does not, for no thing could have been made from nothing or return its being to nothing, and God's justice would be contrary to the act of His dominion as regards all the acts of His Dignities, were the world to lack a beginning. On account of what his intellect had said, Blaquerna's memory remembered that all acts of nature are subject to God's dominion, for some are subject thereto as regards the fact that they operate naturally, in accordance with how they are assisted and permitted by divine dominion, while others are forced and constrained by Him insofar as such dominion performs things miraculously and beyond nature, which performance must needs be in accordance with the act of justice as regards bonify-

---

11. Occ. *passió accidental.* Christ's passibility is 'accidental' as opposed to 'substantial', inasmuch as such passibility is not part of God's essence and is, therefore, not necessary, but rather a response to the contingent fact of man's fallen nature.

ing, magnifying, and so on, in order that it may be known that the act
of the Dignities lies beyond the act of nature. And because the act of
the Dignities which lies beyond nature occurs in regard to greater
things, and with more frequency and more contrariety to the course
of nature, the God of nature is shown more clearly to exercise an act
of dominion over natural things. So Blaquerna's memory remembered, therefore, that God has ordered the seven sacraments, whose
act takes place frequently and in a variety of locations beyond the
course of nature. Blaquerna's will wished to utter the following words,
so it said that divine dominion had very strongly obliged it to love and
fear its God, since it is dependent upon Him for the creation, sustain-
ment and benefits it receives from Him; and, furthermore, that because God wished to become man and to be put to death, he created
a certain man, so that it might become that man's slave and be redeemed through the recreation[12] the latter performed by means of
His agonising Passion.

[18] 'Intellect, my friend', said Blaquerna, 'understand that the
act of God's patience is very great among us, for God has created and
recreated us, and unfailingly and without cease we receive from Him
benefits and grace, yet we are disobedient to Him and obey earthly
lords and worldly matters. Remember, O Memory, how many are the
offences we commit daily against God, and the fact that God's patience awaits our making amends. Behold, O intellect, how many are
the people who fail to know or believe in God and who worship idols,
and how few are those who love and know God. And you, O Will,
weep at the fact that the Saracens are in possession of the Holy Land
of Outremer, where God assumed flesh and died insofar as He was
man; and weep because wicked priests abide in sin, yet handle the
Holy Body of Jesus Christ. But God exercises patience in all such matters.'

Will wept, as did Memory and Intellect, within the eyes of Blaquerna, who said:

'Ah, how patient God is towards the world, despite there being so
many culpable and ungrateful people within it!'

After these tears, they all wept together at length over the Holy
Passion of Our Lord God, wherein God exercised the greatest pa-

---

12. I.e. redemption.

tience. For His Passion was great, insofar as His death was the greatest in terms of the greatest feeling a creature can feel. And it was great because, while being without sin, He was crucified and betrayed, sold, scourged, mocked and put to death by those whom He forgave, and on whose account He had come in order to be man. Yet He exercised patience when He was forsaken and when He saw Our Lady demeaned, assaulted and made tearful by His Passion. And He exercised such patience in all of His deeds that no mind could conceive thereof nor intellect understand.

[19] So day and night, in this and many other ways, using the three acts of his soul, Blaquerna the hermit, a righteous man, contemplated and worshipped the Divine Dignities, by means of which he raised his faculties aloft in order to gain knowledge of the Holy Trinity and the Incarnation of Our Lord God.

# Appendix II

**THE DIVINE OFFICE**[1]

| Hour | Time celebrated | Clock time for 21st March |
|---|---|---|
| Matins | the eighth hour of the night | 2:00 AM |
| Lauds | daybreak | about 5:30 AM |
| Prime | the first hour of the day | 6:00 AM |
| Terce | the third hour of the day | 9:00 AM |
| Sext | the sixth hour of the day | 12:00 noon |
| None | the ninth hour of the day | 3:00 PM |
| Vespers | before dark | about 5:30 PM |
| Compline | before retiring | |

Note: The Romans divided the day and the night into twelve unequal hours each. Consequently, the length of the hour depends on the length of the day (or night). At Rome (lat 41°54′ N), an hour ranges from 45 to 75 minutes in length.

---

1. Information taken from Collamore (2000) in Fassler and Baltzer (2000), 3-11, here 3.

# Bibliography

## Abbreviations

*3 Soc.*  Latin: Théophile Desbonnets, '*Legenda trium sociorum*: Edition critique', Archivum Franciscanum Historicum 67 (1974), 38-144; English: *Legend of the Three Companions*, in *FAED* 2, 61-110.

*ACIV*  Ramon Llull, *Ars compendiosa inveniendi veritatem* (*Brief Art of Finding Truth*), MOG 1 (1721), int. vii, 1-41 (433-473) [+31], Ivo Salzinger (ed.).

*AD*  Ramon Llull, *Ars demonstrativa* (*Demonstrative Art*), ROL XXXII/CCCM 213 (2007), Josep Enric Rubio Albarracín (ed.).

*Blaquerna*  Ramon Llull, *Romanç d'Evast e Blaquerna* (*Romance of Evast and Blaquerna*), NEORL VIII (2009), Albert Soler and Joan Santanach (eds.).

Cat.  Catalan.

*DCVB*  *Diccionari català-valencià-balear: inventari lexicogràfic i etimològic de la llengua catalana en totes les seves formes literàries i dialectals*, a publication initiated by Antoni Maria Alcover, revised and completed by Francesc de B. Moll, with the collaboration of Manuel Sanchis Guarner and Anna Moll Marquès, 10 vols., Palma de Mallorca: Editorial Moll, 1926-68; available electronically at: http://dcvb.iecat.net/.

CCCM  Corpus Christianorum. Continuatio Medievalis.

DRVCR  *The Holy Bible*, Douay-Reims Version. Challoner Revision.

*EL*  *Estudios Lulianos* (Palma de Mallorca, 1957-91).

*FAED* 2  Regis J. Armstrong, J. A. Wayne Hellmann and William J. Short (eds.), *Francis of Assisi: Early Documents. The Founder*, Vol. 2, New York: New City Press, 2000.

*Felix*  *Fèlix, o Llibre de meravelles* (*Felix, or the Book of Wonders*), (Catalan) NEORL X and XIII (2011 and 2014), Lola Badia (ed.-in chief), Xavier Bonillo, Eugènia Gisbert, Anna Fernàndez Clot and Montserrat Lluch (eds.); (English) *SW* 2 (1985), 647-1105, Anthony Bonner (ed. and trans.).

*Gentile*    Ramon Llull, *Llibre del gentil e dels tres savis*, NEORL II
             (1993), 1-210 (*Book of the Gentile and the Three Wise Men*, *SW*
             I, 91-304).

*LC*         Ramon Llull, *Llibre de contemplació en Déu* (*The Book of Con-
             templation on God*), ORL II-VIII (1906-1914).

*Lover*      Ramon Llull, *Llibre d'amic e amat* (*Book of the Lover and the
             Beloved*), in *Romanç d'Evast e Blaquerna*, NEORL VIII (2009),
             428-522.

MOG          Ramon Llull, *Raymundi Lulli Opera omnia*, Ivo Salzinger
             (ed.), 8 vols., (numbered I-VI, IX-X), Mainz 1721-42. Fac-
             simile reproduction edited by F. Stegmüller, Frankfurt, 1965.

NEORL        *Nova Edició de les Obres de Ramon Llull*, Palma de Mallorca:
             Patronat Ramon Llull, Vols. I-XIII (1990-present).

Occ.         Occitan.

ORL          *Obres de Ramon Llull*, 21 vols., Salvador Galmés et al. (eds.),
             (1906-50).

*PL*         *Patrologiae Cursus Completus. Series Latina*, 221 vols, Paris,
             1841-65, J. -P. Migne (ed.).

ROL          *Raimundi Lulli Opera Latina*, Vols I-V: Palma de Mallorca
             (1959-67); Vols VI-XXXVI: Turnhout: Brepols Publishers,
             Corpus Christianorum. Continuatio Medievalis (CCCM),
             1975-present.

*RSB*        Bruce L. Venarde (ed. and tr.), *The Rule of Saint Benedict*,
             Dumbarton Oaks Medieval Library, DOML 6, Cambridge,
             MA/London, England: Harvard University Press, 2011.

*SOED*       *The New Shorter Oxford English Dictionary*, 2 vols, Lesley
             Brown (ed.), Oxford: Carendon Press, 1973 [1993].

*ST*         St Thomas Aquinas, *Summa theologiae*.

*SW*         *Selected Works of Ramon Llull (1232-1316)*, 2 vols., Anthony
             Bonner (ed.), Princeton, N.J.: Princeton University Press,
             1985.

*v./vv.*     versicle/s.


## Primary sources

HUGH OF ST VICTOR (2007): *Hugh of Saint Victor on the Sacraments of the
    Christian Faith* (De sacramentis), Roy J. Deferrari (tr.), Eugene, Or.:
    Wipf and Stock Publishers [Medieval Academy of America, 1951].

LLULL, Ramon (1987 (?)): *Blanquerna*, E. Allison Peers (intr. and tr.), Robert Irwin (ed.), Daedalus European Classics, London/New York: Daedalus/Hippocrene Books; this text is effectively a reprint of Allison Peers' translation, *Blanquerna. A Thirteenth-Century Romance*, London: Jarrolds, 1926.

LLULL, Ramon (2003 [1995]): *The Book of the Lover and the Beloved/Lo libre de amich e amat/Librum amici et amati*, Mark D. Johnston (ed. and tr.), Oxford (U. K.)/Bristol: Aris & Phillips/The Centre for Mediterranean Studies, University of Bristol.

LLULL, Ramon (2005): *Doctrina pueril*, Joan Santanach i Suñol (ed.), Palma de Mallorca: Patronat Ramon Llull (NEORL, VII).

LLULL, Ramon (2006): Raimundus Lullus, *Quattuor Libri Principiorum*, María Asunción Sánchez Manzano (ed.), Turnhout: Brepols (ROL, XXXI/CCCM, 185).

LLULL, Ramon (2007): Raimundus Lullus, *Ars demonstrativa*, Josep Enric Rubio Albarracín (ed.), Turnhout: Brepols (ROL, XXXII/CCCM, 213).

LLULL, Ramon (2007a): *Blaquerna*, Patrick Gifreu (tr.), Fondation Prince-Pierre Monaco, Éditions du Rocher (Collection 'Les Grandes Traductions').

LLULL, Ramon (2009): *Romanç d'Evast e Blaquerna*, Albert Soler and Joan Santanach (eds.), Palma de Mallorca: Patronat Ramon Llull (NEORL, VIII).

LLULL, Ramon (2010): *A Contemporary Life*, Anthony Bonner (ed. and tr.), Barcelona/Woodbridge: Barcino/Tamesis.

LLULL, Ramon (2011-2014): *Llibre de meravelles. Volum I: llibres I-VII. Volum II: llibres VIII-X*, Lola Badia (ed.-in-chief), Xavier Bonillo, Eugènia Gisbert, Anna Fernàndez Clot and Montserrat Lluch (eds.), Palma de Mallorca: Patronat Ramon Llull (NEORL, X and XIII).

LLULL, Ramon (2012 [1995]): *Llibre d'amic e amat*, Albert Soler i Llopart (ed.), Barcelona: Barcino, 2nd ed. (ENC, B, 13), 61-193.

LLULL, Ramon (2013): *The Book of the Order of Chivalry*, Noel Fallowes (tr.), Woodbridge: The Boydell Press.

RICHARD OF ST VICTOR (1979): *Twelve Patriarchs, Mystical Ark, Book Three of the Trinity*, Translation and Introduction by Grover A. Zinn, Preface by Jean Châtillon, New York/Mahwah, N. J.: Paulist Press (The Classics of Western Spirituality).

WILLIAM OF ST-THIERRY (2003): *Guillelmi a Sancto Theodorico Opera Omnia, III: De Natura et Dignitate Amoris*, Paul Verdeyen (ed.), Turnhout: Brepols (CCCM, 88), 175-212.

## SECONDARY SOURCES

ALLEN, Rosamund (ed.) (2004): *Eastward Bound: Travel and Travellers, 1050-1550*, Manchester: Manchester University Press.

ARTUS, Walter W. (1995): 'Ramon on First and Second Intentions. A Basic Ethical Doctrine', in BAZAN *ET AL* (1995), 978-990.

BALDWIN, John W. (1997): 'Paris et Rome en 1215: les réformes du IVe concile de Latran', *Journal des Savants*, n° 1, 99-124.

BAZAN *ET AL* (eds.) (1995): *Les philosophies morales et politiques au Moyen Age. Moral and Political Philosophies in the Middle Ages. Actes du IX Congrès international de philosophie médiévale. Ottawa, du 17 au 22 août 1992 (S.I.E.P.M.)*, Bernardo Carlos Bazan, Eduardo Andujar and Léonard G. Sbrocchi (eds.), II, New York/Ottawa/Toronto: Legas.

BIRKEDAL BRUUN, Mette (ed.) (2013): *The Cambridge Companion to the Cistercian Order*, Cambridge: Cambridge University Press.

BONNER Anthony (ed. and tr.) and BONNER, Eve (tr.) (1993): *Doctor Illuminatus: A Ramon Llull Reader*, Princeton/Chichester (UK): Princeton University Press (Mythos).

BONNER, Anthony (2007): *The Art and Logic of Ramon Llull. A User's Guide*, Leiden/Boston: Brill (Studien und Texte zur Geistesgeschichte des Mittelalters, 95).

BURNHAM, Louisa A. (2008): *So Great a Light, So Great a Smoke. The Beguin Heretics of Languedoc*, Ithaca and London: Cornell University Press.

BUTLER, Alfred J. (1884): *The Ancient Coptic Churches of Egypt*, Vol. 2, Oxford: Clarendon Press.

CHAREYRON, Nicole (2005): *Pilgrims to Jerusalem in the Middle Ages*, New York/Chichester, W. Sussex: Columbia University Press.

COLLAMORE, Lila (2000): 'Charting the Divine Office', in FASSLER and BALTZER (2000), 3-11.

COLÓN, Germà, MARTÍNEZ, Tomàs, and PEREA, Maria Pilar (eds.) (2004): *La cultura catalana en projecció de futur: Homenatge a Josep Massot i Muntaner*, Castelló de la Plana: Universitat Jaume I.

Curtius, Ernst Robert (1990): *European Literature and the Latin Middle Ages*, With a New Afterword by Peter Godman, Willard R. Trask (tr.), Princeton, N.J.: Princeton University Press (Bollingen Series, XXXVI).

Davy, M. -M. (ed. and tr.) (1959): *Deux traités sur la foi: Le Miroir de la foi; L'Énigme de la foi*, Paris: Vrin.

Fassler, Margot E., and Baltzer, Rebecca A. (eds.) (2000): *The Divine Office in the Latin Middle Ages: Methodology and Source Studies, Regional Developments, Hagiography*, Oxford: Oxford Univerrsity Press.

Fidora, A., and Rubio, J. E. (eds.) (2008): *Raimundus Lullus: An Introduction to his Life, Works and Thought*, Robert D. Hughes, Anna A. Akasoy and Magnus Ryan (trs.), Turnhout: Brepols Publishers (Supplementum Lullianum, II / CCCM, 214,).

Grendler, Paul F. (ed.) (2004): *Renaissance: An Encyclopedia for Students*, Vol. 3, New York: Charles Scribner's Sons.

Hames, Harvey J. (2012): 'Through Ramon Llull's Looking Glass: What was the Thirteenth-Century Dominican Mission Really About?', in Ripoll and Tortella (2012), 51-74.

Jenkins, John I. (1997): *Knowledge and Faith in Thomas Aquinas*, Cambridge: Cambridge University Press.

Jotischky, Andrew (2004): 'The Mendicants as Missionaries and Travellers in the Near East in the Thirteenth and Fourteenth Centuries', in Allen (2004), 88-106.

Jotischky, Andrew (2013): *Crusading and the Crusader States*, Abingdon: Routledge [first published by Pearson Education Limited, 2004].

Kibler, William W. and Zinn, Grover A. (1995): *Medieval France: An Encyclopedia*, London: Routledge.

Lawrence, C. H. (2013): *The Friars: The Impact of the Mendicant Orders on Medieval Society*, London/New York: I. B. Tauris, 2nd revised ed.

Leff, Gordon (1999 [1967]): *Heresy in the Later Middle Ages: The Relation of Heterodoxy to Dissent c. 1250-c. 1450*, Manchester: Manchester University Press, 2 vols. [special one-volume edition for Sandpiper Books Ltd., 1999].

Pick, Lucy K. (2004): *Conflict and Coexistence: Archbishop Rodrigo and the Muslims and Jews of Medieval Spain*, Ann Arbor: University of Michigan.

Reilly, Diane J. (2013): 'Art', in Birkedal Bruun (2013), 125-39.

RIPOLL, Maria Isabel, and TORTELLA, Margalida (eds.) (2012): *Ramon Llull i el lul·lisme: pensament i llenguatge. Actes de les jornades en homenatge a J.N. Hillgarth i A. Bonner*, Palma/Barcelona: Universitat de les Illes Balears/Universitat de Barcelona (Col·lecció Blaquerna, 10).

SCHAFF, Philip (ed.), and WEST HADDAN, Arthur (tr.) (2009): *Nicene and Post-Nicene Fathers*, First Series, Vol. 3, Buffalo, NY: Christian Literature Publishing Co., 1887; revised and edited for New Advent by Kevin Knight (2009): http://www.newadvent.org/fathers/130108.htm.

SCHMID, Beatrice (2004): 'El lul·lià *en gràvit* o *engràvit?* A la llum d'un passatge del *Libre de les medicines particulars*', in COLÓN, MARTÍNEZ and PEREA (2004), 459-69.

TANNER, Norman P. (ed.) (1990): *The Decrees of the Ecumenical Councils: Nicaea I to Lateran V*, I, Original text established by G. Alberigo, J.A. Dossetti, P.-P. Joannou, C. Leonardi and P. Prodi in consultation with H. Jedin, London/Washington, D.C.: Sheed and Ward/Georgetown University Press.

TWOMEY, Lesley K. (2013): *The Fabric of Marian Devotion in Isabel de Villena's* Vita Christi, Woodbridge: Tamesis.

VERGER, Jacques (2007 [1973]): *Les universities au Moyen Âge*, Paris: Quadrige/Presses Universitaires de Paris, 2nd ed.